I0843079

Drawn by Light

John W. Otte

Geeky Grace Books

Copyright © 2024 by John W. Otte

All rights reserved.

No part of this publication may be reproduced, distributed, or transmitted in any form or by any means, including photocopying, recording, or other electronic or mechanical methods, without the prior written permission of the publisher, except as permitted by U.S. copyright law. For permission requests, contact [include publisher/author contact info].

The story, all names, characters, and incidents portrayed in this production are fictitious. No identification with actual persons (living or deceased), places, buildings, and products is intended or should be inferred.

ISBN: 979-8-9858103-6-3 (print)

ISBN: 979-8-9858103-5-6 (ebook)

Book Cover by Kirk DouPonce, www. DogEaredDesign.com

Edited by Megan Gerig (MG Literary Services)

To Joel

The Expanse
ELSCONTIN
The Stone
Kolvese Plain
The Edge
The Gold Light Forest
The Vinian Mountains & Highlands
Slewvess
The Sheum Heartland
Belliding
The Far Waters
The Diradco Mountains
The Bearer's Repose
KSANN
Drran
Maoton
Bastion
The Greiid Flats
Weisk
The Right Highlands
The Blood Sea
The Low River Province
The Weyfir Coast
Shols
RIOKA
The Sprenatci Pass
Mountains
Plisk Sanctuary Oasis
Errroan (Ruins)
THE XONTIEL DYNASTY
The Kronin Desert
The Elder Sea
THE DALARK IMPERIUM
The Cradle Bridge
The Pistan Expanse
The Demilitarized Zone
Ufuaa
The Dalark Channel
The Dalark Beachhead
Nexek the Bridge (Ruins)
ERECONE
The Weyfir Sea
TOMMA
The Foundations
PEDREVOR

Dramatis Personae

THE QUEEN'S COURT IN EXILE:

- Everys - Rightful queen of the Xoniel Dynasty, a toratropic mage, and now hiding in the Cold Light forest

- Challix - Everys's assistant

- Trule - Everys's chief maid

- Rewether - Commander of Everys's Queen's Guard

- Oluna Hishi – Wife of Masruq, the Minister of Finance, now separated from her husband

- Favid – Everys's father

- He Who Occupies the Lowest Reaches (aka Occ) – The Diradae who accidentally injured Narius during ritual combat

THE COURT OF THE USURPER:

- King Brencis - Former head of the Dynasty's Military, leader of a successful coup, now ruler of the Xoniel Dynasty

- Queen Viara – Brencis's wife and Narius's ex-wife, supposedly pregnant with Narius's child

- Paine - Narius's Vizier

- Auriel Zammit - Governor-General of Bastion

- Bokil - Minister of Internal Security

- Elamek - Minister of Agriculture

- Istragon - Supreme Prelate of the Dynasty's official religion

- Masruq - Minister of Finance

- Ventios - Minister of Labor

FORMER PALACE STAFF, THEIR FATES UNKNOWN:
- Filamon - Narius's Minister of Resource Management

- Yull - Narius's Minister of Foreign Affairs

- Urett - Narius's assistant

- Zar - Commander of the King's Guard

- Farga - King's Guard and Narius's Swordbound

- Tormod - Narius's Spymaster and secretly a Siporan

- Overturn – Brencis's replacement as head of the Dynasty's military after Brencis turned traitor

OTHER RESIDENTS OF THE DYNASTY:
- Prince Quartus – Narius's brother, declared outlaw but secretly working for Tormod

- Yusra – A beautiful Dalark spy with an unknown master who has helped Quartus

- Redtale - Former head of Everys's Queen's Guard and now leader of the Untested

- Galan - Everys's older sister

- Legarr - Everys's younger brother, now dead

- Ulsa - Everys's mother

- "Auntie" Kyna - Siporan con artist (or maybe something more)

THE COLD LIGHT YOREROOT:
- Stunted Root - Second of the Yoreroot

- Tall Reach - Third of the Yoreroot

- Evergreen - Knowledge Keeper

- Firestruck - Defender of the Forest

- Seed Cluster - Liaison of the Fields

- Yllana - Grafted to Tall Reach

THE DALARK IMPERIUM:
- Tirigian - Emperor of the Dalark Imperium

- Innana - Princess of the Dalark Imperium and Narius's former fiancée

- Kavi – A silent toratropic mage in Innana's employ

- Narius – Former king of the Dynasty, presumed dead, but secretly rescued by Kavi at Innana's direction

The Story Thus Far...

When King Narius's wife leaves him, he needs to find a new one fast to preserve the legitimacy of his reign over the Xoniel Dynasty. A young woman named Everys is brought to the palace and chosen to be the new queen, but this is a disaster for her. Everys is not only Siporan, a marginalized people whose homeland was destroyed by Narius's ancestor four hundred years earlier, but she practices a rune-based magic that is illegal. If anyone discovers her secret, she could be imprisoned, exiled, or even executed.

Everys's first days in the palace are filled with missteps and mistakes as she tries to figure out her place, including starting a riot in her home neighborhood and attracting the possibly romantic attention of Prince Quartus, Narius's younger brother. This leads to clashes with not only Vizier Paine, Narius's chief adviser, but also her new husband as well. Narius and Everys eventually strike an uneasy partnership and even start to respect each other, but everything is put in jeopardy when assassins try to murder them both. Everys saves Narius's life, but she does so with her magic, revealing what she truly is. Quartus is blamed for the attempted assassination. At Everys's request, Quartus's life is spared, and he is declared outlaw and banished from the palace.

In the attack's aftermath, Narius and Everys's uneasy partnership becomes more friendly. Everys teaches Narius about her abilities, while he reveals the Dynasty has been hiding sacred Siporan relics called the Principalities in their archive for the past four hundred years. Their relationship grows stronger when Everys and Narius visit the Cold Light forest, a recently conquered addition to the Dynasty, one controlled by a race of sentient trees. Everys brokers peace between the Cold Light and the Dynasty, ending decades of tension.

At a state dinner held in Everys's honor, Narius and Everys almost kiss, but they are interrupted by incredible news. The Dalark Empire, the Dynasty's chief rival, wishes to formalize a peace agreement between the two kingdoms. To do so, Narius would have to marry Princess Innana, a young woman he has pined for for years. This is everything Narius has wanted, but he doesn't want to lose Everys. She ends their marriage so he can marry Innana and finally have true peace with the Dalark, even though it breaks her own heart.

Narius should be thrilled, but he's miserable. Innana turns out to be a foolish young woman, and he misses Everys. In the meantime, Everys learns more about the conspirators who sent the assassins. Working with Quartus, Everys discovers a secret lab where people are experimenting with her people's runes. One of the test subjects is her younger brother, who dies in her arms. More than that, she learns the conspirators plan to attack Narius at his wedding to Innana.

In the chaos of the attack, Duke Brencis, the head of the Dynasty's military, reveals himself to be a part of the conspiracy. Worse, Narius is severely injured. Everys saves his life, but does so by using his blood to cast a healing spell, something that is forbidden. When Everys recovers from her ordeal, Narius confesses his love for her and asks her to marry him again. She happily agrees. Quartus is sent on an undercover mission to investigate the conspiracy against Narius and Everys, and the newly remarried couple settles into their new life together.

The situation in the Dynasty only continues to deteriorate in spite of Narius and Everys's best efforts. The Dalark Emperor was killed at Narius's abortive wedding to Innana, meaning her older brother, Tirigian, is not only the new Emperor, but he is making moves that could plunge the Dynasty and Imperium into war. Worse, Duke Brencis is fomenting rebellion throughout the Dynasty's holdings, while his co-conspirators are moving behind the scenes. Narius has been challenged to ritual combat by Supreme Prelate Istragon, the Dynasty's spiritual leader, to prove he is still worthy of the throne.

In trying to deal with the mounting crises, Narius's advisers suggest Narius set aside a long-standing law and marry multiple wives, especially after his ex-wife reveals she is pregnant with Narius's child. Everys is horrified, especially when Narius doesn't reject this plan immediately. Everys tries to help ease the situation, but once again, she's unsure how. Things only get worse for her when Favid, her father, who has been gone because of a religious obligation, comes to the palace and disapproves of her marriage to Narius.

In the meantime, Quartus tries to untangle the conspiracy against Narius and Everys. His efforts are frustrated by dead ends and opposition from his adversaries. The only bright spot comes from teaming up with the beautiful Yusra, an intelligence operative from the Dalark Imperium.

During a peace summit with the Dalark Imperium, Narius shocks Everys by offering to once again marry Princess Innana to end the tension between their two kingdoms. The offer is rejected when the Dalark ambassador dies, apparently killed by magic runes similar to what Everys uses. Narius's offer to Innana hurts Everys. Narius can't blame her, but he feels like he has no other choice.

Everys hopes that attending a ceremony with one of her maid's family will be a pleasant distraction, but Duke Brencis disrupts it. He kills one of Everys's guards with an ancient Siporan weapon. He also reveals he has married Narius's ex-wife, Viara.

In the meantime, Narius visits the island province of Maotoa to shore up their loyalty. While he's there, the Maotoan princess, Cosena, tries to seduce him. This prompts an argument between Narius and Paine about what Narius should do to save the Dynasty. But then the Dalark Imperium invades Maotoa. During the invasion, Narius sustains injuries, which prompts Narius and Everys to reconcile.

Narius is able to recover, but he still has to face the ritual combat. Everys tries to find a solution that wouldn't require Narius to risk further injury, but she fails. Narius fights valiantly in the arena, but he is nearly killed in combat. Everys is devastated, but the situation worsens when her father forbids her from using her magic to heal him.

Quartus and Yusra's investigation has led them to a nobleman, who has been conspiring with not only other people in the Dynasty but in the Dalark Imperium as well. They determine it has something to do with the sewers beneath the Dynasty's capital, Bastion. Before they can learn what the plan is, the noble kills himself using toratropic magic like Everys's. This leads them to discover that the mage-kings, the corrupt rulers of the Siporan people, survived the destruction of their homeland and are seeking revenge.

Everys tries to hold the crumbling Dynasty together, but the situation spirals out of control. The Dalark Imperium invades the Dynasty, only to be countered by troops loyal to Duke Brencis. Worse, Narius hasn't recovered from his injuries. When Everys tries to heal him, she's instead given a powerful vision of the Dynasty's past, accompanied by a reminder that "All Empires Fall."

Brencis marches on the capital. In the ensuing chaos, Favid casts a spell that seemingly kills Narius. Quartus and Yusra discover what the conspirators have built in Bastion's sewers: a city-sized rune. As Everys evacuates the palace, the conspirators activate the spell, shattering the city.

Everys flees to the Cold Light forest for refuge. Brencis claims not only the ruins of Bastion, but the throne as well. But what no one realizes is that Narius has not only survived Favid's attempted murder, but he has been pulled out of Bastion and brought to Princess Innana in the Dalark Imperium.

1

For that flickering moment between sleep and wakefulness, she wasn't really alone. Everys's husband slept next to her, separated by a twist of the covers. She could worm her arm through the blockade and touch his arm, caress his cheek, feel his warmth on the pillow, and—

"Blessed?"

Reality settled heavily on her. Narius wasn't on the other side of the bed. He hadn't been for months, and he never would be again. Everys screwed her eyes shut. Her grief had dulled since she'd fled from Bastion as the city fell to Brencis's troops and a gigantic toratropic rune destroyed it. Then, she thought she'd never be able to breathe again, let alone think without being smothered by her loss. Now the grief was just a burn, a constant presence lurking over her shoulder.

"It's an hour into First Watch."

Everys forced herself to sit up. Trule, her chief maid, stood in the doorway, carrying herself with a quiet authority. Pale green scales covered the reptilian Plissk girl, and a mane of black feathers cascaded down to her shoulders. How was this the same skittish girl Everys had met less than a year earlier? But then, crisis had hardened them all.

She rolled out of bed. As she stumbled toward the bathroom, Trule stepped aside to allow three other maids to dart into the room. One went to the closet to pick out potential outfits for the day. The other two followed Everys into the bathroom to offer any help. Everys smiled her appreciation to them. Sometimes it was nice to let the others worry about the minor details so she could focus on the larger ones.

As the girls prepared her shower, Everys reviewed their situation. She and the other survivors from her husband's administration had found refuge in the Cold Light's forest. Their hosts had given them nearly free rein of their entire territory, allowing more and more soldiers and people loyal to her husband to seek refuge in the forests. But although they had plenty of supplies, they were prisoners within the forest. As long as "King" Brencis and the Dalark controlled the rest of the Dynasty's holdings, leaving the forest was dangerous at best, suicidal at worst. And as long as Brencis remained in control, Narius' vision—her vision—for a better Dynasty would remain unfulfilled.

Everys dressed quickly, picking a simple, utilitarian outfit for the day. Now wasn't the time for formal clothing. There was work to be done and she had to be dressed for it.

"Are you looking forward to the Moonslight Festival, Blessed?" Trule asked as she brushed Everys's hair.

Everys grimaced. Every year, the Cold Light celebrated the Moonslight Festival so those who lived in their forest could give thanks for the previous year and look forward to the year to come. She knew she should be excited. But thinking about the previous year dredged up too many painful memories: Being torn from her family home to be forced into what started as a loveless marriage. Surviving multiple assassination attempts. Revealing her long-hidden powers to people who should have killed her. Seeing her husband gravely injured in ritual combat and then succumbing to the wounds. Witnessing the absolute destruction of her home. How could she muster any excitement to remember any of that?

"Do your people have any special celebrations?"

Everys considered it. "*Ez'mazzonal* is coming up soon. Originally, we celebrated it to remember the founding of the Ascendancy when my ancestors laid the first brick for Nekek the Bright. But now, it's a chance for people to celebrate community and the way we're drawn together. Families often have reunions and there's a lot of good food and..."

Her voice trailed off. This would have been the first chance for her and Narius to celebrate *Ez'mazzonal* as a couple. Right before he died, Narius had shared his desire to convert to her faith. He would have enjoyed the celebration and pestered her with questions about everything that went into the holiday. A tear squeezed out of her eye and she swiped it away.

Arms wrapped around her from behind and Trule's cool, scaly skin pressed into her. "It's all right, Blessed. I miss him too."

Trule's caring heart pouring into Everys's, steadying her, strengthening her. Not enough to banish the pain, but to dull it by a small degree. Then Trule pulled away and continued her work on Everys's hair.

Once she was done, Trule handed her a simple breakfast, some sausage rolled in a flatbread wrap, as she left the bedroom. Challix, her assistant, waited for her in the hallway. Everys had worried that Challix wouldn't adjust well to their change in surroundings. She had always struck Everys as a woman used to a more refined existence. But Challix had taken to their new environment with gusto. She, too, wore a simple work outfit, although she'd elevated the homespun outfit into something intimidating, a formal uniform.

"I trust you're ready for the usual litany of problems," Challix said.

Everys offered a wan smile, then took a bite of her breakfast. "Let me guess. More tension between our people and the Cold Light's?"

Challix nodded. Everys chewed harder on the bit of breakfast to keep from sighing. Yes, the Cold Light had been marvelous hosts, but there were still problems. So many of the newest residents in their forest remembered how costly it had been for the Dynasty to conquer the Cold Light some sixty years earlier. Others remembered how some of the Cold Light had resorted to terrorist attacks throughout the Dynasty's holdings. She herself remembered how the people in her neighborhood of Fair Havens had whispered about the wrath of the sentient trees. To suddenly find themselves under the protection of their former enemies was a hard change for many from the Dynasty to make, especially since they had to leave so much of what they knew and loved behind.

"Are plans still proceeding for the Festival?" Everys asked.

"They are. The Yoreroot promises this year's Moonslight Festival will be unlike any that came before it." Challix smirked. "They don't seem to understand that means nothing to us since this will be our first Moonslight Festival."

A slight grin tugged at Everys's lips. Apparently, the Festival was quite the party, attracting people from all through the Cold Light forest. Even though she didn't feel like celebrating herself, she saw this as a strategic opportunity. If the refugees and the Cold Light's people were able to enjoy themselves, they could forge new bonds that could smooth over some of the tension.

Guards suddenly rushed past her and Challix.

"Rewether!" Challix called after one of them. "What's going on?"

Rewether, the captain of Everys's guard, skidded to a halt. "Transports coming out of the treeline!"

"Ours?" Challix prompted.

He nodded, then sprinted down the hall.

Everys frowned. Based on Rewether's reaction, these transports weren't expected. So who would be approaching...?

Her eyes widened. Maybe someone was bringing news about what happened to Narius's body. Or better yet, what if it was Narius himself? Yes, that was possible! Maybe the doctors had gotten it wrong. Maybe he had somehow survived and had been hiding this whole time. Hope swelled within her, shoving away the doubt that whispered around its edges. She glanced at Challix and ran after him.

They sped through the Embassy's halls and out the front door into the settlement known as Tall Reach's Shade, named after the Cold Light who inhabited a copse of trees where the Yoreroot, the Cold Light's leaders, met. When Everys first visited Tall Reach's Shade, it had reminded her of a sleepy rural village. Now it reminded her of a bustling city, with certain areas taking on distinct personalities.

Within ten minutes, they came to an embankment that surrounded the Shade. Soldiers stood on top of the earthen walls, their flechette throwers ready. Everys headed for a break in the wall, ignoring Rewether's shouted protest.

A vast forest stretched out in front of her. But her gaze hitched on the three military transports that sat just outside the treeline. Soldiers clambered out of them, their uniforms disheveled and, in some cases, bloodied. A group of soldiers emerged from behind the rampart, their weapons aimed at the newcomers. They closed the distance. The newcomers raised their hands, showing they were unarmed. A quick conversation ensued, and then the troops from the ramparts signaled an all clear.

Everys left the rampart and crossed toward the transports. When the soldiers saw her approaching, they snapped to attention.

"What happened?" she asked.

One soldier, whose ID tag identified her as Bulwark Uslan, stepped forward. "A few days ago, we encountered a group of refugees entering the forest and we decided to escort them here. Before we could, though, we encountered a unit loyal to King Brencis. Bad firefight. We chased them off, but one refugee got hit pretty bad. We need a medic."

Everys turned to Rewether, who nodded sharply. He bellowed orders at the soldiers on the berms.

"Hope they know how to treat an Ixactl," Uslan said. "He fought like the Warrior's own spawn, but he got shot up pretty badly. I'm surprised he made it this far."

"Where is he?" Everys asked.

Uslan led her over to the second transport, a larger vehicle designed to carry troops into combat. They circled to the back where a group of haggard people, a mix of humans, Plissk, and even an Elbrekkian, were sliding out. When they saw Everys, they all bowed and quickly shuffled out of the way. Uslan pulled the tarp back, allowing the sunlight to trickle into the transport.

A hulking body lay on the transport's floor, his head propped up on the far wall. Like all the hill giants, the Ixactl's skin resembled rocks, but his usual flinty gray was waxy and pallid. His prominent horns swept out from his temples and curled back.

Everys gasped. "Strategist Overturn?"

He smiled weakly at her. "Reporting for duty, Blessed."

She whirled on Uslan. "Why didn't you tell me it was him?"

Overturn waved away her objection. "Ordered her not to. Trying to maintain a low profile."

Her heart hammered in her chest. At her suggestion, Narius had promoted Overturn to oversee the Dynasty's military shortly before Narius died. The Ixactl strategist hadn't been able to escape Bastion with her before a city-sized toratropic rune had destroyed the capital. She had been hoping for weeks now that Overturn would make his way to the forest, but not like this.

As Rewether joined her at the back of the transport, she leaned in closer to him to whisper, "Clear the area."

The guard's eyes widened, but he leaped into action, barking orders to the nearby soldiers. Everys clambered into the transport, careful to avoid Overturn's thick legs. She fished a small vial of amber liquid from a pocket and opened it.

Overturn frowned at her. "What are you doing?"

"Making sure you're okay," Everys whispered. "Now hold still."

She squeezed a bit of the viscous liquid onto the tip of her finger then set to work, drawing a looping pattern onto the bandages covering Overturn's chest.

His eyes widened and he tried to sit up. "What are you...?"

She cut him off with a look. "Status report, Strategist. What's happening outside the forest?"

"Nothing good." Overturn's voice was little more than a bare wheeze. "Bastion's a wreck. A lot of Dalark troops loose in the holdings. Brencis claims he's driven them out, but we know that isn't true."

Everys grimaced but kept drawing. That sounded about right. Shortly before Bastion was destroyed, the Dalark Imperium invaded the Xoniel Dynasty's holdings. While Brencis had blunted the invasion, he clearly hadn't defeated the Dynasty's ancient enemies. Part of her was glad the Dalark were a continued thorn in Brencis's side, but she also suspected that the Dynasty's residents were suffering for it.

Overturn continued his report, rattling off details as she finished the rune's pattern. She took a deep breath and activated it. Light rippled across the pattern, and the glow sank deep into Overturn's chest.

His voice trailed off as the color returned to his skin. Everys smiled to herself. Her family's rune was one of the most powerful healing spells known to her people, the Siporans. She had suspected it would do the trick, but without knowing exactly what had happened to Overturn, using it was a bit of a gamble.

Overturn looked down at his chest, then sat up straighter. He flexed his arms, wiggled his fingers, then looked at her with wide eyes. "You are a toratropic mage."

She tensed. Technically, toratropic magic had been illegal for the past four hundred years, ever since the Xoniel Dynasty and the Dalark Imperium destroyed the Siporan Ascendancy. She hoped that Overturn would be open-minded enough to overlook that little detail, but she couldn't say for certain.

He pursed his lips, then chuckled. "I know I should have you arrested, but I'd much rather serve as your military adviser. If you're okay with having this broken wreck in command again."

"Nothing would please me more, Strategist," Everys said.

Overturn nodded and the two of them slipped out of the transport. As they emerged, a cheer went up along the ramparts. The soldiers must have realized who had arrived. Overturn waved to them. Everys did too, although she wasn't nearly as enthusiastic as he was. She was glad that Overturn had made it to the forest, but she would have gladly traded anything for just another moment with her husband.

2

Narius's heart stuttered, and he paused in the doorway to breathe deeply. That wasn't happening as often, thankfully, but it still occurred often enough to worry him. His recovery was taking too long. He had to regain his strength so he could return to the Dynasty.

He pressed a hand to his chest and sucked in another breath. Three months earlier, he had been severely injured in ritual combat. Just as he was recovering from those injuries, his father-in-law Favid had cast a toratropic rune that had undone every spell ever cast on him. Dozens of wounds had opened up in him and only quick action by a young woman named Kavi had saved his life. He knew he should be grateful, but ever since Kavi had saved him, he'd been stuck in a secret medical facility in Utuaa, the capital of the Dalark Imperium. Over the past few weeks, he'd only interacted with a handful of people.

Narius shuffled into the hallway beyond. The hall was white with silver highlights, clean to the point of gleaming. There were half a dozen rooms like his, all unoccupied, along with a monitoring station at one end of the hall. Next to that was a thick metal door he suspected led to the rest of the building, or maybe even the outside.

Bracing himself, Narius set out down the hall, taking slow, measured steps. The day before, he had completed twenty laps. He was determined to add another ten this time, even though he knew it would wring him out.

With each step, he went through the mental list he had cultivated. Each step was a reminder of what mattered, what he had to do.

Step. *Am I the father of Viara's baby?* Step. *Make amends with Paine.* Step. *What happened with the Dalark invasion?* Step. *Did Brencis succeed with his coup?* Step. *More important: what happened to Everys?* Step. *Most important: reunite with her.*

He kept repeating that list to himself, using each question to motivate himself. The problem was, whenever he tried to broach any of these subjects with his doctors, they claimed the discussion would put undue stress on him. As if keeping him ignorant of these issues wasn't causing him even more stress!

He caught his reflection in a nearby window. He barely recognized the man who stared back at him. A thick beard nearly covered his neck. His coppery hair had grown shaggy as well. His face had shrunk, bags ringed his eyes. Would Everys even recognize him if they saw each other?

Yet one thing gave away his identity: his golden eyes, the mark of the royal family. Sure, lots of nobles in the Dynasty had metallic eyes. The royals' many cousins and other distant relatives shared that trait. But as far as he knew, no one in the Imperium had this feature. Anyone seeing him would instantly know who he was or, at the very least, strongly suspect it.

He kept going, counting his steps, focusing on his gait. Within a few minutes, he approached the large doors and the monitoring station. He recognized the nurse who sat behind the desk. Sylvine was a pretty young woman with large hazel eyes and thick blond hair. She had a habit of chattering as she checked on him, so he had gleaned a lot about her life. Unmarried, although three potential suitors vied for her attention. Second oldest out of four children. Not too close to her father, but she adored her mother. Generous. Warm. The perfect caregiver.

"Are you feeling okay, Master Ancur?" she called.

Narius smiled at the assumed name. While the staff knew who he really was, they all called him "Ancur," a Dalark word that roughly translated to "deliberately anonymous."

"Feeling stronger every day, Sylvine," he replied, wincing at how hoarse his voice sounded. "Just couldn't sleep."

Her features puckered into a frown, and Narius stifled a groan. That would get passed along to her superiors and probably result in more tests. He supposed it made sense for Sylvine and the others to be cautious.

Over the past three months, he had undergone eight different surgeries to patch up the damage done by Favid's spell. From what they had told him, he had nearly died four different times since arriving in

Utuaa. Even though he was the king of the Xoniel Dynasty, the Dalark Imperium's oldest rival, they clearly didn't want to see that happen.

He grimaced as he came to the unmarked line he knew he couldn't cross without Sylvine objecting. Then he turned a slow circle and started back for his room, only to jump as he realized that someone else had appeared in the hallway. A young woman leaned against an open doorframe, her arms crossed. Her brown hair framed her heart-shaped face, and she waggled her fingers at him in greeting.

"Kavi, you know it's bad for me to be startled," Narius grumbled.

Kavi tipped her head to one side, her grin turning lopsided. He chuckled. She didn't buy his protests and they both knew it.

"So, how's your night going?" Narius asked as he shuffled past her.

She fell into step next to him and made a series of gestures, tight and close to her chest. Narius frowned, trying to decipher them. Kavi had tried to teach him the sign language she used, and while he'd picked up enough to understand the gist of what she was saying, there were times nuance eluded him. Like now. As Kavi signed, he understood her night had been boring, but she included some details about what he thought was a royal reception she had attended.

Kavi glanced at his face and stopped signing. She touched his shoulder and then, slowly and deliberately, signed, *How are you feeling?*

"Better every day." Narius forced a smile, but then his chest twinged and he winced despite himself.

Kavi pressed gently on his shoulder. *You need Sylvine?*

He shook his head. "I just need to keep walking. I need to get stronger."

You need rest. Don't ... yourself.

He wasn't sure what she said, but from the context and her expression, he suspected she was warning him about overexerting himself. But what choice did he have? Unless...

"I don't suppose you'd be willing to use your... special skills, would you?"

Kavi shot a look back toward the monitoring station, her eyebrows pinched together. Narius chided himself at his carelessness. He knew Kavi could perform a type of toratropic magic, one that relied on hand gestures instead of written runes and ink. She had helped him with her spells several times. But he hadn't thought of whether people knew what she was capable of.

She steered him into one of the empty rooms. Once again, she was deliberate about her signs.

I have. The spells have done everything they can.

He scowled at the answer, and she offered him an apologetic smile. He shouldn't blame her. That meant that he just had to be patient.

But this line of questioning prompted a new one he had been pondering for the past few weeks. He strongly suspected Kavi was Siporan, although he had never pressed her on the issue. As much as the Dynasty discriminated against the Siporans, he suspected the Dalark Imperium treated them worse. "You're a *zhannoq'uem*, aren't you?"

Kavi blinked in surprise. *Where did you hear that word?*

"Scrivener Tolistan told me about them," Narius said. "He said that they were... the royal guard for the mage-kings, right? Capable of powerful magics, unlike anything other toratropic mages could do."

Kavi snorted. *That's not... true.*

"What isn't?" Narius asked. "That you're *zhannoq'uem* or that they could perform impressive feats of magic?"

Frustration flitted over Kavi's face. She launched into a series of elaborate signs, her hands moving faster than Narius could really track. As near as he could understand, she was *zhannoq'uem*, but if that was because she was a direct descendant or her teachers were, he couldn't be sure. After a few minutes, Kavi caught herself, and she slowed her gestures down.

We have hidden ourselves since then. Few know what I can do, just you and my...

Kavi's hands abruptly halted, and she looked over Narius's shoulder, her eyes widening.

Mistress!

Narius looked over his shoulder. Sure enough, someone stood in the doorway, hands on her hips.

"And what do we think we're doing?" Her voice was teasing yet firm.

Narius sighed and faced her. "Hello, Innana."

Innana offered him a thin smile. He unconsciously took a step back. He was still struggling to adjust his thinking about her. She wasn't the alluring girl he had fallen in love with when they'd met as children at a trade summit on Maotoa. She wasn't the romantic ideal he had created in his mind during their long years apart. She wasn't even the flighty girl who had frustrated him so much in the weeks leading up to their abortive wedding. No, this was the real Innana, cool and calculating, so quietly intense she genuinely scared him.

Her gaze flicked between Kavi and him, finally landing on her. "Have you seen to that matter we spoke of earlier?"

Doubt flickered across Kavi's face. *No, mistress. But I thought that maybe...*

Innana arched one brow. Kavi stilled, then ducked her head and hurried out of the room. Innana watched her go, then turned to Narius and smiled warmly at him.

"Let's get you back to bed, shall we?" Her tone clarified that it wasn't a request.

He groaned. "I was only taking a walk."

"At this time of night?" She clucked her tongue. "I'll have to talk with Sylvine about that. She should know better."

"It's not her fault, Innana."

"I never said it was. You can't push yourself too hard, dear Narius."

She escorted him back down the hallway to his room. He wanted to object, but he knew he couldn't. She was the one in charge. While the medical personnel, or even Kavi, might disagree with her, they wouldn't defy her. So he couldn't either.

Innana gestured toward his bed. "In we go."

He bit back a complaint but did as he was told.

"I know you want to do more, but I need you to rest, Narius," Innana continued.

"Can you at least tell me what you know about Everys?" He winced at how small and pathetic his voice sounded.

She smiled thinly. "Would that I could. But the doctors are quite clear that—"

He groaned and sank into the bed. Of course. Keep him ignorant. Keep him isolated. For his own "good."

Innana perched on the end of the bed. "I know you chafe against these restrictions, but I promise you, a time is coming when you will enter the fight. I intend to open up a second front in this war, one much closer to home. And you, my dear Narius, are the chief weapon in my arsenal. So rest and recover. The battle will be here soon."

3

The medics declared Overturn completely cured. Thankfully, no one asked how that had happened. Everys was relieved at the news, even more so when Challix offered to help the strategist settle in. That meant she was free to check on one of the Shade's most reclusive residents.

Everys wound between buildings shaped out of the forest's trees. She passed by a team of grafted who were moving their hands to slowly twist three trees together to create a new home for a family of Dunestriders. They barely glanced in her direction. That teased a smile to Everys's lips. The legitimate ruler of the Dynasty had just walked by them, and they were more enamored by the trees.

Eventually, the buildings thinned out, and the bustle of the settlement quieted. Everys breathed deeply, savoring the smell of moss mixed with pine needles. Her guards shifted uneasily. She knew they didn't like it when she left the Shade's confines. But she had little choice. Not if she wanted to visit her father.

They followed a barely visible path through the undergrowth until they came upon a little shack. Unlike the buildings in the Shade, this one was constructed out of regular timber and stone, and it only had a few rooms and a few modern conveniences. Everys had insisted the Embassy had plenty of room, but Papa had adamantly refused. While she wanted to give him his space, it hurt that she had to face her grief without any family to support her.

She stepped up to the rough-hewn door and rapped against it. Since leaving the Dynasty, Papa had spent most of his time reading the Siporan ancient texts and praying. She was relatively sure he was eating—a grafted brought him supplies every week. But beyond that...

"Come in!" a feminine voice called.

Everys startled. Who would Papa have visiting him? And then, as she realized the answer to her own question, she smiled and pushed open the door.

A matronly woman bustled around the tiny kitchen, dusting the furniture and straightening the supplies in the cobbled-together cupboards. She paused in her work long enough to smile at Everys.

"Well, hello, Blessed! Has it been another week already?" Oluna asked.

The sadness that had clawed at Everys released her. She'd first met Oluna at a social function at the palace, and they'd quickly become friends. Oluna was one of the few people in the court who didn't feel the need to preen and posture around Everys, and her willingness to be genuine at the expense of her social clout had been so refreshing early in Everys's days as a newly married queen.

"How are you?" Everys asked.

Oluna sighed heavily and dramatically. "Oh, I'm managing, Blessed. Life in the Shade isn't as amusing as it was in Bastion. There aren't many nobles here, so the rumors I can start are limited."

Everys's smile broadened. Oluna specialized in engineering scandals within the nobility. A useful hobby in the royal court, but as she had pointed out, that mostly consisted of the two of them in the Cold Light forest.

Oluna snapped out her rag and returned to work. "Your father is out back by the fire ring. I swear, that man needs a strong woman in his life. And thankfully, he has two."

Everys chuckled and slipped out the back door. Her guards took up posts on either side of the house's back door, where they would be close enough to see her but not so close as to overhear what she or Papa would say.

She picked her way down a gentle slope to an area where the trees and bushes appeared to have been shoved out of the way. A small pit, filled with a pile of white and black ash, had been dug in the center. Seated on a log facing the fire pit was Favid, her father.

Papa wore a simple white shirt with light blue pants. They appeared free of stains and recently pressed, although they hung loosely on his frame. Everys knew from Oluna's reports that his eating habits were a source of constant battles between the two. He was clean-shaven, his graying hair laying neatly. She closed her eyes and hung her head, sending up a silent wish that she could find the right words or the correct actions to fix whatever had broken between them.

"You gonna stand there and stare at me?" he asked without turning around.

Everys jumped, startled at the sudden question. But then she smiled. He might be surly, but she still hoped they could reconnect. If she couldn't have Narius, having her father's love once again would be nice. She picked her way down the slope, coming around the log Papa sat on. A tool kit was open on the log next to him and he hunched over the access hatch of a small data scriber.

"Papa, what are you doing?" she asked.

"This belongs to Shielder Multrin of the 7th Sword Battalion," Papa said, his voice strained from his concentration. "It got a little banged up as his unit entered the forest. I figured since the trees don't exactly have much by way of electronics repair shops, I should help."

Seeing him so focused on his work reminded her of when she would help him in the back room of the Broken Sword. That seemed like such a long time ago, sealed away in a past they'd never be able to revisit. And yet, for just a moment, Everys could pretend like nothing had happened, like they were still the same people they had always been.

He glanced at her out of the corner of his eye. "Don't you have royal things to do?"

And the moment was gone. "Papa..."

He turned back to his work. "Your friend can find better things to do with her time. Call her off."

"That's not why Oluna comes out here."

"She knows I'm married, right?"

"Papa!"

He tried to make an adjustment to the scriber. But instead, he fidgeted with the tool then tossed it back into the kit.

"I wish you had never brought me here," he muttered.

Everys's head snapped back, stung by the venom in his words. "Papa, if you had stayed in Bastion, you might have been killed when the city shattered."

He wouldn't meet her gaze. Her heart froze. Did he wish he was dead? Were things really that bleak for him here?

She reached over and took his hand. "We could go to conclave together."

"Since when have you been interested in anything to do with the Singularity?"

A fair accusation. When she had been younger, Papa had insisted she attend Siporan religious observances, especially when her talent for toratropic magic became clear. In her childhood, she had chafed under the requirement. Once Papa, Mama, and her older sister Galan went on their vigil, she had stopped going altogether. Ever since the Dynasty and the Dalark had destroyed the Siporan Ascendancy four hundred years earlier, many of their people had decided that the Singularity had given up on them, so they should return the favor. That had been Everys's attitude as well. So how could she explain the change?

"I came to realize something recently," she said carefully. "People can come and go. Empires can rise and fall. Even all of this"—she gestured toward the trees—"could be razed to the ground. But through it all, the Singularity will remain."

Papa finally met her gaze, his brow pinched into the smallest of frowns. "That almost sounds sincere."

"It is, Papa. And I've been learning a lot from the Siporans who live in the forest. They have insight into the Singularity and the runes that I've never heard before."

That earned her a snort. "Bunch of heterodox dreamers from what I've seen."

"Maybe, but they're all we have."

Papa pursed his lips, then nodded heavily. "Well, I suppose we could try it."

Her heart leaped at the possibility. It would feel good to spend some time with Papa at conclave. She knew how important it had been to him when she was younger.

He started to rise, but as he did, he paused. He looked up at her, and a hardened expression settled on his face. It was almost as if a door closed behind his eyes.

"But some other time." Papa's voice was gruff, harsher than it had been. "Not today."

Everys fought to keep from letting her disappointment show. "Of course, Papa. I'll see you again soon."

He sat down and resumed his work on the scriber. Everys rose and walked back up to the cabin. Oluna stood near the back door. She wiped her hands on her apron, a sad look on her face.

"He is doing much better," Oluna said.

Everys smiled, deciding to change the subject. "Have you heard anything about Masruq?"

Oluna's expression turned brittle. She was normally so gregarious, untiring even. For her to falter that much meant that she was struggling.

"Not a thing," Oluna said. "Snippets. Still serving as the Minister of Finance for Brencis. I'm sorry for that."

Everys waved away the apology, even though the fact that Masruq had stayed in Bastion to serve Brencis rankled. But she understood. He likely didn't have a choice. Many of Narius's former advisers had probably made similar choices.

"And Zivah?" Everys prompted quietly.

Tears welled in Oluna's eyes. Zivah was her granddaughter who had been deathly ill. Everys had tried using her healing rune to cure her, but she'd never found out if it had worked.

"Nothing," Oluna whispered. "Not a single piece of news. Our house shouldn't have been touched by the disaster, but I..."

Her voice trailed off, and Everys gave her a hug. Everyone had lost so much when Bastion fell. As peaceful as the Shade was, she couldn't lose sight of that. Brencis needed to pay for what he had done.

4

Quartus had never considered himself a violent man. Sure, he had gotten into scrapes when he was a child. Who didn't? And yes, he had joined the military when he was old enough, but he'd served in counterintelligence, mostly leveraging his crisp uniform to attract women. Even after he'd left the service and spent his days carousing through the less reputable parts of Bastion, he'd done his best to avoid actual confrontation and violence.

But now? Violence was his purpose. Death and destruction, all focused on one man: Brencis.

He watched the crowd in the refugee camp going about their business. These people had resided in Bastion before the city had been destroyed. Most of them attributed the city's destruction to an earthquake, but Quartus knew better. He had been in the city's sewers when the giant mechanism that triggered the city's destruction had activated. He was probably one of the only people who had figured out that the greatest threat to the Dynasty wasn't the Dalark Imperium. It wasn't the rebellion in Maotoa. No, the greatest threat the Dynasty faced was hiding in plain sight. Siporan mage-kings, thought to have been wiped out four centuries earlier, had somehow survived the destruction of Nekek the Bright, their capital, and had engineered everything that had happened in the past several months. And Brencis was their puppet. Quartus was sure of it.

If that was all that Brencis had done, Quartus would have left his fate to people far more important than him. But Brencis and his co-conspirators had murdered Narius and Everys, Quartus's brother and sister-in-law.

For that, Quartus was going to kill him.

The conviction surprised him. When they had grown up together, he and Narius had not gotten along. Things had only worsened after Narius ascended the throne. But then Quartus had been accused of trying to assassinate the king and queen—something he now suspected had been orchestrated by the mage-kings. He should have been executed for his supposed crime, but Everys's intervention had saved his life and started him down a different road.

One that led him here.

Someone plopped down next to him. He startled, ready to snap at whoever it was to keep moving, but then he caught a good look at her. Long auburn hair framed piercing amber eyes. And even though she routinely smeared dirt on her face to hide her features, her dusky complexion gave away that she was Dalark. In spite of his perpetual sour mood, he couldn't help but smile as Yusra settled in next to him.

"You're going to need to teach me how you do that sometime," he whispered. "I never saw you coming."

She offered him a smirk. "Leave me some secrets."

Heat flushed through him. When he'd first met Yusra a few months earlier, they had both been hunting the same quarry. He was doing so at the behest of Tormod, Narius's spymaster. She, however, was doing so for someone within the Dalark Imperium. Thankfully, she had agreed to work with him.

"Any luck finding a way out?" he asked.

She shrugged one shoulder. "Several, but none that will be helpful."

"What do you mean?"

"According to the rumors in camp, a pair of guards at the south gate will let people out if you give them eight hundred blades per person or something of equal value in trade."

Quartus frowned. "You have that kind of money on you?"

She smirked. "Nor anything I'd want to trade with either of them."

"Next option?"

"Some Ixactl in the northwest corner supposedly have found access to an old steam tunnel that runs under the camp. I've heard you don't need actual money to get out."

"They're letting people slip out because they're so altruistic?"

"Favors to be named later. That sort of thing."

Quartus nodded thoughtfully. He could probably work with that.

"Anything else?"

"Lots of stories, but I don't think any of them are credible."

He didn't know what he could offer the Ixactl in terms of favors. About the only thing he had of value was his identity as a disgraced former prince. But the Ixactl would likely turn him in if they learned his true identity. However, if it was their only option...

"Take me to the Ixactl."

Yusra stood. Quartus snared a ratty blanket from within the tent and threw it over his head and shoulders, pretending he was trying to stave off the cold. It wasn't much of an act. The temperature had dropped significantly in the past few weeks.

Quartus tried not to look at the refugees as he and Yusra passed. He knew what he'd see: desperate families, children playing in spite of the hardship, people huddled together for warmth, each of them hoping that this crisis would end soon and they'd be able to return to the city and maybe rebuild their lives.

Eventually, they entered a part of the camp that was filled with nothing but Ixactl. He had no idea how they were able to cram into human-sized tents as the smallest Ixactl was at least six feet tall. The hill giants glared at them as they passed. Yusra didn't seem to mind. She held her head high and walked with a spring in her step, as though she belonged there as much as they did. Quartus offered his best winning smile. Unfortunately, his charm seemed lost on them.

"They're right over there." Yusra pointed to a cluster of tents, where at least a dozen Ixactl milled about.

Quartus took a deep breath and headed in their direction.

When the Ixactl saw his approach, they parted to allow him to approach the center of the crowd. Whether that was because they recognized Yusra or figured they were coming to see their boss, he didn't really care. Just so long as...

"Qulinus?"

Quartus felt like he had walked face-first into a brick wall. He knew that voice.

A huge Ixactl with mismatched horns and skin the color of obsidian rose from where he was sitting on an overturned barrel.

Stoophawk guffawed. "Look what tumbled into my tent. You guys remember how I told you about Qulinus? I used to run with a gang he led. Made all sorts of promises about all of us becoming richer than the royals someday but turned out, he was just playing with us."

Quartus gritted his teeth. While there was some truth to Stoophawk's story, he wasn't being completely accurate. Quartus had promised to pay Stoophawk and his gang—something he intended to do!—but then a bunch of them had died when they raided a secret lab. Stoophawk rightly blamed Quartus for the deaths. That, and Quartus's inability to pay him, led to a savage beating at Stoophawk's hands. Just seeing the Ixactl made his body ache, even though he had recovered from the beating months earlier.

He held up his hands. "Look, Stoophawk, I'm not looking for any trouble. We just heard you had a way out of the camp."

Stoophawk laughed. "Oh yeah, I got a way out for you. Gravedigger's way."

The Ixactl leader snapped his fingers, and three of his goons turned on Quartus, flexing their thick arms and snarling at him.

Quartus took a step back, keeping his hands up and open. Even though his heart hammered in his chest, he forced himself to speak slowly and coolly. "You're right. I made a bunch of promises to you and the rest of our gang that I didn't keep. And Hiley, Stickler, and Clovis all died and I regret that. But I need to get out of this camp and I'm willing to negotiate with you."

"Do you remember what I told you the last time we saw each other?" Stoophawk growled.

Quartus swallowed hard. "You said if you ever saw me again, you'd kill me."

"Give me a good reason why I shouldn't keep that promise."

Before Quartus could come up with an answer, Yusra stepped between the Ixactl and him. "How about I give you three good reasons?"

Stoophawk gaped at her, then roared with laughter. Thankfully, his goons stopped where they were, joining their boss's laughter.

"Who's the pebble, Qulinus?" he asked.

Yusra didn't answer his question. "First of all, I have access to significant financial resources. If you show us your exit, I will not only pay you for that information, but also for the wrongs this man has done to you."

That only caused the Ixactl gang to laugh harder.

"Second," Yusra continued, nonplussed, "you should help this man because his name isn't Qulinus. It's actually Quartus, King Narius's brother. I would think having a member of the royal family in your debt would be worth it."

Stoophawk guffawed even harder, but several of his gang stopped, studying Quartus's face. Quartus tried to project a regal air.

"And third, if you don't show us the exit, I will make you stop laughing."

That, finally, caused Stoophawk to stop. He leaned in close to get in Yusra's face. "I'd like to see you—"

Before he could finish the taunt, Yusra elbowed him in the eye.

The Ixactl stumbled backward, clutching at his face and bellowing. Before the others could react, Yusra slammed into one of the nearby goons and shoved him hard enough he tripped into one of his companions. She ricocheted off him into another Ixactl, practically climbing him to plant a solid kick in his jaw.

Quartus gaped at her as she jumped and caught the horns of another goon, yanking him off-balance. His gaze darted around the camp, checking for guards. Thankfully, he didn't see any. But then, why would he? Brencis's troops probably didn't care if the refugees killed each other.

By the time he turned his attention back to the fight, six Ixactl lay on the ground, groaning and clutching different parts of their body. Stoophawk knelt in the dirt, holding his neck and coughing. And Yusra stood over him with her fists thrust onto her hips.

A thrill shot through Quartus. She was amazing. Breathtaking. Spectacular.

"I meant what I said about the payment," Yusra said. "Are you going to show me your exit or not?"

Stoophawk glared at her, but then he laughed again, a bit of blood spraying out of his mouth.

"I like this one, *Quartus*. You have a deal, pebble."

Stoophawk clambered to his feet and headed toward one of the tents. The other Ixactl moved out of the way, clearly keeping their distance from Yusra. Quartus stuck as close to her as he could.

Pulling back the flap of the tent, Stoophawk motioned for them to go inside. Quartus hesitated, not wanting to turn his back on the Ixactl. But Yusra snared his hand and pulled him inside.

The interior was like all the other tents in the camp, with only a human-sized cot. Stoophawk had apparently tried to decorate his tent with a plank underneath the cot and a battered crate for a table. Stoophawk grabbed one corner of the board and pulled it to one side, revealing a storm drain underneath. The bars were too close together for someone to squeeze through, but the lock that should have held it closed was missing. Quartus spotted bits of metal on the ground, probably the lock's remnants.

With one hand, Stoophawk lifted the grate and motioned toward the opening. "Follow the blue arrows. That will lead you to an outlet that empties into a tributary of the Melgor. Wanna be careful there, because the bank's slippery. It's a two-hour walk back to Bastion."

Quartus nodded, motioning for Yusra to go first. Before she could slip through the opening, though, Stoophawk snared her arm.

"How you gonna keep your promise to me, pebble?" Stoophawk asked.

She smiled sweetly at him. "Do you really think making threats is the best way to cement our friendship, Stoophawk? Or do I have to humiliate you again?"

Stoophawk blinked, then laughed. "You got guts, pebble. Lot more than your boy there."

Yusra batted her eyes at the Ixactl, then slipped through the hole. Quartus didn't linger. The last thing he needed was a parting threat from Stoophawk.

Cold bit into his ankles as he dropped into the water. Quartus cringed as the water soaked through his boots and into his pants. His arms pinwheeled. Yusra helped steady him. Once he was sure she was okay too they set out. Sure enough, blue arrows had been painted at the top of the walls, indicating the way they should go.

As they walked, he noticed that Yusra was favoring her right leg. He reached out and touched her elbow. "Are you all right?"

She nodded, wincing for a moment. "Didn't want to show any weakness in front of your friends, but I think I tweaked my ankle when I swept the big one's legs."

Which one did she consider the "big one?" But Quartus didn't ask the sarcastic question. Instead, he stepped closer, putting his arm around her waist and pulling her arm over his shoulders. She regarded him with a lopsided smile.

"Now's hardly the time," she murmured.

His cheeks heated, but he returned her smile with one of his own. "Why not? I find the atmosphere particularly romantic down here, don't you?"

She laughed, a melodic trilling. "I had enough of fetid sewers back in Utuaa, thank you very much."

But Yusra didn't pull away from him, so they hobbled through the sewers in a comfortable silence, following the arrows until they emerged from a culvert near the Melgor River. Quartus took a quick look around. No sign of any soldiers. This might work out after all.

"So now what?" Yusra asked.

"We go back to Bastion," Quartus said.

And hopefully, that would bring him one step closer to killing Brencis.

5

B y the time Everys made it to the Siporan conclave on the edge of the forest, the melancholy that had clung to her had loosened. She made it in time to catch the end of the service itself, a blessing followed by a beautiful song. Once the other worshipers filed out of the building, Everys slipped down a side staircase and into the catacombs beneath the building. While she enjoyed the services every time she attended, what hid underneath the conclave excited her a lot more.

At the bottom of the stairs, she entered a well-lit hallway. Large pieces of parchment hung on the wall, each one covered with looping lines and sworls that formed intricate patterns. Everys paused near one of them. She had never encountered this design anywhere else, and that was because this rune had only been created fifty years earlier. According to a note tacked on the wall next to it, this rune would allow people to see in darkness.

Then she came to the end of the hallway, where someone centuries earlier had carved a promise from the ancient texts: "As the runes of ink undergird His creation, He draws a rune of light to overarch all things."

She followed the curved wall and entered a large room. Lights strung along the ceiling illuminated the rows of tables and large chalkboards. A dozen people of all ages and races hunched over the tables, each one occupied by their experiments. This was part of the reason Everys loved visiting the catacombs. The people who lived here called themselves the *zhanhaydkor'uem*. The name roughly translated to "Illuminates."

She had never heard of this sect before she arrived at the Shade. They were so very different from the Siporans she knew—welcoming proselytes with enthusiasm, regardless of race.

They were also obsessed with toratropic runes, considering it their sacred duty to research them and develop new ones. Whereas her masters had warned her against such experimentation, the Illuminates relished it. But even new runes were secondary to their true goal: to cast a rune with light.

The ancient texts contained several references to "runes of light," and none of the scriveners she knew could say definitively what they referred to. Some believed they were descriptions of the Singularity's incredible power, since only He could draw runes with light itself. Others saw them as metaphors for what toratropic mages were to do with the runes: help people with what the Singularity had given them.

But the Illuminates were obsessed with the idea of runes of light. They took it as a challenge, one that they had never come close to achieving. They displayed their failed attempts along the edges of the room. Pieces of parchment with runes cut in them to allow light to shine through. Prisms with runes carved in their sides to cast light. Even now, they were continuing their research.

Everys smiled wistfully, her eyes prickling with tears. Narius would have loved it here. He had been so fascinated by toratropic magic and runes. She suspected he would have found dozens of kindred spirits among the Illuminates.

A young Kolvese woman looked in her direction, and Everys's melancholy evaporated. She didn't know how Style always knew when she arrived, but somehow she was always the first to greet her.

"Hey, Blessed! I wouldn't come in here for another hour or two. Screj is about to attempt to cast another rune with fiery ink," Style shouted.

That elicited an indignant shout from an Elbrekkian man on the other end of the room. He had ashen skin, with spines jutting from his temples and down the back of his neck. "It's a legitimate line of inquiry! The ancient mages would have had access to flammable oils and other accelerants that could have been used—"

"Have you been able to cast a rune with fire yet?" Style asked.

The spines along his back quivered as his eyes turned into inky black pools. "That's not the—"

"So the answer is 'no,'" Style replied with a smile. "And you think that's going to change today?"

"I'm mixing the accelerant into a batch of Cold Light sap that Firestruck gave me, and—"

"So then, would it be the fire that causes the rune to work or the sap?" Style asked.

Screj's head snapped back as if slapped. "Th-that's... uh, that's a valid..."

"Tell you what," Style said. "If you get your fire rune to do *anything*, I'll cook dinner tonight. But if you fail, you cook."

Screj glanced toward Everys, as if he expected her to step into the argument, but she had learned to keep her distance when these two sparred.

"That's not exactly fair," he finally said. "I've prepared dinner for the past two months!"

"What does that say about your line of research, my dear?" Style retorted.

Screj's mouth screwed into a thin line.

"Hey, you know I'm only teasing," Style called over. "I'll make dinner tonight. You just make sure you don't singe off your spines, okay? I got an itch I'll need you to scratch later."

Screj tried not to laugh, but then he guffawed. He shook his head and turned back to his table. Style shot Everys a smile before she turned back to her research as well.

Everys's gaze roamed the room, soaking in the other Illuminates as they conducted their own experiments and research. Some were mixing inks. Others were poring over ancient texts. Her gaze hitched on one older man, with shoulder length brown and black hair and fiery brown eyes. He had looked up from his research and glared at her across the room.

She clenched her jaw. Hirfan had made it clear that he didn't approve of her presence. But because she was both Siporan and the queen, he couldn't keep her out. That didn't stop him from glaring any time they were near each other.

"Are you all right, Blessed?"

She jumped at the quiet voice behind her. She turned and looked down at the ancient Siporan man, his skin so creased and weathered that he appeared to be on the verge of disintegrating.

Everys offered him a quick bow. "Master Tillmin, it's good to see you."

He waved away her greeting. "I don't have time for empty words, Blessed. I asked you a question: are you all right? You've been dripping sadness through my laboratory since you entered."

A sob rattled her chest so suddenly she almost let it out. She hadn't meant to, but something about the conclave service had stirred up desires she had long left buried.

"Come, come, let's get some tea into you." He motioned for her to join him at his station.

Tillmin's table occupied one corner, far away from the others. Unlike Style, Screj, or the others, his table only had a large prism held in a metal clamp. A pattern had been carved into the prism, one that would shine a rune onto a surface when light passed through it. While the setup looked brand new, Everys knew the truth: this prism-caster had been built in the ancient capital of the Siporan Ascendancy, Nekek the Bright, a thousand years earlier. When she had met Tillmin, the Illuminate master had proudly shown her the prism-caster.

But the caster wasn't the only thing the master had on his table today. Two steaming cups of tea awaited them. With a smile, he pressed one into her hands.

"You knew I was coming?" she asked.

"Call it a hunch," Tillmin said. "But I can't help but wonder, with all your responsibilities, why you visit so often."

That was a good question, one she had never really considered. She pondered his question while he sipped his tea.

She finally found the answer. "Back in Bastion, we're told to hide our runes. We can use them, but we have to be cautious about it. When we're taught how to draw the runes, our masters teach us in hushed tones, almost as if they're ashamed. But here, there's so much enthusiasm. Joy. It's refreshing."

"As well it should be," Tillmin said. "We sometimes get this strange idea that serving the Singularity is supposed to be dour and devoid of any happiness."

"Like Hirfan?" The words slipped out of Everys before she could think better of them.

Tillmin smiled. "He is... a challenge, to be sure. Joy calls to him, but he steadfastly clings to the past."

"Why?"

He hesitated. "That is not my story to tell. But you are correct. Hirfan radiates seriousness. Sometimes that is appropriate. When we remember Downcasting. When we are confronted by our failures. But think of the trust that the Singularity has for us, that He entrusts this world to us. Such love! Such faith!"

"Such a mess that we've made of it," Everys said with a sad smile.

"I suppose so." Tillmin took another sip of tea and his gaze rested on the prism-caster. "Do you know what I love most about the Illuminates, Blessed? Everything we do expresses hope. We know from the ancient texts that light is potentially the most powerful of toratropic inks. In spite of that, no one has ever cast a single rune using light. And yet we don't let that deter us. Even though the task seems impossible, we continue to try. Because we know that if we were to ever succeed, the results would be worth it. After all, the prophet Lonna said, 'With the rune of light, He shall reshape the world.' And reshaping this broken world is worth striving for, don't you think?" He nodded at the cup in her hand. "Now drink your tea, Blessed."

She did, and although the tea had cooled considerably, a warmth trickled through her. Perhaps one day, she could recapture some of that anticipated joy for herself.

6

Bastion wasn't much better than the refugee camps. The mage-kings had destroyed much of the city, and most of the rubble had yet to be cleaned up. Work crews focused on the wealthier parts of town, clearing away what little debris there was. Based on Quartus's estimates, those neighborhoods would likely be back to normal by year's end. But at least half the city had been shattered, and it might be years before they restored everything.

That suited Quartus just fine. Yes, the devastation meant the military patrolled the streets and maintained a strict curfew, but it also meant there were plenty of places to hide. They had found the ruins of a hotel that once catered to the nobility on the edge of Gilded Lock. The entire structure looked on the verge of collapse, but the building was mostly deserted. There were a few other squatters in it, but they had quickly figured out that most of them didn't care what anyone else did, as long as they were left alone.

It took them a week to make sure their room was secure, and that they had access to food and water. Once they were sure that they were safe, he started plotting his next move.

He needed an ally, someone close to the so-called king. And Quartus knew exactly who he should target.

"Elamek?" Yusra asked. "The Minister of Agriculture?"

"Before the coup, Elamek was an outspoken supporter of Everys. From what I've heard, at several parties, he unironically declared his love for her," Quartus said. "Nothing inappropriate, just genuine devotion for her."

"But he survived the purge," Yusra said. "So it may not have been true."

Quartus grunted. That was a good point. After Brencis took the palace, he had dismissed dozens of people from the previous regime. Only a few of the advisers from Narius's council remained: Masruq, the finance minister; Bokil, the Minister of Internal Security; Elamek, the agricultural minister; and Yull, the foreign minister.

"His love for her was real," Quartus said. "I'm willing to bet my life on it."

"And mine too?" Yusra asked quietly.

Quartus's head snapped back, her words stinging. She wouldn't meet his gaze, studying her fingers that twisted together in her lap.

"Yusra, we've been over this. Brencis is part of the mage-kings' conspiracy, the same one that your master sent you here to investigate. Don't you think he'd want you to do something about him?"

Yusra didn't answer, but he had learned how to read the uncertainty in her expression. His question hadn't been fair, and he knew it. Yusra's master had done something to her before sending her to the Dynasty. She had a strange case of amnesia, unable to name her master, and it also meant she couldn't be entirely sure what her master's wishes would be in this circumstance. But this wasn't the first time Yusra had expressed doubts about Quartus's plans.

Maybe if he tried a different approach. "What am I supposed to do, Yusra? He's stolen my brother's throne. He's likely the one who killed both Narius and Everys. Shouldn't he be held accountable for that?"

She finally met his gaze. "Of course he should. But is this really the right way to go about it? Won't this create more chaos?"

It could. Killing Brencis might pitch the Dynasty into even more confusion. But he didn't care. Justice and honor demanded Brencis die.

He waved away Yusra's words. "We'll worry about that when Brencis is gone. For now, we enlist Elamek to our cause."

Yusra pursed her lips into a thin line, but she sighed and nodded. "How do you propose we do that? I doubt he'll be open to a visit from a disgraced prince and a Dalark agent."

Quartus smiled thinly. "We could be surprised there, but you're right, it's not a gamble worth trying. Instead, we'll rely on Elamek's largess."

"How do we do that?" Yusra asked.

Quartus turned on the crier and scrolled through several saved news stories. Once he found the right one, a pleasant-looking Grerid woman appeared on the vidscreen and smiled brightly.

"Considering the suffering of the common people of Bastion, Supreme Prelate Istragon has called on the nobility to observe the practice of *methok rue*. On the first day of the week, those in particularly dire straits are encouraged to go to the manor houses of the nobility to submit petitions for support."

Quartus muted the sound. "I've confirmed Elamek is doing as Istragon suggested. The past two weeks, his house in Gilded Lock has been swamped with petitioners."

"And we're going to somehow get to the front of the line and ask, 'Instead of financial help, could you help us commit some light assassination?'"

He smirked, almost laughing at the joke. "Tempting, but not quite. From what I've heard, the nobles are swamped with petitioners. But they can't just turn them all away or else they could anger the Supreme Prelate and, through him, the king."

"The poor dears," Yusra murmured.

"Indeed. So during the daylight hours, their security forces are completely overwhelmed with trying to keep order. The local constables are strained past their capacity to help as well. And with the military having to maintain order in the refugee camps and the rest of the city..." He let his voice trail off, hoping she'd pick up where he left off.

Her smile brightened. "Elamek's manor will be vulnerable to people trying to sneak in through the back."

His smile broadened as well. This was why he relished working with her. Their thoughts often synced like this. "In two days, the petitioners will be at Elamek's front door, so we slip in the back and wait to see him. Easy as anything."

Yusra's expression faltered for a moment, but then she nodded. "We'll see."

Quartus leaned back, threading his hands behind his head. Yes, they would.

7

K avi appeared in the door of Narius's room and beckoned for him to follow. He levered himself out of his chair, wincing as his back twinged. But he smiled when that was the only pain he experienced.

She led him past the nurses' station to an elevator, which took them up out of the basement clinic. Narius's stomach twisted as they rose. The last time he had felt this way, he was still serving in the military, hunting for Dunestrider separatists. He was deep in enemy territory, and his body wasn't about to let him forget. So he did what he had been taught: take a deep breath, relax his hands, and focus on the mission. The same mission he'd decided on the moment he'd woken up in Innana's care.

He was going to return to Bastion. He would retake his throne. But first, he would make sure Everys was safe.

She had to have survived. He couldn't accept any alternatives. But the only way to know for sure would be to return to Bastion. And the only person who could make that happen was Innana. So whatever her game was, he'd play along. At least, for now.

After ascending at least a hundred floors in the elevator, they emerged onto what appeared to be a circular, open-air balcony. It took Narius a moment to realize thick glass enclosed the entire room. He walked past a long conference table surrounded by high-backed chairs, then past a sitting area with low sofas and looked out the windows. His breath caught in his throat.

Utuaa, the capital city of the Dalark Imperium. The heart of the city was ringed by larger buildings, similar in appearance to the glass towers that filled the Dynasty's cities. But those towers stood watch over a circular section of the city, one made of squat, brown buildings. While they had all been constructed out of similar bricks, they were wildly different shapes. Some had low domes. Other had steeply slanted roofs. Many of them had borders along their top edges made of shimmering blue stones.

Narius frowned as he studied the skyline. He had never seen the city in person, only images. But there was something unsettling about the view. The various shapes blended into an undulating sea of brown stone, punctuated by blue waves. The city's center felt like rippling water, in constant motion. Narius blinked several times, shaking his head to clear it, but each time he looked closer, the sensation grew stronger. Within a few minutes, his stomach twisted inside him.

"You get used to the effect after a while."

Narius jumped. How had Innana snuck up on him like that? He turned to her. She looked out over the city, her face impassive.

"Behold the Navel of Utuaa, built to exacting precision, following the sacred geometry as revealed by the Potentate Kalibanna. Most consider him a genius with architecture." She smiled at him. "I would say madman, but the two are often related."

Innana gestured for him to come back to the sitting area. Kavi had already perched on the back of a chair. Even though she appeared precariously balanced, Narius suspected she was stable as a rock. Narius settled onto a couch.

"The doctors tell me you are ready to be discharged from their care," Innana said. "That is good news indeed."

"So I can return to the Dynasty now?" Narius tried to keep the hope out of his voice, but he wasn't entirely successful.

"Not yet, no," Innana said. She blew out a long breath, then regarded him, her head tipped to one side. "Tell me, Narius, how much do you know about our religion?"

Back when he had attended school at Pellio's Legacy, he had taken the standard theology courses. While most of them focused on the Dynasty's beliefs, a few had discussed the religions of other nations. And he had spent too much time with Innana's brother, Tirigian, shortly before he and Innana were supposed to get married. Tirigian had spent hours pontificating about the superiority of Dalark's beliefs.

"The Dalark believe that, overarching the entire world, are spirits, the divine ideals of concepts such as love, justice, or 'the divine geometry.'" He winced as a bit of condescension laced his voice. "Once every couple of generations, one of these spirits will choose a human as a 'potentate,' who embodies that ideal to teach the Dalark how they can live out that ideal."

Innana's smile broadened. "A succinct explanation. Seven hundred years ago, Kalibanna was inhabited by the spirit of the divine geometry and, as its potentate, passed on the knowledge of how to create 'pleasing' architecture that mollified the spirits to bring prosperity to our people."

"And it worked?" Narius asked.

She waved a hand around the room. "The proof is all around us. Once Utuaa's Navel had been rebuilt according to the geometry, we conquered our neighbors and brought them under our mandate."

Narius frowned. That seemed rather convenient. His teachers used to speak of a logical fallacy: *after, so because of.* Just because the Imperium conquered their neighbors, that didn't mean it was because they had followed this so-called sacred geometry. But then, his people were just as guilty of the same sort of logical errors. How many of them attributed their success in war to the Perfected Warrior's blessing?

"If it were up to me, we would raze the Navel and jettison the geometry. But it comes from the spirits, as revealed by the potentates, so it cannot be changed. And thus it is for so much of our society. Once a potentate has revealed the will of the universe as embodied by the spirits, not even the emperor himself can undo it.

"That is why, for so many centuries, our culture has stagnated. Yes, the spirits have inspired us toward certain progress, but in other places, we have remained as we have been for far too long."

Narius fought to keep from grimacing. While he didn't doubt what Innana said was true, he also knew that in some ways, the Imperium was more advanced than the Dynasty, especially in terms of technology.

"But I intend to change that. And to do so, I will need your help," Innana continued.

He shifted in his seat, uncomfortable at the hungry look in her eyes. "Innana, if you're thinking that my offer of marriage is still viable, I have to tell you, it's not. I love my wife and—"

Innana blinked at him, then guffawed. She clutched her sides and laughed for several minutes, finally swiping away tears from her eyes.

"That is the furthest thing from my mind, dear Narius," she said. "I appreciate your latest marriage offer for what it was: a political gambit designed to avoid conflict between our peoples. I know how much you love Everys, and I would never dream of trying to entice you away from her."

Oh. As much as he was relieved by what she said, her matter-of-fact tone still stung a little.

She must have seen the hurt flicker across his face. "Come now, Narius. Can you honestly say that anything other than political expediency ever motivated your proposals? That was certainly the case with your latest offer of marriage."

Once again, Narius shifted in his seat. That was all too true. To avoid open conflict between the Dynasty and the Imperium, Narius had offered to take Innana as a second or possibly third wife. It had been a spur of the moment, desperate gambit that hadn't benefited him. "I'd like to think that I loved you at one point."

"And I loved you too. When we first met and throughout our clandestine courtship, I loved you with all the passion and ardor of a young girl who has met her first love. But tell me the truth: do you feel any of that for me now?"

"No." The answer came easily enough. "Not like that."

She smiled. "And neither do I. Oh, I would have accepted your offer gladly. We would have made formidable partners, and we could have shaken the world together. But you found your true love. And I have found mine as well."

That caught his attention. He shouldn't have been so surprised. He hadn't exactly been faithful to Innana in the waning days of their hidden courtship when he fell in love with Everys. But this was the first time he had heard anything about Innana having a different suitor.

"Who?" The question slipped out of him.

She nodded toward the window. "The Dalark Imperium."

Narius blinked, his surprise melting away into disappointment. He had actually hoped for something less cliché.

She glanced at his face and laughed again. "I know, every politician says something like that, but it's very true. I don't want my people to languish under outdated beliefs and systems any longer. The spirits and potentates could only bring us so far. Now I want us to go the rest of the way. And I need your help to achieve it."

"How?" Narius asked.

Innana leaned forward and touched some controls on a low table between them. The lights in the room dimmed, and a hologram sprang to life over the table. Narius flinched at the sudden burst of light. Yet another reminder of the Dalark's technological superiority. That Innana took such a marvel in stride was unsettling.

An image formed of a statue of a man in Dalark robes and wraps. His face was elongated and stylized, but Narius could still recognize the distant look in his expression. He stared up toward the sky, a rapturous expression on his face.

"This is the Potentate Senen. He lived two hundred years ago, embodying the spirit of authority. It was his writings and teachings that shaped our modern understanding of the Emperor's role in society. Our government is based entirely on his ideas," Innana said. "But in the middle of his writings, there is a curious statement."

She adjusted the controls, and the image flickered, replaced with an image of an open book. The writing on the page was faded with age, using a script Narius couldn't read but guessed was likely Dalark. Then the letters on the page glowed and rose from the book, which vanished, leaving just the words.

Innana nodded at the text, which rotated in the air between them. "'The greatest of rulers will be he for whom death is just a nuisance, a buzzing fly to be ground under his heel. He will be the one far greater than the spirits, far superior to all the potentates. In his hands will be the power and authority to reshape the world, for he will be the only one who could claim every bit as his own. And as proof of his identity, he shall be the king whom death could not hold.'"

Narius frowned. "That seems a bit... grandiose."

Innana chuckled. "That's how most scholars describe this passage. Many attribute it to Senen imbibing of too much new wine too early in the morning. Others see this as aspirational: 'this is how every emperor should regard himself and behave.' My brother sees it that way, as did my father before him."

"And you?" Narius asked.

Her smile sharpened. "I see this passage as a key. The method by which I will set my people free. All I need to do is create a king whom death could not hold."

A chill swept through Narius. Shattered Spear, she couldn't mean *him*, could she? He hadn't exactly ground death under his foot. He had been rescued by Kavi.

"Now wait a moment, Innana. I'm not this king!"

"In reality, no. But you died. That's the official story coming out of the Xoniel Dynasty, broadcast to every corner of the globe. Everyone in the Imperium knows that you are, for all intents and purposes, dead. But if you were to turn up in the Imperium, alive and well? There are those who would think you are Senen's king."

The chill that encased Narius twisted into a knot in his stomach. "Are you suggesting that we found a cult with me as its leader?"

"Nothing so sinister. Instead, you would be the catalyst that would allow me to achieve the goal I've held for so long: taking control of the Imperium so I might reform it." She rose and stepped toward the window, indicating the city with a sweep of her hand. "My people are ready for change, Narius. They don't approve of the way my father and brother stoked the hostility between our peoples. They want to see the Imperium shed its past and march boldly into the future. But they need a spark. They need a push. They need someone to show them that change is not only possible, but achievable."

"They need me," he finished for her.

"No. They need *me*. But in Dalark society, I am merely a shadow in my brother's house until he can marry me off for political gain. But if Senen's king, whom death could not hold, were to name me the true Empress, they would rise behind me. That is what I need you to do. Be the spark. Be the catalyst. Be that king long enough to unseat my brother."

Narius grimaced, the idea feeling sour as he considered it. He could see the tactical benefit for the Dynasty. Neutralizing the threat of the Dalark Imperium made sense. With an ally on the throne in Utuaa, he could focus on dealing with Brencis without the added distraction of Dalark nipping at his heels. The offer was tempting...

But he shook his head. Destabilizing Tirigian's government could take months, even years. By the time Innana took the throne—if she ever did—Brencis would be so firmly entrenched in Bastion he'd never be removed. If Narius was going to save the Dynasty, he had to go back now.

"I'm sorry, Innana," he said. "But the Dynasty needs me more. I need to go back."

Innana studied him, her face expressionless. The effect was unnerving. He had no clue what she was feeling. Anger? Disappointment? Frustration?

"Very well. Kavi will plan for you to return to the Dynasty's holdings. Just let her know where you want to be sent."

Kavi sat up straighter and signed something so fast that Narius couldn't decipher it. An objection? A question? He didn't know.

He rose and nodded to Innana. "Thank you for understanding."

He started for the elevator. While he didn't look behind him to check, he knew that Kavi had followed.

"Before you go, Narius, I have one question for you. What will your first step be after you return?" Innana called after him.

He hesitated for a moment, then turned toward her. "I'll search out nobles and military units who are still loyal to me. We'll rally our forces, find a place to hunker down and plan—the Cold Light forests, maybe—and then—"

Innana rose from her couch and shook her head. "If that is your plan, may I suggest one that will save you time? Just fly into Bastion and turn yourself over to Brencis now."

His head snapped back as if struck. "Wh-what?"

"I don't think you understand the situation in the Dynasty," Innana said. "I barely have a handle on it either, but from what I've been able to determine, you would be hard-pressed to find people still loyal to you. Half of your advisory council has sworn fealty to Brencis and the other half has been dismissed. There are rumors of an insurgency brewing in Bastion, but it is nascent and not a credible threat. Because of Brencis's status as a genuine war hero, most of the military has sworn loyalty to him as well."

Narius tamped down on a spike of frustration.

His mind landed on a thought. "If I can find Paine, he'll be able to help me. He's always had an innate understanding of..."

His voice trailed off as Innana and Kavi exchanged a look.

"What?" he prompted.

Innana sighed. "It brings me no pleasure to share this, Narius, but Paine has sworn loyalty to Brencis as well."

An icy chasm tore open in Narius's chest. No. That couldn't be true. Paine would never.

But Innana leaned forward and adjusted the controls of the hologram, replacing the image of Senen's prophecy with a video. Narius recognized the throne room in the royal palace immediately. There was Brencis, perched on the throne like a preening fool. And kneeling before him was...

Narius's legs wobbled. Paine knelt before Brencis, his arms open, palms facing the new king. It was a pose Narius immediately recognized. Paine was indeed pledging his loyalty to Brencis.

Before he could digest that, the image was replaced by Paine sitting down with a member of the criers' guild. He recognized her; she often skulked around the palace, hoping to glean information from the bureaucrats.

"You have to admit, Vizier, your shift in loyalty is unusual. Everyone knows how close you were to the previous king," she said.

Paine offered her a thin smile. "I was indeed loyal to King Narius. To a fault, some would say. But that was unwise. Narius meant well. He always did. But we can lay much of the disaster that has befallen the Dynasty at his feet. Had he been more decisive, we may have been able to stave off much of the chaos that has unfolded."

How could he say that? Yes, Narius and Paine had disagreed about the direction Narius wanted to take the Dynasty, especially in those last days, but to so openly admit it like that? How could his friend do this to him?

"And you believe that King Brencis will do a better job?" The crier's tone was a prompt.

Paine's smile twitched, but he nodded. "That is my hope, yes."

Innana tapped a control, and the footage disappeared.

"If you were to return to the Dynasty now, I'm afraid that you wouldn't accomplish much. You would have few supporters and even fewer friends."

Narius's breathing turned ragged. A wave of dizziness crested over him, and he wanted nothing more than to lie down, curl up, and let the world continue without him. But he couldn't. Not until he asked one more question.

"What about Everys?" he whispered. "What about my wife?"

Again, Innana and Kavi exchanged unreadable looks. Then Innana smiled sadly.

"Unfortunately, I could not learn what happened to Everys. We have heard no reports of her death, if that is any consolation, but she has completely disappeared from the Dynasty's holdings. She might be safe. Or she might not."

Heat stung Narius's eyes, and he wanted nothing more than to cry. Even as the urge overwhelmed him, he could hear his father chiding him for showing such childish emotions. Kings didn't cry. They especially didn't blubber, which is what he really wanted to do.

"I am so sorry to be the one to share this information with you, Narius, but I will make you a promise. If you stay and help me, when you return to the Dynasty, it will be with the full might of the Dalark Imperium behind you. Our influence with the other nations. Our military. Our economy. We will not rest until you are restored to your throne in Bastion."

Narius shifted his weight. She had a point, one he wished he could ignore. But he couldn't.

"Please. I've been waiting to bring down my brother for years. This is our best chance. You help me, and I will help you. I promise."

Narius's gaze flicked to Kavi. She offered him a half smile and a shrug, along with a signed message he thought meant, *What do you have to lose?*

He sighed. "All right. I'll do it."

8

Everys took a deep breath and stepped through the door. She was about to enter what the grafted called "the ballroom." It was a gorgeous space. The Cold Light had constructed the Embassy out of seven different trees, their trunks woven together to create the largest structure in the Shade. The ballroom was nestled in the middle, with all seven trunks clearly visible, the individual trees' branches woven together to not only close in the gaps but to create the floor as well. Every time she stepped into the ballroom, Everys could imagine it being used for its original purpose. She could almost hear echoes of music and the murmur of cheerful conversation. She wished she could see it used like that instead of what her advisers had turned it into.

No one called it the ballroom anymore. Instead, everyone, including the grafted and the Cold Light, referred to it by its new name, the war room.

A large table had been set up in the middle of the room underneath a vidprojector. Several aides scurried around the table, setting out glasses of water and digital scribers. Everys drifted to the head of the table and glanced over the data that was already projected on its surface: a map of the forest, each settlement highlighted in bright blue. If she was reading it correctly, the forest was secure with no sign of any interlopers. But it appeared as though Brencis had forces snooping along the western border and Dalark had some units slithering along the southern with a few naval ships in the sea to the north.

She sensed a presence behind her to her right. She glanced over her shoulder. Challix smiled at her.

"Anything I should know before we get started?" Everys asked.

Challix frowned, tipping her head to one side. "Nothing of any import. Strategist Overturn has been introduced to Firestruck through a grafted named Effort. I didn't observe, but it sounds like the conversation was productive."

Everys nodded, a smile tugging at her lips. She was glad that Overturn had finally made it to the forest. When she had first arrived, the Cold Light had promised they would go to war for her. While they had welcomed both her and any Dynasty troops who had defected to the forest, they had yet to give her any sign of when this war might happen. With Overturn here, maybe they would finally get some answers.

"I hesitate to mention this, Blessed, but it has been more than three months now. You really should name a new Swordbound."

Everys bit her lip. She knew she had to, but she didn't want to. Rewether had also been quietly reminding her lately she had to name a new Swordbound, a special guard who carried a ceremonial sword with him or her to fight duels for Everys. Her last Swordbound, Kevtho, had died several months earlier, defending her against Brencis. She knew she had to do it, but a part of her felt like doing so would be a betrayal of Kevtho's memory. She kept putting it off, but she knew she wouldn't be able to do that for long.

Before Challix could say anything else, the door to the war room opened. Yllana, Effort, and two other grafted entered. All four of them were younger than Everys by several years. The youngest appeared to be only eighteen, while Yllana was the oldest at approximately twenty-two. They chatted and laughed together as they walked in. Vines wrapped each one of them, and leaves were woven into their hair. The plant matter even pierced their skin, marking them as grafted.

When Yllana saw her, her smile broadened. She excused herself and strolled over to Everys. "And how are you today, Blessed? Are you looking forward to the Moonslight Festival?"

Everys forced herself to smile. No, she wasn't. Not really. But she knew she would have to preside over the celebration. Yllana had been dropping hints for weeks now.

The grafted must have read the hesitation in her expression. She touched Everys's shoulder. "If this is too much, Blessed, the Yoreroot would understand if you excuse yourself..."

Smudges and splatters, that was the last thing she could do! The Cold Light had been so generous in taking her in. She couldn't insult her hosts by refusing to take part in one of the most important celebrations they had. "No, I am looking forward to it." She tried to force her expression to appear more genuine. "Is there anything I should prepare? Anything that needs to be done?"

Yllana shook her head. "No, the Cold Light have been making preparations for months. And since you are their guest, there technically isn't anything for you to do."

Everys easily picked up on the unspoken prompt. "'Technically?'"

"Well, there is a tradition that if an outside ruler attends the Festival, that ruler presents something that represents their people to the Yoreroot. A gift, a piece of art, something like that."

She was supposed to what? Create some artwork? How was she supposed to do that? Well, she could always draw runes on something, but that she was toratropic mage wasn't widely known in the forest. The last thing she'd want to do was broadcast her abilities and heritage, especially when so many people still mistrusted Siporans.

Challix cleared her throat. "Actually, Blessed, an idea occurs to me. We do know someone who has a background as an artist, and he's been looking for something meaningful to do."

Everys frowned, but then she caught up with Challix's thought. She laughed. Why hadn't she thought of that?

As soon as the meeting ended, Everys practically flew out of the Embassy, with Rewether and another of her guards trailing her. After a few minutes of walking, they reached the edge of the Shade. Once again, the sudden transition from settlement to forest was startling. It was like the trees were barely tolerating their presence, pressing up to the border to reclaim the small pocket of civilization.

Eventually, they came to a gnarled tree. This one was massive, at least a hundred feet around, with roots as thick as she was. It jutted up through the forest canopy, its limbs twisted and creaking. Everys circled around it, picking through the tangle of roots until she came to a depression between two roots. She offered a smile to Rewether and his partner, who took up position. Then, squaring her shoulders, Everys stepped down into the hole.

She had to duck as she descended, but soon, she found herself in front of a round wooden door. She grabbed the iron mallet that hung near the door and thumped on the wood. Everys pushed her shoulder against the wood, forcing it open. Cool air washed over her as she entered the hollowed-out tunnels. She had to stoop in some places, her hair brushing along the dirt ceiling. Her hand ran along the rough walls, her fingers skipping along thick cables that were woven together to hold back the soil. She came to a fork in the tunnel and paused, listening carefully. A faint skittering came from her left, so she headed down that branch.

The floor sloped, and she emerged into a hollowed-out space filled with shadowy webs. The white strands swayed back and forth in an almost hypnotic rhythm. Everys paused. She knew better than to rush into this room. The hollow's occupant had a habit of not paying attention to where he was going.

Sure enough, a large creature scuttled out of a side tunnel. He resembled an enormous spider, walking on his hind four legs. He used his arms, both his larger upper pair and his smaller lower pair, to part the curtain of webs. Two smaller appendages on the back of his thorax vibrated so quickly they appeared to be a blur. As strange as he appeared, though, the most noticeable thing about him was the mask he wore. Everys had never seen his true face, because he always wore the same mask as the rest of the Diradae, an oval shape made of a gray material. The mask's face was an elongated, stylized human face, completely expressionless.

"Hello, Occ!" Everys called.

He whirled around and let out an almost ear-piercing squeal. He hurried forward, making a chittering sound that set Everys's nerves on edge, even though she knew it meant he was excited.

"Oh, Blessed, when I heard the pounding, I hoped it would be you! Come in, come in!" Occ motioned toward the room. "I have chairs in here somewhere!"

Occ shuffled through the room, pulling away webs until he found a wooden chair. He motioned for her to sit, then he settled in next to the chair, tucking his four legs under his massive frame.

"So what brings you to my hovel?" he asked.

"I have a favor to ask," she said. "You used to be an artist, correct?"

Occ ducked his head, his lower arms swiping across his chest in a gesture Everys knew meant he was embarrassed. "I dabbled. If anything, I was more of an art historian. Why?"

"You've heard the Moonslight Festival is coming up?"

"I have indeed!" Occ's hind appendages made a skittering sound. "The grafted have told me so much about it, I can hardly wait. It sounds absolutely delightful!"

"Well, I've just been informed that it's traditional for visiting dignitaries to present the Cold Light with some sort of gift. Art or something similar. Challix suggested that you might create something for me."

Occ stilled, so much so that Everys worried he had somehow frozen. Was this normal? She was still learning to decipher the Diradae's unique body language. But then he flapped both sets of arms and his hind appendages rattled.

"It would be my absolute honor to do so. I'll admit, I've been struggling with finding my purpose since coming here, Blessed. I had feared that I would never find something suitable for me to do. But art, I can do. Here! Let me show you!"

Occ ducked out of the room. Everys wondered if she was supposed to follow him, but just as she rose from her chair, he returned. But he did so empty-handed. Everys frowned at his hands, then looked up to ask what he was doing.

Her words caught in her throat. Instead of the usual expressionless, generic face, his mask now appeared to be a stylized version of Narius's face. Her heart slammed in her chest, cold sluicing over her skin.

"Blessed?" Occ's voice sounded like it was drifting down a long tunnel. "Are you all right?"

No, she wasn't, but how could she explain? In the moments after Narius died, Everys had tried to summon the Singularity to revive him. Instead, she had received a frightening vision, one filled with war and conflict that culminated in seeing a creature that had been stitched together with parts of the different races. But the most memorable part had been the Diradae mask the creature wore, one that was fashioned to resemble Narius's face. And now Occ had recreated that image. Her breath stuttered, and she struggled to keep from vomiting.

Occ hurried to her side and ducked low. Up close, Everys could see that the texture of this mask was different. Where Occ's usual mask appeared smooth, this was rough, like it had been constructed out of layers of rope. Everys wanted to touch the mask, to run her hand along it, at first to see what it felt like, but then because she could pretend it wasn't a mask but her husband, joining her again for one brief—

"Blessed?" Occ asked again. "What's going on?"

His gentle question snapped her back to reality. She realized that her hand hovered over the mask's cheek, so she snatched it away.

"Th-that's a wonderf..." The word caught in her throat. "You made that?"

Occ didn't answer. Instead, he darted out of the room, down the same tunnel, and came back wearing his original mask. He approached her cautiously, making a high-pitched keening with his rear appendages.

"I am so sorry, Blessed. I wasn't thinking. I only wanted to show you what I can create. It's a tribute to my deep respect for your husband. I should have realized it would be too traumatic for you. I am so sorry. I absolutely understand if I've offended you with my insensitive mistake. Please, find someone else to create your gift!"

Everys took several deep breaths to calm her stuttering heart, then forced a shaky smile to her lips. "No, Occ. Narius would be honored. You really made that mask yourself?"

"Using my webbing, yes," Occ said. "Some Diradae artists use the ore we mine from the deeps. Others use fungus or other organic material. But I feel using my own webbing is more personal."

Her gaze roamed around the room. What she had assumed was just a poorly cleaned space took on a new life. Along one wall, Occ had woven a series of triangles into the webbing, all of them different sizes. On another wall, multiple circles intersected to create a soothing pattern. Being an artist must come naturally to him.

"Occ, I would love for you to create a gift for me to present to the Cold Light. I can think of no one I'd entrust this to."

Occ preened, his lower hands rubbing his upper arms. "Very well. I accept your commission. What are you envisioning?"

They spent the next two hours brainstorming. While she initially didn't have any ideas, he was able to draw out her expectations—something that symbolized the coming together of the Dynasty and the Cold Light. A piece that spoke to their future, evoking mutual trust and collaboration. By the time they finished, Occ practically vibrated with ideas, and for the first time in weeks, Everys could honestly say she couldn't wait for the Festival. Hopefully, it would be the start of something wonderful.

9

T hankfully, Elamek was a generous individual with *methok rue*. The Minister of Agriculture was not only trying to live up to Istragon's call, he was determined to exceed it. At least, that's what the rumors on the streets said.

Quartus had always had a talent for whispering the right words into the right ears.

Beggars pressed against the line of Elamek's personal guards and tried to shove past them. The desperation in the air was so thick Quartus almost choked on it. Elamek's protectors had formed a cordon around his house, but even with help from the local constabulary, the desperate outnumbered them.

"We should move before this turns into a full-scale riot," Yusra whispered. "If the military gets involved..."

She didn't have to say anything else. If the military intervened, there'd be little chance they could sneak inside Elamek's house. So he followed her along the edge of the crowd.

One of the house guards spotted them and shouted, "Where do you think you're going? Supplicants remain out front."

Yusra opened her arms. "Do I look like I need your lord's help? We're visiting my cousin next door, and she doesn't want any attention."

The guard looked ready to object, but Quartus shot him a pointed glare. His mouth snapped shut, and he waved them along. Yusra smirked at Quartus and the two of them slipped between the houses.

Once they emerged from the narrow walkway, Quartus scanned the back of Elamek's house. His guess had been correct. Only two guards watched the back of the house, but they were distracted by the chaos out front. He easily boosted Yusra to the top of the wall. Then she helped him up and over. If they'd tripped an alarm, no one responded.

The two of them sneaked across the backyard, past an impressive sculpture garden, and up to the back of the house. The Trickster must have been smiling on them; they didn't encounter anyone. Even better, they found an unlocked door.

Quartus took the lead. Although he had never been to Elamek's manor before, he had been to plenty like it. He led Yusra past the kitchen. A quick check of Elamek's private study revealed no one inside, which left the upstairs.

As they scaled the stairs, Quartus examined the portraits of Elamek's ancestors. All of them were dour faced and scowling except for Elamek and his family. Quartus's stomach flipped. He knew Elamek was married, but he hadn't realized he had three young daughters. Was it right for him to ask the minister to join his plot to kill Brencis?

At the top of the stairs, Yusra tugged on his arm and gestured down one side of the hall, indicating she would check those rooms. He nodded and headed in the opposite direction. He found bedrooms, three of which were clearly set up for Elamek's daughters, the fourth apparently a guest room. All of them were empty. Where was Elamek's family?

He turned around. Yusra had pressed up against a wall, her eyes wide and prompting. She jerked her head toward one open door and nodded vigorously.

Quartus hurried down the hall. As soon as he passed her, Yusra fell into step behind him. He paused outside the door, took a deep breath, and slipped through.

He stepped into a darkened room, a private den by the looks of it. Elamek sat in an overstuffed chair facing a fireplace, but instead of watching the flames, the minister stared out a large window overlooking the front street. Even though the window was closed, the sounds of the crowd easily bled into the room. Gone was the minister's smile from the portrait, replaced by a gaunt and haggard look. He slumped in the chair, holding a glass filled with an amber liquid.

Quartus motioned for Yusra to move past him into the room, then he eased the door shut. Once that was done, Quartus stepped forward and cleared his throat. "Elamek."

The minister nearly dropped his glass. His gaze landed on Quartus and his eyes widened. "P-Prince Quartus?"

"I need help. I think you can provide it," Quartus said.

Elamek shrank away from him. "Me? I'm the last one you'd want to help, given what happened the last time we saw each other."

Bitterness flashed through Quartus's mind. Elamek had been part of the trial where Narius had declared him outlaw and exiled him. As much as that miscarriage of justice still galled him, Quartus shoved the angry thoughts aside.

"Tell me, where do your true loyalties lie?" Quartus asked

A roar from the front of the house punctuated his question. Yusra shot him a wide-eyed look. The whole situation was about to boil over outside, and the last thing they wanted to do was linger. But he focused on Elamek.

"M-my true loyalties?" Elamek asked. "Wh-what do you mean?"

"Come off it, Elamek." Quartus strode forward, trying to loom over the minister. "You made no secret of how much you admired the former queen. And I would have thought you loyal to my brother as well."

"I am. I was," Elamek spluttered.

"Then why are you serving the man who usurped Narius's throne?" Quartus wanted to shout the question, but he knew he couldn't. So he tried to inject as much anger into his whispered words as he could.

Elamek blanched and his whole body trembled. "Y-you don't understand. I didn't want to. But I didn't have a choice."

Quartus snorted.

"I didn't!" Elamek insisted. "Did you hear what happened to Filamon? He's dead, Quartus. Killed by Brencis himself. After he arrived at the palace, he gathered all of Narius's advisers in the throne room and demanded us to swear loyalty to him. Filamon refused, so Brencis drew this strange, broken sword and used it to killed him. And when it was covered in their blood, the sword's blade became this... this *thing*. This otherworldly blade that seemed to draw the life out of all of us. We had no choice, or he would have killed us with it too!"

The man had gone mad. Or he was drunk. Quartus's gaze flicked to the spilled glass. How many of those had he drunk already? Or could it be something more sinister? That blade Elamek described sounded like Siporan magic. Had the mage-kings done something to Elamek?

"I c-couldn't do that to my girls, s-so I did what I had to. I didn't want to. Brencis is a monster. Always has been. Have you heard what he's doing?"

Quartus exchanged a look with Yusra. She shrugged.

"He's sent soldiers to the refugee camps and started sorting the occupants by race. Plissk in one, Dunestriders in another, Weyfir in another."

"Why would he do that?" Yusra asked.

"Supposedly, he's going to deport them all to their home regions. He claims Bastion can't support so many displaced people, but that isn't true! I've seen the numbers. If we're cautious about how we distribute our resources, we can easily help those affected by the disaster. But Brencis won't listen. He keeps ranting about his 'glorious vision for a stronger Dynasty.'"

Quartus stooped down to look Elamek in the eyes. The other man shied away from him.

"Elamek, I'm going to kill Brencis. That will stop all of this. But I need you to get me in the palace."

At first, Quartus didn't think that Elamek had heard him. He continued to stare at the window, his forehead growing more and more slick with sweat. Then he blinked and refocused on Quartus.

"Into the... to kill..." He nodded, his forehead pinched into a frown. "Y-yes... I could do that, I think. They're always looking for new servants. If we got the right uniforms, the right disguise, we could..."

Yusra grabbed Quartus's shoulder and squeezed. He swallowed a frustrated grunt, but stood and allowed her to pull him away from the chair.

"We can't go ahead with this, Quartus," she whispered.

"Why not? He has a way in."

"Listen to him! He sounds like he's barely holding on to his sanity. And if Brencis is killing people he suspects are disloyal, what will he do to Elamek and his family if you fail?"

Quartus turned back to Elamek. "Where are your wife and children?"

"Far from here." Elamek chuckled softly. "We've heard rumors that... well, that if someone needs a safe place, the Cold Light will give them shelter. I sent them to the forest a week ago."

Quartus smiled at Yusra, who shook her head and crossed her arms.

"So will you help me?" Quartus asked.

With a shuddering sigh, Elamek ran his hand through his hair. "I will, but only—"

Elamek's voice pinched into a gurgle, and his eyes widened. He looked down at a dagger embedded in his chest. Quartus dropped into a defensive crouch, making himself as small a target as possible. His gaze snapped around the room. Where had that come from?

Inky smoke boiled out of a spot on the fireplace's black wall, pouring over the still-burning fire. Oddly, the fire didn't seem affected by the shadows. The spilling darkness simply swallowed it up, creating what almost appeared to be a pitch-black hole in the wall.

Quartus backed away from the fireplace. "We need to—"

Someone burst out of the shadows. The attacker wore black from head to toe, including a hood and mask that completely obscured his features. He didn't appear armed at all. Quartus took another step backward, his hands up.

The attacker pulled the dagger from Elamek's chest. The blade was different than Quartus expected, strangely truncated. Blood flowed along the blade into six patterns etched into the side. The moment the blood soaked into those grooves, the color leeched from the room as darkness rushed to the weapon and formed a longer blade.

Quartus's eyes widened. He had heard of such weapons. *Ur-ke-leshen*, the cursed blades used by the Siporan Ascendancy. Absolutely lethal in the right hands, and he suspected this killer had just those hands.

Before Quartus could react, the attacker lunged forward. Quartus dodged, but barely, feeling the blade slice through the air next to his right cheek.

"Move!" Yusra pulled him out of the room.

Quartus tripped over his own feet. A strange pulling sensation grew in his chest and he felt as though his limbs were wrapped in heavy metal weights. He could easily just lie down right there and fall asleep and—

"Come on!" Yusra's voice warbled, like she was speaking to him from a dream.

They practically fell down the stairs. The attacker charged after them, his blade ready to strike.

With a cry, Yusra threw a vase at him. At the last second, the vase's trajectory curved away from the assassin, as if nudged by unseen hands. The attacker leaped the rest of the way, landing nimbly at the bottom of the stairs.

Quartus froze, staring at the blade. The shadow dripped like thick liquid, vanishing before it hit the floor. Once again, Quartus felt drawn to the blade. He stumbled forward a step and the man in black leveled the blade toward Quartus's heart.

Then, with a shout, guards appeared behind Yusra. Their weapons snapped to their shoulders and they opened fire. Yusra grabbed Quartus's shoulders and dragged him to the floor. Flechettes ripped through the air over them. But like with the vase, the projectiles bent around the assassin, thudding uselessly into the walls. Then the attacker leaped at the guards, defying gravity, his body spinning at a dizzying speed as he tore into his victims.

"We need to go!" Yusra shouted over the guard's dying screams.

Quartus didn't argue. They scrambled from the floor and sprinted out the back of Elamek's house. Yusra vaulted to the top of the wall, then paused long enough to help him scale it as well. They dropped to the ground and ran. As they fled, the strange numbness that had encased his mind unraveled, only to be replaced with anger. Another death Brencis had to answer for. And Quartus was all the more determined to make sure that he did.

10

Narius hadn't felt this nervous in a long time. Speaking before the Ethnarch Parliament or in the Hall of All Voices? Not his favorite activity, but he could do it. Facing down a rampaging Diradae in an arena? It had nearly killed him, but he would do it again. Sit down for a strategy session with his council when all of them thought he had lost his mind? A pleasure compared to what he was expecting.

Back when he'd attended Pellio's Legacy, Paine had convinced him and their friend Jesik to perform in a theatrical production. Because of his status, the director had cast him in the lead opposite Jesik. It had been an adaptation of a romantic myth, requiring both he and Jesik to share several intimate moments on stage. That had been awkward enough, and the memory dredged up some secondhand embarrassment, especially given how things had ended between Jesik and Paine. But after that humiliating experience, he had sworn he'd never perform in the theater again. Yet here he was.

As the memories of his last performance washed over him, his mind hitched on Paine. His vizier. His best friend when he was younger. They had fought before he'd been so badly injured, but was that really enough for Paine to betray him? He couldn't understand why that had happened. He clenched his jaw. All the more reason to get home again. He needed answers. He needed Everys. He needed to be there.

There was a soft knock on the door. He turned as Kavi slipped inside, carrying a large box. She set it on the bed next to him.

"What's this?" He gestured toward the box.

Your costume.

Why was she smirking? Before he could ask, Kavi slunk out of the room. He opened the box and nearly dropped the cover. What was Innana thinking?

He picked up the shirt, which was so stiff he could cut himself on the cuffs or collar. It was a horrible teal color with yellow and red ribbons woven through the arms. The pants were made of a light brown leather with elaborate stitching along the pleats and around the waist. The boots underneath the clothes looked functional, even though the toes were blunt and turned up.

Narius sighed. He should refuse just for his outraged sense of fashion. But that wouldn't help matters. Innana's plan, and he had to go along with it. No matter how uncomfortable he might be.

It took close to fifteen minutes to squeeze into the outfit. Technically, everything fit, but the pants turned out to be snug and the shirt had a mind of its own. But when he emerged from the room, he felt like he was ready for whatever came next.

Until Kavi looked at him and started laughing silently.

"This wasn't my idea, you know," he grumbled.

That's what we all keep telling ourselves, she signed.

Who else was Kavi talking about? But she didn't elaborate. Narius adjusted the clothing, only it wasn't the costume that was chafing. Yes, Innana had saved his life, but this felt like a prank.

Kavi led him to the elevator. But instead of taking him all the way to the top of the tower, they only went up three floors to an underground garage. Eight different transports were lined up, all angled to face a ramp that would presumably take them into the city. Narius stopped to admire the transports. They were like the vehicles he knew back home, resting on six tires. But whereas civilian transports in the Dynasty took design cues from their military cousins, these were sleek, with curving lines and silver accents.

Narius turned to the ramp and looked up at the night sky. He took a deep breath. Even though the air was sharp with the smell of fuel, he still relished the coolness. He was outside his room, taking the first step toward his freedom. How could he not savor the moment?

Kavi snapped her fingers and gestured toward a transport that wasn't as flashy as the others, just a simple matte black. She opened the door and motioned for Narius to slide inside.

"So, where are we going?" Narius asked as she settled in next to him.

...in the Navel. That's where this will start.

He didn't catch the first few words, but she didn't take time to explain. Instead, her seat slid up to the controls, and she fired up the engine. Rather than the loud roar Narius expected, the transport purred as they left the garage.

Much to his surprise, it was night, maybe a few hours into Fourth Watch. The buildings they passed were all glass and steel, outlined with bright green and red neon lines. Narius felt like he had been taken to some futuristic place. Most towers in the Dynasty were utilitarian, with sharp right angles that flaunted their concrete like armor. The buildings here flowed, curving gracefully up into the night sky, almost as if gravity couldn't hold them back.

Something *chirruped* next to him, and a vidscreen slid out of a wall. It flickered, then displayed an image of Innana. "Good evening, Narius. Are you ready to make your debut?"

He snorted, then gestured toward his outfit. "I'd be a lot more ready if I didn't look like something straight out of a children's vid. What am I even supposed to be?"

She smiled. "I know it's not what you're used to, but that outfit evokes the fashions common during Senen's day, mixed with a bit of Dynastic flair. Don't worry, you won't have to wear it all the time. We just wanted your first foray as Senen's king to be noticeable."

Well, he certainly was that. "What am I supposed to do?"

"Kavi is taking you to the Founder's Septagon at the heart of the Navel."

Narius waited for her to elaborate. When she didn't, he gestured. "And..."

"And when you arrive, just do whatever feels natural to you," Innana said. "I have confidence the rest will take care of itself."

"I'm surprised you're not here to supervise," Narius said.

Innana laughed. "Tempting. But better for me to remain in the shadows for now."

Before he could respond, the screen went dark. He grumbled and sank back into his chair, staring out the window.

The transition into the Navel was obvious. The buildings' architecture changed from modern to ancient in a blink, the road narrowing to the point where Narius feared they would get stuck between the buildings. Somehow, though, Kavi squeezed through until she pulled over by a large square. She spun in her chair and motioned for Narius to exit the transport.

He hesitated. "What am I supposed to do? Just go out there and walk around?"

Kavi smiled sympathetically, then reached over and patted his knee. *Do you ... will follow.*

Narius frowned. What did that mean? Unfortunately, Kavi only motioned for him to leave once again. Narius took a deep breath, nodded to himself, and slipped out.

The first thing he noticed was the smell. Old sewage mixed with rotting garbage clawed at his nose. He winced, steadying himself against a wall. Even though he wanted to dive back into the transport, he remembered what his drill instructors had told him: if he ever encountered an overwhelming stink, it was better to power through it than run from it. His smell receptors would die soon enough. As far as he was concerned, the funeral couldn't come quickly enough.

Once he felt steadier, he took stock of his surroundings. Two large stone buildings made of brown stone with blue highlights loomed on either side of them. Up close, he realized the highlights were actually brightly colored rocks, thousands of them cemented together in intricate whorls and slashes. A wave of dizziness crested over him, and he lurched a little. The effect was even more powerful close up. He grumbled and shook his head, trying to clear it. Sacred geometry indeed.

There was an open space ahead, brightly lit and apparently filled with people if Narius judged the noises right. That must be the Founder's Septagon. He headed in that direction, still not sure what he was going to do.

When he stepped into the light, he stopped and stared. The space was indeed a giant septagon, framed by the seven buildings around it. Multiple tiers were connected by low ramps. Large planters bordered each level, but rather than holding flowers or bushes, only dead, scraggly sticks poked up. Despite the late hour, the Septagon was filled with people, but a quick look revealed them for what they were. Homeless. Destitute. People who had nowhere else to go.

This was where Innana wanted him to appear? What was he supposed to do? Go in and talk to people? He had nothing to offer them. The ridiculous outfit didn't come with any money. But Innana had insisted. So he straightened his shoulders and headed across the street.

At first, no one seemed to notice his presence. The people who crowded the Septagon were huddled together for warmth and were conversing in closed off groups. A few eyed him as he passed, their gazes raking over him as if evaluating whether he was worth the trouble. Although he got a few curious looks, no one said anything and turned away as he passed.

With no further thoughts on what to do, he kept moving toward the middle of the Septagon, ascending the tiers until he reached the center. There he found a gigantic statue that, much to his surprise, he recognized. It was the stylized sculpture of Senen that Innana had shown him a few days earlier. He frowned. Was this why she wanted him to come here? If he was supposedly Senen's "king whom death could not hold," it made sense for him to reveal himself in Senen's presence.

A helpless feeling crested inside him. What was he doing here? Playing dress-up in a foreign city while his home undoubtedly burned? What kind of a fool was he to trust this plan?

But as he considered his worries, another voice rose in his mind, that of Scrivener Tolistan. Before his supposed death, Narius was preparing to convert to the Siporan faith and Tolistan had been instructing him. Part of those lessons had included reading from the Siporan's ancient writings, and one passage bubbled up in his memory.

You Who spun the stars into rivers, Who carved the channels in the depths, when my steps take me far from Nekek the Bright, when I wander where Your light does not seem to reach, guide my feet to where You want me to go.

He didn't know why that particular verse popped into his head. He had never been to Nekek the Bright, the fallen capital city of the Siporan Ascendancy, and he had no desire to do so. But he was far from his own home.

Narius forced himself to stay still and he glanced up toward the darkened sky. *I don't know if You can hear me all the way here in Utuaa. I suppose You can if You did spread the stars I see. I need Your help now more than ever. If this is what I'm supposed to be doing, let it work? Just lead me where I need to go.*

A sharp cry sliced through the night, startling him out of his reverie. Narius spun. An older woman swung her cane at three young men, who seemed intent on stealing her meager possessions. There didn't seem to be any constables in the area, and the other people clogging the Septagon didn't seem to care.

"Hey!" he shouted. "Get away from her!"

One hooligan looked in his direction but turned back to his victim.

Narius snarled, his fingers spasming into fists. "I said get away from her!"

As he crossed the space, Narius's mind caught up with his body. What was he doing? He didn't know if these goons were armed! And they outnumbered him three to one. If this went badly, he could wind up in a hospital bed again, or worse.

But he couldn't retreat now, not when he had their attention. At the very least, the old woman could slip away.

The three young men laughed as he approached. One of them shouted something in Dalark. Although he didn't understand, the tone conveyed the man's contempt well enough. They advanced on him with a feral light in their eyes.

But then one of them stopped short. His mouth popped open. He shouted something and jabbed a finger at Narius. Narius didn't understand, although he thought he heard his name. Great. They recognized him. That would make him an even more tempting target. He dropped into a ready stance. Hopefully he had healed enough for hand-to-hand combat.

Then, much to his surprise, the leader's eyes widened. He stumbled backward and shouted the same phrase using Narius's name. Tripping over themselves, all three of them fled.

Narius stared after them. What just happened?

The old woman approached him, her eyes wide and her hands trembling. She looked up at him and gasped. Then she turned to the others in the Septagon. She shouted something in Dalark. Once again, Narius heard his name, but he heard another he recognized. Senen.

He looked back at the statue of the potentate, then turned to the old woman. Only she wasn't alone. More people had joined her, all of them gaping at him. One by one, they joined her in shouting his name and Senen's, pumping fists in the air in rhythm to their shouts.

Narius started to speak, but the people cried out in alarm and backed away from him. He frowned. What was going on?

A hand touched his elbow, and he turned. Kavi stood next to him, weaving her hands around a small flicker in the air.

"What?" he whispered.

Time to go. As soon as she finished signing that message, she resumed her gestures around the flicker. Leading the way, Kavi wove among the startled people, all of whom were whispering and buzzing.

Once they were back inside the transport, she relaxed into her chair with a sigh.

"What were they saying back there?" Narius asked.

Kavi winced, a frown flitting across her brow. Then she carefully, deliberately, signed, *Narius, Senen's promised king.*

11

Everys stood behind the doors of the Embassy and took several deep breaths. She should be excited. She had watched from her bedroom window as booths were set up in the plaza in front of the Embassy. Lights were strung between the trees, creating a glowing canopy. And now, at sunset, she was expected to make her entrance. Her arrival would mark the official beginning of the Festival.

"Are you ready to go, Blessed?" Trule asked from just behind her.

No, she wasn't. She knew she should put on a cheerful face, but how could anyone expect her to act like the past year was worth celebrating? She should be here with Narius or with her Swordbound, Kevtho. Or her younger brother, Legarr. And it wasn't just death that had taken people from her. Not that long ago, she had had a falling out with the captain of her guard, Redtale, over a cultural misunderstanding. Plus there was the ongoing rift between her and Papa.

Her breathing turned shallow, and she braced herself against the door. Gray nibbled at the edge of her vision. Her knees wobbled and she stumbled forward.

Four sets of hands steadied her and Trule gently turned her so they could stand face-to-face. "Blessed, you're safe. You're all right. We're all here for you."

Her other maids murmured their agreement. Everys offered them a shaky smile.

"If this is too much, we can go back up to your quarters. I'll send word to Challix that you're sick. Shara can brew some sandwarmer tea and we'll spend the night inside."

Everys laughed, a frantic giggle. "I don't think Challix would let me get away with that."

"She's not the queen, is she?" Trule asked with a twinkle in her eyes.

More laughter, and the knot in Everys's chest loosened. She straightened and shook out her hands. "No, I can do this. I have to do this. But thank you."

"We'll be nearby if you need us," Trule said.

Everys nodded absently. The girls darted forward again, straightening her dress. She didn't know where Trule had found this one. The diaphanous gown flared at her waist, and the tight sleeves reached halfway to her wrist, where they too flared out and hung almost to her knees. The fabric was a shimmering blend of reds, yellows, and oranges, with tiny jewels sewn in intricate patterns along the bodice and down the skirt. When she first saw it, she thought it resembled a sunset, with evening stars emerging from the night. The girls had swept her hair up, leaving two ringlets loose to frame her face. She always marveled at how they could make her look like a queen, even when she didn't feel like one.

Trule offered her an encouraging smile, then two of the maids hauled the doors open. Everys fixed on a demure smile and glided forward onto the front steps.

The activity in the plaza fell silent. Hundreds, if not thousands, of people milled about, and all of them stopped to witness her entrance. As she descended the steps, polite applause rippled through the gathering.

Challix waited for her. Her assistant wore a tight-fitting black dress, nothing flashy but definitely elegant. "Good evening, Blessed. Are you ready for this?"

Everys nodded, resisting the urge to wipe her hands on her dress.

"Let's head to the main stage," Challix said. "Tall Reach is going to offer some opening remarks. Then the food booths will open, along with the art pavilion. There are several musical groups that will perform on the east stage. There might be dancing over there as well, but there's no expectation for you to join. I understand they are expecting you to say some words at moonrise, which will happen in about two hours. Until then, you're free to enjoy the Festival as you see fit."

As Challix continued to explain what was happening, she led Everys through the crowd, which parted for her. She studied the booths as they walked. A wave of delicious smells washed over her, prompting her mouth to water. Roasted meats, sweet treats, even a tart tang, all blended into a wonderful aroma. If she had her choice, she'd spend most of the night here.

"I'm looking forward to the shessu caravan booth myself." Challix nodded to one corner of the pavilion.

A group of dark-skinned Kolvese manned the tables, but behind them was an enormous shessu, the size of a small hill. She had a long, whip-like tail, four legs, two thick arms, and a barrel-shaped head with four large black eyes. Dozens of barrels had been strapped to the shessu's body.

"Apparently U'k-nissa has been wearing those pots for a week now," Challix explained. "She and her team are the best at making three-day stew, although because of the volume they're making, they had to cook it for longer."

Strains of music wafted through the air, and Everys glanced to her left to find a large stage set up. A group of half a dozen musicians were playing what sounded like a traditional Dunestrider march, although they had put a bit of a syncopated twist to it.

"Enjoy that while you can," Challix said. "My understanding is that a group of Ixactl soldiers have an amateur roarcore thundermetal band. That might be the best time to get some food."

Challix led her into a different part of the Festival, an art pavilion. The organizers had erected a wall to display paintings. Many of them portrayed realistic landscapes of thick forests or rambling rivers. A few bordered on the abstract, bright splashes of color that somehow complemented each other in spite of the chaos. A few were simply too strange for her to make sense of. A quick check of the labels revealed that these had been painted by... Trule? Her maid had created this art? Everys made a mental note to tease her about not sharing this talent with her earlier. She'd have to commission some new pieces for her quarters.

Beyond the wall was a sculpture garden. Everys led the way into a cluster of different statues. Some were clearly meant to be specific people or animals, caught midmovement or stoically looking off in the distance. A few were twisted shapes that evoked fury or passion. She looked around. Would this be where Occ had set up her present?

As if reading her mind, Challix gestured for her to follow. They wound through the other displays until they came to the center of the art garden.

Occ crouched in front of a large, Y-shaped tree branch. Alternating bands of color represented the history of the Dynasty wound up the thick base. The left branch was a riot of swirling colors, meant to symbolize the intermingling of the different races, and green leaves and vines, a nod to their hosts, covered the right branch. A complex weave of webbing strung between the two branches and were joined by connecting bands, creating a strangely hypnotic pattern.

"Blessed! I'm so sorry you saw this before it was finished," Occ said, then ducked down to fiddle with some sort of device on the ground in front of the branch.

With a click, the device activated. A pulsating dot of red light appeared in the center of the weave, then traced intricate patterns across the webbing. At first, it was a message, dedicating the artwork to the Moonslight Festival. Then the light turned green, tracing out pictures of the Cold Light's pillar trees. Then strange looping patterns, followed by more pictures. Some were easy to decipher. Others were more abstract. One pattern in particular kept repeating, a blend of lines and angles that Everys found strangely familiar, only she never got a good enough look at it to figure out why.

"This is amazing, Occ!" she whispered. "You outdid yourself."

"I appreciate your enthusiasm, Blessed." Occ wrung both sets of hands together. "I had Chance's own time getting the targeting laser to behave properly."

Everys's head snapped around. "That's a targeting laser?"

Occ nodded. "Off a combat skimmer. I had to make quite a few promises to the technicians who were maintaining it just so I could borrow it for tonight. Plus I had to cobble together my own programming for it to trace the patterns and... Broken Sword!"

He lunged for the laser and started working with it. Everys frowned, then looked at the artwork. The laser had turned green again, drawing the trees over and over instead of shifting to the next pattern.

"Unfortunately, it gets stuck every now and then," Occ mumbled. "And... there!"

The laser made a soft chirruping sound, then the imagery on the webbing shifted, this time sketching out a simplified map of the Dynasty's holdings. Occ rose, but he wrung his lower hands while his upper swiped at his mask, as if he were desperately trying to rub it clean.

"It's fine, Occ. Your artwork is incredible. Everyone is going to love it," Everys said, touching one of his lower shoulders.

"But I wanted it to be perfect for you, Blessed. You deserve so much better," he said.

She wanted to hug him. She definitely didn't deserve someone as loyal and sweet as Occ.

Challix cleared her throat. "I'm sorry to interrupt this moment, but Tall Reach will start his opening speech soon."

Of course. Duty. Responsibility. Those never went away, no matter how much she might wish it.

Challix led Everys out of the art pavilion and to the main stage. Yllana already stood at center stage. The gathered crowd made room for Everys as she approached.

As soon as Everys took her place near the front of the stage, Yllana smiled brightly. But then a shudder passed over her body. Her face twitched and twisted. As the fit passed, she stood up taller and straighter. Her expression became wizened, almost ancient. Everys recognized what was happening immediately. Yllana shared a mental connection with a Cold Light named Tall Reach. Occasionally, the sentient tree could take direct control of her body.

"My friends, it gives me great pleasure to welcome you to another Moonslight Festival. Tonight is a time for us to celebrate how our Hearth has provided for those who seek refuge in our forest. While there is much uncertainty in my Shade because of the ongoing conflict in the larger world, for one night, may we set aside those anxieties and enjoy one another's company. By the end of the night, may we all have been drawn closer together, grown tighter in our mutual bonds. Please, enjoy the Festival."

At first, the reaction was muted applause, but that soon grew into cheers and hoots. The crowd broke up and drifted out to the pavilions. Everys's lips twitched into the barest smile. Maybe this wasn't exactly what she wanted. But hopefully, it would turn out to be what she needed.

12

As much as she hated to admit it, Everys could relax. The food was delicious. She had sampled everything she could, and while the three-day stew was good, she discovered that Weyfir lichen skewers were maybe her new favorite food. She had expected them to be chewy, but instead, they had a sharp crackle that released a burst of salty sweetness.

After eating, she had carefully examined and enjoyed every work of art in the pavilion. Occ, unfortunately, was still trying to get the laser to work properly. It kept locking up at random times, tracing the same design over and over.

The only genuine disappointment was the musical performances. It turned out that all the musicians were amateurs, many of them chosen from the refugees that had recently entered the forest. They all tried their best, but each act turned out to be worse than the first. If she didn't know better, she would have suspected that the entire sequence of musical acts was an elaborate prank by the Cold Light. The last one especially, a roarcore thundermetal band, proved especially heinous. From what Challix whispered to her, the Ixactl music was usually performed by four musicians, a full choir of twenty-five individuals to create the proper droning, and then two lead singers to overlay the melody. This band, Stoneclad Surge, only had one Ixactl and a handful of his friends. They had created the drone as best as they could using synthesizers. Everys didn't know if true roarcore thundermetal was supposed to sound so jarring, but she wished that someone would turn down the volume. While Stoneclad Surge was enthusiastic, their performance made it hard to have conversations anywhere nearby.

By her count, Everys had made at least ten circuits through the Festival grounds. She hadn't really spoken to many people, just acknowledged them in passing. Rewether and Challix shadowed her, quick to intervene if needed.

Everys paused as a small cluster of children waved at her. She smiled, then took a moment to drink in everything she had seen and experienced. She hadn't realized how much she needed this reminder of what she was fighting for. It felt like she was waking up after a long sleep, suddenly aware of the world around her again. Yes, she had known what a threat Brencis and the Dalark were, but she had been so cocooned in her grief she had lost track. It was a minor miracle their enemies hadn't completely overrun them yet.

She glanced at Challix, then winced as another low *thrum* from the music stage vibrated through her.

"What?" Challix asked.

"I know that I say this all the time, but I feel like I haven't sufficiently thanked you for your work," Everys asked. "You know how much I appreciate what you've done for me, right?"

"Of course." Challix's reply seemed oddly muffled, like she was speaking with a clenched jaw.

"Well, thank you. I mean it. You've done so much for me, and I haven't shown you the appreciation that you deserve."

A frown flitted across Challix's face. Her lips pressing into a thin line. She almost looked angry. But why?

"Is something wrong?" Everys asked.

"Is that the best you can do?" Challix asked. "Just a few pretty words? Do you know how much I've had to do the past few months to keep all of this going? Constant meetings, making excuse after excuse for you."

Everys gaped at Challix, startled at her hostility. She had seen her assistant get frustrated with her, but she'd never seen her this angry ever. Challix fixed her with a fiery gaze.

"I-I'm sorry," Everys said. "I didn't realize. I've been grieving and—"

"And you're the only one who lost someone?" Challix's voice could freeze a river. "I don't know what happened to my parents or my sister! Everyone here has lost someone, Everys. And yet we've had to do our best to keep going, to hold things together, to stand against Brencis and Tirigian and everything. I just..."

With a snarl, Challix spun on her heel and stomped off. Everys stared after her, horrified. How long had Challix felt that way?

"Dented Breastplate, what a woman!" Rewether whispered.

Everys gaped at him. He stared after Challix, desire burning in his eyes. But then he blinked and looked at Everys. He stammered an apology, then snapped to attention, his cheeks flaming.

"Are you okay?" Everys asked.

Rewether didn't answer and wouldn't meet her gaze. She studied his face, then turned and started for the main stage. She thought the time was coming for her speech. The sooner she could get that over and end this night, the better. Maybe she and Challix could work things out in the morning.

As she walked through the crowd, she spotted Oluna and, much to her surprise, her father. Papa actually had a bowl of what looked like Plissk sandpoppers, which surprised her. Those had a considerable kick, and he had never been one for spicy food. She made her way over to them and, as she did, another loud *thrum* rattled through her. Everys pressed a hand to her head, suddenly dizzy. Thankfully, the sensation passed quickly enough.

Oluna brightened at her approach. "Blessed! Good evening, or happy Moonslight, or whatever we're supposed to say. Are you having a good time?"

Everys almost said something about what just happened with Challix, but she caught herself. No need to broadcast those sorts of problems, especially not in front of Papa or anyone else who might be eavesdropping. "Enough of one, yes. How about you?"

"Oh, what I've seen has been absolutely marvelous! We only just arrived and haven't even made it to the art pavilion yet. The food has occupied our attention. I can't say that I've enjoyed all the different delicacies offered tonight, but this has certainly been an entertaining evening. Much different from the parties I'm used to.

"I know you had little to do with the planning of this Festival, but this is quite the celebration. A victory for morale, even if it won't count for much else."

Everys frowned at the criticism. That didn't sound like Oluna. Then there was another *thrum* and Everys's knees went weak for a split second. What was wrong with her?

"I have to wonder, though... what are you up to?" Oluna's eyes narrowed, and she studied Everys's face with an almost predatory glint in her eyes.

What did that mean? "I'm not up to anything. I mean, I have to make a speech in a little while, but that's it."

Oluna blinked, surprise flitting over her features. Then she laughed. "Of course, dear! I'm sorry. Probably imbibed too much of that grafted wine. Have you tried it yet? I think their connection to the trees gives them an advantage in vintnery. I think I'll go get another glass. Favid, do you want anything?"

Papa grunted, the first sign he had made that Everys or Oluna were there. Oluna smiled at them both, then sashayed back toward one booth where a group of grafted were handing out mugs of wine.

"How about you, Papa? Are you having a good time?" Everys asked cautiously.

"How can I? I've been kidnapped, held here against my will, and I do not know if your mother or sister are safe. How can you expect me to drink and listen to music and act like everything is fine?"

Everys winced at the venom in Papa's voice, but she wasn't surprised.

"Of course not, Papa. But that doesn't mean you have to be so hostile. None of this was my idea."

"Is that what you're telling yourself? That you're the victim here?" He glared at her. "Whose decision was it to come to this Singularity-forsaken land? Who decided I had to come with you?"

Everys started to answer, but another *thrum* cut through her, stealing her breath. She glared over at the stage. When was that performance going to end?

"And let's not forget that none of this would have happened if you hadn't married that monster!" Papa practically spat the last word. "You know what? I'm glad he's dead. I'm glad he's gone. I had hoped that you would come to your senses if that happened, but now I'm really beginning to understand how truly lost you are."

As each of Papa's words sliced into her, Everys's breathing turned ragged. Numbness swept through her body and she had to choke back sudden tears.

Rewether sucked in a sharp breath behind her. "Sir, you will—"

"Don't you dare tell me how to talk to my daughter, guard," Papa snapped. "This is a private matter, and I'd appreciate you showing some respect for that."

Rewether's hands clenched into fists. Everys stepped between him and Papa.

"Maybe you should go get some more food, Papa." She tried to inject some authority into her voice. "Or just go home."

Papa snarled something at her then stomped away. Rewether made like he was about to go after him, but Everys shot him a glare that froze him in his tracks. The last thing this Festival needed was a fight between the queen's father and chief guard. Inkstains! What was getting into everyone? Was this normal for the Moonslight Festival? She looked around the celebration, trying to see if there was any evidence of strange behavior from the other Festival goers. Everys didn't see any fights, but she thought she saw some people in heated arguments. She spotted Occ running toward the art pavilion, his entire posture screaming panic. What was he doing? She started after him.

Before she could take more than a step, though, a column of shadows erupted in front of her. Everys stumbled back, uncertain what she was seeing.

A figure burst out of the shadows, a plain-looking man with an average body and a nondescript face. But she recognized him immediately.

"Tormod?" she gasped.

Tormod, Narius's spymaster, brushed off his shirt then looked around. His expression brightened when he spotted Everys, but then his face pinched into a frown.

"Why send me here?" he muttered.

A brilliant ball of light erupted from the art pavilion, and a wave of energy rippled through the Festival. Everys threw her arms over her face to protect it, but then a blast of pure toratropic magic tore through her. She staggered backward, then peeked from behind her arms. Nothing had changed as near as she could tell. Everyone looked confused and were...

Wait, who were those people in the black outfits? Four of them stood near her. They wore tight-fitting black clothing with glowing red runes painted on their chests. She stared at one of them, and his gaze locked with hers.

He bit off a curse. "The runes have been broken. Attack!"

13

Rewether bellowed a challenge and charged at the man who had spoken. But before the guard could grab him, the man opened his palm, revealing an almost completed toratropic rune. He swiped a single finger through it, completing the pattern, and flames burst from his open hand.

Rewether cursed and threw himself out of the fire's path, which somehow curved after him. Thankfully, it only singed his boots. Rewether rolled, then popped to his feet, pulling a flechette thrower from his hip holster. He swung it up and fired, a *pop-hiss* sounding as the metallic shard sliced through the air at the attacker. But the projectile somehow bent around the man in black, missing him completely.

"Get out of here, Blessed!" Rewether roared as he continued to fire.

Tormod snared her arm, dragging her away from the people in black and toward the Embassy. Soldiers raced toward the invaders. At least a dozen more people in similar black outfits, were throwing fire and lightning into the screaming crowd. Where had they come from?

Tormod handed her off to another guard who hustled her up the stairs into the Embassy itself. The gigantic building was mostly deserted since the staff had all gone to the Moonslight Festival. But this was too quiet. The Embassy shouldn't have been completely empty. A shiver wormed down Everys's spine. She started to call out for someone, but the guard shook his head sharply and held a finger to his lips. Her stomach twisted. Of course. Don't draw attention.

Her guard—what was his name?—motioned for Everys to follow her and then he started, slowly and carefully, for the stairs that led to her quarters.

The moment he stepped onto the lowest step, two runes flared to life on either side of his feet. Electricity sparked up his body, freezing him in place. Then, a second later, he slumped to the floor, smoke rising from his clothes.

Everys bit back a scream. Where had that come from? Were there toratropic mages in the Embassy?

Then she took a deep breath. She couldn't panic. She had to find out what was going on. She pulled a vial of ink from her pocket and broke it open. With a trembling finger, she sketched an insight rune onto her open palm and activated it. A soft blue glow emanated from her hand, and she raised it up, willing the spell to reveal what was hidden.

Slowly but surely, dozens of runes flickered into view. She sucked in a sharp breath. Whoever had done this was thorough. Half of the runes were scattered across the stairs, traps set for someone blindly charging up them. The others were positioned near doors and windows, ready to catch people as they entered. Everys quickly darted from rune to rune, inspecting each one. They appeared to have been drawn in haste. They were simple, with no fail-safes or surprises. She set to work smudging the patterns, and within five minutes, she had disarmed all the traps.

Something crashed in the upper floors. Everys jumped at the sharp sound. She hurried up the stairs, still giving the spots where the runes had been a wide berth, just in case. When she arrived at the second-floor landing, she saw a door crack open and someone peek through. A moment later, much to her surprise, Hirfan emerged. Everys froze.

He stopped as well, staring at her with wide eyes. He stammered something, looking over his shoulder as if the answer were standing behind him.

"Are you okay?" Everys asked.

Hirfan nodded. "There's a lot of toratropic magic permeating the air here, but otherwise, I'm fine."

Her gaze narrowed. Of course he would notice that, but it still made her wonder why he was in the Embassy in the first place. But then she shook her head. She couldn't get bogged down with that question.

She jabbed a finger at the stairs. "Go for help. Find a guard or a soldier or whoever, and get them to come back here."

Thankfully, he nodded and headed down to the first landing. Everys waited, just to make sure he wasn't caught. Then she set out to find the intruders.

Everys slunk through the second floor of the Embassy, checking each door carefully. Offices composed most of this floor, but she knew there were maps and diagrams about the defenses of the forest. Much to her surprise, those offices were empty. She frowned. Why wouldn't they look for military intelligence? What was their actual target?

Another crash from the floor above her. Her frown deepened. The only thing on the next floor up was a library. The Cold Light had collected hundreds, if not thousands, of books. She had spent many hours perusing their collection, marveling at the many hidden gems they had secreted away. But why would the intruders be there?

She crept up the stairs to a small landing. Sure enough, the door was open and, when she peeked inside, she spotted six intruders, all of them dressed completely in black, all with the same rune painted on their chests. Several bookcases had been knocked over, their contents scattered over the floor. While five of them searched through the spilled books and pages, one stood in the middle of the room, his arms crossed.

"Keep looking! If we don't find that information, the *ar'zhannok* will have us flayed!" he barked.

"Not finding anything over here," one of them shouted.

"Nothing here either. These books seem to be more Plissk travel-ogues," another reported.

The leader snarled something under his breath. "No maps? They have to have records somewhere!"

"Are we sure they'd write down something that important?"

Everys had to stop them. She didn't have any idea what they were searching for, but she couldn't let them keep looking. What if they found it?

She peeked into the room again and spotted a book that had skidded close to the door. An idea stitched together. Hopefully, the Cold Light would forgive her for what she was about to do.

First things first. She painted a rune on the door frame. Once the trap was set, she eased her foot into the room and nudged the book closer. She scooped it up and then used its cover as a canvas, sketching a rune onto it. As soon as the pattern was complete, she activated it, then kicked the book back into the room. A flood of smoke erupted from the book, filling the room almost instantly.

The agents in the library choked and coughed.

"Did one of you idiots set the room on fire?" the leader bellowed.

The smoke billowed out of the room, which was exactly what Everys was hoping for. She pressed up against the wall and waited.

"Get out of here! Go! Before they figure out what's going on!"

Footsteps came toward the door. Everys held her breath.

She could barely make out the first figure to go through the door, but when they crossed the threshold, the trap activated. The agent's legs buckled under him and he tumbled to the floor, unconscious before he even hit. Everys quickly grabbed his arm and dragged him out of the way, tucking him behind a low end table. She crouched down next to him and waited.

More people stumbled out of the library, coughing and cursing with every step. The leader bellowed an order, but then they all heard it: the front doors banging open, followed by Rewether barking an order of his own.

"Too late. We need to leave, now!" the leader said.

There was a strange *whooshing* sound. Then silence.

Everys frowned. Had they gone down the stairs? Surely they would have run into Rewether. She risked a peek into the hallway. There was too much smoke to tell for sure, but it looked like the agents had vanished. She checked to make sure that the one she had knocked out was still there. He was, and he was actually snoring.

Footsteps up the stairs. Then Rewether and half a dozen guards fanned out, their weapons drawn.

"Blessed!" Rewether called.

"Here!" Everys replied.

The guards whirled on her, but then they all holstered their weapons.

"Are you all right?" Rewether asked.

She nodded, but realized he might not see that through the smoke. "I am. I've got a prisoner."

"You what?" Rewether asked.

The guards hurried forward and three of them quickly slapped the sleeping agent in manacles. Rewether gave Everys a quick once-over visually, then nodded to himself.

"I doubt this is what the Cold Light had in mind for tonight, huh?" he asked with a grim smile.

Everys didn't return the expression. No, it wasn't. But a grim determination quickly chased away the last vestiges of fear, and even her sadness. Now she had a puzzle to solve. And smudges and splatters, she was going to figure out why those people had invaded the Shade.

14

The adrenaline rush and exhaustion warred in Narius's body. Maybe he had pushed himself too hard.

He didn't notice until it was too late that Kavi had taken him somewhere new. He frowned as they slid past a well-lit building surrounded by people. The entire scene was painted in garish neon colors that caused the people's clothing to glow in a way that hurt his eyes. A few of the passersby noticed them as Kavi maneuvered into an alley to the back of the building. Narius slumped in his seat. He didn't know if they could see him through the darkened glass, but better safe than sorry. Once they were away from the prying eyes on the street, Kavi shut off the engine and slid out of the vehicle. Narius waited, unsure of what was happening, but then followed her out.

She led him through a back entrance to the building. Discordant music nearly overwhelmed Narius. He could feel the rhythm in his chest. Kavi led him up some stairs in the back to an office that overlooked a crowded dance floor. Lights strobed inside as bodies thrashed in time to the music. Thankfully, the thick glass muffled the music, although he could still feel vibrations from the music and dancing through his feet.

The room itself was an office with a large, glass-topped desk and a cluster of couches facing a fireplace. Innana stood by the window, overlooking the revelers. She turned to him and smiled.

"Is this safe?" he asked. "That looks like a riot in its earliest stages."

"You're not entirely wrong," Innana said. "But I find it's good to give the people of Utuaa an outlet for their aggression and frustration. For now, at least. When the time comes, we'll make some adjustments to the entertainment at my clubs to stoke the fires of resentment when I need them."

Her clubs? As in plural? Narius regarded her with open surprise.

She smirked at him. "Underestimating me is deadly, as my brother will soon learn. How did your first excursion go?"

Narius grimaced. Now that he was away from the Septagon, now that the giddy rush had passed, he realized he actually had done little. Yes, a crowd had seen him stand up for that poor woman, but what impact could that really have?

"Not as well as I'd like," Narius said. "I'm not sure I furthered your plan that much."

"Oh?" Innana's lips quirked into a grin again. "Perhaps we should ask Kavi."

They turned to the young woman. She looked between them and shrugged. *He did what you expected.*

What Innana expected? Narius frowned. What did that even mean?

A door on one side of the room opened, and three men stepped inside. Narius froze. It was the three men who had harassed the old woman at the Septagon.

Innana turned to them. "And you? How would you say King Narius did?"

"Quite well, my lady," one of them said. "He didn't even hesitate."

Another one of them hurried forward, his hand outstretched. "I hope you're not mad at us, Your Strength. It was an honor to work with you."

Work with him? What was going on? He suddenly felt lightheaded, as if he had been exercising for too long. He staggered.

Kavi steadied him and helped him over to the couch. Innana dismissed the men, then sat next to him on a chair.

"So none of it was real?" Narius whispered.

"It depends on what your definition of 'real' is," Innana said coolly. "Were the men who harassed that old woman actors, chosen by me to play that part? Yes. But you didn't know that. Neither did the old woman nor the many people who inhabit the Septagon. You saw a threat and acted nobly. They saw a king who had returned from death to protect them. How can either of those not be real?"

"Because you orchestrated the whole encounter!" Narius said.

"Of course I did. What was I supposed to do, Narius? Send you out on the streets of Utuaa and let you wander around until you blundered into the right set of circumstances? No, we had to make sure that your first encounter with the Dalark people happened properly. The right location. The right audience."

What audience? The only people who had seen him were the homeless denizens of the Septagon. And yes, they had been very grateful for what he had done, but he doubted that the rest of the Imperium would believe a word they said. He knew that that would be the case in the Dynasty.

She must have read the skepticism on his face. With another knowing smile, she scooped up a remote and pressed a button. The fireplace slid aside, revealing a bank of vidscreens. One by one, they each flickered to life. At first, Narius thought they were showing different things, but as he studied the footage playing, he realized they were all showing the same scene, just shot from multiple angles.

There he was, in Senen's shadow, striding forward with anger in his eyes. There he was, advancing on three ruffians, who quickly retreated. There he was, surrounded by people who were chanting his name and Senen's.

Innana set down the remote and turned to him. "Did you really think that I would let your return go unnoticed? I made sure that there were plenty of people with scribers ready to record whatever happened."

Narius stared as the footage on each screen looped over and over. "What is this?"

"Years ago, I grew frustrated with the way my father had a stranglehold on the distribution of information in the Imperium. So I quietly financed a clandestine network that allows my people to share information with one another, away from the prying eyes of the Imperial censors. And right now, the footage of your return is spreading, not just in Utuaa, but all throughout the Imperium. By morning, I would say that half our citizens will have seen this footage. By the end of the week, most everyone will have."

Narius looked at the screens again with a stab of concern. "Won't your brother find out?"

"Undoubtedly, but I wouldn't worry. Tirigian has heard and already dismissed rumors of your presence in the Imperium."

Wait, what? Narius turned to her. "Why would Tirigian have already heard that?"

"Because I started rumors to that effect two months ago."

Narius collapsed back in the chair as Innana nodded.

"When Kavi brought you to Utuaa, I knew I had my opportunity. So when I was sure you were going to survive, I started the rumors. At first, people just claimed to have seen you in their dreams. Then, there were stories about how a friend of a friend or a distant relative claimed to know someone who saw you in the middle of the night. Easily ignored at first, but those stories were persistent. Soon, the sheer number of people who claimed to know someone who saw you became hard to ignore.

"But Tirigian's intelligence agents discounted those stories in official reports, because they insisted you died in Bastion shortly before the city fell."

"Which the agents did at your direction," Narius guessed.

"Of course. My brother is a foolish man, easily misled if he's told what he wants to hear. He wants to believe you dead, so even when this footage is brought to him, he will believe those who told him of your demise."

"And I'll keep making appearances like that." Narius gestured to the screen. "More fake confrontations with the same actors?"

She shook her head. "Don't be silly. If we did that, the wrong people would notice and call this all into question. Instead, we will engineer future appearances to seem natural, but they will all be controlled. Never fear. You will be safe."

Narius frowned. As much as he hated to admit it, he was relieved the confrontation in the Septagon had turned out to be fake. Innana had clearly put a lot of thought into this plan.

"Kavi will take you to a safe location where you will stay until we are ready for your next appearance."

She strode out of the office.

Narius didn't move. He said nothing. And Kavi let him sit there, soaking in the jarring rhythms, wrestling with a question that had been nagging him, only to become sharper with Innana's passionate words. She knew who she was and who she wanted to be. But what about him? When all of this was over, who was Narius? Who would he be?

15

R ewether didn't declare the Embassy secure for a full day. During that time, he insisted Everys stay in a barracks, surrounded by soldiers. Even then, Everys didn't feel all that safe. So many questions chased her through the night that she couldn't sleep. Where had the intruders come from? What had caused them to suddenly appear like that? And what had they been looking for? Unfortunately, Rewether kept her sequestered away from the answers.

The next morning, though, the moment the sun rose, Everys threw off the covers, hastily dressed, and sent a guard to summon Rewether. He met her at the door with a grim expression.

"We're not entirely certain that the Embassy is safe yet, Blessed," Rewether said.

Everys straightened to her full height, which gave her just a couple of inches over him. "You're investigating the use of toratropic magic. Who better to help than me, especially after what I saw?"

Rewether grimaced but quickly hid the expression. He pursed his lips together and led her to the Embassy.

The mood in the Shade had shifted. People bustled from building to building without acknowledging those they passed. Even the surrounding woods seemed muted, like the animals didn't want to attract anyone's attention.

"Status?" Everys asked.

Rewether grunted. "It's a mess. We don't know where they came from or how they got here. The most obvious theory is that they were here to assassinate you, but that doesn't seem likely. As near as we can tell, they had a team shadowing you for a while. Why not strike before they were revealed?"

"Do we know how their invisibility was broken?" Everys asked. "They seemed just as surprised as us."

"Not a complete explanation, no. Tormod has a theory, though."

Tormod? Her brows rose. Rewether sighed and motioned for her to follow him. He walked away from the Embassy and started for the art pavilion. She remembered seeing the flash of light from there the night before, plus a wave of...

Her eyes widened. Toratropic energy. Someone had cast an extremely powerful rune. Had that been what unmasked the intruders? She hurried her pace, almost rushing past Rewether.

The art pavilion was in ruins. The temporary wall lay on the ground, the paintings splattered with mud and dirt. The other sculptures in the garden beyond were knocked over, some of them shattered. Oddly, though, Occ's statue remained standing. Occ stood next to it, wringing his hands together as Tormod looked over the art. As Everys approached, Occ scurried forward, practically crawling across the ground.

"Blessed, I am so sorry! I didn't know that this would happen. I didn't intend to cause so much trouble," Occ said.

"It's all right, Occ. Let's see what Tormod has to say," Everys said.

Tormod turned to her, but there was hesitation in his expression. His gaze shot to some people who lingered nearby, clearly curious about whatever had happened. Rewether caught the look and quickly ordered the pavilion cleared. Within moments, the only people left were Occ, Tormod, Everys, and Rewether.

"Thank you," Tormod said. "First, I'm so thankful to see you alive and in one piece, Blessed."

"Where have you been?" Everys demanded. "We could have used your help so many times over the past few months!"

Tormod ducked his head. "I am sorry, Blessed. I tried to return as quickly as I could, but the situation has been so fluid, I haven't been able to make it."

Everys scowled at him, but then tamped down on her frustration. She knew that was true. Narius had often said that he gave Tormod free rein to do what he felt was necessary. If he hadn't returned until now, there had to be a good reason for it.

"Rewether says you have a theory about what happened?" she prompted.

Tormod nodded. "Based on my admittedly cursory investigation, I believe Occ accidentally cast a rune last night."

Everys's mind went blank for a moment. "H-he what?"

Occ made a high-pitched keening noise. "I'm sorry, Blessed. I didn't mean to, and now I've ruined everything."

Tormod chuckled. "Actually, Occ, I suspect that you may have saved the day."

The keening cut off, and Occ swiveled to look at Tormod. "I did?"

Tormod nodded, then gestured toward the art. "From what I understand, Occ had trouble with this piece. Something about the patterns getting stuck?"

Occ's head bobbled. "That's true. You saw it, Blessed. The patterns didn't always cycle the way they were supposed to."

"According to the witness statements, about fifteen minutes before the attack, the laser stuck on one pattern in particular." Tormod produced a scriber and handed it to Everys. "I pulled this from the device's memory. Does this look at all familiar?"

She looked at the small screen. At first, the pattern was a meaningless jumble of lines and twists. But as she examined it, she recognized bits and pieces. A flourish that would cause the effect to radiate. Another that amplified intensity, making the effect almost unstoppable. The more she looked at it, her suspicion grew. Occ had somehow included a toratropic rune in his design. Her head snapped up.

Tormod nodded solemnly. "You see it too?"

Everys held up the scriber so Occ could see the pattern. "Occ, how did you come up with this?"

Occ studied the screen for a moment and then, much to her surprise, hurried out of the pavilion. Rewether shouted after him, but the Diradae didn't stop. So Everys started after him with Tormod and Rewether in tow. Occ led them to the Embassy, up the grand staircase, and into the library. His sudden entrance startled several of the guards posted there, who swung their weapons around. But when they saw it was Occ, they relaxed.

The room was still wrecked, although someone had moved the fallen bookshelves off to the side. The books and other materials were scattered across the floor, but that didn't stop Occ. He darted through the mess, his head low, before rushing to one of the shelves that hadn't been knocked over. He pulled a large, leather-bound book off a shelf.

After a quick examination, he set it on a table and carefully opened the book. The pages were worn and yellowed, but they were covered in writing, occasionally punctuated with a sketch or drawing. As Occ flipped through them, Everys leaned over, recognition tickling the back of her mind.

Then Occ flipped past a page that snared her full attention: stick figures standing amid eight talon-shaped plinths with a burning ball of light hovering over the whole scene. A crude depiction of a celebrant entering the Scriptotum in Nekek the Bright. She had seen this book before, the first time she had stayed in the Embassy. That seemed like such a long time ago, but this book had been hidden in a pile of garbage in what was now the war room.

But Occ didn't linger on that drawing. He flipped to the back, which contained multiple pages of runes. She thought she recognized some of them—they were variations of the runes she had used throughout her life—but then she realized something. The page on the left depicted the complete rune. The opposite page showed the same rune, but broken into pieces, with notes scribbled under each segment.

And then there it was. The pattern. It was unmistakably a rune. How hadn't she recognized it?

Everys put a hand on his upper shoulder. "Occ, let me see if I understand this correctly. You found this book in the library, found this pattern, and incorporated it into your art?"

Occ's mask bobbled in a somewhat creepy imitation of a human nod. Rewether ground his teeth, and it was clear from his expression that he was about to say something harsh.

So Everys interjected herself. "Why *this* rune in particular, Occ?"

"Well, because of what this says." Occ indicated the notes. "This is a truth-seeker rune. I don't know what that means, but I figured that was an appropriate sentiment to—"

Everys held up a hand to stop Occ from talking. Her mind reeled from what little he had said. He created his art using a book of Siporan runes? One that apparently he knew how to read?

"How do you know that written language?" The question burst from her lips.

"You don't?" Occ asked. "It's the shessu traders' cant. We still use a version to keep track of mining operations. I mean, I can't read all of it. There are a lot of words here that make little sense to me, but I can get the gist of it."

Everys mulled that over. That made sense. The shessu herds had wandered all over Ehun, trading with everyone. From what she understood, they had used the traders' cant to communicate with them all, a common language that anyone could easily learn. The Dynasty had assumed that the cant had been lost when the shessu were wiped out. Narius would have been so excited to see this. He had been so interested in the runes and what they meant...

Her eyes widened. Narius would definitely have loved this discovery. Before he died, he had been doing research on the runes. Well, he had sponsored the research, bringing in Scrivener Tolistan and Professor P'layvo from the Irieling Scholastium to see if they could decipher the runes. As far as she knew, they had learned nothing significant. But this book would have changed that.

She wished she could read the cant herself. If she could read the entry, she'd have a better idea of what the rune could do. Disrupt glamour runes, clearly. Make people more apt to share truths they'd rather hide. That could explain much of what she saw. But was there more? The runes always had little quirks and surprises baked into them. If only they had Scrivener Tolistan and that professor now.

But they didn't, and wishing for them wouldn't change anything. Instead, she had to focus on the crisis at hand. Occ's rune was a puzzle, but it was one that could keep. For now, she had to focus on what the intruders were doing.

"Did we capture any of the other agents?" she asked Rewether.

He shook his head. "No. The others somehow disappeared before we could stop them. The one you captured woke up about an hour ago. We've gotten nothing out of him."

Everys's gaze drifted to the book. A smile tickled her lips.

"Let me try."

Rewether frowned.

Tormod cleared his throat. "I don't think that's a good idea, Blessed."

She knew this was a bad idea. Experimenting with runes, even if they were pictured in an ancient book, was a bad idea. But they needed information. They needed to know what the only surviving intruder knew. And it seemed too serendipitous that they discovered this rune when she needed it most.

"Trust me. I can get him to talk."

Everys paced in a small room in the Embassy's basement. They didn't have a prison or a dungeon exactly, but when they first arrived in the Shade, Rewether and the guards had convinced the Cold Light to reshape the root system of the Embassy's trees to create a makeshift jail. It wasn't much, just a few dank rooms dug out of the ground, with a central guard room connecting them all. There was a bench filled with vidscreens, each one monitoring the same cell.

Still, she braced herself as Rewether ensured the room was secure—trussing up the intruder so he couldn't move, stationing guards who already knew what Everys was capable of, moving people away from the room so no one would accidentally overhear. But she had her own preparations she had to make. Deep breaths, sorting through the questions, prioritizing her thoughts.

Most of all, though, she prayed. A silent plea to the Singularity. For understanding. For insight. And for forgiveness if she was going down the wrong path.

The door behind her opened and Oluna hurried in. Everys blinked, surprised to see her friend. The guards behind her tensed.

"There you are!" Oluna said. "I've been so worried."

A pang of guilt struck Everys. She had been so focused on what had happened the day before, she had given little thought to her other friends.

"Let me look at you." Oluna grabbed her hands and pulled her arms open, her gaze shooting from her head to her toes. "All in one piece, thanks to the guards, no doubt. So what are you doing down here? No one would tell me."

"You know, there's a reason for that, Oluna," Everys said, not unkindly.

Oluna laughed. "Oh, of course. Need to know, security protocols, all the usual excuses. Believe me, Blessed, I can keep a secret better than anyone."

"How did you even get down here?" Everys asked.

Oluna tittered. "Why, I worked my magic, of course. I insisted to the guards that you would need my moral support, and eventually, they saw things my way."

That made sense. Oluna had a way with people. Everys had seen that herself firsthand.

Rewether emerged from the cell. His gaze landed on Oluna and he frowned.

"She stays," Everys said.

He grunted but nodded. "As ordered. We're as ready as we'll ever be."

Everys took one last shaky breath and slipped into the cell.

The intruder lay on a bed, his arms and legs chained to the posts. He was a young man, with sandy blond hair and wide, green eyes. His right shoulder was bandaged heavily. He didn't appear scared so much as overwhelmed, but she saw the disdain in his expression as she entered. Her gaze flicked to the two guards that stood on either side of him. They already had their weapons drawn and trained on the intruder. The door clicked as Rewether took up a position behind her.

Everys forced herself to smile. "Do you know who I am?"

His gaze flicked over her. "Yeah. You're the fake queen, the pretender. Got no business being on that throne."

"Is that why you and your friends were here?" Everys asked.

The intruder snorted. "You're still alive, aren't ya? So what do you think?"

"Then why were you here?" Everys asked.

The intruder laughed, but that turned into a wince. "You think I'm gonna tell you just because you asked politely?"

Everys ground her teeth. No, she didn't. But she thought she should at least give him a chance.

"So what's next? You gonna torture me?" The intruder chuckled hoarsely. "Not exactly your style, is it?"

"You're right. It's not." Everys produced a pen and a scriber. "This is."

The man went still, his gaze locked on the pen.

"You obviously know something about toratropic runes. You had one painted on your chest yesterday. So you know what they can do." She snapped the pen in half. "And I'm sure you've at least suspected I know something about runes. So since I'm looking for information from you, I'll trade with you: I just learned a new rune I'm dying to use."

She called up the image of Occ's truth-telling rune, then daubed a bit of ink on her finger and nodded to the guards. They pushed the intruder down on the bed. He grunted and squirmed, but he couldn't escape. Everys carefully drew the rune on the man's chest. She knew if she didn't get the pattern right, the rune wouldn't work.

While she worked, she kept talking. "I don't know what this will do, exactly. Normally I wouldn't experiment like this, but you're not leaving me much choice." She paused. "Unless you've changed your mind."

The man's eyes were wide, and she thought fear lurked in them, but then he clenched his jaw.

"Have it your way." She resumed drawing. "Like I said, I don't know what kind of effect this will have on you. Hopefully nothing unpleasant."

He still said nothing. She stopped prompting, focusing instead on finishing the rune. Within a few minutes, she added the last bit of detail. Then she activated the rune.

Thankfully, there was no burst of light, no explosion of energy. Instead, the ink glowed a brilliant blue before the man's skin absorbed the pattern. He grunted and squirmed. Everys waited a few moments for the spell to take hold. She studied his skin, his eyes, his posture, looking for some reaction. When nothing happened, she went ahead.

"Let's start with something simple. What's your name?" she asked.

The man clamped his mouth shut, but then a blue light shimmered across his eyes. He whispered, "Hommas Thunn."

"Where are you from, Hommas?" she continued.

Again, he struggled, but the blue light rippled across his eyes. "I grew up in Dreadshore, but I moved to Wrine a few years ago."

Was that true? In some ways, it didn't matter. She just wanted to see if or how the rune worked. It seemed to compel him to tell the truth, so it was time to dig.

"How many of you were here yesterday?" she asked.

More struggling, but then he relaxed. "Eleven. There were eleven of us."

No blue light. Did that mean he told the truth without resisting? Maybe.

"We already know that you weren't here to kill me. Like you said, you could have done that easily enough and no one could have stopped you. So why are you here?"

This time, Hommas tried to resist, and he actually clamped his mouth shut. But the blue flicker in his eyes grew brighter and brighter until the breath burst from his lungs.

"We're looking for something."

He sagged into the bed, clearly relieved. Everys bit down on her own frustration. She wouldn't let Hommas hide behind a vague truth like that.

"What were you looking for? Specifically," she said, leaning in closer.

Once again, Hommas struggled. The blue light built in his eyes, and he thrashed against the restraints. Everys ground her teeth. She was grateful for the spell forcing him to tell the truth, but she didn't know how long it would last. If he fought too long, the rune might run out, and she really didn't want to cast it again.

"Ink!" The word burst from Hommas's mouth. "We were looking for ink."

Everys frowned. That made absolutely no sense. Why would the mage-kings look for that in the Embassy?

"What kind of ink did you think you'd find here?" Everys asked.

"The most powerful there is," Hommas said. "More powerful than anything known for centuries."

That made even less sense. The most powerful ink? That was Cold Light tree sap... No, wait. That wasn't true. According to the ancient texts, human blood was more powerful than that. But the mage-kings could find that anywhere, even from Hommas. So why would...

A chill swept through her. According to the old legends, there was an ink even more powerful than human blood. Blood collected from the dead gods of the Elderreach cult. None of her masters had actually thought that kind of ink was real. They'd said it was a myth, like drawing runes with light.

Hommas couldn't possibly be telling the truth, could he? She didn't think he could lie under the truth-telling rune's effects, but maybe he didn't realize he wasn't telling the truth. Without knowing how the rune worked exactly, she had no way of knowing.

"Why would you find that here?" Everys pressed.

"The *ar'zhannok* does not share that kind of information with us. We are ordered, and we obey," Hommas said.

Everys swallowed her frustration. That made a certain amount of sense as well. "How were you hoping to find this ink?"

Hommas's struggle lasted longer this time, and the light in his eyes was dimmer. The rune was running out.

"Records. Books. Maps that would lead us to what we seek," Hommas said.

That explained why so many of them were in the library.

"Why does the mage-king need this ink? Do you know that?" she asked.

Hommas didn't even hesitate. "So your precious Dynasty will finally be destroyed."

"How?" Everys prompted.

He glared at her, his jaw clenching, but then he laughed. "With the right ink and the Principalities' secret, everything will change."

What was he talking about? The Principalities were eight sacred objects that had once stood in the Scriptotum in Nekek the Bright. She had destroyed five of them before fleeing Bastion. Everys had heard nothing about a secret connected with them.

So what could she do? She could keep asking more questions, but she doubted he could give her much more than that.

"One last question, Hommas. Who is the mage-king?" Everys said. "I want a name."

Hommas's eyes widened. He clamped his jaw shut and thrashed against the restraints. The blue glow built in his eyes, growing brighter and brighter. But then the glow flickered. Everys sucked in an anxious breath. The rune was running out of power.

"Tell me!" she snapped.

Hommas's back arched.

"The mage-king... The mage-king is..."

Then a new rune appeared over his mouth, one made of jagged red lines. Hommas's eyes went wide as the blue light from the truth-telling rune snuffed out. He thrashed against the restraints again and a scream tore out of his mouth. Black, inky lines crawled from the rune across his face, up to his eyes, and down his neck, as if liquid shadow were consuming his body. His struggle became more and more violent until finally, he went completely slack, his breath rattling in his throat before going still.

17

E verys stumbled as she emerged from the Embassy's basement. Her mind reeled. They still didn't know who the mage-king was, but they knew what the mage-king was after: powerful ink. And for whatever reason, they thought they could find it in the Cold Light's forest.

But why?

She was so distracted by her roiling thoughts she nearly collided with Yllana. The grafted danced back a step, offering her an apologetic smile.

"Blessed, we understand that you were questioning one of the intruders. Did you learn anything useful?" Yllana asked.

Everys took a few more deep breaths, trying to banish the image of Hommas's death from her mind. When she realized she couldn't, she forced herself to answer. "We did. The mage-king sent those people here looking for some sort of ink."

Yllana's features froze. "Oh?"

"Do you know what they might have been looking for?" Everys asked.

The grafted hesitated, her eyes darting back and forth as if frantically reading the answer. Then she shook her head. "Unfortunately, no."

Everys blinked. Yllana was lying to her. The grafted were usually so open, the very idea struck her as wrong. But she couldn't deny what she was seeing.

"Do the Cold Light know?"

Again, Yllana's eyes darted back and forth. A strange shudder passed over her face, almost as if Tall Reach were about to speak through her.

But when Yllana met her gaze, it wasn't with the haughty detachment that came from a Cold Light's presence.

"No, they don't. If you would excuse me, please."

Before Everys could press the issue, Yllana turned and scurried away. It almost appeared as if she were fleeing.

Rewether stepped up next to Everys. "That was weird."

It was. She considered following the grafted and demanding answers, but that wouldn't be wise. Given the tension between the forest's original residents and the newcomers, and given how the agents had completely disrupted the Moonslight Festival, pressing the issue would only make things worse. Better to focus on what they could figure out.

"Let's see if they've learned anything up in the library."

As they walked through the Embassy, Everys felt like she was being watched. She was, obviously. The people they passed all turned to look at her, assessing her mood, probably to see if they should be scared or worried. But this was more than just the people she passed. She felt like invisible people leered at her from just outside her vision, like if she could turn fast enough, she'd catch them. A shiver wormed across her skin. She knew that the guards had done their best to secure the Embassy, so she was likely imagining it all.

When they approached the main staircase, she slowed to a halt. Half a dozen people knelt on the stairs, poking at the places where the agents had painted their runes. She lurched forward, ready to warn them away, but then realized that the person at the bottom of the stairs was Screj. A few steps up knelt Style. And overseeing them all was Tillmin. Everys blinked. She had never seen so many Illuminates outside of their catacombs before.

Tillmin turned at her approach. "Blessed. I hope you don't mind. When we heard what happened here, we were curious about the runes and ink used. So we're collecting samples. I hope that's all right."

Rewether started to object, but Everys stepped forward before he could. "Perfectly. We'll be grateful for any insights you can give about what happened here."

Everys headed for the stairs, but something Tillmin had said stuck in her mind. She turned back to him.

"Who told you about this?" she asked.

"Hirfan," Tillmin said. "He said he was in the Embassy when the attack happened."

Unease slithered through Everys. "Did he say why he was here at the time?"

"No, but I suspect I know his reasons." Tillmin motioned for Everys to step away to a more secluded corner. Once they were out of earshot of the others, he leaned in closer. "Hirfan is struggling with your presence here."

Well, that wasn't anything new, but Everys swallowed the sarcastic comment.

"He believes the Cold Light should never have offered you refuge. More than that, the Cold Light should have never submitted to the Dynasty's rule even though you returned their Hearth. He often shares how he believes the Dynasty will bring about the destruction of the forest as a whole and our order in particular."

Once again, Everys had to catch herself before she objected. She didn't want that to happen, but she couldn't guarantee that it wouldn't. The Dynasty was at war with the Dalark Imperium, after all, and they were being hunted by Brencis, a man who had made his opinion about the Cold Light abundantly clear when he had been the head of the Dynasty's military.

"We've tried to dissuade him of his beliefs, but he clings to them most stubbornly. If I had to guess, he was probably in the Embassy snooping for information to confirm his beliefs. I apologize for his indiscretion."

Everys frowned. She could understand why Hirfan would be worried. She even admired his audacity in taking advantage of the situation. But she'd need to speak with Rewether and Overturn about maintaining better security in the Embassy. They couldn't take any chances.

"Is there anything else you need, Blessed?"

She almost said no, but then an idea caught in her mind. "Actually, there is. We have... the body of one of the people who attacked the forest. I know this is morbid, but could you examine him? See what kind of runes or ink he may have used?"

Rewether coughed discretely and she gave him a look. His disapproval was painted clearly over his features.

Tillmin picked up on it as well. "Never fear, guard. We do not approve of the mage-kings or their schemes. We want the truth as much as you. It will be our honor to see what we can learn. Now, if you'll excuse me."

He strode back to the stairs, and Everys passed him and the other Illuminates and headed up to the library.

The room was still a mess from the attack. She knew that probably rankled their hosts but Rewether had insisted on maintaining the room as it was until all the evidence the attackers had left behind could be collected for analysis. Two guards had maintained a vigil since the attack, but now they had been joined by three grafted that Everys didn't know.

"—must insist," one of them said as Everys approached.

"We have our orders, ma'am," the guard replied evenly.

The grafted looked at each other, then turned back to the guards.

"The Yoreroot is most insistent," another grafted said. "They want the library to be restored immediately."

A frown tickled Everys's brow. A strange desperation laced the grafted's words and attitudes. They were too eager to get inside the library, so focused on their task that they hadn't realized Everys was standing right behind them. Rewether started to say something, but Everys motioned for him to keep quiet. She wanted to see what else the grafted might reveal.

"We have our orders," the guard repeated. "The library stays off-limits until Rewether says otherwise."

"But you've had more than enough time to collect your evidence!" The third grafted's voice was an almost petulant whine.

This made no sense. Why would the grafted be so worried about this?

Her eyes widened as the answer occurred to her. The mage-king's agents had been looking for something in the library. Did the Cold Light want the library picked up to keep Everys's people from figuring out what?

A plan quickly formed. She nudged Rewether and whispered for him to get Trule. Then she strode forward, plastering what she hoped would look like a friendly smile on her face.

"What seems to be the problem here?" she asked brightly.

The grafted turned and seemed genuinely surprised to see her there. But then they hurried forward.

"Blessed, we're sorry if we disturbed you. We were just explaining to the guards that we wish to restore the library to its proper condition. They are insisting that we cannot," the lead grafted said.

"I can understand your frustration," Everys said. "Perhaps we have been overly cautious. Allow me to make it up to the Yoreroot."

Thankfully, that was when Rewether returned with Trule. Everys motioned for her maid to step forward.

"This is the head of my personal staff, Trule. She and the rest of my girls will see that the library is cleaned up and restored to its original condition."

The feathers along Trule's scalp ruffled, a motion Everys recognized as confusion, but she didn't say anything.

The grafted glanced at each other, unease flickering over their faces.

"That won't be necessary," the lead grafted said. "The Yoreroot appreciates the gesture, but we don't need you to inconvenience yourself."

"Nonsense!" Everys smiled, making sure to inject some steel into her expression. "I insist."

The grafted paused, their eyes flickering the way Yllana's had not that long ago. Then the leader smiled and bowed. "As you wish, Blessed."

The grafted scurried away. Everys watched them go, maintaining her smile. The moment they had disappeared, she turned to Trule.

"I'm sorry to pull you away from your other duties," she whispered. "But I want you and the girls to carefully clean up the mess in the library."

Trule studied Everys's face. "And?"

"See if you can figure out what the attackers were looking for," Everys whispered. "See if there's any pattern to what they were doing. Then let me know what you find."

Trule nodded, then left to summon the rest of the staff. Everys let out a long breath. Hopefully they would be able to dredge up some answers soon, because she didn't like where her thoughts had been drifting. The Cold Light knew something about why the mage-king attacked the Festival and they weren't sharing. As much as she wanted to trust her hosts, Everys knew she needed that answer more.

18

Everys tried to distract herself with a stack of reports on the military's ongoing efforts to patrol the forest's edge. But try as she might, she simply couldn't focus on the words scrolling by on her scriber. Part of it was that there was nothing interesting in the reports. At least, nothing that required her immediate attention. But mostly, she wanted to head down to the library and see if Trule had found anything.

Finally, just as Third Watch started, the doors to her quarters opened and Trule and the other girls slipped inside. Their clothes were disheveled and stained with sweat and it looked like most of them couldn't move much faster than half speed. But Trule's eyes shone with triumph.

"You found something?" Everys prompted.

Trule nodded. "Yes, quite a bit. First, there is this."

She turned and gestured toward Shara, who stepped forward holding a canvas bag.

"I found this half-buried under a stack of books," Shara explained. "I think the attackers must have left it in their rush."

Everys's eyes widened at the implications. Based on the way Shara hefted the sack, she could tell that there was something inside it. She motioned for Shara to hand it over and dug inside.

Unfortunately, there wasn't much, just several loose papers and three books. She glanced at the books' spines. One was written in a language she didn't understand but thought might be an ancient Weyfir script. The others were collections of ancient mythology—one dealt with Weyfir myths, the other, ancient Dynastic stories. She frowned. Why would the attackers have been interested in those?

The maps didn't seem to have anything to do with the books. Since two of them had to do with the Weyfir, she expected them to have something to do with the Weyfir's territory or their coastline. Instead, the maps were rough sketches of the Cold Light's forest. Not Tall Reach's Shade or any of the paths she had traveled in the past, but instead, they were the eastern woods that crawled up the Spineridge Mountains, the length of the Root River, and a third that had writing she didn't recognize, like crisscrossing scratches that could easily be mistaken for doodles.

"Yes, that one is most interesting," Trule said. "Plissk duneplot notations."

"Can you read these?" Everys asked.

Trule's scales blanched for a moment, then she shook her head. "I'm afraid not, Blessed. That writing hasn't been used for centuries."

Everys tamped down her disappointment. The fact that the girls had found this at all was a tremendous help. She wished that Professor P'layvo was with them. Maybe she would have known how to read them.

"Did you find anything else?" she asked.

Trule nodded. "We were able to reconstruct which books the intruders were interested in."

"How?" Everys prompted.

"We clean up after people for a living, Blessed," Kisa, another of the girls, said with an impish smile. "We have learned how to tell when a person is done with something and when they'll come back to it."

Everys's cheeks heated and the girls giggled. She supposed that was true. How often had she left work out in haphazard piles around her quarters and the girls had left them alone while cleaning up the rest of the quarters?

"They were very interested in books of ancient mythology and maps of the Cold Light's forest," Trule said.

That lined up with what Hommas had told her during the interrogation. They were looking for ink, and they must have believed that they could find it somewhere in the forest. But why would they need books on mythology? Were they looking for clues about the ink Hommas mentioned? But then why steal books on Weyfir and Dynastic mythology? She picked up the one about Weyfir myths and flipped through them. Creation stories, a whole section about a war between gods, plus dozens of heroic journey ballads. Much to her surprise, the book about the Dynasty's mythology had nothing to do with the official pantheon. No stories about the Perfected Warrior or the Water Bearer or any of the lesser deities. Instead, there were ancient myths about the Dynasty's earliest conquests, stories of the Xoniel tribe's founding, but nothing that seemed to connect to forbidden ink.

There was a tentative knock at the door and Challix slipped inside. Everys sat up straighter, setting aside the books. She hadn't seen her assistant since the Moonslight Festival. She didn't know for certain if Challix was trying to avoid her. She did know that she had been avoiding Challix. It was juvenile, but Challix's harsh words still stung.

"I apologize for the interruption, Blessed." Challix wouldn't meet her gaze, instead inspecting the floor near her feet. "But I was asked to summon you to the Illuminate's compound. Master Tillmin believes they have some answers for you."

Everys rose. "Ladies, you have done well. Thank you so much."

Trule smiled, then turned to shoo the other girls back to their chores. Challix motioned for Everys to exit in front of her, still not looking her in the face. Everys left her quarters with Challix several steps behind her.

As they left the Embassy, a weight settled in Everys's stomach. This wasn't right. Yes, Challix had said some harsh things, but Everys could see the truth in them. She stopped and turned toward her assistant, hoping that she would catch up. Challix hung back, shooting a look in Everys's direction. Finally, Everys motioned for her to come closer. Challix flinched—Everys had never seen her assistant do that before!—but she nodded to herself and stepped forward with great determination.

"Challix, I—"

Challix shook her head and held up a hand. "No, Blessed. I must insist that you allow me to speak first. I behaved horribly last night. I don't know why I said those things. I certainly didn't mean them."

But she did. Everys knew that. Occ's truth-telling rune had dredged up feelings and laid them bare.

"You did, and you have a right to feel that way," Everys said. "I have been very negligent, and I've been hiding behind my grief for too long. I shouldn't have done that, not with the threat of both Brencis and the Dalark hanging over us. And now that the mage-king has made this big move, I definitely can't sit out any longer. I'm sorry that I've left you to shoulder so much."

"But that's my job!" Challix said. "I'm supposed to help you to—"

"You're supposed to help me pick out clothes and decorate my quarters, and maintain my social calendar. I've been expecting far too much of you." Everys smiled as an idea occurred to her. "So I don't want you to be my assistant any longer."

Challix's eyes went wide, and tears pooled in their corners. "I completely understand, Blessed."

"I don't think you do. From now on, you'll serve as my vizier."

"You... vizier... *what?*"

Everys nodded, smiling. She could get used to seeing Challix flustered like this. "I am the legitimate ruler of the Xoniel Dynasty. Since Paine isn't with us, that means I need someone to serve as my vizier. I can't think of a better person to do so."

Challix looked like she was about to faint. She kept shaking her head, her hands trembling. Everys caught them and gave them a gentle squeeze.

"You've already been doing this job, just without the authority and the recognition. You deserve this, Challix. I have complete confidence in you."

"But after all that I said..."

"Do you know how many times Paine used to correct Narius and call him to task? More times than I liked. And he was frustratingly right most of the time." She was glad Paine wasn't around to hear her admit that. "I need you to keep me focused."

Challix took a shaky breath, but she nodded. "Very well. I accept."

Everys smiled and pulled her into a hug. At first, Challix was hesitant, but then she returned the embrace. And while this hadn't fixed everything between them, she knew they had at least taken the first step.

Some of the tension lingered as they walked the rest of the way to the conclave. Thankfully, though, Challix walked at her side instead of behind her. They made their way through the hidden entrance and into the lab. Tillmin spotted her arrival and ushered her through the main laboratory, down a twisting hallway, and into a cramped and darkened room.

A large wooden table dominated the center of the room, where Hommas's body was laid out. He had been stripped of his clothing, but a towel covered his waist, another his head. Everys shuddered as she glanced toward his hidden face. The memory of his death clawed at her.

Hommas's clothing had been hung near the far wall, stretched out with what appeared to be wires to expose as much fabric as possible. A person in Illuminate robes adjusted them, then turned, revealing that it was Hirfan. He froze when he saw Everys, then scowled at her.

She shot a questioning look at Tillmin, who didn't seem at all abashed. "I asked for Hirfan's help. He's the best we have at this sort of work."

Everys swallowed her objection. She didn't like the idea of Hirfan helping, but she trusted Tillmin.

Hirfan produced a piece of wood, no more than a foot long and six inches wide. He dipped a finger in a pot of ink that rested on the table, and sketched a rune on the wood. Once it was activated, it produced a blue glow that he ran over Hommas's body. At first, nothing seemed to happen, but then spectral lines appeared over his chest and hands. Hirfan waved the wood over Hommas's clothing, and more lines appeared in the middle of its chest.

Once all of that was done, Hirfan set aside the wood and gently lifted the bottom edge of the towel covering Hommas's face. Everys tensed, worried about what they would see, but he only exposed the mouth, where a ghostly pattern shone in the darkness.

"I just used a rune that reveals previously cast spells," Hirfan explained. "And this body is still practically swimming in toratropic magic. It appears as though he cast at least a dozen spells in the last week or so."

Everys looked down the length of Hommas's body, her gaze hitching on the pattern that hovered just above his chest. At first, it looked like a confused jumble of lines, but it slowly unraveled itself into the truth-seeking rune. She nodded, remembering that was where she had drawn it.

The other glowing lines also resolved into different runes. Most of them clustered around Hommas's right hand. Were those ones that he had drawn himself? She recognized a few of them: the trap runes she had disarmed on the stairs, an insight rune that should have helped him find what he was seeking. But others were alien to her.

"Do we know what these do?" she whispered, worried that if she spoke too loudly, the spell might break.

Hirfan scowled at her but shrugged. "Some, yes."

He pointed at each rune individually, confirming her suspicions about the runes she recognized. But he pointed out three that he said he didn't know, jagged lines and sharp angles that hurt Everys's eyes from looking at them for more than a few seconds.

"And then there's the one over his mouth," Hirfan said. "I don't know that one either."

Everys risked a glance and immediately regretted it. Her stomach lurched and flipped at the sight, a grating sense of wrongness searing through her. She didn't need to know exactly what the rune did to know on a deep, visceral level that this was the product of the mage-kings' corrupt practices.

"Any chance we can figure out what these unknown runes do?" she asked.

Hirfan shrugged again. "I'm drawing images of them using graphite to prevent them from being cast. I can check our records for similar spells, but that will take a while."

"It's too bad that your Diradae friend's book isn't easier to read," Tillmin added. "We might find some insight in there."

"Thank you both for your help. Keep investigating please," she said.

Hirfan looked ready to object, but Tillmin motioned for him to keep silent.

"Of course, Blessed. We are more than happy to help."

As Everys and Challix left the catacombs, Everys's mind pinwheeled through her questions and half-formed theories. They already knew the mage-king was responsible for the intrusion. And now they had a vague idea of what they were looking for: some sort of ink, maybe connected to Weyfir mythology or the founding of the Dynasty, somehow connected to the Cold Light's forest.

She squared her shoulders as they left the conclave building itself. The way Everys saw it, she had two options. She could continue to grope in the dark and hope she could weave together a theory. Or she could go straight to the source.

"Come," she said to Challix. "We need to go have a chat with our hosts."

19

Without waiting for Rewether, Everys walked a well-worn trail out of the Shade. The path twisted around some boulders and shrubs, but then passed between two large trees that almost appeared to be pillars flanking a doorway. And in some ways, they did, for as Everys walked between them, she entered the place where the Cold Light's Yoreroot met.

At first glance, it appeared unremarkable, a small copse of trees in the middle of a larger forest. But a quick examination revealed the oddities, like the dozen pillar trees that were equally spaced around a depression in the ground. The depression housed a mostly green jewel held in place by a cluster of gnarled roots that poked out of the ground. Pale light danced within the gem and the flickers seemed to grow brighter and more energetic as she approached. This was the Cold Light's Hearth, a sacred relic that helped the forest flourish and had been the catalyst for making peace with the recalcitrant trees.

She stepped up to the Hearth and pressed her hands on it. She looked up at the pillar trees that loomed over her and cleared her throat. "We need to talk."

At first, nothing happened. But then, one by one, light flickered beneath the pillar trees' bark. First one tree, then another, and then another, until pale light seeped through cracks and knots on most of them. A few short minutes later, eight people hurried into the clearing, each one of them wrapped in vines and branches. She recognized Yllana and Effort among them. The grafted stood next to the glowing trees, and then the Cold Light inhabiting those trees took control of them. Their bodies twitched and jerked as the ancient intelligences took hold.

"Everys Queen, what is it you wish to discuss?" Tall Reach said through Yllana's mouth, his tone infuriatingly calm.

"As I'm sure you're aware, operatives working for the mage-king infiltrated the Moonslight Festival," Everys said.

"To my great regret, yes," Firestruck said through Effort. "I have failed to protect the forest from interlopers. I am redoubling my efforts to watch the hidden paths."

"I am gratified to hear that, but that is not why I wanted to speak with you. I have been conducting an investigation into what these invaders sought. I've learned they were sent here to find powerful toratropic ink, one that can be found in your forest. Why would they believe they could find that?"

The grafted went still and Everys waited. She knew what was happening. The Cold Light were connected to each other in what they called "the Below." She had glimpsed it once via an insight rune. The Cold Light might not be speaking to her, but they were likely discussing what to say in the Below.

"The intruders were focused on the library, yes?" one of the grafted said. "We have preserved knowledge you fleshlings have lost. They must believe that we have the formula for this ink. Would that not be so, Evergreen?"

"This is true," Evergreen said through an older grafted. "We have many volumes written by toratropic masters who lived and died many centuries ago. Perhaps the mage-kings sought that information."

Everys narrowed her eyes, trying not to glare at Evergreen's grafted. A likely explanation, but also a lie. Trule and the girls hadn't mentioned anything about the intruders gathering those sorts of books.

"Except they were looking for maps," Everys said. "They didn't expect to find what they were looking for here. They thought they'd find it elsewhere. So what was it they were looking for?"

"You can't possibly expect us to know that!" Firestruck said. "Our forest is vast and contains wonders the likes of which your fleshling mind can't conceive. To expect us to understand and know what such vile people would seek is ludicrous."

"You've boasted about the wonders of your forest before, but I don't think they're looking for stunning waterfalls or majestic vistas. They're looking for something very specific, and I think you know what it is." Everys planted her hands on her hips. "And I need to know too, so we can plan how to stop them. Because if we don't, they'll keep trying. They'll keep coming. And who knows what will happen if they succeed? They shattered an entire city not too long ago, and that was with synthetic tree sap! What do you think will happen if they get their hands on something even more powerful than that?"

Again, the grafted fell silent. Everys crossed her arms and glared at them one at a time. They didn't react, although their gazes were locked on her.

Finally, Tall Reach cleared his throat. "Your words have merit, Everys Queen. But what you are asking... You are inquiring about something we have long tried to keep buried. A shameful thing, a history that we would rather not relive."

"As a Siporan, as a descendant of the Ascendancy, I understand that all too well. But a blot on my people's history seems to be seeking something similar of yours. Isn't that reason enough to share it?"

"No," Evergreen said. "Not that we do not trust you, Everys Queen. We do not trust ourselves. We have already made promises to you that many in the forest do not agree with. Sharing this... it could create a breach in the Below, unlike any we have ever experienced."

"We are going to continue the discussion in the Below," Tall Reach said. "I believe we can reach a consensus, but it may take time. If you would give us that, please?"

Everys shifted her weight. Normally, that request wouldn't bother her, but it felt like an evasion. But then she saw the pleading look in Yllana's eyes. Whether that was from the grafted or Tall Reach, she didn't know. But it was enough to convince her.

"Very well," Everys said. "I will return to the Embassy."

She turned and strode out of the clearing. Halfway back to the Embassy, she came across Rewether.

"Good talk with the trees?" he asked as he fell into step with her.

"We'll see. What's going on at the Embassy?" she asked.

He grunted. "Still cleaning up. Your council is waiting for you in the war room."

"Oh?" Everys asked, her heart twisting. The last thing she needed was another crisis.

"Nothing hugely important. Just routine reports. Challix thought—" Rewether's cheeks reddened, and he coughed into the back of his hand. "Challix thought it might distract you."

Everys swallowed a chuckle at Rewether's discomfort. Part of her wanted to play matchmaker between the guard and her new vizier. But that didn't seem like a good use of her time. Maybe she'd suggest it to Oluna and see what her friend could concoct.

And as much as she didn't relish the idea of sitting through another meeting, she knew it had to be done. So she followed Rewether up into the Embassy and into the war room, hoping it would all be quick.

Two hours later, Everys stepped out of the war room again and took a deep, steadying breath. She tried to release her frustration, but she found it was difficult to do so.

It wasn't her advisers' fault. They were clearly as annoyed and frustrated as she was. The intrusion the day before had upset and unsettled everyone. At least there were some bright spots. Overturn reported that Brencis's troops had done nothing at the same time as the invasion. That likely meant that, whatever the mage-king had been doing, he hadn't included Brencis in on the plan. That was a blessing. She shuddered to think what would have happened if troops loyal to Brencis had invaded the forest while they were dealing with the intruders.

Aside from that, though, there was only confusion and questions. What were the intruders after? How had they slipped into the forest? With the Cold Light occupied in their internal discussions, that left the other advisers to speculate and grow more and more frustrated. Finally, Everys put an end to the meeting.

She leaned against a wall and mopped her face with her hands. Why was this so difficult? Yes, she hadn't been trained to be queen, let alone the true leader of the Dynasty. But she knew what she wanted to do was right. She couldn't just abandon the Dynasty to Brencis's tyranny or the mage-king's schemes. So why was she struggling so badly? Shouldn't the Singularity make her job easier? She was trying to do the right thing.

"I need Your help here," she muttered. "Please. Show me what I'm supposed to be doing."

Someone cleared her throat. Yllana waited a respectful distance away and offered her a shaky smile.

"The deliberations have been intense, Blessed," Yllana said. "But the Cold Light have come to an agreement."

"And?" Everys prompted.

"They're willing to explain what the intruders were after," Yllana said. "More precisely, they're willing to show you. Only you. You need to get ready to travel. You're going to the Deep Forest."

20

Everys tried to stretch and twist the knots out of her back. Trying to sleep in the jostling transport had not been enjoyable. If she had known it would take a three day journey over rough terrain, with just her and Tall Reach inhabiting Yllana's body, she might not have agreed to go, no matter how badly she wanted answers.

She squinted out the window. What time was it? Was it even morning? She couldn't tell. The surrounding woods were dark, filled with shifting shadows. It didn't appear to be the middle of the night, but she couldn't see the sun to gauge whether it was morning or still evening.

The transport lurched and came to a stop.

"We have arrived." Tall Reach pushed open the door and gestured for Everys to exit.

She did and came to an immediate halt. The trees were bare and dry, some of them covered with a dull brown moss, but most looking like a breeze would cause them to crumble. All were a melange of grays, blacks, and whites, like someone had completely drained the forest of color. She gaped at her surroundings. What had happened here?

She turned a slow circle and spotted a trail. Tall Reach led the way, easily making his way over the uneven dirt. Everys hurried after him. Loose rocks and roots created tripping hazards, but she managed to keep up with him.

They emerged at the bottom of a hill and Everys stopped short. A huge mound stretched before her, too perfectly sculpted to be a natural hill, even though it was covered in scraggly bushes, twisted trees, and patchy, dried grass. Plus, there was an entryway carved into the side, bordered by thick stones. Two abstract sculptures knelt at either side of the entrance, both vaguely shaped like a human, but their chests and heads were made of boulders, their arms and legs thick branches, everything held together by brittle-looking vines. Even though they knelt, they were taller than Everys by several feet.

"You'll come out whole, Everys Queen," Tall Reach whispered, something she had never heard a Cold Light do before.

He walked through the archway. She hesitated, wondering why he phrased his assurance that way.

They descended a ramp dotted with glowing stones. There were no other decorations or adornments, just pale flickers along the rough-hewn walls.

Then she and Tall Reach emerged into an enormous cavern. A trench had been dug around a large stone, one almost as big as the cavern itself, that rested in the middle of the space. Everys looked up at the ceiling that disappeared into darkness overhead. She spotted rough, rib-like supports that held up the roof. Why had they done all this to house a boulder?

"This way, Everys Queen." Once again, Tall Reach's tone was low and almost reverential. He motioned for her to approach the boulder.

She did so, her mind racing. Was this a holy place for the Cold Light? Is that why Tall Reach was behaving like this? But if that was the case, why was everything in this part of the forest dead or dying? Who would have created this barrow and just for a rock like...

Her eyes adjusted to the dim light, and she suddenly realized that what she was looking at wasn't made of stone, but flesh. A massive creature lay before her, turned on its side. She stumbled back a step. All she could see clearly was its head, large as a house, with a bony forehead studded with sharp spikes and large pincers where the mouth should be. For a moment, she hoped it was an enormous statue, but it wasn't made of wood or stone. It appeared to be made of chitin, the same texture as a crab's shell. This had been a living creature at some point.

A blast of humid air rolled over her, chased by cooler air that smelled of rot and decay. Everys gagged, staggering, before another wave of hot air slithered over her.

Her head snapped up, and she gaped. It wasn't dead. That was its breath. Whatever this creature was, it was still alive.

Her chest heaved as panic stabbed into her mind. She took a step backward and wanted nothing more than to flee the barrow, to dive back into the transport and return to the Shade, seal herself in her room, and—

A firm hand settled on her shoulder.

"Breathe, Everys Queen," Tall Reach whispered. "Breathe. He is no threat. He is in deep hibernation."

Everys heard skittering overhead. She looked up and saw shapes scuttling along the rocky ribs. Whatever was up there stuck to the darkness, but she thought she could pick out spindly legs and matte black bodies wrapped in vines. She shuddered.

"Wh-what is it?" she asked.

Tall Reach sighed. "I cannot pronounce his people's name with this crude tongue, nor would I want to. The dissonance of their speech is more than most fleshlings can bear. Translated into Dynastic, they call themselves the Only True. I do not know if you have a name for them, but you call their devotees the Elderreach. That name may suffice."

It felt as though she had fallen into a deep pit, her mind tumbling end over end. Was this... could this be... an *Elderreach god*? They were real? She had heard many stories about them and the cult they inspired, but she—like everyone else—assumed they were simply myths and legends, nightmares that were thankfully fictional.

"Wh-what is it doing here?" she asked.

"He is our penance." Tall Reach walked up to the Elderreach and rested a hand against its forehead. "They came from the south. Hundreds. Thousands. They burned through us, scattering ashes in their wake. We fought them with what we had, but we nearly lost everything.

"We had to survive. So we did... unspeakable evils, using what weapons we had and what armies we could raise. The war lasted for three centuries and raged across much of what you know as Ehun. The battles changed us in profound ways. We have adapted to them, but we know the cost of war. And we know what it cost them."

Tall Reach fell silent. Everys could hear the clicking of the creatures overhead and, after a while, even the low rumble of the monstrosity's breath.

"What happened?" Everys asked quietly.

"We slaughtered them. Even after we drove them out of the forests, we pursued them. And we killed them all. Every one of them, except for this one. We tracked him to a small village and..." He paused, then turned to her. "Perhaps you would like to see for yourself."

Everys frowned. What did that mean? But Tall Reach headed further into the barrow. She hurried after him, not wanting to be alone. She tried to give the slumbering creature as wide a berth as possible. They rounded the head, and Everys got a good look at the rest of the creature's body. It had to be at least three hundred feet tall, with two thick arms that ended in massive hands with claws as big as her. But it also had thousands of thinner whip-like tentacles that covered its shoulders and arms, each one tipped with a spike. A shudder wormed across her skin, and she pressed up behind Tall Reach.

He didn't seem to be affected by the sight. Instead, he led her to a wall opposite the creature's waist. Unlike the rest of the barrow, the wall was made of smooth bricks. It was dotted with clear crystals, each one of them enclosed in a frame of wire mesh. Everys frowned. She had seen this sort of thing before and recently. But where?

Tall Reach ran a finger along the topmost row, then pulled down the second from the right. He hefted it and turned to her.

"We call these 'memory tears.' Every few decades, the Elderreach will shed one. We collect and examine them, saving the ones that seem significant. This... this will show you. Be open to receive what it offers. A closed mind cannot access what it contains."

He held it out to her. Everys gingerly took it, surprised at how heavy it actually was, at least thirty pounds if she had to guess. The wire was twisted at odd angles, but she found slots where her fingers seemed to naturally slip through. She was about to ask what to do next, but a burning sensation swept across her palms, where her skin touched the metal caging. She sucked in a deep breath...

And suddenly, she was out in the sun. But it felt different. The brightness hurt, the air stung. She was used to the deeper pressure, the insulating cold of brine sloughing past her scales and...

Her eyes widened. She was looking through the Elderreach's eyes, seeing the world as it must have. The brilliant sun, the biting air...

The pains and agony that radiated through her body. Arms and legs, screaming from the cuts that had bitten deep into her. The burning in her chest from sprinting over the blasted land, soaked through with the blood of her kin. Those air-drinking trees! They had done this to her. To them! To all of them! The screeches of her kin, dying in the surf. The taste of dirt and wood in her mouth as she fought her way free.

Stumbling over hills, trying to lose her pursuers. Even now, she could hear them scrabbling behind her. She had to get away. She had to—

She tripped over her tail, spilling into the dirt. She skidded across the ground and came to a rest. Her vision swam, and she could feel her strength flowing out of her.

Then she saw them. Humans. She rested in one of their villages. Slowly but surely, the humans emerged from their hovels. Most hung back, but one crept forward, crouched low, a mix of fear and curiosity. She considered using the last of her strength to lunge forward, gobble him down. One final, defiant act before the trees claimed her...

In a flash of light, the vision ended. She lurched forward, fumbling with the tear. She looked up at Tall Reach, who nodded grimly.

"We found him before he could fully die. The humans had fled, taking his final-tear with him." At her confused expression, he continued. "Shortly before an Elderreach dies, they shed a final-tear, their last memories."

Everys frowned. "But it's still alive. You said it's hibernating."

"Yes, *he* is," Tall Reach said. "But there are telltale signs when a final-tear has been shed. Trust me, Everys Queen. We know very well what those are. He shed his. We brought him here, where we encased him in the ground, where we hold him in sleep."

"But why?" Everys said. "I know the myths my people tell. If even half of them are true, the Elderreach are an evil unlike anything any of us have ever encountered. Why keep it... *him* alive?"

"Because he is the last. Because we made him the last." Tall Reach's gaze dropped. "Because if we let him die, then we will cross the threshold and become like them. Destroyers. Ravagers. A scourge bent on annihilation."

Everys looked down at the tear. This was all too much. Bad enough that she was facing wars and insurrections, the mad plots of mage-kings. To find out that this ancient evil still existed, a living, breathing "god" who...

Her eyes widened as the pieces fell into place. According to the ancient texts, Elderreach blood was said to be the most powerful of inks, capable of creating runes of unimaginable power. Again, none of the scriveners thought such ink was real, just the product of fanciful myths. But here was the proof that they were all wrong.

"This is what they were after," she whispered. "His blood."

"We think so, yes," Tall Reach said. "We, too, pieced together the clues. They somehow know about him and were trying to find out where, exactly, he is. Thankfully, this is a secret we have never written down. Only the Cold Light themselves know about our unfortunate guest. And now, you do too."

Everys held out the tear. Tall Reach took it and set it back in its place. Her gaze skimmed the dozens of other tears. What would she see in each one?

"We should go back, Everys Queen," Tall Reach said. "It is our hope that, with this knowledge, you might be able to stop your enemies."

Could she? She'd have to try, to repay the trust that the Cold Light had shown her by sharing this.

They walked back along the monster's body toward the exit. Even though she didn't want to look, her gaze still flicked to the Elderreach. She couldn't help herself. She could feel the weight of its presence drawing her in, pulling her gaze...

As it looked back at her.

She froze. Had it woken up? The massive eyes, taller than her, were open, a red, metallic sheen flickering over their surface. She stood, transfixed, horrified at what might happen. Would it lunge forward, snatch her up in its jaws?

But then the Elderreach blew out a long breath, and its eyes drifted shut. Everys gagged on the stench, but she couldn't will herself to move.

Tall Reach placed a hand at her back and urged her on. He escorted her back to the transport and helped her board.

They remained silent until Tall Reach released Yllana. But even after Yllana regained control of her body and her bubbly personality returned, Everys remained quiet. She watched the trees of the Deep Forest slowly give way from browns to greens. And she hoped that what she had seen would remain lost in the forest.

21

B y the time Everys returned to the Shade, she had mostly recovered from seeing the Elderreach. She wasn't sure she'd ever
truly be free from the cloying presence of the creature's mind. As she
disembarked the transport, Challix and Rewether met her.

"Status?" Everys asked.

"All secure here, Blessed," Rewether said.

"Did you discover what the intruders were after?" Challix asked.

Everys hesitated. The Cold Light had shown her a tremendous
amount of trust by telling her about the Elderreach. That secret wasn't
hers to share.

"I believe so," Everys said. "And the implications are troubling.
Assemble my advisers."

Challix hurried back into the Embassy. Everys followed her up the
steps and headed for her room. While Challix gathered everyone,
Everys would take a quick bath to wash the journey from her.

Once she was done, she headed for the war room. Waiting for
her were three of the grafted, including Yllana. Strategist Overturn
was conversing quietly with Rewether and Tormod. Occ stood in one
corner, but he perked up when she entered.

"Overturn, any new developments?" she asked.

"Thankfully, no. Brencis's troops are still prowling the border, but
none have made any overtly hostile moves. Were you able to determine what the goal was in infiltrating the Shade?" Overturn asked.

That question again. Everys shot a look to Yllana, who blinked
and returned a puzzled expression. But then a subtle tremor worked
through her, and when she met Everys's gaze again, there was an
ancient presence lurking in her eyes. Tall Reach pursed his lips but
gave her a very subtle nod.

"They were searching for a rare source of extremely powerful tora-tropic ink."

Overturn swore under his breath.

"More powerful than what they used to destroy Bastion?" Rewether asked.

Everys nodded. "Based on my understanding, yes."

While the others digested that information, she looked across the table and met Tormod's gaze. The color had drained from the spymaster's face. He would understand better than anyone else.

"They must be preparing to cast another rune," Challix said. "Something even more devastating than the one that destroyed Bastion."

Everys cleared her throat. "The mage-kings will probably try again to retrieve that powerful ink. They don't have it yet, which is a good thing. That means we can try to stop them. The problem is, we don't know what it is they're trying to do. We know it has something to do with the runes carved on the Principalities. But with the Principalities in the Archives destroyed, we can't..."

Her eyes widened as a thought struck her. She looked across the table at Tormod.

"Narius's translation project. P'layvo would have images of the Principalities, wouldn't she?" she said.

Tormod grimaced. "My understanding is she gave Narius an encrypted scriber with the only copy of their data."

Everys's heart sank.

But then one guard by the door stepped forward, an uncertain look on his face.

"Begging your pardon, Blessed. I bunked with Farga, your husband's Swordbound. He told me that before he fought in the *harsannon*, King Narius gave a scriber to the scrivener."

That information seemed to take Tormod by surprise. But Everys's heart raced along with her mind as she put together the possibilities. If Tolistan had the scriber, that meant he had images of the destroyed Principalities. And she knew how to draw her family's rune. At least, she had been taught it, but she had no way of knowing if what she knew matched what was actually carved into her family's Principality. Then there were two other Principalities that the Siporans had hidden away before Nekek the Bright fell. No one knew what those two looked like except...

A smile burst on her face. Except for the families who cared for those Principalities while on their vigils, just like what Papa and Mama and Galan had left Bastion to do five years earlier. And it was possible that Tolistan would know who to ask to find out that information.

"We have to find Scrivener Tolistan," she said. "We need both the scriber and the locations of the missing Principalities."

Tormod shifted, his expression uneasy, but he didn't object. Everys was glad that Papa wasn't sitting in on this meeting. He would have had a stroke out of sheer rage.

"That's only half the solution, though, isn't it?" Challix asked. "Even if we have all eight Principalities, we won't know what the mage-kings want with them."

That was true. But Everys brightened as another thought occurred to her.

"Maybe we can figure that out," she said. "If we get the scriber with Tolistan and P'layvo's research, maybe we can resume it here. And if we use the book that Occ found, maybe we can translate what the runes say. We'll need Occ or some of the shessu to help translate the book, but maybe that will help us figure out what the mage-king's plan is."

"I'd be more than happy to help!" Occ said.

"We might want to enlist the help of the Illuminates as well," Everys said. "They've been studying runes for centuries. Their input would likely be invaluable."

Tormod nodded grimly. "I will contact some of my agents in Bastion. They'll track down Tolistan and bring both him and the scriber here. P'layvo as well."

Everys shook her head. "No. I have to go."

The room fell silent. Rewether stared at her, aghast.

"Absolutely not, Blessed," he said.

Everys shook her head. "Tolistan won't give information about my people's most sacred objects to just anyone. And he may suspect that any agents you send are part of a trap. No, he would only entrust it to another Siporan, someone he knows and trusts."

While the others mulled over that information, Everys once again met Tormod's gaze. The spymaster had gone ashen. While she knew his true heritage, that he was Siporan, none of the other advisers did.

Tolistan likely didn't either. He finally closed his eyes and nodded once.

"The queen has the right of it," Tormod said. "It has to be her."

"But what happens if there's a crisis here while you're gone?" Challix interjected.

"Let's be honest, I'm not contributing much." Everys held up a hand to stop any disagreement. "We all know it's true. Yes, I sit in on these meetings and I give orders, but I trust all of you to keep things running. Overturn, I know that you and Firestruck will keep the forest secure. Tormod, I know you will continue to work on finding out what Dalark and Brencis are up to. All I do is settle arguments, and Challix, I'm pretty sure you can do that better than me. This is something that I can do. Something that only I can do."

She thought she had convinced them. None of them looked happy, but none of them objected.

"If you do this, you can't go alone," Rewether said. "I'll handpick the best guards we have and send a squad with you."

Everys shook her head. "If I'm accompanied by too many people, I'll stand out. It'd be better for me to go with two people at the most. One would probably be better."

Rewether scowled. "Fine. I'll accompany you."

"Very well. Let's make preparations and get going," she said.

They spent the rest of the meeting discussing what felt like trivial matters. Not that Everys dismissed food supplies and border security. She just knew that she had to focus on what really mattered. She had to be the one to stop the mage-kings. They were a stain on her people's history, something that every Siporan had carried with them, since the days before Nekek the Bright's destruction. She was the only one who could bring together the people and resources needed to stop them.

22

"For the record, Blessed, I feel it would be better for me to go on this mission." Tormod didn't look up from his work.

"Duly noted, Tormod." Ice bled into her voice. "But I need you to continue whatever it is you're doing."

Tormod sighed. He ran a hand through his thinning hair and met her gaze. "Blessed, are you trying to punish me?"

She scowled back at him. "Why would I do that?"

"Oh, I can think of several reasons." He ticked them off his fingers. "I was outmaneuvered by the mage-kings. I could not provide Narius with an adequate warning about the multiple disasters bearing down on him. I could not prevent his death. I've been gone for months, leaving you exposed to the mage-kings. You're right, Blessed, why would you want to punish me?"

Everys squirmed in her chair, some of his words striking a little too close to home. While she had never quite put it that way, she did harbor some resentment toward Tormod for not saving Narius. Someone should have been able to do something. But then she remembered how sorrowful Tormod had been when the city fell. He had taken the failure personally.

"Forgive my sarcasm, Blessed. Back to the matter at hand. I have prepared both you and Rewether a false identity. Your primary identity will be that of Evina Truost, a cousin to a minor house who has provided cover for my agents in the past. Rewether will be your personal bodyguard, Remard. Evina is for when you travel. She has all the correct permits and information in public databases. When you arrive at a location, you'll have a secondary identity of Emerin Bray, a member of a former noble house. In that case, Rewether will be Redarm, your cousin. Should you feel those identities have been compromised, you'll have two backups. Only use those if you're sure you have to; they will not stand up to anything except the most cursory of examinations.

"I have reached out to some people I know who will fly you to Bastion via a roundabout route. Your cover story will be that you and your bodyguard were exploring the islands in the Expanse with the help of an Ixactl guide."

He then set what looked like a bracelet on the table between them. By royal standards, it was understated, just a few gold loops studded with two dozen amber beads. But Everys smiled when she saw it. Those beads were actually ink. They were easily detachable and, with a little bit of friction, would turn to gel. Tormod had given her a similar bracelet months ago, but in the lead up to Bastion's destruction, she had used up all the beads. She quickly snared it and slipped it onto her wrist.

"Use that and your time outside the forest wisely. May the Singularity travel with you and grant you what you need, Blessed," Tormod whispered. "And may we all survive."

Everys looked up from her bag as she heard the harsh buzzing of a skimmer overhead. That had to be the smugglers that Tormod had contacted.

Rewether poked his head inside. "You ready, Evina?"

She forced herself to smile. She could hear the discomfort in his voice. Rewether was always so proper. Pretending she was someone other than the queen might prove too much for him.

She hefted up her bag and nodded. "Let's go."

They started out of the Embassy. As they walked toward the airhub, though, her steps slowed. She turned a circle, drinking in the sights and sounds and smells of the Shade. A pang of longing shot through her. Somehow, this little town had become more than just her hiding place or refuge. It had become a home of sorts. And she knew that, once she boarded the skimmer, there was a good possibility she could get caught or even killed by her enemies. She sucked in a sharp breath to tamp down the roiling unease that had settled in her chest.

"Are you all right, Blessed?" Rewether asked.

She shook her head. She didn't want to leave, even though she had to. But as she stood there, she also knew there was one thing she had to do before she left. She handed Rewether her bag and told him she'd be right back, then took off at a run before he could say anything.

Everys followed the path out of the Shade to Papa's house. She found him sitting outside on a rough chair cobbled together out of thick branches. He frowned as she approached.

She stumbled to a stop and stared at him, not even sure what she could say to him. So many regrets, so many missed opportunities, and while she wished she could stay long enough to patch them all up, it would take too long.

So she settled on the best thing she could think to say. "I'm going to be gone for a while, Papa. I just wanted you to know."

He perked up at that. "You're leaving the Shade? Where are you going?"

Should she lie to him? No, not when that distance remained between them. But he could probably know some details.

"I'm heading to Bastion first. And then..." This part stuck in her throat. "Then I'm going to see if I can find Mama and Galan. I want to bring them here."

"Really? Do you need me to come with you?" he asked. "The road to our family's vigil is dangerous. I can show you how to get there easily."

Oh, how she wanted to agree. Spending that much time with Papa might help heal the brokenness between them, but she also knew he wouldn't be able to move as quickly as she and Rewether needed to. "I'm sorry, Papa. We need to travel light. Can you at least tell me where to go?"

He scowled at her, then sighed. "Hold on. Let me get something."

Papa went into his house. A few moments later, he came out with a scriber. He held it out to her without meeting her gaze.

"This is a map of where you can find Mama and Galan. I was thinking about asking that Ixactl who runs your military to send someone to find them, but I never... I was worried... He would have said no."

Everys's heart tore. "He wouldn't have!"

Papa rolled his eyes. "Oh, of course. Because he'd worry about two Siporans hiding on the edge of the Demilitarized Zone."

So that's where their family vigil was held. She had always suspected, but never knew for sure.

"He would have, especially if I told him to," Everys said. "And I doubt I'd even have to do that. Overturn is a good person, Papa. They all are. I know that you have a hard time seeing that. But while I'm gone, can you please at least try? Oluna can help you."

Papa snorted, but then his expression softened. "I suppose."

That's all she could ask. She tried to think of something else she could say, some platitude she could share or promise she could make. But nothing came to mind. So she hugged Papa, holding him tight while struggling to hold back tears. Then, before she lost her nerve, she hurried back to where Rewether waited for her.

"All good, Blessed?" he asked.

She only nodded because she couldn't trust herself to speak. He seemed to understand. He put a comforting hand on her back and steered her toward the airhub, which was little more than a clearance created and leveled by the Cold Light. Overturn's military had set up tracking and communication equipment in a building made of three pine trees twisted together.

The skimmer they walked toward didn't look like it was in the best shape. The wings were scratched up and dented, as was the fuselage. The paint was garish, chipped and peeling in some places, patched up with mismatching colors in others. The whole thing appeared on the verge of collapse, which wasn't much of a surprise given that it appeared to be forty years old.

But more surprising were the two individuals who stood by the open hatchway. One was a nervous-looking Grerid man wearing a white shirt, open at the chest, with khaki pants. The other was an Ixactl with skin the same color and texture as rose quartz. She had never seen one of the giants with that color skin, but even more unusual was the fact that he only had one horn on the left side of his head.

The Ixactl smiled brightly and bowed when he saw her. "Blessed! So good to make your acquaintance. My name is Cage, and this is my associate, Tattanae Meerdra."

The Grerid man grimaced but waved to her.

"You the pilot?" Rewether asked the Ixactl.

"Thankfully not," Meerdra muttered.

Cage shot his assistant a look, then turned back to Everys with a smile. "No. The actual pilot is preparing for liftoff. Meerdra and I will escort you to Bastion."

Oh. Everys suddenly felt a little better. There was something... off about this Cage that she couldn't quite put her finger on. But if Tormod trusted him...

"So you've done this sort of thing before?" Rewether glared at Cage, his arms crossed.

Meerdra snorted, then covered his mouth.

"Ah, no." Cage rubbed the back of his neck. "This is my first time escorting royalty. But never fear. Meerdra and I have a vast range of experiences. You are in excellent hands. Now, if you'll please board?"

Everys exchanged a look with Rewether. The guard didn't appear happy, but he finally sighed and boarded the skimmer. Cage offered Everys his hand and boosted her inside. Unfortunately, the cabin's interior was just as cobbled together as the exterior. But there was a somewhat comfortable seat for her. Once everyone else was aboard and settled in, the engines roared to life and soon, they were in the air above the forest and heading out to the vast blue of the Expanse.

23

<hr>

Thankfully, Innana didn't insist on the ridiculous costume this time. She actually allowed Narius to choose his own clothing. In the grand scheme of things, that was a minor victory, but it was a win he still appreciated. At his request, Kavi brought him a pair of loose green pants and a comfortable blue-green shirt with sleeves that came down to his elbows. She also brought a bag filled with accessories like rings, bracelets, and even what looked like a hat made of gold and silver wires.

Once he was dressed, he slipped out of his room where Kavi was waiting. She glanced at him, then smiled.

"So what are we doing tonight? Another well-choreographed appearance with cameras that just happen to be there?" He tried—and failed—to keep the frustration from bleeding into his voice.

For the past two weeks, Kavi had brought Narius out to different districts in Utuaa for carefully choreographed appearances. None of them were as dramatic as the first one in the Septagon, but now that he knew Innana employed actors, he could pick them out of the crowd easily enough. Some people who saw him were too quick to identify him, too quick to pick up the chant that echoed behind him wherever he went.

Narius, Senen's long-promised king.

Kavi smirked. *No, she has something more... tonight. She wants you to appear in...*

Narius frowned as Kavi kept signing. Was that a proper name? She must have read the confusion on his face. She smiled kindly and started over.

You'll go to a place where big, important people meet and see each other. It's called...

Again, she signed something, but slower and more deliberately. *K-A-L-I-B-A-N-N-A-S C-O-L-O-N-N-A-D-E.*

His eyes widened. "Kalibanna? As in the insane architect?"

She laughed silently and nodded enthusiastically.

He groaned, piecing together what she was telling him. "Big, important people" meeting in a place called Kalibanna's Colonnade? They must have been the Dalark equivalent of the Dynasty's nobility. "I suppose we can't rely on rumors and shaky vid footage of me forever. We need more credible people to help sell the idea that I'm Senen's king, whom death can't hold, right?"

For a split second, Kavi's expression turned brittle, but then her impish grin returned. It happened so quickly, Narius thought he had imagined it.

"What's the matter?" he asked.

Kavi studied his face, then shook her head and looked away. *It's nothing.*

"No, it clearly is something," Narius said.

Kavi went still. She studied the floor, her face pinched into a frown, before looking up at him again.

Senen. He's ours.

He frowned. What did that mean?

He's one of us. One of me. She sighed, then spelled it out slowly and carefully. *He was a Siporan.*

Narius's eyes widened. "Does Innana know that?"

She shook her head. *Many of us have had to hide who we are. Hatred for Siporans runs deep.*

He winced. That was true in the Dynasty as well.

Senen was a teacher on—he thought the word she used was "government"—*and wrote many thoughts about how it should run. When he died, one of his students found more of his notes and writings, including the promise of the king. When Senen was declared*—he assumed she signed "Potentate"—*the Dalark thought the promise was for them. But we know it was for us. This is our promise, not Innana's. Not theirs.*

Oh. Narius ground his teeth, silently cursing his inability to communicate better with Kavi. He had so many questions. Tolistan had told him about the authors who had written so many of the ancient texts. Did the Siporans in the Dynasty know about Senen? Would they consider his words sacred? What else did he say about this king?

But he couldn't allow himself to be sidetracked. This was just... just curiosity on his part. Maybe after all of this was over, he could sit down and have a more detailed discussion with Kavi and others about Senen's promised king. Maybe he'd be able to facilitate something with the leaders of her faith community and Scrivener Tolistan. Maybe...

He brightened as a new possibility occurred to him. If Innana could wrest control of the Imperium from Tirigian and he could regain his throne, maybe he could try to reunite the scattered Siporans and find them a home, somewhere where they could rebuild their communities and reforge their identities.

Before his supposed death, he had proposed a sweeping collection of laws that would have decriminalized the Siporan faith and practices. Instead of hiding their incredible abilities, they would have been free to pursue them if they wished.

So he made a promise to himself. If he survived this, if he made it back to the Dynasty, he would see this happen. He would see the Siporans have a home.

And if keeping that promise meant he had to play Innana's little game, so be it.

Thankfully, Kalibanna's Colonnade was not nearly as twisted as Utu-aa's Navel.

Once Kavi dropped him off a short walk from the Colonnade, Narius cautiously approached the structure. It turned out to be an open-air pavilion bordered by sweeping marble columns. Unlike the Navel, the design wasn't stomach turning, although the pillars were twisted and curved, looking like they had been melted and reshaped to where they didn't look capable of holding up the partially completed roof.

In some ways, the Colonnade looked like the wreckage of some strange attack, blasted and melted by an intense heat. And yet there was an eerie beauty to the structure.

Even though it was the middle of Third Watch, the Colonnade was brightly lit and crammed with people. Narius kept his head down as he approached the structure. Innana had been very specific about what was supposed to happen: Get into the Colonnade and work his way to the northern portico. Find a way to be noticed by the people gathered there. When the time came for Narius to leave, Kavi would retrieve him, the same way she had after each appearance.

He tensed when he saw a security checkpoint to enter the Colonnade. Would he have to show some sort of identification or be searched? But the guards simply funneled the incoming visitors through what appeared to be a detached doorway. Some sort of security scanner? He practically vibrated as he stepped through, not meeting the gaze of the security guards who lazily waved people through.

A few more steps and he was in. And he had to admit, the entire structure was more impressive on the inside. Strategically placed openings in the roof revealed little swaths of the sky, and oddly placed planters filled with bushes and flowers, even a few small trees, somehow channeled the people who mingled and kept them from tripping each other up.

Narius sized up the surrounding people. He had been correct in his initial guess. Based on their dress and actions, these were the rich and influential citizens of the Imperium. He may not have understood their words, but their attitudes translated easily enough. Several of the passersby shot him snooty looks, clearly judging his outfit. He considered confronting them, but Innana had been very clear about going to a specific place. He took a moment to get his bearings and then headed for what he thought was the northern portico.

At first, he thought he had gone in the wrong direction, slipping through the footpaths and dodging people having quiet conversations or strolling along the promenades. But then he spotted a small knot of people clustered around a raised dais. Was that it? He stepped up to the edge of the crowd and popped up on his toes. There were three people on a raised stage, standing behind podiums. One lectured the other two, although he kept casting looks toward the crowd. Narius frowned. What was this? A speech? A debate? The man's voice was amplified, loud enough for Narius to hear his words, but he couldn't understand them.

Someone nudged his arm. He whipped to his right, almost colliding with a young woman. She smiled kindly at him and then gestured to a low pillar to his left. She said something, then pointed to his ear.

Narius stepped over to the pillar and inspected it. It stood waist-high, having three headsets wired to the base. He frowned, then spotted several other pillars like it, with people holding handsets to their ear. Audio amplifiers? Translators? Only one way to find out.

He picked up the handset and held it to his ear. After a series of clicks, a clearly artificial voice asked him something in a language he didn't recognize. It wasn't Dalark. A second later, the voice asked a question in another unfamiliar language. He waited, then the voice asked, "Do you want Dynastic?"

The option surprised him, but he said, "Yes, please."

There was another series of clicks, and then another synthetic voice with a distinct male tone started speaking. "—what my colleagues fail to understand is that the Dynasty is living proof that the Imperium's policies toward assimilation are correct. Look at all the troubles that our venerable rivals have had with their so-called subjugated races. Because the Dynasty has allowed them too much latitude, they have faced strife for centuries. The Colonial Uprisings, the Cold Light's rebellion, the major crime in their cities, all of this stems from their lax policies. But we of the Imperium have insisted that the races who have joined our Imperium assimilate. They leave aside their cultures so that we all may enjoy greater peace and stability."

"At what cost?" This synthesized voice was slightly higher pitched. "Not just to those who were subjugated, but to us as well? Culture, languages, history, all of it gone in the name of Imperial unity. Think of what Emperor Teggiz did to the Weeping Stones in Batun. Or how, within two generations of their assimilation, no one could speak or read the Hamartin language anymore. Yes, the Dynasty may have its issues, but they have a richness that we lack here."

A murmur rippled through the crowd. It didn't sound like the listeners liked that point at all.

"Think of it this way," the second voice said. "Suppose you take a bunch of food, liquify it all, and then dump it into a glass. Does that help the flavors? Or do we get an unappetizing mush? But suppose we take those same ingredients and put them together in a salad. Doesn't that elevate the ingredients into something better?"

The first speaker guffawed, as did many in the audience. "Such crude metaphors belie the weakness of your argument, Tensin. Are some things lost? Perhaps. But everything worth having has a cost, does it not? Would we rather have a few dusty relics, languages that few speak, and the tensions that have swamped the Dynasty? And given the chaos that has descended on them, how many of the Dynasty's citizens wish their insipid kings had paid similar costs?"

That caught Narius's attention. Was this why Innana had sent him? To interrupt a debate?

"Some might, Angara. Some might. From what I've heard, King Narius was trying to move the Dynasty toward greater tolerance. It would have been interesting to see how his policies would have transformed their society compared to ours."

"An interesting proposition, but a futile one. Now that Brencis has replaced the fallen Narius, we shall never know," Tenson said.

Narius fought to keep from rolling his eyes. Another staged appearance, after all. He should have known. He set down the translator and stepped forward.

"Perhaps not so fallen after all!" he shouted.

Those standing near him turned. Several gasped and shrieked, shying away from him and giving him space. He walked up to the dais and hopped up onto the stage. Much to their credit, Tensin, Angara, and the third man looked positively shocked, so much so that Narius momentarily wondered if maybe they didn't know he was coming.

"I am Narius, the true king of the Xoniel Dynasty. Brencis is a usurper and traitor who has stolen my throne. And I am here to tell you..." What, exactly? That he was still alive? That he wanted to fight? What did Innana expect him to say? He finally settled on the only thing that occurred to him. "...that we do not need to be enemies. That there is greater strength to be found in peace between our two nations. That—"

A woman shrieked in the audience, and Narius froze. He knew that voice. The crowd parted to reveal Innana. She was draped in thick, dark cloaks, which conveniently fell away as she stretched out a trembling hand toward him. She cried out again, saying something in Dalark in a breathy voice. Narius gaped at her. What was she doing?

He started to say something, but the crowd in front of him went still. No, not still. Frozen. It was as if the entire crowd had turned to statues, their frantic whispers and confused cries cutting off in an instant. And then Kavi was at his side.

Time to go.

She led him off the dais and through the crowd, taking a moment to throw a thick cloak over his shoulders and pulling a hood over his head. They made it halfway to the exit before the entire crowd resumed their movement. Guards cried out and rushed toward the dais, but they ignored Kavi and Narius. Within a matter of minutes, Kavi had led him out of the Colonnade and to the waiting transport. He tried to ask her what had happened exactly, but Kavi seemed not to hear him. Or she was deliberately ignoring the question.

Fine. If she didn't want to answer, Narius would have to ask some pointed questions of Innana. If their partnership was going to work, she couldn't keep surprising him like this. He couldn't stay in the dark anymore.

24

After the attack at Elamek's, Quartus and Yusra went to ground for a week. Normally, that was a prudent move, but when facing an assassin that could appear out of nowhere, Quartus suspected it was wasted effort. Still, it gave them both time to breathe and process what had happened.

Why had the mage-kings killed Elamek? The man had sworn allegiance to Brencis and had shown no outward signs of turning traitor. So what did they gain? In some ways, the motive didn't matter. Elamek's murder meant Quartus had to find another ally to help him. But who could that be?

The door to the room creaked open. He whipped around, reaching for a cleaver they had found in the hotel's kitchen. Yusra slipped inside, offering him a reassuring smile. Her arms were full of bags and he could practically smell the grease from across the room. She had gone to the Dunestrider restaurant again. He didn't mind the cuisine, but Yusra had a slight obsession with it.

He didn't relax until she had shut the door.

Her smile broadened. "You know, the ones we're worried about don't need to use the door."

Good point. "Hear anything interesting?"

She flopped onto the end of the bed and started setting out the food. The containers were stained along the bottoms, but despite that less-than-appetizing sight, Quartus's mouth still watered when he smelled hot scamperer thighs, his favorite. He leaned over and snatched up a container, which contained half a dozen honey bombs and a covered bowl of wadi claw dip.

"A few rumors," Yusra said. "One theory is that your brother killed Elamek as vengeance on those who betrayed him."

He snorted at the idea. Narius would have never done that. His brother, while he tried to be stern and gruff, was too gentle. Always had been.

"Others think it's part of the insurrection."

Now Quartus laughed. The few times he'd left the hotel, he'd heard similar stories. According to the rumors, someone was stealing equipment and sabotaging military installations in and around Bastion. It was hard to track down any concrete information about the perpetrators. Understandably, the palace was being tight-lipped about it all.

"Any clues on where we might find them?" Quartus asked. "If they're real, that is."

Yusra shook her head. "Lots of stories, nothing I'd consider reliable."

Quartus nodded thoughtfully, then lunged forward, stealing one of the take-out boxes from Yusra's side of the bed. She shouted a protest and tried to stop him, but he was too quick.

"Can't let you keep all the good stuff." He opened the box and examined his prize. Dunegrub potstickers. He fought to keep the disgust from his face.

She smirked at him. "I heard one interesting story."

"Oh yeah?" He picked the smallest potsticker from the box. Whoever cooked them hadn't breaded them properly. He could still see the grubs' sickly white flesh.

"Supposedly, there's some sort of vigilante protecting the people of Fair Havens," she said.

"What?"

Yusra nodded. "Apparently, for the past few weeks, someone's taken on a bunch of the gangs and petty criminals and chased them out of the neighborhood."

Huh. Maybe that would be worth looking into.

"Feel like taking a trip to Fair Havens?" he asked.

She smirked at him. "Only after you eat the potstickers."

His stomach soured. He forced himself to eat the first grub on the skewer. It was all too chewy, probably undercooked, and the sour taste gagged him.

Yusra's smile broadened as she produced a container of hot scamperer thighs and dug in. He was tempted to scowl at her, but the sheer delight in her eyes at his discomfort made the horrible taste worth it.

Somewhat.

Quartus hadn't been to Fair Havens in months, not since he was nearly caught in a riot that Everys had accidentally started. Before that, he'd never visited. The neighborhood was a notorious ghetto, a blight on Bastion's reputation. So many people from so many races, crowded together in shoddy buildings. Local politicians kept promising to do something about the squalor, but no one ever had. No one had even tried, not until Everys.

As Quartus and Yusra descended from the skyrail, he surveyed the neighborhood. Somehow, the giant rune that destroyed the rest of the city had left Fair Havens untouched, but he couldn't be absolutely sure. The buildings were all in various states of disrepair and neglect. Half of them could have been damaged by the mage-king's rune, and no one would have ever been able to tell. Trash clogged the alleys, the stench rolling through the streets.

"Any idea where we should start looking?" Quartus asked.

Yusra shook her head.

"All right then." Quartus set out down the streets, weaving through the crowd with his head ducked so no one would get a good look at his features.

Without really intending to, he led Yusra straight to the hole where the Broken Sword shop once stood. He stood on the edge of the pit, staring down at it. This had been where Everys and her family had lived. She had intended to build an outreach center on this site, but then all the crises had upended her plans. Now all that was left of her good intentions was a hole in the ground with rancid water pooling at the bottom. His face twisted into a scowl. Everys deserved a better legacy than this.

They spent the rest of the day skulking through Fair Havens. They found little to nothing that actually helped them, just people who had heard stories about the vigilante from their neighbors who heard them from friends who heard them from relatives. As Third Watch wore on, Quartus suspected the rumors weren't true. Yes, things seemed calmer and safer in Fair Havens, but that could be attributed to many things.

Had he really become so desperate that he jumped at a ridiculous tall tale?

As they left the market the third time, Quartus spotted a crier pillar at one corner. The reporter on the screen's voice was badly distorted, but then an image of Governor-General Auriel Zammit appeared on the screen. She was clearly giving a statement and, from the information that scrolled along the bottom of the image, it was an update about the insurrectionist activities in Bastion. Quartus stumbled to a halt, watching the images.

"What are you doing?" Yusra asked.

The quiet question startled him out of his reverie. "Sorry. I haven't seen Auriel in... well, a while."

"'Auriel?'" Yusra repeated with a glint in her eyes. "Should I be jealous?"

"No!" Quartus snapped, then winced as he realized he'd answered too quickly. "It's stupid. She was my first crush."

Yusra looked between him and the crier. He knew what she must be thinking. Auriel Zammit was a beautiful woman, with bright white streaks in her blond hair. Her stern eyes were accentuated by tiny lines. But Quartus could look beyond her age and remember how she used to look. So vibrant, so compelling, so—

Yusra poked him in the ribs with a laugh. "C'mon, Your Strength. Let's keep looking."

She dragged him away from the corner and he followed, but he did shoot the crier one last look.

They finally stopped at a tea shop near Fair Havens's market. Like the rest of the neighborhood, it was run-down on the outside. But the folks who owned it, an elderly Grerid couple, maintained the inside. They kept their cups filled the entire time they were there, watching the passersby.

"So what do we do now?" Yusra finally whispered.

As much as he didn't want to, he knew it was time to admit defeat. "Let's head back to the hotel. Maybe we can come up with something better tomorrow."

She patted his hand. He tossed some blades on the table, far more than what they owed, and headed for the door. But just before they could leave, cold crept up his back, setting the hair on the back of his neck on end. His hand froze on the doorknob as darkness crept into the corner of his vision.

"Quartus..." Yusra whispered.

He nodded. She must have felt it too. He carefully, turned around. The Grerid couple stood frozen behind their counter, caught in the middle of an animated discussion. But Quartus's gaze was drawn to a pillar of shadows that filled one corner of the room. The liquid darkness spilled onto the floor.

Then two figures burst from the shadows, both of them dressed in black outfits. Quartus dropped back into a crouch. He sized up his opponents. Neither of them looked to have the same shape or size as the one who killed Elamek, but that didn't offer him much comfort. Not now that there were two of them.

"Hello, Quartus," one of them said, her voice like brittle glass.

"Our master sends his regards. You're a loose end that we need to—"

The taunt cut off as Yusra threw a teacup at the man's head. He ducked, but then Yusra swung around, throwing boiling water from a pot into his face. He shouted and clawed at the fabric of his mask.

Quartus took the momentary distraction and charged the woman. But she saw him coming and leaped over him, rolling down his back and onto her feet. She swept his legs out from under him and he slammed into the floor with a grunt.

The assassin chuckled and pulled a broken blade from her belt. Quartus flinched at the sight. If that was the same kind of weapon that had killed Elamek, this situation had just become much more dangerous.

He rolled out of the way as she brought the blade down. It only sliced through the fabric of his sleeve. Still, that was too close for comfort. He popped back to his feet and scanned his surroundings for a weapon, anything he could use to defend himself.

Quartus snatched up a chair. It was far too bulky to be used with any finesse, but he had little other choice.

The female assassin laughed. "Really? That's the best you can do?"

"Whatever works, right?"

"Keep telling yourself that."

She lunged at him, and he barely blocked the slash with the chair. The blade embedded itself in one of the wooden legs. He tried to twist the chair to rip the dagger out of the woman's hands, but she didn't let go. Instead, she grabbed a leg and yanked. He fumbled the chair and dropped it, allowing the female assassin to rip her dagger free.

But instead of attacking, the female assassin flicked her wrist in the Grerid man's direction. The man staggered, suddenly free of whatever had held him, and looked down at the smaller throwing dagger embedded in his chest. He gurgled something, then collapsed to the floor. His wife, also freed from the spell, shrieked in horror.

Before Quartus could react to the sudden murder, the assassin tackled him to the floor. Quartus grabbed her wrist with both hands, fighting to keep the weapon away from his chest, but Shattered Shield, this woman was strong! His arms trembled with the effort.

"Time to die, Prince."

But then a massive hand closed around the woman's head and pulled her off Quartus. The female assassin flew across the room and slammed into the wall. Quartus gasped and rolled away from his rescuer.

The female assassin popped to her feet, then froze. She bit off a curse, then slapped at her arm. In a burst of shadows, she vanished from the tea shop.

Quartus looked over and saw that Yusra's attacker had vanished as well. Yusra, whose shirt was torn and sweaty, didn't look the worse for wear. She met Quartus's questioning gaze and nodded. She was okay.

So he turned to face their rescuer. He tensed when he realized their savior was an Ixactl, who turned slowly and met his gaze. At first, based on the sheer contempt in the other's expression, he was convinced he had run afoul of Stoophawk again. But then he realized he was very wrong.

"You," he whispered.

Maybe, just maybe, he hadn't been saved at all.

25

Narius paced the room, resisting the urge to glare at Kavi once again. After they had arrived at the safehouse, his frustration had boiled over and he had demanded that she summon Innana as soon as possible. He didn't like this new turn of events at all. Why hadn't Innana warned him she was going to be in the Colonnade?

As he paced, his anger kept growing. That she hadn't warned him about what she was planning was a sign she didn't see him as a true partner. He was a prop, a pawn, just like the actors she had hired for him to confront in the Septagon. If she overthrew Tirigian, would this define the relationship between the Imperium and the Dynasty going forward?

"Any word?" he finally asked.

Kavi pulled out a scriber and glanced at it. She shrugged, then signed, *Nothing yet.*

And that was another thing! Keeping him waiting like this. Yes, he had nothing else to do, and yes, he was sure that she had to be careful where she went and who she was seen speaking with. But this was disrespectful. He wasn't some lackey or hireling who could be forced to wait for Innana's good pleasure. Narius was the rightful king of the Xoniel Dynasty! He was apparently an integral part of her plan. To not warn him and then to leave him waiting like this?

By the time Innana finally arrived, Narius's whole body shook with barely contained anger. He clenched and unclenched his hands, still pacing in a tight circle. Innana breezed into the apartment, her gait fast and her face pinched into a frown.

"What is it, Narius?" she asked. "I had to sneak out of the palace to come here, and—"

He whirled on her. "Do you want to explain what games you're playing now?"

Her frown sharpened. "What do you mean?"

"Showing up at the Colonnade? What was that about?"

"I often put in appearances there, especially during the lectures. It helps me cultivate an image of a woman whose interests range beyond the traditional," she said coolly. "Why was that a problem?"

"You keep springing these surprises on me!" he said. "First the actors at the Septagon, and now you at the Colonnade. If I'm really your partner, shouldn't you tell me what you're planning?"

Innana chuckled. "Why are you so upset? You did what you needed to perfectly. We couldn't have planned that any better."

Frustration welled up inside Narius. "But what did you say? Why were you there? What aren't you telling me?"

Innana shot a look toward Kavi, whose face remained impassive. Then Innana crossed her arms. "Fine. If you must know, I not only called you by name, but I also referred to you as my 'beloved.'"

A pit opened in Narius's stomach. His head spun. Hearing her use that word dredged up old memories he thought he had buried long ago. He thought she had too. "Wh-what? Why would you do that?"

She shifted her weight, her hip popping to one side. "For the sake of the larger story we're telling. The people who witnessed my outburst will wonder why I called you that and will start making discreet inquiries amongst their friends about why I may have said that."

Narius gaped at her. "And we want that?"

"Of course. Everyone knows that we nearly married not that long ago, but I've recruited some of the palace staff to 'accidentally' let it slip that you and I were carrying on a clandestine romance for years, ever since we met as children at the summit on Maotoa. Once that rumor reaches the right ears, it'll spread throughout the aristocracy in Utuaa and beyond. I expect the story will transform along the way into that of two lovers separated by distance and hostility, cut short by your untimely death. Coupled with the rumors that you have returned from the grave, people won't be able to resist sharing it."

"Again, why?"

"For two excellent reasons. While the reports of your return are spreading, this will ensure they are retold even faster. And second, it will help explain why you will hand over the reins of the Imperium to me when the time comes. If we were simply two people who nearly married for political convenience, the Imperium's citizens might wonder why you chose me. But if we're former lovers? Not only does it make sense why you would do so, it serves as a fitting and satisfying conclusion to the entire story."

Narius frowned. He supposed it did, but the thought still bothered him.

"I don't understand what the problem is," Innana continued. "You agreed to help with my plan."

"To overthrow your brother, yes, but not this... this theatrical farce. What if the story doesn't take? Will you expect me to marry you as well?"

Innana smirked, but there was a moment of hesitation before she did. Blunted Blade, she actually was considering it!

She must have caught his frustration, for she quickly said, "Of course not! And even if we did, it would be a sham, just to shore up the narrative."

So she was considering it! For a brief moment, Narius's mind spun through that possibility. What if she insisted? What if Everys found out?

"Trickster's duplicity, what is wrong with you?" Narius thundered.

Innana blinked, but then her cheeks flushed. Her eyes flashed. "Nothing is wrong with me. I am committed to doing what I must to free my people. I thought you were willing to help me do that."

"Not if it means... not if it means pretending. Acting. This isn't what I signed up for!"

"Oh?" Innana shot back. "Are you saying that you've never done a bit of acting as the Dynasty's king? Never had to put on a smile and pretend what a person at a gala is saying is so fascinating? Never had to hide your true feelings of disgust, as you had to play nice with someone you despised?

"Or maybe this will sound more familiar: 'Innana, I'm so glad that we can finally get married. I'm looking forward to building a life with you.' Or 'Innana, despite what happened at our wedding, I'm willing to try again if you are. I'll set aside Albanon's Compromise and take you as my second wife for the good of the Dynasty.'"

Narius's stomach dropped into his feet. While most of what Innana had said was simply playing politics, and while he may never had said those exact things to her, he recognized the way he had treated her. As a prop. As part of a scheme. He had played a role, just like an actor.

"Yes, I am expecting you to be an actor in a story that I am telling," Innana continued, her voice quiet but fierce. "But it shouldn't be anything you're not used to, Narius. You were raised in a royal family, just like I was. How many times did we have to set aside our personal feelings and play a part? By all the spirits, I don't think I could even count. So why should this be any different?"

She had a point. As much as he chafed against it, there were many times that he had to put on the clothing the servants laid out, go to a party or gala or function that he wasn't interested in, and pretend he was thrilled to be there. But this situation felt different.

He latched on to that idea. "And how does it make you feel to act so differently from the way you truly are? Wouldn't you rather be yourself, your true self?"

Innana frowned. "Of course I would. Do you think I enjoy pretending to be a vapid princess?"

"Of course not. But wouldn't you rather take the throne as yourself?" His thoughts fell together and he stood straighter. "If we follow through on this plan, even if we unseat your brother, people will always see you as a pretender."

She looked ready to argue, but he held up a hand to stop her.

"Yes, I can play the part of Senen's king, and I can eventually name you the true ruler of the Dalark, but you'll only have your throne because of me. Even if the people accept your claim, there will always be people who doubt you should have it."

Innana's mouth snapped shut, and a thoughtful look crossed her face. Narius pressed his advantage.

"Wouldn't it be better if we forget about all of this pretending and focus on getting what you want, what your people actually need?"

Innana went still, her face still pinched into a frown. Narius could practically feel her thoughts wrestling. Then she sighed, her face softening.

"And how do you suggest we go about doing that?" she asked.

He swallowed a sigh of relief. "First, no rumors about our former relationship. That'll just confuse the issue in ways that I don't think will be helpful. Second, no more appearances by me as Senen's promised king. From what I've learned, that promise wasn't meant for this situation, and I feel like we're cheapening someone else's story by using it."

Kavi's froze. Her eyes widened. Then she offered him a small, almost shy, smile.

"After that, we need to find the right people to approach. Allies. Key supporters. People who will back you when it comes time to replace your brother."

Innana nodded thoughtfully. "I'll consider this. For now, we will pause your appearances. I won't spread any new rumors. And in a few days' time, we'll meet again and plan this further. Does that sound acceptable?"

Relief flooding through him. Innana turned on her heel and marched out of the apartment.

As soon as she had left, Kavi approached Narius. *So now what?*

"Now I need your help," Narius said. "We need to figure out who we need to talk to so Innana can overthrow her brother."

Because the sooner that happened, the sooner he could go home.

26

T hankfully, the trip to Bastion had been uneventful. Cage and Meerdra proved excellent distractions. The Ixactl had regaled Everys with stories of their adventures, most of which sounded too outlandish to be true, especially given Meerdra's sour reactions to each retelling.

At one point, the skimmer banked around an immense column of smoke. Everys couldn't tell where it was coming from. Cage and Meerdra couldn't explain it. Their pilot had no idea either, but someone had apparently ordered her to give it a wide berth. The inky smoke rising into the sky caused Everys's stomach to twist. What had happened?

That feeling grew when they finally approached Bastion. As their skimmer circled for a landing at the only functional airhub, a small military encampment just outside the wreckage of the city, Everys inspected the capital city. Large sections of the city were still buried in rubble, the few remaining buildings devoid of life, as if Brencis had left his capital to rot.

After landing, they had to pass through a security checkpoint. Seeing the heavily armed soldiers checking each passenger's identification caused a spike of panic in Everys's stomach. But when it was her turn, the guard who glanced over her papers barely looked in her direction before waving her through the checkpoint. The same thing happened with Rewether. Before she knew it, they were standing outside the military encampment, saying goodbye to Cage and Meerdra.

Tears stung Everys's eyes. Returning to Bastion should have felt like coming home. This was where she had grown up, after all. For most of her life, she had never ventured outside of the city. The soaring towers, the hustle and bustle that permeated the air, the almost electric buzz that seemed to weave its way through every moment had defined her world. Yes, Bastion had always had its faults. What city didn't? But whether she lived in Fair Havens or the palace, this city was home.

That hollow feeling slithered after her as they were driven through the streets toward Fair Havens. She frowned as she looked around at what appeared to be a mostly untouched neighborhood. Had the mage-kings avoided ruining Fair Havens? Was that because this was where most of the Siporans in the city lived?

The driver appeared relieved to drop them off on the edge of Safe Havens, pulling back onto the road so quickly the tires screeched. Rewether glared after the retreating vehicle, then turned to Everys. "Lead the way, Evina."

Everys smiled at the discomfort in his voice. She had tried to encourage him to act more naturally with her, but Rewether clearly couldn't see her as anything other than his queen.

She took the lead, weaving into the crowd. A few of the people they passed gave her unfriendly looks. Nothing overtly hostile, but their postures stiffened as she walked past, and they shied away from Rewether. She was used to distrust in Fair Havens. This was even more intense.

She was tempted to stop by the former site of the Broken Sword, but she knew she wouldn't find anything except a hole in the ground. They had barely made any progress in constructing her outreach center before the disaster. She'd have to add it to the ever-growing list of projects she'd complete if—no, *when*—she removed Brencis from the throne.

Everys led them into the marketplace where she met another surprise. Normally, the Fair Havens market was a bustling place, barely restrained chaos, with so many deals, both legal and illegal, being completed out in the open. Now, only a handful of people darted from stall to stall, gathering what they needed before retreating. The vendors, who normally did everything they could to cajole or entice their customers, remained strangely quiet.

They eventually came to Scrivener Tolistan's conclave. Nothing on the outside proclaimed its identity. The faded signs for the restaurant that used to use the building hung slightly askew. She tried the door, only to find it locked. She blinked, surprised. Yes, Tolistan would lock the front door, but only for part of Third and all of Fourth Watches.

Otherwise, he left the door open to make the space available for the community.

She motioned for Rewether to follow her around the building. Everys knew a side entrance led into what had been the kitchen, but that too was locked tight. She threw her weight against it and the door didn't even budge. That left only one other option. Around to the back, to a hatch cut into the alley's pavement. She knew this entrance would be locked, too, but she had the key.

"Make sure no one sees us," she whispered to Rewether.

He turned to scan the alley. While he did that, Everys knelt and plucked a bead from her bracelet, rolling it between her fingers until the ink had turned to gel. Once it had, she quickly sketched a rune onto the side of the hatch. It wasn't complex, just a quick circle with an octagon inside it, the whole pattern bisected by a curvy line. But the spell sealing the hatch recognized it and released, allowing her to open the hatch.

A ladder led down into the restaurant's basement. She scrambled down, with Rewether following. As soon as he had entered the shaft, he pulled the door closed over him.

"Do we have to do anything to lock it?" he whispered.

She shook her head. The restaurant's basement had been where she had learned to cast runes. The masters had cast a powerful rune on it years ago to make sure that no one could open that hatch. Only people who knew the key rune, like she did, could temporarily open it. In a minute or two, the locking rune would take hold and seal it shut.

Everys looked around the basement. There were still the three sets of tables, one lower than the other two, where students would sit and painstakingly copy runes until they became second nature. The tops of these tables were covered in faded stains, the results of mistakes or spills. Her gaze slid over the empty shelves. Blank pieces of paper and vials of inks once covered the shelves, but they were all gone now. When she looked closer, she realized everything was covered with dust. She frowned. Where were the students? The masters?

They headed upstairs and found a similar scene in what had been the main dining room. The same rows of mismatched chairs faced the center of the room, where the host's podium had been set up for the scriveners. But many of those chairs had been knocked over, and the entire room smelled musty and abandoned.

"Hello?" she called. It was possible that Tolistan wasn't there, but she knew he maintained an apartment above the old restaurant. If he was home, hopefully her voice would carry upstairs.

A moment later, she heard hurried footsteps overhead. Then a door that had been sloppily cut into the dining room's wall banged open. A rail-thin, middle-aged man with thinning brown hair rushed out.

"I thought I told you not to come back here until tonight!" His voice was an anxious whisper, his face twisted in a frown.

But then his gaze landed on Everys. His eyes widened, and the color drained from his face. He stumbled, catching himself on the back of a chair. Rewether rushed to his side and steadied him. Tolistan looked at the guard, and recognition blossomed on his face.

"Bl-Blessed!" he whispered. "Everys, is it really you?"

She nodded, and tears filled her eyes. Tolistan hurried past Rewether and pulled her into a tight hug. She let a single sob escape, rattling her chest, as she hugged him back.

"I'm happy to see you," Tolistan whispered, but then he pulled away from her. "But it isn't safe. Brencis's troops have stepped up their patrols in the past week."

Her heart seized. Then they should probably keep moving. "We won't stay long. We're just here for two things. First, I understand Narius gave you a scriber with the research that you and Professor P'layvo did?"

Tolistan frowned, but nodded. "I have it hidden upstairs. Why?"

As quickly as she could, Everys explained what had happened to her since she'd left Bastion: the Illuminates, the mage-kings' infiltrators, the truth-telling rune, Occ's discovery of the book. The only thing she held back was the existence of the Elderreach, glossing over that and hoping that Tolistan wouldn't pry.

He didn't. Instead, he sank into the nearest chair, his eyes wide with wonder. "Y-you mean... you mean it's possible? The king was right? We could translate the runes?"

"Possibly. The only way we'll know for certain is if we can get the research and try to build on what you and P'layvo started."

"Of course, of course." He smiled wistfully. "I wish she could know that this was happening." He frowned. "Do you think I'd be able to go to the forest? I want to see that project through."

Everys hesitated. She supposed it was possible. People were still finding ways into the forest all the time and technically, Tormod had put together a plan for her and Rewether to return when their mission was completed. But she wasn't sure she could give him much guidance.

"We'll come back to that. We have one other thing we need: the locations of the missing Principalities."

Once again, the color drained from Tolistan's face and he looked ready to deflate. "Wh-what?"

She nodded. "Papa has already given me instructions on how to find our family's. But I need to know where the other two are. We need to get images of their runes, and we also want to make sure that they don't fall into the hands of the mage-kings."

Tolistan ran a trembling hand through his hair, but he nodded absently. "Of... of course. That makes sense. I can reach out to the elders who remain in the city. They should be able to give you the right information to—"

Something banged against the front door. Rewether whirled around, reaching for a weapon at his waist that wasn't there. Tolistan's head snapped around, and he bit off a curse under his breath.

"What's going on, Scrivener?" she whispered.

He mouthed several words, but he didn't actually say anything. "Better for you to not know. Hopefully, this is..." He faltered, his face twisting into a worried expression. "You remember how I said that Brencis's troops were increasing patrols in the neighborhood? They've taken to randomly 'inspecting' the conclave to make sure I'm not hiding any fugitives here."

Everys's heart sank. If they caught her...

"What can we do?"

Tolistan hurried to the podium and pulled out two lengths of fabric. Everys recognized them immediately: mourning shawls, the type used by traditional Siporans to express mourning at the death of a close relative. He quickly threw one over her head and shoulders, then tossed the other to Rewether. Tolistan jabbed a finger at the first row of seats.

"Sit there," he hissed. "I'll tell them you lost a child in the disaster."

"Shouldn't we hide?" Rewether replied.

More banging on the front door, and somehow, it sounded angrier, more insistent.

Tolistan shook his head. "No, they might search the building, and if you're hidden, they'll be suspicious. They've interrupted me giving counsel to people in the past. They're more interested in harassing me. Hopefully, they'll leave you alone."

That wasn't much comfort, but what else could they do? Everys grabbed Rewether by the hand and steered him to one chair. She made sure his shawl was draped properly, then sat down next to him, pulling hers into place. She bowed her head and offered a silent prayer to the Singularity for protection.

A few moments later, the front door scraped open. "Yes?" Tolistan asked.

Footsteps. It sounded like at least three or four people hurried inside, whispering something to Tolistan.

"I thought I told you not to come during the day! And definitely not to bring..." Tolistan's voice trailed off. "Smudges and splatters!"

"You can see why this couldn't wait," a low female voice said.

Everys's eyes widened. She knew that voice.

"A pleasure to meet you, Scrivener. I'm hoping you'll be able to help me." This voice, a male's, was also much too familiar to her.

Tolistan stammered, then said, "Get inside."

More shuffling footsteps. Everys wanted to peek, but she didn't dare. What if she was wrong?

"You already have someone here? We don't want to interrupt." Another woman's voice, strangely accented, but very pleasant.

"You want us to leave?" the man said.

Hearing his voice again confirmed what she suspected. As soon as she heard the door shut, Everys threw off the mourning shawl. Rewether hissed an objection, but she ignored him.

Sure enough, Quartus stood in the conclave, his copper eyes wide and his jaw hanging open. He stood next to a beautiful woman with clear Dalark features. This must have been the "Yusra" he had been partnering with before Bastion's destruction.

Everys looked past them to where Tolistan stood with an Ixactl woman. She was nine feet tall, with gray skin like flint, deep set black eyes, and a red line tattooed across her face. But her most prominent feature was her missing horns. Unlike other Ixactl, her horns were nothing more than ragged stumps.

Redtale gaped at her, then chuckled. "I should have known I'd find you in the thick of trouble, Everys."

27

"Everys?" Quartus whispered. "You're alive?"

Tingles swept across Everys's skin at that too-familiar voice, so similar to her husband's that it caused an ache in her chest. And while Quartus's hair and eyes were a different color, the rest of his face was similar enough that the pang opened into a bleeding chasm. A sob rattled up her throat, and before she could think, she rushed forward and caught Quartus in a crushing hug. He wrapped his arms around her and held her tight, his own chest shaking. Neither of them spoke as they clung to each other.

"What about Narius?" Quartus whispered to her.

She shook her head, wishing she could bury her head in his shoulder, but she was too tall to do that. "He died right before the city was destroyed."

Quartus groaned, and his grip tightened.

They clung to each other for several minutes, neither speaking, just sharing their wordless grief. As much as Everys needed that moment, she realized they couldn't do this forever.

"I'm so glad to see you." She gently pulled free of his embrace, rubbed his shoulders, and then turned to his female companion. "This must be Yusra."

The woman dipped into a curtsy. "Blessed. It is an honor to meet you. Quartus speaks highly of you."

Everys arched a brow at her brother-in-law, and he blushed! Quartus actually blushed.

"Really." Everys turned to Redtale. "Redtale. It's been a while."

That was putting it mildly, and they both knew it. The last time they spoke was during Narius's *harsannon*, the ritual combat that led to his death. Two of her followers had fought him in the arena. They would have seriously injured Narius, but Everys had convinced Redtale to call them off. She'd promised to meet with Redtale and other representatives from the races the Dynasty had conquered to listen to their grievances. Everys never had the chance to make good on that promise thanks to the chaos that erupted after the *harsannon*. Hopefully, Redtale wouldn't hold that against them.

Now Tolistan stepped forward, his hand raised to catch everyone's attention. "While I'm glad for this reunion, I feel it's better for us to move to the basement. It's more secure and we're less likely to attract the attention of the locals. If they see that we have the queen, the prince, and..." He gestured toward the others.

Everys grimaced. That was a good point. "Lead the way."

They left the gathering space and went back down the stairs into the teaching area. Tolistan quickly hustled through the room, brushing off the dust and straightening the benches. As soon as he had cleared the most comfortable chair in the room, the one that Master Igway had reserved for himself back when Everys was a student, he signaled for Everys to sit down. She did so and immediately understood why Igway had claimed it.

The others took up seats on benches and other chairs, although Redtale remained standing near the door. She probably wouldn't have been able to fit on any of the chairs anyway. Silence fell on the room with everyone looking at each other, no one apparently wanting to be the first to speak.

Finally, Everys leaned forward and caught Quartus's gaze. "So you and Yusra survived the destruction of the city?"

"We were fortunate," Quartus said. "We found a public disaster shelter right before the quake happened. Afterward, Brencis's troops took us to a refugee camp. What about you? Where have you been?"

Everys took a moment to order her thoughts. "Shortly before the rune destroyed the city—"

"The what?" Tolistan gasped.

"—I evacuated from the palace. We headed to the Cold Light's forest."

"So why come back?" Quartus asked.

"The mage-kings sent operatives into the forest to steal something valuable. We stopped them, but we learned they're after an extremely powerful ink to cast a specific rune. We think. Rewether and I came to Bastion to retrieve some research Narius sponsored on the runes. And we're going to go find the missing Principalities as well."

"The missing what?" Quartus asked.

Everys winced. She shot a worried look at Tolistan, but he shrugged. "When the Dynasty and Imperium destroyed Nekek the Bright, they thought they destroyed all eight Principalities in the Scriptotum. But they didn't. Instead, the Dynasty captured five of them and held them in the archives. I destroyed those before I left Bastion. But the other three were removed from the Scriptotum before Nekek the Bright's destruction. Rewether and I are going to track down the missing three to make sure that the mage-kings can't get them. But what about you, Quartus? Why are you still in the city?"

Yusra shot a pointed look at Quartus.

He wouldn't meet her gaze. "I'm going to assassinate Brencis."

Everys's eyes widened at the simple declaration. No anger, no fury. She shot a look over at Yusra, who wouldn't meet her gaze.

"He needs to be stopped," Quartus said.

She hesitated. She didn't disagree with him. The only way he'd be stopped was if he was dead. But there was something deeply unsettling about the way Quartus discussed it.

"Is that why you're here?" Everys asked Redtale.

Her former guard grunted. "Not exactly, although I'm open to the possibility. Brencis definitely has to pay for what he did to The Stone."

Everys remembered seeing the smoke on their flight to Bastion and her stomach sank. "What?"

Redtale's scowl deepened. "You remember how I told you that Rockflow was finally willing to work with the Untested?"

Everys frowned. Rockflow was the Ixactl ethnarch, and the Untested were a group of discontented Ixactl youth who had been stirring up trouble. Redtale had been one of the Untested's leaders, and while Rockflow and the Untested hadn't gotten along, that had changed shortly before Bastion's fall.

"After the *harsannon*, what with all the chaos from Dalark invading the Dynasty and Brencis marching toward Bastion, we thought it might be time for the Ixactl to stand on their own. Two months ago, Rockflow declared our independence from the Dynasty."

Everys's head snapped back. Why hadn't they heard about that? News that momentous should have made its way to the Shade.

Redtale must have read her confusion. "The minute Brencis found out, he completely isolated us. He sent a division of troops to surround the city and refused to allow anyone or anything in or out."

"A siege," Rewether muttered.

Redtale nodded. "At first, yeah. Rockflow thought we could outlast them. We had plenty of supplies, and Brencis was up to his horns in Dalark interlopers. There was no way he'd be able to maintain the siege. That was especially true when the Dalark found out about it and started harassing the Dynasty's troops.

"After a month, Brencis ordered the military to use sub-orbital incendiary bombs from Vetranio's war against the Cold Light. Burned The Stone to the ground. Rockflow officially surrendered, but the Untested didn't. Brencis has troops in The Stone, trying to root out the resistance, but they're not making it easy on them. But we all know it's just a matter of time before Brencis wears us down. So that's why I'm here. I'm looking for help.

"However, after seeing the state of Bastion, after learning what's been happening throughout the holdings, I've realized as long as Brencis is king, none of us will be safe," Redtale said. "That's why I came here with Quartus and Yusra. We need to stop him."

"Not just him, though," Yusra said. "Quartus and I learned Brencis is just a puppet for the mage-kings. Even if we were to eliminate him, there's a good chance their schemes would just continue, yes?"

Quartus snorted quietly. He even leaned away from Yusra by a small faction. "We can't leave him in power, though. If you can stop the mage-kings, Brencis will still be around to bomb Dynasty cities and kill people."

"So it's not an either-or, it's a both-and type of thing," Rewether added.

Everys nodded, then looked up and realized that everyone was looking at her. Was it her turn to talk? Oh, inkstains. They were expecting her to figure out what to do. As they should, since she was the queen. Her mind raced as she tried to piece it all together.

"We have three different priorities right now," she said. "Most immediately, we have to get Scrivener Tolistan and the research back to the Shade so he can begin work on translating the runes. Hopefully,

Tormod can retrieve Professor P'layvo as well, but that's outside our control. Second, we need to locate the missing Principalities and make sure that the mage-kings can't learn their runes. And third, we have to stop Brencis."

No one objected. She kept thinking out loud.

"This is what I suggest: Redtale escorts Tolistan back to the Shade. Rewether and I will continue to the Principalities' hiding places. And Quartus, you and Yusra will continue your efforts to neutralize Brencis."

Quartus's lips twitched into a grin. Yusra shifted in her seat, a worried look flashing across her face.

Tolistan blew out a shaky breath. "I'll need to speak with the elders. And I'll need to pack. I think we can leave in the morning."

He directed that last statement at Redtale, but the Ixactl frowned and shook her head.

"I'm not going to the forest."

Everys's heart sank. She knew that, theoretically, Tolistan could make it to the Shade on his own. But given that he was carrying such valuable information, it'd be better if he had an escort. And Redtale could make sure that he was safe.

"Instead, this is what I propose: Rewether, you escort Tolistan back to the forest. I'll accompany the queen."

Everys's breath hitched. Was Redtale really offering to help her? A momentary thrill shot up her spine. Would it be like when they first met, when they had been on the same side? Was that too much to hope for?

She turned to Rewether. "No offense, Rewether, but we both know you're not the right person for this type of mission. You're good as a deterrent. This needs a more subtle touch."

"An Ixactl can be subtle?" Quartus asked, only to have Yusra elbow him.

Redtale shot a glare at Quartus, but Rewether held up a hand.

"She's right. You know she is, Blessed. I'll only get in the way if I accompany you."

While Everys agreed, she couldn't help but be concerned. It was good to see Redtale again and maybe this time together could patch up the rift between them. But Everys could still feel the hurt lurking between them.

Tolistan cleared his throat. "Why don't you all stay here for the night? I'll give my apartment to the queen, Yusra, and Redtale. We three will bunk down here for the evening."

Everys nodded. That sounded like a good plan. If nothing else, she'd need a night to recover from these surprises.

28

It felt strange, looking out over Fair Havens at evening once again. Tolistan's apartment had a better vantage point than hers ever had. Everys could see the Melgor River flowing beyond a wall of buildings, and in the dimming twilight, the polluted river almost appeared beautiful. Thanks to Brencis's curfew, the neighborhood was more peaceful than she had ever experienced. She could almost pretend like her life had turned back to a simpler time. This wasn't the scrivener's apartment. It was hers. The next morning, she wouldn't head out to find Mama and Galan and their family's Principality. She would open the shop and help her customers and make what money she could. Same as the day before. Same as the next day.

The door to the apartment squeaked open, and Everys turned. Yusra slipped inside, a sheepish look on her face.

"I hope you don't mind the intrusion, Blessed." Yusra hung back by the doorway.

"Not an intrusion at all. Tonight, this is your room too."

A room was all that Tolistan really had. Everys thought it may have been the office for the restaurant's manager at one point, a cramped space that could barely contain a bed, a sofa, a comfy chair, and a small kitchenette. How she, Yusra, and Redtale were all going to fit in there was a mystery. Thankfully, they'd only have to cope with the small space for one night.

Yusra sidled through the cramped space and sat on the edge of the couch, her hands folded in her lap. She looked like she was on the verge of saying something several times, but each time she caught herself. Everys smiled. How would a Dalark spy and the Dynasty's queen start a conversation with each other? What could they safely discuss? Everys understood Yusra's struggle all too well.

"Thank you for what you've done for the Dynasty," Everys said. "I imagine you would be in trouble with your superiors back in Utuaa if they knew what you were doing."

Yusra smiled, her lips a tight line. "Not at all, Blessed. My master sent me here to investigate our common enemy. I doubt he would object to my helping you."

Oh? That information caught her attention. "So your master is open to working together with the Dynasty?"

"I couldn't say for certain." Yusra winced. "I know he wishes for our two kingdoms to be on friendlier terms. He uncovered a conspiracy that involved both our governments and sent me to investigate, if not stop it. I'm afraid that I didn't accomplish my goal."

"Nonsense," Everys said. "You and Quartus warned me about the existence of the mage-kings. If you hadn't, I might have left the Principalities where they were, allowing them to fall into enemy hands."

Yusra smiled shyly. "You're too kind, Blessed."

Everys wanted to keep asking questions about Yusra's mission, maybe dig into who her master was. But she could read the unease in Yusra's posture. She had probably probed enough already. A different topic then?

"So..." The word caught in Everys's throat. "How has Quartus been?"

Yusra looked away, her cheeks flaming red. Everys arched a brow. What prompted that?

"He is... good. Very consumed with finding justice for both you and his brother," Yusra said.

Everys's head snapped back in surprise. She knew that, when they were growing up, Quartus and Narius had not gotten along at all. And Narius had declared Quartus outlaw several months earlier.

Yusra must have read the surprise in Everys's expression. She smiled. "I was in the Dynasty's holdings when your husband punished Quartus for his supposed crimes. I can assure you, Blessed, I know for a fact that he is innocent of your attempted assassination."

Now Everys's cheeks burned. "I know that."

"And while I doubt he would ever admit to this, I think Quartus's outlaw status has benefited him. Because he is no longer trapped in his role, he has discovered who he was truly meant to be. He has become a better person."

"I think you contributed to that as well," Everys said.

Once again, Yusra's cheeks blazed red, and she looked down at the floor, coughing.

"It's all right," Everys said. "Quartus is handsome and charming. And I've seen the way he looks at you. I'm glad for you. For both of you. It's wonderful when two people find each other like this."

Everys's throat closed up on her last words, memories of Narius washing over her. She remembered how, one night shortly after their second wedding, she had insisted he teach her about the trade network between Elscontin, Rioka, Tomma, and the Dynasty. Narius had tried, but all of the details were so complex and, in some cases, so mind-numbingly stupid, that they wound up in an argument that suddenly turned to laughter as they realized what they were doing. Tears stung her eyes, and she took several quick breaths.

Yusra leaned forward. "I'm sorry I never got to meet your husband."

"I am too," Everys whispered, then she laughed. "He probably would have pestered you for information about your culture for hours, maybe even days."

"I would have been honored to answer his questions," Yusra said with a sad smile. Then she tipped her head to one side. "Tell me about him. Please."

Everys hesitated at first. After all, sharing personal information with a Dalark spy was probably not the wisest choice. But Yusra prompted her with simple questions, little details that couldn't hurt anything. Before Everys knew it, she was telling Yusra all about her and Narius's unorthodox courtship, some of her favorite memories, their hopes and plans that would never come to fruition. There were moments of sadness but more of laughter, and within an hour or two, Everys had grown so relaxed that both she and Yusra drifted off to sleep in the middle of a story, lulled by both the pleasant if bittersweet memories and the warmth of finding, if not a future sister, then a good and trustworthy friend.

The next morning came too quickly for Everys's liking. As she woke up, still sitting in the same chair near the window, she stretched and glanced over at the couch, where Yusra was curled up. She smiled, a warm haze cocooning her. For a fleeting moment, she wished she could just stay in the conclave, if only to get to know Yusra better. But then she realized that the bed was empty. Where was Redtale?

She bolted out of the chair, startling Yusra awake. The other woman looked around the room and must have come to the same question. Without saying a word, the two of them hurried down the stairs.

They found Redtale sitting on a chair next to the stairway. She glanced at them as they came out.

"Sleep well?" she asked.

"Did you?" Yusra asked.

Redtale shrugged. "Slept on worse in the past. At least I had a chair this time."

"We had plenty of room upstairs," Everys said.

"Bad idea," Redtale said with a shake of her head. "There are only two of us here to guard you, Blessed. Rewether had to get an early start—he and Tolistan say goodbye, by the way—so that leaves me to keep watch."

"So you sat here the entire night?" Yusra asked.

Another shrug. "Ixactl don't need as much sleep as you humans. I should be good as long as I get a full night's rest within a week."

The basement door screeched open, and Quartus slipped through, an apologetic look on his face.

"Sorry. If the scrivener was still here, I'd offer to oil the hinges for him," he said. "Hard to keep a secret training facility secret if it screams like the Sun's own fury every time you open the door. You ready to go?"

For a moment, Everys thought he was asking her. But then Yusra stepped past her, nodding.

"Tolistan's given me a lead on some people who might help us get to Brencis," Quartus said. "We need to meet up with them and see what help they can offer."

An uncertain look flitted across Yusra's face, but vanished quickly.

Everys stepped over to him and gave him a quick hug. "Be careful out there, Quartus. Don't do anything stupid."

He chuckled and pulled free from her. "That strategy's always worked for me in the past. I don't know why I'd change it now."

She grabbed his shoulders. "I mean it. When this is all done, I want us to be a genuine family."

His eyes widened, and he looked ready to say something, but then he nodded once, sharply, before pulling free of her grip. He cleared his throat, but his voice still shook. "C'mon, Yusra. We need to go."

Yusra offered Everys one last smile, then the two of them slipped out of the conclave.

That left Everys with Redtale, who pulled out a scriber and handed it to her. "Before Tolistan left, he gave this to me to give to you. He said it has everything you'll need to know to find the missing Principalities."

Everys thumbed on the device and scrolled through the information. Thankfully, the location of her family's vigil matched what Papa had shared with her. Much to her surprise, one of the Principalities was apparently hidden in Fort Wyne. That wasn't far from Bastion. At the very least, it was closer than the other two. That would have to be their first stop.

"Are you ready to go?" Everys asked.

Redtale nodded, but as Everys headed for the door, Redtale didn't follow. Instead, the Ixactl wouldn't meet her eyes.

"I have something I need to say to you first, Blessed. It's something I didn't want to say in front of the others."

That got Everys's attention. She turned toward Redtale.

Redtale still wouldn't meet her gaze. "I owe you an apology."

Everys's head snapped back as if Redtale slapped her. She started to object, to say that she needed to apologize to Redtale for so much, but Redtale didn't let her speak.

"When I served as the captain of your guard, I had thought it would just be another assignment nannying a spoiled noble. That's all it ever was when I had to guard Viara." She said the name of the former queen like it was a curse. "You were a bright dawn over the mountains, Blessed. You were different in the way you treated the servants, in the way you spoke your mind. I came to admire you greatly. More than that, I considered you a friend."

Everys's throat closed up. She wanted to tell Redtale that the feeling was mutual, but when she tried to speak, Redtale held up a hand to cut her off.

"That's why it hurt so much when I found out about the royal archives. I was still carrying so much anger from when I was younger without realizing it. And... I forgot my place. Even if we were friendly, we couldn't truly be friends. It was wrong of me to expect you to do more than you could. As queen, you have secrets, and it was wrong of me to—"

Everys rushed forward and caught Redtale's hands in hers. Redtale looked down at her in surprise.

"Redtale, you were my friend, and I hope you still can be. I couldn't have survived those first days in the palace without you. I am so glad we're back together again. And from now on, there won't be any secrets between us." She hesitated, realizing she had one left to share. "Starting right now."

With that, Everys plucked a bead from her bracelet and rolled it between her fingers. Without giving it much thought, she sketched a quick rune on her open palm and, with a double tap, activated the spell. A globe of light appeared, hovering just above her hand. After only a few seconds, it sputtered and winked out.

Redtale stared at Everys's hand with wide eyes, but then she blinked. "Well, that answers a lot of questions."

Everys bet it did. "I am sorry I didn't share this and so much more right away, but—"

"But you were right to do so," Redtale said. "If I had learned this while I was still officially your guard, I'd have had to report it. Did the king know?"

Everys nodded. "And now, so do Rewether, Challix, and several advisers."

Redtale nodded thoughtfully. "Good. One last thing."

Redtale knelt in front of her.

"I heard what happened to Kevtho and given that you're traveling with only Rewether, I suspect you haven't chosen a new Swordbound yet. So, Queen Everys, true ruler of the Xoniel Dynasty, I am Redtale of the Prominent Ridge clan. I pledge my life and limbs to you and your honor. My 'sword' is yours." There was a hint of laughter in her voice, though her expression remained serious. "If any should challenge, it is my blood that shall shield you. By the *ma-se-kranna* itself, I swear this to you now."

A chill swept over Everys. When she'd first married Narius, Kevtho, her former Swordbound, had spoken very similar words to her.

Everys's eyes stung, and she swiped away some tears. "I know I'm supposed to give your sword back to you to accept, but you don't have one..."

They laughed, uncomfortably at first, but then genuinely.

"Then tell me this instead: can you forgive me for what I did?" Redtale asked.

Everys smiled at her old guard, her new Swordbound, and her friend. "I already have."

29

I nnana didn't return to the safehouse for close to a week. That was fine, as far as Narius was concerned. It took him that long to calm down and focus his thoughts. While some of his anger and frustration had faded with time, his determination hadn't.

Kavi waved at him to get his attention. *She's on her way.*

Narius nodded his thanks. She had been invaluable to him over the past week. They still struggled to communicate, but they had spent enough time together that he could fill in the gaps from her mood and attitude when his vocabulary failed him. She had listened patiently as he'd outlined his idea, simple as it was, and then helped him do the research and figure out the best way to proceed.

The elevator pinged and Innana stepped out. This time, she wore a subtle outfit made of bright pastel bands that were wrapped around her legs, torso, and arms, covered with a long white coat. Narius couldn't help but chuckle as he observed her outfit. He had spent too much time in the Imperium. In any of the Dynasty's cities, that outfit would have been the focus of everyone's attention. But here, that outfit would barely attract a second glance and probably be written off as understated.

"Well?" Innana asked coolly. "What is your grand master plan, dear Narius?"

He forced himself to keep smiling despite the subtle sarcasm in her tone. No doubt she was frustrated with him. He would be too if someone swooped in and refused to play along with his intricate plan.

"I can appreciate what you were trying to accomplish by having me pose as Senen's king," Narius said. "You had to think creatively to bypass the constraints of Dalark culture to—"

Innana rolled her eyes. "I can recognize diplomacy when I see it. You didn't like my plan, and you were supposed to come up with a new one. If you keep talking like this, I'm going to think that you have nothing to offer."

Narius's gaze flicked to Kavi, who beamed at him and signed, *Tell her.*

He took a deep breath and squared his shoulders. "The more I've thought about it, the more I've realized that there are other flaws in your plan. It's not just built on a series of lies, but it's also too incremental. An appearance here, a surprise there, it would take years to build enough momentum to bring about genuine change."

Innana scowled at him, but she didn't object. He took that as a minor victory, so he kept slogging forward.

"And what happens if people see through the story?"

"What do you mean?" Innana's frown deepened.

"Let me give you an example. When I was in school, I heard a story about a rogue prelate who claimed to have locks of hair taken from the Water Bearer herself. Supposedly, if one slept in the presence of these hairs, one could commune with the goddess herself. And if the prelate whipped you with the hair, you'd receive a special blessing from her."

Innana gaped at him, and Kavi flared her hands that showed she was laughing.

"It was probably more solemn than I'm making it sound," Narius added hastily. "The point is, this prelate amassed quite the following in a very short amount of time. Thousands of adherents, all of them professing to be 'the Water Bearer's Tide.' The prelate kept his messaging apolitical, but a new movement with that many believers was worrisome, especially since the Dynasty was dealing with the Colonial Uprisings.

"The prelates tried to combat the new beliefs with theology, but they weren't able to make inroads that way. So King Pellio attacked along a different vector. He had an agent from Internal Security steal one of the hairs and had it tested. The hair was most likely that of a long-tailed crag jumper.

"Now that information wasn't enough to completely discredit the prelate, but once they knew what the relic truly was, they could chase down the people who helped the prelate create it, along with accomplices who had lied about seeing visions or receiving blessings from the hair."

"And I suppose that, as soon as it was brought to light, the cult just disbanded?" Innana said.

Narius grimaced. "Not entirely. Some of the prelate's adherents abandoned their faith. But the prelate himself decried the government's supposed lies. Then he and his followers holed up in their compound. When the Dynasty's military put them under siege, the cult fought them to the last."

Innana looked away, but Narius could practically feel her sorting through his words. Kavi gave him a subtle, encouraging nod and flashed him a thin smile.

"Is that what you fear will happen? That we'll all die in a standoff with the Imperium's military?"

"I would hope not, but it's still a warning we should heed," he said. "Yes, some may believe the story, but others won't. They'll start investigating the sightings, and eventually, they'll find a thread they can pull to unravel the entire scheme. The longer we have to maintain the fiction, the more likely it'll happen. Can you honestly say that no one could find out about how Kavi got me out of the Dynasty? Or the secret medical facility or the actors? When the truth comes out, will those who bought into the rumors accept being lied to?"

Innana glowered at him, but he could tell that he had scored some points with her. She couldn't say those things and she knew it.

"So what do you suggest?" she asked.

"Instead of relying on flimsy lies that could unravel and leave us exposed, I suggest we act more tactically. Have me meet with carefully chosen individuals, people who can have a real influence in Dalark society. I'm assuming you've tried to meet with these people in the past?"

Innana said nothing, but the way her eyes twitched told Narius that she not only had, but she had also failed.

"I'd be willing to bet that they wouldn't turn me away, especially not with the rumors swirling. I go to them, I speak to them, I convince them to listen to you." He took a step closer to her. "Innana, I truly believe that you are the Imperium's best chance. I want you to be the Empress or whatever you want to call yourself. Let me open the doors to make that happen. That way, no one can accuse you of deceiving them to get the throne."

Innana's eyes narrowed, and he could feel her gaze dissecting him. He stood tall, trying not to waver.

Finally, she sighed. "Do you have someone in mind?"

Narius nodded. "I've been working with Kavi, and I think I have a likely candidate."

Kavi stepped forward and handed both Innana and Narius scribers that held the information.

"I want to meet with Seminal Tensin Bakun," Narius said. "He was in the Colonnade when I made my last appearance, taking part in the debate. He actually sounded open to peace with the Dynasty. And Kavi tells me that he's one of the greatest minds the Imperium has produced in this generation, a true leader among the intelligentsia. If I can persuade him, that's a good start."

Innana frowned. "Those chosen for the debates are picked specifically because they can present viewpoints fairly, not because they necessarily believe them."

"That may be, but according to Kavi, Seminal Bakun has been investigated four different times by the Imperial Secret Police on suspicions of dissident thought," Narius countered. "That has to mean something."

Innana studied his face. Narius fought to keep his anxiety from showing.

Then she smiled. "Very well. Let's try this and see what happens."

Narius blew out a sigh of relief as Kavi flashed him an excited sign. It would work. It had to.

30

Quartus tried to leave behind the uneasy feeling that had settled on him overnight. Not that he regretted seeing Everys. Far from it. Just knowing she was still alive had reignited the smallest flicker of hope within him.

But he knew that ember guttering inside him was dangerous. He could already feel some of his anger at Brencis loosening. The day before, he believed Brencis had murdered both Narius and Everys. But now he knew Everys was not only alive but fighting back. That knowledge alone prompted a quiet voice inside him to question his intentions. Maybe Yusra was right.

He shoved the doubts aside. He was being ridiculous. What was he supposed to do, arrest Brencis? He wasn't a constable. Even if he could somehow capture Brencis, what would he do with him? Drag him to a prison in chains? Hope that the troops loyal to the so-called king would lay down their arms and surrender? No, the best way to defeat this evil was to lop off its head.

They met Tolistan's contacts in an abandoned apartment complex. Quartus had a feeling they weren't the only ones in the building. That much available space was bound to attract squatters and others who needed shelter. But no one challenged Yusra or him as they entered the building, proceeding to an apartment on the third floor. Inside, they found half a dozen people waiting for them. Two were Ixactl, one Plissk, a Weyfir, and two Siporans. Quartus suspected those must have been Tolistan's contacts. Bloodshale, one of the Ixactl, made introductions, a flurry of names that Quartus knew he'd probably struggle to remember, then motioned for Quartus and Yusra to take a seat on a badly stained couch.

"We hear you want to eliminate Brencis, is that right?" Bloodshale asked.

Quartus nodded. He liked that. Straight and to the point. "That is my plan. I hear you might have a way to get me access to do so."

The group exchanged a look. Then the other Ixactl, Lastdew, cleared her throat. "We think we have an opportunity to strike at Brencis."

"Excellent. Why do you need me?" Quartus asked.

The others exchanged looks before Arssick, the Plissk, flicked a tongue across his eyes. "Opportunity, yes. Knowledge of how to exploit it, not so much. Having to move in circles we aren't a part of and don't know how it works, yeah?"

Quartus pursed his lips. That made sense. "What's the opportunity?"

"You're familiar with the Day of Accountability ritual, I assume," Karliss, the Weyfir, asked.

Quartus leaned back, chuckling. Oh, he was aware of it, all right. "Four months after taking the throne, a newly crowned king of the Dynasty must go on a personal retreat where he is confronted by those who will serve as his advisers. They share their personal thoughts and, hopefully, pledge their undying loyalty. I remember when my brother had to go through his."

He stopped sharing there, but his mind filled in the rest. As Narius's younger brother and a potential successor, Quartus was supposed to take part. Instead, he went on a pleasure cruise out of Bluerest.

He sat up straighter as his mind made the connection. "They never announce where the Day takes place. You found out?"

Ifamin, one of the Siporans, nodded. "My brother and I work in Ethnarch Chilyana's manor in Gilded Lock. At least, we usually do. But for the past three weeks, she has sent many of our coworkers to her private villa in the Westerhold to prepare for some sort of secret event."

"But the other day, I was able to wheedle it out of the house steward," Eleeman, Ifamin's brother, said. "The king's Day is going to be held there in two weeks."

Quartus nodded thoughtfully. The Westerhold was one of Bastion's satellite cities, far enough away that people could pretend they had escaped the capital, but not as far as to have left its orbit entirely.

Hosting the Day would be a good way for Chilyana to prove her loyalty to Brencis during a fraught time.

"Ifamin and Eleeman have persuaded the house steward to hire us as temporary staff to prepare the villa for the Day," Bloodshale said. "Lastdew and I are working security. Karliss is part of the landscaping team. And Arssick is supposed to work the cleanup crew afterward."

Yusra leaned forward, frowning. "So we have a way in with you two. Karliss can help stash equipment we need, and Arssick is our exit route. So why do you need Quartus?"

The others once again shot uncertain looks at each other before Lastdew spoke up. "We know the Day is happening there. We know the layout. And you're right, we have routes in and out, but—"

"—but you don't know what's actually going to happen during the Day itself," Quartus finished for her. "Or when Brencis would be vulnerable."

Lastdew nodded.

Quartus did as well. "Well, there would be lots of opportunities. I'm assuming they've built the hut?" He directed that last question to Karliss. Once the Weyfir confirmed, Quartus continued. "So Brencis will sit in a hut in the middle of the grounds. One by one, anyone he considers significant for his reign will enter the hut and share their honest opinion of him. Once that's done, they're to leave the king alone in the hut to ponder whatever it is they've told him. According to tradition, the king is supposed to be alone for hours on end, with guards pulled back far enough to respect his isolation."

"So we strike then," Bloodshale said. "When he's alone and vulnerable."

Quartus scoffed. "He'll be alone, but not vulnerable. They won't have guards stationed in or by the hut, but they'll be watching it carefully. That means there's no way for anyone to sneak into the hut once the Day has started. They'd notice. And that also means that whoever actually did the killing wouldn't be able to leave the hut without being noticed either. To strike at Brencis there, someone would have to hide in the hut for several hours if not days. They would also have to accept they'll be caught and executed afterward. Any of you ready for that?"

Yusra glared at him, and he could almost hear her asking if he would sacrifice himself like that either. He shifted in his seat, then forced himself to smile.

"But there is good news." He turned to the Siporan brothers. "I'm also assuming that the steward has been sending a lot of alcohol to the villa as well?"

Eleeman and Ifamin exchanged surprised looks before the former said, "She has, yes."

Quartus smirked. "That's part of the Day as well. Those who have spoken to the king are expected to wait for the king to emerge from the hut. And then there will be a feast where drinking and debauchery are encouraged and expected."

Bloodshale gaped at him. "Why would they do that?"

"Because it's believed that doing so helps smooth over any wounds that might have been opened during those conversations. Strengthen the bonds of those who serve the king. Forge lasting friendship that will carry the king and his advisers through any crisis." Quartus snorted. "You'll be expected to take part as well."

The rest of the people in the room shifted in their seats. While Quartus had never experienced one of these parties himself, he had heard rumors. According to the palace staff, Narius's celebration had been tame in comparison to those of their father and grandfather.

"That's our opportunity," Quartus continued. "While Brencis is in the hut, he'll be untouchable. But once the party starts and the drinks flow, everyone will relax and assume they're safe. Then it's just a matter of getting Brencis alone long enough. As long as the assassin can keep his wits about him, escaping should be relatively easy as well."

The others exchanged looks and nods before Bloodshale turned back to him. "So, will you help us?"

"Of course I will." Quartus couldn't help but feel Yusra's gaze bore into the side of his head. "We're going to make Brencis pay for what he's done."

31

T hankfully, Everys's ID allowed both her and Redtale to purchase high-speed rail tickets out of Bastion to the city of Fort Wyne. The soldiers guarding the boarding gates only gave them a cursory examination before waving them through. Within an hour, the Bastion skyline was behind them as they climbed out of the Melgor River basin and up into the Grerid Flats.

Everys studied the countryside as it slipped by. At first, she thought that she could forget about the crises and enjoy the scenery. But during the train's four-hour trip, they whizzed past destroyed military vehicles and scars from recent battles. She couldn't get a good look at anything—the maglev was simply moving too fast—but based on the blur of colors, most of them appeared to be Dalark. That made sense. Before she had abandoned Bastion, the Dalark had landed thousands of troops along the Dynasty's western shore. Brencis had blunted that invasion with troops loyal to him. Apparently, some of those battles must have taken place along this rail line. How many soldiers died on each side?

When the conductor warned them they were only an hour away from their destination, she pulled out the scriber Tolistan had given her. The Principality in question was under the care of a family known only as "The Shadows." According to the notes, the elders had tried to contact the Shadows and warn them of her arrival, but communication between the major cities was still unreliable. They might know they were coming, but then, they might not either.

A short time later, the maglev pulled into the Fort Wyne station. Redtale and Everys lined up with the rest of the passengers to disembark. They stood behind a family of Grerids, parents with three kids. The youngest kept peeking at them. At first, Everys thought she had been recognized, but then she realized the young girl was staring wide-eyed at Redtale. The Ixactl, who wore false horns, tried to ignore her, but eventually glanced in the child's direction and returned her wide-eyed stare until the kid looked away. Everys caught a laugh before it slipped free.

The soldiers checking the passengers in the station all wore the livery of the Leedeke family. Everys tensed as they motioned her and Redtale forward, scanning their ID documents. Everys offered them what she hoped was a disarming smile. The soldier checking her ID frowned at her, then motioned for another guard to join them. Everys could feel Redtale tense next to her.

"If you could come with us, please?" The soldier's tone made it clear that it wasn't a request.

"What seems to be the problem?" Redtale's voice was a rumbling threat.

The soldier didn't answer the question, which set Everys's heart slamming against her ribs. Had they been caught already?

He ushered them into a room with only two chairs sandwiched behind a long metal table. The soldier indicated they should sit, then took up station by the door. Redtale tried several times to engage him in conversation, but he simply stared at the wall over Everys's shoulder.

A few minutes later, an official in a well-tailored outfit stepped into the room, consulting a data scriber as he walked. He stood next to the soldier, merely reading the scriber without so much as glancing in Everys's direction. She wanted to laugh. He was obviously trying to make her nervous. Unfortunately, his tactics were working.

Finally, after several uncomfortable minutes, the man looked up, his thin face pinched into a scowl. "So who do we have here?"

Was he hoping she'd slip up? She sat up straighter. "Evina Truost. Why are we being detained? If you don't explain yourself, my uncle—"

The official waved away her words, focusing instead on Redtale. "And you?"

Redtale sat up straighter. "Cragline. Hired by Madam Truost's uncle to accompany on her trip."

Everys tensed. Redtale's tone was calm, almost bored, but she could read the tension in her friend's posture. Redtale was getting ready to do something, most likely violent. She tried to signal to her to remain still.

"I see... yes, Madam Truost's travel documents do list a bodyguard." His gaze sharpened and drilled into Everys. "Only the bodyguard is listed as male and not Ixactl."

Everys tried to laugh lightly, waving away the details like a pesky insect. "Ah, yes. I was supposed to be traveling with Remard, but he took sick back in Bastion. Thankfully, Uncle Sillam was able to acquire Cragline's help at the last moment."

The official stared at her, his face blank. Did he believe it? Everys tried to keep her breathing calm, but she worried she'd start sweating. Dropping her hands into her lap under the table, she tugged a bead free from her bracelet and started rubbing it between her fingers. Just in case.

"Indeed. That does seem perfectly reasonable, and under other circumstances, we could easily process the change for a modest fee," the official said.

Everys could translate that easily enough. They didn't have many blades on them, but maybe they could scrape together enough for an adequate bribe.

"But the Dynasty is currently at war. Dalark scum roam our holdings freely and their agents could be anywhere." The official glared between Everys and Redtale. "The smallest error could be evidence that spies or saboteurs sit before us."

Redtale chuckled, the sound of rocks shifting before an avalanche. "Let's be reasonable."

"Oh, I will be." The official smiled, a predatory grin. "Once I've assured myself of your true identities."

Everys glanced at Redtale, who shrugged. Then Redtale burst from her seat and slammed into the guard, driving him into the wall.

Did that mean Everys had to deal with the official? Inkstains! The bead had liquified, but what could she do?

"Keep back!" Redtale barked. "I can handle this."

Redtale could definitely handle two people, but more would be on their way. The interrogation room was undoubtedly monitored. Before too long, it would flood with more soldiers. They'd be overwhelmed.

Everys's gaze shot to the door. If they left that way, they'd only run into the reinforcements that much faster. No, they had to exit in a more unconventional way.

She hunched over, trying to shield what she was doing from any prying cameras. Then she frantically sketched a rune on her open palm, the same one she had used to flush the mage-king's agents out of the library back in the Embassy. As soon as she cast it, smoke burst from her hand and quickly filled the room. Redtale grunted as she backhanded the official, but the smoke filled the room so quickly Everys didn't see him hit the floor.

"Nice, but now what?" Redtale asked from somewhere in the opaque mist.

"Now we make a new exit."

Everys hurried to the wall opposite the door. She had to work from memory without seeing what she was doing. Thankfully, she knew this rune well enough that she quickly sketched it out on the wall and activated it.

With a loud *crack*, the wall shattered. Thankfully, it was an exterior wall, leading to an alley behind the transit hub. The smoke poured out, obscuring the pavement below. Everys quickly slipped through the hole and dropped down. Redtale grunted as she squeezed through. As soon as she was free, Redtale led Everys out of the alley and onto the streets. Much to Everys's surprise, no one seemed at all interested in the smoke belching from the transit hub, making it easy for them to simply disappear into the crowd.

Sirens blared in the distance. Probably local constabulary or maybe even military, responding to what happened. Everys picked up the pace, trying to put as much distance between them and the transit hub as possible.

Once they were several blocks away, Redtale touched her shoulder. "Now what?"

That was the problem. Everys had no idea.

By the time the sun started to set, worry had settled on Everys like a heavy cloak. Thankfully, they hadn't attracted any attention from passersby as they made it through the streets of Fort Wyne.

But what could she and Redtale do now? Sure, they could find a quiet corner of the city and hole up for the night, but that seemed incredibly unwise. They needed more than just shelter. They needed safety, security. They needed the Shadows.

Redtale steered her down a side street away from a crowded pavilion. That was smart. Less chance she'd be recognized. Everys offered a weak smile to Redtale. She was glad they were together again, but maybe she had been too overconfident. Maybe she should have listened to Tormod and allowed him to handle this part of the scheme. Did she really need to be the one to find the missing Principalities and ensure their destruction? Maybe, but probably not. So why had she been so insistent that it had to be her?

Because she wanted to escape. Because she wanted to be useful. Because she knew she was failing as a queen, but this mission gave her something she could do.

And now she was going to fail this too.

Well, maybe that was overstating the case. They hadn't been captured, and they knew that the Siporan family guarding the Principality was in Fort Wyne. All they'd have to do was find them... somehow.

"Everys, keep facing forward," Redtale murmured.

A jolt raced down Everys's spine at her friend's tone. Calm, but laced through with threat and danger.

"Someone's been following us for the past two blocks," Redtale continued.

Everys almost whipped around, but Redtale's warning kept her from doing so. Her shoulders tensed, and she forced herself to keep walking. "So what do we do?"

"There's an alley coming up on our left. We enter it, then see who this is."

She nodded, her gaze locking on their destination. She tried to keep from hyperventilating as they took those last steps, then turned carefully into the alley. Once they had, Redtale maneuvered her to a crouch behind a stack of crates, then shielded her.

Everys held her breath as a young woman appeared in the alley's entrance. She hesitated, then crept into the alley. She held what looked like a scriber in front of her, consulting its screen as she took each step. A tracking device? Had the soldier tagged them somehow at the transit hub?

Before Everys could puzzle that out, Redtale burst from her hiding spot and slammed into the woman. The scriber clattered across the pavement and came to rest at Everys's feet. Only it didn't sound like it was made out of metal but... wood?

Everys picked up the scriber. Only that wasn't what it was. Instead, it was a piece of wood with a glowing symbol drawn on it with...

Everys's eyes widened.

"Redtale! Get off her!"

Redtale looked up, then rose to her feet. "You sure?"

Everys nodded, showing her the plank of wood. "This is a seeker rune. It allows the person holding it to track toratropic magic. She's Siporan."

The woman rose to her feet and dusted herself off. "I am indeed. My name is Taffinia. I work for the Leedeke family. We've actually met once before, Blessed, when you met with Lady Leedeke before the king's *harsannon*."

Everys wracked her memory, but she couldn't remember. That was months ago, and she had been so focused on procuring Annada Leedeke's help, she hadn't noticed any of her retainers. "I'm sorry, but—"

Taffinia waved away her apology. "I understand. Functionaries like me are meant to blend into the background. It's what we do."

"And what are you doing now?" Redtale gestured toward the plank.

"Looking for you both. When I saw the footage of you from the transit hub, I knew you must be here for an important reason. That's why I had the security records erased and I retrieved this." She held something out.

Everys carefully took it and realized it was their IDs and travel documents.

"I've taken the liberty of issuing new travel permits for you. The terms are broader and should help you avoid future entanglements," Taffinia continued.

"Thank you." Everys pocketed the ID.

"If I may be so bold, Blessed, why are you here?"

Everys hesitated, preparing herself to lie. But as she did, she looked down at the plank of wood. The seeker rune slowly fizzled, the glow winking out. Taffinia was obviously a Siporan. Maybe she could help them find the right family.

"We're looking for someone from the local Siporan community," she said.

"Oh?" Taffinia's head tipped to one side. "Anyone in particular?"

"Probably a well-established family. Members of the family have probably... disappeared for an extended period of time." Everys winced at the uncertainty in her tone.

A broad smile split Taffinia's face. "I know exactly who you're looking for."

"You do?" Redtale asked.

"Yes. My family. I just received a message from the elders in Bastion, saying that someone—they were very cagey about who—would be arriving to visit our Principality. That means it's time for you to visit the ruins of Elregan, Blessed."

32

Taffinia had a transport waiting for them not far from the alley. During the drive, Taffinia filled Everys in on her family's history. Like Everys's, her family had cared for their Principality back when it stood in the Scriptotum in Nekek the Bright, removing theirs before the city's destruction. But where Everys's had opted to hide out in the wilderness of the former Siporan Ascendancy, Taffinia's had taken their Principality to what had been the heart of the Dynasty itself. When Elregan fell and the Leedeke's took over the stewardship of the ruins, her family continued their vigil by pledging their loyalty to the noble house. Since no one lived in the ruins anymore, it served as a perfect hiding place.

During the drive, Everys explained what her mission was, about the threat that the mage-kings posed, especially if they could find the missing Principalities. At first, Taffinia was skeptical, but then she seemed to piece together what was happening. While Everys couldn't tell if she was okay with the plan, she at least didn't argue about it.

Everys had never been to Elregan, although she had seen pictures and heard the stories. Elregan, the home of Heronus, who destroyed her people's homeland. Elregan, the fallen jewel of the Dynasty. Even though the buildings had been unoccupied for more than three centuries, Everys still felt her breath catch as Taffinia led them through the streets past buildings that felt like they were mere shadows of their former selves.

"We don't have to worry about tourists," Taffinia said, her voice so loud that Everys winced. It felt like sacrilege. "Ever since the quake at Bastion, the Leedekes have closed access to the ruins. We're the only ones here."

She led them past the wreckage of the royal palace, the only building that had been destroyed when the city was abandoned. They walked quietly past the abandoned buildings which stood sentry over their fallen comrade, until they came into a part of the town that comprised squat buildings made of dull brown bricks.

"The tourists usually don't visit this far back into the ruins," Taffinia said. "This was known as the Scribblers' Quarter. My ancestors were some of the first to emigrate to the city, mostly to prepare for our Principality's arrival. When the refugees from Nekek the Bright arrived, they found us waiting as well. When Elregan fell, a great terror drove out most of the inhabitants, but our people were spared. Come. I'll show you where the Principality rests."

They approached a building with rounded walls and a squat dome. Everys glanced at a nearby sign that labeled this building as a grain warehouse. Taffinia led them to a section of blank wall, counted bricks from one corner, and then pressed her hand against the wall.

No, she didn't press it against the wall. Instead, her hand slipped through it as if it wasn't really there.

"A glamour spell," she explained.

Without another word, Taffinia slipped through the illusion.

"That safe?" Redtale asked.

Everys had no idea. But if Taffinia could do it, she could too. She took a deep breath, closed her eyes, and stepped forward.

She felt nothing unusual as she passed through the illusion, maybe a tingle that swept over her arms and down her back. But then she was through, entering a dimly lit tunnel where Taffinia waited. A few seconds later, Redtale stepped through the illusion as well.

Taffinia gestured for them to follow her, and they headed down a sloped tunnel that looped around the edge of the building. They emerged into a round chamber and there, standing in the middle of the room, was the Principality.

At first glance, it didn't look like much, just a ten-foot-tall stone plinth roughly shaped like a talon. But about two-thirds of the way up the outside curve, a small square area had been smoothed down, and a single rune had been carved in the center of that space.

Everys took a tentative step toward it, then glanced at Taffinia for permission. When the other woman nodded, Everys stepped closer. She had never seen this rune before, which wasn't a surprise. The families that safeguarded the Principalities kept these powerful designs secret. Everys couldn't help but compare this rune to her family's. Where her family's reminded her of a fern unfolding, all languid loops and swirls, there was an almost mechanical precision to this one, triangles and circles interlocking in an almost gear-like fashion. She considered tracing the rune with her finger to see if she could get a better sense of it, but she stopped herself. Yes, this was a sacred moment, but it was one that would have to be brief.

"Can you tell me what it does?" Everys whispered.

"Of course, Blessed. It's a storytelling rune. Once cast, the storyteller can weave a person into the story, leading them to believe that they are a part of it, that they are experiencing it all firsthand."

"My father used a similar rune recently. He used it to show me... well, something deeply personal." The memory of Papa's intentions for their family still weighed heavily on her.

Taffinia nodded. "That's probably a variation on this one. But this rune is so powerful, a person can literally lose themselves in the story."

Everys's eyebrows shot up. She thought that her family's healing rune was impressive. This was incredible. She turned and nodded to Redtale, who pulled out a scriber. Then Everys turned back to Taffinia.

"We're going to take several images of the rune and then..." She swallowed hard. "Then we're going to shatter it."

Taffinia went still. She stepped over and ran a hand along the side of the Principality, tears welling in her eyes.

"This has been a part of my life for as long as I can remember," she whispered. "It's defined my family for generations. But I also trust you, Blessed. Do what you have to."

33

Narius's feet bounced as the transport wound its way through the streets of Utuaa. Once again, Kavi was escorting him. This time, his nerves were more jangled. His body brimmed with energy and felt as if it would rattle apart. The sensation was almost intoxicating. Broken Spear, he hadn't felt like this in months! Not since...

Not since he realized he had fallen in love with Everys.

That quiet thought stilled him, but only for a moment. That was part of the reason he had to succeed. The sooner he helped Innana overthrow her brother, the sooner he could return to the Dynasty and find out what happened to his wife.

Kavi glanced at him from her seat, and a worried expression flitted across her face. *Are you okay?*

He smiled at her. "Just a little worked up. I should be fine."

She tipped her head to one side with a sad smile, then wove her hands together in an intricate pattern before thrusting her open palms at him. He braced himself, expecting a wave of energy to crash over him. But nothing seemed to happen. He frowned, then realized that his legs had stilled. His breathing had slowed. He raised his eyebrows and blinked, then looked at Kavi.

"Thank you," he said.

She smiled, then signed, *You're welcome. Relax. You'll do fine.*

Narius frowned. Some gestures Kavi had made while she signed to him seemed similar to the motions she made while casting the rune.

"Kavi, I'm curious about something. You both communicate and cast runes through gestures."

She nodded, her brow pinching into a curious frown.

"When you cast the runes, do they mean anything? Is it like using words?" He winced at the strange wording. Maybe if he gave an example. "When Everys drew her runes, there were definite patterns that differed from rune to rune. I thought that maybe the runes were a language. Do you have any insight into it?"

Kavi's frown deepened. When she finally started signing again, her motions were slow and deliberate.

Yes, my signs and my magic are similar. I use words when I cast my spells.

Narius wanted to crow in triumph. He knew it!

Don't get too happy. She signed something else, but whatever she was trying to say was too complicated for Narius to follow. Something about the signs and the spells being together.

He finally shook his head. "I'm sorry. I didn't understand that at all."

Kavi sighed and pinched the bridge of her nose. She produced a scriber, tapped away at the keys furiously, then handed it over to him.

The zhannoq'uem *developed our sign language from the spell gestures, not the other way around. So my signs and spells are connected, but not in the way you're thinking.*

Oh. Narius sank back in the seat, disappointment crashing over him. That could have been a good avenue to explore.

Kavi waved at him, a sympathetic smile on her face. She started signing again. *My magic and Everys's magic are the same but different. Pretend Innana, you, and I see a beautiful sunset. We want to catch it. But you paint. I write poems. Innana writes music. We all catch the sunset. Will what we make all be the same?*

Narius shook his head.

Magic is the same. My magic, Everys's magic, they're the same sunset. The way we catch it is different.

Narius mulled that over. That made a certain amount of sense, but it still disappointed him to learn that. He had been so sure there would be a connection. But then, maybe he had been wrong about it all. Maybe the runes weren't a language. Maybe that was a wild theory that came from his imagination.

He sighed. "Well, let's go visit this philosopher, shall we?"

Kavi nodded with a smile. Narius turned back to the window, watching as the buildings slid past them.

Narius glanced around the neighborhood as he approached Tensin Bakun's house. He didn't live in Utuaa itself. Instead, the seminal lived in a modest neighborhood of small houses, crammed so tightly together they almost sat on top of one another. The buildings were all the same uniform dull blue. There was very little to differentiate them save for an identification code painted in bright red over their doors. The entire effect was unsettling. Narius almost expected all the doors to open at the same time, copies of the same resident stepping out simultaneously, their motions in perfect sync.

He shook off the sensation that scuttled up his back. At the door, Kavi pressed a button in the frame. As they waited, Narius tried to keep from bouncing on his toes. Focus. Remember the objective. He was here to gauge Bakun's receptivity.

The door slid open, revealing Bakun. He was shorter than Narius expected, barely over five feet, with a horseshoe of wiry black hair and large, green eyes. He gaped at Narius for a second, and then chuckled.

"I'm starting to wonder why the dead keep visiting me." Bakun's voice was a resonant bass. His eyes twinkled with silent laughter.

"May I speak with you, Seminal Bakun?" Narius asked, trying to keep his tone formal.

Bakun leaned forward, scanning the street. "And where are the secret police hiding before they swoop in, hmmm?"

"If you fear this is too dangerous..." Narius motioned toward the transport.

The other man guffawed. "Now that is an interesting question. What is 'danger' indeed? A person thrust into combat might fear the situation is too dangerous, but a soldier, trained for war, would not. That same soldier might fear the danger of professing his love to a beautiful young woman." Bakun winked at Kavi. "Whereas the first man would do so to a dozen women in one night. The real question, my good sir, is what kind of danger are you?"

Narius hesitated, unsure if he was supposed to answer.

That only prompted Bakun to laugh even harder. "Come in, come in. Let me assure you, I am no danger to you, friend Narius, if that is who you really are."

Bakun ushered them into his home, which turned out to be just as modest on the inside as it appeared on the outside. There wasn't much to look at, just a collection of couches and chairs in one corner, a kitchenette in another corner with a small table, and then an arch that Narius assumed led to his bedroom and other facilities. The only notable feature was a large painting of a windswept prairie at sunset. Bakun motioned toward one of the couches. Narius went and sat down, but Kavi took up station next to the door.

"Some might see you as an ill omen," Bakun said. "Instead I am curious. What brings Senen's long-promised king to my doorstep?"

"I wanted to discuss what you said in the Colonnade, sir. I found much of what you said very persuasive."

Bakun snorted and flicked a hand at him. "Oh, that. Yes, Angara and I fulfilled our roles quite adequately, didn't we?"

Narius's heart sank. More acting? Had he misjudged the situation?

The seminal must have caught his worried expression, for he smiled and leaned forward. "But truth be told, I insisted I take that side of the debate. What is a seminal for if not to provoke questions and growth in his hearers? And how better to do so than with something you believe?"

Narius nodded thoughtfully. Rather than dive in the way he planned, maybe he should be more circumspect. "I often find that growth is necessary in both people and institutions."

"Indeed?" Bakun's eyes narrowed.

"For example, during my time as the Dynasty's king, I came to understand that we have not been fair to our subjugated races. Our treatment of them has been harsh and, in many instances, cruel. It was my goal before my... well, my death, to take steps to correct that."

Bakun didn't respond. He stared at Narius, having gone so still that Narius worried that he had offended him.

Best to keep going. "And while I've learned as much as I could about the Imperium's history, I am an outsider. I wonder, sir, what insight you might offer. Purely from an academic perspective, of course."

He still didn't say anything. His gaze flicked to Kavi, then back to Narius.

"Dangerous indeed." He rose, heading for the kitchen. "May I offer you something to drink, Your Strength? You haven't lived until you've sampled our *kathekk*."

Narius shot a look at Kavi. She nodded warily. *A sweet drink. Should be safe.*

Bakun must have caught his uncertainty. He produced a large bottle and brought it over for Kavi to inspect. When she nodded again, he went back to the kitchen and poured two glasses, then shot a questioning glance at Kavi. She shook her head. Bakun brought Narius a glass, then took a long gulp from his before sitting down again.

Narius took a tentative sip. The flavor exploded in his mouth; a blast of sugary sweetness chased by a strange bitterness that caused him to choke. But once the initial shock passed, he found a pleasant tingle dancing across his tongue.

"This is very good," he said.

Bakun smiled and finished his glass. "I suppose. I personally find the sweetness too overwhelming. If I had my choice, I would offer you some Dalark goldwine or, better yet, a well-aged Ksann whiskey. But alas, Potentate Yrelin, the embodiment of the spirit of moderation, decreed that we may only imbibe on seven different days of the year and today, sadly, is not one of those seven."

Really? Narius shot another look at Kavi, who shrugged.

"Never mind that we all know that 'moderation' looks different for each person. Like danger does. Although we all agree it is true danger to question the wisdom of the spirits as shared by the potentates."

Narius took another sip of the *kathekk*, then said, "I understand how you feel. I've come to think that the Dynasty's insistence on military might and prowess has become a cage that is holding us back. As long as we continue in that vein, seeing people as those who can feed our military or be fed to it, we won't be able to grow."

Bakun raised his glass. "To the self-made cages we seek to escape."

"Oh?"

Bakun studied his glass without drinking. Then he set it aside. "We Dalark pride ourselves on the strength that our adherence to the spirits and potentates give us. We have no room in our lives for doubt. And why would we? We have the truth of the spirits as distilled through the potentates. They give shape to all that we are."

He turned and indicated the painting. "What do you think of this, Your Strength?"

Narius looked it over, trying to be as critical in his evaluation as he could. But then, art had never been his strongest subject. "Very nice. Um... very pastoral?"

Bakun snorted. "Would you be interested to learn that this is one of only a hundred paintings that the Dalark are permitted to display in their homes?"

Narius's head jerked to one side, as if Bakun's words had knocked him off balance. "Wh-what?"

"It's true. Potentate Gokh, speaking on behalf of the spirit of art, said that paintings depicting nature in its simplicity promotes harmony and clear thinking. Before any art may be distributed to the masses, it must undergo a rigorous check by seminals like me and other experts to make sure it adheres to Gokh's standards. Those that do not are hidden away, rarely seen by the ordinary Dalark. Too dangerous, you see."

Narius gaped at Bakun, his mind reeling. For years, he had heard stories of the Dalark masters like Bolatar or Vrakun. Their masterpieces were hoarded by the Imperium, said to be too valuable to be seen by outsiders. He had always assumed that meant that the Dalark got to enjoy them instead.

"And this is true of so much of our society. The food we eat, the way we interact, our government, our entertainment, our culture, all carefully orchestrated and constrained. And while we tell ourselves that we are so enlightened and advanced, certainly compared to the vicious and backward Xoniel Dynasty, many of us know that simply isn't true."

Bakun seemed to collapse in his chair, his eyes wide and his mouth pressed into a thin line, as if he was holding back more to his rant. Narius understood his hesitation. He suspected that if the wrong person heard what he had just said, Bakun would be in serious trouble. And yet, in spite of that, he knew he had to keep pressing.

"So you think the spirits and potentates are..." He couldn't bring himself to finish the sentence, if only to keep from frightening Bakun away from his honesty.

"Untrue?" Bakun's gaze turned distant, then he shook his head. "No. There is truth to be found there, but only once it's been stripped of its feathers and leaves."

Narius frowned, prompting Bakun to laugh.

He leaned forward on the couch, his eyes alight once again.

"Many generations ago, in a place not too far from here, a group of travelers came across a most unusual sight: a great column, thousands of feet high, jutting up out of the vast plain. Made of a substance they had never seen, this structure could withstand the strongest storm, would not even sway in the mightiest of tremors. And these people, long without shelter, realized they had found a safe haven. For you see, these travelers were clever. They quickly learned how to attach their homes to the column, and thus anchored, they knew they would be safe for years to come.

"Soon many homes dotted the sides of the column, with the most prestigious and important claiming the highest vantages for themselves. And many decided to decorate their new homes in ostentatious ways, their shelters sprouting embellishments like leaves on a tree or feathers on a brightly colored bird. Within three generations, the column was a riot of these embellishments."

Narius risked a glance at Kavi to see if this was normal. She gave him a playful scowl and motioned for him to pay attention.

"One day, messengers arrived from the north. A great storm was coming and would arrive at the column in two weeks. The residents scoffed at the news. Their homes had weathered storms. Then more messengers: the storm was unlike any seen in the whole of the Imperium, coming in a week! And still they scoffed. Even as the clouds loomed on the horizon, ominous as war, they went about their lives without fear.

"The storm crashed down upon them. Wind and rain, so strong the ground itself shook. The people huddled in their homes, still confident they would weather it all. But those leaves and feathers that had once been such a source of pride were caught by the storm, ripping the houses themselves from the unshakable pillar. And so what had taken years to build was destroyed in less than an hour."

Bakun fell silent and hung his head, almost as if he was grieving for these clearly fictional people. Narius wasn't sure if he was supposed to say something or not, so he just sat there and gave the other man space.

Finally, Bakun looked up with a sad smile. "That is a story that we tell our young ones when we first teach them about the spirits and potentates. And we patiently explain the allegory to them. The column is the truth revealed to us from the spirits via the potentates. We of the Dalark nestle firmly against such truth to weather the greatest of storms.

"But many of us know that much of what we consider 'truth' is nothing more than the leaves and feathers we have added ourselves. And when the storm comes—and I do believe that a storm greater than any we have weathered is imminent—so much of what we have sheltered in will be ripped away."

Once again, silence hung between them, but this time, Narius knew not to break it. Instead, his thoughts turned inward. He saw the truth in what Bakun had told him, but not for the Dalark. For the Dynasty. For himself. His people had clung to so much that they all knew wasn't true. And now, the storm had come. He had no doubt that much was being ripped away from the Dynasty's people. The same could happen to him. What truth did he cling to?

His mind spun back to his first lesson with Scrivener Tolistan and the words that he had shared with Narius what felt like a lifetime ago: *O Siporans, remember: the Singularity is supreme, the only, the whole. In Him and through Him and for Him, all was made. And we are His people, the servants of His will.* As he remembered those ancient words, a warmth and certainty spread through him. He knew what his column was. He knew what truth he clung to. And He had brought him this far. How could he doubt whatever path lay before him?

Narius leaned forward. "Seminal, I can tell that you are a man of deep thought and wisdom. The sort who sees what is and does not flinch from it. A true potentate."

Bakun smiled indulgently. "I'm no Varsillin, but I thank you for the flattery."

Narius wasn't sure what that meant, so he pressed on. "I appreciate your candor and I find much we have in common. We both want our respective kingdoms to be better, to grow, to flourish. What if I told you I knew of someone who wanted the same thing for the Imperium. Someone who was passionately dedicated to bringing about the kind of change I suspect you yearn for."

Bakun didn't reply. Instead, he stared at Narius with such intensity that Narius grew uncomfortable. He wanted to squirm. But he held the other man's gaze, praying that he hadn't just made a costly mistake.

"Dangerous indeed," Bakun murmured, then he smiled. "Tell me more."

34

Once they returned to Fort Wyne, Taffinia helped Everys and Redtale on the next leg of their journey. She bribed the commander of a military convoy, telling him that the two women were looking for their loved ones who had disappeared during the invasion. He bought the stories, and before long, Everys and Redtale were seated in the back of a supply transport, bracing themselves against every bump and dip in the road.

The drive took twelve hours, and thankfully, the troops left them alone during most of that time, only occasionally checking on them when the convoy stopped. They were all polite enough, but Everys knew that the sooner they could get away from them, the better.

Toward the end of the drive, Redtale scooted over to Everys and nudged her. "What's our next step when we arrive?"

Everys tried to rub the exhaustion out of her eyes. "According to Papa, there's a man in Longwatch named Treskin. He used to bring my family supplies. He'll know a way into the Demilitarized Zone."

Redtale grunted thoughtfully, then said, "Small problem, though. The Demilitarized Zone doesn't exist anymore."

"I know," Everys said, not wanting to pursue that line of thought.

Redtale hesitated, then said, "A lot of troops went through the Zone in the early days of the invasion. Maybe your mother and sister won't be there anymore. They may have had to flee or they could've been captured or..."

Everys winced as Redtale's voice trailed off. Yes, that was definitely possible. But she had to hold on to the hope that Mama and Galan would still be there. Otherwise, she'd just curl up and stop entirely.

After another hour, the convoy arrived at Longwatch. The commander ordered Everys and Redtale out of the transport and sent them on their way.

She and Redtale slipped out of the supply depot into a town that appeared to be little more than abandoned ruins. Crates dotted the streets, and most of the buildings were damaged or had collapsed into rubble. There were civilians who apparently were trying to go about their regular lives, heading for the local market or trying to fix up their badly damaged homes, but they had a haunted look to them, as if they were merely going through the motions.

According to Papa's notes and corroborated by Tolistan, Treskin worked in a nearby rock quarry. Everys and Redtale made their way there, only to learn that the owners had shut the quarry down for the past month and a half. Thankfully, the man guarding the gates knew Treskin and directed them to a nearby bar. The establishment looked like a pile of rubble with a front door. As they approached, Redtale put a hand on Everys's shoulder and motioned for her to stay put. Then the guard darted inside.

Everys tried to remain calm while she stood on the street corner by herself. Thankfully, her discomfort didn't linger as Redtale emerged and beckoned her to come in.

Large cracks in the interior wall painted jagged sunlight across the dirty floor. A few men and women slumped at their tables with half-empty glasses strewn around them. But one man with short-cropped dusty hair sat in a back corner, clearly alert and watchful. In some ways, he reminded Everys of her brother, Legarr. Even though he never looked directly at her, Everys knew he had examined her the moment she walked in. He sat up straighter as she approached his table.

"Well, hello, little lady, what can I..." His voice trailed off as she sat down across from him. Then he leaned forward and got a good look at her. "Inkstains, it's you!"

Well, that would make this a lot easier. Everys smiled. "My father sends his regards."

Treskin snorted. "I bet he does. What are you doing here? I don't think this is exactly safe!"

"I know, but I need you to take me to my family's vigil." She hesitated, then added, "Have you been out there since the hostilities started? Are Mama and Galan...?"

"They're hanging in there, but just barely," Treskin whispered. "I tried to get them to leave after the Dalark stormed across the Zone, but they refused. Stubborn as your father, that's for sure."

Everys smiled sadly. "How soon can we go?"

Treskin rubbed his chin thoughtfully, then said, "We can head out in two hours. Sound good?"

Everys nodded, trying to keep herself from getting too excited. She didn't know what they would find. But she was one step closer to reuniting her family.

Two hours later, Treskin met them on the outskirts of the supply depot. He stood next to a transport that vaguely resembled a military vehicle, only Everys quickly realized that the camouflage pattern on the sides was a bit off. Treskin had also changed into an outfit that appeared almost military at first glance.

"Have to blend in," he explained.

Within a matter of moments, they rolled out of Longwatch and into what had been her people's homeland.

Everys resisted the urge to hang outside of the transport and soak in the air. Yes, she had visited the edge of the Demilitarized Zone once before, but to actually be there? She drank in the rolling hills, the wild trees, the way the wind carried an odd scent that was both strange and yet familiar at the same time. Was this what it was like for people to return to their actual home?

"How close will we get to Nekek the Bright?" she asked Treskin.

He shook his head. "Nekek's on the other end of the Zone. You wouldn't want to go there."

"Why not?" she asked.

Treskin hesitated, then sighed heavily. "Trust me, Blessed, your curiosity is understandable, but it's best to leave that alone."

Oh. Everys supposed that was wise. But still, a little part of her wanted to see the city spoken of so fondly in the ancient texts, just to walk those streets and see what might have been. Another dream to set aside, along with so many others.

They rode in silence for close to an hour, but then Treskin seemed to tense behind the controls. When Everys tried to ask what was wrong, he motioned for her to keep quiet. She clenched her jaw, tamping down her frustration. A skimmer roared by overhead, but even after the sound faded, Treskin didn't relax.

They continued on like that for another hour before Treskin steered the transport into a small copse of trees and killed the engine. He slid out of the cabin and took a quick look around before motioning for Everys and Redtale to join him.

As Everys slipped out of the transport, she soaked in the surroundings. The trees were thick but gnarled, poking out of the dry dirt. Brown rocks jutted from the soil as well, creating a snaking and chaotic wall.

Treskin led them through the underbrush until they came across a large piece of metal that lay haphazardly against a hill.

"Help me out here," he whispered, nudging Redtale.

The two of them walked to one side, where Treskin pulled a chain out from under a bush. With Redtale's help, he pulled on the chain. The piece of metal slid to one side with a low grinding sound, revealing a hole bordered with worn tan stones. Treskin poked his head in, then signaled for them to follow him.

Everys dropped into a narrow stone tunnel. Treskin led the way again, confidently slipping through a winding passage until they came up to another chain hanging from the ceiling. Treskin motioned for them to stop, and he pulled on the chain.

"Sets off a quiet bell in the residence," he explained. "That way we don't sneak up on them."

Everys's heart leaped. They were that close? Did that mean that, at any moment, she'd see her mother and sister again?

A section of wall scraped and groaned, the stones shifted to the left, and an open doorway was revealed. Everys pushed past Treskin and hurried down a set of stairs into a well-lit room. A short table was pushed into one corner, bordered by well-worn cushions and pillows. One wall had carved stone shelves in it, dotted with cannisters and bowls. Another had a small counter jutting into the room. Dozens of pieces of paper were tacked to the wall over the table, each one covered with sketches.

And there she was. Mama's hair had gone completely gray, and she wasn't nearly as plump. She stirred something in a bowl, but her motions were almost frenetic. Everys felt a pang of guilt. Mama always got intense when she was annoyed, usually by something one of her children did. The last time Everys had seen that posture and sharp motions was when she had skipped conclave again to sneak out to the market.

Mama turned toward the door, but then she froze. Her eyes widened, and her legs wobbled a bit.

"Ev-Everys?" she whispered. "Is that really you?"

Everys rushed forward and caught Mama in a hug. Mama whispered questions, but her words blurred together. And Everys wanted to say something, but her throat tightened and she couldn't muster more than a ragged sob. Soon Mama started crying, and before too long, Everys joined her. They clung to each other, and Everys quietly thanked the Singularity that she had found her safe and sound.

"What are you doing here?" Mama finally whispered.

Everys laughed, so many words and questions and memories clogging her mind. She had so much to say, to ask, to tell, that she hardly knew where to start.

"Where's Galan?" she asked.

"Where else? The Wall." Then Mama cocked her head to one side. "You have no idea what I'm talking about, do you?"

Everys smiled. "Papa's told me about it."

Mama's eyes widened. "He found you? He's okay?"

Everys winced. Found her, yes. Okay, that was debatable. "He did. He evacuated Bastion with me when the city fell."

"And your husband? The... the king?" Mama said, her voice uncertain.

A brief pang shot through Everys, but she braced herself. Papa had been so disapproving of Narius. Would Mama be any better? "He... he didn't make it."

Mama stared at her, then pulled her into another hug. "I'm so sorry, dear. I wish I could have met him."

A sob rattled through Everys's chest. "I do too, Mama. But this will have to wait. We need to get Galan and get you out of here."

"Our vigil is over?" Mama asked.

That was one way of putting it. "Pack up your things. Redtale, help her, please. I'll go find Galan."

Mama gave her some basic instructions about how to navigate through their sanctuary. Everys slipped out of the living quarters into a large tunnel that stretched into darkness in both directions. She headed to her left, staring up toward the ceiling that was obscured in shadows. What was this place?

That mystery would have to keep. She rounded a corner and came to a halt. Her sister, Galan, knelt in front of a section of wall, running her hand over a series of glyphs carved into the stone. Everys froze to study her. In some ways, her sister hadn't changed. She had black hair that fell to her shoulders, with narrow green eyes that darted across the wall. Everys had always envied her sister's good looks. Most of the people in Fair Havens had noticed Galan before Everys, and that sometimes hurt. But Galan had ignored the fawning attention. She had always been too focused on her studies.

Her face was scrunched in concentration. Then Galan glanced in her direction, a relaxed smile on her face. But when Galan actually saw her, she froze. Her mouth popped open in a tiny circle. Then she laughed.

"Well, look what the chakrut dug up!" Galan rushed forward and nearly knocked Everys over as she embraced her.

The two sisters clung to each other and half-laughed, half-cried.

"So I hear congratulations are in order," Galan said. "And a king, no less."

Everys's happiness shattered. But she swallowed the brief stab of grief. "H-he's..."

Galan pulled away, studying Everys face. Then she pulled her into an even tighter hug. Nothing else had to be said.

Finally, Everys pulled out of the hug and swiped away her tears. "So Papa told me about this wall. Just a bunch of names, right? He says that you're always out here."

"And probably frustrated because he doesn't know why, right? It's the way I've coped out here, Everys. Five years with only your parents and the occasional visit from Treskin? It wears on you after a while."

Galan led Everys over to the wall. "But here I have hundreds of names, people who have been in this space before me. I know nothing about them, so I make up stories, who they were, why they were here, whether we'd get along. Sometimes I pair them off or create little families."

Sadness for her sister smothered Everys's own grief. "That must have been difficult."

"It was something I had to do, y'know? It was that or start licking the walls, and I figured Papa would be more worried if I started doing that. This one?" She pointed to one glyph. "He and I get into philosophical debates every other day. This one loves to bake muffins in the morning. And this one... well, he knows me better than anyone. My one true confidant." Galan trailed off, then offered her a shaky smile. "So, why are you here?"

Everys motioned for Galan to sit down and, as best as she could, explained everything that had happened over the past year: her first marriage to Narius, how they had fallen in love, the conspiracy against them, Viara's pregnancy, the war with Dalark, and the mage-kings' plot. Galan listened, but she also peppered Everys with dozens of questions, especially when it came to Tolistan's project to translate the runes. Everys wasn't able to answer those to either of their satisfaction, but with each question, a quiet certainty grew within her.

Finally, she said, "Galan, I was intending to send you and Mama to the forest as soon as I finished here, but now I know you have to go. I think you'll be able to help them with the project."

Galan blinked, clearly surprised, but then a brilliant grin split her face. "That sounds amazing. I'll go pack!"

Galan leaped to her feet and started toward the living area. But then she skidded to a halt and hurried back to Everys.

"I should show you where the hiding place is first. It's tricky to find."

Galan snared her hand and dragged her down the tunnel, running her hand along the rough wall. Then she stopped at a small crevice in the stones and gestured, as if inviting Everys to step through a door.

Everys braced herself and stepped forward. Once again, there was a strange rippling sensation as she walked through the glamour spell. And then there it was. Her family's Principality, the one that they had been charged with protecting for generations.

It wasn't any different from the others she had seen. Made of the same stone, conforming to the same basic shape, with little irregularities that came from the masons who carved it. But seeing her family's healing rune on the curve caused a flutter of recognition in her heart. She stepped forward and caressed the stone, savoring the rough texture underneath her fingers until she reached up and traced the familiar lines. Tears stung her eyes as she plucked a bead from her bracelet, rolling it between her fingers to liquify the ink.

"Thank you for everything you've given me," she whispered.

And she traced the shatter rune on its surface.

35

Much to Everys's relief, Treskin promised to escort Mama and Galan all the way to the Shade. He had joked that his part of the vigil was over as well, so there was nothing keeping him in Longwatch. Everys thought she sensed a bit of relief in his joking demeanor and she couldn't blame him. Mama and Galan were definitely happy to leave their hiding place. After Treskin led them back to town, they went their separate ways, with Galan and Mama both giving Everys long hugs before they boarded a skimmer with Treskin.

Once she was sure they were gone, Everys set out with Redtale. According to the notes from Tolistan, the final Principality was in Breakwater, a little fishing town on the southern shore of the Water Bearer's Repose. Getting there proved to be tricky. There was no major airhub traffic leaving Longwatch or arriving in Breakwater, nor was there a high-speed rail connection. Thankfully, Redtale pieced together a series of shorter legs that, after nearly two full days of travel by skimmer and public transport, had them arrive in Breakwater in the middle of Second Watch. When Everys stumbled off the public transport, she wanted nothing more than to find a hotel or a hostel or some place where she could freshen up. But she had a feeling that time was of the essence. They had been lucky with the first two Principalities. She knew she had to find the last and get back to the Shade as quickly as she could.

According to Tolistan's notes, the elders referred to this family as "The Tide." There wasn't much else in the notes, except that the Tide worked at the local fishing docks. Once Everys and Redtale got their bearings, that was where they headed.

"Rough town," Redtale said as they walked through the streets.

That was an accurate assessment. The city had clearly fallen on hard times, but from her cursory examination, Everys suspected it was a slow decline rather than a recent problem. Most of the buildings they passed looked like they had been neglected for years, with chipped or peeling paint and obvious issues that hadn't been fixed in years. The people, too, seemed neglected. Most of them looked tired and haggard, as if they had been working for months or years with not enough pay. Everys frowned. What noble house took care this town? Why had they neglected their people so badly? She couldn't do much about it now, but she made a mental note to look into that when she returned to the palace.

Redtale grunted quietly, and Everys glanced in her direction.

"We've picked up a tail," Redtale said. "Don't look behind us, but we've got three people following. And I spot two more ahead that are going to ambush us."

Everys resisted the urge to look over her shoulder, but she easily spotted two young men, a Grerid and Kolvese, standing near an alley mouth. Although they were trying to pretend like they weren't watching them, they clearly were. They had turned toward each other, their heads lowered like they were whispering to each other, but the Grerid kept shooting covert looks in their direction.

"So what do we do?" Everys whispered back.

"Keep walking. Maybe they'll think twice if they see I'm with you," Redtale said.

She nodded, but Everys's heart betrayed her growing unease. It slammed against her ribcage faster and faster until she worried it would burst from her chest. Sure enough, as they approached the alley, the two young men straightened and fixed them with a pointed look.

"Hey, c'mere," one of them said.

"Eat rocks." Redtale's voice was icy enough to freeze the Plissk's Sanctuary Oasis.

Apparently, the young men weren't intimidated. They both flashed flechette throwers at them. "Get in the alley. Now!"

Everys was about to object when someone rushed up behind her and shoved her into the alley. Redtale's shout was cut off as she was pushed in after Everys. Everys whirled around and faced five young adults, the two who had threatened them, plus two Ixactls, a male and female, and a well-muscled Elbrekkian. Redtale tensed to leap into a fight, her hands balled into fists, but the non-Ixactls all produced weapons and aimed them at Redtale.

"We don't want any trouble," the Grerid said. "We just want your valuables. Blades, tech, jewelry. We can all walk away from here in one piece. We just gotta keep cool and calm, and no one will get hurt."

Redtale grumbled something, but Everys put her hand on her shoulder. She held up her hands in surrender, and thankfully, Redtale did likewise.

The Grerid nodded, and the Kolvese and Elbrekkian darted forward, checking their pockets. Everys winced as they confiscated their IDs and the loose money they had. That was worrisome, but hopefully, they wouldn't need any of that.

But then the Elbrekkian pulled out the scriber with Tolistan's notes. Everys tensed, ready to object. That had all the images they had taken of the two Principalities. If that were to fall into the wrong hands...

Before she could say anything, the Elbrekkian yanked her bracelet off her wrist. Everys squeaked. Bad enough to lose the scriber, but losing the bracelet would effectively disarm her.

The Grerid whipped his weapon around to aim it at Everys. "I said, don't move."

"I'm not planning on it," Everys said, surprised she could sound so calm. "You can have everything else, but please, the scriber won't get you much. Same with the bracelet. That's a family heirloom, but its only value is sentimental."

"Metal's probably worth something if we melt it down," the Elbrekkian retorted. "Plus, we can always pawn the scriber. Plenty of call for those."

Everys's breath stuttered. She couldn't lose those. Not like this!

Redtale snorted and tensed. Before Everys could stop her, she charged with a loud bellow.

The Grerid shouted something and fired, but he must have missed, because Redtale slammed into him hard enough that he flew back into the far wall, crumpling to the ground. Redtale backhanded the Kolvese, dropping him as well. The Elbrekkian fumbled with his weapon, unable to juggle it and the stuff he carried. That made it easy for Redtale to knock him out with a head butt, one that resulted in a loud crack from the Elbrekkian's face.

But that left the other two Ixactl. The female guffawed. "You're pretty spry for an elder. But you've got rocks between your horns if you think you can take both of us at the same time."

Redtale chuckled as well. "You whelps aren't a threat."

The two younger Ixactl charged, the male going for Redtale's legs, the female aiming for her chest. Redtale spun out of the male's path, but the female caught her arm with one of her horns. Redtale hissed and grabbed at her arm. Everys gasped. Blood welled up between Redtale's fingers. Everys's gaze flicked to the female's horns, and she realized the female had sharpened the tips. So had the male.

Redtale sneered at them. "Can't win with what the ancestors gave you? You gotta cheat?"

"This ain't the arena, old lady. You gotta do what you need to to win," the male said with a shrug.

Redtale glared at him, then lunged for the Elbrekkian's dropped weapon. But the female was faster, kicking it out of her reach. She then kicked Redtale in the face hard enough that one of her false horns fell off. The female laughed as she picked it up and flaunted it at the male like it was a trophy.

"Better sharpened horns than falsies!" the female crowed.

Redtale clambered to her feet, blood trickling out of her nose. She twisted her neck, resulting in an audible crack that sounded like a tree limb snapping. Then she set herself and raised her fists.

"I'm not getting any younger, and you two definitely aren't getting any smarter," she muttered.

The female threw down the false horn and charged. This time, Redtale stood her ground. She snared the other woman's horns and, with a sharp twist, tossed her over her hip. But the male was right there, clubbing Redtale in the side of the head with his meaty fists. Redtale staggered.

A snap-hiss sliced through the alley, a puff of air that Everys immediately recognized. She whipped her head around. The Kolvese had recovered, and he held his flechette thrower in a shaking hand.

Everys turned back to Redtale but then stopped with a gasp. Her guard's eyes were wide as well, dark purple blood blossoming in the middle of her chest. She staggered, then collapsed to one knee.

"Get out of here!" the Kolvese shouted.

Apparently, that was all the others had to hear. While the male Ixactl helped the fallen Grerid, the female roused the Elbrekkian. Then the two of them scooped up what he had dropped, and they all scrambled out of the alley as quickly as they could.

Everys snapped out of her paralysis and rushed to Redtale's side. Redtale collapsed to one knee. Her skin was turning a strange ashy color and her eyes were glazing over. Going into shock? Probably. Redtale tried to say something, but she fell onto her back with a groan.

"No, no, no!" Everys cried. She dropped next to Redtale and looked over her injuries. The cut in her arm from the female's horn wasn't all that deep, but would normally require stitches. The chest wound, though, was more worrisome. Everys didn't know much about Ixactl physiology, but from the way Redtale was fading, she had to assume this wound could prove fatal.

Everys screamed for help, but no one seemed to hear her. She looked around the alley, trying to find something, anything, that could help. Then she realized that, in his hurry, the Elbrekkian had dropped some of what he had stolen. She spied the scriber—thank the Singularity for that!—and a few loose blades, but unfortunately, she didn't see her bracelet.

Could she find a substitute ink? She spotted nothing she could use, just mud and what looked like fetid garbage water leaking from a nearby bin. Neither would make for good enough ink.

But then her gaze fell on Redtale's own blood. Her stomach twisted. She had used blood to heal someone once before. It had worked, but at a steep cost. The rebuke had put Everys in a coma for nearly a week. Something like that could happen here as well, but what choice did she have? She couldn't let Redtale die!

"Promise me you'll make sure I'm safe," Everys whispered, and she dipped her finger in the blood pooling near Redtale. "I don't know how long I'll be out."

Redtale's eyes drifted in her direction, and it looked like she was trying to say something, but only an indistinct mumble slipped through. Everys gritted her teeth and set to work, tracing out the powerful healing rune that was her family's legacy. Her hand trembled as she worked, mostly because she knew what would happen when she activated the spell.

By the time she finished drawing the rune, Redtale had gone dangerously still. Everys took several ragged breaths, braced herself, and then activated the rune.

For a moment, nothing happened, and Everys worried she had gotten it wrong, or worse, it was too late. But then the pattern on Redtale's chest lit up with a blaze of red light. The Ixactl woman gasped, her back arching, as the glow seeped into her body. The wounds in Redtale's chest and arm closed up and the ashy color disappeared from her skin. Redtale's eyes became alert, and she sat up.

"What did you—"

A blazing pain erupted in Everys's chest, mirroring where she had drawn the rune on Redtale. Everys bit back a cry and doubled over, wrapping her arms around her body as if to hold herself together. The pain snaked through her chest and down her arms and legs before pulling together in a knot of agony that perched right between her eyes. The world was awash in a blaze that forced Everys to squeeze her eyes shut.

But then, in an instant, the feeling faded. Everys sat there, her eyes still closed, stunned. This made no sense. Why was she still conscious? Had she somehow developed a tolerance for rebukes? Was that possible?

"Everys, are you okay?" Redtale whispered.

She had no idea. She gingerly loosened her arms and uncurled, waiting to see if there was going to be another wave. Nothing happened. She took several ragged breaths, looking down at her own body. Why hadn't the rebuke been as strong as she'd expected?

"I-I think so," Everys whispered.

"Are you two all right?" a voice called from the alley's mouth.

Redtale whipped around, dropping into a fighting stance. Everys shied away behind her.

An older Kolvese man stood in the alley. He was well dressed, with a shock of white hair and a concerned look on his face.

"Keep walking," Redtale said through a snarl. "We're fine."

"My friend, the amount of blood around you and the frightened look on your companion's face tell me you are anything but." The man held out a hand. "I mean you no harm. Why don't you come with me? My home isn't far from here. You can contact the constables."

Everys shook her head. "No constables."

The man frowned. "I understand your hesitation, but I can only assume you're both the victims of some sort of assault. They should—"

"No constables." Redtale's voice carried a threat.

"As you wish," the man said.

Everys frowned. There was something familiar about this man, but she couldn't quite figure out what. It didn't set her at ease, but it was enough to pique her curiosity.

"At least come with me and recover," the man said. "My wife can make you both some tea. You look like you could use it."

That did sound nice, and the man's smile was definitely disarming. Everys decided she needed to take the risk. She rose. "Thank you. I appreciate it..."

The man smiled at her unspoken prompt. "Vessel of the Wandering Profit clan. Come, let's get you taken care of."

He turned and motioned for them to come out of the alley. Everys started to follow, but Redtale snared her arm.

"What?" Everys asked.

"You don't recognize the name?" Redtale whispered. "Wandering Profit clan? That's Paine's clan."

Everys's head whipped around and she looked at Vessel. Suddenly, the pieces fell into place. She saw the similarity. That's why he seemed so familiar.

"Forgive me for hesitating, but I have to ask. Are you somehow related to Vizier Paine?" Everys asked.

The man's face turned stony, but he nodded once, sharply. "I am. He is my son. But let me assure you, no matter what you may think of him, you need my help and I am more than happy to offer it."

Redtale clearly didn't like that answer, but Everys didn't know what else they could do. They needed a moment to collect themselves, and tea sounded nice. She made a quick decision. She scooped up the dropped scriber and the scattered blades and headed after Vessel. Maybe it wasn't the smartest idea, but in that moment, it felt like the right one. And that would have to be good enough.

36

Vessel's home turned out to be close to the alley. It wasn't much to look at, but it was definitely better maintained than the neighbors', painted a vibrant blue. The front yard was a carefully cultivated rock garden, with the stones arranged in swirls and pinwheels as opposed to just dumped haphazardly. Vessel escorted them through a foyer and living area. Everys wished she could slow down and inspect the house, to soak in the details of Paine's childhood, if only to decipher him a bit. A Kolvese woman, thin but muscular through the shoulders with lighter skin than her husband's, turned as they entered, and her eyes widened as her gaze fell on Everys and Redtale.

"More strays?" she asked, her tone teasing.

Vessel clucked his tongue. "People in need of refuge, my dear. Who am I to turn them back on the trail?" He turned to Everys and Redtale. "This is my wife, Freedom. I did not catch your names."

"We didn't give them," Redtale grumbled.

Vessel's mouth clicked shut, but he recovered from his surprise quickly enough. "No matter. It wouldn't be the first time a Kolvese has shared the trail's bounty with anonymous strangers. They usually turn out to be on the most important business. Please, have a seat. Freedom, I was thinking some Lady Night if we still have it."

Everys perked up. She had only had Lady Night tea once before, when she was younger, from a Kolvese merchant who had been passing through Fair Havens. She had loved the rich sweetness.

Freedom nodded, and soon, she and Vessel were working together to brew the tea. While they did, Everys drifted along the edge of the room, her gaze drifting from decoration to decoration. There were images of Vessel and Freedom together at various stages of their life. One was a wedding portrait. Another was of Vessel with a large Kolvese man who appeared to be a relative. Then Everys's gaze hitched on one picture in particular: Paine when he was a young teenager with three Kolvese children, a boy and two girls, practically climbing up his arms with wide smiles.

"Ah, you have found our joys," Vessel said. "Yes, those are our children. Trail and Stars, the twins, and then Solstice. And I'm sure you recognize Paine."

At the mention of her son's name, Freedom muttered something under her breath. Everys didn't know the Kolvese language, but from the tone and vehemence, she suspected it was a curse. Vessel snapped something at her in the same language, and then he turned to Redtale and Everys, an apologetic smile on his face.

"I'm afraid our eldest is a sore point for Freedom," he said.

"'A sore point?'" Freedom repeated, her tone incredulous. "That monster steals his friend's throne and what does Paine do? Play lackey to the tyrant?"

Vessel's expression turned brittle, and his gaze flicked toward Everys and Redtale. Everys could read the fear in his eyes. Her heart lurched. While she had no love for Paine, she knew how much Narius had loved him. That made Paine's actions so inexplicable. In some ways, she was glad that Narius had never found out how fickle Paine's loyalty actually was.

She held up her hands. "We have no love for Brencis."

"That's for sure," Redtale muttered.

That seemed to help, but Vessel didn't relax by much. "I admit, Paine's actions have us confused. I thought we had raised him to be more loyal, especially to someone who has done so much for him. But I also trust my son. I'm sure he has his reasons for what he's done. But enough about him. What brings the two of you to Breakwater?"

Everys and Redtale exchanged uncertain looks. Obviously, they couldn't give the real reason. As friendly as Vessel and Freedom were, she had no way of knowing how they would react. But Vessel was looking at them with such intensity, she was sure that he somehow would see through their poorly constructed anonymity at any moment.

"We're trying to track down some of her relatives," Redtale blurted. "Inheritance issues."

Everys gaped at her. What was she doing? Redtale offered a tiny shrug.

"Those can be tricky, yes. But I know most of the people in Breakwater. I'm the local schoolmaster, so it's likely that I've either taught them or their children. What are their names?"

And there was the problem. Everys grimaced. "We don't know."

Vessel took that in stride. "A mystery! Makes the story even better. What do you know?"

"They're fishermen," Everys offered.

Freedom laughed near the stove. "That narrows it down."

"And they're Siporan."

That caused both Vessel and Freedom to pause. They glanced at each other, then Vessel smiled. "I think I know who you're looking for. Good people, but they keep to themselves. Problem is, they're probably out on a job right now, and they won't want to talk to anyone when they get back. Tell you what. Spend the night here. In the morning, I'll bring you to them and introduce you."

"We couldn't possibly," Everys said.

Vessel leaned forward, his expression serious. "It's the least we can do. As Kolvese, we believe that to share one's shelter with others is the highest of obligations. It is a chance for us to make our guests... blessed."

She jolted at the gentle insistence of his final word, a slight smile flitting across his face.

"You will be safe with us, my unnamed guest," Vessel continued. "I promise it. And I, unlike others I know, keep my word."

Tears stung Everys's eyes. "Then we accept. With the deepest of gratitude."

She turned back to Freedom and smiled as the older woman offered her a steaming cup of tea. She took a tentative sip. At first, the tea was sweet and fruity, only to be chased with a mossy undertone. It was perfect, the best counterpoint to their time so far in Breakwater. And she knew she had made the right choice.

When Everys woke the next morning, she felt more rested than she had since she left the Shade. And the breakfast Vessel prepared certainly helped. A hearty mix of fruits, sausages, and pastries, Vessel described the meal as a traditional Kolvese breakfast for people heading out on a long journey. Everys devoured everything they put before her, and even Redtale seemed to enjoy it as well. Thankfully, Redtale had fully recovered from her injuries, and Everys hadn't experienced any further rebukes.

Once they finished eating, Vessel led them down to the docks that jutted into the Water Bearer's Repose. When she saw the sheer number of docks, she understood why Freedom had laughed. If they had simply shown up, looking for the Tide, they would have never found them. But now, at least, Vessel had helped them narrow down the search.

Vessel led them to a well-maintained dock with three fishing boats tied to it. Dozens of people were clearly getting ready to head out for the day, but they paused their work when they saw Vessel approaching. They greeted him warmly, and then Vessel introduced Everys to an older woman named Feltys. When Feltys saw Everys, her gaze sharpened, but she nodded politely.

Once Vessel had left, Feltys pulled out a rag and wiped off her hands. "We got word from the elders at Bastion to expect you, Blessed. How can we help?"

Everys breathed a sigh of relief, and she explained what she was there to do. Feltys listened to it all, her brow pinched in a frown.

"Can't say I'm thrilled to hear about what you're planning to do, but the elders said to cooperate, so I guess I have little choice," she said. "But I suppose not much will change for us after you're done."

That prompted a question for Everys. "How can you maintain a proper vigil in the middle of a town?"

Feltys smiled enigmatically. "Because we have our Principality in a safe place. C'mon. I'll show you."

Instead of leading her back into town, she made her way to one boat. She whistled at the crew, who stopped what they were doing.

"Change of plans, everyone. Passenger charter, my family only. You know how it works."

There was some grumbling, but the crews between the three boats shifted their stations, some of them boarding the boat Feltys indicated while others took their place on the other boats. Within a half hour, Everys and Redtale were on the boat and heading out into the middle of the massive inland sea. Everys frowned. Had they stashed their Principality on an island?

They sailed out for half the day before Feltys whistled again. The boat sloughed to a halt, and the crew dropped the anchor. Everys frowned and looked around. They weren't near any land. There weren't any other boats close by either.

Feltys stepped up next to her. She held a piece of wood that had a bowl balanced on top of it. From the rancid smell, it was clearly filled with ink produced by the Dynasty. Feltys handed the bowl to Everys then dipped her finger in the ink, tracing a rune on the wood.

"How familiar are you with the legends, Blessed?" Feltys asked as she worked. "For example, the story of Delman's Treasure?"

Everys frowned. The legends were little more than bedtime stories, not part of the ancient texts the Siporans held sacred. But her father had told those tales to her, Galan, and Legarr plenty of times. Legarr loved this one. "King Delman had a beautiful daughter, the envy of the entire court. Many vied for her hand, but Delman didn't want to betroth her to just anyone. So he took a necklace his daughter wore and had it thrown into the depths of the Gravebalt Sea. He proclaimed that any who could retrieve the necklace would win his daughter's hand."

Feltys nodded, continuing to sketch a rune on the wood that appeared to be a combination of interlocking swirls. "And what happened?"

"The young men who claimed to love the princess tried everything they could think of, but none could swim into the depths of the lake to retrieve the necklace. But one young man, an apprentice scrivener, was determined to claim the princess's hand." Everys's eyes widened as her mind raced ahead to the end of the story. Her gaze latched onto the rune that Feltys was sketching.

Feltys nodded. "And the Singularity came to him in a dream and showed him a new rune, one which would allow him to plumb the depths of the lake. And thus armed, he succeeded where others failed."

As she finished the story, Feltys tapped the rune on the wood to activate it. Then she tossed it over the side of the boat.

The moment the wood hit the water, a loud thrum rattled the boat. Everys could feel the deep vibration through her legs. She immediately latched onto the railing, trying to steady herself. A loud roar drowned out the thrum.

"All stories have a kernel of truth to them, Blessed," Feltys said. "I don't know if King Delman had a daughter or if the Singularity truly gifted that rune to an apprentice scrivener, but..."

She gestured over the side of the boat. Everys clung even tighter to the railing and risked a peek over the side.

There was a hole in the middle of the water, twenty feet across, plunging down into the fathomless depths. Did it reach all the way to the sea floor? Everys couldn't tell for sure from her vantage point, but it appeared to be a possibility. The eeriest part of this was that the walls of the hole were perfectly still, as if the water had merely frozen in place, unmoving.

A cranking sound came from behind her, and Everys turned. The crew swung a winch out over the hole. At the end of the rope was a lit lantern and what appeared to be a harness she could sit on.

"I've gone down there dozens of times this way, Blessed," Feltys said. "You'll be perfectly fine. Plan to be pulled up in ten minutes, okay? Don't dawdle."

The crew set to work, strapping Everys into the harness. Redtale looked ready to object, but she thankfully didn't. Once Everys was secured, Feltys gave a signal with her hand and the rope went taut, lifting Everys from the deck. The winch swung her out over the sea until she dangled over the water. Then Feltys shouted for her to be lowered, and slowly but surely, Everys dropped to the level of the sea and then into the hole itself.

She didn't know how long it took to reach the bottom. In some ways, it felt like agonizing hours, slowly dropping in the perfectly circular column of air amid the water. In others ways, it went by too quickly. Beyond the impossibly smooth walls, Everys could see the shadows of fish darting back and forth. A few even ventured close to the hole, but then fled. Eventually, Everys spotted a small circle of ground below her.

Her feet landed in the squish of sand and rock. The wooden plank with the rune lay near her, the ink slowly burning away as the spell did its work. Judging on what she saw, she didn't have that much time.

Water dribbled down the Principality's sides, but it didn't appear any the worse for wear. She took images of the rune chiseled into its side, noting how this one had a blocky feel to it, all right angles and straight lines, but intersected with looping circles that seemed to hold the whole thing together. She took at least a dozen images of the rune. But when she got ready to draw the shatter rune, she hesitated. This was the last Principality, the last connection between her people and their past in Nekek the Bright. Once it was gone, that chain to the past would be severed. In some ways, she knew it was the right thing to do. At least, she thought it was. But in that moment, her doubts reared up.

"I know You gave these to us so long ago," she whispered. "And while this feels right to me, what You think matters more. So if this isn't the right thing to do, give me a sign. Show me a different way to go."

Everys closed her eyes and waited. She didn't know what she expected or even hoped for. An upwelling of certainty from within or maybe a flash of light from above? But nothing happened. All she heard was the slow drip of water from the plinth and a muted shout from up above. She realized she didn't have any time to waste. If she was going to do this, she had to do it now.

Using the ink that Feltys had given her, Everys sketched out the shatter rune on the Principality's side. As soon as she activated the spell, the Principality shuddered and then dissolved into small chunks.

Everys looked down at the pile of rubble and waited another second to see if the Singularity would rebuke her or offer her some assurance she had done the right thing. She finally sat down in the sling and waited.

True to her word, Feltys pulled her out of the hole. Shortly after Everys's feet touched the deck, the spell holding open the column ended and the sea gently returned to its original place. Everys looked over the railing as the waters swirled together. She had hoped she might catch a glimpse of the Principality's remains being swallowed by the sea, but it was no use.

"Did you get what you needed?" Feltys asked.

Everys nodded. "One more question. What does that rune do?"

Feltys smiled wistfully. "We call it the homeseeker. No matter how far you may roam, no matter how lost you may become, using that rune will help bring you home again. I've used variations of it while out here on the Repose plenty of times. It's handy."

Everys didn't doubt it. And, as the boat turned back to Breakwater, she wondered what would happen if she tried casting it now? Where would it lead her? To Bastion? To the Shade? Or to wherever home was without Narius?

37

K avi studied Narius's face, concern painted over hers. *Are you sure you want to do this?*

No. He didn't. Not even a little. "Yes."

She glanced out the transport window, squinting against the bright noonday sun. People wandered past their vehicle, only a few glancing in their direction with open curiosity. There were so many of them, taking a stroll through what the locals called the Emperor's Shadow. The park was lovely, with a large lake in the center bordered by large swaths of grass, bushes, and flowers. Under other circumstances, Narius might have wanted to spend some time savoring the beauty. But not in the middle of the day. And not when the Imperial palace literally loomed over everything. Narius could almost feel Tirigian glaring down at him from some high tower.

But he didn't have a choice. This was the only way he'd be able to approach his next target.

He checked his outfit one more time. Appearing in public like this was a risk, but he and Kavi had mitigated it as much as they could. She had acquired the robes of a Pathworn mendicant. He had never heard of the order—another frustrating gap in the Dynasty's understanding of their rivals—but according to Kavi, the mendicants were expected to wear rough-spun brown robes that completely concealed their bodies. Everyone knew to give them wide berths and not to speak to them unless spoken to first. While Narius appreciated the anonymity the costume would provide, the one thing he hadn't anticipated was how itchy the fabric would be.

Taking one last bracing breath, Narius slipped out of the transport. He pulled the robe's hood over his head and shambled forward, trying to adopt the correct gait as best he could. Kavi had shown him footage of how a mendicant walked, an unsteady lurching that looked like they were perpetually about to trip over their own feet. He didn't know if he was doing it right, but the people got out of his way as he headed into the park.

As he walked, he reviewed what he knew. Their target was a man of strict routine. Every day, at this time, he left the palace to spend an hour by himself in the park. Narius wound his way through the paths until he found the appropriate bench. Sure enough, a solitary man approximately Narius's age sat alone, staring out at the lake, his hands folded in his lap. He sat with a stiff posture, his red military uniform crisp. His face, rugged and handsome, was clean shaven, although there was a sorrow lurking behind his hazel eyes. Narius nodded to himself. This had to be Wullis Planka.

Narius shuffled to the bench and lowered himself onto it carefully. Planka glanced at him out of the corner of his eye, confusion flitting across his face for the briefest of seconds. Then he turned away from Narius ever so slightly, whether out of deference for a mendicant or a desire for his own privacy, Narius couldn't tell. They sat quietly, both regarding the gentle lapping of the water.

Taking a deep breath, Narius murmured, "Hello, Dawn Ixket."

Planka whipped around as if he had been slapped. He stared at Narius, his eyes wide. "Excuse me?"

When Kavi had shared Planka's school nickname—and how she learned it in the first place, he didn't know—Narius didn't understand the reference. Kavi had explained that an ixket was a type of hawk found in Ksann. Given Planka's reaction, there was probably a good story behind it.

Narius carefully turned toward him and adjusted the fabric to reveal his face. "My apologies for being so forward, but I didn't know how else to get your attention."

The color drained from Planka's face, and he stumbled to his feet. "Y-you!"

"Indeed. So what happens now?"

Planka glared at him, and Narius held his breath. Would Planka do his duty and try to arrest him? Or would he actually listen to what he had to say? Kavi had seemed very certain it would be the latter, but Narius braced himself for the former.

Much to Narius's relief, Planka sank back down on the bench, turning away from him to stare out at the water. "Why are you here?"

Narius chuckled. "That's an excellent question. I shouldn't be in Utuaa at all. I should be in Bastion, fighting the war between our peoples." He paused, then added quietly, "And so should you."

Planka stiffened, but he didn't look in Narius's direction.

"You have quite the reputation," Narius continued. "Wullis Planka, Hero of the Imperium, exemplar of loyalty and the finest military mind the Dalark has produced in three generations. Our military was so sure you would be the one leading the charge against the Dynasty, we had multiple plans to neutralize you."

Planka didn't respond, didn't so much as twitch.

"I understand how difficult it is to carry such a reputation. My family, the Xoniel, have lived with something similar since time immemorial. We were known throughout Ehun for our savagery in combat. So many tribes and peoples told whispered stories about the 'shining eyed ones,' how our eyes were the harbingers of death and destruction. Quite frankly, I never really cared for that weight either. And yet, here we both are. So why is it possible for both of us to meet in Utuaa?"

Still no answer. Narius hadn't really expected one. That Planka still listened was a minor victory. All Narius could do was soldier on and hope he could provoke him into revealing the answer.

"One thing I've discovered about the Dalark over the years is that they love drama," Narius said. "Elaborate costuming, showy displays, playacting. So I can't help but wonder if that's it. Have you been acting this whole time? They claim you're so courageous, but the truth is, you're still here because you're a coward."

Planka whirled on him, fire flashing in his eyes, and for a brief moment, Narius thought Planka would punch him. They started at each other before Planka raised a quaking finger and jabbed it in Narius's direction.

"You have no idea what you're talking about," Planka whispered.

"Then what is it?" Narius pressed. "Why would the Hero of the Imperium pass on a chance to finally put the Dynasty in our place? Why would you shun the glory you could claim for yourself?"

"I wouldn't expect someone from the Dynasty to understand."

"You might be surprised," Narius replied, leaning forward. "Why don't we make this a fair exchange? If you answer my question, I'll answer yours."

Planka studied him, his expression skeptical. Narius almost suggested that they use karabek sauce to make their discussion more interesting. It had worked when he and Everys were getting to know each other. But that memory only caused him a pang.

The other man finally sighed and looked down at his hands. "They asked me to go. Insisted, really. 'You are the sword in the Emperor's hand. Your presence will bolster the troops and spur them on to greater victory. We need the Protector...'" His voice caught. He winced, then ground out the rest. "'The Protector of the Southern Expanse.'"

Narius frowned. He knew from maps of the Imperium that the Southern Expanse was a strip of land along their border with Erecone. He considered prompting him to keep talking, but from Planka's attitude, he suspected he should let him explain at his own pace.

"Have you ever heard of the Eternal Blossom?" Planka asked, his voice a bare whisper. When Narius shook his head, Planka chuckled. "I'm not surprised. They're a tiny tribe who used to roam the foothills of the Cradle Ridges. When the Dalark expanded north a hundred fifty years ago, we displaced them from their hunting grounds and forced them to resettle in the Southern Expanse. At the time, Emperor Meklin proclaimed, 'A blossom that is eternal can bloom in any environment.'

"To their credit, they did. The Eternal Blossom went into that barren land, one that no one else wanted, and while they didn't thrive, they adapted. They survived. They made the Expanse their own. And the Imperium, for the most part, left them alone."

So many questions bubbled up within Narius, but he shoved them back down.

"Twenty years ago, prospectors discovered rare metals and other valuable resources in the Southern Expanse. The Imperium tried to convince the Eternal Blossom to leave, but they wouldn't. The clanhead refused, saying that Meklin had gifted the land to the tribe in perpetuity.

"Then three years ago, the situation came to a head. The Eternal Blossom refused to vacate. Every Imperium official left their encampment frustrated. So finally, Emperor Devroshan sent a detachment of troops to clear them out of the Southern Expanse. And I was put in charge of the operation for what he thought were valid reasons."

Planka fell silent, staring out at the water. Narius waited for him to speak. He already suspected that this story wouldn't end well.

"I was so young, so inexperienced. So ready to prove myself and my loyalty to the Emperor. My troops and I approached the encampment carefully. We had heard rumors that the Eternal Blossom had acquired weapons from the Dynasty, from your Duke Brencis."

Narius bit back a curse. Knowing what he did of Brencis, it wouldn't have surprised him if he had done something like that.

"So we were all on edge, weapons ready, just in case." Planka took a deep breath. "I approached their barricade to speak with their clan-head, who turned out to be twelve. Twelve! Who appoints a leader that young, that inexperienced? And I presented Emperor Devroshan's orders. He refused. We argued. And then I heard the shot."

He winced, screwing his eyes shut. He took several ragged breaths, and Narius wanted nothing more than to put an arm around him. He recognized battlefield trauma when he saw it.

"My troops, convinced one of the Blossoms had fired at me, charged the barricade. And once they broke through, they swept into the encampment and killed everyone. Hundreds of people, their entire tribe, killed within fifteen minutes. And I stood there and watched it all happen.

"Only it turned out the Eternal Blossom didn't have any weapons. They hadn't fired the shot. One of my troops overreacted and fired first and I..." He screwed his eyes shut again. "The Imperium covered up what really happened. Declared it a victory for the Emperor. And I was lauded as a hero. Me. The one who, in a panic, ordered the extinction of an entire tribe.

"*My* entire tribe."

A chill swept over Narius and his stomach flipped. Surely he didn't mean...

Planka tugged his left sleeve up enough to expose his wrist. Faint green lines wrapped around the wrist and, when Narius took a closer look, he saw the ghostly outline of ten-petaled flowers, at least a dozen of them, studding the vine-like pattern.

"When I was a child, my people thought that if they were to send one of their own to serve the Imperium, it would lessen the tensions. So I was selected, sent to the Imperial War College, rigorously trained. That is why the clanhead argued with me. He thought our kinship would mean I would shirk my duties. And when I returned to Utuaa, I was lauded for placing loyalty to Imperium over my blood relatives. I was feted. Praised. And all the while, I had to carry the guilt of what I had done to my own people.

"That's why I'm not in the war. If I had gone, they would have put me in charge. And I couldn't do it. I couldn't betray the Eternal Blossom again."

Narius's stomach twisted. He could scarcely imagine what that was like. For a moment, he tried to take comfort in the fact that the Dynasty hadn't done anything like that, but then he realized they had. When his grandfather had invaded the Cold Light's forest. When they had conquered the Ixactl to use them as shock troops. Or the Diradae to mine their mountains for visium. Maybe their atrocities weren't fresh, but they did exist, leaving a complex legacy that he had to both bear and acknowledge. Maybe this was why he was here instead of in the Dynasty. So he could see. So he could understand.

So he could help both nations take a step away from what they had been.

He scooted closer to Planka. The other man either didn't notice or didn't mind.

"I wish I could say I understood how you feel," Narius said. "But I don't. I never could. While I served in the Dynasty's military, I never saw active combat. This may sound insincere, but I'm glad you were able to stay here rather than be on the front lines of this ridiculous war."

Planka glanced in his direction, a frown flitting over his face. "I never thought I'd hear someone from the Dynasty say that any war is ridiculous."

Narius smiled sadly. "Understandable. But that's an attitude I wanted to change. That, and the relationship between the Dynasty and the Imperium. I need help to do so. Yours."

"If you're trying to recruit me as a spy, I won't do it."

With a chuckle, Narius shook his head. "I wouldn't dream of it. No, there's someone who I think would want to hear your story and make sure that something like that will never happen again."

Planka finally turned to look him directly in the eyes. "Who?"

Narius leaned closer. "Princess Innana."

Something sparked in Planka's eye, a flare of recognition or understanding or hope. "The princess? Really?"

"Would you be open to hearing what she has to say?" Narius pressed.

He looked out at the water again, but then Planka nodded once, sharply.

Narius breathed out a soft sigh of relief. He had known that approaching Planka would be a gamble. For all he knew, Planka could have ignored what he had to say and captured him. Best to withdraw now before that thought occurred to him. He rose and started his shuffling walk back the way he came.

"Wait."

The word froze Narius in his tracks. He gritted his teeth and slowly turned back.

"You said we would make a fair exchange. A question for a question," Planka said. "You asked yours."

Narius straightened. "Of course. I apologize."

Planka looked away, his eyes darting back and forth as if they were trying to find the individual words hidden in the grass.

"How..." He turned his attention back to Narius with an intensity that knocked him back a step. "How did you get her to love you?"

The look on Planka's face was filled with an intense longing that he clearly was trying to hide. For just a moment, Narius thought he meant Everys. But no, that couldn't possibly be the case. With a start, he realized what he was actually asking, and it made sense. The Hero of the Imperium undoubtedly crossed paths with the royal family on numerous occasions.

"Ours was a love born out of youthful naivete. We never loved each other, not really," Narius said.

Planka frowned. "But in the Colonnade, she said—"

Blunted Blade, this again? Narius stepped closer. "Our history is complicated, but believe me, we are only friends." He winced. That seemed like an overstatement. "Colleagues. Partners." Another wince. "If you are true to yourself, I have no doubt you'll have much in common with her."

Relief and disappointment warred across Planka's face, but he nodded once. "A pleasure to meet you, Your Strength."

"You as well, Wullis Planka."

Narius turned and shuffled off before he could be drawn back into a conversation. He didn't know what might result from this particular conversation, but he hoped that in some way, it would bear fruit.

38

Normally, with this much drinking and celebrating going on around him, Quartus would find himself with a drink in each hand and a pretty young woman willing to hop into his bed. He had plenty of reasons to do so. The stress from sneaking into the manor was bad enough—Ifamin had smuggled both of them into the house in a crate labeled as fine wines—but it kept mounting with each passing moment. And as the servants circulated through the manor's hall, Quartus was sorely tempted to snatch a goblet and drink deep of whatever was offered. It had been months since he had attended a party like this, filled with the finest members of the Dynasty's upperclass.

Strangely, when he actually considered joining the revelry, his stomach soured. Part of it was because he had to remain sober. If he drank as much as the other partygoers, he would likely either miss his opportunity to strike or he'd fumble the attempt. But what surprised him most was that as he thought back on all the times he had indulged, he found the memories didn't hold the appeal they once did. It was strange. Before Narius had banished him, all he lived for were parties like this one. Now that he had lived outside the palace walls, he realized what a colossal waste of time this was. These overstuffed fools, congratulating each other with slurred, nearly incomprehensible words, while the Dynasty crumbled around them. So he stuck to water, sipping it slowly and hoping that no one would notice.

Thankfully, no one did. They were too busy downing their own drinks and talking to each other so loudly, they likely could have roused everyone in the Gravedigger's domain. Quartus circulated through the crowd, identifying the people he passed. There was Masruq, the finance minister, a goblet of wine in each hand. His chubby face was blotched, but he smiled and laughed at everything his companion, the newly minted Duke Korran, Brencis's successor, had to say.

"So what did you tell the king?" Masruq asked.

Korran snorted. "Not supposed to tell, remember? 'S supposed to be private."

"I won't tell anyone." Masruq guffawed. "I probably won't remember what I said in a couple hours!"

That caused both men to laugh uproariously. Quartus fought to keep from rolling his eyes, sticking as close to the wall as he could.

"Fine, I'll tell you." Korran stumbled forward and laid a hand clumsily on Masruq's shoulder. "I told him I was glad he was king. We need someone like him on the throne. But I also told him he needs to tread more cautiously. He's trying to change too much at once. If he goes through with his plans for the Siporans—"

Masruq scoffed. "It won't come to that."

"I've seen the plans, Masruq. It could. It really could."

Masruq looked ready to say something, but then looked past Korran and apparently spotted Quartus. Quartus quickly spun away from the conversation, pretending like he hadn't been eavesdropping.

He moved through the crowd, passing by other ministers, nobles, and a few ethnarchs, all of whom were similarly inebriated. The only other sober people were Yusra, who watched the party from one corner of the room, carefully hidden behind a standing plant, and Queen Viara, who glared at the rest of the partiers as she sipped water from a crystal goblet. Seeing her with her swelling belly caused a pang in Quartus's heart. That was supposedly his niece or nephew she carried. At least she wasn't jeopardizing the baby. He caught himself staring at her, idly wondering if the child would favor Narius or her. He shook his head to clear it.

He spotted Bloodshale and Lastdew standing sentry by the entrance to the kitchen. Even though both wore security uniforms, they, too, held drinks, which was problematic.

A low gong sounded, and the party stilled. Then Brencis arrived, the doors bursting open as if kicked. Two men rushed in with heraldic trumpets, playing a military charge. Then Brencis strutted into the room, his arms raised as if in victory. He wore silken robes over a loose-fitting shirt and pants. The others applauded as he entered. He basked in their adulation, then signaled for them to stop.

"My friends, I have meditated on what you told me. And I appreciate your honesty. Some of you shared deeply personal things with me, concerns that you have, and I promise, I will take them all to heart."

More applause.

"But now is not the time for brooding and recriminations! Now is a time for us to grow closer together. After all, you will help me shape our Dynasty for the better! So continue to enjoy the night. I know I will."

With that encouragement, the partygoers resumed their conversations. Sprightly music, provided by a trio of musicians, began playing. And Quartus nodded to himself. *Keep drinking, you fools. Numb yourselves.*

Sure enough, as the night wore on, the party grew more and more raucous. Married men were openly flirting with their friends' wives and the other women present. A few even approached Viara herself, who dismissed each one with an annoyed flick of her hand. Within a few hours, some flirtations became more intense, and soon, couples were slipping away from the party and heading up a flight of stairs, presumably to find some privacy. When Quartus saw that, he smiled to himself. That was how they would get Brencis away from the party. But they'd need the right bait.

Observing the party for a little longer provided the right opportunity. One server, a young Hinaen woman in her early twenties, was clearly taken with the new king. Every time she circulated through the partygoers with a tray of appetizers, her gaze would inevitably drift to Brencis. Then she would stare at him, her eyes wide and her cheeks flushed. Quartus recognized the signs of an enamored server almost immediately. He had encountered plenty of girls like that in the palace back in the day.

He sidled up to her. "Fancy the king, eh?"

She fumbled the tray she was carrying but didn't drop it. "I don't know what you mean, sir."

"It's all right," he whispered. "No one would judge you for noticing him. And he's noticed you as well."

Her eyes widened. "He has?"

Quartus nodded sagely. "He has been discreetly enjoying your presence. He can't be too open about it seeing as the queen is right over there, but I believe he reciprocates."

The girl took several gulping breaths. "Really?"

Quartus nodded again. "So this is what I would do. Bring him something to eat and then ask him if he'd like to show you the upstairs."

She blushed furiously, then shot a nervous look toward Brencis, who was regaling several partygoers with some ridiculous tale of his exploits. "I couldn't possibly!"

"Of course you can," Quartus said. "You're part of the celebration as well. Be bold! Be brave! He'll like that."

A smile flitted across her face, and she tucked a stray lock of hair behind her ear. Then she turned and hurried in Brencis's direction. Quartus fought to keep from grimacing. He had no way of knowing if this would work, but she was pretty and young enough that Brencis would at least be flattered.

The young girl strode right up to Brencis and thrust her tray at him, saying something to him as she did. Brencis looked surprised, but then his gaze slithered up and down her body. He smiled wolfishly at her, then took the tray and handed it to one of the others. He put an arm around her waist and led her to the stairs.

Quartus blinked. All right, then. Time for the next part of his plan.

He made his way across the room to where Yusra was waiting. She shot him a withering look as he approached.

"What do you think you're doing?" she hissed at him. "Why would you do that to that poor girl?"

"I didn't do anything to her, and if we act fast enough, neither will Brencis," Quartus shot back. "Now act like you actually fancy me."

She glared at him, but then favored him with a fawning smile, one that was probably a bit overdone. He returned the expression, then offered his arm to her. She took it, and he led her toward the stairs as well.

There were two royal guards standing sentry at the bottom. They signaled for him to stop, then gave both him and Yusra a quick glance. Quartus held his breath. They were in elaborate outfits designed to draw attention to the clothing rather than their faces. But he couldn't hide his eyes or Yusra her Dalark features. But the guards had clearly been drinking, so their screening wasn't exactly thorough. Then they motioned for them to head up the stairs with a sloppy wave.

"How do you plan on finding him?" Yusra asked as they approached the landing. "By my count, there are at least twenty people up here."

"Twenty-two," Quartus said. "But only one of them will have guards posted at his door."

As they arrived on the top floor, they found a long hallway bordered with dozens of doors. And sure enough, only one of them had guards flanking either side.

Yusra nodded. "So now what?"

He didn't answer, instead pulling her close and laughing like he was drunk. She leaned into him and giggled, running a hand over his chest as they stumbled forward. The guards glanced in his direction, but they quickly ignored them. Quartus led the way to the room next to the one the guards watched. Thankfully, the door was unlocked. Quartus shoved it open with his shoulder, allowing him and Yusra to fall through.

The room appeared to be an office, but someone had removed most of the furniture and replaced it with a plush bed. Quartus snorted. Clearly Ethnarch Chilyana had understood what kind of party this would be. More importantly, there was a window in one wall. He pushed it open, poking his head out. He had guessed correctly. To his left was another window, and it had to be the room that Brencis was in. Even better, a narrow ledge ran along the length of the building, just underneath both windows.

"Found our way in," he said.

Before he could climb out the window, though, Yusra caught his arm. "Quartus, wait."

He shot her an annoyed look. "I thought you didn't want Brencis to do anything to that girl."

"I don't, but I'm not sure that what you're planning is right either."

He growled, closing his eyes. Not this again. "What better chance than now?"

"I don't disagree, but are you sure this is right? Are you sure this is what you should do?"

"Who else? Yusra, who else? You saw those sycophants downstairs. None of them have the courage to even say that what Brencis did to my brother was wrong! None of them can see that he'll only lead the Dynasty into fresh disasters. He has to be stopped, and we're doing that right now."

She looked like she was ready to say something else, but she fell silent. Quartus hauled himself out of the window and onto the ledge.

Guards patrolled the grounds below, but they didn't seem concerned about what might be happening above them. He inched along the side of the manor until he was next to Brencis's window. He glanced to his right and saw that Yusra was clambering out of the window as well. Good. As annoyed as he was at her hesitation, he knew he wouldn't be able to do this on his own.

Carefully, he reached over and tested the window. Much to his delight, it turned out to be unlocked. He eased it open, careful not to make a sound. Low voices spilled out of the window, the girl's high-pitched giggles and Brencis's throatier chuckles. Quartus winced. He could have gone his whole life without hearing that.

He slid along the ledge and then up and into the room. Brencis had the young girl on a bed, his bulk on top of her, kissing her cheeks and neck. She ran her hands along his shoulders and through his hair, whispering encouragements.

Quartus spotted what he needed: a heavy metal vase sitting on an end table next to the window. He hefted it up and smashed it across Brencis's head. The king collapsed onto the girl, who gasped. But then Quartus slapped a hand over her mouth.

"Not a sound or I'll kill you too," he growled.

Yusra shimmied through the window and hurried to the bed.

"Take the girl, gag her, and tie her up in the closet," Quartus said. "I'll deal with the king."

Yusra glowered at him, but she didn't argue. She pulled the young girl out from under Brencis and dragged her over to the closet. The girl remained quiet, but tears streamed down her face.

Quartus rolled Brencis onto his back. This was going to work out perfectly. He would strangle the king, and then he and Yusra could escape back to their room. No one would dare interrupt the king's assignation, so it would give them plenty of time to slip out of the manor and make their escape.

He tossed the vase aside and flexed his fingers, savoring the way they stretched. Then he slid them around the unconscious man's throat and... and...

He hesitated.

No, focus! Now wasn't the time for doubts. He had to act. He had to end this miserable creature's life. For his brother. For what he had done to Everys. For all his crimes.

He still couldn't do it.

What was wrong with him? Pity? Cowardice? It really didn't matter. At any moment, the fool could wake up. He was already stirring. Quartus had to act!

He grit his teeth, leaned in, and—

The door banged open, and someone marched in.

"Your Strength, reconsider what you're about to do with that young woman."

Quartus froze. He knew that voice. He turned toward the door, and sure enough, Vizier Paine stood in the entryway.

Paine froze as well. They stared, both of them clearly shocked to see the other. Paine's gaze darted from Quartus to the hallway. He shot an angry look at Quartus, then took a deep breath, clearly getting ready to shout.

He didn't get the chance. Yusra snared his arm and yanked him off balance, chopping his throat with the side of her hand. He gagged, his eyes bulging. Then Yusra flipped him onto the floor, punctuating the move by kicking Paine across the face.

She shut the door carefully, then whirled on Quartus. "Follow me!"

With that, she shimmied back out the window and crawled back to their room. Quartus stepped over Paine, who groaned quietly, and followed Yusra. He was suddenly all too aware of how precarious this route was. His heart lurched at the height, the way the cold air tugged at his hair. The moment they made it into the room, Yusra took several gulping breaths, then started crying before bursting through the door back into the hallway.

Quartus stared after her. He hurried after her, looking up and down the hall. She was already headed down the stairs, and the guards at Brencis's door were watching her and laughing. He shot them a sheepish grin and then followed.

She didn't stop at the landing, heading for the kitchens. That was their exit vector. Bloodshale waited by the door, ready to let them through. Quartus squared his shoulders and—

"Guards!" Paine's voice was unmistakable, filled with a mixture of rage and fear.

That was his cue. He hurried past Bloodshale into the kitchen.

"What do we do now?" Yusra whispered.

He didn't know. If the guards saw what had happened to Brencis, they would lock down the entire manor. His mind locked up as he tried to sort through the options. Hide? No, they'd comb the entire place. Were they trapped? Had their luck run out?

Someone grabbed Quartus by the shoulder and spun him around. He found himself face-to-face with one of the cooks. The man glared at him.

"What are you doing here, Quartus?" he demanded.

Quartus stammered, trying to dredge up the right excuse. But then two details slammed down on him, cutting off his words.

For one, the cook had called him by name.

For another, he recognized him. The bulbous nose, the unruly red hair, the watery blue eyes.

"Urett?" he whispered.

The man scowled, confirming Quartus's guess. Urett had been Narius's personal assistant, his constant shadow, always overlooked by most people because of his unobtrusive nature. Why would the former king's assistant be working as a cook at the Day of Accountability for his usurper?

Urett's face twisted into a snarl. "You need to get out of here. My transport is out back, the green one with silver highlights. Steal it. There's an access road that the guards don't know about that will take you around the lake and then off the property. Follow it and then abandon the transport once you're back in Bastion. Provided you don't get caught, meet me at The Shessu's Burden in Gilded Lock in six days' time right at the start of Second Watch. Now go!"

He pushed Quartus away, and Yusra dragged him out the back door. They found Urett's transport easily enough. By the time they pulled away from the manor, the building had lit up, every light snapping on at once. Yusra hunkered down behind the controls as they slalomed down the road and onto the path that Urett mentioned.

Yusra relaxed. "That was too close!"

Quartus's hands spasmed into fists. If Paine hadn't interrupted him, this would have all been over. Maybe he had another target to add to his list.

39

It took Everys and Redtale several days to make it back to the forest. At first, the trip had been easy, but about halfway through, something happened that riled up the constables and military. Suddenly, there were checkpoints everywhere. Thankfully, they escaped the guards' scrutiny and could continue on their way. Eventually, they entered the forest's southern border. From there, friendly troops found them and transported them back to the Shade.

When they finally rolled into the Shade, all Everys wanted to do was get out of the transport, go up to her room, and take a long, hot bath. Surely she'd be able to chisel out an hour or two to collect herself before she tackled whatever problems had stacked up in her absence. But Challix was waiting for her. Her vizier hurried forward and caught her in a hug.

"You can't believe how happy I am to see you back, Blessed," Challix said, then turned to Redtale. "You as well, Redtale."

"Good to see you too, Challix," Redtale said with a thin smile.

"Anything significant happen while I was gone?" Everys asked.

"It depends on what you mean by 'significant,'" Challix said. "In some ways, no. The forest's border remains secure. Just the usual flyovers by Brencis's troops, plus we've seen evidence of the Dalark navy off the northern shore. Overturn's worried about a potential amphibious landing, but we haven't seen any evidence of that.

"We had new refugees arrive as well. One group included Minister Elamek's wife and daughters. We're getting them settled in. But some of them have been busy since arriving, and I think you'll want to hear what they've been up to."

Oh? Challix had imbued her words with a hint of excitement, enough to propel Everys forward. The bath could wait.

Challix led her back to the Embassy, climbing up through the levels until they came out on one of the uppermost areas. Everys froze at the top of the stairs. A large bank of computer terminals had been set up on one side of the room and looked completely out of place against the walls of woven tree branches. At least a dozen people were gathered around tables, upon which were books, papers, and drawings of all kinds. She recognized some of them immediately: Occ, Galan, Tolistan, members of the Illuminates, and...

"Professor P'layvo?" she said with a smile.

The researcher who had worked on Narius's project looked up from where she fiddled with one of the computer terminals. She smiled brightly. "It's good to see you again, Blessed! I'm so glad Tormod fetched me. When he said you had some new data for the project, I couldn't wait to help. And I have to tell you, Blessed, we're close. We are very close."

Everys brightened at this. "You are?"

P'layvo nodded. "Your Diradae friend has been helpfully translating the notations in that book. We're still missing a few key phrases, but we have the AI already analyzing what's missing and we're confident we'll be able to piece it all together soon. And, once that happens, the rest should fall into place.

"That book was what we were missing. It's the bridge between the written language used in your ancient texts and whatever language the runes use. At least, there's enough in the book to help us extrapolate the rest. This is exciting, Blessed. Very exciting indeed!"

The professor's enthusiasm was contagious, but as much as Everys wanted to hear what else the professor had to say, she needed to check in with everyone else as well. She hurried to Galan, who crushed her in a big hug.

"You and Mama made it safely?" Everys asked.

Galan nodded. "No genuine problems to speak of... well, except Papa. What happened to him?"

Everys winced. "I don't know. He's been so angry for the past several months and I don't know why."

"I've tried to get him interested in what we're doing here. This is the sort of thing you'd think he'd want to tackle—a gigantic puzzle—but he practically accused me of being an *ar'zhannok* when I suggested it."

Everys pursed her lips, trying to swallow her sadness. She had hoped that Mama and Galan's presence would have helped changed his attitude. But instead, it sounded like he was taking out his anger on them as well.

"I'm sorry."

"Don't be. Mama and Oluna have been keeping him company while I'm up here working on this." She giggled and squeezed Everys's shoulders. "This is amazing, Everys! I don't know how much I'm helping, but I'm learning so much and it's all so much fun."

"Nonsense," Occ said from across the table. "Lady Galan has been most helpful. Her insights into Siporan naming conventions have saved us from following many false veins."

Everys shot Galan a teasing look. "'Lady' Galan?"

Galan shrugged. "I guess that's what I am since I'm your sister. Everyone is calling me that. Although, truth be told, I think it's because Occ is sweet on me."

Everys blinked, her mouth popping open. He was what?

Occ made a strange chittering sound under his mask. "Blessed, let me assure you, I have done nothing untoward at all! I would never dream of scandalizing your family or position."

Galan laughed. "It's all right, you big bug. Maybe I've got it backward and I'm just sweet on you."

That caused even more chittering. "I hesitate to correct someone of a greater social standing, but I'm not exactly a 'bug,' Lady Galan. I have more in common with spiders than insects, although the Diradae's closest relative in terms of genetics is actually the Chance squid!"

Galan chuckled. "I love teasing him. He gets so flustered."

Everys laughed, but she stifled it as Tormod approached her.

"Welcome back, Blessed. I trust your trip was successful?" he prompted.

She produced the scriber and set it on the table. "Images of the missing Principalities, plus notes on what the runes do. And I wouldn't have been able to do this without your help."

Tormod chuckled. "Oh, I'm sure you would have managed."

"I lost my bracelet. Stolen in Breakwater."

"Problematic, but not terribly so," Tormod said. "Unless they experiment with the beads, they shouldn't discover what it actually is. They'll probably dispose of them once they realize that they're not valuable. But I can make you a replacement easily enough."

"Have you heard anything since I've been gone?"

Tormod sighed heavily. "Unfortunately, my network of informants, both here and in Dalark, is still in chaos. I've been able to glean some interesting information, but I'm not sure that any of it will be helpful. I'm preparing a detailed report that will be ready for you to read tomorrow morning."

"Anything I need to know now?" Everys asked.

He shook his head. "Nothing I'd consider credible: reports of a new cult forming in Dalark around one of their potentates. Stories of Riokan troops in Weyfir territory. Rumors that Brencis was nearly assassinated. That sort of thing."

Oh. She started to say something, but her words blossomed into a yawn.

Tormod chuckled. "Why don't you get some rest? The Dynasty can survive for another twelve hours."

Everys wanted to argue, but a wave of exhaustion crashed over her. She nodded and left the room, heading down to her quarters.

Trule squealed when she stepped through the door. "Blessed! Welcome home!"

She smiled tiredly as Trule hustled her into the room, barking orders at the other girls. Before too long, they had her dressed in a comfortable robe and two of the girls were preparing a warm bath for her. Trule peppered her with questions the entire time, and Everys held nothing back, sharing what she saw in Fort Wyne, her family's vigil, and in Breakwater. Much to her amusement, Trule didn't seem interested in the Principalities or what happened to them. Instead, she quizzed Everys on the sights she had seen during her trip, the people, the cultures. Everys made a mental note: at the first opportunity she had, she would send Trule on a long vacation so she could see all of those things for herself.

The bath itself was a blessing from the Singularity Himself. As she soaked, she could feel the tension from the road melt away. She likely could have fallen asleep there, but eventually, Trule helped Everys from the tub and dressed in comfortable pajamas. Trule and another girl offered her their arms. At first, Everys was somewhat insulted. She was perfectly capable of walking on her own. But when she discovered that her legs had grown heavy, and she stumbled, the girls quickly caught her. They helped her to her bed and settled her in.

As Everys snuggled into the covers, Redtale appeared above her, a bemused grin on her face. "Don't worry, Blessed. I'll check in with Rewether, and then we'll make sure you're not disturbed for the rest of the night. See you soon."

Everys wanted to respond, but she found she couldn't. She was already drifting away.

The next morning, Everys looked over the gathered advisers. As strange as it felt to admit it, she had missed all of them. Even though she had just brought Mama and Galan back from their vigil, seeing everyone around the table in the war room felt like a true family reunion. Seated to her right were Overturn, Rewether, and Redtale. Across the table stood Tolistan, P'layvo, and Galan. To her left were Yllana and two other grafted, Effort and Daniu, representing the Yore-root. Oluna sat along one wall, practically beaming like a proud mother watching her kids at play. And as always, Tormod had found a corner to lurk in, watching everyone with a relaxed smile.

"We're all curious. What did you discover while you were out there, Blessed? Any little detail can help," Overturn said.

"We've debriefed everyone as they have arrived and we have a much better picture of what is happening in the Dynasty's holdings," Tormod added. "So why don't you start and we'll ask questions as you go."

Rewether brought her a chair, then Everys launched into an account of everything she had experienced since leaving the forest.

It took her several hours to go through all the details. Now and then, one listener would interject a question to tease out more details or clarify something she said. At one point, Oluna asked if she had heard anything about Masruq. At another, Overturn asked her to describe what she had seen in the military base where they met Treskin.

But the one moment that seemed to capture everyone's attention was when Everys described the attack in Breakwater and how Redtale had been injured.

Overturn chuckled and nudged Redtale. "For someone who got shot, cousin, you look remarkably hale."

Redtale snorted. "You can thank the queen for that. She healed me with one of her runes."

"Is that so?" Tormod left his corner perch and approached the table. "Didn't you say that your attackers stole your ink in Breakwater, Blessed?"

Everys's stomach fluttered. She had hoped that she wouldn't have to share this detail. "They did, yes."

"Then how were you able to heal Redtale?" Tolistan asked.

Everys and Redtale exchanged a look. "All I had on hand was her blood."

The Siporans at the table gasped, as did Yllana.

"I know the Singularity forbids it," Everys said.

"I, for one, am glad you did it anyway," Redtale said with a grim smile.

Everys pursed her lips together. A thought occurred to her, a question she had carried in the back of her mind ever since she was able to heal Redtale in Breakwater. When she had used blood to draw her family's healing rune on Redtale, the rebuke had been severe, but it had only lasted a short time and hadn't caused her to black out. So why, when she used Narius's blood to draw the same rune, had she been rebuked so severely?

"Blessed? What is it?" Overturn asked.

"Just trying to figure something out." She looked up, and her gaze flicked from Tolistan to Tormod, then to Yllana and Galan. Maybe one of them would have some insight into this particular puzzle. "I really don't want to admit this, but when Brencis shot Narius a few months ago, I did the same thing with him. I used his blood to cast our family's healing rune. Only that time..."

Challix's eyes went wide. "Is that what happened? It was a rebuke?"

Everys nodded.

"Some of you may not be aware, but the queen spent several days in the infirmary recovering. I didn't know that rebukes could be so severe," Challix said.

Tolistan leaned forward, his face twisting into a puzzled frown. "They aren't. Not usually. You're sure it was a rebuke?"

Everys chuckled mirthlessly. "I'm positive."

"Is it possibly because the king is a human and Redtale isn't?" P'layvo asked, then she held up a hand as if to placate Redtale. "No offense."

Redtale grumbled something under her breath but settled back in her chair, scowling at the researcher.

"That wouldn't be it at all," Tolistan said with a shake of his head. "The ancient writings are clear: it's not just human blood that's forbidden, but blood from any sentient race. So the queen would have experienced a rebuke whether she had used human blood, Plissk blood, Weyfir blood, or even..." The scrivener blinked, then turned to the grafted. "Isn't Cold Light tree sap the same as blood?"

"Of a sort, yes," Daniu said. "But why would that matter?"

"Because sap from a Cold Light tree, especially one from a seed pod, is the most potent ink Siporans have ever had," Galan explained. "But the Singularity doesn't rebuke a mage who uses it."

Yllana nodded sagely. "The seed pods are ungerminated. And when the Cold Light supplied sap to the Siporan Ascendancy, they were very cautious to not overharvest. I could summon Tall Reach or ask Evergreen to join us. They might know better than me."

"That isn't necessary," Everys said, although she had to admit a little curiosity.

Oluna suddenly stood up, her eyes wide. She met Everys's gaze, then hers dropped away.

"Excuse me, please. I need to..." Oluna's voice trailed off, and she hurried out of the room.

Everys watched her go, then motioned to Rewether to lean in closer.

"Have someone make sure she's all right," Everys whispered.

Rewether nodded and made a hand signal to a guard, who slipped out the door after Oluna. Everys turned her attention back to the discussion. Different people offered explanations for what may have caused the reaction. Galan suggested that Everys's near panic when healing Narius had heightened the rebuke's effects, but Redtale pointed out that Everys seemed panicked when she had been injured as well. Tolistan speculated perhaps Everys had made a mistake while drawing the rune, leading to the rebuke to be stronger or weaker. Everys didn't think that was the case.

For a while, Tormod had the best suggestion out of the bunch, that the stronger rebuke was because of Everys's stronger emotional tie to

Narius than to Redtale. "Perhaps your estrangement offered you a bit of insulation."

Everys winced at the reminder, but Tolistan objected, saying that there was nothing in the ancient texts that suggested that would be the case.

The debate wore on for close to a half hour. During that time, the guard Rewether sent to check on Oluna came back and reported that Oluna was fine, she just needed some air. For a moment, Everys thought the guard seemed a bit off, but Rewether sent the man back to his post before she could ask if he was okay.

Finally Everys held up a hand. "Does anyone have a new theory? We keep circling back to variations on the same themes."

No one offered anything, so Everys moved the discussion on. She didn't know if anything she was sharing would actually help, but as long as her advisers wanted to hear it, she was willing to share.

"Blessed? Blessed, please wake up."

Trule's voice sounded like it was drifting across the top of a placid lake, causing gentle ripples along the surface. Everys sighed and rolled over, burrowing deeper into the pillow. What was it now? She had spent the entire day being debriefed and then listening to updates from everyone on what she had missed while out of the Shade. When she made it back to her quarters, she had wanted nothing more than to sleep, to catch up on the rest she had missed. Apparently that wasn't to be.

"I'm sorry. I know I said we would let you sleep, but he's most insistent about speaking with you, and your sister is with him, and—"

Wait, this wasn't a dream? Someone really needed to talk to her? She groaned and sat up, the covers clinging to her arms like vines on a grafted. She shook them off and rubbed her eyes.

"What time is it?" she mumbled.

"Almost the end of Fourth Watch," Trule said.

Everys opened her eyes. Her chief maid stood at the foot of the bed, wringing her hands.

"I'm so sorry, Blessed. Normally, I would never dream of waking you. But he was so sure I should!"

"Who?" Everys asked, her mouth feeling like it was stuffed full of fabric.

"Occ. He says it's urgent."

She frowned. Occ was here? But then the last vestiges of sleep fled from her mind, and she sat up straighter. "Urgent? Did he say why?"

Trule nodded. "He said that they've made a breakthrough."

40

The next time Innana showed up at the safehouse, Narius knew that something had happened. Something good. As much as she tried to hide her excitement, he could see the lightness in her step, the light in her eyes.

"Well?" he asked.

Innana struck what he thought was an overly dramatic pose, then favored him with a smirk. "I have had several rather interesting discussions as of late. Seminal Tensin Bakun wishes to have a private discussion about the 'philosophical underpinnings' of the Imperium's authority. And the Hero of the Imperium himself, Wullis Planka, has asked me to dinner."

"Really?" Narius struggled to keep his voice calm so he wouldn't crow about his success.

Innana's smile sharpened. "I have to say, Narius, I'm impressed. You can be quite persuasive."

Kavi stepped up to Narius and patted him on the arm. He smiled at her in return.

"Now..." Innana's smile turned predatory. "Now we aim higher."

Unease twisted in Narius's stomach. There was something unsettling about Innana's attitude, but he couldn't quite place what.

"Have you heard of a man named Varsillin the Elder?" Innana asked, her tone light.

Kavi's head snapped back as if someone had slapped her. She started signing something so frantically that Narius couldn't understand her. Innana must have followed it, for she sighed through her nose.

"What's going on?" Narius asked.

"Kavi is worried that I am too ambitious," Innana said.

Kavi's face twisted in a scowl, and she made several emphatic gestures that Narius didn't need translated. He could read her frustration easily enough.

Narius held up his hands in what he hoped was a calming gesture. "Let's start slowly. Who is this Varsillin?"

"A member of the upper echelon of Dalark society," Innana said. "Most call him 'the Living Potentate.'"

Narius glanced at Kavi, who added, *He is very respected. I've heard he's wise.*

"What spirit is he supposed to embody?" Narius asked.

Innana chuckled. "Unfortunately, that has yet to be determined. But despite that, he is well regarded by most in the Imperium. The public believes that if Varsillin were to whisper, even my brother would strain to hear his words."

"I don't suppose there's any truth to that," Narius said.

"No. But that is what many believe, and that's why it's important you talk to him."

Narius frowned. Given what Innana had shared, someone with that much influence and respect in Dalark society could rally even more support to Innana, but only if Narius could convince him. Knowing nothing about Varsillin's politics or loyalties, that seemed like a big gamble. He shifted his weight and ground his teeth as he considered it.

"Are you sure we should speak to someone so prominent?" Narius asked.

Innana smiled indulgently. "We could accomplish so much if we can convince him to side with me. Yes, we could form a coalition of different influential people. But if we can convince Varsillin? That would go a long way to rallying support. Why, just his name alone would legitimize what I am trying to do."

Do we even know where he is? Kavi asked.

"My informants have found his retreat," Innana said, then explained to Narius. "Varsillin is a bit of an ascetic. He's rarely seen in public."

Narius mulled over Innana's words. After a few moments' consideration, he nodded. Though speaking to him was a gamble, Varsillin could secure their victory that much sooner.

"Take me to see him," Narius said.

"And I'll accompany you," Innana said.

Kavi's head snapped back again, and she signed furiously. This time, Narius could decipher her frantic gestures easily. She didn't think this was a good idea. Neither did he.

"Why?" he asked.

"For two reasons. First, getting an audience with Varsillin is difficult. You can't arrive uninvited."

"Not even the revivified king of the Xoniel Dynasty?" Narius asked.

"Perhaps," she allowed with a smile. "But in the time it takes for you to get an audience, someone could report your request to my brother's secret police. No, it's better if I arrange for the meeting. He wouldn't turn away the Emperor's sister. And besides, if I truly am ready to rule the Imperium, I have to go out on the front lines, as you Xoniel might put it."

Narius frowned. He didn't like this, but she had a point. So he finally nodded.

"Excellent. We'll depart for Varsillin's retreat at once." At his surprised look, she added, "I've already made the appointment. He's expecting me—and by extension, you—in just a few hours."

With that, Innana breezed out of the room.

Kavi turned to Narius. *Are you really okay with this?*

He shook his head. He wasn't, but he also knew that in a war like this, sometimes you had to gamble.

Varsillin's retreat overlooked the Lake Corcola, an inland sea to the northwest of Utuaa. Innana spent the drive out to the retreat peppering Narius with information about Varsillin's childhood, his education, his significant accomplishments, anything that might give him an opening. Narius could understand why Varsillin was so respected. A child prodigy and a polymath, Varsillin had dabbled in science, philosophy, and economics, dazzling those who had interacted with him. He had written dozens of treatises on those subjects and more, earning him countless accolades. Narius felt a little intimidated at the thought of trying to mentally spar with the man. Would he be able to convince someone who could clearly outthink him at every turn? True, he had held his own when talking with Bakun, but this challenge was several orders of magnitude larger.

The retreat itself was a walled compound with a thick tower that rose above the hill it perched on. Narius sank back in his seat as armed guards approached the transport to verify that Innana was inside. Once they had, they waved them through a heavily armored gate.

"Why all the security?" Narius whispered.

Innana smiled at him. "Gifts from my father. When people first started whispering about Varsillin becoming a potentate, Father insisted on making sure he was safe. It wouldn't do for a potentate to die on his watch."

That made sense, but seeing so many armed individuals made him nervous.

Once the transport was parked, a house steward met Innana. The man made an elaborate show of greeting her with sweeping bows and other sycophantic gestures. Innana brushed past him with a high-pitched giggle, insisting that he didn't have to make such a fuss. Narius and Kavi trailed behind her. Thankfully, the steward's attention was completely on Innana.

The tower itself was functional, with few decorations and even fewer luxuries. Instead, they passed a simple kitchen and then followed a winding staircase that hugged the exterior wall of the tower. The steward led them to the topmost floor. They entered a semicircular room that was lined with shelves, each one crammed with books, data scribers, and much to Narius's surprise, dusty scrolls. A large wooden desk, covered with loose pages, had been shoved off to the right.

But Narius's gaze was immediately drawn to one corner of the room, where four chairs had been set up. An older, short man with spindly legs and arms and a long, scraggly beard sat in the second largest. He rose as they entered and smiled broadly as Innana entered, saying something in Dalark that caused her to smile.

"Thank you for seeing me, Varsillin." Innana dipped into a curtsy.

His head tipped to one side, his brow pinching into a frown. His gaze flicked toward Kavi, then Narius. "It is I who should do obeisance to you, Princess. And who are your companions?"

"This is Kavi, my personal attendant." Innana gestured to Kavi, then turned to Narius. "And this is..."

Her voice trailed off, her tone prompting. Narius sucked in a breath, hoping that it would calm his jangled nerves. He stepped forward and drew back the hood of his cloak.

"I am King Narius of the Xoniel Dynasty, Varsillin. I'm the reason Princess Innana wanted to meet with you."

Varsillin leaned back, his eyes wide. Then he chuckled. "So the rumors are true. Senen's king has indeed arrived, has he?"

Narius grimaced. "Not exactly, sir."

The old man chuckled. "'Sir?' You show me too much respect as well, Your Strength. Come, sit down. Perhaps you would like to explain what your 'not exactly' means."

Innana didn't hesitate. She swept to the largest chair and settled into it. Narius hesitated, then chose one of the other chairs for himself, leaving Varsillin the second largest. Kavi apparently decided not to sit, instead lurking near the staircase.

"You call me Senen's king, and I know that a lot of other people do as well," Narius said. "But I have to confess, I am not the fulfillment of a potentate's prophecy."

"Oh? Then what are you?" Varsillin asked.

"A friend to the Imperium. I have been most of my life." He resisted the urge to glance in Innana's direction. "My fondest wish has always been peace between our peoples, and I'm hoping you can help me achieve that."

Varsillin laughed. "And what could an old man like me do?"

"You have influence in Dalark society. People may mistakenly call me Senen's king, but they also call you the Living Potentate."

"Perhaps they are as mistaken about me as they are about you."

"I couldn't say one way or the other," Narius admitted. "But the princess has shared how important you are. If you call for change in the Imperium, people will listen."

"Maybe they would, but what kind of change do you think I could bring about? I could speak out about the costliness of war, the futility of bloodshed and continued animosity, and some may listen. But I doubt highly that Emperor Tirigian would be one of those. He seems very determined to prosecute this war against your people."

"Then perhaps you would support someone who would seek peace."

Varsillin went still. He studied Narius's face through squinted eyes. "Your Strength, I understand why you are being oblique in your wording, but I am an old man who doesn't have time for verbal games. Speak plainly. What is it you want me to do?"

Narius glanced at Innana, who nodded subtly.

"I want you to pledge your loyalty to Princess Innana as the Empress of the Dalark Imperium."

The room went unnaturally silent. Varsillin's brow pinched into a frown, his gaze flicking between Innana and Narius. Narius held his breath, his hands clenching into fists.

Then Varsillin sighed, sagging back in his chair. "I see."

He fell silent again. Kavi took a step forward, her mouth in a grim line.

Varsillin looked up, his eyes hard. "I feared that this might be why you wished to see me, Princess. I wish to all the spirits and potentates that I was wrong."

Kavi started to move, but before she could, the door to the other room burst open and five heavily armed men rushed inside, military weapons in their hands. A man in a stiff-looking uniform, black with silvery buttons, followed them. He sneered at them.

"You are all under arrest for treason against the most noble Emperor Tirigian." His voice, though thin and reedy, carried an unmistakable undercurrent of menace.

Innana snapped something in Dalark. Kavi's eyes widened and she looked upset, but then she nodded sharply. She twisted her hands together, her fingers dancing, and she vanished in a blur. The soldiers shouted and fired where she had been standing, but the flechettes tore through empty air and thudded into the wall.

One man shoved Narius out of his chair and, while two others covered him with their weapons, wrenched his arms behind his back.

"We do not know how you cheated death in Bastion, *King* Narius." The man spoke the title like it was an insult. "But when the Emperor is done with you, you will wish you had stayed dead."

41

Occ kept yammering as he led Everys back up to the makeshift lab. He hadn't stopped talking since she'd emerged from her room. Maybe she was still half asleep, but she hadn't been able to make sense of anything he was saying. Something significant had happened, and he needed her to see it right away.

When they arrived in the lab, it surprised Everys how many people were already there. Didn't anybody sleep?

Professor P'layvo hustled over to her. "Excellent timing again, Blessed. Wait until we show you what we've found, and it's all thanks to you!"

"What are you talking about?" Everys asked.

"The AI's done it. We're able to translate the runes."

Everys went still, a chill sweeping over her. "Y-you... you what?"

P'layvo nodded.

"But just last night, you said that you still had a lot of work to do with the bridge. How could the AI have made that much progress so quickly?"

"Honestly, we're not entirely sure," P'layvo said. "But last night, we fed the AI the images of the missing Principality runes so it could add them to the dataset. And somehow, that did it. It was like those eight runes came together and unlocked the entire puzzle. If I didn't know any better, I'd almost chalk it up to divine intervention."

Pins and needles chased the chill across Everys's skin. Her breath turned shallow and her head swam. "Show me."

P'layvo led her over to a larger vidscreen. A rune was displayed on the screen, one that Everys didn't immediately recognize. She knew she had seen its pattern before, but she couldn't quite place it right away.

"I believe your Diradae friend uncovered this one. According to the book, it's a truth-seeker rune. With the translation of the shessu cant and the data from the Siporan ancient texts, we could break down this rune into... well, see for yourself."

P'layvo touched the screen, and the rune appeared to unravel, different portions stretching or breaking apart. Then the bits and pieces transformed into words in Dynastic:

What [[untranslated]] in shadows are
Reveal, [[untranslated]] truth-that-lives.
Make plain what others fear.

Everys frowned and pointed to the boxes on the screen. "What is that?"

"An unfortunate necessity, Blessed," P'layvo said. "While we can read the runes, we don't have a full vocabulary for them yet. We could make guesses based on context. Given what this rune does, I suspect the first unknown is 'hidden' or some related synonym. The second might be a vocative, but it could also be an adjectival modifying the proper noun the AI rendered as 'truth-that-lives.'"

"Oh." Everys tried to keep the disappointment out of her voice. "So I suppose we couldn't start writing our own runes?"

"Moons above, no!" P'layvo said. "Even with this breakthrough, there is much we don't understand about how this language functions. For example, the grammar appears to be spatial on a two-dimensional plane. There is no other written language that I'm aware of that uses such a structure. Until we can discern the rules that govern the runes' grammar, anything we attempt to write would be gibberish. Plus, there's the fact that each rune appears to be a poetic incantation. Unless we find detailed instructions about how to write one of those incantations correctly, I'm not sure we could accomplish much."

A frown pinched at Everys's brow as her disappointment crested. Her shoulders sagged.

P'layvo chuckled. "Your frustration is understandable, Blessed, but this is a process. It always has been. Granted, it goes much faster with the AI to help us. Without that, we may have struggled with this for years. Decades, even."

She supposed that made sense. While all of that was true, the mage-kings had generations—centuries, even—to work with the runes. This was a major advance, definitely, but they were still trying to catch up.

"Never fear, Blessed. The good thing about the AI is that it doesn't need to sleep. And I have enough people helping that we can monitor it through every watch. We already have partial translations for close to thirty runes, including the Principality runes, and we're discovering more about the vocabulary and grammar with each one."

Everys nodded and turned to leave. But then she hesitated. "You said that you've translated all the Principality runes. Can I see my family's?"

P'layvo smiled warmly. "Of course, Blessed. Let me call it up."

The professor made some adjustments to the screen, and a second later, her family's healing rune appeared. Seeing it rendered so starkly, with so many people nearby, made Everys feel unsettled. A glowing line passed over the rune, and once again, the design pulled apart into individual squiggles, moving around the screen before transforming into words:

The [[untranslated]], deep and [[untranslated]]
Heal what in my soul is certainty and delight
Sick and broken, [[untranslated]] completer-of-[[untranslated]]
Mend and bind and make whole again.

Everys frowned, repeating the poem several times in her mind before saying, "This doesn't make any sense."

P'layvo made an inquisitive sound and looked over at the vidscreen.

"'Heal what in my soul is certainty and delight?'" Everys pointed to the line on the screen. "That doesn't make any sense. And this rune has four lines instead of three. Is that normal?"

P'layvo squinted at the poem, her mouth moving as she reread it several times. Then her face settled into a determined glare. She called up another rune and had the AI show its translation. Three lines. Another rune. Three lines. The homeseeker rune that Feltys had shown her. Four lines.

"That is... certainly an interesting puzzle," P'layvo murmured. "Perhaps Principality runes have four lines because they are more powerful?"

Everys ignored the speculation, instead leaning in to read the translation which, unfortunately, was spottier than her family's:

[[Untranslated]] far from [[untranslated]] I wander

Seek me, [[untranslated]] dwelling-place!
Show me give me what I [[untranslated]]
Desire where my steps [[untranslated]] me.

"This doesn't make any sense either," Everys whispered.

P'layvo inspected the translation. "Trickster's guile, what is this?" Then she whirled toward one of the research assistants. "Find Tolistan and Galan." She turned to a different assistant. "Double-check the AI's translation matrix. Make sure that it's not hallucinating. If that's optimal, prioritize the AI's efforts to decipher any untranslated words or phrases in the Principality runes." Orders given, she turned back to Everys. "I'm sorry we didn't notice earlier, Blessed."

Everys chuckled. "You only made this discovery a few hours ago, Professor. I think it's understandable."

"Still. You have entrusted me with one of your people's greatest secrets and treasures. I should be more diligent in my work with them."

Everys smiled and touched the professor's shoulder. What she had said was true. This was her people's greatest treasure. That wasn't a perspective she had often encountered in the Dynasty. Even though she hadn't experienced as much hostility in recent months, every time she found that acceptance, it was like a deep breath of crisp air.

Her eyes widened as a thought occurred to her. The book! The book she had found in the Embassy, the one that Occ had used in creating his art. Maybe that might have an explanation for what was happening with the runes.

"Have you finished translating the book that Occ found?" she asked.

P'layvo blew out a breath between pursed lips. "Yes, we have. After I arrived in the Shade, I worked with two very helpful shessu in translating the cant. Why?"

"I know they have drawings of the Principalities in the Scriptotum. Maybe they also have something in there about the Principality runes, something other than how to translate them."

P'layvo frowned. "There were many mentions of the Principalities themselves, but not necessarily about how their runes were construct-ed. Still, you may find something in here that I overlooked." She walked over to a worktable and retrieved a scriber. "We were able to digitize the contents of the book, meaning you should be able to search for specific words or phrases. The AI has also built a cross-referencing web for the text as well, meaning that you should be able to rapidly search related topics. I'll let you know if we figure out what's happening with the Principality runes."

Everys thanked her, found a corner of the room, and called up the book. Rather than jumping to random points throughout the book, she read the first few pages, if only to understand what this book was all about.

Unfortunately, whoever wrote it didn't share many details about their motivation or what they hoped to accomplish. The author didn't even identify who they were. Instead, after dedicating their scholarly work to "divine potential," the author launched into an elaborate explanation of the medicinal properties of plants that could be found in the Cold Light forest.

With a grunt, Everys activated the search and entered "Principality runes." Much to her surprise, that brought up dozens of passages. Most of them weren't all that helpful. The author had apparently interviewed several toratropic mages at some point and recorded verbatim what their answers were to the same questions. Much of what had been written was information she already knew: how each Principality was assigned to a family, how they represented the most powerful runes the Singularity had gifted the Siporans, how the Principalities stood in the Scriptotum in Nekek the Bright...

But then Everys found a statement that caused her to pause:

One master, who showed me no small amount of trust, related a strange legend to me. She said some toratropic scholars believed that, hidden within the runes carved into the Principalities, was a powerful spell. One that, if pieced together, could bend the very fabric of reality to the caster's will. I asked if the rune had ever been cast. She said that it had not, that many had tried to discern the spell's shape, but none had succeeded. In fact, she shared that most considered the possibility of such a spell ludicrous, for why would the Singularity share His authority in such a matter? But she admitted that in her weaker moments, she was tempted to try. For the legends said that with such a rune, one's will could match that of the Singularity Himself.

Everys sat back in her chair and watched as P'layvo and her assistants worked on the computer terminals. A rune that would allow someone that much power and authority was mind-boggling. She had never heard of such a thing. Was that possible?

Before she could fully consider it, Tolistan and Galan entered the lab. Tolistan headed straight for P'layvo, but Galan hesitated in the door when she saw Everys. After tapping a fist against her thigh, she walked over to her.

Everys looked up at Galan, her heart stuttering at the worry painted over her sister's face. "What's wrong?"

"Have you talked to Mama or Papa since you got back?" Galan whispered.

Everys winced, then shook her head. She had been meaning to, but hadn't been able to.

"Go see them as soon as you can. Mama's worried about Papa. She says something's wrong with him."

42

The Dalark secret police had a lot more confidence in Narius than he did. They had shackled his arms and legs. Then, for good measure, they forced a helmet over his eyes and clamped a plate over his mouth. He could barely breathe through his nose, and anything he could hear was muffled. He was dragged out of Varsillin's tower, stumbling and tripping the entire way, before he was heaved into the back of transport.

He didn't know if he was alone. He couldn't hear anyone and found that he couldn't easily get off his stomach, not with the way he was bound. And the way the driver steered the vehicle didn't make it easier either. He slammed into the walls and floor, once with enough force that stars burst in his vision. He finally tried to curl up into a ball, if for no other reason than to make himself as small as possible.

After what felt like weeks of being thrown about the transport, the vehicle came to a halt. A few moments later, rough hands grabbed him and hauled him out. They set him on his feet, but he couldn't get his bearings, stumbling and almost collapsing to his knees. Someone shouted something, punctuating it with a blow to his head. The helmet blocked the pain, but the metallic clang rattled Narius's teeth. He straightened, then was shoved forward.

He shuffled his feet so he could sense anything that would trip him. His captors shouted abuse at him and jostled him as he moved. Then the muffled sound around him changed, as did the air. It became cooler, drier. Had he walked into a building?

Two people grabbed his arms, and a third wrenched the helmet from his head. He blinked at the bright lights that bathed him. Dark figures stood in front of him, silhouetted by two massive lights. He spotted movement to his left and glanced in that direction. Innana stumbled to a halt. She, too, was bound and gagged, but her hands were manacled in front of her and her gag was cloth, not metal. But then the guards removed both of their gags. Narius worked his jaw, wincing at the taste of metal that lingered on his lips.

"Somehow, I should have realized your death was a trick."

Narius turned back to the silhouetted individuals. He knew that voice. Sure enough, Emperor Tirigian strode forward, a sneer etched on his face. Like most Dalark, he was pale skinned with wispy blond hair. But even though he was only a few years older than Narius, his face was lined and wrinkled, as if he had aged drastically. Narius could sympathize. Ruling had a way of aging a person, especially during a war. Instead of wearing his usual ostentatious ribbons and wraps, Tirigian was dressed simply in black pants with a black overcoat, the cuffs and collars bordered with gold piping.

"When I heard the reports you died in Bastion, I thought such news was too good to be true. After all, no one ever claimed to find your body. But you remained missing for so many months I thought perhaps the stories were accurate. Then the rumors began: King Narius, back from the dead and walking the streets of Utuaa. Narius, perhaps the once-dead king that Senen promised? And here you are!" Tirigian laughed lightly to himself, then turned his attention to Innana, saying something to her in Dalark.

"I fear you do not know me very well, dear brother," Innana said.

"Speaking Dynastic for your one true love, are we? Very well, I shall play along." Tirigian turned back to Narius. "She is still quite fond of you, you know. Despite the cruel way you used her."

"I could say the same thing about you," Narius retorted. "As a prop when she—"

Tirigian waved away his words. "Oh, yes, yes. It doesn't matter, you know. For now, I have caught you conspiring to overthrow my reign. How wonderfully delicious it will be to see you die! Why, I'm planning the most excruciating of deaths for you, King Narius."

Narius sighed. "And I suppose that's going to happen tomorrow?"

"Of course not!" Tirigian chuckled. "Where would the fun be in that? No, I have plans. Parades. Public humiliation. Spectacle and drama, all to show my people and yours that you are no longer any sort of threat to me."

Narius considered what Tirigian had to say, then burst out laughing.

"What? What is so funny?" Tirigian demanded.

"I'm not sure how much of a threat I've ever been to you," Narius said. "You thoroughly took me by surprise when you invaded Mao-toa—congratulations on that, by the way. Hopefully, the Maotoans will be just as much of a dagger in your back as they were to me. You capitalized on the chaos at my wedding to Innana by seizing the throne.

"And now? I'm still nothing. You have to contend with Brencis and I suspect he's making you fight for every gain and pay for it with blood." Narius leaned forward. "And from what I understand, no one knows where Everys is. She's the one you should be worried about."

"Your little Siporan pet?" Tirigian scoffed. "Why would I ever fear her?"

"Because most people don't realize it, but she's so much stronger than me. Smarter too. She may be in hiding right now and focused on Brencis, but I guarantee that when she can finally pay attention to you, she will burn your empire down around you."

Narius let the threat hang between them for a few moments.

Doubt flickered across Tirigian's eyes. Then he scoffed again. "Yes, yes, your bravado is most intimidating. You almost convinced me to spare your life just now."

Tirigian laughed, and the others in the room quickly joined him. None of the others sounded genuine, and Narius thought he detected a note of fear in some of their voices. Maybe he had rattled them. Those seeds could bear fruit later. Unfortunately, he doubted that he'd ever find out.

"Take my sister to her accommodations." Tirigian smiled.

The guards snared Innana's hands, and she cried out as they dragged her away. Narius twisted, trying to make sure she was all right, but one of the guards standing near him cuffed him across the head. This time, stars exploded in his vision and he staggered.

"So gallant, are we?" Tirigian said. "Still worried for your so-called love? Let us see if we can cure you of that weakness, hmmmm?"

Narius regained his balance and stood taller, just in time to see one of Tirigian's sycophants handing him a club. The Emperor regarded the weapon, spinning it in his hand, then focused a vicious gaze on Narius.

"Let us see how strong you truly are."

By the time Tirigian was done, Narius's entire world was agony. Pain radiated through his arms and legs. He didn't think anything was broken. But he couldn't focus his mind long enough to really assess his injuries.

The guards hauled him to his feet and tried to get him to stand, but he couldn't. With a strangled cry, he collapsed to the ground, new pain shooting through his body. The guards laughed then snared his arms, carrying him between them. Narius tried to focus on what was happening, the route they took, any details, but everything was wrapped in a haze.

They descended multiple flights of stairs into a dank hallway. Narius's head lolled to one side, and he saw prison bars sliding past. A dungeon? That seemed right.

The guards came to a halt and tossed him through an open doorway. Narius skidded across the floor and came to rest in a heap. His captors followed him in and roughly removed his shackles. They said something in Dalark that Narius was sure was some sort of insult. Then, laughing, they left the dungeon, the door slamming shut behind them.

With a groan, Narius rolled onto his back and tentatively stretched out his arms and legs. Pain shot through him, but he was able to extended them fully. Nothing broken then. Good. He gingerly inspected his chest and head. Maybe a cracked rib.

"Narius?" a voice called, sounding as if it drifted down a long tunnel.

He rolled on his side and looked toward the door. Innana stood at the bars of the cell across from him, worry painted across her face.

"Are you all right?" she asked.

He chuckled, pain lancing through his chest. "Not really, but I'll live. Your brother needs to work on his technique. You?"

Innana offered him a shaky smile. "They only hurt my pride. Although I may be a traitor, none of them would dare abuse the Emperor's sister."

If only they were as respectful of foreign kings. He rose to his feet and took a moment to regain his balance. His body protested every move, but he didn't collapse. He turned a slow circle, taking in his surroundings. A filthy cot, a moldy sink, and a toilet whose stench sliced through the haze cocooning his mind. No window, just a flickering light in the hallway outside his cell.

"Any idea where Kavi went?" he asked.

"No," Innana replied. "I merely told her to escape. She'll go to ground, avoid the places we've been. I suspect she has some safehouses set up for herself that I don't know about."

He nodded. Good. "Do you think she'll try to rescue us?"

Innana chuckled ruefully. "She may want to, but she'll know better than to try. This is the Peltun, the most secure prison in Utuaa. No one escapes from here. That's why our rulers have always used it to house their most dangerous prisoners."

"And their most valuable," another woman added.

Narius started. He knew that voice! A mixture of honey and heat, the sort that could set men's ears prickling at a mere whisper.

"Cosena?" he said.

Across the way, in the cell next to Innana's, a woman stepped up to the bars. It was Cosena! The last time Narius had seen the princess of Maotoa, she had been dressed in a gauzy skirt and top, colorful like most of the outfits the islanders wore. But even though she wore plain rags, even though her hair was a tangled mess, she still carried herself with a dangerous sensuality.

She smiled sadly at him. "The same. Are you wishing that you had taken me up on my offer?"

Narius fought to keep from glaring at her. Several months earlier, Cosena had not only tried to seduce him, but she'd also proposed to him as well. His refusal had apparently triggered the Dalark invasion of Maotoa. Narius and his vizier, Paine, had nearly lost their lives during that invasion.

"Not even for a moment," he said. "What are you doing here? The last I heard, your stepfather had married you off to Tirigian as part of their new relationship."

Cosena scoffed. "In name, I am Tirigian's wife, but in reality, I am his hostage. As soon as our nuptials were completed, he had me taken here. I haven't seen him since."

For a moment, Narius felt a guilty pang. Yes, Cosena had been an unnecessary distraction during the middle of a crisis and her stepfather and mother had betrayed him. But he didn't feel like she deserved this harsh of treatment.

"And I don't know what you think this 'Kavi' can do, but let me assure you, the princess is right." Cosena leaned against the bars of her cell. "There is no escape from Peltun. You're stuck here until Tirigian gets bored and has no more use for you. Might as well settle in, Your Strength. You aren't going anywhere."

Everys found Mama and Oluna sitting on the front porch of Papa's house. For a moment, seeing the two of them together felt odd. Maybe even wrong. It wasn't the first time that people from her life before being queen had invaded her new world. But it still felt strange to see these two women together. She motioned for Rewether and Redtale to wait.

Mama rose as Everys approached. "Galan said something. I wish she hadn't."

Everys searched her mother's face for some hint about what was happening. She didn't see panic, so the knot in her chest unwound a little. "I'm glad she did. What's going on?"

"Your father is acting very distant. Withdrawn." Mama groped for the right words. "He was happy to see Galan and me when we arrived, but after that passed, he went for a walk and didn't come back for hours. When he finally did, he seemed angry when I asked what was wrong."

Everys snared Mama's hands and squeezed. "Papa has been very upset ever since he came to the palace in Bastion. He didn't approve of my marriage to Narius."

That was an understatement. The way Papa had carried on while they were in Bastion, he thought that Everys's love for Narius was some sort of betrayal or blasphemy.

"I told your mother that," Oluna said. "He's always been a bit stand-offish with me as well."

Mama shook her head. "I've known Favid for close to forty years now. I know when something is bothering him."

"Have you asked him?" Everys asked.

"Of course. He practically screamed at me to leave him alone."

Everys blinked. She couldn't imagine her father screaming at Mama.

Tears welled up in Mama's eyes. "I don't know what to do. I'm almost feeling like it was a mistake to come here."

"No..." Everys pulled Mama into a hug. "This is the best thing for all of us. He needs you, Mama."

Mama sniffled and nodded, but she wouldn't meet Everys's eyes. "I suppose."

Everys's eyes stung as well. She wished she could fix this. There had to be something she could do to bring whatever was bothering Papa out into the open so they could fix it.

Her eyes widened as an idea occurred to her. Maybe there was a way...

"Are you sure this is a good idea, Blessed?" Rewether said. "Isn't there a chance you could get—what-do-you-call-it—rebuked?"

Everys tried to push the question out of her mind. Yes, that could happen. Granted, when she used the rune on Hommas, she hadn't been rebuked, but these circumstances were different. However, she didn't know what else to do. So she stirred the bowl of tree sap and continued painting the rune on the outside of Papa's cabin.

She had already drawn her family's healing rune, changed so that the effect would focus on emotional and spiritual health, its power centered inside the house. Now she sketched out Occ's truth-telling rune, using similar flourishes to modify the core spell. She wasn't entirely sure what would happen if she combined the effects of these two different runes, but she figured it would be good for Papa to be honest about whatever was bothering him and, by doing so, maybe find some healing. At least, that was what she was hoping for.

Mama had gone to keep Papa company while he chopped wood. She hadn't been completely comfortable with Everys's plan, but as Everys explained what she hoped to accomplish, Mama had tentative- ly agreed. Oluna had volunteered as well. At first, Everys didn't want her there. This situation was too personal, too private. But Oluna had pointed out she had been with Favid for months now and wanted to help both him and Everys. When Mama had accepted Oluna's offer, that put an end to the discussion.

Once the truth-telling rune was done, Everys activated the runes. A wave of toratropic energy rolled past her then faded. She hoped it would be subtle enough that Papa wouldn't notice.

Everys walked around the cabin where Papa swung an ax with determination, splitting logs with a grunt and snarl each time. Mama stood nearby, her fingers laced together in front of her. She spotted Everys's approach and gave a tiny shake of her head. Papa apparently hadn't said anything to her.

Papa looked up from his work as Everys stopped next to Mama. His lips twitched into a frown.

"You come to stare at me too?" His voice was gruff, tired.

"Papa, I was hoping we could talk. It's important." Everys tried to hide her wince. She couldn't be too open with him. If he was suspicious, he wouldn't go into the cabin and the runes wouldn't be able to do their work.

His gaze sharpened, then he gave the ax a last swing, burying it in a log. "Fine. Let's get this over with."

The three of them walked up to the cabin. With each step, Everys grew more and more tense. Would he notice the rune's effects? Would he say something? But Papa strode up to the back door and shoved it open. When he stepped through, though, he paused and Everys sucked in a sharp breath.

But then Papa turned back to her and jerked a thumb over his shoulder. "What's she doing here?"

Everys and Mama stepped up behind him, and Everys spotted Oluna standing sentry near the front door, just like she was supposed to.

"Oluna's worried about you," Everys said.

"Of course she is." Papa sighed.

Mama shot Everys a worried look, then followed Papa into the cabin. Everys breathed a silent prayer that this would work. She marched into the cabin and shut the door.

Papa dropped into his chair, his posture slumped and a scowl etched on his face, the same one she had seen so many times. Everys's stomach twisted. Was the spell even working on him? He didn't show any outward signs. But she couldn't hesitate. The effects wouldn't last forever.

"Papa, we're all worried about you. Ever since we left Bastion, you've been so hostile. Mama and Galan have noticed it already. Something is bothering you and we want to know how to help."

Papa glared at her, his gaze so venomous she actually stumbled back a step.

"You really have to ask? I thought I made myself perfectly clear!" He leaned forward. "What's bothering me is your apostasy. The way you turned your back on your community, your family, and your faith. You married a direct descendant of the monster who destroyed our homeland."

Everys pursed her lips. Papa's words stung. But nothing he said was new. He had already said all of this before they fled to the Shade. But none of this explained why he had been so sullen since them.

"Favid, how can you say that?" Mama whispered.

"How can I not?" Favid snapped. "Don't you see what happened? Our daughter has betrayed us all! She wants us to call what is clearly evil good, the same way that the Dynasty has always done."

"Narius was a good man, Papa." Even though Everys had made this argument many times, she wanted Mama to hear it, to see how Papa reacted. "He was different. He wanted to change things—"

Papa exploded out of the chair, his motion so sharp and sudden that Everys flinched. He wouldn't actually hit her. Would he?

He didn't move any closer, just glared at her. "The Dynasty has remained unchanging for hundreds of years, drunk on bloodshed and conquest. How could one man ever think to change that?"

Again, Mama gasped. Even Everys was taken aback by the vehemence in Papa's tone. Was that a result of the runes? Was the magic drawing the venom out, forcing him to vent his anger? Was the healing rune helping at all?

"Don't look at me like that, Ulsa! We left her in charge of the shop, told her to keep her brother out of danger, and what happened? She jumped into the bed of that monster, razed our family's heritage, and let her brother die."

Everys blinked back tears. All of that was true and she still carried the weight of her bad decisions with her, especially when it came to what happened to Legarr and the Broken Sword. She swallowed hard, trying to blunt the spike that drove into her heart.

"And when I confronted her about it, what did she do? She shoved me off into the hands of her husband"—He jabbed a finger at Oluna—"who took me to one debauchery after another. This is what our daughter is trying to defend, Ulsa. This is how badly she was corrupted. That's why I had to do what I did!"

Cold swept over Everys and her skin pebbled. What was he talking about? She leaned back, taking a few ragged breaths.

"What did you do?" Mama prompted, her voice a whisper.

"I did the only thing I could to set Everys free." His cheeks flushed and he took several deep breaths. His eyes widened and a blue shimmer danced across them. He balled his hands into fists, his knuckles white.

Everys's stomach twisted inside her. "What did you do, Papa?"

"I nullified all the runes you ever drew on him."

The color drained from Mama's face. "Favid, you didn't."

"What did he do?" Everys fought to squeeze the words out of her tightening throat.

Mama glanced at her, then turned her gaze away. She twisted her fingers in her dress, and her next words came out choked and choppy. "The heads of the Principality families are taught a secret rune that only they know, one that enables them to nullify any rune that's been cast, no matter how long it may have been. Once that rune is drawn, it erases the others from existence."

The chill grew into a shard of ice, stabbing right into her lungs. Everys tried to take several breaths, but she couldn't. A vision of Narius lying still in the infirmary bed taunted her. She barely squeezed out a question: "And if someone had been healed multiple times with our family's rune?"

"All of his wounds would have come back," Mama whispered, tears streaming down her cheeks.

"And if those injuries were fatal?"

Mama didn't say anything. Papa wouldn't meet her gaze. That was all the answer she got, but it was all she needed.

The ice in Everys's chest melted in a flash of heat, one that burned from her heart down her arms and up to her scalp. "He was my *husband*! I loved him, Papa. I truly loved him, and you killed him!"

Papa began to cry. "I thought I knew what to do. To save you from yourself."

She spluttered, trying to find the right words, the right thing to say. She had hoped that once Papa's secret had been revealed, the healing rune could do its work. But this. How could any of them heal from this?

Instead, she settled on the only word that made sense. "Guards!"

Rewether came in through the front door, Redtale through the back. Both of them had their hands on their weapons, but hadn't drawn them. Rewether's gaze ricocheted through the cabin before settling on Everys.

"Arrest my father." The words nearly caught in her throat. "For murdering King Narius."

Mama started to say something, but Oluna rushed to her side and put an arm around her shoulders, hushing her.

"Blessed?" Rewether said. "I'm sorry, did you say..."

"Arrest him now." *Before I lose my resolve.*

Redtale moved quickly. She stepped up to Papa and nudged him. "Let's go."

Papa obeyed, and Redtale marched him toward the door. He stopped as he passed her, trying to meet her gaze, trying to say something. But then his shoulders slumped and he allowed the guards to escort him out of the cabin.

The moment they left, Everys's legs buckled and she collapsed to the floor, her body wracked with sobs. How could he have done that? How could he be so broken as to kill the man she loved? Why had the Singularity allowed such a cruel thing to happen? But no answers came, even as Mama knelt and wrapped her arms around her. Instead, Everys curled up on the cabin's floor and let the grief swallow her whole.

44

Quartus and Yusra didn't return to their safehouse for several days. Instead, they spent that time in any hiding spot they could find. Theoretically, no one should have been able to find the hotel. How would they know to look there? But given what had happened at the Day of Accountability, it was better to assume that everything was compromised. Quartus knew they'd have to live on adrenaline and little sleep for a few days. If they hadn't been caught after four or five days, they could maybe think about returning to their makeshift headquarters.

When the time came, they didn't rush back into the hotel. Instead, they set up in another nearby abandoned building, one with a good view of the hotel. They took shifts watching it for any unusual activity. The last thing they'd want to do was walk right into a trap set by Brencis or his cronies. After two more days of seeing nothing out of the ordinary, they risked going back to their room.

Quartus checked the thread tied between the room's doorknob and frame. Still intact. He motioned for Yusra to wait, then pushed the door open. He stepped into the opening and took a quick visual sweep of the room. There was the pile of seemingly dirty clothing, but with different colored sleeves poking out of the pile in an alternating pattern. There were the used take-out containers, stacked from smallest to largest with a twisting pattern. The left door of the wardrobe appeared to be open just a thumb's width. He looked down at the floor, checking the white powder he had spread across the carpet for any obvious footprints. Sure, a truly determined intruder could easily recreate any of those signs, but not all of them and not the six other indicators he had created before they'd left for Chilyana's.

"I think we're good," he said.

Yusra brushed past him. She looked over the room and then cast a smirk in his direction. "This hotel has horrible maid service."

He grunted. "I'll be sure to mention it when we finally depart."

Yusra flopped down on the bed, pushing the pile of dirty laundry off onto the floor. "So are we going to talk about what happened?"

Quartus gnashed his teeth. He didn't want to talk about this. His failure had haunted him every step while they were hiding. Not talking about it was simple enough. They were too focused on survival the last few days to have deep conversations on anything. But he had known that, once they had found relative safety, Yusra would bring it up.

"What do you want me to say? That I failed my brother?" Quartus spat out the question like a curse.

"No!" Yusra leaned forward. "I don't think that's the case at all. You didn't fail him. Do you really think that Narius would have wanted you to kill Brencis?"

Quartus almost said he would, that any of the Dynasty's citizens would say that was their way. The Warrior's Meditations made it clear: "As much as it is within your power, do not let the Sun set before your family's honor is avenged." By that logic, Brencis had to die.

Except...

Except Yusra hadn't asked if the Dynasty would understand. She had asked if that was what Narius would have wanted. As much as his brother had tried to live out the Dynasty's ideals, Narius hadn't been a typical king. When Quartus had been framed for an assassination attempt, rather than execute him, Narius had declared him outlaw and exiled him. Quartus knew that Everys had encouraged him to do so, but Quartus had come to realize that Everys had drawn so much goodness and mercy out of his brother, allowing him to become who he truly was meant to be.

"He wouldn't have." The admission almost stuck in Quartus's throat.

"So by not killing him, you're honoring your brother's memory better," Yusra said. "And now we have a new possibility, this Urett."

Quartus grunted. That was true.

Yusra frowned. "Is there something wrong? Do you not trust Urett?"

It wasn't that. Quartus didn't trust Urett or distrust him. He had never really interacted with him. Urett had been one of Narius's tutors when the brothers had been younger, then transitioned into being Narius's assistant. He had been Narius's near-constant shadow in the palace, easily overlooked and ignored. He didn't know how many times he and Urett had been in the same room without Quartus realizing it.

"He's loyal, I'm pretty sure of that much."

"To Narius? Or to the throne in general?" Yusra prompted.

Quartus would have considered Paine loyal to Narius, but apparently he had misunderstood the vizier's allegiance. Was Urett the same way?

"That's a good question," Quartus said, hesitation bleeding into his voice.

"So do we meet with him or not?"

Quartus considered it. "I don't see that we have much of a choice. It's either that or let Brencis go about whatever he has planned, and I can't do that. We should at least hear Urett out."

Yusra nodded, then stretched, pulling her arms behind her head. Quartus's gaze locked onto her lithe form and his heart stuttered. He quickly averted his gaze. Now wasn't the time for such thoughts, as sweet as they were.

"I'm going to see if we still have water. If we do, I'm going to wash up." Yusra gestured toward the bathroom. "Unless you'd rather go first."

He had other ideas of what he'd rather do, but he kept them to himself. He could still feel the uncertainty between them, and a flirtatious suggestion might not be welcome. So he shook his head.

Yusra slinked off the bed and headed for the bathroom, casting one more smile at him. "I'm proud of you, Quartus. It takes a strong person to realize they were on the wrong path and turn back. I'm glad you did."

With that, she slipped through the door. He stared at the closed door, chewing on what Yusra just said. She was proud of him. Those simple words soothed some of the anger inside him. Rusted Greaves, that woman bewitched him and he didn't mind at all.

Quartus took a seat on the bed and switched on the crier. He doubted that the palace would say much about his attempt at killing Brencis, but he had been among public relations types long enough to know how they might shape the narrative.

He didn't recognize the person on the crier, a trustworthy looking Weyfir with brilliant teal skin, shimmering white hair, and dark eyes. Quartus was surprised to see a member of a subjugated race at all; he knew how much Brencis distrusted nonhumans. Maybe the criers guild was trying to provide cover for the king by having a nonhuman deliver the news. Whatever the case, the man cheerily recounted a story about a celebrity hosting a charity event for Bastion refugees.

But then the reporter said something that caught his attention: "...and while cities like Wrine are still under active threat by Dalark forces, others, like Sholn, face a long reconstruction period after the... incident there."

Quartus frowned. Incident? He caught the subtle hesitation in the reporter's voice, the tension that flickered across his face, as if he said something he shouldn't have. What happened in Sholn? And then the crier's feed cut off, almost midsentence.

He snared the remote for the crier and pulled up the search interface, asking the device to pull up any stories about the Sholn "incident." The device hummed, then reported that there were no stories.

So what could "the incident" have been? Sholn was the Weyfir stronghold city. That might explain why the reporter knew about whatever had happened. And if there were no stories on the crier network, the government was trying to hide it.

Thankfully, Quartus knew how to dig up the information in spite of the censorship. He retrieved a scriber and used it to connect to the Trickster's Eye, a clandestine computer network that operated without official sanction. During his time in the Dynasty's counterintelligence service, Quartus had monitored the Eye for threats. If anyone would have information on what had happened in Sholn, it would be the Eye.

At first, he didn't find anything other than recommendations for illegal establishments in Sholn itself. But then he tumbled across a series of messages that someone on the Eye had somehow obtained. He scanned through them, and as he did, his stomach twisted and a sour taste flooded his mouth.

Apparently Sholn had been spared during much of Dalark's invasion. That made sense, given the city's location. While a lot of trade flowed through Sholn's ports, the fact that it was tucked away in the southeast corner of the Dynasty's holdings meant it was isolated from the fighting.

But then, about two weeks earlier, an entire legion of Dalark troops had approached the city, but not to attack it. Apparently the legion had tried to attack a Dunestrider city on the edge of the Kronin Desert, only to be rebuffed by not only the city's defenders, but a sizable Plissk militia. They had retreated and somehow wound up in Sholn. Lady Akina Palbury, the mayor, had offered them refuge as long as they disarmed.

Everything was fine until Brencis found out. The king ordered Lady Akina to turn over the Dalark troops and she had refused. After several days of tense negotiations, Akina apparently made some sort of snide comment about Brencis's reign.

The next day, Brencis ordered the city destroyed.

Quartus's skin turned clammy. He didn't know how accurate the information was—the Eye was notorious for carrying both fact and fiction in equal measure—but if even half of what he read was true, then tens of thousands of people had died. The military units carrying out the destruction had been told that Dalark had captured Sholn. Once the bombing was complete, Internal Security had swept in and covered up the true reason for the destruction.

He read report after report, story after story, many of them conflicting, but all pointing in the same direction. Sholn was in ruins, destroyed because of Brencis. Thousands of people dead. And this was only one story. How many more were out there that no one would ever hear?

Quartus's fingers tightened around the scriber, just as they had around Brencis's throat. He had had the opportunity to stop more tragedies like this and he hadn't taken it. He wouldn't make that mistake again. He would meet with Urett, find out the other man's plans, and then he would use them to make sure that Brencis would die.

45

Even though Everys gave herself two days to recover, she didn't feel any more rested when she called her council together. She wished she could seal herself in her room, sleep for at least a month, and try to find the peace that eluded her. But no matter how hard she tried, she couldn't calm her roiling thoughts. Her father had murdered her husband? How could anyone expect her to live, let alone function, after something like that happened?

But she couldn't hide in her room forever, no matter how much she may have wanted to. Eventually, she had to face the reality, both of what Papa had done and what was happening in the rest of the Dynasty. She was still queen. So she pulled herself out of bed, dressed, and headed for the war room.

A larger crowd than usual waited for her. There was Yllana and two other grafted to represent the Cold Light. Overturn was conversing quietly with Rewether and Redtale. Professor P'layvo, Galan, and Tolistan stood with representatives from the Illuminates, Tillmin and Hirfan. Challix stood at the head of the table, with Tormod lurking in one corner.

As Everys approached the table, she beckoned for everyone to come closer. "Thank you all for indulging me. I needed a few days... well, I needed a few days."

Most of the people nodded sympathetically, and P'layvo put a hand on Galan's shoulder.

Yllana raised a tentative hand. "If I may, Blessed? The Cold Light are deeply distressed about what you learned about Favid's crimes. What is to happen with him?"

That was something she had agonized about over the past two days as well.

"I'm not sure yet," Everys said. "From what I understand, according to the Dynasty's traditions, I should preside over a trial and pass sentence on him immediately. But..." Her voice trailed off. She couldn't bring herself to say what would likely happen, not in front of Galan.

"If we may be so bold, Blessed, the Yoreroot has a recommendation," Yllana said.

Everys pursed her lips. While she knew that most of her advisers would expect her to handle this, she was willing to entertain other options. So she gestured for Yllana to continue.

Instead of speaking, though, Yllana shuddered as Tall Reach took control. He straightened up and looked at her, his eyes brimming with sympathy.

"Give your father to us, Everys Queen. We will cultivate him," Tall Reach said.

Everys shifted uncomfortably.

Redtale cleared her throat. "That's not a euphemism, is it?"

Tall Reach smiled. "Not at all. As you know, we have extended our hospitality to many over the centuries. Some have indulged in violence and crime in spite of our welcome. We have developed ways of working with them to cultivate their minds and souls, to help them see the error of their ways."

"You'd be willing to do that?" Everys asked.

"We would consider it an honor to be given this task."

Everys exchanged a look with Galan, who stared back with wide eyes. Finally, her sister shrugged one shoulder.

"Very well. I accept your offer."

Yllana shuddered as Tall Reach withdrew his presence.

An uncomfortable silence hung in the room before P'layvo cleared her throat.

"I have good news to report," she said. "The AI may have solved the puzzle about the strange interpolations in the Principality runes."

Everys perked up at this. While she hadn't been able to give much thought to that mystery, she was interested to hear what the Professor and her team had found.

"It turns out that there are random phrases inserted into each of the Principality runes," Tolistan said. "At first, Professor P'layvo thought there was an issue with the AI, but once we had found all eight phrases, we discovered it creates a poem of its own..."

P'layvo produced a scriber and clicked a few buttons on it. A vid-screen lit up and a series of lines scrolled across the screen:

I see the lack [[untranslated suffix]] that fixed needs be
Overpower brokenness [[untranslated suffix]]
Give me what I deepest desire (70% certainty)
So long as [[untranslated - walking metaphor?]]
In my soul is certainty and delight
To (46% certainty) what you call me.
Unleash (60% certainty) your power, your strength,
Reshape (82% certainty) the world to my (25% certainty) will.

Everys leaned forward, reading the lines several times.

"So... there was a poem hidden in the middle of those runes?" Rewether's voice betrayed his skepticism. "That's neat."

P'layvo offered the guard commander a thin smile. "It's more than just a poem. Every rune is a poem, albeit a shorter one."

Tingles swept down Everys's spine. "Are you saying that this is a rune?"

Tolistan nodded, and P'layvo pressed a button. The translated words were replaced with computer-generated drawings of the eight Principality runes. A segment of each glowed blue, then pulled out of the rune itself, all of which faded away. The segments then moved together, the pieces locking together to form a new rune.

As Everys stared at it, a low heat settled in her stomach. Even though she had never seen it before, she knew, deep in her soul and mind, that this rune had power. The way the lines swirled around each other, bisecting and turning away, twisting into the most elaborate pattern she'd ever seen. This wasn't just a rune, this was a work of art. She could practically hear this rune's heartbeat, feel its breath on her cheek.

Apparently the others in the room, even the non-Siporans, could sense the difference as everyone shifted positions and murmured.

"Wh-what does it... y'know, do?" Rewether's voice was tiny, like that of a child.

"An excellent question," P'layvo whispered. "And unfortunately, it's not one that we can answer."

Tolistan cleared his throat. "If I may? So far, all the runes we have translated have turned out to be a type of poetic prayer, one that requests the Singularity to do what the rune is supposed to do. At least, that's held true in all the runes that we've been able to translate so far. Given what we've been able to translate in this... well, puzzle rune, for lack of a better term, it would seem that it can somehow unleash the Singularity's own power and, as it says, 'reshape the world' according to the caster's will."

Once again, an uncomfortable silence descended on the room, and Everys remembered what she had read in the translation of Occ's book. Could this be what the author was describing?

"Do we have any idea if that's true?" Redtale asked quietly.

Galan, P'layvo, and Tolistan exchanged sheepish looks before Tolistan said, "We're not entirely sure, but..."

"...we tried casting it," Galan said with a wince. "Nothing happened."

Everys's head snapped back. They had what?

"Our guess is that this rune would need a supremely powerful ink to actually be cast," Galan said.

That made sense. While the runes Everys knew could be cast with any ink, the ancient texts told stories of mages casting incredibly powerful spells. In many of those stories, they couldn't use common inks but special ones, like Cold Light tree sap.

"Can you call up the translation again?" Challix asked.

P'layvo did so, and Challix walked around the table to get a closer look at the words. Then she pointed to some of the notations. "What does all of this mean?"

"While the AI has cobbled together a loose translation, some of it is guesswork. My professors at the university referred to them as 'trusses of trust,'" Galan said. "In some cases, like the fourth line, the AI simply can't make any determination what the translation should be. In other cases, it can make inferences based on context, grammatical cues, and related words."

With that, Galan launched into a mini lecture about the AI's progress in deciphering the puzzle rune. Everys couldn't understand half of what she was saying. At first, she was delighted to watch as her sister dazzled the room with her knowledge. But then a wave of sadness crested over her. Not long ago, Papa had shared his hopes for their family. He had hoped that Galan would be a professor. Instead, she had hidden in the Demilitarized Zone for five years and now had to hide herself in the Shade. That didn't seem fair.

Once Galan was done, Everys smiled her thanks to her. "On a related topic, have you fed the runes used by the mage-king's agents to the AI?"

P'layvo exchanged an uneasy look with Tillmin.

"Y-yes, we did," Tillmin said. "It was... most illuminating."

Everys wanted to chuckle at what she assumed was an unintentional pun. "And?"

Another uncertain look, but then P'layvo used her scriber to call up an image of another rune. Unlike the ones shared earlier, this one was jagged, harsh in its shape and construction. Everys could feel its wrongness slither across her skin, leaving a trail of puckered flesh behind.

"This is the rune the agents had on their clothing," Hirfan said. "And it's fairly easy to translate."

P'layvo hit a button. The rune pulled apart into words: *Blind my enemies to my presence.*

"We're fairly certain that this one is what rendered the attackers invisible," Hirfan said.

Another rune presented itself, only to be translated: *Fill my prey with fear of my blade.*

"This most likely is designed to sow panic among people."

Another. *Take me to my desired destination.*

"We think this is a teleportation spell of some kind."

Everys shuddered. The harsh wording didn't sit right with her. The other runes, like the Principality runes, were poetic prayers. These were just demands.

Before Hirfan could say anything else, though, a guard rushed into the room, his face pale.

"Blessed, word from the comms office. They've picked up a broadcast from Bastion and they said the crier guilds are saying it has something to do with you. They're routing the signal here now."

Everys frowned. What could this be about? Challix adjusted the controls, dismissing the image of the rune for the signal in question. Everys recognized the image immediately—the press room at the palace. There was the podium where Narius, Paine, or a member of the public relations ministry would interact with reporters. No one was there yet, but from the buzz of the reporters' voices, she suspected something big was about to happen.

Sure enough, a few moments later, Vizier Paine approached the podium.

Everys's stomach twisted. She thought of the pain in Vessel and Freedom's voices as they talked about their son, but she tamped down on the memory.

"Thank you for joining me today," Paine said. "For many months now, I have heard speculation about the former king and queen's fate. Despite the earliest reports that both Narius and Everys died in the disaster that overtook Bastion, we now have information to the contrary."

Everys gasped. Did that mean... Did that mean that Narius was still alive?

"Even though we have never found Narius's body, we have multiple attestations that the former king did indeed die from his injuries from the ritual combat. However, the fate of the former queen has been more uncertain. We never found adequate proof of her demise and we recently received reports of her and her former Ixactl bodyguard traveling throughout the Dynasty's holdings, including here in Bastion. What she was trying to accomplish, we do not know."

Now Everys's heart stuttered. Who had reported her? She doubted it was any of the Siporan families who'd helped her. Were they safe? Or what about Paine's parents? Were they in trouble?

Paine didn't betray any emotion as he continued, "Previous to these reports, King Brencis learned some disturbing information about the queen. When he first learned of it, he remained silent in the interest of the Dynasty's stability. But now that we know Everys is still alive, he wishes to make these allegations public."

Everys frowned. What allegations? What could Paine possibly be talking about?

"That is why I am inviting Minister of Finance Masruq to join me."

Paine stepped aside, and Masruq, Oluna's husband, waddled up to the podium. He was a short man, with a large gut and ruddy cheeks. Everys gasped when she saw him. Dark bags hung under his eyes while his hair frizzed out like a cloud. She wasn't all that surprised. She'd always suspected that Oluna was the one in charge of their relationship. He'd probably been lost without her.

"Good afternoon." Masruq's voice was hoarse, barely more than a wet whisper. "It brings me no pleasure to bring this information to light, but as a member of the king's council, I feel I must.

"Many of you may not know this, but I have a granddaughter. Her name is Zivah. She has lived with my wife and me for most of her life, and for most of that time, Zivah has been bedridden due to what we believed was an incurable disease."

The people around her started whispering, but a chill swept over Everys. She had met Zivah shortly before Bastion fell, when Masruq and Oluna hosted her for dinner. And there was only one reason Masruq would bring that up now.

"Go get Oluna," she whispered to Redtale. "Now!"

Redtale quickly left the room.

"Several months ago, something miraculous happened. For the first time in her life, Zivah showed signs of improvement. She still has a long way to go, but the doctors are confident that she will make a full recovery."

The reporters listening to Masruq's stories made sympathetic noises, but Everys felt like she was being crushed by an incredible weight.

"At first, I thought this miracle was a gift from the Water Bearer herself, but then I discovered the truth. This was not something done by the Water Bearer, but by Everys using foul toratropic magic."

The reporters gasped.

Masruq nodded grimly. "Because of Zivah's condition, my wife and I had installed a surveillance system in her room to monitor her. Shortly before Bastion's fall, we hosted the queen and, during said dinner, this happened."

He made a vague gesturing motion. The camera pivoted, showing a vidscreen. Everys's body turned to ice as she watched herself slink into Zivah's room, pluck a bead from her bracelet, and then painted the healing rune on Zivah's chest. Thankfully, the camera angle was such that no one could see what exactly she was doing. But Everys knew. And clearly, Masruq had figured it out as well.

On the screen, Everys pulled away from Zivah. The camera caught a glimmer of light as the spell took hold. Then the camera angle shifted to one right over the bed. As the footage replayed, there could be no doubt. There it was, her family's rune for everyone to see. Gasps echoed through the chamber as the rune flared to life.

Just as the footage ended, the war room's door opened and Oluna stepped inside, a quizzical look on her face. Redtale marched in after her, then steered her to a place closer to Everys.

Masruq reappeared on the screen. "While I appreciate what the former queen did for my Zivah, she used toratropic magic, a practice that has been outlawed since King Heronus destroyed Nekek the Bright four hundred years ago. I debated what to do with this information for a long time, but I finally realized I had an obligation to report this to the king."

Paine took Masruq's place and glowered at the reporters. "This information is obviously concerning, especially given the rumors of how so many Siporans fled Bastion before the city was destroyed. That Everys was so brazen in using illegal magic suggests that other Siporans may do the same. While Everys may have escaped justice, King Brencis is determined to investigate the ongoing use of toratropic magic fully. He thanks Minister Masruq for bringing this information to light, and..."

Paine kept prattling, but no one in the war room was listening. Everyone had turned to Everys. But Everys could only stare at Oluna. Her friend watched the vidscreen, her brow pinched into the tiniest of frowns.

"Oluna?" Everys asked, her voice frail.

Oluna turned to face Everys, her expression neutral.

"Why did Masruq do that?"

Oluna's expression twisted, taking on a vicious glee. "Because I told him to."

46

Everys gaped at Oluna. She couldn't possibly have heard her correctly.

"Why are you so surprised, *Blessed*?" Oluna spat the word like a curse, her eyes alight with malicious glee. "Why else would my dear Masruq do anything? I've had him on a short leash ever since he first laid eyes on me. Who do you think steered him to the heights of power? Whose family has been hard at work to bring justice to the Dynasty? Did you really think that your anemic magic was the only one to survive Nekek the Bright's fall? Oh, no. The true inheritors of toratropic magic have thrived in the shadows all along. Isn't that right, Rewether my dear?"

Rewether's head snapped forward and his expression went slack. Two runes blazed into existence on his temples. Red light flared in his eyes. With a roar, he drew his flechette thrower and whirled on Everys.

"Down!" Redtale barreled into Everys's chair.

Flechettes sliced through the air, and Redtale grunted as she collapsed on top of Everys. Screams and shouts broke out through the war room. She couldn't see what was happening from underneath Redtale, but she thought she heard Overturn bellow, then thunderous footsteps.

"Stay down, Everys." Redtale's voice was a rumble in her ear.

Everys nodded, her whole body trembling. Redtale jumped to her feet and screamed a challenge. She dropped her shoulder and took two steps forward only to freeze in position, the air vibrating around her.

The room went disturbingly quiet. Even though she had just promised to stay down, Everys realized she couldn't. She was too vulnerable. So she carefully peeked over the table.

Everyone had frozen in place. Overturn was tackling Rewether, both of them at such a strange angle that they should have tipped over, but they didn't. Oluna circled the table, picking up scribers and then, after inspecting their contents, tossing them away. Then she picked up one in front of Professor P'layvo, looked at the screen, and chuckled to herself. She turned, as if to leave, and her gaze fell on Everys. Her eyes narrowed.

"How are you still moving?" she muttered.

Shadows erupted in the corner. Tormod hurtled out of the darkness, two blades in his hands. He slashed at Oluna, who somehow slipped to one side, sliding under the blade. Then she raised an open hand, revealing a crude rune painted on her palm. A blast of force drove the smoke away and knocked Tormod off his feet. He dropped one of his daggers, which skittered across the floor and came to rest next to Everys.

"You can't stop me, Tormod," Oluna said. "No one can. We will reshape the world."

Reshape the world? How did Oluna know about that? Then Everys realized how often she had sat in on council meetings, silently listening as they talked about these incredible secrets they had uncovered.

Everys snatched up the dagger and lunged for Oluna. Without even looking in her direction, Oluna held up her left hand, revealing another rune. The pattern flared red and it felt as though Everys ran face-first into a wall, slamming to a halt and freezing in midlunge.

Oluna advanced on Tormod, but the spymaster spat something in a foreign language, then slipped a hand up his shirt sleeve. Smoke billowed around him and he disappeared into the haze. Everys stared at the spot where he had stood. Where was he going? Why would he abandon her like that?

"Coward." Oluna turned back to Everys, a gleam in her eyes. "I should thank you, Everys. We have been trying to unravel the mystery of the Principalities' secret for generations. Thanks to you, we now have what we need. Well, almost. But I think you have the rest as well."

The rest? Everys's eyes would have widened if they could, but she was stuck fast. The Elderreach!

Oluna tugged the dagger from Everys's hand, then used it to prick her own finger. She drew something on Everys's dress. Everys tried to twist away, to stop her, but she couldn't move, couldn't so much as wiggle.

"You have been most helpful indeed," Oluna murmured.

Red light sliced through Everys's vision, chased by a flame that burrowed into her chest. Suddenly her mind was awash in secrets, things she had tried to hide for years. Skipping lessons at conclave, the time she kissed Boril Clegwether in the marketplace, her false promises made to scrivener after scrivener, so many others. But as each of those rose to her mind, they were shoved away until finally, an image formed, clear as crystal: a great barrow in the Deep Forest, the entrance flanked by silent statues, and deep within, trapped in an eternal slumber...

No!

Oluna reared back, her eyes shining with blue light, her smile triumphant. "And there it is."

Just as quickly as the onslaught started, it cut off, so completely that Everys felt her body jolt in its invisible restraints.

With a chuckle, Oluna knelt and drew a rune on the floor next to them. A pillar of smoke billowed up from the floor. Oluna straightened, squared her shoulders, and stepped through.

Everys tried to thrash against the power that held her, but it was no use. Oluna had probably just transported herself to the Elderreach's barrow and there was nothing that she could—

Then she tumbled to the floor, catching herself on her hands and knees. Sharp pain jolted up her legs and arms. She looked around.

Much to her surprise, Hirfan stood behind her, his fingers stained with ink. His chest heaved as if he had run a great distance. "You know what she's after?"

Everys nodded.

His mouth pulled into a grim line. "Stop her. I'll try to free the others."

She didn't want to. She had never felt toratropic magic so overpowering before. There was no way she could ever hope to defeat Oluna. But she realized she had to try.

Hirfan offered a hand to help her up. She turned to the pillar of shadows, which seemed to grow smaller and smaller with each passing second. If she was going to act, she had to do so now.

With a shout, she charged the pillar. The moment the inky blackness enveloped her, she felt like she was tumbling head over heels through a void, only to come crashing down on rough stone. It took her a moment to realize that she was back in the Elderreach's barrow. There was the monstrosity, wreathed in shadows. She had emerged from the portal close to its—his!—chest. Oluna stood next to the creature, her dagger out and poised to start cutting.

"Oluna!" Everys shouted. "Stop!"

Oluna whipped around, her face twisting into a snarl. "How did you—"

A low moaning, emanating from all around them, cut through Oluna's question. A chill scrambled up Everys's spine and she froze. What was that?

Large objects fell from the ceiling, slamming into the ground hard enough to knock Everys off-balance. The dark shapes rose up around her, monstrous, misshapen creatures wrapped in vines and branches. They vaguely resembled Diradae, with scythe-like claws instead of hands and gnashing mandibles that looked sharp enough to sheer through a tree. The creatures bellowed an ululating challenge, then they charged.

Everys scrambled backward as the closest creature slashed at her head. She barely managed to duck in time. "It's me! I'm Everys. I was here with Tall Reach not that long ago."

The creatures didn't seem to understand. They scrambled after her, three of them working in concert to herd her away from the sleeping Elderreach. They snarled and snapped at her, but they didn't press their attack. Had they understood her words?

She risked a peek past them at Oluna. She had rolled away from the Elderreach and fire wreathed her hands. She tossed fireballs at the creatures that circled her, but she couldn't seem to hit any of them.

"Please, let me help," Everys said to the creatures near her. "I don't want her to get to the Elderreach either. I can help stop her."

She tried to pass through them, but they closed ranks and chittered at her angrily. She gritted her teeth, weighing her options. They clearly weren't happy to have her in the barrow, but they appeared content to herd her away from the Elderreach. But if she tried to go after Oluna, they likely would attack her. But what could she...

Then Oluna slammed a fist to the ground. Lightning exploded from the point of impact. The bright slashes lit up the Elderreach in an eerie white light, but then the bolts slammed into the creatures surrounding her. They spasmed and shrieked as fire danced over them, then collapsed into smoking heaps. She glanced in Everys's direction and smirked.

"Far too timid, Everys." Her voice somehow cut through the dying moans of the creatures. "There's no way you or your kind could ever stop us. And once I have this thing's blood, we'll finally set everything right."

Everys had to act. But she didn't have any ink on her. She looked around for anything she could use as a weapon. Her gaze hitched on a sharp rock jutting out of the ground. Could she pry it free? She winced. Even if she could, how could she use that against Oluna?

Wait. There was a way. Her stomach curdled as she weighed the possibility. What else could she do?

She knelt and drew her fingertip across the rock's edge. She hissed as it tore the skin open and a bit of blood welled up from the cut. Before she could change her mind, she sketched out one of the few combat runes she knew, a fire-throwing spell, and then activated it.

A tingle started in the soles of her feet. The sensation grew, slithering up her legs, through her chest, and then down her right arm. What felt like molten iron burst from her hand as a thick rope of flames sliced through the air toward Oluna. Everys gritted her teeth, trying to aim the stream between the creatures advancing on her. They still snarled and clacked their mandibles at her.

Before the attack could land, Oluna snapped up a hand and somehow redirected the fire away from her. The stream of flames split, consuming the creatures near Everys.

Oluna cackled. "How did it feel, using your own blood to cast a rune? Exhilarating, isn't it? The power that can be summoned from within you at a moment's notice. You and I may be more alike than you realize."

Everys started to answer, but then the rebuke struck, slicing up her arm with a sudden, sharp agony. She staggered, grabbing at her chest. But just as it hit, it faded.

"And the rebuke? They fade quicker the more they happen, Everys," Oluna said. "Eventually, you're able to shrug them off like nothing.

Why do you think I haven't been stopped by your precious Singularity? He can't stop me. No one can."

Not if Everys had anything to say about it. She charged forward, hastily scribbling another combat rune on the back of her hand. It might be a futile gesture, but she had to try.

At the last second, Oluna snapped up a hand, revealing another rune on her palm. How was she drawing those so quickly? The rune flared with harsh purple light.

An invisible force slammed into Everys and threw her across the space, pinning her to the wall. She wasn't paralyzed this time, but she couldn't free herself.

"That's enough out of you. As your rightful ruler, I order you to stand down."

Everys's mind hitched on Oluna's words. Rightful ruler? Did that mean...?

The other woman must have read her confusion. Oluna laughed. "You still haven't figured it out yet? I'm no mere scribbler. I am the *ar'zhannok*, the heir to the throne in Nekek the Bright."

She was *what?* Everys gaped at her. She was a mage-king? The mage-king, the leader of the conspiracy? This whole time? How had Everys missed that?

"But I've wasted enough time on you as it is. Time to collect what I came here for." Oluna turned to the Elderreach and pulled the dagger from her belt.

"Please," Everys whispered, her voice straining against the force that held her. "Please, don't let her..."

The ground rumbled, and Oluna stumbled to a halt. Gigantic vines erupted from the ground on all sides of the Elderreach. They reached up, almost to the ceiling, but then bent back down, covering the creature's body completely. More and more burst from the ground and, within seconds, the entire creature was wrapped from head to foot in vines. Then, with a loud rumble that shook the entire barrow, the vines pulled the Elderreach underground. The ground closed over the hole, kicking up a cloud of dust that rolled over Oluna.

The other woman stared at the now-empty space, then whirled on Everys.

"Where did they take it?" she screamed.

Everys sucked in a breath. "I don't know."

Oluna shrieked and threw the dagger into the shadows. She clawed at her hair, then calmed.

"Fine. We'll go with our back-up plan." Oluna fixed Everys with a look. "Goodbye, Everys. We'll see if you survive long enough to see our new world."

Oluna knelt and drew another rune. Shadows burst from the floor into a pillar that Oluna stepped through.

As soon as Oluna disappeared, the force holding Everys to the wall vanished and she dropped to the floor. She looked around the empty barrow and shuddered. She was stranded and alone.

47

Movement caught her attention out of the corner of her eye. More of the creatures scuttled down the walls, all of them headed toward her. She winced. Just what she needed. Within moments, the creatures encircled her, snarling and snapping at her.

"And where were you?" she demanded. "Maybe if you had taken the threat more seriously, we could've stopped her."

Much to her surprise, the creatures didn't attack. Instead, they stayed ten feet away from her, shifting back and forth.

"*... Everys Queen...*"

She jolted at the whispered words. Where had that come from? She looked around, hoping that maybe someone had come to get her.

"*... Everys Queen...*"

No, that voice was closer than she thought. Right in front of her? The creatures?

"Who's there?" she demanded.

One of the creatures shambled forward, its gait uncertain. Then it dipped its massive head, and somehow, a rasping voice emerged from its maw.

"You may call me the Last, for that is what I am."

Everys's eyes widened. Was a Cold Light speaking to her through this creature? It seemed likely, given how it was wrapped in vines like a grafted and the voice—the Last?—had referred to her the way the other Cold Light did.

"Have we met before?"

The creature made a hacking sound. Everys realized it was trying to laugh.

"No, Everys Queen. The others isolate me. I have only the slightest connection in the Below. A few, like Firestruck, keep me informed of what happens elsewhere. But they want my attention focused here."

Everys frowned. "Why?"

"This is my cultivation for nearly destroying us."

"The Cold Light?"

"Indeed." The creature shuffled a bit closer. "You see, I am the only living Cold Light who was there for the war."

A chill swept over Everys. According to Tall Reach, the conflict between the Cold Light and Elderreach happened eight thousand years earlier. Could a Cold Light really live that long?

"I remember it well. The burning of the forest. The pitched battles. How close we came to extinction." The Last sighed, causing the creature he controlled to shudder. "That was why I suggested what I did. Why I did what I did."

She couldn't help herself. "What?"

"Before the war, we used to bond with animals in the forest. Small rodents. The occasional wolf. They assisted us in clearing underbrush, maintaining the complex dance of life. But when the Elderreach came, I suggested we bond with the intelligent peoples beyond the forest's border. Humans. Ixactl. Plissk."

Why would he be punished for that? "Did you give them a choice?"

"No. I said it was necessary. A way to protect us. But it damaged us. Made us more like them." The Last's voice was flat. "Once the threat was over, my people were horrified at what we had done. Because I was the originator, I was given the task of safeguarding the last living Elderreach."

Everys considered what the Last had told her, but her mind hitched on a question. "But they still use grafted today."

"Volunteers, not forced." The Last's ghostly voice carried only a trace of bitterness, and Everys suspected that was due to speaking through the creature. "There are those who feel that even this is a step too far. They are the ones who insist on my banishment."

She looked around the cavernous barrow, now so empty without its sole inhabitant. She frowned, then turned back to the creature.

"So where are you?" she asked. "I don't see a pillar tree in here."

The Last didn't answer, but then a faint glow worked its way through one of the barrow's ribs, a pale red light that rose from the ground and up toward the ceiling. But then rib after rib lit up, dozens of them glowing at once. Everys stared at the sight, her mouth open. Was the barrow made out of the Last's pillar tree? She had seen the Cold Light construct incredible structures using ordinary trees. Why couldn't they do the same with the trees they inhabited?

"What will happen now?" Everys asked.

The creature shuffled closer and leaned in close enough that she could smell its rancid breath. "Do not inquire of this further, Everys Queen. The Yoreroot made an exception to show you this, and the result is that this sanctuary was breached. We will maintain our vigil as long as we must. Now go."

Everys's skin went clammy and she stuttered. "B-but I can't. I don't have transportation."

"Don't you? I know what you are. I know what your kind is capable of. You have the ink."

She looked at her finger. And she had seen the teleportation rune. The question was, could she remember how to draw it? She didn't see much choice.

She squeezed her finger, drawing out a red bead, and knelt to draw the rune's pattern. As she worked, more details filtered into her mind, almost as if the rune itself were somehow prompting her on how to finish it. In spite of that, her skin still crawled as it came together. This was wrong. Not just using the blood, but the rune itself.

With a trembling finger, she activated the rune. At first, nothing happened, and she relaxed, just a bit. There was nothing forbidden about drawing a rune that didn't work. But then sharp claws dug into her mind, trying to sift through her thoughts for information. No, a command. A destination. She pictured the war room in the Embassy.

The rune erupted in shadow, flowing into a pillar. She felt a tug at her heart, as if it was trying to pull her into the void. With one last look around the barrow, she rose and stepped through.

She emerged in the war room. Her own guards leveled their weapons on her, and she froze until they recognized her and relaxed. Redtale rushed to her side.

"Are you all right?" she demanded. "Where were you?"

Before Everys could answer, though, a burning sensation flashed up her arms, lodging at the base of her neck, like a severe burn but underneath her skin. As quickly as it flared up, it faded. She froze. Was that it? If so, what did that mean? Was it like Oluna said, that she was becoming immune to the rebukes?

She dropped to the floor, landing hard enough to send a shock up her spine. She tucked her knees under her chin and hugged her legs. Her body's warmth and strength drained out of her as everything she had just seen and heard crashed down on her. Oluna was responsible for all of this? She was the mage-king? Everys thought of all the times Oluna had sat in on strategy sessions, how many secrets she had heard. And she had been with Papa for weeks! Had Papa been telling the truth about what Masruq did with him? Had Oluna encouraged Papa to kill Narius?

It was too much. Too much! As her advisers flocked around her, peppering her with questions, Everys closed her eyes and tried to blot out the noise, the confusion, all of it. What were they supposed to do now?

48

No one complained that Everys hadn't moved since she returned from the Last's barrow. If they had problems with it, they wisely kept those thoughts to themselves.

Not that she would have noticed if someone said something. Everys felt as though she were wrapped in a thick woolen blanket. The world seemed muffled and distant, insulated as she was from everyone else. Her mind simply couldn't stop ricocheting from everything that had happened. The fact that Oluna hadn't gotten the Elderreach blood was little comfort since she had stolen the Principalities research. Worse, Everys's secret had been broadcast throughout the Dynasty. Would anyone want her to be queen now? Everything had fallen apart and she had no idea what she could do to fix things.

The doors to the war room banged open and Tormod ran inside, with Style, Screj, and half a dozen other Illuminates in his wake. They all had bandoliers studded with tiny vials crossing their chests. Their gaze swept the room, their postures tense as if ready for a fight. When they saw that there were no enemies to face, they relaxed and drifted into the room, offering to help.

Tormod, though, stepped over to Everys and knelt next to her. "Blessed? Are you all right?"

She looked at him and her brow furrowed. Heat cut through the chilly cocoon wrapped around her body and mind. "Where did you go?" She could barely muster a whisper.

He grimaced. "When Oluna bested me, I realized we needed reinforcements. I withdrew to the Illuminate's compound and asked for their help."

She sat up straighter, grinding her teeth as she did. "Then what took you so long? The conclave isn't that far away!"

"Very true, but we had to cross a battlefield to get here."

What? Everys tipped her head to one side, as if that would help her understand his words better.

He nodded grimly. "I believe Rewether wasn't the only victim of Oluna's corruption. There was a firefight outside the Embassy."

Another wave of cold sluiced through Everys. "Was anyone hurt?"

"Minor injuries, thankfully. And when we arrived, the Illuminates were able to put them all to sleep," Tormod said

Everys looked around the war room, suddenly aware that she hadn't seen Rewether, Redtale, or Overturn since her return. "What happened to Rewether?"

Challix cleared her throat from nearby, catching Everys's attention. "Redtale and Overturn were able to subdue him while you were away, Blessed. He's being held in a cell now."

That information didn't comfort her as much as she hoped.

"Come, Blessed." Tormod stood and offered her a hand. "I'm sure you've been through much and we will all want to hear what happened, but for now, let's start with getting up."

"It's all gone so wrong," Everys whispered.

"As happens sometimes, yes," Tormod said, then smiled sadly. "Those are the times when we lean on Him hardest, yes? Each other as well. Start with me and we'll figure this out together."

She took his hand and, with his help, rose. Her legs protested, pins and needles sweeping through them. She winced, but waved off Challix's offer of help. She'd be okay. She had just been wallowing too long. She approached the table on unsteady legs, then looked around the room again, realizing that aside from the Illuminates, only Challix and a handful of guards remained.

"What happened to everyone else?" she asked. "Are they okay?"

"Shaken, but not injured," Challix said. "As soon as Oluna vanished, we evacuated them to safety. I believe your sister, Professor P'layvo, and the scrivener are being checked out by the medics. I would suggest we do the same with you, Blessed."

That made sense. Everys nodded, and Tormod escorted her out of the room, steering her around the overturned chairs and spilled scribers. They left the war room and carefully made their way to her quarters. The minute they entered, Trule and the girls swarmed her, guiding her to a nearby couch.

"I leave you in better hands than mine, Blessed," Tormod said. "I'll look in on Oluna's victims and see what we can do with them."

Everys smiled her thanks. As Tormod left the room, a medical team arrived. They conducted a thorough physical, one that lasted close to an hour. When they were done, they had noted the nicks and cuts from when she had used her own blood to cast runes, along with a number of scrapes and bruises. But the lead medic prescribed one thing, namely rest.

She would have objected, but from the expression on Trule's face, that was a fight she would have lost. So she surrendered, allowing the girls to tuck her into her bed. Not that it would do her any good. Her body may have been fine, but her mind simply wouldn't leave her alone. She wrestled with everything that happened until finally, mercifully, exhaustion overwhelmed her and she tumbled into a deep sleep.

Everys spent the next two days sequestered from the world. By the third day, Everys realized she couldn't hide anymore. Yes, Challix had things well in hand—not at all surprising—but Everys knew she couldn't hide any longer. She emerged from her quarters, finding Redtale standing guard outside her room.

"How are you feeling, Blessed?" Redtale asked.

Everys considered lying, but decided against it quickly. No need to resume that bad habit with Redtale. "Not great, but a little bit better."

"Small steps conquer tall mountains," Redtale said. "Where are we heading?"

She thought it over. She could stop by the war room and see what else she had missed. Or maybe check in with Professor P'layvo? Or she could visit with Mama and Galan. But no, she realized she had to take care of something else first.

"Let's go see the Illuminates. I need to thank them for their help."

Redtale nodded sharply, then motioned for her to lead the way.

Everys started out, but then hesitated long enough to fall into step with Redtale. "And how are you doing?"

"All things considered, I'm okay," Redtale said. "Good thing I don't have my horns anymore. I think Rewether would have torn them off if I did."

"And he's doing better?"

"Mortified at his behavior. Ready to resign his position by way of apology. But yes. Whatever Oluna did to him stopped about the same time Oluna and you jumped into that portal." Redtale glanced at her out of the corner of her eye. "Let's not do that again without one of us to protect you, okay?"

Everys smiled sheepishly. "I'll do my best not to jump into toratropic portals without an escort."

Redtale smirked. "That Hirfan examined all of the people Oluna bewitched and he thinks they're clean now. He and a team of Illuminates are conducting a sweep of the personnel in the Embassy to make sure Oluna doesn't have any other unwitting accomplices. So far, they haven't found any."

Good. That was good. They left the Embassy, and as they walked to the nearby conclave, she noted the signs of what had happened: flechettes embedded in trees, spots of blood on the grass, the cordon erected around the Embassy, patrolled by soldiers. Everys hurried her steps. The sooner they arrived, hopefully the sooner she'd start to feel like things would be better.

Much to her surprise, she wasn't greeted as she walked through the gallery. She soon found out why. The Illuminates were gathered in the lab, talking excitedly. She wondered if any of them could understand what the others were saying. She carefully edged up to the crowd, trying to determine what had them so excited.

Then she spotted what was in the center of the gathering: a large tree branch, shaped like a Y, with gossamer webbing strung between the forks. She blinked. Occ's artwork?

Then Master Tillmin noticed her. He whistled twice, the shrill noise cutting through the chatter. Once the rest of the Illuminates had calmed down, he opened his arms.

"Blessed, I'm sorry no one greeted you properly, but we... well, we have much to discuss right now," Tillmin said. "For starters, we have determined that most of your staff was untouched by Oluna's spell. A truly diabolical rune, that one, but one that shouldn't trouble us again."

That was a relief, but it didn't explain why they had brought Occ's art here.

Tillmin noticed her attention on the branch, and he chuckled. "Yes, that. Your Diradae friend may have helped us solve a puzzle that has eluded us for generations! Come, come!"

He motioned for her to step closer to the artwork. Much to Everys's surprise and relief, the intricate web weaving appeared to be intact.

"We've been most eager to study Occ's art, but we had the worst time trying to get our hands on it. Strategist Overturn and your guard, Rewether, insisted that we couldn't even look at it because of its potential as a weapon." Tillmin scoffed. "As if we were interested in weaponizing the runes."

"Not an unusual attitude, Master," Style interjected.

Screj elbowed her, and she glowered at her husband.

Tillmin waved away the words. "Yes, yes. But Occ's accident raised some fascinating questions. At first, we thought maybe we had stumbled across a new form of ink. To my knowledge, no one has ever tried to make ink out of Diradae webbing before."

Everys frowned. "Would that even be possible?"

Screj cleared his throat. "My hypothesis was yes, Blessed. I reasoned that the heat from the laser liquified the webbing, causing it to run together and activate. If that were true, and given how powerful the spell's effect was, it would mean that we had discovered an ink even more powerful than Cold Light tree sap."

Style shot him a glare. "Don't waste her time. Was your hypothesis correct?"

With a sigh, Screj said, "No, it wasn't. I obtained a sample from Occ, and the art piece shows no sign of liquefaction."

"Then what was the ink in the rune?" Everys asked.

"Well, once my hypothesis was proven false, we thought that maybe someone spilled something on the artwork or Occ used some sort of resin to protect the weaving. But further investigation—"

Style clamped her hand over Screj's mouth, then motioned for Tillmin to speak.

His eyes lit up. "It was the laser, Blessed. We're almost sure of it."

A tingly wave crested over Everys. "Wh-what?"

Tillmin nodded emphatically. "It's the only explanation. We've taken numerous samples—carefully, I assure you—and we can't find any other form of ink in the weave at all. It can only be the light!"

Everys stared at the Illuminate master. She understood his excitement. This was something his sect had been chasing for centuries. To suddenly find out that what they sought was not only possible, but they had experienced it? That had to be exciting.

"But how?" she asked.

"Do you remember how Occ set up the laser?" Tillmin prompted. "The light traced the rune's pattern so quickly that, to the naked eye, it appeared as if the rune had been drawn by light. A complete circuit. It has to be the laser. Occ cast the rune with light!"

Everys stumbled back a step and collapsed onto a nearby chair. The Illuminates resumed their animated discussion, and this time, she understood their excitement. But that raised a question.

"Don't the ancient texts say that only the Singularity can paint runes with light?" she asked.

Screj shook his head. "That's one interpretation. But we believe the Singularity would permit us to cast a rune with light, which is confirmed since Occ didn't suffer any sort of rebuke."

He hadn't, had he? And Everys knew how bad a rebuke for using forbidden ink could be. If the Singularity didn't want them to use light, Occ would have been rebuked.

The more she thought about it, the more hope swelled within her. If Everys had access to light-drawn runes, that might be enough to counter whatever the mage-kings had planned.

"What do you need for me?"

The discussion died. Tillmin smiled grimly.

"We need you to talk to Strategist Overturn. He won't let us access the laser Occ used for his artwork. But if you asked..."

"Consider it done." Everys rose from her chair. "Make this your top priority. We may need it sooner than we realize."

Tillmin drew up to his full height, even though that meant he only came up to her shoulder. "We will undertake this with the utmost seriousness, Blessed. Never fear, we will determine what this discovery means."

49

The military had commandeered a large building near the Embassy to serve as their headquarters. It was the only site the Cold Light had allowed the newcomers to change substantially. Like most buildings constructed by the Cold Light, it had been made of woven-together trees. It had originally served as a boarding house for newcomers to the forest. Upon arriving in the Shade, Overturn's people had built fortifications around the perimeter, shoring up the tree trunks with armor they had stripped from broken transports. The overall result was a garish blend of organic and patchwork metal.

The soldiers guarding the perimeter came to attention as Everys passed with Redtale in tow. As she approached the building itself, she could hear raised voices.

"...need to give me some sort of estimate!" Overturn's voice sounded like an avalanche.

They entered the building, allowing them to hear what the grafted was saying.

"We are making progress in raising our army." That was Effort's voice, but clearly Firestruck was speaking through him. "But the process is arduous, for both the troops and for us. We need more time."

"We don't have more time! According to the reports I've seen, either the Dalark or Brencis's forces could be at our door at any time. We can hope they will erode each other's strength, but even then, I fear we will not be able to repel them for long. We need more troops and quickly," Overturn replied.

Everys entered the strategist's office. The room itself was a cramped space, with a small desk overflowing with scribers and maps. Three vidscreens dominated the walls, displaying tactical maps, satellite imagery, and scrolling logistical data. Overturn towered over the grafted.

Effort looked ready to reply, but Overturn noticed Everys's arrival. He straightened and turned to her, his expression abashed. "Blessed. I'm sorry that..."

"Is there anything I can help with?" Everys asked.

Overturn shot a dark look at Effort, who faced Everys with the imperious expression of Firestruck.

"Not unless you can control the passage of time, Everys Queen," Firestruck said. "The strategist's argument is with the forces of nature, not me."

Overturn looked ready to object, but Everys held up a hand.

"You're sure there's nothing else that we can do to help?" Everys asked.

Firestruck's expression faltered, and it looked like he was about to release control of the grafted. Doubt flickered across his face, but then he nodded slowly, thoughtfully.

"There is indeed something that would assist us." He turned back to Overturn. "It would be immensely helpful if you were to join with us, Overturn Strategist."

"A joint command structure?"

"No. I would bond with you, bring you into direct communion with me." Firestruck paused. "You and I would graft together."

Overturn blanched and he stumbled back a step. "I... you... what?"

Firestruck nodded. "There is a barrier of misunderstanding between us, Overturn Strategist. Of mistrust. We know of only one way to tear down that wall. Be a part of us, and we promise we will address your doubts."

Overturn took several ragged breaths, then nodded weakly. "I will... I will consider your offer."

The grafted bowed, then he shuddered as Firestruck released him. When he straightened, he offered Overturn a sympathetic smile. "If it is any consolation, Strategist, every grafted feels overwhelmed when a Cold Light chooses us. And there is no shame in declining. But consider their offer."

That said, the grafted glided out of the room. Overturn took several shuddering breaths, then turned to Everys fully. He gestured toward a chair in the office, which she sat in. Redtale stepped up behind Everys on her right.

"What can I do for you, Blessed?" Overturn asked.

Everys considered just asking for the laser right then, but that didn't feel right. Overturn was clearly rattled, and she couldn't blame him. "Are you okay?"

He chuckled mirthlessly. "No, Blessed, I am not. When King Narius appointed me to be head of the Dynasty's military, I knew I faced an uphill battle. But that was all right. Ixactl fight uphill all the time. Right, cousin?"

Redtale smiled.

"I knew dealing with Brencis and Tirigian would be difficult, but I relished the idea of the challenge. But I have locked horns with the Cold Light every day over their support. I do not doubt that they are stalwart allies, but they are so slow in their thinking. If I did not know better, I would think them unconcerned about what is happening. They promise they are raising an army, but they are unwilling to let me inspect these troops or share their strategy for deploying them. They expect me to craft a battle strategy with one eye swollen shut and one arm bound."

Everys pursed her lips, feeling his frustration bleed into her. She could understand where he was coming from.

"And the only way to find out what they are doing is to become one of their thralls?" Overturn winced, then corrected himself. "Grafted. I know that is the correct term. But I have to admit, old fears die hard. I do not wish to lose my autonomy."

"I don't think that actually happens," Everys said. "Not unless you allow one of the Cold Light to speak through you. From what I've seen, you would remain yourself."

"Even still." Overturn sighed heavily.

She considered what he said, then leaned forward in her chair. "You know that when I first became queen, it wasn't by choice. Redtale scooped me out of Fair Havens and practically dragged me to the palace."

Redtale winced, then touched one of her horn's stumps. "That's not entirely accurate, Blessed."

Everys smiled. "Maybe not, but it definitely felt that way. I didn't want to be there. But eventually, I came to understand that maybe I had to be. Maybe I was being given an opportunity to bring my perspective to a place where it needed to be. I realized that, in spite of my misgivings and discomfort, and yes, even anger, I had to set aside those feelings for the greater good."

Overturn's brow furrowed, and he fiddled with the tip of his right horn. "Are you ordering me to become a grafted?"

She shook her head. "I would never do that. The choice has to be yours. I know it would be a lot, maybe too much. All I am asking is for you to consider their offer."

He stared at the desk. But he nodded. "Very well. What else can I do for you?"

"I understand that the Illuminates have been trying to borrow a targeting laser from one of your skimmers."

Now he looked up at her. "You want me to give them one."

"I do."

He ground his teeth. "I'm very hesitant to do that, Blessed. When that Diradae borrowed the laser, he fiddled with it. It took our technicians two weeks to fully repair it. We don't have many to spare."

"I suppose that's true," Everys allowed. "But what the Illuminates are doing is important. I would consider it a personal favor if you give it to them."

He guffawed. "Blessed, you are my queen. If you say they need the laser, they'll get the laser. I'll put in the order right now and—"

The vidscreens behind Overturn lit up, an angry red flashing, and a siren wailed in the distance. Overturn bolted out of his chair, and Redtale stepped forward, putting a hand on Everys's shoulder.

"What is it?" Everys asked.

Overturn consulted the vidscreens then bit off a curse. "Dalark incursion over the forest, coming in from the north. They'll be overhead in about ten minutes. Our skyscan didn't pick up on their presence until just now."

Cold swept over Everys. She knew the Dalark were more technologically advanced than the Dynasty, but this was a frightening reminder of what that actually meant.

Overturn watched as reports scrolled by on the vidscreen, and he grunted several times. Each one sounded more frustrated than the last.

"What is it?" Everys prompted.

"None of this makes sense. It looks like the skimmer deliberately tripped our skyscan, like they wanted us to know they're coming. And near as we can tell, it's only one bomber. No escorts."

"One bomber can do a lot of damage with the right type of ordnance," Redtale said.

He nodded, then turned to Everys. "I'm going to have to insist you get to shelter, Blessed."

Everys wanted to object, but Redtale clamped a hand on her shoulder and dragged her back to the Embassy. On the way, Dynasty personnel scrambled to more defensive positions. As they approached the Embassy, engines roared as two Dynasty cloudskimmers launched into the air, presumably to intercept the Dalark bomber. Then Redtale hustled her into the building and down into the cellar, where she found herself surrounded by dozens of people. Trule found her quickly and the two of them sat side by side, holding hands as the seconds ticked by.

After so many tense minutes, the door to the shelter opened, and a guard called for the people to come out.

As she emerged, Everys found Overturn waiting for her, his expression grim.

"What's the situation?" Everys asked.

"We tried to intercept the bomber, but by the time our skimmers caught up to it, it had already dropped its payload, a single piece of ordnance that impacted in the middle of the Shade."

Everys felt numb. "A bomb?"

"We thought so at first. But we had a bomb disposal unit inspect it, and they report that there are no explosives on it at all. Instead, it seems to be a message meant for you."

What did that mean?

"Best come see for yourself." Overturn gestured for her to follow him.

"Is that safe?" Redtale asked.

"As safe as we can make it."

Overturn's reply did not fill her with confidence, but she followed him anyway.

The area around the impact site had been evacuated, and Overturn's soldiers had hastily erected a wall of sandbags around the unexploded bomb. A group of men stood nearby, taking off padded armor. They flashed Overturn an affirmative gesture, and the strategist nodded.

"The area is secure, Blessed, and you're safe. Come with me."

He led her to the bomb, which jutted out of the ground. It was a cylinder taller than she was, with what appeared to be most of it buried beneath the ground. Portions of the black metal casing had been removed, exposing the inner workings. But although some of the exterior panels had been removed, she could still see a message, written in crisp black lettering, on its side: FOR QUEEN EVERYS'S EYES ONLY.

As she stepped up to the bomb, another panel dropped open, revealing a series of lenses. The device clicked and whirred, then made a strange chittering sound. The topmost part of the bomb fell off, hitting the ground with a clang. Everys jumped back and Redtale interposed herself between the bomb and Everys.

But the device didn't explode. Everys peeked around Redtale. A new device had been revealed, one that looked vaguely familiar. She had seen something like this before, but where?

More chittering, then the top of the bomb glowed. Ribbons of light wove through the air and coalesced into an all-too-familiar image. A hologram of an imperious Dalark man stared down at her.

"Greetings, Queen Everys," Emperor Tirigian said.

50

Everys stared up at the Dalark emperor. She knew she was supposed to be impressed, both with the holographic technology and with Tirigian's dramatic appearance. But she wasn't. Not with the theatrics—Narius had often said that the Dalark were addicted to making grand gestures that ultimately proved worthless. Not with the technology either—Tirigian had pulled a similar stunt at supposed peace talks a few months earlier. And she definitely wasn't impressed by Tirigian's appearance. Oh, he tried to project strength and power. He wore an intricately woven suit of chain mail, the individual links crafted from bronze, gold, and silver. A long cape hung from his shoulders, the most brilliant shade of purple Everys had ever seen. And the crown on the man's head was studded with dozens of precious jewels.

But Everys she saw past the illusion. It was hard to miss the dark circles under his eyes, the gauntness in his cheeks. This was a man who was slowly being consumed. For a moment, she felt a stab of pity for him.

That feeling quickly evaporated as he sneered down at her. "I heard you had retreated to live amongst the trees. I had hoped that this was but a rumor, but I see now that it is reality."

She crossed her arms and popped her hip to one side, hoping that he'd interpret that as boredom. "What do you want, Tirigian? Are you really this desperate for attention?"

He chuckled. "Hardly. I have much that could occupy my time and attention. Subjugating your precious Dynasty, for example. We have nearly brought all of it under our control, you know."

She resisted the urge to snort. That was far from the truth. She had seen Tormod and Overturn's reports. She suspected he wanted her to argue, so she ignored the provocation and waited for him to speak. Let him fill in the silence.

He shifted his weight, and a perturbed expression flitted across his face. "I suppose you wonder why I am contacting you like this?"

"Because you felt like handing over some advanced technology to us?" She flashed him a smirk. "Thanks for the holographic projector, by the way."

Tirigian glowered at her. "You would do well to moderate your tone, witch."

"You would do well to remember that I am the rightful ruler of the Xoniel Dynasty, Tirigian," Everys shot back.

"Indeed? Then why are you cowering in a forest, surrounded by savages, while Brencis rules from Bastion's ruins?"

"Not cowering. Waiting for my opportunity."

Tirigian laughed. "That, sadly, may have passed you by."

She arched a brow. What did that mean?

He smiled indulgently. "I must admit, you have impressed me, witch. When I first learned Narius had married you, I thought you had somehow seduced him through your foul magic. When my spies said he had come to genuinely care for you, I thought him foolish. But when I saw his shameful behavior when he was to marry my dear sister, I realized his affection for you was genuine, as was yours for him. I must admit, you are an impressive woman. But you are still a Siporan, the descendant of foul mages. You do not deserve to have any form of power in this world, not after what your kind has done to good people."

Everys wanted to laugh. Given how xenophobic the Dalark were, she knew what his definition of "good people" was.

"I had hoped King Brencis would put an end to you, but clearly, he is incapable of doing so. And while I could simply wait to deal with you once my forces are victorious, I do not feel comfortable allowing a Siporan witch time to scheme. So I am going to give you a chance to do what is right."

"And that is?" Everys asked.

"Unconditional surrender. I will send a skimmer to collect you from the forest and bring you to Utuaa. There you will be my... guest." The way he said that last word left no doubt what she would actually be.

"You wouldn't execute me?"

"Not until you have stood trial for your people's crimes," Tirigian said. "We are a just society in Dalark, after all."

She had no doubt he believed that. She also knew that no matter what, any trial would end in her execution.

"I'm not doing that, Tirigian. I'd be a fool to give up now."

"Not a fool at all, dear 'queen.'" Tirigian leaned down, his eyes flashing. "For if you surrender, I will reunite you with your lost love."

Her body went rigid at the obvious threat and Redtale growled next to her.

"How dare you mock my grief." Everys forced the words through her clenched throat. "This conversation is over!"

She looked over the bomb, trying to find an off switch or something she could yank to end the transmission. Before she could move, though, Tirigian held up a hand.

"Why do you think I am mocking you?" Tirigian tipped his head to one side. "This is no insult. No jest. I can and will reunite you with Narius. See?"

He stepped aside, and they shoved someone into view. The man stumbled and fell to his knees. But then Tirigian reached into the image and snared the man's hair, pulling his head up so Everys could see him. Cuts bled on the man's cheeks and lips. One eye was blackened and swollen shut. But the other...

Everys gasped. She knew that face. Bruised and swollen though it was, there was no mistaking him.

"Narius?" she whispered.

Her legs buckled underneath her. Redtale grabbed her by her elbow and steadied her. Was this a trick? An impostor or impersonator? Was Tirigian trying to fool her?

But then the man's eyes focused, and his gaze locked with hers. Recognition bloomed on his features. He tried to say something, but Tirigian cuffed him across the face. He collapsed to the ground with a pitiful moan.

A fire ignited deep in Everys's chest, burning through her body, into her hands, her feet. The world swam with flames and a righteous fury rose inside her.

"My sister somehow plucked him from Bastion and thought to use him to overthrow me. He has been my guest for the past several days. I do not think he has enjoyed his stay, yes? And now we are about to have a parade together, he and I, to show my people what happens when I am defied."

The image shifted to Tirigian, and Everys's heart stuttered. She wanted to scream at him to show her Narius again, so she could talk to him, tell him she loved him. Tell him anything, but she couldn't form the words. How was he still alive? How had Innana gotten him out of Bastion?

"You can ease his suffering. Surrender to me, and I will reunite you. You will be my personal guests. You will stand trial together. You will share the same fate. Refuse me, and you will never see him again. If you truly love your husband, Everys, end his suffering and shorten yours. Surrender."

A tremor wormed through her. She tried to contain it, but her hands trembled. Her breathing became ragged, and she briefly considered trying to tear the holographic projector apart with her bare hands. Redtale whispered something to her, but Everys couldn't hear her words over the roar in her ears.

But then, all of it vanished in an instant. Cold certainty settled on her. She looked up at Tirigian and set her jaw.

"You know, Tirigian, I've heard a lot about you," she said, her voice flat.

"Oh?" He actually seemed flattered.

"Yes. The palace staff talked about you for weeks after you left Bastion, and they all said the same thing. You're a vacuous, egotistical, vapid fool. They all laughed at you. Now I understand why."

His eyes flashed, and he drew up to his full height. But she didn't let him speak.

"And now I've also learned one more thing about you. You are an idiot."

His head snapped back as if she had slapped him.

"You accuse me of being a Siporan witch. If you thought that was true, why did you ever think it was a good idea to threaten me?"

Tirigian's eyes widened, and he stammered, as if trying to find the words.

"Because the rumors are true. I am a toratropic mage. I am the rightful ruler of the Xoniel Dynasty. And you're right, I love my husband. But my love for him is not so shallow that I would betray him. I will not surrender. Not to you, not to Brencis. Not to anyone.

"But I promise you this: you will regret what you did to my husband. I love him more than you could ever understand. Because of what you've done, I am going to make you suffer."

51

"**S**hut it off!" Tirigian's voice was laced with panic. "Shut it off!"

An ache radiated from Narius's jaw where Tirigian had slapped him. But in spite of the sleepless nights in the dungeon, in spite of the beating the guards had given him before dragging him to the throne room, Narius felt better in that one moment than he had in months.

Everys was alive.

That was all that mattered. Aches and pains he could endure. Beatings, he could weather. Knowing that Everys was still alive? He hadn't really doubted—he knew how strong she was—and what he saw just then confirmed it. The fire in her eyes. Her regal posture, greater than anything the Perfect Warrior could have hoped to be. He could endure. He could survive. And one day, they would be together again.

Tirigian whirled on him, fury blazing in his eyes. "Do not believe your woman's pretty words. She is far from here and she will never touch me."

Narius couldn't help but smile. "I've seen my wife do amazing things, Tirigian. I wouldn't be so sure you're out of her reach."

Fear flickered in Tirigian's eyes. But then the rage burned brighter. He backhanded Narius across the jaw again, and sparks flickered across Narius's vision, pain punching through his skull. Before he could recover, Tirigian followed with a sharp kick to Narius's stomach that sent him back to the floor.

Tirigian whirled on his advisers. "Prepare him for the parade! I will not allow the witch to intimidate me!"

One of the advisers—Narius thought his name was Utulgal—stepped forward, his hands fluttering in front of his chest. "Are you sure that's wise, Radiant One? Given how... agitated the populace is at present, this might be an unnecessary provocation. Perhaps we should contact Brencis instead. Perhaps we can use Narius as a bargaining point for concessions. We could trade him to Brencis for, if not outright victory, then lucrative concessions during peace talks. I'm sure King Brencis would love the chance to eliminate his rival himself."

Narius coughed, trying to make sense of what he was hearing. Why would Utulgal suggest something like that?

Tirigian rose up to his full height, his eyes indignant. "Nonsense! Why should I deprive myself of the chance to dispense my imperial justice on this pitiful wretch? I will not send him to the Dynasty. Prepare my sister and the Maotoan barbarian to join Narius on display. My people will be reminded of how strong I truly am."

Utulgal bowed sharply, then spun to relay the Emperor's orders. Two guards stomped forward and hauled Narius to his feet, but he didn't have the strength to stand on his own So they dragged him out of the throne room. Tirigian continued to bark orders at his sycophants regarding costuming and crowd control. As his voice faded, Narius was more and more convinced that Tirigian had made a colossal mistake.

Narius just hoped he would survive it.

As the hologram of Tirigian fizzled, the fire that burned inside Everys dimmed, but only a little. She may not have been able to see Narius anymore, but just the fact she knew he was still alive somehow lent her a strength she had missed for months.

But at the same time, she knew he might not be alive for long. Not with the way Tirigian had beaten him. Not with the obvious threat lingering. She had to do something to rescue him and do it now.

She marched back toward the Embassy. Redtale led the way and the soldiers once again parted to allow her to pass. She scanned their faces as she did. Thankfully, she didn't see any judgment. Many of the troops appeared to be on the verge of tears, and a few were swiping their eyes. When she was about halfway through the crowd, a cheer went up. It took her a moment to realize what the troops were saying.

"Everys! Narius! Everys! Narius!"

The chant grew louder and more boisterous. Soon, the entire Shade thundered with the soldiers' voices. By the time she reached the Embassy, Everys was walking even taller, and she felt more confident and self-assured than she had in months. She was even more determined to march through the Dynasty, across the Dalark Channel, to the gates of Utuaa itself. And she suspected that every one of the people calling her and her husband's names would be at her back.

Only she wouldn't need them. She wouldn't need to march. She had a more direct route in mind.

Challix waited for her at the Embassy. She peppered Everys with questions, but she didn't stop to answer any of them. She couldn't. Her plan was too time sensitive and her boldness too ephemeral. If she was going to do this, she had to do it now. Rewether and Redtale paused to fill Challix in. Everys climbed the steps into the Embassy and headed straight for the translation lab.

Only P'layvo was in the lab, which really didn't surprise her. From what she'd seen, she suspected that the professor had ignored the warnings and remained at her work. She looked up from a stack of scribers and smiled, her eyes bright. But her expression sobered once she got a good look at Everys.

"Blessed, is there something I can do for you?" she asked.

Everys nodded, fixing her attention on the computer terminal that housed the AI. "Has the AI learned enough to create a rune yet?"

P'layvo hesitated, her gaze skipping toward the device. "Not with any certainty or precision. Tolistan and Galan have cobbled together a few, and we're hoping to persuade the Illuminates to test them out in a controlled environment. But it is theoretically possible now. Why?"

"Show me," Everys said.

The other woman didn't hesitate. She headed over to the terminal and turned it on, bringing up a prompt.

"Anything else?" she asked.

"Show me the runes that the mage-king's agents used."

P'layvo hesitated, but she did as she was told.

"Now please leave." Everys fought to keep her expression neutral.

P'layvo gave her one last curious look before she left the room. Everys released her held breath. She knew she wouldn't be able to do what she needed to if someone was watching.

She flipped through the runes the mage-kings had used in their attack. It turned out that Hirfan had also identified the runes that Oluna had used in her escape. All of them had been collated and duly translated. She skimmed over the translations, noting the terse wording, the harsh syntax, the direct nature of those spells. While P'layvo had said that they couldn't create runes like those Everys used, she suspected that she could cobble together something like what Oluna used. These were blunt and simple. She knew that what she wanted to do would require something that brutal. She paused over the teleportation rune, reviewing its shape, its composition, noting where she hadn't gotten it quite right in the empty barrow.

But once she was certain she had seen enough, she turned to the AI's controls. Carefully, deliberately, she entered what she needed:

Make my enemies face justice.

52

The guards forced Narius to change into little more than a loin-cloth for the parade. This exposed the bruises and cuts from the beatings they had administered. Once he was in his costume, they chained him hand and foot and led him, stumbling and tripping, out of the prison to a platform hitched to a transport. The platform itself had three levels, constructed out of plain wood, shaped like a lopsided stepped pyramid. The guards forced him onto the topmost platform, where they chained him to a large ring in the floor. They cinched up his chains, keeping him in an awkward hunched position. An ache grew in his back, setting off a storm of pain from his bruised body. He finally, tentatively, knelt onto the platform, hoping that the chains would allow him to find a semicomfortable position. Much to his relief, he was able to curl into a ball even though the chains chafed at his knees.

He let out a tiny groan. The thrill of seeing Everys drained out of him, chased away by the pain that radiated through his body. Yes, she had threatened Tirigian and the Emperor had taken her seriously, but in reality, what could she do? She was all the way in the Cold Light's forest and he was here, trapped in Utuaa. Even if Everys started planning a rescue now, it could be days, maybe even weeks, before the operation could be launched. During that time, he would be at Tirigian's mercy.

So who could he count on? The people he had connected with? Maybe, but he doubted they would step in at this point. Too dangerous. Kavi? She might try, but even with her abilities, this might be too much for her.

The Singularity? He nearly dismissed the thought, but then latched on to it. Yes, the Singularity could do something if He wanted. But would He? Narius didn't know. He couldn't presume to guess. All he could do was trust.

"If You could intervene, that would be great," he murmured. "But if not... take care of the Dynasty please. Take care of Everys. Make sure they're both safe."

Footsteps rocked the platform and Narius risked a peek. He sat up when he realized that Innana and Cosena had been shoved onto the lower platforms. Innana wore a plain dress that wasn't at all regal. Cosena wore what amounted to rags that barely protected her dignity. Neither woman looked like they had been beaten, but they were covered in dirt and grime.

"Narius!" Innana called as the guards locked her chains into a loop. "Are you all right?"

That was a difficult question to even think about. So he shrugged a shoulder and winced at the lance of pain. "Been better. You?"

Innana squared her shoulders and shot a glare at the guards. "About the same."

"Any idea what's about to happen?" he asked.

She nodded grimly. "Unfortunately, yes. We're about to be the guests of honor for a full military triumph, paraded through the streets of Utuaa as conquered enemies of the Imperium."

Narius chuckled, setting off a riot of pains in his chest. "Seems a bit premature. I know for a fact that he hasn't caught Everys yet."

Innana quirked a brow in his direction, a light gleaming in her eyes. But that died quickly. "The Imperium doesn't let little details like that get in the way of its spectacle. Neither will my brother. This will let everyone know that his power is unmatched and unchallenged. And, if he follows protocol, he will put us all on trial for our supposed crimes and then carry out sentence shortly thereafter."

Cosena groaned.

"Meaning?" Narius prompted.

"We may only have a week to live. Maybe less."

Cosena moaned, louder. Narius sighed and offered up another prayer that somehow, this would all turn out all right.

By the time Everys emerged from the translation laboratory, she had everything she needed. She had memorized both the teleportation rune and the one she had created. Now all she needed was ink. Thankfully, she had a few vials, mixed from Cold Light tree sap, in her room.

When she reached her quarters, Trule and the other girls looked up, worry painted across their faces. Before they could ask anything, Everys pointed to the door. Although Trule appeared like she wanted to object, she ushered the rest of the staff out of the room.

Everys took a steadying breath. She went to the cabinet where she had stored the ink vials. Once they were in her hand, she turned around and froze.

Redtale had followed her into the room, her fists on her hips. "Where are you going, Everys?"

She straightened. "I don't answer to you."

"You don't," Redtale said. "But it's hard to protect you when I don't know what you're planning."

Everys's lip twitched, Redtale's cool condescension dredging up memories of her earliest days in the palace. "I know what I'm doing."

"Never said you didn't. Just need to know what's about to happen so I can make sure you're safe."

"But I'm not!" Everys snapped. "None of us are. Not as long as Oluna is out there. And Narius isn't safe either. I have to do something. I have to go get him. I have to... I have to..."

Her throat tightened around her words, her eyes burning as tears threatened to spill down her cheeks. Redtale studied her face, hers pinched into a frown, then she stepped forward and wrapped Everys in a tight hug.

"And if you're going after him, I'm coming with you." Redtale's voice was a comforting rumble.

Everys pulled back, surprised.

"We did just talk about this, didn't we?" Redtale said with a surprisingly gentle smile.

The objection died in Everys's throat. She had promised. And if she was about to transport herself to Utuaa, she would want someone to protect her if things went wrong. So she nodded, then opened a vial of ink. She set to work, drawing the teleportation rune in the middle of the floor. Redtale watched her, shifting her weight from side to side.

Everys couldn't blame her. With every stroke, every line, she could feel her stomach twisting and flipping. The wrongness of this rune unsettled her, but what other choice did she have?

As soon as the pattern was completed, Everys braced herself and activated the spell. Even though she knew what to expect, she still winced as the invisible claws sliced into her mind, demanding to know where she wanted to go.

A shiver slid down Everys's spine and a part of her recoiled from the prompt, as if a stranger whispered in her ear, his breath hot on her cheek. She closed her eyes and tried to picture Narius in the grips of Tirigian. Utuaa. The Dalark Imperium. That was where she wanted to go. To her husband.

The rune burst with black smoke, which rose up into the all-too-familiar pillar of inky darkness. Everys shot a look at Redtale. Her swordbound's face flickered with uncertainty, but she nodded.

Everys squared her shoulders and, with a deep breath, entered the portal.

The parade transport rumbled to life and pulled out into the streets just outside the Imperial palace. An entire legion of Dalark troops waited for them, arrayed in their sharpest dress uniforms, flechette throwers slung across their backs. They snapped to attention as the transport came up behind them, then they marched down the street, their steps like cracks of thunder. The transport and platform lurched forward, almost knocking Narius off-balance. Within a few moments, the soldiers escorted them onto a city street. The citizens of Utuaa lined each side in straight, ordered rows, like they were statues, their expressions unreadable. Were they happy? Frightened? Narius couldn't tell.

A voice speaking in Dalark boomed behind him, echoing off the surrounding buildings. While Narius couldn't understand the words, the speaker's tone was clear enough. Exultant, especially when he said the names of Narius, Innana, and Cosena.

Narius craned around and spotted another transport at the end of the procession, festooned with audiocasters. But between that vehicle and the platform was Tirigian himself, riding on a platform of his own, one trimmed in gold and pearl, bedecked with flowers and piles of what appeared to be a vast treasure. He wore gleaming armor, the kind that ancient warriors might have used. He stood tall and proud, waving to the gathered citizens. And yet they still didn't react, watching the spectacle in silence. Was that normal? Narius would have thought that a military triumph would be met with at least a little enthusiasm.

In the end, it wouldn't matter. Narius was on display for the entire Imperium to see and eventually, he knew that this would end in his death.

The frigid void whipped past Everys, yanking her hair before shoving her forward into a bright morning light. She blinked against the sun, confused for just a moment. It had been almost the end of Second Watch just a moment ago. Where had the spell taken them?

Squinting, shading her eyes with an upraised hand, Everys turned a slow circle. They stood on a tall building overlooking a city she didn't immediately recognize. The towers were oddly shaped, mostly glass and twisted in ways she didn't think would work but clearly did. And off to her left was a large, walled-in complex of some kind, with buildings that loomed over the cityscape like menacing soldiers.

Her eyes widened. The royal palace of the Dalark Imperium. They were in Utuaa. The rune had worked!

The realization hit her like a punch to the chest, but then her heart spasmed inside her, a tightening sensation that momentarily stole her breath. She gasped and staggered as pain radiated through her body, but then it flitted away. A rebuke? She had never experienced one that was so gentle.

"You okay?" Redtale asked.

Everys waved her off, then stepped to the edge of the roof. The citizens lined the streets in orderly rows, all of them turned to face the same direction. What were they waiting for?

And then she saw it: soldiers marching in unison, their right arms swinging in wide arcs, their chins jutting toward the sky. They turned a corner onto the main thoroughfare beneath Everys, never breaking stride and remaining in perfectly straight rows. Hundreds of them, maybe even thousands, strutting through Utuaa.

Following them came a military transport, painted in drab grays and greens, pulling a platform with three people kneeling on it. Two appeared to be women and the one on the topmost was...

"Narius." His name caught in Everys's throat, and she fought back an onrush of tears.

He looked so small, so broken, kneeling on the platform, his head bowed.

Then another transport turned the corner, pulling another platform. Given how ostentatiously that one was decorated, all gilding and purple banners, she knew that had to be Tirigian on display as well. A voice drifted up from below, blaring the identities of Tirigian's captives.

"So now what?" Redtale asked. "Head down to street level and hope we can find a place to get him?"

No, that wouldn't work. Everys had always known that. They'd need a way to incapacitate everyone between her and him.

She knelt and daubed more ink onto her finger. She set to work, drawing her new rune. She didn't know with absolute certainty that it'd work—and if it didn't, she didn't have a backup plan—but in her heart of hearts, she *knew*. She knew this would do what she needed it to. Even as her skin crawled as the jagged rune came together, she continued working.

"Everys..." Redtale's voice was a warning rumble.

She ignored her. Once the rune was completed, she gritted her teeth and activated the spell.

At first, nothing happened. No shimmer of light, no outward sign that the spell had done anything. Everys fell back onto her heels and stared at it. She had been so sure, so convinced that this would work, that this would—

Then a strange presence slithered up her sides, like tiny claws digging into her skin. She shuddered and twisted, trying to escape the feeling, but they only dug in deeper.

justice, yes? on those who wronged you and him and all of you, yes?

Was she imagining the voice? She might have been, but it felt so real.

"Yes," she whispered. "Justice on Tirigian. On anyone who would keep me from Narius."

The presence hesitated, then she felt a malicious glee well up inside her.

they will pay they will pay they will pay

The mantra echoed in her mind and she felt the heat drain from her body, siphoned through her chest as if being consumed by the rune. She tried to back away from it, but she found herself held in place.

"Wait..." Her voice was sucked away as if caught in a windstorm.

they will pay they will pay they will pay they will pay they will pay

Redtale shouted her name, but the sound barely registered. Everys's arms and legs felt like they were encased in metal, held in rigid place. And then unseen hands lifted her from the roof, the heat pouring from her body into the rune.

they will pay they will pay they will pay

Someone shouted from the street below. At first, Everys thought that it was a cheer, but soon, the cry was joined by another voice. Then another. And another. As more voices joined in, Everys realized they weren't happy. They weren't celebrating. They were screaming, agonized shrieks.

and they will die

53

N arius sighed and shifted his weight, trying to regain the feeling in his legs. Over the past hour, he had discovered the most comfortable position available to him was to kneel, his back bowed so that his forehead almost touched the rough wood beneath him. He considered simply collapsing into a tiny ball, but one of the guards who marched alongside the platform snapped at him when he tried. So he remained hunched over, his back radiating with agony, his knees rubbed raw by the platform.

Then someone in the crowd shrieked. Narius's head snapped up and he looked around. It was so sudden, so sharp, unexpected, but he couldn't spot the offender. The guards on either side of the platform drew their weapons and scanned the crowd.

Then there was another scream. And another. People on both sides of the road wailed in apparent pain. Narius thought he spotted one of them, an older woman who clawed at her neck as if being strangled. Narius sucked in a sharp breath. What was happening?

Then Innana collapsed to the platform in front of him, her fingers bent like claws. She thrashed against the chains, as if trying to free herself or tear at her body. An inhuman scream bubbled up from her. Narius gaped at her, then realized that Cosena was convulsing as well. And was that... was that *smoke* rising from the Maotoan princess? It looked like it, black steam rising from her body.

One of the guards shouted something and whirled around, running back toward Tirigian's platform. Only he didn't make it, stumbling and collapsing to the road. Narius twisted to see what had caught his attention. Tirigian was writhing, his back arched and his legs twisted at odd angles. The same black miasma rose from his body. Narius's mouth popped open. What was going on?

He craned his head around, trying to examine as much of the crowd as he could. More and more people were succumbing to whatever this plague was, including the soldiers marching at the front. So why wasn't it affecting him?

No, wait, there was someone else in the crowd who didn't seem to have been struck down. An individual threw aside a cloak and raced up onto the platform. Narius shied away from whoever it was, worried they were about to attack him, but then he realized who it was.

"Kavi!" he gasped.

She shot him a thin smile as she knelt next to Innana, looking her over. *You all right?*

"I think so. What's going on?"

Someone cast a rune. Powerful. Evil.

Narius's eyes widened. Like the mage-kings? Why would they be here? Why would they attack the Dalark like this?

He scanned the crowd again. Every victims' body smoked, the vapors swirling together and rising above the street and converging at the top of a nearby building. And at the top...

His eyes widened. A figure hovered over the roof, arms wide, head tipped back as if exulting in what he was doing. That had to be the person responsible.

"Kavi!" he shouted. He jerked his head toward the building when she looked. "Can you do something to stop this?"

Kavi glanced at Innana, and then nodded grimly. *I'll try.*

With that, she slid off the platform and hurried toward the building. Narius wished he could urge her on, make her move faster. Because he suspected that if she didn't, soon the streets would be filled with corpses.

"Everys!" Redtale's voice was barely perceptible over the maelstrom's roar. "Stop!"

She would if she could, but she didn't know how. The rune held her in place, a gnawing void that stormed in front of her. She had only meant for Tirigian and his lackeys to be affected, but this rune attacked everyone, its hunger expanding with every second, claiming more and more victims. Although she couldn't be absolutely certain, she somehow knew that its effect was radiating out further and further into the city.

But she couldn't stop. It wasn't just that the rune had somehow locked her into place. The echoes of pain, agony, and terror of each victim poured through her into the rune. The spell was using her as a lens, a focal point, dredging up all of her anger toward the Imperium. Not just for what Tirigian did to Narius, but for the way they had nearly killed Narius on Maotoa. How Innana had almost stolen Narius from her. How their animosity toward the Dynasty had shaped so much of her life. How they had helped to destroy Nekek the Bright. They would face justice for it all.

Her justice. Her wrath. Her anger.

Only she didn't feel that anger anymore. But the spell wouldn't stop. Not until it, not she, was satisfied.

Strong hands grasped her legs. Redtale? Had to be. But when her Swordbound pulled, Everys didn't budge. Instead, she felt a fire blaze across her legs and suddenly, Redtale let go and cried out.

The spell's focus split. No longer just the Dalark. How much pain had Redtale caused her over the past year? Her condescension when Everys first arrived at the palace. The way she abandoned her when she needed her most. Her betrayal by founding the Untested, supplying fighters for Narius's *harsannon*. She had to face justice for what she had done as well. And she would.

Redtale's startled shout turned into a strangled scream. Everys struggled to break free, but she couldn't. She was trapped. By the anger. By the hatred. By the pain that she had clung to for so long...

Then she spotted motion out of the corner of her eye. Something flickered through her peripheral vision and it sounded like there was a puff of air near the rune.

The draining sensation disappeared instantly and Everys dropped to the roof. Her knees buckled, and she collapsed into a heap. With a groan, she sat up. The world swam and juked around her and she pressed both hands to her head to dispel the dizziness that washed over her. Someone towered over her. Not Redtale; she groaned nearby. Everys squinted and willed her eyes to focus.

"H-Hirfan?" she whispered.

The Illuminate stared down at her, his mouth pressed into a grim line.

"Let's get you out of here, Blessed." He spat her title like it tasted sour.

She was in no condition to argue, so she nodded. Hirfan helped her to her feet, then stepped over to Redtale and did the same. Then he produced a vial of ink and drew a rune on the roof. Everys shied away from it when she realized he was sketching out a teleportation rune.

"Is that a good idea?" Her voice was raw, as if she had been screaming for hours.

He snorted. "Unless you have a skimmer waiting on standby, it's really our only option, isn't it?"

She wanted to scowl at him, but he ignored her. She shuddered as he worked, then looked over at the plague rune. Much to her surprise, the pattern was still there, but it was coated in a strange gray dust. She took a step closer to examine it, but before she could, what felt like a spike made of ice drove itself from the top of her head down through her neck and into her chest. A painful chill, like her body was being flash frozen, snapped through the rest of her body. She nearly collapsed to the roof, her arms wrapped around her middle. Redtale caught her and kept her steady as the pain grew and sharpened, then vanished. Tears streamed down her face and she looked up at Hirfan.

"If you're looking for sympathy for getting rebuked, you won't find any from me," he muttered.

He cast the rune and the pillar of black smoke burst from the roof. Hirfan didn't wait to see if she followed. He merely stepped into the portal and disappeared. Redtale helped Everys stagger toward the pillar. As she stepped through, she heard the door to the roof bang open. She glanced over her shoulder to see a young woman with a heart-shaped face burst out of the stairs. The other woman's eyes widened. She bared her teeth, then rushed at them.

Redtale pushed Everys through the portal and stumbled in after her.

They tumbled into Everys's quarters in the Embassy. Hirfan adjusted his clothes, and then winced, his face twisting with pain, most likely a rebuke from using the teleportation spell.

Redtale helped Everys sit on one of the couches. Everys smoothed her hair and then gave Hirfan her full attention.

"Thank you for your help." She winced at the sound of her voice. She needed something to drink.

"I didn't do it out of loyalty, Blessed," Hirfan shot back. "I was only doing my duty."

Redtale bristled, taking a step forward, but Everys waved her back.

"What duty would that be?" Everys prompted. Maybe she could finally figure out why Hirfan was so hostile.

He considered her, peering down his nose, then sighed. "Have you ever heard of the *zetlashab'uem*, Blessed?"

She frowned. She recognized the Siporan ancient language, just not the word. She shook her head.

Hirfan scowled. "Of course not. It means Shadowbreaker and your kind drove us out of Nekek the Bright two thousand years ago."

"'My kind?'" Everys repeated.

If Hirfan picked up on that, he didn't let on. "Siporans who recklessly use the runes without thinking through the consequences. Or did I misunderstand what you were doing?"

Everys glowered at him, stung by the accusation.

"When the Singularity first gave the runes to the Siporans, He also charged some of us to police their use. That was us, the *zetlashab'uem*. We reviewed what the scholars researched. We supervised what the celebrants did in the Scriptotum. We made sure that the runes were used in a proper way, one that pleased the Singularity. But after Annaeus discovered the *ur-keleshen*, he drove us from Nekek the Bright."

"So a mage-king did it," Everys countered.

"But none of the others objected. They were all too pleased to send us away. We wandered Ehun until we found refuge here, in the forest. When the Illuminates arrived several centuries later, we struck a partnership with them. They could experiment. We would stand ready to intervene if needed."

Everys shifted in her seat. That explained much of his animosity toward her. But it didn't change the fact that he had saved her and stopped her from doing something incredibly evil.

"I understand. And while I can't change what happened to your ancestors, all I can do is thank you for how you helped me," Everys said. "And I promise to do better."

Hirfan studied her face, then snorted again. "We'll see."

With that, Hirfan strode out of the room. As soon as he left, Trule and the girls peeked inside. They quickly scurried in and fretted and fussed over her. Everys let them, trying to shake off the last vestiges of what the rune did to her. But she couldn't quite, because a small part of her was upset that Hirfan had stopped her. A part of her had loved every second of that plague rune and what it could do to the people who had wronged her. A part of her wished she could go back and finish what she started. Show them her power. Show them her anger. Show them her justice.

No. She shook her head, trying to dislodge the thoughts. But they stubbornly remained. Finally, she shuddered. What would Narius think of what she'd done?

54

Narius pulled on his chains, trying to slip his hands free, but he just couldn't quite squeeze them out. Kavi had been in that building for so long—it'd felt like hours—and still the people on either side of the street convulsed and thrashed, the strange black miasma rising from their bodies like they were all smoldering. Their shrieks and cries had become a deafening cacophony that assaulted his ears...

And then the sound ended.

He stopped struggling. Narius risked a look at the surrounding crowd. Whatever plagued them had apparently released them. They were swaying back up to their feet, shaking out their arms and legs, gingerly touching their heads and chests. A few had bloodied faces or hands, having scraped them on the road. Some staggered and collapsed, clutching at knees and feet and elbows, crying out with new pain. Innana and Cosena recovered as well, picking themselves up from the platform, although they couldn't straighten completely due to their chains.

He twisted and saw that, unfortunately, Tirigian was recovering as well. He had clearly been shaken by the experience, his costuming askew and his impeccable hair mussed. But the moment they locked eyes, some of the fear vanished, replaced by fire in the Emperor's eyes.

Tirigian shouted and order. He tried to stand up, but he was tangled in his robes and nearly tripped. He barked the same words at the nearby soldiers again. The guards hesitated, glancing at each other, but then hustled to surround Tirigian's platform. The transport slowly backed away from the parade as the guards clambered onto the platform, assuming defensive positions around the Emperor.

Narius's breath turned ragged. Tirigian wasn't even going to make sure his people were all right? He was going to retreat behind the walls of his palace?

"Do you see?" The question burst from his mouth before he could think about it. He knelt so he could take a deeper breath, and then bellowed, "Do you see?"

The crowd went still, all eyes on him.

"Do you see what kind of a man your emperor is? His people suffer, and he flees. Is this really the man you want to lead the Imperium?"

Did they understand what he was saying? He wished he could speak Dalark, but hopefully enough people could translate. From what he could see, some in the crowd were translating what he said, passing the message on.

"You have a better choice right here: Princess Innana! I have seen her heart. I have seen her passion. I have seen what she values, and that is you. All of you. You don't have to have a leader who preens and postures and then runs when things become difficult. You don't have to have a leader who doesn't care about you."

Innana looked over her shoulder at him, her eyes wide. Narius gritted his teeth. He couldn't stop now, even though her eyes screamed a warning to him. If he was going to die, he'd rather do it now on his own terms than as Tirigian's plaything.

"You have a choice," he shouted. "It's yours. Not mine. Not his. What kind of Imperium do you want? Now is your chance. Seize it!"

Silence fell over the street. Narius hung his head and closed his eyes. There was no point in trying to make eye contact, no point in trying to read the crowd's reaction. His entire future was in the hands of the people who stared at him.

No, not just them. The Singularity's too. And while Narius knew that should give him comfort and encouragement, it didn't. Not as much as he thought it should. He bit his lower lip and squeezed his eyes shut.

Someone shouted.

Far ahead of the platform, a man with a somewhat familiar voice barked what sounded like a command, then repeated it several times. Narius looked up, frowning. Then ice lodged in his stomach. The soldiers who had been marching in front of his platform snapped to attention, then readied their weapons. As one, they turned to face

Narius. He gritted his teeth and closed his eyes again, waiting for the flechettes to rip through him.

Instead, the ground thundered as the soldiers charged, the platform rocking hard enough that Narius was almost knocked off-balance. Narius flinched, then sank to his knees. He bowed his head and closed his eyes, ready for death to finally claim him. The crowd screamed and shouted, roaring in anger, and yet the soldiers still didn't act. What were they waiting for?

"Narius."

Wait, he knew that voice. He looked up and realized that Wullis Planka stood over him. Soldiers surrounded them, but their weapons were pointed outward. No, not outward. Toward Tirigian's platform. Planka turned to one of the soldiers and shouted an order in Dalark. That soldier hurried forward, produced a small laser cutter, and burned through Narius's chains. When the chain broke with an audible clank, Narius nearly toppled over. Planka caught him and helped him up before stepping down to Innana, personally cutting through hers. He helped her to her feet, then held out a hand. A soldier handed him a blanket, which he threw over her shoulders. After several of his troops surrounded her, he returned to Narius's side, his face grim.

"I apologize for my tardiness, sir. Seeds planted deep take long to sprout."

"I'm glad for the harvest, regardless of timing," Narius said. "What are you doing here?"

"Tirigian wanted the Hero of the Southern Expanse to lead the troops in his triumphant parade. His mistake. As was putting you on display." Planka motioned around them. "Your harvest is larger than you think."

Narius looked around, frozen in absolute wonder. The crowd wasn't paying attention to him. Instead, they had turned on Tirigian, throwing rocks or trash or whatever they could find at the rapidly retreating Emperor. Some members of the crowd surged after him, but many others were chanting something over and over. It took Narius a moment to realize what they were saying:

"Innana! Innana! Innana!"

A laugh bubbled up his throat. He took up the shout as well, pumping his fist in the air. Innana stared at the crowd with wide eyes, then schooled her features and stood taller. Even though she was wrapped in a blanket, she looked more regal than Tirigian could ever hope to. More than Narius had ever been, he was certain.

"While I appreciate your enthusiasm, sir, we should really get you off the street," Planka said. "Her as well. I have no doubt Tirigian will send troops to put this down."

Narius nodded. "You have a safe place in mind?"

Planka grimaced. "Not yet, but I have some ideas. You ready to go?"

"Not yet," Narius said. "I sent a... a friend into that building. We'll want her to come with us."

Planka glanced where Narius indicated, then nodded. "We can't wait forever. Two minutes."

Narius wanted to object, but he had no authority, and Planka was correct. If Kavi didn't emerge soon, they'd just have to hope she'd catch up.

But then Kavi burst out of the building. She scanned the street, clearly taken aback at the brewing revolt. She shook it off and slipped through the crowd, ducking and weaving around the people until she made it to the platform. The soldiers tried to stop her. At Narius's prompting, Planka ordered her through.

Kavi's chest was heaving and her face was covered with sweat. She met Narius's questioning gaze and shook her head. She tried to sign something, but Narius couldn't follow most of what she was trying to communicate.

"Did you see who they were?" Narius asked.

It was an— She grimaced, then carefully spelled out. *I-X-A-C-T-L with no...* Another sign he didn't understand. When she saw the confusion, she drew large shapes at her temples.

"Horns?" he prompted.

She nodded.

An Ixactl with no horns? His eyes widened. Redtale? Sure, there were probably more than just one Ixactl who didn't have horns, but how many would have a connection with toratropic magic. But if that was Redtale...

"Did you see anyone else up there?" he asked.

Kavi waggled her hands. *Thought I did, but didn't get a good look. Maybe a woman?*

"What did she look like?" Narius's voice was insistent, almost harsh, but he couldn't help it. He had to know!

Kavi stepped back, worry flitting across her face. *I didn't get a good look at her. I'm sorry.*

He ground his teeth. A woman, capable of toratropic magic, in the presence of an Ixactl with missing horns? His mind made the connection almost immediately. But his heart rejected it. Everys would never use a rune to cause this much suffering. It had to be someone else. A coincidence. Or someone was trying to frame her. That had to be it. Whoever was behind all of this was trying to tear Everys and him apart, make him doubt the only person he could completely trust.

"Sir?" Planka prompted. "We have to go."

Narius jolted at the quiet words, but then nodded. "Of course."

Planka turned to his troops, calling out orders and motioning for the soldiers to form a protective cordon around the platform. Narius sat down hard, his face pinched into a frown. He had to get home. He had to prove to himself that Kavi had been mistaken. Because she had to be mistaken.

Right?

55

Mama opened the door to the cabin almost immediately after Everys knocked. Her eyes widened, and she stepped aside without a word. Everys felt like she was slinking back home after breaking curfew. She ducked her head as she stepped inside.

As Everys did, Galan jumped out of her chair, her surprised expression mirroring Mama's. Galan started to say something, then caught herself. Everys winced. The researchers must have figured out what she had done. Galan had probably seen the plague rune. And Hirfan wouldn't have hesitated to tell everyone what she had been doing in Utuaa.

Galan's expression hardened. She crossed her arms. "Is anyone still alive in Utuaa?"

The question stung, especially since Everys didn't really know the answer. She didn't think anyone had died; she was pretty sure that she would have felt that through the rune. But who knew what had happened in the aftermath?

"Galan..." Mama's voice carried a familiar warning.

"No, Mama, she doesn't have an excuse. Do you know what she did, what she tried to do?"

"I wasn't trying to..." The excuse died in Everys's mouth. She did want to hurt people, just not that many.

"There's a reason why we've had to hide what our people are still capable of for so long. And what's the first thing that you do after Masruq revealed what you are? You went to Utuaa and tried to kill everyone!" Galan said.

Everys's cheeks burned. She was grateful that Redtale had elected to stay outside of the cabin. Everys wasn't sure how she would have reacted to their queen getting scolded by her older sister.

"Galan, enough." Mama turned to face Everys. "Were you rebuked for what you did?"

Everys winced at the memory of the icy pain shredding her from the inside out. "I was."

"And are you sorry for what you did?" Mama continued. "Do you recognize the wrong and do you intend to avoid it in the future?"

"I am." She tried to shove down the quiet voice that insisted that it wasn't that big of a problem, that she could do it again and be more focused.

Mama turned back to Galan. "Anything else?"

Galan gaped at her and made a vague gesture toward Everys. "Mama!"

"What would you have me do, Galan?" Mama asked. "Send her to bed without her supper? Tell her advisers that she's been a naughty girl and can't go to any meetings for a week? Besides, I understand why she did it. I heard what that awful Tirigian said about her husband. If something similar had happened to your father and I had the resources and abilities, I might have done the same."

Galan tried to protest further.

"Enough!" Mama's voice rose to a shout. "Legarr is dead and Favid has been taken by the Cold Light. I can't lose anyone else!"

Everys winced at the pain woven through Mama's voice. Galan's mouth clicked shut.

"I never said I approve of what Everys did. I said I understand it. There is a difference." Mama smoothed her dress. "Now I've made kretsel and there's more than enough for you, Everys, and your guards."

Everys brought Redtale into the cabin and they all sat down around the table. The kretsel, a traditional Siporan dish consisting of pan-fried fish topped with a tangy sauce, was delicious as usual, but the meal was profoundly uncomfortable. Galan picked at her food, not meeting anyone's gaze. Redtale didn't say much, but whether that was out of duty or politeness, Everys couldn't tell. Mama tried to fill the void with tales of what she had been doing. Apparently she had volunteered to help new refugees settle into the Shade. As for Everys, she felt the weight of both Mama and Galan's disapproval throughout the meal. What should have been a warm experience had turned into a reminder of how close she had come to becoming the very thing she was supposed to fight against.

When dinner wrapped up, Everys decided she wanted to stay in the cabin rather than return to the Embassy. After everything that had happened, she wanted to be close to her family, if only for one night. Redtale went to coordinate the guard, leaving the three women to find a way to share a space that had only been designed for one person. Eventually and at Everys's insistence, Mama and Galan took the bed while Everys tried to make a nest on a wooden bench.

Within an hour of their turning in, Mama and Galan had drifted off. Sleep eluded Everys, but not because of the bench. She had found the right amount of blankets and pillows to get comfortable. No, the memories of what happened in Utuaa bubbled through her mind all night. The screams. The insatiable hunger of the plague rune. Galan's revulsion and judgment. Worse, those memories wove together with Oluna's words. How rebukes would become more bearable, how casting forbidden runes or using blood would become easier. And she realized how true it was. Even now, a part of her wanted to go back and finish the job.

And why shouldn't she? They were at war with the Imperium. Yes, attacking civilians wasn't right, but from what she had seen while traveling with Redtale, the Dalark hadn't been careful with the Dynasty's civilians. They had sown fear and chaos throughout the Dynasty's holdings. Why shouldn't they get a taste of what they had brewed?

Besides, she had gone there to rescue her husband. How could anyone fault her for that? He would know how to end all of this. Wasn't that what needed to happen? If she had succeeded, the war, the crisis with Oluna and her co-conspirators, all of it would have been over and they could have finally found peace. She had heard Overturn and other strategists talk about "tolerable losses." Maybe this was just another example of that.

Maybe she had gone too far in Utuaa. But she had been trying to do the right thing. That had to count for something.

Everys didn't know when she drifted off to sleep, but all too soon, Mama was bustling through the cabin to make breakfast, not just for them but also for the guards stationed outside the cabin. While she worked, Galan clambered out of bed and glowered at the room. Everys stifled a chuckle. Her sister had never loved mornings.

Their gazes met across the cabin. Galan frowned, but then she stumbled over to Everys.

After several minutes of studying the floor, Galan looked up. "I'm... I'm sorry, Everys. I thought a lot about what Mama said, and she's right. I don't know what you're experiencing or how I would respond. I'm just worried about you."

Everys smiled and squeezed her sister's shoulder. "Thank you. I appreciate it."

They fell silent, which was an odd mixture of both awkward and comforting at the same time. Finally, though, Galan offered her a small smile.

"So what are you going to do now?"

"I don't know how, but I'm getting my husband back."

"I'm not trying to drop rocks on you, Blessed. Honest," Overturn said. "But there's nothing we can do."

Everys's fingers curled into fists as the strategist gestured toward the map table. She glared at the displayed information as if it was the map's fault. She had hoped that they could figure out a way to rescue Narius using conventional means.

"This is the latest intelligence we have about troop deployments within the Dynasty's holdings," Overturn continued. "As of right now, there are three major fronts in the ongoing conflict between Brencis's troops and the Dalark invaders: the Plotan Expanse, the Grerid Flats, and the Edge and Shessu Heartland. The first two are easy enough to understand. The Dalark have pushed up through the Demilitarized Zone into the Expanse and they continue to land troops from Maotoa in the Flats. We're not sure where the armies came from in the Edge and Heartland, but this effectively cuts off any land route we could take to the Dalark Channel. We would encounter troops from both sides of the conflict. And if we were to march out of the forest's southern border through the Right Highlands, we'd likely catch the attention of Brencis."

"We couldn't cross through the Water Bearer's Repose?" Everys asked.

Overturn shook his head. "We don't have enough ships to transport our troops. Even if we did, we're hearing reports of Maotoan piracy in the Repose. Not sure how they got there, but they're there."

"Could we find mercenaries to rescue him?" Challix asked.

"That is a possibility, but not a wise one," Tormod said from his perch in the room's corner. "I have contacts with several. A few might be able to accomplish what we want. But once they realize they have the Dynasty's rightful king in their clutches, I couldn't guarantee they wouldn't return him to Tirigian or hand him over to Brencis for a greater reward."

"How about international pressure?" Everys asked. "We go to Elscontin or Tomma and ask them to put pressure on the Imperium to return Narius."

This time, it was Challix who objected. "I don't think that would work. The other major nations have shown a great deal of reluctance to say anything in this conflict. The best we could expect is silence."

Everys ground her teeth, scowling at the map. A few of her advisers whispered to each other and she could feel the weight of their stares on her. Did they know what she had done? Did they approve? In some ways, it didn't matter if they. She was queen, after all. And they should all want the same thing, for Narius to be brought home. She couldn't leave him in Utuaa. There had to be a way for her to—

Her eyes widened, and her head snapped up so she could stare at Tormod. Maybe there was a way.

"Thank you, everyone, for your input, but I don't want to give up just yet. I want you to keep working on this problem. If there's a way to rescue Narius, I want to find it. Dismissed." She kept her gaze locked on Tormod, communicating silently that he should stay.

The rest of her advisers filed out of the room, and thankfully, Tormod seemed to have gotten the message. He watched the others leave.

As soon as the room was empty, Everys circled around the table, heading for Tormod. "When the mage-kings' agents attacked the Moonslight Festival, you teleported into the Shade. And you did it again when Oluna attacked me. You've been able to do that this whole time!"

Tormod sighed, then he nodded. "But it's not as simple as you're thinking it is, Blessed."

"What do you mean?"

Tormod rolled up his left sleeve, then set his arm on the table and twisted it so his palm faced up. "Are you familiar with the *reshi'zhad* oath?"

Everys frowned and shook her head. Then she spotted what Tormod must have wanted to show her: a tattoo, almost nestled in the crook of his elbow. It was old, faded, but she still recognized the loops and whorls of a rune.

"In ancient times, some toratropic mages would undergo a ritual where a rune was etched into their skin. It was a way of dedicating themselves fully to the Singularity and his will. For some, the *reshi'zhad* was a temporary thing. For others, like me, the oath is permanent. Because I am *reshi'zhad*, I am given a unique ability few others have, but to use it, I must forgo certain aspects of life. Marriage, for instance.

"When activated, I am sent almost instantly to where I need to be. A handy quality for a spy to have. I've used this rune to serve two kings and, now, one queen, and I can honestly say I wouldn't be the master of shadows without it." He rolled his sleeve down again, obscuring the rune.

"So you could use your tattoo to get him?" she prompted.

Tormod sighed and hung his head. "I wish it were that simple, Blessed. But I don't think that will work for two reasons: First, I've never tried to bring someone with me. I don't even know if that's possible. But more importantly, there is no guarantee I would be able to help Narius."

Everys frowned. "But you said that sends you where you need to be."

He nodded emphatically. "Yes, Blessed, where I need to be. As determined by the Singularity, not by me. That's been my challenge when using this for the Dynasty. Where I think I need to be is rarely where I wind up."

What did that even mean? Her brow furrowed as she tried to decipher what he was saying.

"Perhaps I can explain it best with this story. When I was a young man, I secured a job in the Bastion constabulary. I was able to use my tattoo to bring me to key pieces of evidence or even locate criminals. As a result, I gained a reputation of being a miracle worker, which brought me to the attention of the Ministry of Shadows. I was officially recruited by Lord Tiyson Samag, my predecessor, in the early days of King Girai's reign.

"During those days, there was increased tension between the Dynasty and Rioka. While it never truly became public knowledge, most inside Girai's administration expected the situation to turn to all-out war."

Everys frowned. What did this have to do with anything?

Tormod offered her a thin smile and held up a calming hand. "Lord Tiyson heard that Rioka was developing a fleet of submersibles capable of positioning short-range ballistic missiles anywhere in the ocean. With that technology, they could devastate Bastion with little to no warning.

"As you can imagine, Lord Tiyson was frantic to find any information about this fleet, the technology, the Riokan plans, anything. I was stationed in Rioka and I had my orders: find out whatever I could. I used my tattoo, expecting that I would jump into Riokan high command. Instead, I found myself in Gliaton, a major port city in Tomma. I returned to Rioka and tried again, only to wind up in Gliaton again."

"Why?" Everys asked.

Tormod chuckled. "I wondered that too. I worried that I had made some sort of mistake. But eventually, I remembered the terms of my *reshi'zhad* oath. The tattoo will take me to where I need to be. So why did the Singularity think I needed to be in Gliaton? Rather than return to Rioka, I stayed and did some digging. Do you know what I found?

"It turned out the Tomman government had fed the intelligence on this Riokan missile system to Lord Tiyson's agents. The Tommans were hoping to sell submarine hunting technology to our navy. All in the interests of helping us protect ourselves from the Riokan threat, of course. Never mind the substantial markup they had engineered because of our desperate need."

Everys gaped at him.

"When I returned to Bastion with that information, Lord Tiyson passed it along to King Girai. He shared it with the Golden Revolution to prove that both the Dynasty and Rioka had been manipulated. As a result, the Riokans backed down, and relations between us and them normalized." Tormod chuckled ruefully. "Rioka fought a very brief war with Tomma over what happened, but that ended when the Tommans handed over the responsible parties so the Golden Revolution could execute them personally."

She winced, even though she knew the Tommans deserved it.

"If I hadn't trusted the Singularity's guidance in bringing me to Gliaton, the Dynasty and Rioka might well have gone to war. And that's a lesson that's been borne out repeatedly in my career. I don't always understand why I jump to where I do, but there is always a reason. His reason, not mine."

"But don't you think that the Singularity would want Narius to be safe?" Everys insisted.

Tormod studied her face and she could feel her cheeks burn. Did he know? Had someone told him? Would he refuse because of what she did?

"Perhaps He does. But if there's one thing I've learned in my many years of serving both the Dynasty and the Singularity, what I consider important often isn't the same as what He does."

Everys started to object, but Tormod raised a hand.

"I am not saying no, Blessed. I am open to the possibility. But I'd like some time to reflect. Can I please have a few days?"

Everys sat up straighter. "He may not have a few days!"

Tormod sighed. "I understand the urgency, Blessed. I do. I will do my best to hurry my preparations, but I do need that time. Please."

She ground her teeth. She wanted to go now, to have Narius home by the end of the day or the next at the latest. But she nodded curtly.

He rose. "Then I'll take my leave. I'll have my answer in a few days. Be patient, Blessed. I don't believe the Singularity is done with either of you yet."

56

When the time came, Quartus and Yusra went to Gilded Lock. But instead of arriving at the beginning of Second Watch, they did so at the beginning of First Watch, taking up positions near The Shessu's Burden to see if they could spot Urett's arrival. Yusra had pointed out that this could easily be a trap. Quartus didn't think it was—Urett didn't seem clever enough to pull off something like that—but it wouldn't hurt to be cautious.

At the end of First Watch, Yusra met him at the mouth of the alley. "Anything?"

He shook his head.

"Me neither," she whispered. "So do we go in?"

He considered it, then nodded. "I think it's worth hearing him out."

They didn't bother checking the front doors of the abandoned restaurant. Instead, they stole around to the back and tested a door in the alley. It turned out to be unlocked. Quartus eased it open and Yusra slipped through first. A second later, she quietly beckoned him inside.

A thick layer of dust covered everything in the kitchen, which surprised Quartus. He had assumed that The Shessu's Burden had closed shortly after the cataclysm, but it looked like it hadn't been open in years, maybe even a decade.

One wall of the kitchen was an empty fish tank, allowing Quartus a view of the dining room. About a dozen round tables were scattered through the room, each one with chairs stacked neatly on top, as if whoever had abandoned the restaurant had expected to open it again soon. A solitary figure sat at the center table, his back to the kitchen. Quartus smiled grimly. Bad operational security. That had to be Urett.

He and Yusra quietly slipped into the dining room, then approached the man. Sure enough, it was Urett.

"So how'd you get here?" Quartus asked when he stood just behind him.

To his credit, Urett didn't flinch at the sudden question. He turned and looked up at Quartus, then gestured to the two chairs opposite him. "I have my own way in. Please, join me. I'd offer you refreshments, but the kitchen is closed."

Quartus stalked around the table and sat down. Yusra stood next to him, but didn't sit. Instead, she scanned the room, her features pinched into a frown.

"So what were you doing at Brencis's Day of Accountability, Urett? Looking for a new master?" Quartus asked, his tone harsh.

Urett glared at him. "Hardly. I would never serve anyone but your brother."

"So why were you there?" Quartus demanded.

"Looking for allies. You and I aren't the only ones dissatisfied with Brencis's reign."

"Like the insurrectionists?" Yusra commented.

"Like them, yes." A smile flickered across Urett's face. "I have found a few who want to act and are making plans to do so soon. A group of nobles are planning to approach Brencis and request he abdicate the throne."

"'Request?'" Quartus quirked a brow.

Urett shrugged. "They know he likely won't be willing, so they're planning to offer him certain concessions to entice him."

"Concessions?" Heat flashed through Quartus. The nobles thought they could negotiate? Were they stupid? No, he already knew the answer to that question. Not stupid, just incredibly short-sighted.

"The rumors I've heard suggest something like a pardon from the new ruler, followed by a swift exile to a foreign nation."

"And if Brencis abdicates?" Yusra asked. "Who would replace him?"

"A few names have been suggested. Trin Samag. Johenrath Japaul. Possibly Klamont Wendly. The most likely choice, though, is Arkid Gardan."

Quartus groaned. None of those possibilities were good. He didn't know much about Lord Johenrath, and that obscurity made him unlikely to succeed. The others would all make horrible kings, although Gardan might at least be a tolerable disappointment.

Urett smiled sadly. "Yes, I am aware how lacking those choices are."

"There are so many better options," Quartus said. "Perhaps Anadda Leedeke?"

"Lady Leedeke died when the Dalark tried to conquer Fort Wyne," Urett said.

He hadn't heard. How many holes had been blasted into the Dynasty's hierarchy? Who would rise to take those places?

"If those options are so bad, there has to be someone," Yusra said.

"There is," Urett said slowly, his gaze settling on Quartus.

Quartus's eyes widened. He looked between Urett and Yusra, then held up his hands. "Absolutely not. I will not be king."

"You'd be a good choice," Urett said. "Narius's brother and legal successor, the last son of King Girai."

Quartus laughed. He'd make a horrible king. He had wanted nothing more than to escape the palace with all of its demands and expectations. How could anyone expect him to go back there?

"Absolutely not!" Quartus snapped.

"We felt we had to ask before we put forward a different candidate," Urett continued.

Wait, who was "we?"

The room exploded with activity. A dozen people emerged from under the covered tables, flechette throwers at the ready. Quartus froze, his hands up at his side. Yusra dropped into a defensive crouch. Urett, for his part, didn't even flinch.

"You set us up?" Quartus demanded.

"Not at all," Urett replied coolly.

Quartus froze, but then he recognized the soldiers who surrounded them. That was Zar, the head of Narius's King's Guard. And Farga, Narius's Swordbound. Many of the people surrounding them were members of the royal guards who had served Narius and Everys.

Then he realized that a person standing before him wasn't armed. Instead, her hands were tucked behind her back, her posture rigid. Like the soldiers, she wore simple clothing, but she still radiated authority and calm. And he instantly recognized her.

"Auriel Zammit?" he breathed.

She tipped her head back and regarded him coolly. Then her lips twitched into a slight smile.

"At ease," she said.

Immediately, the soldiers put up their weapons and relaxed their postures. Zammit turned a critical eye to Quartus, and he felt like he was about to wither under her scrutiny. He tried to sit taller, prouder, to impress her, but then realized what he was doing. So he purposefully slouched.

She chuckled. "Still the same Quartus."

"I'm surprised to see you here," Quartus said. "Aren't you still Governor-General of Bastion?"

"Of course," she said, pacing a circle around him. "But if Brencis knew what else I was doing, he'd have other labels for me. Like 'saboteur.' Or 'traitor.'"

Yusra's eyes widened. "You're the leader of the insurrection?"

Zammit nodded. "I found plenty of people who are dissatisfied with Brencis's reign, people who were ready to act. Some, like Zar and Farga, are doing so out of loyalty to King Narius and Queen Everys. Others are fed up with Brencis's ineptitude. We even have a contact inside the palace who is feeding us intelligence for our operations. We've made ourselves quite the nuisance."

"And now you're going to become queen? Is that it?" Quartus asked.

"Not exactly," Zammit said. "I am not a noble. If anything, I would serve as regent or maybe steward until a suitable ruler is found."

"Such as if Queen Everys were to return," Zar said.

"If that should happen and the nobles were to accept her, yes," Zammit said. "If not, then another of the nobles' choosing."

Quartus nodded thoughtfully. That was a pretty good plan. The nobles would likely bicker and argue over who should claim the throne, with negotiations and betrayals flying back and forth until, finally, one family wore down and outlasted the rest. But that was a process that could take weeks at best or years at worst. Given the threat of Brencis, they had to act fast. Having Zammit hold together the Dynasty in the interim would be a good move.

"So why do you need me?" he finally asked. "It sounds like you have everything you need."

"We do, yes, but then Urett spotted you at Brencis's Day of Accountability, and we realized we could make an even stronger case to the nobles," Zammit said.

"If you were to endorse Auriel as acting regent, we believe the nobles will be even more likely to agree," Urett added.

Quartus stroked his chin as he considered it. That also made sense. If the Dynasty's former prince supported her, the nobles were indeed more likely to fall in line.

"Okay. I'll do it," Quartus said.

Zammit smiled, and for the briefest moment, Quartus saw why she was the best choice. She looked regal, brimming with true authority. If it were up to him, he would gladly leave her on the throne. But then, he also knew that Everys was working on her own plans to overthrow Brencis. He would have no problem backing her to be queen once again either.

With his agreement, Zammit and Urett outlined the rest of what he needed to know: where and when this meeting with the nobles would take place, how he could get inside, and so on.

As they left The Shessu's Burden, Quartus could practically feel Yusra's excitement boil off her. Of course she backed this plan. But with every step, Quartus grew more and more disconcerted. Yes, Urett and Zammit had put together a workable solution, one that might even pull the Dynasty out of this dangerous spiral. But there was one component missing: true justice. Letting Brencis walk away from the death and destruction he had caused? That didn't sit right with Quartus at all.

Eventually, a determined frown settled on his brow. He'd play along. He'd help Auriel Zammit. But he was going to make sure that Brencis would still face justice for what he had done.

57

Morning light trickled into Narius's room and he tried to roll away from it. His entire body erupted in pain. He groaned. He had barely gotten any sleep. Part of it was because of the lingering pain from so many beatings. But the larger part was the memories of the previous day.

Images of what he had seen at the parade had haunted his dreams. So many people suffering, their bodies smoking. No matter how hard he tried to banish the memories, they crept back to needle him all night. Worse, Kavi's description of the perpetrators assaulted him as well. A human woman and a hornless Ixactl. It had to be Everys and Redtale. But why would his wife have done such a horrible thing? That was like something out of the old legends about Siporan mage-kings and their cruelty. Yes, Everys could cast powerful spells with her runes, but there was no way she would ever stoop so low and do something so needlessly evil.

He squeezed his eyes shut. He had lost so much over the past months. He had lost his kingdom to Brencis. He had lost his best friend when Paine betrayed him. He had nearly lost his life at Favid's hands and then again at Tirigian's. He had temporarily lost his identity as Innana tried to mold him into Senen's long-awaited king. Had he finally lost his wife as well? What more could he possibly be asked to sacrifice?

Narius snorted and chided himself. Wallowing wouldn't help anyone, and right now Innana might need his help. He gingerly sat up.

Only to freeze when he spotted two Dalark soldiers looming near the room's entrance. Their gaze flicked in his direction, then one of them stepped out of the room. The other's expression didn't waver, but he didn't look at Narius again. Was the guard making sure he was safe? Or was he a prisoner once again?

A moment later, the other guard returned, accompanied by Planka. With a sharp wave, the Dalark officer dismissed the guards.

"How are you feeling?" Planka asked.

Narius shrugged, but winced as pain lanced down his back.

Planka smiled sympathetically. "Do you need me to get the medics?"

Narius waved away the offer. A doctor had looked him over the previous day and declared that all he needed was time and rest. He doubted he would get much of either, not in the way he truly needed. He couldn't. There was still too much to do.

"What's been happening?" Narius asked.

"There are riots all through Utuaa, at least in a dozen districts. Tirigian is mobilizing the local garrisons to quash them, but his forces are outnumbered. He's also tried to cut off communication with the rest of the Imperium, but word is slowly filtering out. We've received unconfirmed reports of similar riots in other cities."

Narius soaked in the information. Encouraging, but too early for anything to be definitive. Yes, the local garrisons could be over-whelmed by the rioters, but there was only so much civilians could do against soldiers. And if Tirigian brought in reinforcements? This could all be short-lived.

With a grunt, Narius leveraged himself to standing. Planka reached out to steady him, but Narius waved him off. Taking a deep breath, he headed out of the room.

They were hiding in a basement of some kind—Narius thought it might have been a library, but he hadn't gotten a good look at the building when they arrived—one filled with soldiers. The sight of so many people in Dalark uniforms sent a momentary surge of worry through Narius, but he pushed down the fear. He knew intellectually he was safe, but his instincts were harder to convince.

Planka motioned him toward a table, where a paper map of the city was spread out. Notes written in Dalark had been scribbled all over it, and while Narius couldn't read them, he could interpret the information: troop movements, the location of riots, possibilities and probabilities written in different colored inks.

Narius turned to Planka and motioned for him to step closer. While he didn't know how many troops spoke Dynastic, he didn't want to risk anyone overhearing.

"What do you think the chances are of this working?" Narius asked.

Planka hesitated, working his jaw like he was chewing on Narius's question. He shrugged one shoulder. "Not great at present, but if we're able to coordinate with other citizens? If we can rally more troops to our cause? We might be able to become more than just a temporary nuisance."

Narius looked over the map again, reassessing his opinion. This could be the first step toward changing the Imperium provided everything Planka said happened. With reinforcements, logistical support, not to mention support from the general public, this could be the end of Tirigian's reign.

"What do you need me to do?" he asked.

Planka's jaw dropped open, and he laughed, once, then covered his mouth. "Forgive me, Your Strength. You have been instrumental in bringing us to this point. The princess has told me about everything you've done. But this really is an internal matter for the Dalark people. While we are grateful for your help, I fear that your continued influence would be... detrimental."

Narius couldn't help but notice how the way Planka said "influence" made it sound like he wanted to say "interference." Even stranger still, hearing someone say they didn't need him anymore, something that he had been wanting for weeks, left a bittersweet feeling.

Best not to dwell on that lest he wind up volunteering for more missions. "It's too bad that the Dalark troops in our holdings can't be here to help. After fighting the Dynasty's forces for so long, I wonder who they would side with."

"No doubt," Planka said, his tone almost condescending.

Did he think that the Dynasty wasn't a challenge? That couldn't be the case. Clearly the Dynasty had to be putting up something of a fight or Tirigian would have declared victory sooner. Or maybe there was something about how the Dalark achieved their invasion that—

Narius's eyes widened as that stray thought dredged up a memory. How could he have forgotten about Dalark's bizarre invasion of Maotoa? Yes, he had gone through so much since that morning on the island, but thinking of Dalark's invasion of the Dynasty's holdings reminded him of sitting in the guest room in Dreah, Maotoa's capital, having fought with Paine. And then some sort of portal opening in the fountain in his room, allowing Dalark soldiers to stream through.

"Dented Breastplate and Broken Sword!" he muttered.

"Your Strength?" Planka asked.

"Where's Cosena?"

Planka gestured toward another room, and Narius headed in that direction immediately. He strode past other people who snapped to attention as he walked. He ignored them, his mind locked on a single question.

There she was, sitting in a quiet corner, conversing with Innana. Kavi perched on a nearby stool, watching the action around her with what appeared to be detached amusement. Innana looked up at Narius, concern spreading across her face, but he ignored her, focused solely on Cosena.

"You have a way to send me to the Dynasty, don't you?" he said.

Cosena looked up at him, her expression unreadable. She quirked a brow at him but didn't respond.

Innana looked between them, then her eyes widened as well. "Is that how my brother was able to move so many troops to the Dynasty so quickly?"

Narius nodded. "When I was visiting Dreah, Dalark troops came through a portal in a fountain in my room. And, come to think of it, that would explain how you got into my room that night. You were able to open one of those portals in the water."

"When she got into *where*?" Innana repeated.

Cosena sighed. "It's true. We call them the chantways or the Bearer's Blessing, a gift she gave us to rule the seas and oceans. Wherever there is water and one of her statues—or a specific kind of substitute—we can travel there."

"So you can send me home," Narius said.

Cosena's eyes narrowed. "And why would I do that?"

Narius's mind locked up. The arrogance. The defiance. There were so many answers he could give. Because her people had betrayed the Dynasty. Because she had tried to seduce him all those months ago. Because Tirigian had made her a prisoner rather than a partner. But he tried to let go of the angry spike pulsing in his chest.

"Because it's the right thing to do. I've done what I can here. Now I need to go fight for my throne." He turned to Innana. Maybe if she took his side. "Please. You promised."

Innana studied his face, then turned to Cosena. "Sister, if you're able, I would ask that you do this."

Cosena looked between them, then shook her head with a sigh. "And once again, Maotoa is a pawn between Dalark and the Dynasty. As we always are. I'll ask it again: Why should I? How does helping you regain your throne help me? Help my people?"

Irritation flashed through him. A thousand retorts, many of them vulgar and demeaning, boiled in his mind. But he tamped down on his frustration. He couldn't really blame her for what she was doing. Maotoa had always chafed as the last of the Dynasty's colonies, even though they ironically had started the Colonial Uprisings that freed all the others. She had something he needed. Why would she give that away freely?

"Fine." He forced the word. "If you return me safely to the Dynasty's holdings, preferably in Bastion or its environs, I will renounce the Dynasty's claims on your home."

Cosena's lip twitched into a snarl. "That's only worth something to me if you succeed in overthrowing Brencis."

"Do you think you can convince Brencis to make a similar promise?" Narius countered.

Cosena tipped her head to one side and Narius could practically hear her weighing the option. In truth, she probably could persuade Brencis if she got him alone, but he wasn't about to point that out.

"Fair." She turned to Innana. "But I'll only agree if you make the same promise."

Innana's head snapped back as if struck. "I can't possibly... That is, I'm not sure I would be able to follow through on such a..."

Narius fixed her with a stern gaze. He needed this. And she owed him. But he also knew it would be unwise to challenge her openly.

Finally, Innana sighed. "Very well. I will take it under advisement."

Much to Narius's surprise, that seemed to be enough. Cosena rose in a smooth, almost slinky motion. She headed for the nearest door.

"Let's see if we can find enough water to do the trick," she said, her voice a seductive purr.

Narius shivered as he followed her.

"Sending you home is no easy task," Cosena said. "First, we need a body of water large enough to create a gateway. And second, I can't just send you anywhere. I need a bridgestone to open the portal on the other side."

"A what?" Narius asked.

She sighed dramatically, like an exasperated teacher. "Do you remember the statues of the Water Bearer in Dreah, how they held gems? Those are bridgestones. I need one close to a large enough body of water to open a gate. The only bridgestones I know are in Maotoa. I doubt you want to go there."

True enough. While that would be closer to the Dynasty, it would still be in territory occupied by the Dalark. And he didn't think he'd find a way to the mainland from there.

"Do you have a way of finding a 'bridgestone' in the Dynasty's holdings?" he prompted.

A grin tugged at her lips. "Perhaps."

Innana summoned Planka and whispered something to him. He, in turn, snapped an order to two Dalark soldiers, who escorted Narius, Innana, Kavi, and Cosena through a back door, up some stairs, and into the city.

Narius could hear sirens in the distance, punctuated occasionally by explosions or shouting. A palpable tension hung in the air, and Narius felt like he should crouch down, move carefully, treat this like an active combat zone. It probably was.

The soldiers appeared to feel the same way. They signaled for everyone to hurry but keep quiet at the same time. They hustled through a deserted street to a nearby park that was similarly empty. A large fountain burbled in the middle. The soldiers took up station near the park's entrance.

Cosena slunk to the fountain and settled on the edge. She dipped her hand into the water. Humming a meandering tune, she closed her eyes, and her brow pinched in concentration. Then her eyes flashed open. She sang, her alto voice thrumming. Her eyes glowed, a similar sheen rippling across the water's surface. Then the fountain churned, the water rising into a mound with a vortex in its side. The water spun away, revealing another place, a rocky shoreline with a city off in the distance. The towers jutting into the sky were blunt columns, unlike the buildings he had seen in Utuaa. Narius thought it looked like the Dynasty, but he couldn't be sure.

He glanced at Cosena. She smiled at him, but that did little to ease his apprehension. So instead, he turned to Innana.

"I have to admit, I have grown used to your presence here," Innana said, a slight quaver in her voice. "You've helped me achieve something that I thought would only ever be a dream. Thank you, Narius."

"No, thank you," he said. "You saved my life. If it wasn't for you, we wouldn't have this chance to make things right. Everything right."

He took a step toward her. The soldiers tensed, some of them readying their weapons. Innana shot a sharp look at them, and they stepped back, their expressions chastised.

Narius closed the distance and tentatively pulled Innana into a hug. She stiffened in his arms at first, but then she returned the gesture. It was an awkward feeling. Maybe it wasn't the best choice. But he didn't know how else to express his gratitude.

"You'd best go," Innana whispered.

He released her, then turned to Kavi. She tipped her head to one side and shooed him toward the portal.

"As soon as this is over, we'll have to get together to discuss the Dynasty's relationship with the Imperium," he said.

Innana chuckled. "Stop stalling, Narius. She's waiting for you."

He swallowed hard, then waded into the ankle-deep water. The cold bled through his shoes and he sloshed forward. He took a deep breath and pushed a hand into the portal. There was no outward sensation that indicated he was interacting with something magic, but suddenly, his hand was warmer than the rest of his body. With one final breath, Narius stepped through.

Dizziness crested over him, and he stumbled forward, dropping into knee-deep water. He clambered forward, away from the vortex, and spun around in time to see the vortex spinning shut. Then he lurched toward shore, finally pulling himself up onto a concrete barrier.

He stood on a jetty that stabbed into a vast sea. Docks peppered the water in the distance. A city skyline loomed in the darkened sky, but he didn't recognize it. Not Bastion, but the architecture was familiar, the sort of thing he would expect to see within the Dynasty's holdings.

A smile tickled his lips. He had made it. He was home. Time to see if he couldn't take back some of the things he had lost.

58

A few days after her misadventure in Utuaa, Everys received an invitation to visit the Illuminate's enclave. Based on the way the messenger practically vibrated with excitement, she had a feeling they had made a breakthrough. She found Tillmin waiting for her at the bottom of the stairs, wearing a wide grin.

"Come with us, Blessed, and be prepared to see something truly revolutionary." Tillmin made a sweeping gesture with his arms, as if he were ushering her into some sort of theatrical production.

A giggle burbled up her throat, high-pitched and girly. Everys blinked, surprised. She hadn't laughed like that in years.

Tillmin's eyes sparkled. "My apologies, Blessed. Aftereffects of a most illuminating experiment."

What had happened here? The deeper they went into the Illuminate compound, the giddier she felt.

They entered the lab where, once again, the Illuminate researchers had gathered in an excited crowd. Much to her surprise, Occ stood in their midst. They jostled each other and joked. Even Screj smiled and laughed as Style teased him.

Style turned to her. "Blessed! Thank you so much for getting us that targeting laser. We have already learned so much in a short period."

That was wonderful to hear. The Illuminates parted, ushering Everys into a seat. They had set up the targeting laser to point at a blank metal plate. They had also wired the laser into a computer terminal with a broad screen.

"Once we got the targeting system, we tried to modify it, but we couldn't. Thankfully, your friend Occ could assist us. As a result, we named him a member of our order," Tillmin said.

Occ ducked his head and batted at his mask with his lower hands. "It was my pleasure to do so."

Tillmin waved away his words. "Too modest, Occ! Too modest! When you assist in a breakthrough that someone has waited a thousand years to achieve, you're allowed to boast a little."

Now Occ ducked even lower, looking like he was about to slink under a table, but the Illuminates next to him caught his shoulders and pushed him upright.

"So what we've done here is create an interface that allows a mage to draw a rune on this screen." Screj showed the computer console. "The computer then deciphers the pattern and feeds the proper movement patterns to the laser. And Blessed... you would not believe the results we've seen."

"Show her!" Style said with a giddy giggle.

Screj mirrored his wife's expression and produced two vials. One was a dark blue, almost black, in color. The other was a syrupy yellow.

"Ordinary ink, and this is ink made from Cold Light tree sap. I'll draw a simple illumination rune with both." Screj walked over to the metal plate and drew the same rune twice. The darker ink was runnier, but Everys knew that wouldn't matter for the spell to work. "Lights!"

The lab was plunged into darkness. A second later, the regular ink rune glowed a sickly green. But then, the light grew brighter until a small circle of light, the same intensity of a campfire, blazed into existence. After a few moments, the light faded and disappeared. After another moment, the second rune blazed into existence, glowing a bright blue, but then the light flared so quickly that Everys squinted against it. Her eyes quickly adjusted. This time, the light was almost as bright as the lab's normal lights. Once again, the conjured light faded and disappeared.

"Style, would you do the honors?" Screj asked.

"With pleasure, my love."

The computer made some soft *boops* and *beeps*. Then a single point of bright red light appeared on the metal plate, approximately halfway between where the other two runes had been. Then the light moved, slowly at first, meandering in what appeared to be an aimless pattern. But with every passing moment, the dot moved faster and faster. Soon, Everys could see the rune's pattern take shape in the afterimages left by the laser. But the dot continued to move, faster and faster, until it seemed to elongate, stretching into a line that looped and swirled, doubling back on itself until it appeared as if the entire rune had been drawn in a single line of light.

"Brace yourself," someone whispered with an excited giggle.

A ball of light blossomed in front of Everys, bright as the sun itself, so bright it felt like the light tried to shove her off her perch. She gasped and covered her face with her arms as the Illuminates hooted and jumped up and down around her. Even though her eyes were tightly shut, she could still see the light filtered through her eyelids.

Just as suddenly, the light vanished. Everys risked opening her eyes, blinking against the darkness. Even after Screj called for the lab's lights to be turned on again, she felt like she was sitting in deep shadows.

"Isn't that amazing, Blessed?" Style asked. "Drawing runes with light is possible, resulting in power we'd never dreamed of before."

"We've confirmed the results with at least fifteen different spells. Our last one was to try a joy-caster rune. The effect was only supposed to last a minute or two." Screj laughed. "That was three hours ago."

The other Illuminates laughed and Everys joined in, and not just because of the rune's effects. This was an amazing discovery. Her mind positively reeled at the implications. They could draw her family's rune on the side of a hospital and heal everyone within. With the right rune and the laser, they could potentially clear the rubble out of Bastion in moments instead of months.

She stopped laughing as her mind continued down that path. With a device like this mounted on a cloud skimmer, they could draw a rune onto a battlefield and wipe out an opposing army in a matter of seconds. Using this to draw Occ's truth-seeker rune would make people incapable of lying, forcing them to share their deepest, darkest secrets.

Everys remembered what Oluna had said about the rebukes getting easier each time they happened. With every step forward, it would become easier and easier to push the boundaries and do things they were never intended to do. No wonder the scriveners often said that only the Singularity could draw runes with light. It wasn't just because doing so was impossible until now. It was because only He could be trusted with this kind of power.

She looked up and spotted Hirfan standing in one corner of the lab, his expression grim. Even though he didn't say anything, she could read his concern across the room. Tillmin nodded soberly to her. He touched her elbow and beckoned her to leave the group.

"I can tell by your expression that you've probably had the same realization that I did. While this is a triumph for our order, we have only stumbled across a thorny ethical quandary. Is this too much power for our people to have?" His voice was quiet.

"What can we do about it?" Everys asked. "Do you want me to return the laser?"

Tillmin chuckled sadly. "I'm afraid it's too late for that. Too many of us have seen what's possible. Even if we didn't have the targeting laser, how long do you think it would take for someone to engineer a similar system? No, this is a dilemma that we must face as an order and determine how best to proceed. I plan to swear them all to secrecy later today. I would ask that you show the same level of confidence."

"Of course," Everys murmured.

"Thank you." He continued walking. "There is something else we need to share with you. I asked Hirfan to do some research into a question that you recently asked."

"Oh?"

He looked her full in the eyes. "Why were you rebuked so strongly when you used your husband's blood as opposed to your own or Redtale's?"

It felt like ice slithered down her back. "How did you know about that?"

"People talk and people listen. Thanks to Hirfan, I can provide some answers for you."

He led her out of the lab to a conference room of sorts, with bare stone walls, a long wooden table, and a dozen mismatched chairs. He motioned for her to be seated first, then settled into a seat across from her.

"While the Illuminates have primarily focused on drawing runes with light, we have had members who have delved into the most obscure aspects of toratropic magic. About a hundred years ago, one researcher focused on what contributed to the intensity of a rebuke." Tillmin dropped into the chair on the opposite side of the desk.

Everys blinked. "You're kidding."

"Not at all. We know from our masters that several factors dictate a rebuke's intensity: the level of harm done to the target of the rune, the intentions of the caster, plus the details of the Singularity's commandments and dictates. This researcher, a young man named Pallion, wondered if part of it might have to do with the ink used." Tillmin rummaged through the stacks of paper until he pulled out a leather-bound book. "As disturbing as his research was, he was meticulous in his notes."

"How would you even test that?" Everys asked.

"Oh, the same way we test the efficacy of a new ink. We use the same rune but with different inks and record the results. Here, though, Pallion recorded what the rebuke felt like, how long it lasted, and if there were any lingering effects." He handed the book over to Everys.

Frowning, she opened the book and skimmed the contents. What she saw was shocking. Pallion must have repeated his experiments hundreds of times, always recording the results in charts in cramped, neat handwriting. She flipped past page after page, gawking as she kept finding more notes to skim.

"How did he ever do this without someone realizing?" she asked.

Tillmin's expression soured. "Unfortunately, people did, and several of his fellow Illuminates volunteered to be test subjects."

Everys's head snapped up and Tillmin nodded grimly.

"The pursuit of knowledge can be seductive if it's not tempered with wisdom," he said somberly. "He never drew a rune that would harm someone permanently, only cause them minor pain or discomfort. And he never asked anyone to draw a forbidden rune or use forbidden ink. He would only do that himself."

"Even still..." Everys's gaze dipped back to the page, skimming down the notes.

"As regrettable as Pallion's research was, I think it may hold the answer to your question. Hirfan has reviewed his findings and, based on his own experience, confirms what he discovered. Pallion's research indicates that the type of ink used in a rune can intensify the strength of a rebuke."

Everys nodded. That made sense. But then that just led her to the true puzzle:

"So why was the rebuke so intense when I healed Narius?" she asked. "I understand I healed him using his own blood, but it didn't hurt nearly as bad as when I did so for Redtale."

Tillmin pursed his lips. "I would think the answer would be obvious, Blessed. The issue isn't the rune or the circumstances. The issue is your husband's blood. Something is different about it, something significant."

Everys looked down at Pallion's research again. Again, that sounded logical. But what could it be? What could be so different?

Maybe there was a way she could find out. She handed the book back to Tillmin. "Thank you. And please congratulate everyone on their discovery. They should be proud."

"I hope they feel the same when we're done discussing the ethical ramifications. Let's be honest, Blessed, new discoveries are sometimes not as worthy of celebration as we might first believe."

She froze, then studied the Illuminate master's face carefully. Was that a subtle rebuke? Maybe. Hirfan probably told him about what she had done. But she didn't see any recrimination in Tillmin's expression. She brushed aside the thought and took her leave.

She ascended from the Illuminate's compound and exited the enclave building, where Redtale fell in step with her. Redtale gave her a questioning look, but Everys marched straight for the Embassy. She didn't want to risk the possibility of Redtale questioning anything that they were doing. She had to keep moving.

Thankfully, Tormod was still in the Shade. He sat in the war room, considering the map. When she entered, he looked up and offered her a smile.

"Blessed, I was just about to go looking for you." His smile faltered. "But it looks like you may have orders for me."

"I do. I need to know who I would speak to about the royal family's blood," she said.

Tormod tipped his head to one side, frowning. "Now, why would you need information about that?"

She considered telling him. As a Siporan, he would understand where Redtale wouldn't. But she didn't feel like she could share, not when all she had was speculation. "It's a personal matter. Is there anyone who might have that information?"

"Besides the royal physicians?" Tormod asked. "I would think if there was something unusual about the family's blood, they would know."

"Can we get those records?" she asked.

He nodded thoughtfully. "I have a few agents still in place in the palace. I think they should be able to obtain what you're looking for."

She hoped so. At least that might give her a clue. "Thank you. What did you have for me?"

Tormod took a deep breath, bracing himself against the table. Then he offered her a shaky smile. "I've given this a lot of thought and meditated on the possibilities. Given my understanding of what my oath is capable of, I think I could take someone with me if I were to use it."

Everys's eyes widened, and her mouth popped open. Before she could say anything, he held up a hand.

"There are a few things I need you to remember, Blessed. First, I can only make a jump once every few days. It takes a lot out of me to travel in that manner, and I'll need time to recover. Second, the journey can be unpleasant. Third, and most importantly, while we can jump together, it is the Singularity who will determine where we land. Do you still want to do this?"

Everys stood up straighter and nodded. She was certain that the Singularity would want her to find her husband. Narius could help her make sense of all of this. He would know what to do about Brencis. And even if they didn't find him, a slim chance was better than none.

"Then I suggest you get your sleep, Blessed," Tormod said. "Because at the midpoint of First Watch, we will begin our hunt for your husband."

59

"**N**arv! We're not paying you to gawk at the scenery."

Narius jumped at the captain's bellow. Even though the man was a Weyfir, he had a set of lungs like an Ixactl's, able to strip the hide off a lazy crewmember with little or no notice. Narius quickly shoved his mop into the bucket and scrubbed at the same patch of deck that he had cleaned the previous three days. The other deckhands near him also focused on their work, pretending like that's what they had been doing the whole time.

As soon as the captain returned to the wheelhouse, the deckhands relaxed. A few even offered Narius sympathetic smiles. They had all been the target of the captain's ire. Narius returned their smiles but kept working. If he continued attracting attention, someone might see through his assumed identity of Narv, a drifter looking for a ride to Bastion, and turn him over to the authorities.

But even as he tried to concentrate on mopping the deck, his gaze kept being drawn to the passing scenery. Cosena's portal had deposited him in Suwell, a port city on the Melgor. He had signed onto this boat's crew in exchange for passage upriver. The trip had been illuminating for all the wrong reasons. What had happened to his Dynasty?

He had never really spent a lot of time in this part of the Dynasty's holdings, but he knew what it should look like. While this area wasn't as fertile as the Cold Light's forests or the Right Highlands, this had always been farmlands that helped supply Bastion. Most of those fields should have been harvested and bare, ready for winter, but crops still stood in many of the fields. When the wind came in from the north, it carried the stench of rot and decay. Other fields were barren, but they had been burned. And quite a few of them were studded with destroyed or abandoned military vehicles.

"Pretty grim, ain't it?" a gruff voice asked.

Narius looked to his right. Another deckhand had joined him at the railing, surveying the damage. He was a broad-shouldered Maotoan, which wasn't a surprise. The Maotoans had a tendency to stick close to the water if they could. His name was Siaku, and he had been a part of the crew for the past few months.

"I remember when the shooting was still going on." Siaku jerked his chin toward the fields. "We carried soldiers and equipment from Bastion down to Suwell right before the invasion."

"Hey!" Another deckhand shouted. "Papa Siaku is tellin' stories again."

Siaku ignored the small cluster of crew that gathered around him. "We were about two-thirds of the way there when the Dalark land-ed from Maotoa and started pushing inland. Suddenly, we've got flechettes zipping past us and heavy artillery sending up geysers in the Melgor. Military ordered us all below 'for our safety' while they opened fire from the deck. Scariest three Watches of my life. Thought for sure the Gravedigger was going to drag us all down to him, but we somehow made it. Took us close to a month to fix up all the damage."

"Thank the Warrior for King Brencis then, huh?" one of the other crewmembers said.

Narius's stomach twisted and he grimaced. Then he ducked his head, worried that someone might recognize him through his reaction.

Except Siaku snorted and shook his head. "You'd think someone who's supposed to be such a great warrior like Brencis would've ended things by now. Found a solution or ended the conflict. Instead, he's just prolonging things so he can grab as much glory as possible. You hear what happened to the crew of *The Shessu's Glory*? Every one of 'em got conscripted into the navy."

"That's because you Maotoans stabbed us in the back, Siaku!" someone shouted.

Rather than get angry, Siaku chuckled and nodded. "That we did, I suppose. But can you blame us? When things get tough like this, you gotta protect your own. That's something Brencis doesn't understand."

Now Narius perked up. In spite of himself, he offered a small grin to Siaku.

"Of course, Narius wasn't much better." Siaku spit over the rail into the river.

Some of the gathered crew groaned, but Narius could tell that it was good-natured. None of them were genuinely upset. They nudged each other, their expressions eager.

"You hear the latest about him? That whole 'Fallen Sword' fiasco?" Siaku asked the crowd.

Narius's jaw dropped open. Falling Sword, not fallen. He had been working on "Falling Sword" before the war broke out. But that had been highly confidential.

"Narv obviously has," Siaku said. "King Narius had this goofy notion to send robots out into space and drag asteroids back here so we could strip them and use the minerals and such. Supposedly, it was going to supercharge our economy and inject so many blades into the Dynasty that everyone would live like nobles."

A few of the crewmembers chuckled. Narius didn't. While Siaku had relayed his plan mostly accurately—if a bit crudely—he could tell from the big man's attitude that he had issues with it.

"But do you really think that's the way it would've worked?" Siaku asked. "Of course not! Where would that money have actually wound up? Not in our pockets. In the government's coffers. In the hands of the nobles who contributed to it. It would've wound up in TelleGlin's bottom line since that Gaines lady was helping. Eventually, we may have gotten a drizzle of money if we were lucky. But most of it would have stayed far away from us and far away from anyone who actually could use it."

Narius frowned. That wasn't true at all! The whole point of Falling Sword was to make things better for the people.

"Maybe you should become king, Siaku!" someone suggested.

The crowd laughed and Siaku joined in, but then he waved away the laughter and shook his head.

"Can you imagine how the nobles would react if one of us ever made it to the throne? Didn't you see how they treated that poor Siporan girl? Branded her a witch, blamed her for everything, and then killed her!" Siaku leveled a finger at one of the deckhands. "And don't even bother with that nonsense about her still bein' alive, Obligation. I've heard the rumors, too, but that's all they are. I don't care what your mom's neighbor's cousin claims to have seen in Breakwater."

The others laughed, and Obligation, a Kolvese worker, raised his hands in good-natured surrender.

"Nah, they don't want any of us anywhere near power or influence." Siaku's tone became serious. "If they did, they'd risk losing what they have. They call us traitors or dust-drinkers or scribblers or *kathartin*. They keep us down because that's the only thing they know. Unless someone actually comes along and forces them to change, that's the way it'll always be as long as the Dynasty has kings."

The others grumbled in agreement, and once again, Narius ducked his head. No one had commented on his metallic eyes, but those were a clear mark that he had at least a little noble blood in him.

"Story time's over, folks," Siaku said.

Sure enough, the captain was descending from the wheelhouse, screaming about laziness and insubordination. After berating the crew, he ordered that they be given emergency rations for supper that night. While the others grumbled, Narius paid little attention to the punishment. As he finished his work, he couldn't help but wonder if it was worth it to reclaim his kingdom at all.

60

E ven though her stomach had been rumbling since she'd awakened that morning, Everys refused to eat breakfast. After Tormod's warning the day before, she didn't think it'd be a good idea for her to attempt this on a full stomach. The last thing she'd want to do is vomit when they arrived wherever it was they were going.

Once she was dressed, she left her quarters, where she was met by a very dour Redtale.

"I don't like this at all," Redtale said. "Tormod is capable in the field, but I'd feel a lot better about this if I was coming with you."

"I understand. But Tormod told me he's not sure how many people he could bring with him. If we find ourselves in Utuaa and we have to bring Narius home, we don't want to make hard choices."

What she didn't tell Redtale was that she had already made that decision for herself. If it came down to her or Narius, she would send her husband home with Tormod without a moment's hesitation.

They made their way through the Embassy to Tormod's room. The room was mostly empty except for a single candle on a wooden stand. As they entered the room, the aroma of the candle washed over her, sweet with a hint of pepper. She choked on the odor initially, but after taking a few breaths, Everys relaxed.

Tormod sat in a single chair, wringing his hands together over and over. He smiled at her, the expression clearly forced. "Are you ready to go, Blessed?"

Ready to use a spell that could throw her halfway around the world? Not even close, but she couldn't say that. Tormod might decide not to attempt this, or worse, she might convince herself not to try. So she squared her shoulders and nodded.

Tormod studied her face, then turned to Redtale. "I'll have to insist that you stay out of this room until we return."

Everys could read the hesitation in Redtale's expression. She offered her a shaky but reassuring smile. With one last grunt, Redtale stepped out of the room with Rewether close behind.

Once the door closed, Tormod turned to her. "We'll see how this goes, Blessed. You must follow my lead and listen to any directions I may give you without question."

She nodded soberly. He studied her face for another moment, then nodded. He rolled up his sleeve and pressed a hand over the tattoo. Then he closed his eyes and whispered something. She recognized her people's ancient language, but she couldn't understand any of the words.

So she closed her eyes and took a deep breath, focusing her mind on Narius. That was who they were looking for, after all. She offered a silent prayer to the Singularity, *Please, bring me to my husband. Let him be all right.*

The surrounding air turned frigid, a shiver worming through her. A breeze swept through the room, jostling the hem of her dress a bit at first, but then tugging on it with more force. She tried to use her hands to hold it down, but before she could, Tormod lashed out and snared her arms. He continued to whisper, but a low buzz surrounded them, growing so loud it felt like it would rattle her teeth free.

Then, in an instant, the floor dropped out from under them.

Everys gasped, but the sound was snatched away. Hot and cold waves lashed at her and the wind tore at her hair. She screwed her eyes shut and fought to keep from screaming, but a squeak escaped her lips and she was convinced that if they were to come to a stop, they would simply shatter against the ground.

Then, with a lurch, the strange sensation passed. Tormod stumbled into her and the two of them almost toppled, but she planted her feet and kept him upright. Gulping down breaths, she opened her eyes and looked around.

They stood in the center of a darkened office. The room was small, almost cramped, with a single desk shoved in one corner with a powered-down computer terminal pushed up against the wall. Even though she had never seen this room before, Everys felt like she recognized it somehow. A familiarity to it she couldn't quite place.

"Oh dear," Tormod whispered, looking at their surroundings with wide eyes.

"What is it?" Everys whispered. "Do you know where we are?"

He nodded. "This is my office in the palace, Blessed. We're in Bastion."

Everys's gaze jumped to the door, and she braced herself. What if someone had heard their arrival? At any moment, someone could open the door and find them.

Tormod must have sensed her worry. "No one will find us. The entrance is hidden, and only Narius and I knew where it was." He chuckled ruefully. "Not where we wanted to wind up, but this was a successful test. And this saves me some time."

Everys frowned. "How so?"

"We wanted to procure Narius's medical records. They're stored here in the palace. Why send an agent when I can get them myself?"

Tormod produced a vial of ink and popped off the top. He daubed some on his finger and pulled Everys's arm toward him. "I'm going to go down to the infirmary. I want you to stay here, Blessed. There are far too many people in this building who would recognize you, and we can't guarantee that any of them would still hold even a shred of loyalty for you."

As he talked, he drew a rune on her wrist. It was extremely simple, resembling a stylized half-shut eye.

"I don't want to take any chances, so I'm going to cast this stealth rune on you. It's similar to the one that Oluna's agents used, only this one won't set off a rebuke. As long as you don't move too quickly, no one will see you. I don't expect anyone to look into this room, but we can't be too careful. Once I'm back from the infirmary, I'll trigger the return spell."

"Will we be able to try again?" Everys whispered.

He shook his head. "Definitely not today, and I may need an extra day or two to recover. No offense, Blessed, but while bringing you with me is possible, it drained me more than I expected. I'll need some time to rest."

With that, he finished the rune with a little flourish, then activated it. Nothing seemed to happen, but she trusted Tormod. He took a long, shuddering breath, then slipped out of the room, leaving Everys alone in the dark.

How long was he going to be gone?

Everys's legs bounced a chaotic rhythm, and she stared at the door. She had no idea how long it had been since Tormod left. As far as she could tell, her stealth spell was still working, but that meant little. Tormod had never told her how long it would last. Had something more important distracted him? Worse, had he been captured? If he had, how was she going to get out of here?

At first, she could keep those worries at bay. But the longer her wait dragged out, the more frantic she grew. She got up and paced the cramped room, turning endless circles if only to burn the nervous energy out of her body. But that was a half measure. Her anxiety continued to build.

She had to do *something*, even if it was just to take a peek and see if she could find out if Tormod had been caught. She touched the wrist where Tormod had drawn the stealth rune. It felt like the spell was still working, but she had no way to know for certain. With a deep breath, she pushed the door open.

Much to her surprise, she found herself inside the royal library. She hadn't spent much time there when she was queen, mostly because there wasn't much to see. Just empty rows of shelves, the books long removed. Suddenly, though, it made sense why no one had repurposed the room. If they had, Tormod's secret lair would have been found.

She grabbed a small statuette from a nearby table and stuck it in the door to make sure it didn't close all the way. A risk, but it would be worse if the door shut completely. She had no idea how to open it again. Once she was sure that was done, she listened for noises from the hallway outside the library. As far as she could tell, everything was normal. She took a few breaths to steady herself, wiped her hands on her dress, and crept for the hall.

Poking her head out of the door, she glanced in both directions. No one was coming, so she slipped into the hallway. Her heart hammered in her chest, and she smiled at the thrill. In some ways, it felt strange to be in these halls again. On the other hand, it felt like she had come home.

She heard the guards before she saw them walking down the hall in front of her. She quickly pressed up against the wall. If the stealth rune had worn off...

But the guards tromped past her, discussing some recent sporting event. One of their gazes flickered in her direction, the guard's brow pinching into a frown, but they didn't say anything or hesitate as they walked right by her, close enough she could feel the breeze of their passing.

As soon as they were out of sight, Everys released her held breath and fought to keep from laughing. Exhilaration coursed through her. Objectively, she knew she should go back to Tormod's office, but in that moment, shrouded by the rune, she wanted to keep looking. Let Tormod get Narius's medical records and whatever else he found. Maybe she could glean some intelligence with some careful snooping as well.

She set off, this time with purpose. Where should she go? The Amber Office? The throne room? No, that didn't seem wise. While she might find some helpful information, she was just as likely to get caught. She headed up to the royal quarters. The staff there had a habit of gossiping. Maybe she could overhear something juicy.

It was slow going, and she had to stop three times to let guards and servants pass her. But eventually, she came to the doors of the queen's quarters. Everys made a split-second decision. Rather than risk going to the king's rooms on the floor above, she could use the secret passageway between the queen's and king's quarters. There would be less chance of her being spotted if something happened to the rune.

She eased the door open and slipped inside. Then she stopped short.

The room had been transformed in her absence. All the furniture was gone, replaced with garishly colored sofas and chairs. The fireplace had been completely transformed into a metal and glass sculpture with green flames dancing within it. All of her decorations had vanished as well. Everys's stomach turned. She shouldn't have expected Viara to leave everything the way Everys had left it, but seeing the drastic changes made Everys feel even sadder. This had been her home, her true home, where she and Narius had—

The door rattled behind her. Everys jumped and hurried away from it just as it opened. Two guards stepped inside, and for a brief, heart-wrenching moment, Everys thought she had been caught.

But then they stepped away from the door, taking up station on either side, and Viara stepped through. Everys gaped at her. The queen wore too much makeup, probably to look enticing in spite of her puffy facial features. Her clothing, a bizarre riot of colors and patterns, did little to hide her swelling belly.

"...know that we just got done renovating, but none of this feels right to me," Viara said, gesturing broadly at the room. Five girls trailed after her, most likely her assistant and some of her maids, none of whom Everys recognized. "So I want to get rid of everything. Repaint the walls a neutral color. Then bring in that Waterpath interior designer I've heard so much about. Let's see what he can do with the space."

The girls nodded and agreed with everything Viara was saying, but when her back was turned, they exchanged mocking looks, one of them silently mimicking Viara's haughty expression.

Viara continued to rattle off her ideas about what to do with the rooms, then glared at two of the girls and jerked her head toward the kitchenette. They sprang into action, preparing a small meal for Viara. Everys's stomach rumbled at the sight of the food. She slapped a hand over her belly, grimacing as she waited to see if anyone had heard. Didn't look like it.

Within ten minutes of their arrival, Viara had settled onto one of the couches next to the bizarre fireplace, glaring at the girls as they tried to make her comfortable. Once she had been given her snack, she snapped for everyone to leave her. The others did, rushing through the door.

Viara glowered at the door, then took an experimental nibble on a slice of cheese. She blanched and frowned, dropping it onto the plate. She tossed the snack onto the floor, the plate shattering and the food spilling everywhere.

How could she be so wasteful? How could she—

Then Everys heard it: the quiet sniffle. She slowly came out of her corner and circled around the couch. Viara swiped at her face, smearing her makeup onto her hands. She shook them out, as if that could get rid of the stain. When she saw they were still dirty, more tears flowed, and soon, she was sobbing quietly to herself.

Everys froze in place, both horrified and fascinated. She knew how much Viara despised her. Narius's ex-wife had made that abundantly clear. And Everys had used that as an excuse to think of Viara as a monster, a force of evil. But now, seeing her so miserable, Everys was struck at how small she was.

How human.

"This isn't what I wanted at all," Viara whispered, her voice hoarse.

Everys tensed. Had Viara seen her?

"Not for me. And not for you." Viara touched her belly, running a hand along its swell. "When I found out about you, I was so angry. At myself for being careless. At him for not caring about me anymore."

Him who? Everys wanted to scream the question at her, but she clenched her teeth shut.

"And when Brencis offered to marry me, I thought that this was it. This was my way back to what I deserve. I thought I'd finally have what I had been missing for so long." Viara's head dropped back, and she looked up at the ceiling. "But nothing has turned out the way I wanted it to. I'm still just a pawn in everyone else's schemes. First Daddy's, then Narius's, and now Brencis's."

Everys's heart twisted and she wanted to cry with Viara, as insane as that felt. She knew what it was like to be used. And while, objectively, she knew that must have been what it was like for Viara as well, she had never really thought about what that must have felt like.

"So I'm going to promise you something." Viara sat up and wrapped her arms around herself. "No matter who you are, no matter what people expect you to do, I will never use you. Not anymore. All I'm going to do is love you and be there for you."

Viara tried to keep talking, but her shoulders heaved, and she wept again. Everys sucked in a sharp breath. She suddenly wished she had stayed in Tormod's closet like she was supposed to. This wasn't something she should have heard, even though she was glad she had. At that moment, she decided.

She hurried as quietly as she could and crouched down next to Viara's couch. She produced a vial of ink and used it to sketch out her family's healing rune on the wall, adding flourishes that would promote healing of mind and spirit. Once she activated it, she carefully nudged a decorative vase over to hide it from view while it worked. The rune wouldn't last long, only a few hours, but maybe that would be enough.

Once that was done, Everys headed for the door. She'd have to be careful since Viara's guards were likely stationed right outside, but she could—

Viara sighed heavily, then mumbled, "I only wish your father could have met you before he died."

Everys whirled around. The baby's father was dead? Did that mean... did that mean the father was actually Narius?

Before she could do anything, though, she felt a sharp tug on her legs, as if someone was trying to pull her through the floor. Then, with a lurch, she dropped, shooting through the alternating waves of cold and hot. Something rammed into her from behind, then hands clamped onto her arms. Tormod? Hopefully. They shot through the strange void until, with another jolt, they dropped back into the empty room in the Embassy.

Everys steadied herself, only to be turned around. She came face-to-face with Tormod, who stared up at her with an angry expression.

"I thought I told you to stay in the office," he said.

She tried to explain, but no words came. Everys finally squeezed out, "I'm sorry."

His eyes narrowed. He fished a scriber out of his pocket and held it up. "I was able to get Narius's medical records. Did you find out anything of interest?"

Everys once again found herself at a loss for words. In some ways, yes, but if she said that out loud, she felt like she would sully Viara's grief. So she finally sighed and shook her head. "Personal matters."

Tormod tipped his head to one side, then nodded curtly. "Let's get this to the doctors and see if they can figure out what you're looking for. And then I need to rest up if we're going to do this again. And I suspect you need some time to recover as well."

She nodded absently. Yes, she probably did, but she also knew that in some ways, she would never recover from what she had overheard.

61

B y the time Narius reached Bastion, he wasn't sure he could take any more surprises. The destruction and desolation only grew worse the closer they got to the capital. More wrecked vehicles, more evidence of fires and explosions, and sometimes, Narius was pretty sure he saw bodies in the fields. Guilt chased him down the river. So much of this was his fault

The time he spent with the rest of the crew only soured his thoughts. They were all accepting of him, even if they did resort to teasing him about his metallic eyes from time to time. But that was clearly not out of spite, more like hazing. During meals and downtime, Narius got to know some of them better, and what he learned sickened him. They all told the same story: struggling to make ends meet while growing up, taking whatever jobs they could, and then their lives being disrupted by the war between the Dynasty and the Dalark. While none of them were as outspoken as Siaku, Narius easily picked up on the undercurrent of resentment toward the nobility and the royal family.

Once the barge had docked outside of Bastion to take on new cargo, the captain called together the crew and paid them their wages. Some he invited to stay on for the next trip. He didn't make that offer to Narius, instead dismissing him with a thin smile.

As soon as he was away from the docks, Narius found a spot where he could see the Bastion skyline. While he had heard the stories of Bastion's destruction from Innana and members of the barge crew, he wanted to see it for himself. From that vantage point, though, he couldn't see much, just glass towers stabbing into the sky. Some familiar towers might have been completely missing, but he couldn't say for certain.

He caught a ride with a transport delivering foodstuffs. The driver, a hulking Ixactl, wasn't the chatty sort, and that suited Narius fine. The silent ride allowed him to soak in the sights as they drove.

So what did he do now? As much as he hated to admit it, he hadn't given much thought to what his next steps would be if he made it back to the Dynasty. He had assumed that when he made it home, he would have more help from Innana or he could find allies. Realistically, though, who did he have left? Not Paine. Not any of his council. He didn't even want to think of Everys in that moment. But now he was entering his capital, and he didn't know what he was going to find.

"You okay?" the Ixactl asked, his voice little more than a grunt.

Narius smiled. "Yes. I'm just trying to figure out where to go when we reach the city."

The Ixactl grunted again. "You ain't comin' home with me."

"I would never dream of asking," Narius said with a chuckle. "I do appreciate your help in getting me to Bastion."

Yet another grunt. "Times like this, we gotta stick together, right?"

He supposed that was true. That was the ideal that the Dynasty preached, after all. Loyalty to the throne, loyalty to your comrades-in-arms, and loyalty to...

His eyes widened. He knew where they had to go.

"Can you drop me off in Cliffside?" he asked.

"Yeah. Why?"

Narius smiled grimly. "I've got family there."

At least, he hoped he still did.

Even though the driver left him on the outskirts of Cliffside, Narius still had a good distance to walk. Plenty of time for Narius to second-guess himself. Yes, he did have family in Cliffside, but would he be welcome?

His parents had only had two children, an endless source of scandal or gossip. Narius hadn't understood until he was older. The nobles, all of whom had identified potential sons and daughters to marry off to the royal family, were disappointed when there were only two options. The Samags had scored a victory when Father betrothed him to Viara, and Father would have eventually forced Quartus into a similarly loveless union.

But their grandfather had fulfilled his duty with gusto. Before he died, King Vetranio had sired a grand total of sixteen children, six legitimate, the others not. Father had despised most of his siblings as leeches and hangers-on. He couldn't ban them from visiting the palace, but Father had made his disdain obvious enough that by the time Narius assumed the throne, most of his extended family ignored him. Only Uncle Galio, one of Vetranio's illegitimate sons, had weathered Father's hostility.

Uncle Galio's home wasn't much to look at, a mere three stories tucked into a modest property with a small pond. Being the illegitimate son of a king twice removed offered little in terms of financial security, especially given Galio's spending habits. He had few staff, too, just an automated watch system at the front gate. The moment Narius hit the call button, the front gate to the property popped open.

As he approached the house, Narius eyed the overgrown and poorly kept grounds. He was surprised that the local constables hadn't written him up for the lack of upkeep, but then, Galio had always been quicker to pay a bribe than a salary.

When he reached the porch, the front door swung open. An elderly man toddled out onto the porch, hunched over and grizzled with age. His head swayed as if perched on a loosened spring, and Narius wondered how he could navigate at all, given how bleary his eyes looked. Could this really be Galio? When had his hair gone so white, his beard become so scraggly?

"Y-yes?" the man rasped. "Who is it?"

"Uncle Galio?" Narius whispered.

The old man paused in the doorway, then cranked his neck upward to get a better look at Narius. "N-Narius? That can't be you, can it?"

"It is, Uncle. What happened to you?"

The man hesitated, then popped upright. He quickly whipped off a wig and fake beard, his movements so quick that Narius jumped back into a defensive crouch. In that quick motion, though, the old man somehow transformed into the man Narius remembered.

Galio was taller than Narius, with a tightly trimmed black goatee that was shot through with blond streaks. In the same way, Galio's hair was mostly black but with an almost white streak that ran from above his right eyebrow and back along his scalp. Any bit of frailty had vanished in an instant, and Galio gaped at Narius.

"I thought you were dead!" Galio whispered, then seemed to recover from the initial shock and quickly ushered Narius into his house.

Narius hadn't been there in years, but Galio's house was unchanged. There was a sickly sweet tang to the air, like that of spilled brandy, that permeated the rooms.

"I was, at least for a little while," Narius said.

"I bet that's a story and a half." Galio guffawed. "Gotta say, I love how you've taken after me. Your grandfather would've popped a blood vessel if he heard you married a scribbler. And here you are, sneakin' around Cliffside like a criminal? Love it! So why'd you come to an old warrior like me? You really this desperate?"

This time, honesty seemed like the best plan of attack. "I am, Uncle. Very few people know that I'm still alive, and they aren't here in Bastion. I wasn't sure where else I could turn."

Galio smiled broadly and enveloped Narius in a tight hug. "You did the right thing, kid. I've kept so many secrets over the years, Dalark intelligence would love to crack open my skull and sift through them all. Come in, come in!"

Despite the clutter and chaos of his house, Galio navigated them from the front door into the kitchen, where he whipped up a pretty decent meal, even though Narius suspected many of the ingredients had expired. He didn't care. It was the first good meal he had had since returning to the Dynasty.

As they ate, Galio quizzed him about where he had been and what he had been up to since his apparent death. Narius told him most of the tale—after all, who would believe him that a nonspeaking Siporan mage had somehow saved him from death or that he had worked with the Emperor's own sister to overthrow Tirigian?—but left out some details just to be absolutely safe. Galio hung on every word before he finally asked what Narius had been dreading.

"So now what?" Galio asked. "What are you going to do next?"

Narius glowered at the remnants of his meal, as if his indecision was the food's fault. He just didn't know. Returning to the Dynasty, making it to Bastion, finding shelter, those goals had all been obvious. But how could he go about anything else? Rallying support? Finding his way to the forest? Reuniting with Everys? He didn't have the first idea of how to proceed.

Galio chuckled and settled an encouraging hand on Narius's shoulder. "Hey, kid, this is going to be okay. You've just got what Dad always called 'strategic paralysis.' Hits the best military leaders. Huge objective, unsure conditions. How do you do it all, right?"

Narius nodded, even though he always found it strangely disconcerting to hear Galio refer to King Vetranio as "Dad."

"Take Dad's campaign against the Cold Light. How many people have tried to conquer the trees? Dozens? Hundreds? Who knows? But Dad was determined to do it. So he overcame his strategic paralysis by defining his goal. What was it he wanted to achieve? Specifically, mind you. It wasn't enough for him to say 'conquer the Cold Light.' No, he wanted to subjugate them and claim their fields for the Dynasty's glory."

Galio almost sounded proud as he talked, causing Narius to squirm in his chair. That definitely wasn't the attitude Narius would have taken toward a military conquest that ended with Vetranio firebombing the forest.

"You just need to do the same thing. Set aside the big picture stuff for now and define what your goal is!"

Narius nodded as though Galio had just dropped the Sun's own wisdom before him. What was a manageable goal? Maybe getting out of Bastion, although where he'd go after that, he had no idea. With very few resources, there was no way he'd be able to travel all the way across the Dynasty's holdings to the Cold Light's forest. So what did he need immediately?

"Allies. As many as I can get. People who are still on my side, who might be ready to take a stand against Brencis," he whispered.

Galio crowed in triumph and clapped him on the back. "There you go, kid! That's the path forward."

Narius nodded enthusiastically, but then his shoulders slumped. How could he get those allies? Go door-to-door, begging each of the noble houses individually?

Galio's eyes twinkled. "And, as Chance would ordain it, I've heard rumors of just the place where you might find them."

62

Three days after their first jump, Tormod was ready to try again. But when Everys met him, he practically radiated exhaustion.

"Are you all right?" she asked.

He smiled wanly. "I could lie and say that I am, but this recovery has been difficult."

"Do you need more time?" Everys asked.

"No, I am ready." His expression hardened. "I suspect, Blessed, that part of the reason this was so difficult is because I had to 'pull' you away from whatever you were doing in the palace. I insist we stay together. If we can't, you must follow my instructions to the letter. If I have to exert myself like this again, I'm not sure I'd be able to continue."

Everys winced. She nodded soberly.

Tormod studied her expression, then nodded to himself. He rolled up his sleeve and activated the tattoo. Everys once again offered a silent plea to help her find Narius and quickly.

The spell took hold, dropping Everys into the strange void. This time, the effect wasn't nearly so disorienting. Maybe it was because she knew what to expect. Or maybe she had built up some immunity to the effects. Whatever the case, Everys could hold it together as she dropped through the heat and cold, ignoring the roaring in her ears, until she staggered forward, losing her balance for half a heartbeat. Once she had regained her footing, she took stock of her surroundings.

They had dropped into what appeared to be a canvas tent, the walls and ceiling stained and poorly patched. The fabric shuddered and flapped in the biting wind, which snuck along the floor and clawed at her ankles. Everys took an inadvertent step toward Tormod, as if she wanted to steal some of his heat. But then she noticed Tormod was doubled over, his chest heaving. Sweat slicked his brow.

"Are you okay?" she whispered.

He shook his head. "Not really, no. But I will be eventually. Let's see where we've wound up."

Tormod crept to the tent's entrance and poked his head out. He pulled back in and motioned for Everys to follow him outside.

She emerged from the tent into a sprawling camp, hundreds of tents crammed together, bordered by a high fence topped with razor wire. Everys turned a slow circle. The ground was nothing but mud, dotted with brackish puddles. The tents were barely holding together, their fabric threadbare or torn. There were half-rotten crates set up outside some of the tents, all of them obviously empty. She practically drowned in the despair that pervaded the atmosphere. The hopelessness was overwhelming, almost as powerful as the stench that assaulted her. Based on what she could see and smell, this camp had poor sanitation. Where were they?

"Let's take a cautious look around, Blessed," Tormod whispered. "Stay close to me in case we need to make a quick escape."

He didn't need to remind her. She felt no desire to head off on her own. As they crept through the camp, Everys couldn't help but wonder where all the people were. Based on where the sun was in the sky, she suspected it was toward the beginning of First Watch. The air was cool and crisp, so maybe everyone was hiding in their tents?

Then they rounded a corner and discovered a group of children. They kicked a half-deflated ball between them, chasing it and laughing. A group of women watched them, slouched on crates or barrels. Everys couldn't help but stare. It wasn't their haggard expressions or resigned postures. It wasn't their threadbare clothes or the grime caked on their arms, legs, and faces.

No, what gave her pause was the fact that all the children and adults were clearly Siporan. It felt strange to see so many of their people gathered in one place with none of the other subjugated races present.

Before she could process this information, a woman noticed them. She whispered something to the others and soon, everyone had stopped what they were doing and were staring at them. Even though these were her people, Everys felt a distinct urge to retreat or to ask Tormod to send them back to the forest.

But then one woman rose and walked over to them. She smiled, her expression still tired, and asked, "Newcomers?"

"Yes indeed," Tormod said quickly. "We just arrived."

"Where'd they find you?" the woman asked.

"At the main airhub. We were being picked up by friends after a long journey," Tormod said.

Every fought the urge to gape at him. He sounded so natural, so honest, and yet she knew none of that was true.

The woman snorted. "Were those 'friends' the ones who turned you in?"

"No, not at all," Tormod said. "Just our bad luck to wind up here."

"Well, if it's any consolation, you're safe here. For now, anyway." She shot a worried look at the children. "We try not to talk about what might happen in front of the kids. They're scared enough as it is."

Everys looked at the children too. One of them stopped playing long enough to offer her a wave and a toothy smile. She returned the gesture.

"We usually only get one meal a day, so show up on time at the south gate. That's where the troops hand out the ration packs," the woman continued. "If you're needing other supplies, you can put in requests there. No guarantee you'll get it, but sometimes we're lucky. If you somehow find yourself with extra clothing or blankets or even food, bring it to Scrivener Sebash. He'll make sure that it gets to people who need it."

Tormod nodded with a smile. "Have you been here long?"

"Ever since the city fell," the woman said. "My family's home was burned down in the rioting before that, but the camps weren't set up until most of Bastion was destroyed."

"And they only rounded up Siporans?" Everys asked.

The woman frowned at Everys's question. "Not at first, no. This camp used to hold many different people. But over the past couple of weeks, they've been releasing the other humans and nonhuman races to go elsewhere."

Everys fought to keep from grimacing. Tormod chuckled and snared her hand.

"You'll forgive my niece. She's just in a bit of shock. We were overseas, visiting relatives in Elscontin, when all of this happened," he said. "When we arrived at the airhub, they arrested us and sent us here. She's a little confused."

The woman grunted. "You probably should have stayed in Elscontin."

"Perhaps we should have," Tormod said.

Before the woman could say anything else, one of the little boys, no older than seven, ran up and tugged on her arm. "Isn't it story time yet, Mama?"

The woman smiled and nodded. "Probably. Should we go see if Auntie is ready?"

The boy nodded enthusiastically and ran back to his friends, spreading the word. The kids quickly abandoned their game and gathered. The other women herded them away from their play area.

"You should come with us," the woman said. "Auntie always wants to greet the newcomers."

Was that a hint of suspicion in her voice? Everys chided herself for asking too many questions. She should have let Tormod handle it.

As if sensing her thoughts, Tormod nudged her. "Don't be too hard on yourself, my dear. This is an unusual situation. Anyone would have difficulty adjusting."

She offered him a shaky smile. Hopefully, she hadn't revealed too much with her ignorance.

The women and children led them through the tent city, past other clusters of people who stopped what they were doing—mostly talking, from what she could see—to openly stare at them. Everys pulled her scarf up and over her head. They probably had noticed how clean both she and Tormod were. That alone made them stand out.

Eventually, they came to a knot of children, sitting in a semicircle facing a tent. They practically buzzed with excitement, which only grew as the group joined them. A few moments later, the tent flaps burst open and an older woman jumped out, a wide smile on her matronly face. She threw open her arms and greeted the children, all of whom shouted their greetings back. Everys smiled at their enthusiasm as the woman sat down on a crate with an exaggerated sigh.

Tormod chuckled. "Why am I not surprised?"

Everys glanced at him. Surprised about what?

"Don't you recognize her?" Tormod asked.

Everys looked back at the storyteller. What was he talking about?

Prompted by the children, the woman launched into a story about how the Singularity once protected a group of Siporans from Ixactl warlords.

As the woman spoke, a growing sense of recognition blossomed inside Everys. There was something familiar about this woman's face, but there was something wrong, something missing. Like a scarf. No. A blindfold!

"Kyna?" she whispered.

"My sister always had a flair for the dramatic," Tormod said.

That was an understatement. Kyna was a Siporan woman that Everys had known from Fair Havens. She insisted that all the residents call her "Auntie," and she made a nuisance of herself. For as long as Everys had known her, Kyna had pretended to have different ailments, acting like she was blind or deaf or unable to walk. Kyna claimed that the Singularity wanted her to behave like that as a lesson to the Siporan community, but Everys always had her doubts.

But there was no sign of disability anymore. Kyna was animated as she told the story, changing her voice for each of the characters, creating vivid descriptions of the family's adventures, so much so that Everys almost could set aside her shock. Eventually, though, Kyna wrapped up the story, emphasizing that although not all the members of the family survived, they had clung to their faith in the Singularity and that had brought them through the crisis. Everys shifted uncomfortably. A good message for the children, but hearing a story where royalty sacrificed themselves to protect others didn't sit well with her.

The children clamored for another story, but Kyna chided them for being greedy. She promised them another story the next day, shooing them. The kids grumbled, but did as they were told. The woman who had spoken to Everys and Tormod quickly darted forward and whispered something to Kyna, jabbing a finger in their direction. Kyna looked over at them and smiled. She offered a jaunty wave, which Tormod returned.

"Nonsense, Silva!" Kyna stood up. "These aren't government agents. I know this one all too well. He's my brother!"

Kyna hurried over and hugged Tormod. Then she pulled free and beamed up at Everys.

"And how are you, dear niece?"

"A bit confused," Everys admitted.

"No doubt you are. Let's spend some time catching up in my tent." Kyna smiled once more at Silva, who glowered at them. "Thank you for bringing them to me, Silva. I relieve you of your *hospitality*."

Silva snorted and stomped away.

Kyna shook her head. "I wish she would look past her own greed. We haven't starved yet. But come, come."

Kyna ushered them into the tent, which contained nothing more than a cot and three boxes, arranged like chairs. Everys frowned. Why three?

Tormod looked over the interior. "Did you know we were coming?"

His sister stepped over to the crate and sat down. "I may have been warned to expect company, yes. I didn't realize that I'd be entertaining royalty or I would have gone to Sebash to ask for some extra food."

Everys held up her hands. "I'm glad you didn't. These people need that food a lot more than I do."

"So they do." Kyna turned her attention to Tormod. "So what brings you stumbling into my little corner of the Dynasty, brother?"

"What else? My oath."

"And the Singularity thought to bring you here? I wonder why that is?" Kyna motioned for the two of them to sit.

"I thought most of the Siporans had left Bastion," Everys said. "I tried to warn them that something like this could happen."

"Many did, but they couldn't make it far without the proper transit papers," Kyna said. "Unfortunately, Brencis saw our people's flight out of the city as an admission of guilt. So he had his troops round up our people and bring them here."

"Has the Singularity said what will happen to them?" Tormod asked quietly.

Kyna shook her head. "Not directly."

"But you have your suspicions," Tormod pressed.

Kyna closed her eyes and her head drooped, as if she were tired. "Some, yes, but I don't know if it is my fear speaking or the promptings of the Singularity. The last clear thing He said to me was this: 'The time for blindness is over. You, mortal, are still to speak to my people. Bring hope. Bring comfort. Bring peace. For the light will soon dawn.'"

A shiver danced across Everys's skin, Kyna's words resonating deep within her.

"So I've done what I can." Kyna shrugged. "Telling stories to distract the children. Reminding the adults of the Singularity's promises. Reminding them that, no matter how the world may change around us, He does not."

Everys leaned forward. "I'm going to fix this, Auntie. I'm going to make it better."

Kyna chuckled and patted her on the knee. "That may not be what you're called to do."

There was a shout outside the tent, then a young man popped his head inside. "Soldiers are coming, Auntie."

Kyna's lips pursed together into a thin line. "I would go."

Everys wanted to object. They had just gotten here, and she felt like they hadn't learned anything important or done anything significant. But Tormod didn't hesitate. He rose, hugging his sister once more while whispering something to her. She patted him on the shoulders.

Then Tormod turned to Everys and extended a hand. "We'd best go, Blessed."

She rose and took his hand. She looked at Kyna and, much to her surprise, wished they could talk more. Everys had never had much time for Kyna in the past. But now, she felt a distinct urge to hug her or drag her with them or...

The ground dropped away from beneath her feet, and she slid through the void. Then they were back in Tormod's room in the Embassy.

He braced himself and took a few shuddering breaths. He nodded tentatively. "Better, but I'll still need a few days to recover, Blessed."

With that, he left her to stand in the shadows, plagued by worries about what she had seen. Finding Narius and stopping Brencis seemed to be even more important. Because if they didn't, she had no idea what was going to happen to her people.

63

Everys considered sending a messenger to Tormod to see if he was ready to try another jump. True, they had only returned two days ago, but she wanted to try again. Seeing the worsening conditions of her people had only motivated her. Unfortunately, speaking with his sister seemed to have the opposite effect on Tormod. He dragged himself back to his quarters the moment they returned to the Shade. As much as she didn't want to, she gave him his space. She knew he'd be ready to try again soon. If he needed some extra time, she should give it to him.

While she waited, she tried to occupy herself with matters of state. Thankfully, it turned out that there wasn't much that demanded her attention. After delivering the holographic projector, the Dalark military had withdrawn from the forest's edges. No one knew why.

Worse, Overturn wasn't there to explain it either. When Everys had returned from the internment camp, she had learned that the strategist had taken the Cold Light's offer. Within an hour of his decision, the grafted had whisked him out of the Shade to some undisclosed location to "prepare him" for his new role in the coming war. Everys tried not to think about how ominous that sounded.

Since the rest of the forest didn't require her help or supervision, she returned to Professor P'layvo's translation team and the Illuminates to see how their research projects were proceeding. What she found was surprising, but not in the ways she expected. Neither team could report much progress in their individual tasks. Galan confided in her that P'layvo was growing frustrated by the lack of data they could feed to the AI. While they had refined their translation of the puzzle rune, they still couldn't determine its exact meaning. And Style shared that Tillmin had shut down any further experiments using lasers to draw runes. Given what Tillmin had shared with her, his decision did not surprise her. She suspected Hirfan had pushed for that and she didn't really blame him.

But what did surprise her was how the Illuminates and the translation team had intermingled. In some ways, it made sense. The Illuminates regularly used runes in their work, which meant that they had insights the translation team needed. And apparently sharing that information had an invigorating effect on the Illuminates in return. When Everys stopped by the translation team's room in the Embassy, she was surprised to see that there were half a dozen Illuminates chatting with the linguists, laughing and sharing stories and ideas.

The conversation died when she stepped into the room, though. She frowned, especially at how Tolistan and Screj looked guilty the moment they saw her. Something was going on.

Galan stood up, looking at Style, who nodded. The two of them approached Everys. Everys winced at the look Galan gave her. Yes, she had apologized, but Everys was sure she still saw a bit of judgment lingering in her sister's gaze.

"We need your help, Blessed," Style said.

"We want you to go talk to Tillmin. We have an experiment we want to conduct, but we need his permission to do so," Galan continued.

Everys frowned, her mind parsing through their words. If they needed Tillmin's permission, that most likely meant that the Illuminates wanted to cast more runes with light. But why would that interest Galan and her team unless...

Her eyes widened. "You want to cast the puzzle rune with light?"

Galan nodded.

"Absolutely not!" Everys said. "We don't know for sure what it does. And we've seen how powerful a rune drawn by light can be. You really want to experiment with that?"

Galan nodded grimly. "I think the risk is worth it."

Everys crossed her arms. She knew from firsthand experience how dangerous experimenting with unknown runes could be. She didn't want to inflict another plague on anyone. But she recognized Galan's expression. She had seen it often enough when they were growing up. Galan was completely serious. And Everys knew how intelligent and cautious Galan was. She wasn't one to take unnecessary risks. "Convince me."

"You've already stated why we need to do this. We don't know what this rune does, and we need to. Oluna stole our research before she escaped, right? That means the mage-kings have the puzzle rune too. What if they use it? Shouldn't we know what it's capable of doing?"

That was a good point, but Everys still frowned. "I thought you said it couldn't be cast without a powerful ink."

"That's our theory, yes, but we don't know for certain if it's true," Style said. "From what Galan tells me, they used regular ink when they tried casting it the first time. It didn't work."

"So use Cold Light sap instead," Everys said.

The two of them exchanged a look, one that Everys could easily decipher. She pinched the bridge of her nose. "You already did, didn't you?"

Galan nodded sheepishly. "Just yesterday. The rune still didn't work."

"Then maybe the rune just doesn't work," Everys said.

Galan shook her head. "You know that's not true. I knew it, too, the moment I saw the puzzle rune."

Everys frowned. Yes, she knew that as well. She still remembered how she felt when she first saw it.

"The problem, Blessed, is that the mage-kings have access to an ink more powerful than sap," Style said. "I doubt they'd hesitate to use blood to cast it."

She sighed, seeing Galan and Style's point. How would they ever know unless they determined what the puzzle rune did? And if regular ink and tree sap hadn't worked, that really left only one last option.

"I can't believe I'm going to do this," Everys muttered. "I'll speak to Tillmin."

"Thank you!" Galan beamed at her.

Everys held up a finger. "But I'm going to insist that we talk to the Cold Light about this as well. No more sneaking around. If this rune is really powerful, I don't want to set it off in the middle of the Shade. We need to take precautions, whatever Tillmin and the Cold Light demand."

Style nodded. "Perfectly reasonable."

Everys blew out a long breath through her nose. Hopefully, she hadn't just made a huge mistake. But there was really only one way to find out.

64

The night before the nobles' gathering, Urett sent word to Quartus that the Humrices, a minor noble family, would host the meeting at their family compound to the south of Bastion. Thankfully, Yusra found them a ride with a group of entertainers who had been hired to perform at the Humrices' estate. Normal people wouldn't hire entertainment while they were planning a sedition. But that wasn't a surprise to Quartus at all. The conspirators wouldn't want to be uncivilized, after all.

The Humrice estate wasn't much to look at. They didn't have any grounds to speak of, just a squat, single-level house with a tower in one corner. The transport drove around to the back of the house so the musicians could unload. They said their goodbyes, mostly to Yusra, and then worked on moving their equipment into the house.

"Shall we go inside?" Yusra asked.

Quartus nodded, and they slipped through the back entrance. That let them into the kitchen, where several servants bustled back and forth, with one very harried steward shouting orders at them all. When she spotted Quartus, she snarled and walked up to him.

"You a guest or a worker?" she demanded.

"Uh... guest," Quartus said.

She jabbed a finger at the exit. "No guests are allowed back here. You go back out front and enter with the rest of them. Don't think you're gonna bypass security like this!"

Yusra offered an apologetic smile and pulled Quartus back outside. As annoyed as he was, Quartus appreciated the way the steward was taking security seriously. He and Yusra followed the pavement back to the front of the house, where several nobles were queuing up to enter the manor.

A handful of security guards checked them for weapons, then motioned for them to enter the house. They followed the hallway to a large ballroom. Quartus took a moment to study the layout in case they had to leave quickly. Risers lined the two long walls with three levels of chairs and tables facing a central open area. The musicians they had ridden with were setting up their instruments along another wall. Only a handful of people meandered through the room.

Yusra tugged on Quartus' hand, leading him up toward one of the topmost levels. Once they were there, they settled in for what Quartus was sure was going to be an interesting night.

For most of the night, Quartus worried either he was the only one who understood the gravity of what was happening or that Urett had lied to him about the purpose of this gathering. Once all the nobles had arrived—by his count, at least forty of them from almost as many families—the servants moved into the ballroom with trays of food and wine. As the musicians played, the nobles mingled with one another, chatting and laughing as if this were any other social event. A few even took to dancing in the narrow area between the risers. For a moment, Quartus considered taking Yusra down to the floor and showing them what true dancing looked like. He knew from experience how graceful she could be.

As he scanned the crowd, he was pleasantly surprised at who had attended. Not just minor houses, but major ones as well, a good cross section of the Dynasty's aristocracy. He recognized most of them, although there were a few he didn't know, like the man who almost looked like his Uncle Galio except for the long, scraggly beard. But there were enough powerful people here to actually threaten Brencis's reign. At least, they could if they would only take this seriously.

After an hour of socializing, a beautiful woman with bright red hair stepped to the center of the room. Quartus recognized her after a moment. Jesik Hollowbrook. She signaled to the musicians, who wrapped up their song and quickly cleared out of the ballroom. The others took it as a signal to take their seats.

"Friends, thank you for coming tonight," she said. "While we may wish circumstances were different, we all recognize the abysmal conditions of our beloved Dynasty. And so, at great personal risk, we have come together to have an honest discussion about how we may best move forward."

Quartus shifted in his seat. No doubt the nobles were taking a risk, but so many of them had behaved like they didn't understand that.

"When the Dynasty has been on ruinous paths in the past, the nobility have been the ones to call the royal family to account," Jesik continued. "This is something I know all too well. Before I married into the Hollowbrook family, I was a Dwellin. It was our family who intervened in the civil war which led to the creation of Albanon's Compromise. At other times, the nobles have used our collective voices to correct the overreach of kings in the past. We need to do something similar today.

"I wish it had not come to this. Brencis is my uncle, after all. But despite my connection to him, I have come to the inescapable conclusion that he is going to ruin the Dynasty if he is not reined in now. I hope that tonight, we will take the first steps toward fixing this unfortunate situation."

Quartus frowned. First steps? Jesik was speaking like this was some toothless committee, not a conspiracy to overthrow a tyrant. Were they going to follow formal parliamentary procedures? Conduct public opinion polls? Take votes? They had to act, and they had to act now!

Yusra put a hand on his knee and squeezed. "Relax," she whispered. "Let them figure this out."

He blew a breath out of his nose and settled back in his chair.

One of the nobles clapped his hands on his knees, then ponderously rose from his chair. He wasn't that large of a man, although he did try to compensate for his aging body by hiding it behind as much clothing as possible. The outfit made him look like he was too cold, although his flushed cheeks gave him the opposite appearance. He tucked his hands behind his back, probably trying to look like he was a stern military commander, but overall, he looked more like an overwhelmed parent. Quartus bit back a groan and mopped a hand over his face.

"What?" Yusra whispered.

"That's Arkid Gardan," Quartus murmured.

Yusra turned back to Gardan, and Quartus could practically hear her doing the mental calculations as she evaluated him. Then she slumped in her chair, a frown flickering over her expression.

"My friends, let us slice to heart of the matter, shall we?" Gardan's voice was surprisingly strong and resonant. "Lady Hollowbrook is right. Brencis is a poor king and we all know it. He has blundered his way through the current war and is far too focused on prosecuting old vendettas and prejudices. What we need is a ruler with the strategic vision to steer the ship of our beloved Dynasty through this storm and to a peaceful oasis."

Quartus winced. If the man ruled the way he mixed his metaphors, they were all doomed.

"And you're the one to lead us?" a woman called.

Gardan shot a smile in the direction of the question. "Of course, my dear. Who else? You all know my family's venerable history. Why, King Heronus was married to a Gardan, after all."

That wasn't much of a claim. Back then, the Dynasty's kings were all polygamous. Half the nobles in the room could claim that one of their ancestors was married to a king before Albanon's Compromise.

"And my family has produced more than our fair share of military leaders over the past few centuries. We take pride at being the primary patron of The Trench, and we all know that school has produced many fine strategists and thinkers," Gardan continued. "With that resource at my disposal, this war would be over quickly."

Quartus frowned at the logic. Just because the Gardans funded The Trench, a notorious military academy in the Kronin Desert, that didn't mean that he'd be good at military strategy.

"I would also pledge three-quarters of my family's financial holdings to the restoration of Bastion, The Stone, Wrine, and all of the cities that have been devastated by this crisis." Gardan clasped his hands over his heart. "We have spent so many years accruing those blades through our vineyards, ceramic factories, and computer labs. It is time for us to put that to work for the Dynasty."

Murmurs rippled through the crowd. Everyone knew that the Gardans were an extremely wealthy family, second only to the Samags. If he was willing to do that...

"Oh, please, Arkid. Now is not the time for lies." The voice that interrupted the whispers was even deeper than Gardan's.

Quartus strained to see who spoken. Much to his surprise, a short man hopped down from his chair. He couldn't have been more than four and a half feet tall, with a wild shock of blond hair. His face appeared as if it had been smashed flat, but there was an incisive gleam in his bright blue eyes. Quartus looked him up and down. He didn't recognize him.

Yusra sucked in a sharp breath. "Do you know who that is?"

Quartus shook his head, but then his gaze snapped to Yusra. Wait, *she* knew? It appeared as though she might be the only one.

"That's Kutnik Zavoleny," she whispered back.

"How do you know that?" he asked.

Uncertainty flickered over Yusra's face. "I-I don't know."

He ground his teeth. That probably meant it had something to do with her memory block. But then the name she said registered.

"That's the Zavoleny patriarch?"

She nodded, her eyes wide, and Quartus understood her wonder. The Zavoleny family was something of a mystery among the Dynasty's nobility. They were easily one of the wealthiest of the major noble families, although no one knew exactly where they ranked. The only thing anyone knew for certain was that the Zavolenys had invested heavily in entertainment, primarily for children. The history books were filled with stories of Zavoleny bards traveling the Dynasty's holdings, sharing stories with whoever would listen. How they had parleyed that into a fortune was the subject of endless speculation among the nobles and conspiracy theories among the commoners.

Kutnik marched down to where Arkid Gardan stood. He smiled up at the other man, who scowled in return.

"You dare accuse me of lying?" Gardan asked. "I should challenge you to a duel, but I hardly think that would be fair. My reach clearly exceeds yours."

The other nobles laughed.

Kutnik smiled easily. "Without a doubt it does, but then, the Gardan reach has always exceeded their grasp. How many times has your family nearly gone bankrupt due to poor investment decisions? I know of at least eight."

The color drained from Gardan's face and he stammered. The amusement in the room died, replaced by looks of shock. Quartus had no idea if that was an accurate number, but based on Gardan's reaction, it probably was.

"I find it fascinating that the Gardans always managed to pop back up onto their feet again," Kutnik continued. "So I wonder, Arkid. How many promises did you have to make to Sellafus Coran this last time?"

The room practically buzzed with horrified voices. Quartus and Yusra exchanged their own shocked looks. They knew that name all too well. Sellafus Coran was a crimelord with whom they had crossed paths not that long ago.

"H-how did you..." Gardan's voice trailed off as his legs buckled under him.

Kutnik waved a hand in Gardan's direction. "Is this really who we want to take over the Dynasty? Someone who can barely keep track of his own house's finances? Or would you rather have Trin Samag, who would use the crown to merely glorify himself? Or possibly Klamont Wendly? Yes, I'm sure a Wendly kingship would be delightful for us all."

The gathered nobles shifted in their seats, but then one of them called, "Who would you choose? Yourself? The Dynasty would be a laughingstock!"

Kutnik's smile broadened. "Undoubtedly we would. Of course, if we were to choose you and your, shall we say, 'proclivities' were to come to light, we would still be an endless source of mirth."

The noble who shouted sank back in his chair, his face turning several shades of red. His wife glared at him, whispering furious questions at him. Quartus would hate to be that man.

"No, I am clearly too easy to overlook," Kutnik continued. "But then, how many times in the past few months have we in the nobility been surprised by what should have been obvious? Why, I suspect that we are overlooking several important factors right now."

As he said this, Kutnik's gaze passed over Quartus, only to hitch on him for just a second. Quartus froze. Had Kutnik recognized him? Was he about to reveal his presence to the gathering?

Thankfully, he didn't. Instead, he turned a slow circle, staring at each one of his colleagues in turn. "We are at a unique crossroads, my friends. We have been brought here by our stubborn insistence on tradition and maintaining the status quo. Do you really feel that we will solve this by simply doing more of the same?"

He let the question hang in the air. Then he nodded to Jesik Hollowbrook, who cleared her throat and stepped forward.

"Thank you, Lord Zavoleny. You have given us much to consider. Does anyone else have something to offer?"

No one said a word. Quartus swallowed a groan. If this was how the night was going to go, they were in for a rough time.

65

Narius tried to sink deeper into his chair, glancing around at the nobles who surrounded him. No one had questioned it when he showed up and claimed to be his uncle. Most of them had never met King Girai's eccentric half brother, so they had no idea what he looked like. A few had shot him curious glances, but none had deigned to speak with him. But now he felt exposed.

Jesik Hollowbrook stood in the middle of the room, trying to prompt more discussion. Narius took a moment to study his old friend. Even though it was only a little more than a decade, it felt like a lifetime ago since he'd last seen her. She had been one of his closest friends, but after what happened between her and Paine, they had drifted apart. As much as Narius had wanted to reignite the friendship they had all shared, he had refrained. Too much to do, and he doubted Paine would have appreciated the effort. Still, it was nice to hear her voice again.

Hers was apparently the only voice that would be raised at this meeting, though. Kutnik Zavoleny's challenge had clearly left them stunned. A few offered half-hearted suggestions that prompted limp debates, but nobody offered a solution that had any real merit.

After a full hour, Narius shifted in his chair, frustration mounting. They were all just posturing, rearranging the units on the battlefield to make them look more intimidating instead of attacking. But then, this is what the nobility had been conditioned to do. They made noise. All flash, no fight. Despite Jesik's attempts at uniting them, they wouldn't actually accomplish anything, unless something forced them to act.

No, not something. Someone.

He braced himself, ready to stand. He'd whip off the disguise, reveal his presence, and take charge of the meeting. Surely with this many people here, ready for change, they'd be glad to help him.

A servant, a young Plissk man, raced into the room and headed straight for Jesik. He whispered something to her, and she straightened, worry painted across her face. Narius froze and waited to see what was happening.

"My friends, we may have a situation. Apparently, a number of armored transports are heading here as we speak. We're not sure who they work for."

Worried whispers rippled through the room, and Narius tensed. Internal Security? Brencis's troops? This close to Bastion, he doubted they were Dalark, but there was no guarantee.

"Please, friends! There is no need to panic. What we are doing technically isn't illegal," Jesik continued. "Brencis hasn't outlawed social gatherings, and that is what this is. As long as we remain calm, these new arrivals will be none the wiser."

Jesik's words had their intended effect. The whispers ended, and soon, the musicians returned and began playing light music. Within a few minutes, the servants returned, circulating among the guests with food and drink, and the gathered nobles began laughing and chatting amiably.

But Narius couldn't relax. While the rest of the people gathered here could claim to be innocent party guests, he couldn't.

Before he could move, the doors to the ballroom burst open and armed soldiers marched inside. Narius sank back into his chair, eyes fixed on the weapons the soldiers carried. Military issued flechette throwers. But then he noticed what the soldiers wore. Not uniforms. It looked more like they had cobbled together soldier-like outfits. Then his gaze caught on what one soldier was wearing, the overcoat from the King's Guard. He should have recognized the shoulder patch immediately! He looked to the man's face and his breath caught.

"Zar?" he whispered.

The captain of his guard scanned the gathered nobles coolly. His weapon wasn't up, but he was ready.

Narius looked at the other troops and recognized another immediately. Farga, his Swordbound. His heart stuttered. Maybe this was a good thing. Zar and Farga had never given him reason to doubt their loyalty. If he could reveal his presence to them somehow...

Then, much to his surprise, Urett strode into the room. His former assistant was dressed smartly in a dark suit, his head tipped back imperiously. His arrival sent a wave of whispers through the guests. From what Narius could tell, none of them knew who he was. That wasn't a surprise. Urett had usually remained in Narius's private quarters, rarely seen by the public. The nobles might know his name, but not his face.

"Hello, my friends!" Urett called. "Never fear. We do not wish to stop your conversation. Instead, we want to add to it. I have arrived with someone who will make a worthy leader for our Dynasty, one much better than Brencis."

He swept his arm toward the door, and then Auriel Zammit entered the room, flanked by more of Narius's King's Guard. She wore her full uniform, a dazzling reminder she was the Governor-General of Bastion.

Narius sank back in his chair, deciding to let this play out. Better to remain an observer.

"My friends, I am sorry to interrupt your gathering," Zammit said. "But when I heard that so many illustrious nobles were meeting together and why, I knew I had to attend. For you see, I am in full agreement. King Brencis must be deposed. The Dynasty needs a firm hand to guide it through this crisis. And I believe I am your best choice to do so."

"There's no way anyone will accept you as queen, Auriel," one guest shouted. "You're not even a noble."

"True, I'm not," Zammit shot back coolly. "But did my husband care when I defended him and his staff against Riokan terrorists? Did King Girai care when he named me the Governor-General of Bastion? Did King Narius care when he kept me in that role? Wake up! The Dynasty is crumbling around you. Now is not the time to bicker about nobility. We need decisive action. I, for one, will break with tradition if it means saving what we all hold dear. Are you so bold?"

Grumbling erupted around him, but Narius couldn't help but be impressed. Auriel stared at the gathered nobles, but she offered a small smirk to Urett, who blushed furiously.

Jesik finally waved down the nobles, then turned her full attention to Zammit. "If we were to back you, what would your plan be?"

Zammit nodded to her graciously. "Provided we can persuade Brencis to step down, our first goal should be to end the war with the Dalark Imperium."

"What of the reports that Queen Everys is lurking in the Cold Light forest? Shouldn't we worry about what she might be up to? She's a toratropic witch, after all!" another person shouted.

Narius bristled at the insult, but Zammit waved it away.

"Have you spent any time with Everys?" Zammit asked. "She isn't a threat. If anything, she could be a potential ally. No, our focus must remain on Brencis."

With that, Zammit launched into a speech in which she outlined her plans for not just what they might offer Brencis to entice him to step down, but also how to bring the war to an end and then rebuild the Dynasty. As the gathered people listened, many of them started nodding and murmuring in agreement.

Narius couldn't blame them. Zammit had clearly given this a lot of thought. Not just that, but the solutions they had crafted made sense. Some of them, such as increased taxes, would be hard to sell, but given the promises she made about greater autonomy among the nobles and future concessions to the common folk, she might just be able to convince the right people to support her. Narius certainly felt more optimistic after hearing her.

But that optimism came at a heavy price. Zammit made it sound so simple, as if governing the Dynasty would be easy. So why had he struggled with it so much?

As he mulled that over, he noticed that Zar frowned and touched his ear, probably listening to a report over a hidden comm. His eyes widened, and he hurried over to Zammit. He whispered something to her. Her expression flickered with uncertainty, then she nodded brusquely and turned to the gathered nobles.

"My friends, we may have a situation brewing. I suggest we continue the ruse that this is a social event for the time being. Music, food, and drink, friendly conversation." She turned to her guards. "Make yourselves scarce."

Jesik barked orders and, within moments, the musicians had returned, along with the servers, who circulated through the room to freshen people's drinks and offer them more food. Narius waved them away, watching the tension build among the guests. The door to the room banged open and Vizier Paine strode into the room.

66

Narius felt like he had been dipped in ice water. What was Paine doing here? He had sworn loyalty to Brencis, after all. Did that mean the gathering was about to be raided? No, Paine had arrived by himself. If Brencis was making a move against the guests, he would have sent troops, maybe even accompany them himself.

Paine's gaze flicked over the guests and Narius held his breath. Uncle Galio's disguise might have fooled everyone else in the room, but Paine knew him too well. He'd see right through the fake beard and wig. But thankfully, the vizier's gaze swept past him without pausing.

The conversation in the room died, as did the music.

Jesik stepped forward, her expression frosty. "Paine."

Paine actually faltered. Narius had never seen his friend look so rattled before. He wouldn't even meet her gaze. "Jesik."

"I don't believe you were invited to this particular gathering." Jesik's voice caused the temperature in the room to drop at least fifty degrees.

"Indeed I wasn't." Paine glanced at her, then turned his attention to the gathered nobles again. "Such an eclectic collection of guests."

"What can I say? I've been known to have unconventional friends." Jesik's eyes flashed. "You of all people should know that."

Narius winced in spite of himself. That was an underhanded cut.

Paine, for his part, only quirked a brow. "Indeed. So, what is the occasion for this... forum?"

One of the nobles gasped. Narius closed his eyes. The fool. Paine had clearly chosen that word to goad them, and that idiot, whoever it was, had fallen for it.

Jesik drew herself up to her full height. "If you have something to say, Paine, just do so and then leave."

"As you wish." Paine tucked his hands behind his back and strode toward the center of the room. His gaze flitted from Auriel Zammit, who had been pretending to talk to Kutnik Zavoleny, then toward the musicians, and then over the rest of the guests.

Narius hated to admit it, but he was impressed. Even now, he could almost hear Paine's thoughts tumbling together. This stalling tactic was clearly designed to ratchet up the tension. Given the way so many of the guests were squirming in their chairs, it was working.

"It may interest all of you to know that, about three weeks ago, the people of the Nobility Commission began hearing rumors of a clandestine meeting, one that was going to be held by a group of nobles for purposes unknown. Normally, such rumors are ignored, but this one kept resurfacing, so often that the head of the Commission thought it best to pass word of this meeting to Internal Security as a possible threat."

Frantic whispers broke out in the room. Sweat beaded along Narius's brow. If Internal Security was involved, that could mean a group of thugs might come smashing through the door at any moment.

"As Chance would have it, though, before the reports of this potentially treasonous get-together reached the ear of Minister Bokil, it first came to me. And I was able to assure the Commission that I would see it was dealt with." He stopped his meandering, glancing around the room again. "Fortunate for all of you. You seek to replace King Brencis. It may surprise you to learn that I am in agreement with you. King Brencis must be removed from power, the sooner the better."

Narius's heart stuttered, and he sucked in a sharp breath. Did that mean...?

"Says the person who betrayed King Narius!" someone shouted at Paine.

Paine winced. He actually flinched! "It's true, I did. I wish I didn't have to, but given what was happening in the Dynasty at the time, I felt I had no other option."

Narius sat up in his chair, his mouth dropping open. What did that mean?

"You all know King Narius was my oldest and dearest friend." Paine glanced in Jesik's direction, then looked away just as quickly. "I owe much to him, both personally and professionally. And I applaud many of the initiatives he intended to champion. I have no doubt that, had he ruled during a more stable and peaceful time, he could have been remembered as one of the greatest kings the Dynasty has ever known. But that wasn't the circumstances he found himself in, and for that reason, I fear history will judge him harshly."

Jesik sucked in a sharp breath. "Paine! How can you say that? He loved you!"

Paine pursed his lips and turned to her. "And I him. But even when the three of us were students at Pellio's Legacy, people saw his shortcomings. Do you remember what Preceptor Ulris said in his final evaluation?"

Jesik's expression remained sour, but there was a flicker of doubt. Narius understood why. Preceptor Ulris had been an exacting teacher, and in that final evaluation, he had said that Narius lacked the pragmatic cruelty needed for the throne. At the time, he had taken his teacher's criticism as praise.

"And I know that there were others who saw the same lack in Narius. For the sake of propriety and... old promises, I will not reveal everything I know. But these doubts have followed Narius for most of his life."

A chasm tore open in Narius's chest. He knew what Paine was referring to. Not that long ago, Paine had revealed he had found notes from Paine's predecessor that suggested Narius's father was considering setting Narius aside as heir and trying to have more children in the hopes of producing one Girai felt was worthy of the throne. He was thankful Paine hadn't revealed that detail, but it still stung.

"As flawed as Brencis is as a king, Narius was flawed as well. I'm sure many of you saw it." Paine gestured at the guests. "I suspect many of you have discussed it in your own homes or in parties like this one."

Hesitant whispers rippled through the guests. Narius looked around, not at all surprised to see the nobles nodding at one another. Of course they talked about his supposed flaws. That's what the nobility did! They were never satisfied with anything the king did. That had been true for Narius's father and grandfather. But to hear Paine speak so bluntly about this wrenched Narius's heart.

"Governor-General Zammit, you worked closely with King Narius." Paine faced her. "What is your honest assessment of his rule?"

Zammit stepped away from Zavoleny, her expression uncertain. She studied Paine, who regarded her calmly, then motioned for her to take the floor again.

"I had my issues with Narius," Zammit said, her tone even. "He meant well. He wanted what was best for the Dynasty. But his energy was misplaced. He fought the wrong battles."

Narius gaped at Zammit, his heart cracking. While he hadn't considered her a friend, she was his colleague, a trusted adviser and helper. Why had she never said anything? He would have listened! He sank back in his chair, his mind reeling. The nobles didn't approve of him. The common folk didn't want him. Even if he did reclaim his throne, he would never be able to forget what he had seen and heard. Maybe he wasn't supposed to be king any longer. But if he wasn't king, then what was he?

Paine nodded sagely, then faced the gathered nobles. "That is why I came here today. I too see the need for change. That is why Governor-General Zammit has my full support."

Muted cheers and applause erupted in the room. Narius hung his head. He didn't have anything anymore, did he? No kingdom, no crown, no friends, no family. What did he have left? Nothing.

He scanned the room, looking for an escape route, but his gaze hitched on one corner. Why did it appear darker than the others? His eyes widened as the shadows deepened, as if they were slowly consuming the rest of the room. The darkness swirled and frothed. A chill settled in Narius's stomach. What was going on?

Three figures emerged from the roiling shadows, all of them dressed head to toe in black, their faces completely obscured. The one in the lead surveyed the gathered nobles.

"What do we have here?" The man's voice was muffled beneath the mask. "A gaggle of traitors? King Brencis sends his regards."

Everys hadn't been able to convince Tillmin. At least, not right away. They went round and round, discussing it for hours before the Illuminates' leader reluctantly agreed, but not before he gave her a lecture about how dangerous this idea was. When he suggested that Hirfan accompany her to observe, she didn't object.

The Cold Light were more understanding. They arranged for a clearing to be set up half a day's journey from the Shade, giving them a place where they could "set off" the rune far away from any civilians.

Challix had stepped in at that point, working with the military to arrange for transportation for the equipment and people. She was cooperative until she learned Everys wanted to observe the experiment. Redtale objected as well, but Everys insisted. If this was going to happen, she needed to know the results.

And so, within a few hours, a caravan of four transports rolled out of the Shade and headed deeper into the forest.

They eventually reached the clearing. The Cold Light had shoved away the trees in this part of the woods, leaving only bare dirt punctuated by the occasional shrub or log. Even the animals had somehow been redirected away from this part of the forest, meaning that the area was strangely quiet. Once they were parked along the tree line, the researchers from both teams set to work. The Illuminates set up a simple metal sheet that they would use as a surface for the laser to draw on. The translation team checked and double-checked the pattern that was inputted into the laser's control, dickering over the placement of each loop and flare.

The teams finally finished their preparations, and Galan and Hirfan trudged to where Everys waited.

Galan smiled at her. "We have everything set up as best as we can."

"We have scribers to capture video of whatever happens," Hirfan said. "We also have two volunteers who are going to stay near the laser to observe the experiment. If anything seems to get out of hand, they'll kill the power to the laser."

"Who volunteered?" Everys asked.

"Screj and Style," Galan answered.

That figured. Hirfan and Galan exchanged another look, then handed a scriber to Everys.

"What's this?" she asked.

"The controls for the laser," Hirfan explained. "We thought it best if you activate the rune."

Everys's head snapped back. "Why me?"

"The rune's translation suggests that whoever activates it will be able to 'reshape the world,' right?" Galan said. "That might be a metaphor, but that made us really think about who we wanted to entrust that kind of power to."

And they were going to entrust it to her? Really? She knew what both of them thought of her and what she had done in Utuaa.

"It was Tillmin's suggestion," Hirfan said, as if that explained it all. "Don't make him regret it."

Everys took the scriber and cradled it, thinking about what she would do with that kind of power. Stop the mage-kings, definitely. End the war, without a doubt. Remove Brencis from power, without a moment's hesitation. But most of all, she would bring Narius back to her.

"So what do I do?" she whispered.

"We'll signal Style and Screj, and then you can activate the rune whenever you're ready," Galan said.

"Just give us a countdown," Hirfan added.

Within a few minutes, Screj and Style signaled they were ready. As suggested, Everys counted down from five out loud and, with a deep breath, she activated the laser.

Even though they were half a mile away, she could still see the bright blue light against the metal plate as it traced the pattern. Hirfan, monitoring the video feed from the site, called out updates on how the process was working.

Light flashed near the metal plate and Style shouted something over the comms, but static suddenly distorted the channel. Then a blast of air pulsed over Everys, followed by a distant thrum. Her heart stuttered, and she sucked in an anxious breath. Another gust of wind pushed at her, not enough to knock her off-balance, but enough to make her worry, followed by a louder thump.

Then the clearing erupted with light, a new sun blazing at the center. An invisible hand pushed at her, and a roar sliced through her chest. She closed her eyes and threw her forearm over her face, but somehow, she could still feel the light burn through her.

Pins and needles swept over her, chased by a heaviness she knew all too well. She had experienced this sensation twice in her life. The first time had been when she had drawn runes at Narius's wedding to Innana. The second had been when she used the same runes in an attempt to save Narius's life. The Singularity had arrived, His presence overwhelming.

But in spite of the substantial weight that bore down on her, she was suddenly aware of someone standing next to her, a comforting presence, familiar. She risked a peek to her right, and in spite of the brilliance that washed out the world, she could see the vague outline of a person, shorter than she was, but male and...

"Narius?" she whispered, hope rising within her.

Then, with an audible pop, the onslaught ended. The light vanished, along with the pressure and the noise and, worst of all, the shadowy figure she had seen. She stumbled forward, looking around. Galan and Hirfan did so as well, but they appeared disappointed. But why?

"Probably for the best that it failed," Hirfan said.

"I suppose so," Galan said.

Everys stepped toward them. "But it worked! Didn't you see the light? Hear the sound? Didn't you feel... Him?"

They gaped at her.

"What are you talking about?" Galan asked. "Nothing happened. The laser drew the rune and just... nothing."

No, that didn't make any sense! Something had happened. She knew something had happened. She turned to her right, where she had been so sure Narius was standing, but there was nothing to show he had. And as she looked around at the rest of the clearing, she couldn't spot any sign that anything had happened.

"Are you all right?" Galan asked.

"I... I don't know," Everys said. "I could have sworn that the rune did... something."

That got Hirfan's attention. He stepped closer. "What happened? Did you experience something? What did you see?"

Everys explained about the light and the blast and the sound and the presence, her words a jumble as she tried to sort through everything. She left out the shadowy man who had stood next to her; the rest of it was weird enough as is. As she talked, more and more people from the teams gathered around her, asking her clarifying questions or for her to repeat details. By the time Style and Screj joined the group, everyone was chattering about different possibilities, almost as if Everys wasn't there.

She looked at Hirfan. "Did I imagine that?"

He considered it, then shook his head. "I don't think so. We've had experiences like this before. Although not to this extreme. One time, Screj tried to cast a spell using his burning ink as a prank on Style."

From where he stood, Screj groaned. "Not this story again."

"Sorry, Screj, it's relevant," Hirfan said. "Anyway, the glamour was supposed to create a ghostly image of a monster. Only Style didn't see it. None of us did, except for Screj. And he only half saw it before the rune failed with an audible pop, like you described."

"It was hilarious!" Style added. "Had him freaked out for close to a month."

"You didn't have to share that part!" Screj said.

"Academic integrity," Style said. "She needs all the data."

He groaned, but he motioned for Hirfan to continue.

"The point is, we realized afterward that the rune almost worked, but failed at the last moment. I suspect that's what happened here," Hirfan said.

"But why?" Everys prompted.

"Hard to say." Hirfan stroked his chin. "In Screj's case, it was probably the ink. When we repeated the experiment with real ink, it worked fine."

"And wasn't all that scary either," Style interjected, earning her a hurt look from Screj.

"Here, we know the 'ink' is good, so it might be a flaw in the rune's design." He held up a hand to stop Galan's objection. "Or it's possible there's an unknown factor at play here."

"So it's a failure?" Everys asked.

"Technically, I suppose you could say that, but look at it this way: if we're having trouble with this, the mage-kings probably are as well. And at least we're all still in one piece!"

That was true, Everys supposed, but as they packed up the equipment, she was all too aware that a piece of her was still missing and, at the rate they were going, probably always would be.

68

Quartus stared at the men in black as the shadows roiled behind them. He recognized them immediately. That was the same outfit worn by the assassin who killed Elamek and the two that had attacked them in Fair Havens. Yusra bolted out of her chair. The rest of the guests seemed confused, but no one seemed to understand the threat.

Two of the assassins snapped something in half, and an acrid smell flooded the room. Quartus's eyes went wide. Ink! The Dynasty always tainted their ink with a foul smell as a way to supposedly combat toratropic magic, to keep supposed mages from hiding what they were doing. Only these men didn't want to hide. No, they clearly wanted people to know what they had.

"Don't worry. This will all be over soon," the assassins' leader said

Two of the assassins swiped their fingers across the backs of their opposite hands, then thrust them at the nobles in unison. Quartus slid out of his chair, dropping to the floor. Yusra dove for cover as well. Fire and lightning shot from the assassins' open palms, slicing through the gathered nobles. People shrieked and screamed, but below it all, Quartus could hear the maddening laughter of the attackers.

Quartus risked a peek at the lead assassin. He had knelt, drawing something on the floor. Oh, that couldn't be good. Clearly the other two were meant to keep everyone at bay while he did the real damage. But what could they do? If they charged, they'd be killed.

But then, a rippling wave of energy passed through the room. The three assassins staggered. The flames and lightning guttered out, and the leader rose to his feet, looking unsteady.

Even more bizarrely, someone else stood in front of the assassins. A young woman, petite with short-cropped hair, wearing an outfit that screamed Dalark fashion. She looked around the room, confusion spreading over her face. Her mouth hung open, and she made a flurry of sharp, intricate gestures.

A thrill shot through Quartus. He had no idea what just happened, who the young woman was or how she got there, but this was the opportunity they needed! He glanced over at Yusra. Fear shone in her eyes, but when she met his gaze, her expression became determined and she nodded. Good. There was no way he would be able to do this without her.

They nodded together, a silent countdown, and at three, they scrambled forward, staying low to avoid the magical onslaught. They closed the distance to the attackers, then in unison, launched themselves at them.

Only the third assassin stepped into their path and raised his hands. Runes flared to life on his palms, and the two of them slammed into an invisible barrier, one that sent a flash of pain through Quartus's entire body. Given the way Yusra bit back a shriek, she must have felt the same thing.

"Help him!" a familiar voice shouted.

Quartus lay on the floor, his head swimming. Was he dying? He didn't think he got hit that hard, but why else would he have heard Narius's voice?

Then a figure leaped over him, and he realized it was the mysterious young woman. She interposed herself between Quartus and the lead assassin, gesturing broadly, then thrusting her closed fists toward the dark-clothed man. He stumbled backward and the runes on his palms winked out. When he regained his balance, he guffawed.

"Could it be? I've often dreamed of testing my mettle against one of you," he said. "Let's see who has mastered our arts better."

The woman tipped her head to one side, the stomped her foot and slashed her arms down. All three assassins were knocked backward. She stuck her tongue out at them, then whirled toward Quartus to...

No, not Quartus. Yusra. The other woman helped Yusra to her feet. Yusra stared to say something, but her face froze in confusion when she saw who was helping her.

"I know you," Yusra muttered. "Why do I—?"

Before Yusra could finish asking, the other woman wiggled her fingers in an intricate pattern, then pressed her hands on Yusra's temples.

Both women's eyes blazed with light and then Yusra staggered away, gasping for breath. Quartus scrambled to his feet, shoving the young woman aside to check on Yusra. She took deep, gulping breaths and clawed at her own head, then she looked up at Quartus.

"I remember," she whispered. "I remember *everything*."

Quartus frowned, searching her face for some explanation of what, exactly, she remembered. She didn't explain. Instead, she moved past him and grabbed the hands of the young woman.

"Kavi?" Yusra whispered. "What are you doing here?"

The young woman—Kavi?—jerked a head toward the three assassins, who were scrambling back to their feet. Yusra cast a glance over her shoulder at Quartus, and he gasped at the ferocity in her grin.

Then the two women turned and launched themselves at the two assassins. Quartus froze, gaping as they fought. They appeared like mirror images of each other, using the same jabs, kicks, and feints almost in unison. The two assassins broke off their attack to meet Yusra and Kavi, almost blow for blow. But Quartus could read the surprise and hesitation in their stances. They hadn't expected anyone to fight back.

"You are proving to be a nuisance, Prince Quartus," the lead assassin growled.

Quartus got to his feet and shrugged. "You're not the first person to say that."

"But I will be the last."

The lead assassin whipped two daggers from sheathes on his belt and spun them in his hand before dropping into a ready position. Quartus crouched, cursing the fact that he hadn't brought a weapon.

But then two men charged the assassin. Quartus belatedly recognized Zar and Farga, the latter ripping his ceremonial sword free from its scabbard. Farga waded in, slashing with his blade while Zar hung back, peppering the assassin with flechettes. In spite of being outnumbered, the assassin held his own. Zar's projectiles somehow bent around him, never hitting him, while the assassin was able to deftly parry Farga's thrusts and slashes.

"Mind giving us a hand, Quartus?" Zar snapped.

The guard shouting his name jolted Quartus out of his stunned reverie. He ran to Zar's side and pulled a smaller flechette thrower from a holster. He tried to get a bead on the lead assassin, but he and

Farga were moving too quickly. If he fired, he'd likely hit the wrong person.

Then Farga cried out and staggered back, blood pouring down his chest. Zar shouted in surprise, but then the lead assassin leaped forward and planted a firm kick in Zar's chest, knocking him backward. The assassin seemed to bounce off Zar, spinning through the air to land in front of Quartus. He slashed with his daggers and ripped the flechette thrower out of Quartus's grasp.

The assassin chuckled. "Did you really think you could stop us?"

"Then why don't you just kill me?"

"Not a bad idea."

The assassin lunged. Quartus tried to dance out of the way, but then he realized that the man wasn't coming after him. And one of his daggers had vanished.

Then he heard the anguished cry behind him. He whipped around and froze.

Auriel Zammit lay on the floor, one of the assassin's daggers sticking out of her chest. Urett knelt next to her, cradling her head in his lap. He wept bitterly, calling her name and shaking her shoulders gently.

Cold sluiced through Quartus as he turned back to the assassin, who chortled.

"We can't have someone actually competent ruling the Dynasty," he said. "That's the last thing she needs."

Fury chased away the numbness, and Quartus roared, charging the assassin. The other man hesitated, apparently surprised, but he danced out of the way, shoving Quartus off-balance as he passed. Quartus almost tripped over Farga's sword. At the last second, though, he scooped up the blade and spun back around, skidding to a halt in a defensive stance. His gaze flicked over to the corner where Kavi and Yusra had cornered the other two assassins. Yusra met his gaze and her eyes widened.

The assassin straightened and cocked his head to one side. "You can't be serious. Do you really think you're a threat to me?"

Quartus clenched his teeth. "I'm not. But she is."

Just as he spoke, Yusra raced past him. Quartus tossed her the sword. She caught it, slid under the assassin's defensive slash, and then stabbed into the assassin's gut before rolling out of his reach.

The man staggered, looking down at the blade. He choked, his voice nothing more than a wet burble. With shaking hands, he pushed up the sleeve on his left arm, exposing a rune tattooed on his wrist. He fumbled at the rune, but then it flared red. Shadows boiled up out of the floor, and the man staggered back a step, the inky tendrils enveloping him. The other assassins summoned their own shadowy pillars and stepped into them.

Quartus growled. No. He wasn't going to get away. Not this time. He charged and slammed into the man, Yusra screaming his name as the two of them tumbled through the dark. The assassin grappled with him, trying to twist away. Quartus wouldn't let go. He snared the man's arms, groping against him until his fingers brushed the sword's hilt. He grabbed it and, with all of his strength, twisted. The assassin grunted.

Then the two of them tumbled out of the void, rolling across a hard surface. Quartus slammed into a hard wall with a groan. But he shook off his dizziness and clambered to his feet. No way he was going to let a knock on his head make him an easy target.

The shadowy portal vanished, as if being sucked in on itself. They weren't in the ballroom anymore, but he didn't recognize his surroundings. A noble's house, that much was obvious from the dark wood paneling, rich decor, and large hallways. He shot a glance at the assassin, who had rolled onto his side, his fingers brushing against the sword's hilt. Satisfied he wasn't a threat, Quartus crept down the hall.

Then he spotted it: a massive painting near a staircase. It was of an older couple sitting with a teenage girl. He recognized them immediately. How could he not? It was the Minister of Finance, Masruq, and his wife, Oluna, with a young girl. Was that Zivah? The criers had been carrying stories lately about how Everys had healed Zivah using her magic. Was this their manor? Why had the assassin brought them here?

"Who are you?" a crackly voice asked.

Quartus spun and saw a young woman, no older than eighteen, standing at the bottom of the stairs. She stared at him, horror painted across her face. He looked down and easily understood why. His clothing was askew and covered in blood. He held up his hands to keep her calm.

"Please..." A weak voice drifted from Quartus's right. "Don't hurt her."

Quartus turned. The assassin sat slumped against a wall, blood pooling beneath him.

"Grandfather?" The girl shrieked, pushing past Quartus to rush to the assassin.

The assassin coughed, but then tugged the mask off, revealing Masruq. Quartus gaped at him. Masruq was a middle-aged bureaucrat so badly out of shape that walking the perimeter of his office would have winded him. *He* was the assassin?

The girl blubbered as she knelt next to him. She touched the sword, looking like she might try to pull it out, but Masruq moved her hands away and cupped her face with his.

"It's too late for me," Masruq said. "But not for you. That's why we're doing this. For you."

"What? Grandfather, no!" the girl sobbed.

Masruq's eyes went out of focus and his body slackened.

"Nekek... Nekek shall shine again..." The breath wheezed out of his lungs and he collapsed.

The girl fell on top of him, crying bitter tears. Quartus heard shouts of surprise from elsewhere in the house. He took two steps back before turning and dashing for the front door. While he had no doubt in his mind that Masruq deserved what happened to him, he also knew that if anyone caught him there, he'd be just as dead. He burst through the door and escaped into the night, racing as fast as he could.

69

"Q uartus!" Narius shouted his brother's name as he and the assassin fell into the shadows. He started down the steps, but then the shadows pulled in on themselves and vanished. No! He couldn't lose him, not like this. Where had the attackers taken him? He scanned the floor, hoping they had dropped something, a clue he could use to find Quartus. But he couldn't get a good enough look since the nobles were rushing around the room.

Pandemonium reigned in the ballroom. Many of the nobles had already fled, but many more lay where they had fallen, twitching and groaning as smoke rose from their bodies. He had no idea how many were injured or how many had died. More than should have.

Auriel Zammit's skin had turned waxen and gray, but she was being tended to by three of the guards. Urett stood nearby, tears streaming down his face. Kavi stared at the room, confusion painted across her face. Narius felt the same confusion, especially after her sudden appearance at the beginning of the fight. The other Dalark woman stood where Quartus had vanished, her eyes wide and wild.

But then Narius's gaze fell on Paine. The vizier stood near the front of the room, his features ashen. He looked like he was about to collapse.

Narius cast another look around the room. The nobles who had escaped the initial attack crowded near the exits, their voices high-pitched and frantic. The rest of the people milled about, clearly in shock.

There was a gentle prompting at the back of his mind, a nudge that he hadn't felt in what seemed like years. He tipped his head to one side and, as he did, a voice bubble up in his memory.

O Siporans, remember: the Singularity is supreme, the only, the whole. In Him and through Him and for Him, all was made. And we are His people, the servants of His will.

Not that long ago, Scrivener Tolistan had drilled him on this saying from the Siporan ancient texts. Narius had memorized it easily enough, but that hadn't been enough for Tolistan. The scrivener had kept asking what those words meant to him.

At the time, Narius hadn't been able to answer. But now, he understood. If the Singularity was supreme, if He was the only and the whole, then it didn't matter what Narius had to give up as long as he had Him. More of what Tolistan had taught him tumbled through his mind, how the abiding love of the Singularity would never release him or let go of him. As long as Narius had the Singularity, he had enough. No matter what else he had lost, he was still a servant of the Singularity's will. Even now, in the midst of all this confusion and chaos.

"What do You want me to do?" he whispered.

Another nudge. Another prompt. Time to stop sitting out the battle. Time to take charge. He nodded to himself. Maybe this wouldn't lead him back to the throne, but if the Singularity wanted him to step forward in the here and now, so be it.

He ripped off the beard and wig and strode down the risers to the main floor. "Stop panicking! You are citizens of the Dynasty and members of the nobility. Act like it!"

His voice cut through the chatter, and a few turned to see who was speaking. One woman who spotted him shrieked and clawed at her husband. Others went still, gawking at him as he passed. Then many of them dropped to their knees, hastily bowing. Narius hated to admit it, but he felt a bit of satisfaction.

He strode over to Kavi. "How did you get here?"

She made several tentative signs, then shrugged. *I have no idea. I was listening to Innana and Cosena argue, then I was dragged here by powerful magic.*

Narius blinked. He had felt something trying to tug at him at the same time, but he had attributed it to the adrenaline in the moment. It was a mystery that could keep. He turned to the soldiers next.

Zar's mouth hung open. "Y-Your Strength?"

Narius nodded grimly. "Farga?"

His Swordbound groaned from where he lay on the ground. "I'll live, Your Strength. I apologize for losing your sword."

"It was put to good use." He signaled to another guard to tend to Farga, then turned toward Auriel. "How is the Governor-General?"

One guard looked up. "Not well, Your Strength. She's lost a lot of blood. We've stopped the bleeding, but her pulse is thready."

That wasn't good. In spite of what she had said about him, Auriel was a good person. Those were in short supply in the Dynasty.

"Do we have anyone here with better medical training?" Narius shouted.

No one volunteered. He grumbled to himself. Figured. None of the nobles were willing to take the risk. They were only interested in protecting themselves.

"Kavi?"

She stumbled forward, gingerly making her way to Zammit's side. Narius watched her to make sure she made it, then turned to the other woman.

"You were with my brother," he said bluntly.

The woman nodded. "My name is Yusra, Your Strength. He and I have been working together for the past few months."

Narius frowned. "Dalark intelligence?"

"In a roundabout way. On paper, I am one of their agents, but in reality, I answer to Princess Innana." Her tone was uncertain at first, as if she wasn't sure of what she was saying.

Narius swallowed a laugh. He should have known. Innana had clearly been six steps ahead of everyone. It shouldn't have surprised him to find one of her agents in the Dynasty's holdings.

"Do you have any idea who those men are? Where they might have taken Quartus?"

Yusra winced and shook her head. "We've faced them a few times before this, but no, I have no idea."

That didn't sit well with him, but he wasn't sure what he could do in that moment. He would have liked to focus on that puzzle, though, because he wanted to avoid what had to happen next.

"Zar?" he said quietly.

Zar stepped up next to him. "Your Strength?"

"Arrest Vizier Paine for treason," Narius whispered.

Zar smirked. "With pleasure, Your Strength."

Narius finally turned to meet Paine's gaze. Paine's mouth popped open, as if he was about to say something, but Zar moved too quickly. The guard wrenched the vizier's arms behind his back. That seemed to jolt Paine out of his surprise.

"Your Strength, wait!" Paine cried.

"For what?" Narius closed the distance between them. "Excuses? Lies? Or are you going to confess how you betrayed me?"

"That was never my intention" Paine said.

"You're serving as Brencis's vizier!" Narius roared. "Innana showed me what you said to the criers. And I heard everything you said here just now. How stupid do you think I am?"

"Not stupid," Paine said. "Dead."

Narius blinked. What?

"You were dead! I saw you with my own eyes. What was I supposed to do?" Paine yanked himself free of Zar's hands and straightened his robe. He took a deep breath, and then continued to speak, now calm. "Once you died, I realized how precarious our position was. Brencis would storm the capital, resulting in who knew how many casualties. And the Dalark were almost at the gates. Faced with the choice between Brencis on the throne or Dalark razing the city, I chose the lesser evil, intending to make Brencis's reign as short as possible."

"By siding with him?"

"By *pretending* to side with him." Paine turned to Zar. "Tell me, Zar, was the code name for Governor-General Zammit's contact within the palace 'Caravan?'"

Zar's flinched as if he had been struck. He started to say something, but Paine turned back to Narius.

"Yes, I pretended to betray you. I handed Bastion over to Brencis, thinking I would spare the city greater harm. That was before the cataclysm shattered it. And yes, I served Brencis as his vizier as well, but only so I could feed intelligence to Zar and his resistance. Only so I could buy myself more time to find a suitable successor for you. What else was I supposed to do?"

Narius glared at him. "You were supposed to protect my wife."

"And I did, as best I could," Paine said. "When the queen's skimmer left the palace, I sent word to Brencis's troops and claimed I was sending a courier to Rioka to secure their support for Brencis's reign to ensure they wouldn't shoot it down."

Narius frowned. He had no way of confirming that. But given the uncertainty painted across Zar's face, Narius had his doubts now as well. He wanted to be angry at Paine, to blame him and punish him and make him pay for what he did. But as he looked into Paine's eyes, he didn't see a traitor.

He saw his friend.

No. He couldn't think like that. The Dynasty was being ripped apart by war, both from within and without. The nobles had clarified that they thought he was too soft, too weak, to rule the Dynasty. And maybe he had been. But he could fix that, starting right now. All he had to do was give the order—any order—and Zar would carry it out. Imprison Paine. Execute him. Show that he could be the harsh ruler the Dynasty expected, that the Dynasty deserved.

Narius hardened his expression and stood up straighter. Paine must have read the shift in his thoughts, for his shoulders sagged and he closed his eyes. Zar, too, readied himself, adjusting his stance so he could do whatever Narius said. And Narius was ready. Ready to say the word. Ready to see justice done.

Except...

Was this really who he wanted to be? Yes, the Dynasty had always expected their kings to be militant, to be ruthless, to be unswerving in their quests for glory. Conquest. Bloodshed. That had been the hallmark of the Dynasty's entire history. His grandfather had lived by it. His father as well. And everyone apparently expected that of him. But as he stood there, contemplating the execution of a man he had considered his best friend, a little thought nudged him, nagged at him, wouldn't let him go.

Is this what the Singularity would want?

Narius stared at Paine, searching those familiar features for any sign that he could still trust him.

Paine, apparently sensing his hesitation, said, "Narius, I once made a promise to you. I would always support you. I would always be your friend, your partner, your greatest supporter. I truly believed that was what I was doing. But if you don't trust my promise anymore, then do what you must."

Narius's scowl deepened. In spite of everything, a part of him still trusted Paine. Even though he knew that might turn out to be foolish, he couldn't ignore that gut instinct.

"Stand down," Narius mumbled.

To his credit, Zar didn't hesitate. He took a step back and turned away, giving them the smallest amount of privacy. Narius moved closer to Paine hoping only he would hear what he had to say.

"I remember those promises. And I remember I made them as well. I want to trust you. I do. But a lot has happened that I need to sort through. For now, I want you to stay at my side. Be my supporter. And we'll see if we can make it the rest of the way."

Paine nodded, tears glistening his eyes.

Narius turned to the others. While two of the guards worked with Kavi to stabilize Zammit, the others fell silent, their expressions expectant.

"First things first. We need to withdraw from this location. We don't know where the assassins wound up." His gut twisted at that. He didn't know where Quartus was either. "It's safest to assume that they'll report our position and then strike even harder. The faster we can evacuate, the better."

"We've got a command center set up in the city," Zar said. "We can go there as long as it isn't compromised."

Paine winced at that last statement as it was clearly directed at him. "I wasn't aware of its location. As far as I know, Brencis is ignorant as well."

"Good." Narius turned to Yusra. "If my brother survives whatever happened to him, is there somewhere you think he'd go?"

"We've set up a safehouse," Yusra said. "Do you want me to go there?"

Narius shook his head. "Not until we've made it to Zar's command center." He turned to the others. "Move."

As the guards set to work, helping the wounded and each other, Narius took a deep breath and tried to calm his roiling thoughts. A good first step? Maybe. For now, all he could hope for was that the people he loved were safe. Quartus. And especially Everys.

70

Thankfully, after the disappointment of the experiment with drawing the puzzle rune, Tormod contacted Everys and said that he was ready to try again.

As she walked to Tormod's makeshift office, her stomach fluttered. She hoped that this time, the Singularity would send her to Narius. Oh, she understood why He'd sent them where He had. Knowing what was happening to her people in the Dynasty's holdings was important. If anything, it lent urgency to her task. She had to find her husband and bring him home. Only with him at her side could she actually bring an end to all of this madness. She just knew it.

So as she stepped into the empty room where Tormod waited, she offered a silent prayer to the Singularity. *Please? Let me find him.*

Tormod's gaze swept over her. She expected he would activate his tattoo and they would be off, but he hesitated. It almost appeared as though he were chewing on his bottom lip.

"What?" she prompted.

"I've been reflecting," Tormod said. "In particular, the difficulty I've experienced. At first, I thought it was because I was trying to bring a second person along. But then I remembered: I've experienced that sort of traumatic jump in the past. Every time it's happened, it's because I was seeking to impose my agenda on the rune."

Everys shifted her weight, suddenly feeling too hot. She tried to hide her discomfort, but Tormod's gaze bore right through her.

"I told you the tattoo doesn't send me where I want to go, but where I need to. The same is true for you as well. I suspect the reason these attempts have been so uncomfortable is that you're fighting where the rune was trying to send us," Tormod said, his voice gentle but firm.

Her cheeks burned. She wanted to argue, but she knew from his tone that Tormod wouldn't listen.

"I want him back too. Maybe not as fervently as you, but I do." He tipped his head to one side. "But I have to also acknowledge that in this moment, the Singularity may be whispering—or even screaming—'not yet' to my desires. It's possible that the Singularity is trying to say that to you right now."

She started to object, to argue that he couldn't possibly understand, to point out that the Singularity would want her to be with her husband, that He wouldn't want the Dynasty to be ripped apart because of all this chaos, but Tormod held up a hand.

"We can keep trying, Blessed. For as long as I am able. All right?"

Tears prickled her eyes, but she refused to let them fall. She nodded, clenching her teeth. Why couldn't the Singularity give her what she wanted? She needed her husband back. It had been so long since she saw him in Utuaa. He could be anywhere. He could be hurt. Or worse. This had to work!

"Try to let go of your desires." Tormod rolled up his sleeve. "Let's see where He sends us this time."

A frigid wind whipped past her, yanking at her hair. She felt like she was being pulled in dozens of different directions, and she knew she didn't want to go in any of them. She struggled to pull herself into a ball to better weather the storm, but she couldn't move her arms or legs. They felt stretched out, becoming thinner and more fragile. She tried to cry out, but the breath caught in her throat and she choked—

Then she lurched forward, almost slamming into a wall. As she staggered, Tormod collapsed to his knees, his chest heaving. He wobbled back to his feet, but his face was covered by a sheen of sweat. A tremor wormed through his body. She took a step closer to him, trying to steady him or comfort him or whatever he needed. He started to say something, but then his mouth clicked shut and he looked around, his eyes wide.

Everys glanced at him, confused as to what distracted him. He stared at the surrounding room, his face pale. What was the problem?

Then Everys examined their surroundings, and the breath froze in her lungs. She recognized this room. Although it had been repainted and redecorated, there were certain features that couldn't be changed: the lavish sink, the sumptuous shower, the layout of the room.

Inkstains, they were standing in the king's bathroom in the royal palace!

"Now why would You send us here?" Tormod muttered.

At first, Everys's heart stuttered at the familiar surroundings. She knew that just through that door was the king's bedroom, where she and Narius had spent so many sweet moments together. For a split second, she wondered if they had maybe traveled backward in time. She'd find Narius on the other side of those doors and they could redo everything and make sure the disasters never happened. But no, the thought was ridiculous. Toratropic magic could do amazing things, but it couldn't do that.

"Let's just go," she whispered.

Tormod clucked his tongue. "I know this is difficult, Blessed, but we're here for a reason. Maybe Brencis left something in his quarters we're supposed to find? Or we're supposed to see someone in here who—"

A door banged open in the main part of the quarters, and Tormod clamped his mouth shut, his eyes wide. A muffled voice followed, clearly Brencis's. There was no mistaking the haughty tone or the anger that burned underneath his words.

"—do you mean he's dead?" Brencis thundered.

Someone replied, but Everys couldn't recognize the voice or understand the words. But Brencis's response was straightforward enough, an inarticulate roar punctuated by something metal clattering against a stone wall. A serving platter, if Everys had to guess.

"You were supposed to be her best agents! It only took one of you to kill Elamek. You're telling me that three of you couldn't assassinate Zammit?"

Everys froze. The Governor-General was dead? No, wait, they'd tried to kill her. But Elamek was dead? Killed by Brencis?

More incoherent words, this time from another voice. So two people with Brencis, plus who knew how many guards. Would Brencis speak so openly about assassination in front of guards? She didn't think so.

Whatever the third person had to say was long. Everys stepped closer to the door, straining to hear whatever she could. She thought she caught a word or two: "opposition," "Dalark," "countered." She frowned, trying to piece together such scant clues.

But then she heard a word she recognized, one that caused a jolt to travel down her spine.

Whoever was speaking had said Narius's name.

Another scream, followed by a crash.

"You had the chance to kill Narius, and he slipped through your fingers?" Brencis's rage bled through the door. The assassins said something else, only to be interrupted. "I don't care if she wants him captured. I want him dead!"

But Everys didn't care. Whoever he was speaking to had seen Narius! She had no idea if they had seen him in Utuaa or within the Dynasty's holdings, but she didn't care. They knew where he was. And he was still alive. She needed that information, and she needed it now.

She produced a vial of ink and painted runes on the door. One to shatter it, one to create a loud bang. Then more runes on the floor: a paralysis rune to hold whoever was in the other room in place, one to generate smoke.

"Blessed, what are you doing?" Tormod asked, his voice a hiss.

She ignored him. She ignored the muted conversation on the other side of the door. More runes, these painted on her arms. Tormod tugged on her shoulder, but she shrugged him off. She took a deep, steadying breath, and then activated all the runes.

The effect was immediate. One rune on the floor belched acrid smoke just as the door broke with a loud bang. As Everys strode through, the other spells took hold. When she cleared the cloud, she found Brencis and two young men dressed in black on the other side. All three were frozen in awkward positions, clearly trying to dive for cover from the explosion when the paralysis rune snared them.

"Where is he?" Everys's voice boomed, amplified and transformed by the runes she wore on her arms. She wanted to sound like a vengeful Elderreach god and the effect seemed to work.

Brencis's eyes widened. She knew what he was seeing. The other rune she wore was a glamour, changing her appearance so she would appear like something the Gravedigger conjured up. Like death incarnate, come to claim his miserable soul. The color drained from his face.

"Where is he, Brencis?" she repeated. "Where is Narius?"

The two assassins' breathing had turned ragged. One of them appeared on the verge of tears. The other whispered a single word.

"*Ar'zhannok.*"

Everys froze at the title. Did they think she was Oluna? She didn't look anything like her. Or were they reacting to her terrifying appearance, her overwhelming presence, the way she was using the runes to get what she wanted?

Her mind hitched at the thought. Oluna had said that they were alike. She hadn't wanted to believe it, but maybe there was some truth to that, more than she wanted to admit. She looked between Brencis and the assassins. All three were clearly terrified. Was this what she wanted? To inspire terror or to be revered?

No. She wanted her husband back. She wanted Brencis and Oluna defeated and the Imperium to leave them alone. She didn't want this. How had she gotten to this point?

"Blessed, are you all right?"

Everys's breath hitched at Tormod's quiet question. The paralysis rune suddenly broke, and the assassins snapped their hands outward. Something whistled through the air, slicing past Everys. Behind her, Tormod grunted.

She whirled around. Tormod staggered out of the doorway, clutching at the dagger that had embedded itself in his chest.

"No!" she cried.

"Get them!" Brencis shrieked.

Everys's heart seized. She took a step toward Tormod, frantic to help him...

Then she felt a tug at her chest, as if a thread was being pulled tight. Everys lurched forward into a dark void. This time, lights whirled around and past her just as a rebuke sizzled through her body. She clenched her teeth against the pain as echoes of the men's fear burned through her.

Then she lurched and collapsed to her knees in the darkened room back in the Embassy. Tormod slumped against the wall, his breathing shallow as a bloodstain spread through his shirt.

Everys kicked the door open. "Medic!"

Redtale peeked into the room, then repeated the shout. Everys turned back to Tormod and fumbled with her vial of ink. She had used almost all of it up creating the illusions. Did she have enough to actually help? Only one way to try.

She tried to daub some on her finger, but she was trembling so hard she wound up dribbling some of the ink onto her palm. She gritted her teeth and tried to draw the rune. But her mind kept locking as echoes of the rebuke rattled through her. Why couldn't she remember the shape? She had drawn it so many times. She should be able to do this now.

How could she have been so stupid? And now, Tormod could die and it would all be her fault. She had been so sure of herself, so certain she was doing, maybe not the right thing, but something she could live with, and now she had ink all over her hands and Tormod was still bleeding. Was he even breathing anymore?

A hand dropped onto her shoulder and Redtale gently pulled her away. She gasped and tried to pull free, but then two medics rushed past her and set to work.

"Is... is he g-going to be okay?" Everys whispered.

"We'll see, Blessed. We'll let you know."

Redtale helped Everys stand and steered her away from the medics. Everys didn't object. All she could do was swipe at the ink on her hands in a vain attempt to clean them. Her fingers were stained, not just with ink, but with blood. Blood to make ink, blood from her victims, now Tormod's blood as well.

"Hey. Everys." Redtale's gentle voice was barely able to cut through the dissonant thoughts. "Sit down. Breathe. He'll be okay. You'll see."

But he might not be, and that was her fault. *Her fault!*

Gentle hands guided her onto a chair, then Redtale squatted in front of her.

"What happened?" Redtale asked.

Everys hiccupped, then the story tumbled out, a torrent of words and thoughts and fears and guilt. Redtale's brow furrowed as she listened to it all.

"I made a mess of everything," Everys whispered. "First Utuaa, and now this. I've been trying to hold it together, and I've been trying to do what's right, but all I've been doing is breaking things and—"

She scrubbed at the stain on her hands. Redtale caught them in hers, forcing them to be still.

"Look, I'm not going to sweeten this. Yes, you've been making mistakes. Some big ones. I saw what you did in Utuaa, and I'll be honest. It scared me."

Everys tried to pull her hands free, but Redtale held tight.

"And yes, we don't know what's going to happen with Tormod. But I've known him for a while. He's a lot tougher than any of us realize."

As Redtale spoke, the medics hustled past them, Tormod on a stretcher between them, a mask strapped to his face. Everys barely noticed. Her gaze was fixed on the hilt of the dagger jutting from his chest.

"The question now is, what new direction are you going to walk?" Redtale asked.

Every met her Swordbound's gaze. "Wh-what do you mean?"

"We Ixactl have an old saying. 'When you're lost in the mountains, the first one to turn back is usually the smartest.' You're lost right now. How are you going to turn around?"

She considered Redtale's question. Her breathing evened out and her heart stopped stuttering.

"I don't want to be like Oluna. I don't want to use fear or pain against people."

"Good. What else?"

"No more blood. No more forbidden runes or inks."

"Better. And?"

Everys thought it over some more. "When you're lost in the mountains, the best thing you can have is a guide."

"So what will yours be?"

That was a good question. All this time, she had been following her grief over losing Narius or her fear of never finding him again. She had been following her own whims and desires, so convinced she knew what was best. She needed something better. No, *Someone* better.

She nodded. "The Singularity."

"Excellent." Redtale rose and held out a hand to her. "Now, let's get you cleaned up."

Everys sniffled, flinching when she realized that she had just smeared ink across her face. She looked up at Redtale. "That's it? No lecture? No dressing down?"

Redtale tipped her head to one side. "Why? You need one?"

She shook her head.

"Of course, if you start wandering off in the mountains again, we'll have this conversation again, and if that happens—"

"You'll break my horns?" Everys said with a small smile as she stood.

"For starters."

Everys looked up at her Swordbound—no, her *friend*—then lunged forward, catching her in a hug. "Thank you."

They started for Everys's quarters. As they walked, a thought occurred to her. Turning in a new direction was one thing. Following her guide was another. But there was one more step she knew she had to take. She had to start working to make things better.

"Once I'm cleaned up, I'm going to check on Tormod. I'll use my family's healing rune on him to make sure he's okay. While I'm doing that, can you go ask Yllana for a favor?"

Redtale glanced down at her. "Of course. What?"

"I need to go see Papa."

On his way back to Bastion, Quartus came across an untended guard post, one that had a small two-man barracks attached. He slipped inside and quickly replaced his clothing with a uniform. Maybe that would give him the extra layer of camouflage that he needed. Once he had disposed of his bloodied clothes and made sure his "borrowed" uniform was adjusted just so, he continued on his way.

As Third Watch shifted over to Fourth, the streets emptied and Quartus had to become even more cautious. Even though he wore the uniform, he knew that an uppity officer or jumpy squad could stop and question him. While they may not know exactly what he had done, they would detain him until they could pin some crime on him.

When he arrived at the safehouse in Gilded Lock, Quartus couldn't wait to fall onto the couch and rest his aching back and feet. Staying tense and creeping through the city for hours took more of a toll than he'd expected. He unlocked the door, checking the frame for any signs of tampering. Once inside, his gaze roamed over the room, checking the multiple tells he had set up to alert them to intruders. The threads he had tied across the entrance had been snapped. The dirty clothing pile had been disturbed. Someone had been here.

As Quartus considered what he should do, Yusra stepped out of the bathroom, wearing a silky robe. They both froze. Quartus's gaze shot down her exposed body, his mouth going dry as heat flashed over him.

Then she rushed forward, slamming into him and wrapping her arms around him. "Quartus! Thank the spirits you're all right. You are all right, aren't you? Did they hurt you?"

He didn't answer. Instead, he closed his eyes and breathed in the soapy smell, his hands brushing her warm skin. His breathing turned ragged, and he didn't know if he was going to start laughing or crying.

And then she grabbed his face with both hands and kissed him, hungrily, deeply, clinging to him as like she was scared, as if she let go he'd vanish.

Shock sliced through Quartus. He and Yusra had flirted, but they had never acted on their obvious mutual attraction. While he had kissed other women in the past, it never felt this raw, this visceral.

This right.

She finally pulled away and he gulped the air, a laugh bubbling through him.

"What was that?" he whispered.

Yusra laughed and pushed at his shoulders. "I would think you'd know by now, Your Strength."

"But why?"

"Because you're alive." She leaned in closer. "And so is your brother."

It felt like the floor dropped out from under Quartus. His legs buckled, and he collapsed to the floor, Yusra holding on to him as he fell. His jaw dropped open, and a chill swept over his body.

"He... he... what?"

"He was at the Humrice's estate, Quartus. In the meeting the whole time. He sent me to find you."

He stared at her, having trouble understanding her words. The grief, the anger, the righteous fury he had carried with him for the past few months twisted violently in his chest and then it felt like it popped. Tears streamed down his face and he sobbed, his body collapsing in on itself. All of his regrets over lost time, the various hurts and sleights they had piled on each other, he could finally lay them all to rest. They could heal. He didn't know if they'd ever be close, but at least that was possible instead of being a lost opportunity.

Yusra cradled his head against her, stroking his back and whispering something in Dalark. It almost sounded like a lullaby. He had no idea what she was saying, but he didn't care. He let everything pour out of him in one gigantic burst.

When his tears subsided, Yusra kissed the top of his head and pulled him back up to standing. "C'mon, let's get out of here."

He chuckled, swiping at his eyes. "Planning to show up in a robe? He might get the wrong idea."

She laughed and slugged his shoulder, then slipped back into the bathroom. Once she was gone, Quartus looked around the room, trying to categorize the items they had accumulated. What would they need going forward? The scribers, certainly. Some of the clothing, although the dirty pile was made up of items he had scavenged just to check for intruders. But maybe Yusra would want some of them. Who knew? Now that she had her memory back...

He froze, the memory of that strange girl grabbing Yusra and how Yusra had changed afterward. The way she had moved and... well, smiled as she fought those two assassins sent a shiver marching down his spine. Yes, he had seen her fight in the past and he knew how good she was at hand-to-hand combat. What he had seen earlier, though, was enjoyment. Delight. Sheer glee. In that moment, she had changed. Was she the same woman?

He shook his head and shoved the scribers into a sack, deciding to ignore the clothes. By the time he was done, Yusra had emerged from the bathroom, wearing the same outfit she had to the party, a pair of tan pants with a loose white blouse. Instead of a belt, she had tied a brightly colored shawl around her waist. Only this time, he noticed that the shawl was tied on her left instead of on her right. She had twisted the material to create a flair on the opposite side. And she had left the top of her blouse unfastened, something she had never done as long as he'd known her.

She caught his stare, and a smirk flashed across her lips. "Enjoying the view?"

He winced, but not because he had been caught. He had seen a lot more of her just a few moments earlier. Was this another indication that she had changed?

Her smile evaporated. She took a hesitant step forward. "What is it?"

Quartus tried to figure out a diplomatic way to approach it, but he couldn't stitch together the words. So he finally blurted, "Are you still you?"

Her head tipped to one side. "What do you mean?"

"For so long, you've had that memory block, and it looked like that woman took it away. I'm worried that..." His mind raced, trying to put words to his fears. "That you're not the same person. That the you who I've worked with for so long was just a ghost who's been replaced by the real you. I don't even know if Yusra is your real name or—"

"Yusra is my real name," she whispered. "Quartus, I—"

He held up a hand. "Please, let me say this. I know that we've flirted and bantered and Sun only knows that I've pictured the two of us together in so many ways."

Her lips twitched into a knowing grin.

"No, not like that." He winced. "Well, maybe a little. But I mean... as a couple. Meeting your parents. Building a home together. That sort of thing. But now I'm worried that you're not you, that the person I knew and grew to—"

"Will you shut up?"

She closed the distance between them so quickly that he flinched into a defensive stance. But she grabbed the front of his short and pulled him into another kiss, one so urgent it surprised him. She clung to him, holding him so tight he could feel her heart thudding against his own.

"Kavi's memory spell only suppresses information, not personality," she murmured in his ear. "I'm the same woman you danced with at Coran's party. I'm the same woman who has crawled through Bastion's sewers more times than I'd care to admit. I'm still the same woman who has bested you in hand-to-hand combat more times than you should ever admit. I'm still the woman who loves you."

Her words lit a fire deep in Quartus's chest. He kissed her again, but this time their teeth clacked together. He bit back a curse while she laughed. Then she cupped his face and carefully drew him in. Her lips brushed his, a gentle tease, one that stoked the fire even hotter. He held her tight and kissed her, savoring the feel of her in his arms, the raw desire that passed between them.

"I am so glad I found you," he murmured.

"I am too," she whispered.

72

Yllana shot a worried look at Everys. "Are you sure you want to do this?"

Everys took a deep breath and nodded, even though that wasn't entirely true. She knew she had to. But she didn't want to. Curiosity, obligation, and even a little bit of stubborn love she couldn't quite shake. Blocking her path was righteous horror, indignation, and sorrow. The two emotional mixtures were held in almost perfect balance. If she didn't do this now, she'd be stuck. Or worse, she'd walk away.

"Take me to him." She offered up a silent prayer of thanksgiving that her voice didn't betray her conflict.

Yllana led her away from the Embassy to a waiting transport, similar to the one that had taken her to see the sleeping Elderreach the first time. The irony of using it again was not lost on her. Redtale offered her a hand to boost her up then clambered in after her. She wished they would let her make this trip on her own, but she knew why Redtale had insisted.

The transport left the Shade and headed south. Within an hour, the road turned uneven, jostling the vehicle randomly. Each jolt sent another pang of uncertainty through Everys. She shouldn't be doing this. It was a distraction, unnecessary, self-indulgent. She should be speaking with her advisers, inquiring after Overturn, consulting the Illuminates or translation team.

In spite of her misgivings, though, there was a persistent voice that urged her on. So she did her best to brace herself, trying to hold both her body and her resolve in place by sheer will.

Finally, the transport bumped to a halt and the door wrenched open. Yllana waited on the other side, joined by three other burly grafted, two Kolvese and a Weyfir. They nodded solemnly to her as she and her guards slid out of the transport.

"Welcome, Queen Everys," one of the Kolvese said, his voice a bass rumble. "It's rare that we have willing visitors here, even rarer for them to be royalty."

"I suppose not." She forced herself to smile. "Shall we?"

The three grafted led the way, with Yllana falling into step next to Everys. They pointed out the limited landmarks: the dormitories, the dining hall, the vast fields dotted with workers. As they walked, they kept up a running commentary, explaining their philosophy, their precautions, everything she might be remotely curious about.

As they talked, Everys's gaze roamed over the fields, studying the people who worked on harvesting the grain. The stalks were almost taller than the people. They used large scythes to mow through the plants, others following behind to gather what had been harvested.

Redtale grunted. "That wise, giving them sharp implements?"

One of their guides chuckled. "It may not seem so, but only those who have shown sufficient progress are allowed to use them. And we have plenty of safeguards in place in case there's an incident."

They wouldn't trust him with a scythe this early, would they? No, that didn't make sense.

As if he could sense her confusion, the grafted smiled. "But you're not here to inspect our operation. Let's take you to him."

They didn't lead her to the fields, nor to the dormitories. Instead, they took her to a building that appeared to have been carved out of a nearby hill, half of which appeared to have been sheered away. An oval-shaped door was flanked by round windows.

"Newcomers are always held in this facility to help them acclimate," another of their guides explained. "They sometimes find it hard to adjust to the simpler life they experience here. Some try to challenge our hospitality."

One of the guides opened the door and motioned for her to enter.

She entered a long, dirt-floored hallway, the length of which was dotted with round doorways. Much to her surprise, they were all open. As a matter of fact, none of them appeared to have actual doors.

Redtale made a *tsk*ing sound. "Doesn't seem that secure. What kind of prison are you running here?"

"Not a prison at all," one of the guides said. "Cultivation is not about punishment. This is a chance for offenders to reflect on what they've done, how their actions have broken peace within our community, and how they might adjust their attitudes and actions. We believe that humiliating such individuals is counterproductive to our goals."

Redtale made another skeptical sound and looked ready to argue, but Everys held up a hand. There was a time and place to debate incarceration and rehabilitation strategies. This wasn't the time.

"Please," she said. "Where's my father?"

The guides made a sweeping gesture toward one of the doors to the right. Everys forced herself to cross the distance. She hesitated by the doorway as Redtale took up position outside, then with one last, shuddering breath, she stepped through.

Papa sat on a stool in a mostly empty room. He glanced in her direction, then looked down at the bare dirt floor. He appeared well enough, cleaner than he had been, his cheeks not quite as gaunt. His beard was neatly trimmed, and he wore simple clothing, beige pants with a matching shirt. There was a cot, a bronze basin set in a wall, and a window near the ceiling that allowed a trickle of sunlight inside.

"Come to use that splattered rune on me?" Papa asked, his voice a growl. "Violating my privacy once wasn't enough?"

Fire flashed through Everys. "Papa, you tried to kill my husband."

He looked up, confusion spread over his face. "What do you mean, 'tried?'"

"Narius is still alive," she said. At least, he had been, but she decided not to dwell on the other possibility.

Papa frowned. "How?"

"That's really not the important part," she said, although his question resonated so strongly with her. She hoped she would find out someday.

"Then why did you come here? To make sure your tree friends didn't stick their twigs through my skin and make me a thrall? To lord your apostasy over me some more?"

Everys stepped into the room and sank down onto the cot. She twisted her fingers together, studying her knuckles, as if her reasons for coming were written in the creases and wrinkles there.

"I wanted to see if you were sorry," she whispered.

Papa's head snapped back, surprise flitting across his face. But then he scowled. "If I say I am, will they let me go?"

"I don't know." The admission sounded hollow. "That's really not up to me."

He snorted. "Some queen you are."

His words slammed into her gut, and she looked down, trying to figure out what to say next.

Papa sighed and leaned back, resting his head against the wall. "It really isn't bad here, all things considered. The food's not as bad as I would have expected. Not as good as your mother's. And folks are nice enough here. Even the other convicts. They say I'm going to help with the harvest in the next couple of days, then they might send me to another colony to work on resource reclamation, whatever that means. And we have two sessions in the morning and afternoon to discuss our thoughts and feelings."

That might be a good opening. "Are you comfortable sharing with me what you've told them, Papa?"

His expression turned rigid. "What, you're hoping that I've told them that I did something wrong, that I hurt my daughter? That sort of thing?"

"You did more than hurt me, Papa. You hurt the Dynasty. If you had helped him or just left him alone, things may have turned out different."

"And you know that for sure?" Papa retorted. "For all you know, your precious husband could have steered us into an even bigger mess than we're in."

Fire flashed behind her eyes and she clenched her hands into fists. It would be so easy to get into a fight with him. It'd feel so good, so *right*. She didn't understand how he could be so blind to what he had done.

But as angry words boiled within her, she realized that his face had turned red and his hands were balled into fists as well. Something Mama used to say flitted through her mind. When Everys and Papa would argue back when Everys was a teenager, Mama used to say it was because they were so alike. As much as Everys hated hearing that, she had come to recognize how true it was. Papa was always the one who saw the injustice around them and pointed it out. He was always the one who was trying to help their neighbors make their lives easier when he could. He was the one who taught her that it wasn't enough to see that the world was broken; a person had to act as well.

So why had he tried to kill Narius? Because he hated him? Maybe, but that felt like an incomplete answer. Instead, she remembered what he had said in the cabin under the influence of the truth-telling rune. He had lost Legarr. He had lost her. He had been afraid. Afraid of what it meant for his daughter to have married the king. Afraid that he had lost her, similar to how he had lost Legarr, but without the finality and closure. A lingering loss, one that would simply bleed for years and never close over.

In his fear, Papa had done what he'd thought was right. No, what he *knew* was right. Rather than trust that the Singularity had brought Everys and Narius together, Papa had tried to take the Singularity's place, to decide what was the right course of action.

"And you are so like your father." Mama's voice, floating out of her childhood.

And she was. Not just in how she was expressing her anger. She thought of her attempts with Tormod, trying to use his rune to find Narius. Even though Tormod had told her how the *reshi'zhad* vow worked, what it meant, she had stubbornly tried to force her will on the process. And she had done the same in Utuaa. She had given into her fear time and again.

As much as she wanted to remain angry with Papa, she realized she couldn't. She was just as guilty as he was, and in her fear, she had nearly killed hundreds, maybe thousands of people. Thankfully, she had been stopped. And somehow, Papa hadn't been able to kill Narius either.

She forced her fingers to uncurl. She blew out a long breath through her nose, then smiled.

Papa's frown deepened. "What?"

"You asked why I was here. I'll be honest, I didn't really know. But now I do. I forgive you, Papa. I forgive you for what you tried to do. I just hope you're able to eventually realize what you almost did. And maybe, just maybe, you can come to see the Singularity's grace in the fact that Narius survived."

He scowled at her, then turned away, crossing his arms. She waited for a few more seconds to see if he would say or do anything else. When he didn't, she reached out and gingerly touched his shoulder.

"For what it's worth, Papa, I still love you. So does Mama and Galan. We just want you to be okay."

His shoulder sagged a bit, but he didn't say anything. So she rose and left the room.

Redtale settled a massive hand on Everys's shoulder.

"You okay, Blessed?" she asked quietly.

Everys blinked back tears and shook her head. No, she wasn't. And she might not be for a long time. But as she walked down the hall, it felt like she was shedding a heavy coat. For the first time in weeks, she felt almost normal. And if the Singularity willed it, maybe that could carry her to someplace good.

73

Narius was impressed. While Zar's command center wasn't nearly as sophisticated as the Amber Office back in the palace, what the guard commander had set up was definitely effective.

Zar and his men had commandeered the basement of an old medical clinic on the edge of Fair Havens. Racks for weapons and tactical gear hung along one wall, and the wall to the left of that displayed a large map of Bastion, the different neighborhoods shaded with reds and greens and blues, with pins stuck into the map to denote troop placements. He couldn't help but smile. The setup reminded him of the map he had seen in Planka's headquarters in Utuaa. A table filled the center of the room with a dozen chairs around it. Doors led to bathrooms, a cramped barracks, and an emergency medical unit. Narius resisted the urge to poke his head in there again. The last time he'd checked, Zammit was still dangling over the Gravedigger's palm.

So what was their next step? They were safe for now, but he didn't know how long that would last. Once Brencis heard what happened, he would likely send out troops to track them down. Or he might punish the civilian population, venting his frustration on them. Could they do anything to protect them?

As Narius mulled over that question, a light flashed overhead. The activity in the room stilled, and Narius held his breath. When they had arrived, Zar explained that was a signal that someone was approaching the clinic. The lookouts upstairs would assess the situation and alert them if there was any reason to...

The lights flashed again, and a palpable sense of relief swept through the room. Narius didn't know for sure, but he guessed the second flash meant everything was fine.

Zar turned to Narius. "We'll be ready for the briefing in just a moment, Your Strength. Just getting some last-minute intel on the map."

Narius nodded grimly. He knew the others would look to him for guidance, but he wasn't sure what he could offer. He didn't have boots-on-the-ground knowledge of what was happening in Bastion, let alone in the Dynasty. What territory did Dalark control? Were parts of the Dynasty's holdings in open rebellion against Brencis? Were there any other rebel cells they could ally themselves with? He could make suggestions, but he suspected that anything he said would be inaccurate at best or plain wrong at worst.

The door leading to the ground level swung open and two people stepped through. The Dalark spy was in the lead, her hands up in a nonthreatening posture. And behind her...

Narius froze. Quartus's gaze met his.

That couldn't really be his brother, could it? Narius was so used to Quartus being swathed in the height of fashion, put together and suave. The man who entered the basement wore dirty and torn clothing. A smattering of stubble lined his chin and jaw. He looked tired, slightly gaunt, as if he hadn't had a good night's sleep in years.

Before Narius could say anything, Quartus rushed forward and enveloped Narius in a hug so tight he struggled to breathe. Narius froze, surprised at the sudden embrace. He and Quartus had never been friends and had rarely been friendly. In spite of that, though, relief and happiness sluiced through him so strongly that he threw his arms around Quartus and hugged him tightly.

"I thought you were dead!" Quartus's voice was thick.

"I actually was," Narius said.

Quartus pulled away and gaped at him. "You what?"

Narius chuckled. "It's a long story. I suspect we both have those."

He pulled his brother back into a hug, and the two clapped each other on the back. While Narius knew they had a lot to work out, as much as he had with Paine, he was glad for this moment. Maybe, if they all survived whatever happened next, they could be brothers in reality rather than just in name.

"And I have some news. I've seen Everys."

Narius's heart stuttered. "Y-you have?"

"It's been a while, but she seemed to be doing well."

He knew Quartus meant it to be a comfort, but it wasn't. After what happened in Utuaa, could Everys really be doing "well?"

Zar cleared his throat. "I hate to break up the joyous reunion, but we should probably start the briefing."

Narius hid a smile behind his hand. Even though the guard commander was trying to project a gruff attitude, Narius had known him long enough to know that he had been moved as well. Zar's expression had softened, even though his lips had pulled back in an exaggerated snarl.

Everyone gathered around the table, except for Kavi. She remained at her perch even after Yusra tried to coax her into joining them. Zar surveyed the people with a grim nod.

"Normally I would hand this over to King Narius, but given that the king and prince have just joined us, I feel it best that we compare notes," Zar said.

Narius nodded in a way he hoped hid his relief, and the guard commander continued. "But before we do that, do we have an update on the Governor-General?"

One medic nodded grimly. "She's hanging on. I don't know what the king's companion did, but it appears she helped stabilize the Governor-General. She'll need more blood, and I'd prefer if we could find a more modern facility for her, but we'll make do with what we have."

"Kavi, can you do something to help?"

She sat up straighter, started to sign something, but then her gaze darted to the soldiers around the table. Her hands went still and she tucked them into her lap. A few of the troops cast wary glances at Kavi. Narius could read the unease plainly enough.

He held up a hand. "I want to make this clear: I will not tolerate any suspicion of Kavi. She is the only reason I'm still alive as well. She has my full confidence and should have yours as well."

Some of the soldiers relaxed, but not enough of them.

Zar cleared his throat. "Perhaps, Your Strength, you should explain further. Where have you been?"

"As I said to Quartus, I really died after the *harsannon*, killed by my father-in-law," Narius said.

The troops mumbled, glancing at each other skeptically.

Dented Breastplate, this was going to be difficult to explain. "I am not entirely comfortable sharing this information, but Queen Everys does indeed practice toratropic magic, and she—"

"We know that already," one soldier said.

"Yeah, Minister Masruq had this big reveal about it a while back."

Narius blinked. He did? He glanced at Quartus, who nodded grimly. Well, that made things easier.

"Favid used a rune on me that undid the healing spells that have been cast on me over the past year, including the one that Everys cast on me after Brencis shot me at my wedding to Innana," Narius explained. "I nearly died, except Kavi intervened and saved me."

"Yeah?" a soldier asked. "And where did she come from?"

Oh, this wasn't going to go well at all. "She was sent to help me by Princess Innana of the Dalark Imperium."

More murmurs and skeptical looks. A few glanced at Kavi, who smiled impishly and waved at them.

"Kavi somehow transported me to Utuaa, where I worked with Innana in hopes of destabilizing her brother's reign so she could take over." He figured he wouldn't go into all the gory details. "We were caught by Tirigian, but we escaped and they sent me back here. When I heard about the meeting, my uncle helped me infiltrate it." He shrugged. "That's about it."

Zar nodded thoughtfully, then turned his attention to Quartus. "What about you? Aren't you supposed to be outlaw?"

Quartus grimaced. "Yes, I suppose I am."

"A status I hereby void," Narius interjected.

Quartus's jaw popped open. His gaze met Narius's, and Narius was sure he saw tears in the corner of his brother's eyes. Quartus stammered for a moment, then cleared his throat. "After being accused of plotting against my brother, I stayed in Bastion and tried to find evidence that could clear my name. The queen and I were able to uncover a conspiracy against Narius, and after Narius's remarriage to Everys, Tormod sent me to unravel the conspiracy. In doing so, I've discovered that there is a direct descendant of the Siporan mage-kings who has been working for years to bring down the Dynasty. The mage-kings are working directly against not just us, but Everys and the larger Siporan community. They have operatives everywhere. One such individual was Viscount Lorent, who is directly responsible for the destruction of Bastion."

"He's what?" someone gasped.

Quartus nodded grimly. "I don't fully understand how it worked, but he was able to construct a city-sized rune that was responsible for the cataclysm."

"Did you ever determine who this mage-king is?" Narius demanded.

"Oluna Hishi," Quartus said.

All eyes turned to him.

"How could you possibly know that?" Paine asked.

"The assassin who killed Elamek and who tried to kill Auriel Zammit turned out to be Masruq," Quartus said. "What? You thought I was just another pretty face?"

The soldiers exchanged looks that made it clear that yes, some of them thought of Quartus as just that. Narius fought to smile. It was good to have his brother back.

"Do we know their endgame?" Narius prompted.

Quartus and Yusra exchanged a look, then shook their heads. He glanced at Paine, who repeated the gesture. Narius swallowed a grumble. That would have been too easy.

"Then we have a new mission."

"Which is?" Quartus asked.

"Finding Oluna Hishi and the rest of her mage-kings," Narius said. "So we can put a stop to their plans."

74

Everys looked up at the gentle knock on her door. Much to her surprise, Tormod stood in the doorway, a gentle smile on his face.

"What are you doing out of bed?" she asked.

He tipped his head to one side and his smile grew broader. "The doctors proclaimed me fully recovered. A veritable miracle. They said that you may have had something to do with it?"

She couldn't help but return his smile.

"Thank you, Blessed," he said.

"It was my fault you were injured. I had to make things right."

"And you have." He took a step closer. "So what happens now? Do we try again?"

She could hear the hesitation in his tone. He wouldn't argue with her. She was his queen, after all. But she knew he didn't want to.

"About that," she said. "I need to say something. You're right. I haven't been cooperating the way I should. I've been trying to force the Singularity's hand. Not just in our jumps, but in so many other ways as well."

Tormod's face pinched into a frown. She didn't think it was a disapproving look, but more one of evaluation. So she continued her confession.

"You have indulged me far more than I deserve. But I've come to realize that this isn't healthy for me. I can't control this, and I worry that I'll only grow more and more frustrated if we keep trying. I have to entrust this to the Singularity. If He wants Narius and I to be reunited, it'll happen. On His timetable, not mine. We need to stop."

Tormod's expression didn't change for close to a minute, but then he smiled sadly. "Are you sure, Blessed?"

No, not really. She didn't want to stop at all. Now that she knew he was out there, she desperately wanted to find him. But she had to keep walking this new direction. She had to let whatever the Singularity had in mind play out. So she nodded.

"I'm impressed with your maturity." Tormod's smile turned gentle and encouraging. "I know that if our positions were reversed, you would be hard-pressed to convince me to do something similar."

"Thank you. And I am sorry for what happened to you."

Tormod laughed and swatted away her words. "Oh, this? Believe me, I've had worse injuries and visited the Gravedigger's front porch more often than I'd care to mention. You won't be rid of me anytime soon. So. Shall we?" He swept a hand toward the door.

Everys blinked at him. "But...I just said..."

"Oh, I heard. You don't want to try anymore." He leaned in closer. "But I do. One more time."

She hesitated, pursing her lips. As she considered it, she offered up a quick question to the Singularity. *Should I?*

Much to her surprise, a peace settled on her, deep and genuine. A warmth flowed through her as she found herself nodding and saying, "One more time."

They made their way to the darkened room. Redtale shot her a questioning look as she passed, but it was Tormod who motioned for Redtale to follow. The Swordbound grunted and did as she was told, escorting them to the darkened room.

Once they were inside, Tormod rolled up his sleeve. As he did, he met Everys's eyes. "I genuinely hope that we find him this time."

She blinked back tears. She hoped so, too, but there was already a gnawing certainty they wouldn't succeed. So she pressed her lips together and nodded.

He activated his tattoo. Everys closed her eyes and offered a silent prayer to the Singularity. *Take me where You need me.*

A warm breeze caressed her cheeks, sending a shiver down her spine. She braced herself for the jump, knowing that it would be unpleasant yet again.

Tormod patted her hand. "Blessed? We're here."

What? She opened her eyes. The darkened room in the Embassy was gone. Now they stood on a balcony facing a city that seemed vaguely familiar. She could hear voices in the far distance, along with the usual hustle and bustle of a large city. She stepped to the railing to get a better look at their surroundings. The balcony overlooked a neighborhood that looked old, the buildings made of tan bricks. But as Everys studied them, her stomach lurched, and it felt like her mind filled with static. There was something unsettling about the view, and she turned away from it.

"Where are we?" she asked, even though she suspected she knew the answer.

She stopped when she saw Tormod. The color had drained from his face as he stared out over the cityscape. How could he stand the disturbing effect of those buildings?

"Utuaa," he whispered. "I would recognize the Navel anywhere."

Everys's stomach flipped. Her palms itched as she remembered how she had drawn the plague rune not that long ago. Was Narius still here? She supposed that was possible; Brencis's assassins may have tried to kill him here and failed, then reported that to him. She spun on her heel, ready to leave the balcony and at least see if they could figure out why they were there.

"Hold on, Blessed," Tormod said. "We are deep in enemy territory. Let us proceed carefully."

He motioned for her to stay put, then slipped through the glass door into the building. Everys clenched her hands into fists as she waited, trying to keep calm, trying not to let her thoughts and hopes race ahead of herself.

Tormod popped out of the door and motioned for her to follow him. She did so, trying to remain as quiet as possible.

They entered a lavishly decorated suite with plush furniture, impressive paintings of bold colors and slashing strokes, and a highly polished floor that at first appeared to be glass. She took several tentative steps before realizing that she wouldn't slip. Whoever owned this must be wealthy.

"—the protests are spreading," a female voice, rich and sultry, said from an adjoining room.

Everys and Tormod froze. His gaze immediately tracked the voice to an open doorway. He motioned for Everys to stay. She clamped a hand over her mouth, but she was pretty sure whoever it was could hear her heart as it slammed against her ribs.

"Can the coordinators keep them focused?" Another woman's voice, firm and confident, although strangely familiar. "We need a peaceful march to the Navel, not a riot that burns half the city."

"They think so. Seminal Bakun reports that more students are trying to reach Utuaa to join the protests. According to the criers—"

"We don't call them that."

A pause. "According to the criers, there are at least ten thousand people in the streets."

The second woman laughed. "Given Tirigian's stranglehold on the press, I'd be willing to bet that the actual numbers are five to ten times more than that."

"Do you think we'd be able to see the mob from here?"

"Perhaps. Shall we see?"

Everys's eyes went wide. The voices were getting closer. She frantically searched for a place to hide, somewhere they could duck. Tormod had produced some ink and was quickly sketching a rune on his open palm, one she didn't recognize, but whatever it did, he had to hurry.

Two women strode through the open door and Everys gasped in spite of herself. She recognized both of them immediately. How could she not? Both of them had vied for Narius's heart at one point or another.

Cosena of Maotoa and Princess Innana were chuckling to themselves as they stepped into the room. Cosena spotted them first, stumbling to a halt, her eyes wide and her mouth gaping. She stuttered something unintelligible. Innana walked for another two steps before she noticed. But unlike Cosena, who wore her shock openly, Innana didn't appear at all surprised. The only change in expression was a single upraised brow.

"I wasn't expecting company," Innana said. "Welcome, Queen Everys. It's good to see you again."

Heat painted Everys's cheeks, and she bit back a retort. The last time they had been in the same room together was at Innana's abortive wedding to Narius, when he nearly died at Brencis's hands. The memory was far from pleasant and definitely not something to be glossed over.

"What are they doing here?" Cosena hissed.

Innana raised a hand, not taking her eyes off them. "And you must be Tormod? I understand that our Counterintelligence Bureau is often stymied by your antics."

Tormod bowed, a gracious smile on his lips. "Not how I would characterize my operations, but I am flattered all the same."

"To what do I owe the pleasure?" Innana asked. "I presume this isn't merely a social call, Ev—may I call you Everys?"

"That's fine." Everys forced the words through clenched teeth.

Innana smiled pleasantly. "Thank you. I know that is presumptuous, but I hope it won't be for long."

"And why is that, *Sertanjinon?*" Tormod asked.

Innana laughed, a melodic sound filled with delight. "You flatter me, sir."

"Not at all. I believe that is the correct appellation, is it not?" Tormod replied.

She wagged a finger at him. "I see why you have earned your reputation."

Everys shot a questioning look at Tormod. She wanted to smack him for taking over the conversation, but she couldn't help but be curious.

He smiled serenely. "*Sertanjinon* is a technical term for a person who is soon to ascend to the Imperial throne. With some flare to acknowledge her beauty and grace."

Everys fought to keep from rolling her eyes.

"It is true, though. Within two days, three at most, my brother will be deposed by the will of the people and I will assume the throne," Innana said, her tone cool and dispassionate. "Your arrival here is fortuitous, Everys."

"Oh?" Everys struggled to keep her frustration bottled up, but it was growing. "How so?"

"You are one of the legitimate rulers of the Dynasty. Thus, it would be good for us to discuss an important matter, the first item of my agenda for when I take control of the Imperium."

Enough! The thought shot through Everys. Enough of the flattery, the games, the cool detachment. "Where is Narius? I know he was here not that long ago and with you. So where is my husband?" She emphasized her words to remind them both who he belonged to.

Cosena seemed to catch the implication. She coughed and looked away.

Innana, however, didn't appear abashed at all. "I'm afraid we don't know for certain."

"What?"

"We returned him to the Dynasty," Innana said. "We haven't had contact with him since."

Despair welled up inside her. He was already gone? Back in the Dynasty? Then what were they doing here?

Tormod touched her hand, catching her attention. His eyes were wide, and she understood what he was trying to convey almost immediately.

She sighed, biting back a sharp retort. If the Singularity sent them here, He had his reasons.

"Was he... was he okay when he left?" Everys asked. She had to know that much, at least.

Cosena nodded, and Innana added, "He was still recovering from the beating my brother's minions inflicted on him, but otherwise, he was in good spirits. Very hopeful to be reunited with you. That hasn't happened yet?"

Everys shook her head.

"I am truly sorry to hear that," Innana said. "I know how much you love each other."

It stung, hearing that from her of all people, especially since she said it in front of Cosena, who had tried to seduce him not that long ago. But Everys took a deep, cleansing breath. She had to set aside her personal feelings and focus on what was best for the Dynasty. That would be Narius's wishes in this situation, she was sure.

"You mentioned something about your agenda?" Everys said.

Innana gestured toward one couch. Everys went over and picked a spot to sit. Tormod stood at her right while Innana and Cosena settled into their own seats.

"One of my dearest wishes is for there to be peace between our nations," Innana said. "I had hoped I could achieve this by marrying Narius, but that did not work out. Now I hope to bring it about as Empress of the Dalark Imperium, and I hope you will take the first steps toward that with me today."

"Not that I wish to contradict you, *Sertanjinon*, but how is it you find yourself about to ascend?" Tormod asked. "Call it professional curiosity."

"The people of the Dalark Imperium have recently learned some disturbing information about my brother. He has been making some very foolish decisions without thinking through the full ramifications," she said. "Not only has he forced us into a war that very few of our citizens actually wanted, it has recently come to light that he had me secretly arrested and that he had been holding his new wife in prison as well. Those revelations have led to protests throughout our territories, along with severe condemnations by our satellite nations."

"Oh?" Tormod said. "That seems rather... convenient."

Innana smiled demurely. "I may have had a hand in fanning the flames."

Everys wanted to gape at her. Based on what Narius had told her about their near marriage, Innana was nothing more than a vacuous beauty. Clearly, she had fooled many people.

Cosena rolled her eyes. "She didn't do it by herself."

"That is true." Innana looked directly at Everys. "Your Narius helped to bring this about. If it had not been for him, I would likely still be biding my time for the opportune moment. I will soon be Empress, and that is because of him."

Cosena glowered at Innana, and Everys suspected that the Maotoan princess had contributed as well.

"The other thing that has become increasingly clear is that many within the Imperium are already tired of the war between our peoples. Not just the common citizens, but many in the military have whispered about how poorly this war has been conducted. I intend to end it. Tirigian never should have invaded."

"Oh?" Tormod's gaze sharpened. "If I may be so bold, *Sertanjinon*, do you know if anyone influenced his decision to invade?"

Innana frowned. "Yes. I believe that his left hand, Utulgal, was most insistent that he invade."

Tormod's expression darkened.

"What?" Everys asked.

He hesitated, shooting a look at the other women. Everys understood immediately. He knew something that he didn't want to share in front of Innana or Cosena.

"You can tell them," she said. "If we're trying to end the hostilities, showing trust is important."

His expression soured, but he bowed. "At your order, Blessed." He turned to Innana. "Over the past few months, there was a conspiracy at work in the Dynasty to overthrow Narius. At my request, Prince Quartus went undercover to investigate my suspicions. He learned that people who claim to be the direct descendants of the ancient mage-kings infiltrated our government at the highest levels. Shortly before Bastion was destroyed, he sent me a report saying that he had also learned that this Utulgal was part of this same conspiracy."

Innana gaped at Tormod, and, for a moment, Everys savored her surprise.

"That... is quite the accusation. Do you have proof?" Innana asked.

"Beyond the prince's word, no. Although my understanding is that he was working with a Dalark intelligence agent named Yusra."

Now Innana gasped, but she quickly composed herself. "I see. That lends credence to your accusation."

Cosena looked positively sick.

"What is it?" Everys prompted.

She looked at Innana, who nodded. Cosena flinched, but then said, "Dalark has encouraged Maotoa to rebel for years. We've never taken them seriously, but then a few months ago, Tirigian sent Utulgal to meet with Trevik and my mother. Suddenly, both of them were in full agreement. Trevik killed my father shortly thereafter and married my mother."

"That is strange," Innana said. "Narius told me that not long ago, Utulgal urged Tirigian to make peace with the Dynasty."

Everys blinked. "He did what?"

Innana nodded. "Before we escaped, Utulgal urged my brother to send Narius back to the Dynasty, to make a trade of some kind with Brencis. Why would he push for war only to backpedal?"

That didn't make any sense. Why would Utulgal want to send Narius back to the Dynasty? No, not back to the Dynasty. To Brencis. Could it be that he was in league with the mage-kings as well? Given what she heard in Brencis's quarters, that seemed likely.

Wait. When she had been in Brencis's quarters, he had said that "she" wanted to capture Narius. That had to be Oluna. And if Utulgal wanted him sent back to the Dynasty, it was probably so she could get her hands on him. But why?

She turned to Tormod. "We need to go back. Now."

Tormod nodded. "I was thinking the same."

"Wait!" Innana said. "We still have much to discuss."

Everys rose from her seat. "We really don't. You want to end the war. I do too. So do it. Take the throne and recall your military."

"But we have to discuss terms. Where will the borders fall, will there be any economic repercussions, that sort of thing."

"All of that can wait!" Everys snapped. "Don't you see? The real threat are the mage-kings. Provided that we hold on to our thrones, we can hammer out all the details then. Borders and economics, Maotoa's role, both governments' treatment of minorities like the Siporans or the Elbrekkians, all of it can be on the table. For now, though, I need to find my husband." She almost added *before Oluna does*, but she knew that would only lead to more questions.

Tormod stepped close to her.

"Wait!" Innana held up a hand.

Everys signaled for Tormod to do so.

Innana leaned over to Cosena and whispered something to her. The Maotoan princess didn't look happy. She tried to object several times, but then sighed and left the room. As she did, Innana turned back to Everys.

"If this situation is as dire as you claim, I feel it is best if we work more closely together," Innana said. "Before the war started, the Maotoans helped my brother set up a network that would enable him to move troops quickly throughout the Dynasty's territory."

Everys's eyes widened. She remembered Narius telling her about how the Dalark troops had nearly killed him while he was visiting Dreah, how they had appeared through a portal that opened in the water of a fountain in his room. If Dalark had set up similar portals throughout the Dynasty's holdings, that would explain how they had invaded so quickly.

Cosena returned, carrying a crystal the size of her head and a comm device.

"This crystal will allow you to use the network," Innana explained. "When you return to wherever it is you came from, place the crystal near a body of water. Then use the comm to contact me. I will send Maotoans to help you use this to your benefit."

From Cosena's sour face, Everys doubted these Maotoans were all that loyal to anyone but her, but she wasn't about to refuse an advantage like this. She accepted the crystal.

"Thank you." Everys directed her words to Cosena, not to Innana. "I appreciate this, in spite of our history."

Cosena met her eyes, and a small smile tugged at her lips. She nodded, then stepped back.

"May all the spirits and potentates imbue you with their wisdom, knowledge, and strength," Innana said.

Everys had no idea how to reply to that, especially since it sounded like a formal blessing. So she nodded to Tormod. He tapped the tattoo on his arm.

Once again, the shift was subtle. One moment, they were standing in Innana's room, the next, the world had gone dark as they returned to the Embassy.

Tormod took a deep breath, then smiled. "I know that wasn't what you were hoping for, Blessed, but—"

"—but it's exactly what I needed," Everys said.

She knew Narius was back in the Dynasty, hopefully still free. Now all she had to do was find him.

"What happened with the medical records you retrieved from the palace the first time we were there?" Everys asked.

"I gave them to a pair of doctors who serve in a military unit and asked them to look them over," Tormod said. "Why?"

"Go get them. I want to find out if they've learned anything."

"You think Narius's blood might have something to do with why those assassins wanted to capture Narius or why Utulgal wanted to send him back to the Dynasty?"

"It's as good an explanation as any for now," Everys said. "Have them meet me up in the war room."

They stepped out of the darkened room, where Rewether, Redtale, and Challix were waiting for her.

Everys hesitated when she saw Rewether. "How are you?"

He grimaced, ducking his head. "I apologize for my... well, my attempting to murder you, Blessed."

She waved away his apology. "That's hardly your fault. Are you doing better?"

He nodded. "The Illuminates have given me a clean bill of health. No one has noticed any unusual behavior in me or anyone else Oluna corrupted. I'm fit to serve again. If you'll have me, that is."

Everys smirked at him. "I'm not letting you out of your duties that easily. Let's go."

She set out for the war room, and they quickly fell into step with her.

"What happened?" Challix asked. "Did you find the king?"

Everys shook her head. "No, we didn't. But we found some surprising allies."

"Who?" Redtale asked.

Everys explained about Innana and Cosena. The others were silent, although Rewether scowled through the entire story. When she finished, he shook his head angrily.

"You really think we can trust the Dalark? After all that they've done?" he asked. "And we're supposed to trust the Maotoans as well? After the way they almost killed the king? Absolutely not!"

"We haven't exactly been good neighbors to them either," Redtale countered. "Lots of blame to go around on all sides."

Everys offered a smile to her friend. Redtale nodded grimly.

Rewether grimaced, but he nodded. "My apologies. What are your orders?"

She handed him the crystal and the comm. "Take these. Then get a squad of soldiers and take them down to the stream near Papa's cabin. Contact whoever is on the other end of that comm and have them send us whoever they're sending. Once they're here, bring the crystal back here again." Hopefully, if the Maotoan's network needed water, taking the crystal away from the water would stop them from using it without their knowledge.

Rewether set out, and Everys continued on to the war room. Two medics in uniform waited for her. One was a middle-aged Hinaen woman with short-cropped gray hair and a dour expression. Based on her insignia, she was the senior of the two. The other, a younger Kolvese man with a shaved head, had a patch on his shoulder that designated him as a nurse and the doctor's chief assistant.

"Blessed, my name is Doctor Arnitaj Colesynn, and this is my assistant, Heartland. We've reviewed the king's medical records, and as far as I can tell, there is nothing remarkable about him," Dr. Colesynn said.

Everys frowned. How could that be possible? The only explanation that made sense was that there was something different about Narius's blood. Why else would she have been rebuked so severely when she used it? "Are you sure?"

Colesynn nodded. "Quite. Both Heartland and I have reviewed the records twice. Aside from a few unusual incidents where the king recovered more quickly than expected, I cannot find anything that might be deemed unusual."

Heartland smiled sympathetically at Everys.

Everys tried to process that. Obviously, those incidents Colesynn mentioned were times that she had used runes on Narius. But for there to be nothing else? She couldn't accept that.

"I'm not trying to be difficult, really, but there isn't anything about his blood specifically that sets him apart from everyone else?" Everys insisted.

The two medics exchanged a look. While Colesynn looked certain, a bit of hesitation flickered across Heartland's features.

"Well, there is the septeracyanosis," Heartland said.

Everys perked up. "The what?"

Colesynn's lip twitched. "That's hardly unusual."

"But it sets the king apart from other people."

"By which you mean commoners."

Heartland shrugged. "It fits the parameters of the queen's question."

"Fine." Colesynn turned back to Everys. "You truly don't know what septeracyanosis is?"

From the doctor's tone, she thought Everys should. But she had never heard that term before.

"Very well. Septeracyanosis is a condition that can be found in a small percentage of the Dynasty's population." Colesynn's tone was that of a rigid lecturer. "More specifically, the royal family and most noble families as well. But I would hardly consider this unusual. In certain circles, it's fairly common and even desired."

"A blood condition is desirable?" Everys repeated. "What does it do?"

Colesynn looked ready to answer, but Heartland jumped in. "Not that much, actually. The blood from people with septeracyanosis is better at holding oxygen. Some severe cases can cause digestion issues with certain foods. Transfusions can be tricky in those cases as well. And then there are the eyes."

Everys frowned.

"Septeracyanosis's most prominent symptom is a metallic coloring of the iris," Colesynn said, her tone irritated.

Comprehension dawned on Everys. Everyone knew that metallic eyes was a sign that a person was somehow related to the royal family.

"So if Narius and I were to ever have children, they would have this condition?" she asked.

"Most likely not," Colesynn said. "It is a recessive trait. Unless you have noble blood in your family history, it would be surprising if it happened."

Everys fought to keep from frowning at her tone. Heartland shot a look at the doctor and offered Everys a reassuring smile. She smiled back and asked him the next question that occurred to her. "How severe is Narius's case?"

"Fairly, which is understandable, given he is a member of the royal family. In past generations, they sought metallic eyes as a sign of royalty," Heartland said. "Has he ever shown any discomfort when he's eaten dairy?"

She frowned. She couldn't think of any times. So was this the answer? Why would this condition be important? "So where does this come from?"

"There are two possible explanations," Colesynn said before Heartland could answer. "For many centuries, the prelates taught that the metallic eyes were a sign of the Perfected Warrior's blessing upon the royal family. A divine gift, if you will. More recently, though, researchers have suggested that this results from a mutation that has been passed down through certain families."

Everys's frown deepened. She felt like this might be the right answer, but she couldn't see how the pieces fit together.

"Well, there is one other theory," Heartland said.

Colesynn glared at him. "You know full well that that has been discredited."

"Only because no one was willing to finish the research," Heartland replied calmly.

"What was the theory?"

Heartland started to answer, but Colesynn slammed a hand on the table, the *bang* cutting him off.

"I will not allow you to waste the queen's time with nonsense!" Colesynn barked.

Heartland's eyes flared, but he snapped his jaw shut.

"Except it's my time to waste." Everys injected ice into her words. "What is the theory?"

Drawing a breath, Heartland started to answer, but before he could, Colesynn shoved away from the table and stormed out of the room, muttering under her breath about insubordination.

"What was that about?" Everys asked.

"This theory is distasteful, especially to those who take pride in having septeracyanosis." Heartland offered a wan smile. "Such as Dr. Colesynn. You didn't see the silver flecks in her eyes?"

Everys frowned. Colesynn had nearly black eyes. She thought she would have noticed a metallic tint, but that probably explained why she had been so upset. "No, I didn't."

"Don't worry. Nobody does." Heartland shared a laugh with Everys, then his expression turned sober. "What Dr. Colesynn said is accurate. Most researchers would say septeracyanosis results from a mutation that must have developed several thousand years ago."

"But you believe otherwise?" Everys prompted.

He smiled. "Maybe. About sixty years ago, some researchers suggested septeracyanosis could have resulted from crossbreeding with a nonhuman race."

Everys blinked. What?

"Human hybrids aren't completely unheard of in the Dynasty. Most of the nonhuman races can interbreed with humans with varying degrees of success, with Plissk hybrids being the least possible and Elbrekkians being the most probable. The only real exceptions are the Diradae, the shessu, and the Cyklins." At her confused look, Heartland smiled sheepishly. "I find the subject interesting on an academic level, hence why I know about this research at all.

"At any rate, the researchers put forward a theory that this condition resulted from interbreeding. For example, every known Plissk-human hybrid have a skin condition. Ixactl-human hybrids can develop heart and lung anomalies depending on if their mothers receive the right nutrition during their pregnancy."

"So which nonhuman race would lead to this?" Everys asked.

"That's the problem. While this theory explains some aspects of septeracyanosis's origin, it doesn't fit exactly because, as you've just guessed, there isn't a single case of it developing in hybrids with any of the known nonhuman races. It's something that's only found in humans. The researchers suggested that it's possible a tribe of humans interbred with a nonhuman species that has since gone extinct, like the shessu supposedly did. If that's the case, then the bearers of septeracyanosis are the only evidence of such interbreeding. And given that most of those bearers are nobles who shudder at the thought of being 'filthy hybrids,' that research was shut down quickly, especially when King Vetranio heard about it."

Everys nodded. From what she had heard of Narius's grandfather, that didn't surprise her at all.

So did this explain anything? Could a mutation prompt such a strong rebuke? Possibly, but why? Could it be because the Dynasty taught that this condition was a gift from the Perfected Warrior? Maybe. The ancient texts had condemned using blood connected to the Elderreach cults as ink. Since most scriveners believed the Elderreach gods didn't exist, they assumed that the prohibition against Elderreach blood was a blanket condemnation of using blood connected to a false religion. If that were the case, then maybe the Dynasty's belief would be enough to prompt a rebuke.

She frowned. While the Perfect Warrior wasn't real, the Elderreach "gods" definitely were. She had seen one with her own eyes. She shuddered as she remembered its hot, foul breath, the way the keepers scuttled overhead, the way its eye...

Its enormous eye. Its metallic eye that had seemed so familiar at the time and she couldn't understand why.

But now she did. That gigantic eye had been reminiscent of her husband's. Could septeracyanosis mean that the royal families were connected to the Elderreach? That would explain why the rebuke had been so severe when she'd used Narius's blood in a rune. But how would that have happened? Why didn't anyone know this?

"Blessed?" Heartland leaned forward, concern etched on his face. "Are you all right?"

In some ways, she was. This would explain so much! But this was all based on speculation and maybes. She needed more evidence.

"This research. Whatever happened with it?" Everys asked. "Could I find a copy?"

"I doubt it. Like I said, the theory was extremely unpopular with the nobility. There were condemnations from the prelates, an investigation by Internal Security, and pressure from the palace to make everything go away. Even after the research was ended, the sponsors were pariahs for close to a decade."

"Who sponsored it?"

"The Trentwether family."

Everys laughed. That didn't surprise her at all. The Trentwethers were oddities in the noble family hierarchy. They were very interested in education and research, eschewing the usual political jockeying to focus on their own interests. She had briefly met Spanica, the current Trentwether patriarch, just a few months earlier. Would he have a copy of the research? Given his interest in esoteric subjects, he thought that was entirely possible.

She turned to Heartland. "Thank you so much for your help. I think you've given me the missing piece to a very important puzzle."

"I'm glad to have helped."

Everys excused herself and sent for Rewether, excitement shooting through her. She could feel the anticipation building. Could this be it? Could she have finally found the answer?

Rewether stepped into the war room, his expression expectant.

"Did the Maotoan arrive safely?" she asked.

"He did. Much more cooperative than I expected, but he is here. Name's Tanakept."

"Good. We need to see if he can help me take a little trip."

"To where?"

"The Trentwether estates." And hopefully, to some answers.

76

N arius had put this off for far too long.

He had tried to distract himself, studying the map of Bastion, conferring with Zar's team leaders, checking up on Auriel's health. He had engaged in important things, like spending time with his brother, getting to know Yusra, and making sure Kavi was treated well. All the while, the burden loomed over him, taunting him, needling him. Finally, he realized he had to do something.

He found Paine sitting by himself in one corner of Zar's headquarters. Two soldiers always stood nearby, keeping watchful eyes on him. He had traded his robes of state for a simple uniform, one devoid of ranks and honors. He looked smaller than Narius had ever seen him.

Narius watched him quietly, studying him, assessing him, trying to figure out what he should say. But then Paine looked up and noticed him. He started to say something, but then snapped his mouth shut and hung his head.

Oh, this was ridiculous! Narius had known Paine for half of his life. He wasn't going to ignore him now. He strode over and motioned for the soldiers to back off, which they thankfully did, then sat down across from the vizier.

"We need to talk," Narius said.

Paine sighed heavily. "I suppose we do, yes."

"Did you mean what you said? You saw me as a bad king?"

With another sigh, Paine leaned back and ran his hands over his scalp. "The truth?"

"I think you owe me that much at least."

"I do indeed." Paine pursed his lips into a thin line. "I spoke the truth at the Humrices'. I really do believe that under the right circumstances, you could have been one of the best kings the Dynasty has ever known."

"But..." Narius prompted.

"But. But you were shackled to the Trickster's own harridan, Viara. You were stymied in your efforts to secure peace by marrying Innana. And marrying Everys..." Paine's voice drifted off and he frowned. "Your Strength, I know how much you love her, and I envy your relationship. But her presence in your life and the palace added so many complications to an already fraught situation. Too often, you allowed your heart to lead you when you should have tempered that impulse with your mind."

Narius supposed that was true. But then, that had been Paine's responsibility as his vizier, to shore up his flanks and make sure he didn't overlook anything. Rather than point that out, though, he decided to take a different approach.

"Except if it wasn't for Everys, we wouldn't have realized that people were still practicing toratropic magic. We would have never known about the mage-kings' continued existence and threat. If it wasn't for her, both you and I would have died who knows how many times over." Narius leaned forward. "Now I have another question to ask you: are you still my *lecona*?"

Paine sat up straighter. Narius understood why. The word *lecona* referred to a trail partner, one of the most unbreakable bonds in traditional Kolvese culture. Many years earlier, Narius and Paine had taken a vow declaring that they would be each other's *lecona*.

"If you will still have me, I will be," Paine said. "I know I have not supported you as you wish I had. I know that I have failed you time and again. But I promise that as long as I live, I will strive to live up to the trust you have shown me and the trust I hope I will be able to earn once again."

Narius nodded. "I will accept, but on one condition."

Paine quirked a brow.

"When..." He swallowed hard. He had almost said *if*. "When we find Everys, I need you to accept her. Treat her with the respect she deserves as queen. No, the respect she deserves as a person. If you can do that, we will be well on our way to restoring our relationship."

Paine's mouth popped open, but then he snapped it shut again. He nodded solemnly.

"By Wind and Storm, by those we meet on the trail and those who welcome us home again, I promise I will, Your Strength. Narius."

Narius nodded as well. He was tempted to hug his old friend, but he knew that Paine would never accept it.

"Your Strength!"

Zar's voice jolted Narius. The guard commander skidded to a halt near Paine's corner, his chest heaving. Narius looked past him and saw people rushing through the headquarters.

"What's going on?"

"News on the criers," Zar said. "There's been a coup in Dalark."

A thrill shot through him. Innana had succeeded? He sprinted for the war room.

People had gathered around a crier, hushed and focused. As Narius approached, Zar barked an order to make room. At first, they appeared annoyed, but when they saw who was coming, they quickly moved aside.

The crier, a harried looking Grerid woman, tried to speak calmly, but it was clear she was having a hard time doing so. "—receive word from our correspondents in Utuaa. Ordinary citizens have risen all across the Imperium, demanding that Emperor Tirigian abdicate his throne. While the Emperor resisted these demands, a riot that recently broke out in Utuaa seems to have tipped..." The woman looked off camera and then turned back. "We are now receiving a video feed direct from the palace in Utuaa. Please stand by."

A second later, the footage flickered, and Innana replaced the reporter. Narius sucked in a sharp breath. She looked positively radiant, wearing a dress that rivaled anything Tirigian had ever worn. It seemed to be woven of ribbons of silver and gold, studded with precious jewels. Similar ribbons had been woven into her auburn hair, and her green eyes radiated strength and assuredness. She was surrounded by a number of people he assumed were her advisers, although he did spot Planka lurking near her.

She started speaking in Dalark, but a second later, a female voice translated her words into Dynastic. "Rejoice, my people, for the spirits and potentates have heard your cry for justice and they have answered. Earlier today, soldiers loyal to your will stormed the palace and took my brother captive. He and his inner council are being held in a secure location until they can stand trial for their crimes against our beloved

Imperium. These soldiers have also named me to be his successor. By their acclamation, by your overwhelming will, I have accepted.

"As my first official act, I will undo the greatest mistake my brother committed. Effective immediately, all Dalark forces must withdraw from the Xoniel Dynasty's holdings. I will also reach out to the leadership of the Dynasty to see if we may set aside the hostility that has existed between us for centuries. I hope that those who truly have the Dynasty's best interests at heart will see this for the opportunity that it is."

She continued speaking, focusing more on domestic policies and issues. In other circumstances, Narius might have listened if only to see what reforms were possible now that Innana was on the throne.

But now, he needed to focus on the problem this presented. Brencis had been fighting a war on multiple fronts. With Dalark no longer a threat, Brencis could bring the remnants of his forces to bear on the rebels and on Everys.

He turned and found Paine in the crowd. The vizier nodded gravely. He had likely seen the same issue. Innana had created an opportunity for them, but they would have to act quickly to take full advantage of it.

Narius faced the rest of the crowd. "This is good news, but if we don't act swiftly, we are going to lose an opportunity given"—He winced as he realized he was about to attribute what was happening to the Perfected Warrior. Old habits he still had to break—"given to us. This new situation will put Brencis off-balance. We need to move quickly and try to end this now. How do we best take advantage of this opportunity?"

"Isn't it obvious?" Zar asked. "We strike and we strike hard. Right for the head. We hit the palace and reclaim it."

While the others made approving noises, Narius considered the possibility. There was definitely some logic to this. If Brencis was in the palace, they could capture him and all of this would be over. For another, controlling the palace wouldn't just be a symbolic victory. So many of the Dynasty's important decisions were routed through the palace. If Narius could claim it before anyone knew what was happening, they could wrest control from Brencis's supporters as well.

"That has merit," Narius said.

"Merit, yes, but not so much feasibility," Paine said. "The palace was next to impossible to breach during peacetime. Brencis has spent much of his time fortifying it against any sort of assault."

"That's where I come in," Quartus said from the back of the crowd. "Literally. I hesitate to bring this up since I'm sure the guards here would love this reminder, but I found several ways to sneak in and out of the palace with no one noticing. Handy when you're trying to maintain your reputation as a hedonistic narcissist."

Zar scowled at Quartus, but Narius could hear the self-deprecating tone in his brother's voice. He was putting on a front.

"We wouldn't be able to use these secret entrances to move an entire division of troops into the palace, but a smaller, more agile force?" Quartus continued. "That could easily be done."

Yusra frowned and turned to him. "Why didn't you tell me about this before? Why not use this to get to Brencis?"

Quartus grimaced. "Because this would have only given us access to the palace. Getting close enough to Brencis would have taken more than just an open door."

They stared at each other, their expressions unreadable. Narius shifted, suddenly uncomfortable at the silent argument they were clearly having.

But then Yusra blew out a long breath through her nose before she turned back to Narius. "Regardless, Your Strength, this is an opportunity. And, if I may be so bold, we have a saying in Dalark: 'When you want to steal the eggs, distract the farmer.'"

"We're taking advice from Dalark intelligence now?" one of guards muttered.

Narius shot him a disapproving look. "I'll take whatever help we can get. Go on, Yusra."

"Brencis will probably expect some sort of move against him," she said. "If you just show up in the palace, he might be ready for you. But if you were to convince him that your strike was coming from another direction, you might catch him unawares."

That made sense too.

Zar nodded thoughtfully. "One plan Governor-General Zammit was working on was to raid a military supply distribution center just outside of Dropport. We were just going to steal the supplies for future operations, but we could launch an assault on the center instead. If we make enough noise, that'll keep the palace's attention on us and not you."

The others nodded grimly, and Narius understood why. There was a big difference between stealing supplies and actually assaulting a fortified building. Whoever went on that mission could die. But then, those were the risks they had to take if they wanted to stop Brencis.

Zar must have sensed his hesitation. "This is what we volunteered for, Your Strength."

The other soldiers nodded, a few even shouting their agreement.

He knew that, but it still didn't sit well with him. How many people had already thrown away their lives in this useless conflict? How many more would have to die before it was all over?

He squared his shoulders. With any luck, the number would be low.

"All right." He turned to Quartus. "How do we get into the palace without being seen?"

Quartus offered him a lopsided smile. "I'm sure you'll love this, brother. When's the last time you went to an armory service?"

77

Tanakept, the Maotoan sent by Cosena, turned out to be a wizened little man. His leathery brown skin was creased, and he looked so frail Everys worried that if a single leaf fell on him, he'd crumble. But in spite of his withered appearance, he seemed wholly unconcerned, even though he was surrounded by half a dozen soldiers.

As she approached, Tanakept bowed. "Blessed One, it is my great honor to serve you. Where is it you wish the Water Bearer to take you?"

She motioned for Redtale. The Ixactl pulled out a map and spread it out on the ground in front of Tanakept, who squatted down to study it.

"We wish to go to the Trentwether estate in Wrine," Everys said. "Is that possible?"

"Possible? Yes. Achievable? That has yet to be seen." Tanakept squinted at the map and then nodded to himself. He turned and shuffled to the stream.

"Do you need us to put the crystal back in the water?" Rewether asked warily.

Tanakept waved away his question. "The crystal is one end of the chantway. I am the other."

He waded into the stream, which only came halfway up his shins. Then he knelt and plunged his hands into the water.

"When we struck the alliance with the Dalark, they arranged for approximations of the crystals to be strewn throughout your waters, which were replaced with true chantway crystals when they invaded. Let us see if there is one close to where you wish to go."

He took a long breath, then closed his eyes and began to hum a jaunty tune. His face twitched into a frown and his head jerked to the side, the tune modulating with every motion. But then he smiled and finished his melody.

"I have found what you seek, Blessed One," Tanakept said, his eyes still closed. "I will open the door for you now if you are ready."

Everys glanced at Redtale, who nodded gravely. She then touched the vials of ink she had in her pockets, just to reassure herself that they were there. "We are."

Tanakept repositioned himself, and then began to sing, a low droning that started softly but then grew loud enough that Everys could feel it in her chest. As Tanakept chanted, the water in front of him frothed, forming a vortex that somehow stretched across the length of the stream. Then the water rose, lifting the vortex until it was perpendicular to the stream. The water in the vortex faded, revealing a city on the other side.

With one last glance at Redtale, Everys squared her shoulders and stepped through.

A chill swept over her as she passed through the doorway, a prickle of ice that sent a delicious shiver down her spine. But as she stepped out onto pavement bordering the canal in Wrine, a nagging thought occurred to her. The sensation of traveling via the chantway was like what she experienced the last time she and Tormod had jumped using his tattoo. Could the two be related?

Everys peered over the edge of the canal and thought she saw the glint of the chantway crystal in the water, but she couldn't be sure.

Redtale grunted. "When all of this is over, we're going to have to get rid of those things."

Everys agreed. But she couldn't focus on that right now. They had a much more important mystery to unravel.

Wrine was oddly quiet. While Everys had never visited the city, she knew its reputation. Wrine had a been a stronghold for the Dynasty during its earliest expansion, a place where the Dynasty had launched fleets into the Water Bearer's Repose to first control the inland sea and then conquer the territory that bordered it. In more recent years, it had been a commercial hub, where cargo vessels could come from the far-flung corners of the Dynasty's holdings to off-load their merchandise. From all accounts, Wrine was supposed to be a bustling town, always on the move, always changing, so alive that people from Wrine were stereotypically said to have a frenetic energy that wore others down.

But as Redtale and Everys crept through the empty streets, she didn't feel that hum of life and vitality. What few passersby they saw hustled to their destinations after casting suspicious looks in their direction. There was a somber pall that hung over the city.

She soon realized why. Wrine was little more than ruins. Very few buildings had glass in their windows. Thousands of flechettes were still embedded in walls and vehicles.

Finally, they heard voices coming from down the street. Redtale shot her a questioning look, and Everys nodded. They might as well see what was going on. They crept down the street, sticking as close to the buildings as they could, until they came across a large open area, one that may have been a decorative plaza at some point but was now filled with trash, rubble, and burned-out vehicles.

But it was also filled with people, hundreds of them, all of them looking haggard and tired. They stood in line, chatting quietly amongst themselves. Everys's gaze hitched on the soldiers that kept a watchful eye over the crowd, standing on top of ruined transports or makeshift platforms. They didn't wear Dalark uniforms, thankfully, but they weren't wearing the Dynasty's uniforms either. Instead, their markings identified them as being a militia raised by the Trentwether family.

"If you're here for aid, get in line!" one soldier barked, and it took Everys a moment to realize he was speaking to her. "The Trentwethers will continue to observe *methok rue*, but you need to remain orderly!"

Redtale tensed next to her, but Everys touched her arm and motioned for them to take a place at the end of the line.

The line moved slowly, which gave Everys plenty of time to eavesdrop on nearby conversations. Everyone's story was mostly the same. All the people in line were residents of Wrine, trapped here when the Dalark attacked. They didn't have the financial means or the opportunity to flee the city, as many of the nobility had. They had weathered the Dalark's siege as best they could, hunkered down in their homes or wherever they could find shelter. All of them had celebrated when the Dynasty's troops finally pushed the Dalark away from the city, but the Dynasty hadn't stayed, moving on to the next battle, leaving the citizens to fend for themselves.

But thankfully, Spanica Trentwether had stepped in. He had apparently been stockpiling supplies for just such an occasion, and ever since the end of the battle, he had opened his stores to help. The people were grateful, but Everys heard the same doubt repeated many times: how much longer could he continue the efforts? He would run out eventually, and then what would happen?

As Everys and Redtale neared the front of the line, a man's voice boomed over the square. "My friends, I'm sorry, but we have run out of today's allotment. We will resume distribution tomorrow at the middle of First Watch. The soldiers will give tokens to those who have not received their rations, allowing them to go first tomorrow. Thank you."

Everys touched Redtale's arm again. She recognized Spanica's voice. Sure enough, as the crowd dispersed, she spotted him standing in the middle of a cluster of soldiers, overseeing the crowd through his thick glasses. He had always been a small man with thinning red-and-gray hair, but in the intervening months, he had grown more gaunt, as if he hadn't had a good meal since the war began.

"So now what?" Redtale asked. "I doubt he's going to stay here for long."

"We get an invitation to his house," Everys said, then raised her voice. "Lord Trentwether, may I speak with you?"

One soldier standing near him stepped forward and tried to wave her away. "You can come back tomorrow."

"I'm not interested in rations," Everys called out. "Instead, I'm hoping we can continue the discussion we had before the king fought in the *harsannon*."

The soldier looked ready to order some troops to advance on her, but Spanica held up a hand. He squinted at her, then his eyes widened. He clambered off his perch and hurried to her.

"What are you doing here?" he asked in a low voice. "This isn't safe!"

"I realize that, but I've come on a matter of great importance, something that only you can help me with," Everys said.

Spanica shot a worried look at the people who still milled about. He motioned for Everys to follow him. Once they were away from the crowd, he turned back to her.

"I don't know what help I can offer," Spanica said. "My house isn't exactly known for our military might or economic power."

"There are other sources of strength. Such as knowledge. Such as research into septeracyanosis."

Spanica didn't react. "Oh?"

She nodded. "I think the research your family did might hold the key to everything right now. I know that, before the *harsannon*, I promised I would give you access to the palace's archives and libraries, and now I'm asking you to assist me again before I can fulfill that promise. But please, will you help me?"

They had walked a fair distance from the square, where several heavily armored transports waited. The soldiers watching over them snapped to attention as they approached, but Spanica stopped and stroked his chin. Then he turned to Everys.

"I understand why you weren't able to keep your word earlier, Blessed. But words are easy to say, harder to back up. If you want my help, you must give me an honest answer to the next two questions."

Everys braced herself and nodded.

"First, are the accusations that Minister Masruq leveled against you correct? Are you a toratropic witch?" Spanica asked.

Everys grimaced. "We prefer the term 'mage,' but yes. I am."

Spanica's eyes narrowed as he processed that answer. Several of the soldiers with him shifted their stance, readying their weapons. Redtale took a step forward, as if getting ready to interpose herself between Everys and them, but Everys stopped her.

"I appreciate your candor, but this makes my next question even more necessary. Are you somehow responsible for Masruq's death?"

What? Everys's stomach turned cold, and she felt like she might collapse. Masruq was dead? That sweet man who had done so much to welcome her into the palace? Who had been so kind to her and... No, wait, he was married to Oluna and was likely a part of her plans as a willing participant or otherwise. She couldn't lose sight of that. But hearing that he had died still hurt.

"No," she said. "I didn't even know he had died."

Spanica studied her face, then nodded. "I believe you. Let us depart. I hope what I can tell you will help."

She did too. Far too many people had lost far too much already.

"How has no one ever found out about these tunnels?" Paine asked from beside Narius.

The transport went over a bump, jostling the occupants, and Paine and Narius bounced off each other. Paine grunted but didn't look in Narius's direction. Kavi quickly grabbed the sides of the bench and steadied herself with a sour look.

Quartus smirked at them from across the cabin. "That's a great question, Vizier. I wish I knew how to answer it. Maybe a previous supreme prelate had a mistress he liked to sneak into his office. Or maybe he was engaged in some nefarious activities. All I know is, one day, when Father dragged the family to the armory for the morning rituals, I slipped away from everyone during one of Istragon's ridiculous homilies. As Chance willed it, I found myself down in a long-forgotten storeroom where they kept spare ceremonial weaponry. When I tried to pick up one mace, lo and behold, it turned out to be a switch that opened a secret door. I was so scared that I'd get in trouble I raced back to Father's side just as the homily ended."

Narius fought to hide a smile. He could envision his brother behaving like that easily enough.

"Well, I tried to forget about what I saw, but you know how it is when you're young. At least, I'm assuming you did. I can't picture you as a child. But the idea of a secret passageway kept nagging at me. The next time I got the chance, I slipped away, found the same room, and thought that it was a fun little secret just for me," Quartus continued.

"Until...?" Yusra prompted from his side.

Quartus shot her a nervous glance, and he actually blushed! When was the last time Narius had seen his brother blush? Then he cleared his throat and said, "Well, I became absolutely smitten with a pretty young noblewoman who promised... well, I won't go into specifics. Only that she wanted to see me far away from watchful eyes. So I claimed I was going down to the armory to meditate or some such nonsense and slipped out of the palace."

Yusra studied his face and Quartus looked away. Narius had no doubt what that little adventure had consisted of. What was so strange was how embarrassed Quartus was behaving. And why was he so chatty all of a sudden? It was as if he was trying to hide something behind a barrage of words.

His eyes widened as Yusra poked Quartus in the side with a knowing smile. Broken Sword, was it possible? Quartus was so embarrassed by his past exploits because of Yusra! Narius wanted to laugh and pepper him with questions. Who was this woman who had transformed his womanizing brother into this blabbering mess?

Before he could pursue this development, the transport pulled to a halt. Someone pounded on the cab and one guard shoved the door open. Once again, Narius wished that Zar or Farga had come with them. Not that he didn't trust the troops at his side; Zar had vouched for all of them, and he trusted the commander's judgment. But they had insisted on going to the military supply center and nothing could dissuade them.

They had parked at the bottom of the hill the palace complex perched on. A high wall, one that had probably been functional when the palace was originally built but was now little more than a tall decoration, bordered the entire hillside. Quartus jogged over to a section of the wall, studied the bricks for a moment, and then pressed his hand against one of them. He leaned heavily into it. With a deep grinding sound, a portion of the wall slid aside.

"Glad to see it still works," Quartus muttered, then stepped aside and made a grand sweeping gesture. "After you."

Six of the troops trotted through the doorway into the darkness beyond, then everyone else followed, the remaining four troops taking up the rearguard position. The hidden door ground shut behind them.

The tunnel snaked through the darkness, the floor uneven and leading further and further up. They tried to maintain silence, but there were plenty of times that someone tripped or bumped into a rough wall. Eventually, though, they emerged into a musty room, one crammed full of crates and objects wrapped in cloth. A bit of light filtered through a tall window.

Quartus took the lead. "This is it. Follow me."

They emerged in a hallway that Narius didn't recognize, but then, he had never been in the backstage area of the Grand Armory before. They could traipse right by Supreme Prelate Istragon's personal study and never know it. They crept down the hall until they came to an unassuming door.

"This will take us to the utility outbuildings on the palace grounds," Quartus whispered. "From there, we can slip into a service tunnel that will bring us into the second subbasement."

That meant they would enter the palace through a rarely visited corner. No wonder Quartus had been able to come and go as he pleased.

But before Quartus could open the door, Narius paused. He thought he heard... Yes, there it was again. A shout? A scream? Definitely a person crying out, but whether in anger or pain, he couldn't tell. Where was that coming from? He held up a hand and turned a slow circle. It took him a moment to zero in on the sound, but he was pretty sure he could follow it.

"What are you doing?" Quartus whispered. "We need to go this way."

"We will. But I want to see what's going on," Narius said.

Several people hissed their objections, but Narius ignored them and crept back down the hallway. Following the sound, he went up a flight of stairs and found himself standing before a large wooden door he thought he recognized. Another shout. Whoever was in trouble was definitely on the other side. He shouldered the door open as quietly as he could.

He emerged into the sanctum of the Grand Armory. The bejeweled statues of the Perfected Warrior and Water Bearer soared over the central dais, but in the dim light, they appeared vengeful, ready to strike him down. Or maybe not him. Maybe they were preparing to attack the figure who had been lifted off the ground between them, his arms and legs splayed apart as if invisible hands were trying to tear him in half. The man writhed in pain, whimpering, then cried out again, but he sounded like he was more frightened than in pain. It took Narius a moment to realize who it was.

"Istragon?"

It wasn't surprising he hadn't recognized him. He had rarely seen the man not wearing his robes of office. Instead, he wore the tattered remnants of a naval uniform, which had been shredded at the sleeves and legs. Something held him four feet off the ground, where he spasmed and thrashed, trying to break free. Narius thought he saw something glowing on the floor underneath him.

Without thinking, Narius rushed into the room toward the dais. Then someone caught his arm.

Kavi stepped around him. *Powerful runes at work here,* she signed. *Stay here so I can look.*

Narius followed Kavi with Yusra, Quartus, and Paine right behind him.

As they approached Istragon, Narius got a better look at what was glowing underneath him. Just as he suspected, it was a rune, a jagged collection of lines and sharp angles that looked like the floor had shattered. Each time Istragon so much as twitched, the harsh red light flared.

Kavi edged forward, crouched low, her gaze locked on the rune. She made several tentative gestures, as if probing the edges of the effect. Then she squared her shoulders and began a series of motions. Much to Narius's surprise, the rune flared even brighter and Kavi skidded backward two feet. She pushed herself forward as if walking against a strong headwind, then tried again. The rune flared even brighter, so much so that it hurt Narius's eyes. He wished he could lend Kavi some strength or encouragement.

Her chest heaving, Kavi made one final, large gesture, a sweeping movement like she was throwing open curtains. And with an audible crack, the rune vanished, and Istragon tumbled to the floor. Kavi staggered back. Sweat slicked her hair, and she looked like she had somehow lost thirty pounds in an instant. Yusra rushed to her side and steadied her as she took several deep breaths.

"Are you okay?" Narius asked.

Kavi shook her head. Her fingers trembled as she signed, *Very powerful. I barely broke it.*

Even though Istragon was free of the rune, he still writhed on the floor.

Kavi waved her hands over his body, then rocked back on her heels and slowly stood. *Again, powerful runes. I think I've undone them all, but I may have missed one, so be careful.*

Narius nodded and took a tentative step forward. "Istragon? Can you hear me?"

Istragon twitched, then his eyes fluttered open. He groaned. "Y-your Strength? Is that you?"

"It is," Narius said cautiously.

The Supreme Prelate scrambled across the floor, bawling, and tried to snare his ankles. Narius danced back a step, and Kavi stepped between them.

"Forgive me, Your Strength. It wasn't my fault. They made me do it!"

"Do what?" Narius demanded.

"Say such evil things about you. About the queen! After you married her, they started visiting me and they... they drew things on me. Things that made the words burn inside me. I had to let out the bile or it would have consumed me! And every time I did, I felt so good. The more horrible, the better I felt and... and... I couldn't stop. I couldn't control myself! Please, forgive me!"

Narius stared at Istragon in shock. Was that possible? Had someone made Istragon so spiteful, so venomous, so hateful to Everys? His gaze flicked to Kavi, his expression an unspoken question.

She shook her head subtly. *The runes made his hate louder.*

That made sense, but it only raised a different question. "Why?"

Paine nodded sagely. "I had a similar thought. If this was done by the mage-kings, why would a group of Siporans encourage hatred against their own kind?"

The room fell silent for a moment until Yusra gasped.

"They came to him *after* you got married," she said. "The problem wasn't Siporans. The problem was Everys."

Narius's eyes widened. The mage-kings had worked in the shadows for decades, maybe even generations. No one had ever noticed, and probably wouldn't have, until he married Everys. Until he had brought her, a toratropic mage, into the palace, where she could have uncovered everything. So they weaponized Istragon's hatred and unleashed him. Against Everys. Against him. Against the Dynasty.

His face hardened. "Let's go. We need to finish this."

He turned and headed back for the door. He had to remain focused. This needed to end. And he would make sure it did.

The palace grounds should have been filled with the activity of normal life, even during a crisis. Instead, the air hung thick over everything, heavy and silent.

As the squad crept through the maintenance outbuildings, Narius braced himself for their inevitable discovery. By the time they reached the servants' entrance, Narius's nerves were screaming that something was wrong.

One soldier tested the door. He signaled it was unlocked. All eyes turned to Narius for the final decision.

Swallowing his mounting worries, he nodded. "Let's go."

That was all the soldiers needed. Half of them went through, allowing Narius, Paine, Quartus, Yusra, and Kavi to go in before the rest brought up the rear.

They found themselves in a large storage room filled with stacked boxes and crates. A quick sweep of the area revealed it safe, then they crossed to another door and entered the palace proper.

"Where to?" one soldier whispered.

"We'll try the Amber Office first," Narius replied. "Then we'll check the throne room, and if we have to, we'll go up to the royal residences."

The soldier nodded, and they headed out, not hurrying but definitely not lingering either.

Narius's sense of unease grew stronger the further they went. He could excuse the lack of activity outside the palace, but the inside was strangely deserted as well. They passed the kitchens, the servants' quarters, the workrooms, all of which were empty and silent. The loudest sounds were the rustle of fabric as they moved and his own breathing.

They finally made their way out of the servants' area. Still no sign of life. There should have been guards stationed at various corners, functionaries hustling from one office to another, but there was nothing. The palace felt more like an abandoned museum than a seat of power.

"Your Strength!" one soldier hissed by the doors that led to the main ballroom. "You need to see this."

Narius crept over to him and peeked into the room. He nearly jumped back when he saw all the people gathered, facing something in the center of the circular room. But then he realized no one had noticed them. So he took another look.

Judging by their outfits, the crowd was an even mix of servants, bureaucrats, and other functionaries. They stood in ragged circles, facing the center of the room, their bodies swaying and their arms loose at their sides. A few lolled their heads from one side or the other as they moved. Narius looked over the rest of the room. He quickly spotted them: glowing runes painted on the walls at seemingly random points. All of them were different, but they each gave off the same menacing aura.

"What should we do?" the soldier asked.

He didn't know. He beckoned for Kavi to come take a peek. She did so, then shuddered.

"What is it?" Narius whispered.

I've heard of this but never seen it. They are... She frowned, then motioned for Yusra to join them. Kavi asked her to translate, then launched into a quick flurry of signs that Narius didn't understand.

"She says that they are serving as 'rebuke proxies,'" Yusra said. "The mage-kings can use runes to shunt the rebukes they receive to other people. It allows them to act with impunity without fear of the Singularity's reprisal."

Narius's eyes shot back to the room. So many people! What were they planning on doing?

"Can you free them?" Narius asked.

Kavi hesitated, then turned back to him and signed, *It could take hours, maybe even longer, and I don't know for sure if I can.*

Narius grimaced. He didn't want to leave them like this. But helping might take time they didn't have. They had to keep moving and come back once they had captured Brencis.

They eventually made it to the Amber Office, which was empty. Narius's heart ached when he saw the trashed interior. The decorative panels had been smashed, the furniture upended, and ink splattered on each wall. Brencis would never have done this.

Paine peeked into the room as well and his expression turned grim. "This is most unsettling, Your Strength."

Of course it was! All the history that had been made here, the important decisions, to be treated so poorly...

"The mage-kings have always operated from the shadows. They never did anything as flagrant as torturing Istragon, trapping people in some a whatever-proxy, or destroying a room. They aren't worried about stealth anymore."

That was a good point, one that Narius should have seen too. He motioned for the team to move on.

When they arrived at the throne room, two guards eased the doors open and slipped through. A few seconds later, one of them bit off a loud curse. Narius exchanged a look with Quartus and hurried inside.

Close to a dozen people were suspended in the air, hanging by their wrists in invisible manacles. They were alive but unconscious. Some of them, like Bokil, the Minister of Internal Security, or Yull, the Foreign Minister, had been Narius's advisers. The rest were nobles that Brencis had probably elevated to take the place of the people he had executed. Quartus crept by them, his face turning a brilliant crimson. He mouthed several curses under his breath before Yusra squeezed his shoulder.

Narius frowned. This felt like a waste of time. Yes, they could claim the palace as theirs, but would that accomplish anything? With all of the inhabitants incapacitated, it was an empty gesture that wouldn't do anything significant.

"Where's Brencis?" Quartus asked. "I haven't seen any sign of him yet."

"Not just him, but Viara as well," Paine said. "I haven't seen her either."

A cold weight settled in Narius's stomach. He had no affection for his ex-wife, but the thought of her being tortured still twisted his mind. It wasn't just that she might be carrying his child. The thought of anyone harming a pregnant woman couldn't be tolerated.

"New plan," he whispered. "We go to the queen's quarters."

They set out again, through eerily quiet hallways, up into the private residence. Once again, the hallways were deserted.

When they arrived at the queen's quarters, a soldier hustled to the front of the line and tried to pull the door open. A rune suddenly appeared in the middle of the door and flared a brilliant blue. Lightning sliced through the soldier and tossed him against the far wall.

Two soldiers jumped between Narius and the door, their weapons raised, while another pair checked on their comrade. Kavi darted forward and inspected the door. She frowned.

Just a simple trap spell, easy to disarm.

She made a few gestures, then passed a hand over the door. The rune sputtered, then blinked out of existence. Once she had stepped out of the way, another soldier tentatively touched the door and, when nothing happened, pushed it open.

Much to Narius's surprise, Viara's room looked normal. Or what passed for normal with Viara. The furniture was the height of what was fashionable and expensive. Narius held up a hand and went in first, in spite of the whispered protests of the soldiers.

"Viara?" He tried to keep his voice low enough that it wouldn't be overheard but loud enough that it would carry through the rooms. "Are you here?"

Something clattered in the bedroom. Then Viara emerged, her eyes wide.

He froze. He hadn't seen his ex-wife in months. Her eyes were puffy and ringed with dark circles, her hair tangled in knots. She wore a simple robe, one that almost hid her swelling belly. His gaze locked on that. Was that really his child?

"N-Narius?" She stared at him, her lips trembling.

He braced himself, unsure how she would react. If she called for the guards, he didn't know if anyone would actually show up. But she didn't move, just gaped.

"It's me. I wanted to make sure that you and... our baby are safe."

Viara gasped, then rushed forward. Narius tried to drop into a defensive stance, sure that he was about to be attacked, but Viara caught him in a tight hug.

"Narius! When Brencis told me you were still alive, I thought he was teasing me." she wailed. "I thought I'd never see you again! I thought I'd have to raise our child on our own! This has been so horrible!"

"I'm sure it has." For a split second, he felt a jolt as he realized what she had just admitted. The baby was indeed his. How would Everys take this news? What would he have to do to make sure this child—his child—was all right and safe? Why had she waited to tell him for so long? But he pushed those questions aside. She was too scared to think straight. He couldn't imagine what it would be like living in the palace as the mage-kings slowly transformed it.

"I've been locked in my quarters for the past three days! Brencis sent me up here and then someone locked the door. And I've heard the most horrible things day and night and no one would come to help me and I've been so scared..." Her words descended into an unintelligible torrent as sobs overtook her.

Narius stiffly put his arms around her, shocked at the physical contact. He never thought he would feel this much relief at seeing Viara again, let alone hold her in his arms. But it still felt awkward.

"Three days ago?" Quartus repeated. "Where's Brencis?"

"I-I don't know." Viara hiccupped. "When he sent me up here, he said the time had come to strike. A few hours ago, I heard a skimmer leave the palace airhub. I think he might have gone with it."

Strike? Strike where?

"Did he say anything else, Blessed?" Paine prompted.

Narius glared at him, his mind hitching on Paine using the honorific for Viara. Paine shrugged in reply, as if to say that she was still queen, even if Narius didn't like it.

Viara's face scrunched in concentration, then she nodded. "He said something about finishing what Vetranio started."

Narius's breath caught in his throat. His grandfather, Vetranio, had been the one to annex the Cold Light's forests into the Dynasty. If Brencis was going to finish what Vetranio started, that could mean he was heading for the forest...

Where Everys was hiding.

He whirled around. "I want two of you to stay here and guard Viara. Make sure nothing happens to her. The rest of you, come with me back to the Amber Office! Maybe we can find battle plans or some indication of where exactly he plans to strike."

They started for the door, but Yusra didn't move. Instead, she stared at Viara, frowning.

"What?" Quartus asked.

"Why didn't the mage-kings do something to her? They tortured Istragon and hung Brencis's advisers. Why not do something to her?"

Narius frowned at the question.

"Because we needed someone to serve as bait, dearie," a woman's voice said.

Narius whirled around just in time to see the fireplace wall disappear. Oluna Hishi, dressed in crimson robes with elaborate golden embroidery, was flanked by half a dozen people in dark, form-fitting outfits, their faces covered.

The soldiers leveled their weapons just as Kavi launched herself forward, her hands already moving with a speed Narius had never seen before. But before anyone could actually attack, Oluna and her minions held up their hands, revealing glowing red runes that had been inked on their palms. A flash of light sliced through the room, momentarily blinding him.

When the brilliance faded, nothing had changed about the room, but Narius realized he couldn't move. An unseen force held him in place, and he was barely able to do more than breathe and move his eyes. He tried to say something, but his mouth simply wouldn't move.

Oluna dropped her hands, but the others kept theirs raised. She strolled forward, and as she did, pure terror slithered down his back. She wore thick crimson robes made of a fabric with an intricate woven pattern. The end of the sleeves, the high neck, and the end that dragged along the floor were brocaded with silver thread. But his eyes locked on the patterns embroidered in two columns down the front and streamed down the arms. Each one was a toratropic rune, jagged and harsh in their design. He recognized her outfit from images in history books: the raiment of a mage-king. In spite of her compact frame, Oluna radiated menace and power, so much so that it felt as though something was slowly pushing Narius away from her. She flashed him a predatory smile.

"I knew your nobility would prompt you to check on Viara in spite of your history." Oluna's voice had taken on an oily edge. "So honorable. So valiant. So predictable."

She spat the last word, and the invisible force spasmed, crushing the breath out of his lungs. As it did, one pattern on Oluna's robe flashed. How had she cast a rune like that? Did ink infuse the embroidery?

"I will admit, I enjoyed the time I had in the palace after Brencis scurried off to fulfill his dreams of glory," Oluna said as she circled Narius. "But now that we have you, playtime is over. We finally have what we—"

Suddenly, three of the people holding up their hands staggered. Narius thought he saw movement out of the corner of his eye. He tried to crane his neck to see what was happening. Kavi stood to his right, still frozen. No, wait. Had her position shifted?

Oluna turned to her and hissed. "So you're the *zhannoq'uem.*"

The minions flinched again, one of them grunting, and Kavi lurched forward, only to be caught in the invisible snare again.

"Training, skill, and determination. A dangerous combination," Oluna said. "Very well. While I would like to twist the dagger more, we clearly don't have time. Take that one where he's supposed to go. I'll handle Narius personally."

Who was she talking about? Who was going where? Two of the people in black suits strode past Narius, and he felt a blast of cold behind him. Then Oluna stepped close, smiling up at him.

"Don't worry, 'Your Strength.' It'll all be over soon enough."

Then she latched onto Narius's shoulders. Darkness tore at his clothes and hair, and he dropped through a frigid void.

80

At first, Everys thought Spanica was trying to stall. They had left Wrine entirely, slowly ascending into the foothills of what she assumed had to be the Speartip Mountains. Was he actually going to help them? She had no idea. He hadn't said a word since they boarded the transport back in the city.

But the further they drove, a change came over the nobleman. As soon as they left the city, he relaxed, and when the road leveled off, Spanica turned to her and offered a shy smile.

"I apologize for my earlier demeanor, Blessed," he said. "Ever since the Dalark invaded, I've found myself thrust into the position of Wrine's defender. So many of my peers fled the city at the first sign of trouble. Whenever I'm actually in the city now, I absorb the tension and carry it with me."

"I appreciate what you've done, especially helping those people back there," Everys said. "Provided I'm able to, I'll make sure that you and your house receive a commendation."

He chuckled. "That is unnecessary. Others may chase that sort of recognition. I do it because it is right. Now, let's discuss why you're here. You said you wanted to learn more about my father's research into septeracyanosis, yes?"

She nodded.

Spanica considered her, his head tipped to one side. "Why?"

"Excuse me?"

"Why do you want to know this information, Blessed? It seems like a fairly straightforward question. You want information that only I can provide, information that was used to humiliate my family. So I'll ask it again: why?"

Everys exchanged a look with Redtale, then said, "I recently learned about my husband's condition. Some medical personnel I consulted said your family had conducted research into it and I thought maybe—"

Spanica sighed and hung his head. When he looked up at her again, disappointment flashed across his face. "Blessed, you wouldn't travel halfway across the Dynasty's holdings out of idle curiosity. Do you remember what I said I wanted when we met in the palace conservatory?"

Everys thought back. It seemed like such a long time ago when they had met before Narius's *harsannon*. "You said you wanted to see the reality of the world, the truth that is often overlooked or concealed."

He smiled. "Not exactly how I phrased it, but accurate. We are told one thing, but the true reality is something different. We are told from childhood that the Dynasty and Dalark Imperium slaughtered every toratropic mage and ended the practice, and yet here you sit, in defiance of that so-called 'truth.' So many truths hidden behind so many lies, making our lives so complicated and difficult. So what is the truth you are holding back from me?"

Everys winced, but she nodded. He deserved to hear it all. "I don't know how familiar you are with how runes work, but the type of ink we use determines a spell's power. Are you familiar at all with rebukes?"

Spanica shook his head, but his expression turned eager.

"If we misuse the runes or use ink that's been forbidden, our God, the Singularity, will chastise us. These rebukes can range from mild irritation to fairly severe agony."

"Ink can be forbidden?" Spanica prompted.

She nodded. "There's only one forbidden ink: blood. If a mage uses blood to draw a rune, she can expect to be severely rebuked. That's what happened to me a few months ago. I used Narius's blood to draw a healing rune on him, and the rebuke left me unconscious for several days. But then, more recently, I've used Redtale's and my own blood on different occasions, and while I was rebuked for it, they weren't nearly as intense. This has led me to believe that there is something different about my husband's blood, something important. The only lead I have is septeracyanosis and your father's research. Can you tell me what he found?"

Spanica sat back in his chair and regarded her, his expression neutral. Then he pushed his glasses back to the top of his nose and nodded. "We are already heading to the answers you seek, Blessed. I just wanted to make sure you were being honest with me."

Relief sluiced through Everys. But then a thought occurred to her. "What would have happened if I hadn't answered your question?"

He smiled. "We would have found a place to turn around, head back into the city, and I would share the research with you, but not what prompted it. And something tells me that is what you are really looking for."

He lapsed into contemplative silence, and Everys respected that, even though every fiber of her being screamed with questions.

After an hour, the transport shuddered to a stop. Spanica slid over to the door and slipped out. Everys and Redtale followed.

They stood on a vast plateau. The Speartip Mountains rose in the distance, a stunning sight, but Everys's attention was drawn to a series of buildings that stood in a tight cluster in the middle of the grassy expanse. Spanica gestured toward them and started in that direction.

"While my family maintains a residence in Wrine, this is where my father spent most of his youth. He was an amateur archaeologist. Following some leads he found at the Wrine Scholastium, he came out here and discovered... well, it's probably better to show you."

He led them to the largest of the buildings and opened a metal door, ushering them inside. They stood on a metal balcony overlooking a great pit dug into the ground. Lights clicked on overhead, illuminating a multilevel excavation that sank deep into the ground, revealing rectangular shapes built out of rough stone.

"What is this?" she asked.

"An ancient city." Spanica's voice was reverent. "One of, if not the, oldest human settlement in the Dynasty's holdings. Please, follow me."

As they descended into the dig site, Everys looked over the ruins with a mixture of curiosity and frustration. Yes, this was fascinating, especially if what Spanica said was true. But at the same time, she couldn't help but wonder what this had to do with her question.

Spanica took on the role of tour guide. "My father first found traces of this city when he was a young man. The moment he did, he purchased all the land surrounding this area to preserve whatever was here. He never looked for anything else. What he found was more than enough to occupy his imagination."

"Why?" Redtale asked.

"My father believed—and I agree with his assessment—that this is the cradle of the Xoniel Dynasty. This is where everything started. My father found carvings in that building there." He gestured toward one of the stone foundations. "Most of them are in languages he couldn't translate, but he found tablets written in the shessu trade cant that referred to this city as 'the home of those with the shining eyes.'"

This was all fascinating, and Everys could feel a thousand questions percolating in her, but one rose above them all. "How does this answer my question?"

"Because they built this city here for a reason. At least, that's what my father thought."

He led them deeper into the excavation. The ground sloped as they proceeded, but metal handrails had been added where the slope was difficult. She finally spotted their destination at the bottom of a pit: a large cave mouth.

"My father believed this was always the center of the city," Spanica said. "He found evidence of a very primitive village at this level. As the city grew, the ground rose around the cave as more and more layers were added over the centuries."

Redtale stooped to fit through the cave's opening and Everys swore her hair brushed the top of the entrance. Spanica flipped a switch, and with a loud *click*, lights illuminated the cave's walls. Spanica motioned for them to step to the right, and so Everys did, studying her surroundings. She had never been in a true cave before, but for a moment, it reminded her of the Elderreach's barrow back in the Deep Forest, which prompted a shudder down her spine.

"When my father found this cave, he knew he had found something special," Spanica whispered. "Because of that."

He gestured to a far wall. Everys turned and gasped. The cave walls were a mottled collection of whites and tans, but figures were drawn onto the walls in stark black lines. The images were stylized, little more than stick figures, but she could understand what she was seeing easily enough. A group of humans stood around a fire, holding primitive weapons. A few had been drawn as if they had been caught in mid-dance, their arms and legs at odd angles.

She wanted to study the imagery closer, but Spanica beckoned for her to keep moving. They went deeper into the cave, where she found more paintings. Some depicted the humans hunting large animals. Others were of the animals on their own.

"Again, impressive from a scholastic point of view," Spanica said. "Father's research led him to believe that this was some of the oldest artwork in the Dynasty's holdings."

"Then why don't we know about this?" Everys whispered. "Why keep this hidden?"

"You'll see."

They rounded a bend, where they found a flat section of wall covered in drawings from floor to ceiling.

"Take your time to examine this," Spanica murmured. "I'll be waiting at the other end."

With that, he strolled through the chamber without even looking at the walls.

Everys stepped closer to the wall, drinking in the images painted there. At first, it appeared to be a mural depicting a large crowd gathered around a tall figure who stood on a dais in the center of the mural. The people were all stick figures, with featureless faces and lines for arms and legs. Two red crescent moons, embedded in a dark cloud, hovered just above the leader's head, and he held a chalice at shoulder height, catching what might be rain. No, not rain. A crimson streak fell into the cup and overflowed, splashing onto the people closest to the leader.

She frowned and looked at the crowd again. The people walked past the leader from the left to the right, passing through the overflowing liquid from the cup as they did. And then Everys spotted a key detail: all those to the right of the leader, those who had passed through the outpoured liquid, had gray splotches on their featureless faces where their eyes would be. She looked up at the leader and finally noticed that he did as well.

Everys took a step back to reexamine the mural. As she did, she noticed two more things: the crowd on the right was all standing in what could best be described as hostile postures, with brandished clubs and spears. She followed that crowd back to the leader, then up to the moons in the dark cloud. No, those weren't moons. They were positioned almost like... almost like...

Like eyes. Two enormous, scowling, red eyes in a shadowy figure looming over the leader with the cup.

A shudder wormed through her. What did this depict? An ancient legend? Did the prelates know about this at all? Is this why they had objected to the research into septeracyanosis?

Spanica beckoned to her. "There's more to see."

Everys followed him on shaky legs deeper into the cave. There wasn't any art down this passage, but that suited Everys just fine. Her breathing had become sharper, somewhat more ragged, with each step.

She stumbled to a halt as she came face-to-face with an Elderreach god.

They had entered a large chamber, one that appeared to have started as a natural part of the cave but had been expanded and reshaped to be more circular. On the far wall, someone had painted with careful detail the face that Everys had seen in the Last's barrow, the face of that monstrous creature. While the other art in the cave had been crude, someone had spent a great deal of time creating this image. When she stepped closer, she realized it was more than just a painting, though. Someone had carved the Elderreach's features into the wall and then painted over them, adding depth and detail to the image.

Just below the image was a stone slab that vaguely resembled an altar, but one with a large divot cut into its center. Was this... was this a temple? Dedicated to worshiping the Elderreach gods?

"What is that thing?" Redtale whispered, her voice laced through with threat.

"Nothing good," Everys replied.

"When my father saw those images and then this chamber, he questioned the origin of septeracyanosis," Spanica said, approaching the supposed altar carefully. "I'm sure you were told what the prelates say about the royal family's eyes. A gift from the Perfected Warrior, a sign of his blessing. But those images suggested something different. My father wondered if maybe those images told the actual story, but fancifully. The ancient Xoniel 'mixed the blood' of another race with theirs and the metallic eyes were the result.

"No one took him seriously. The nobility who heard about his research were insulted at the implications that they were all hybrids with some sort of nonhuman race. And eventually, the supreme prelate conspired with King Vetranio to shut it all down."

Everys tried to calm her stuttering heart, but she couldn't. She looked up at the carving of the Elderreach face and her mind careened through question after question. Since she couldn't get them in any semblance of order, she picked one.

"Did something used to sit on that?" She pointed to the notch in the altar.

Spanica glanced at it and smiled. "Very good, Blessed. Something did. Here, let me show you."

He produced a scriber and scrolled through the contents before handing it to Everys. A picture was displayed on the small screen, a grainy image of the chamber they stood in, most likely when it had first been discovered. A man who resembled Spanica grinned at her, his arm sweeping toward the Elderreach visage. His arm partially obscured the altar. She squinted and tried to make it out anyway. There was something resting in the divot, an object made of crystal? No, a crystal enclosed by...

She almost dropped the scriber. Although she hadn't gotten a good look at it, she recognized it. An Elderreach memory tear, just like the ones she had seen in the barrow.

"Where is that object now?" she whispered.

"That's the thing, Blessed," Spanica said. "It was here when Father excavated the cave, but the next morning, it was gone. He suspected one of the local workers stole it, although he could never prove it. He hunted for that object for the rest of his life."

Everys tried to tamp down on her roiling emotions. She was both disappointed and relieved it was gone.

"However, earlier this year, I hired a retrieval specialist. He and his partner were finally able to track down the object and return it to me."

He led Everys to a table where an object sat covered with a cloth. Spanica pulled back the cover to reveal an Elderreach memory tear, so similar to the ones that she had seen in otte barrow, only the crystal in this one was green instead of clear. She remembered what Tall Reach had told her about how the final-tear shed by an Elderreach was different. Could that be a final-tear?

With a shaking hand, she reached out to touch the wires encasing the crystal. In this better light, she saw the wires had an organic look to them, like they were originally sinew that had somehow transformed into metal. Her fingers brushed the slots where she knew she could access the memories within. She knew she had to. Something deep within her prompted her. This had the answer. But she knew that the moment she saw what was inside, even though she already suspected what it was, everything would change.

Redtale took a step forward. "Blessed? What are you—?"

Everys threaded her fingers into the metal and opened her mind to whatever lay within.

Once again, she stood on the plain, her body riddled with wounds, her precious blood seeping from so many injuries. Cursed trees!

She towered over the tiny ones, those frail creatures the Cold Light had deemed worthy of protection. These insignificant creatures. Most knew to cower, though one had stepped away from the fire, adopting a challenging pose. She wanted to laugh. She wanted to bellow, shaking the hills and mountains. But she didn't have the strength. That oozed from her body as well.

She fell to her knees and then forward onto the ground, the impact shaking the primitive huts those mewling vermin had constructed. A few even collapsed. Again, she wanted to laugh, but she couldn't find the breath.

As the other vermin screamed and scampered, the brave one stalked forward, holding out a rough stick like a weapon. He stepped forward, curiosity, fear, and bravado warring in his expression. Then he carefully set aside his weapon.

She knew he touched her, but she couldn't feel it against the cold that seeped into her. Then she saw him step back and her heart seized. The filthy creature had scooped up some of her blood! He sniffed at it, and then, much to her surprise and horror, drank deeply.

What was the fool thinking? She knew how toxic her blood was to the lesser beings. But this one didn't care. He stood taller, stronger, jabbering at the others like he had accomplished something incredible.

But then he spasmed, his arms wrapped around his stomach, and he collapsed to the ground, shrieking. The other creatures shrieked with him, shying away. She exulted at the sight. A petty victory, but at least she could claim one more life before hers slipped away.

Only the man didn't die. Instead, after thrashing on the ground, he stood on wobbly legs. He looked at his own hands, touched his face.

And when he looked up at her again, she was startled to see her own eyes staring back at her. His had turned gleaming, a metallic silver with the same sheen as her eyes.

The man turned, his posture now confident, and beckoned the others to come forward. One by one, all the adults were cajoled, threatened, or enticed to drink of her blood, and one by one, they were each changed. Their eyes were all different colors, but they all had the same metallic glint. This went on long into the night. She wanted to groan. Why was death lingering? Why wouldn't it take her from the abominable sight?

As the humans dispersed to their huts in the darkness, she sighed, hoping that she would finally be released from this pain. But instead, she felt cold tendrils wrap around her arms and legs, piercing her skin. And a presence flooded her mind, an overwhelming force that spoke to her.

"The war is over. We will take you to where you may rest."

Everys lurched away from the table, landing in Redtale's out-stretched arms. That voice. It was the Last's, whispering into the ears of the Elderreach as he was carried away, presumably to rest inside the barrow.

"Are you all right?" Redtale demanded.

She nodded, tucking her sweat-drenched hair behind her ear and smoothing it from her eyes.

"What just happened?" Spanica's eyes were wide, his glasses making them comically large.

"You just gave me what I was looking for," Everys whispered. "I know the truth now."

He jabbered questions at her and she felt a flash of the Elderreach's irritation again. But she couldn't answer, because she had such a hard time processing the truth:

In the ancient past, her husband's ancestors had consumed Elder-reach blood, which had transformed them. That had to be why she had been rebuked so strongly when she used Narius's blood. It wasn't just because she had used blood. Instead, it was because his blood was that of an Elderreach.

And in that instant, she realized what she had to do next. She had to find Narius before the mage-kings did. Because if they did, they would have the most powerful ink ever known to her people.

81

Strong hands clutched at Quartus as he slid through a frigid void. He closed his eyes as what felt like claws raked his arms and back. He wanted to scream or cry or fight back. But he couldn't move. All he could do was endure the torment and hope that it would end soon.

Then, with a lurch, whoever was holding him let go, and he stumbled forward. His stomach heaved, and he retched. But he couldn't even vomit. What had just happened to him?

"What's the meaning of this?" a gruff voice demanded.

Quartus froze. He knew that voice. His eyes snapped open, and he looked up.

Brencis sat in a chair in front of him, dressed in military fatigues, glaring at Quartus with sheer contempt. Quartus didn't hesitate. His hand went to his belt, where he drew a knife and lunged. Before he could connect, though, Brencis kicked him hard in the chest, sending him sprawling backward into two men in those maddening black clothes. They caught him and wrested the knife from his hand, then searched him for other weapons.

Once he was disarmed, the men forced him to kneel. The cool barrel of a flechette thrower pressed against the back of his head.

"The *ar'zhannok* sends this one to you with her compliments," one man said, his voice honeyed oil.

Brencis snarled and rose out of his chair. Quartus risked a glance at their surroundings. They were in a cramped but luxurious room. Brencis had been sitting in a plush chair that was bolted to the floor, as was the table beside him. A vibration wormed through Quartus's knees. Were they in a skimmer? His eyes widened. Oluna's lackeys had transported him via magic onto a moving skimmer? As much as he hated to admit it, he was impressed.

"Why would I want him? Narius is the threat!" Brencis growled.

"The *ar'zhannok* has use for your predecessor." The man's voice made it sound like a taunt. "But this one is yours."

Again, Brencis snarled. "She seems to forget who is king in the Dynasty!"

"Oh, she is well aware," the other man interjected with a voice that sounded like ground glass. "It seems you have forgotten the terms of your agreement with her."

Brencis froze, his eyes bulging. For a split second, Quartus saw the fear shining in his eyes as a single drop of sweat beaded on his upper lip. Then Brencis shook his head sharply, as if trying to dislodge his fear.

"Why would she think I'd want Quartus? He's a useless dilettante!" Brencis snapped.

Quartus glowered at him, stung by the insult. Give him his knife back and they'd both see how "useless" he was.

"Perhaps you would be interested to know what Prince Quartus has been doing," the first assassin said. "He was there when our master killed Elamek. He was trying to recruit the minister in a plot to assassinate you."

That caught Brencis's attention. "Oh?"

"Indeed. Not only that, but he was present at the meeting where Governor-General Zammit was conspiring against you. And we believe he is the one who is responsible for the death of our master."

Brencis glanced at Quartus again, realization dawning in his eyes.

"Tell me, Quartus," Brencis rumbled. "Were you at Chilyana's estate for my Day of Accountability?"

Quartus glared his answer at Brencis, but he didn't speak.

"Again, the *ar'zhannok* gives his life to you," the second assassin said. "Now we must take our leave. Do with him as you will."

With that, shadows burst from the floor and swallowed the two assassins.

Crack! Pain exploded across Quartus's cheek, and he collapsed to the floor with a grunt. Before he could recover, Brencis stomped on his chest, driving the breath from his lungs. Quartus rolled onto his side with a groan, wanting nothing more than to cradle himself.

"Guards!" Brencis called. "Bind the prisoner!"

Rough hands twisted his arms behind him and slapped manacles onto his wrists. Brencis's guards tossed him onto a couch as Brencis stepped over to a bar and poured himself a drink. Quartus shook his head, trying to clear it. There had to be a way to escape, but his mind was flooded with pain and it was so hard to string together his thoughts.

"I had hoped that I would have the pleasure of Narius watching me as I destroyed everything he worked for, but if that scribbler wants—Ah!"

Brencis flinched as a rune blazed to life on his temples, angry red lines that twisted across his skin. He doubled over, his hands clutching at his head, then the rune faded and he took several deep breaths. He picked up his drink, but his hand shook so badly that some of the liquor sloshed out of the glass.

"But if *Oluna* wants him, I suppose I will have to content myself with you. Do you know where we're going, Quartus?" Brencis asked as he poured himself a drink.

"To the Cold Light's forest," Quartus said, his teeth clenched against the pain.

Brencis actually looked upset that he knew. "That's right. I'm going to burn those trees to the ground. Then no one will ever be able to oppose me."

"Except for the ones actually holding your leash."

Brencis snorted. "The mage-kings? Please. The Dynasty has destroyed them before. We can do it again."

Quartus gaped at him. "Were you not paying attention to what just happened? Those men could transport themselves from Bastion to wherever we are now. Oluna can discipline you for calling her a scribbler without even being here! Do you really think you stand a chance against her?"

"Oh, but I do! For I still have one of the greatest weapons her kind has ever produced."

Brencis picked up a sword from the counter and showed it to Quartus. It looked like a sword that had been broken in half.

"You see these six runes? When I activate it with someone's blood—say, your blood—this becomes a weapon that is terrible to behold. With this weapon, I slaughtered the queen's Swordbound. This weapon led me to victory against the Dalark countless times over the past few months. And with this weapon in my hand, I will end the threat of the mage-kings once and for all!"

Quartus stared at Brencis. Couldn't he hear how ridiculous he sounded? Why would Oluna allow him to have a weapon that could be used against her? The so-called king was delusional at best or insane at worst. But then, Quartus knew from his own family's history that madness amplified violence instead of preventing it. He tested the manacles and found that he was stuck tight. While Brencis might eventually die by someone else's hands, he could do whatever he wanted until then. And it appeared that Quartus had no other choice but to go along for the ride.

Narius lurched forward as someone pushed him from behind. He tried to take stock of his surroundings, but found himself too disoriented. One moment, he had been in the queen's quarters. And now they were... He looked around, forcing himself to concentrate even though everything juked and shimmied. He spotted tents and soldiers, military vehicles and... Were they in a camp? Who were these people?

Oluna stepped up next to him and he flinched away from her, surprised at how brazen she was. Wouldn't the soldiers recognize her for what she was? Wouldn't they recognize him? But they kept about their business as if two people appearing in their midst was a regular occurrence. Then Narius realized that it very well could be.

"Brencis was kind enough to provide this unit to escort us to our final destination," Oluna said. "As much as I would like to take you directly there, we can't. The ancient wards are still too powerful."

"Where are you taking me?" Narius asked, thankful his voice didn't betray the fear that roiled within him.

She smiled up at him. "Why, Nekek the Bright, of course. Where else would we go?"

Narius frowned at her. "Why would you want to go there? There's nothing left but ruins."

"Ah, but that's where you're wrong, 'Your Strength.'" Oluna spat his title like it was an insult. "The buildings may have been destroyed, but you cannot destroy the idea of the city, what it truly means. The heirs of Nekek the Bright have kept that alive for the past four centuries, even when those who call themselves Siporans abandoned us, blamed us for what happened. And nothing you have ever done has dimmed that light for us."

He stared at her, suddenly struck by how odd this was. According to four hundred years of Dynastic history, the mage-kings had been wiped out with their capital city. King Heronus and his Dalark allies had boasted about this. Everys and Tolistan had also believed the mage-kings were extinct. And yet, here was a woman claiming that very title.

"What?" Oluna snapped. "Stop looking at me as if I'm *katharin*!"

Narius snapped his mouth shut. "Forgive me. I'm just very curious about how any of this is possible."

Oluna snorted. "What you mean to say is this: 'In our arrogance, we assumed we had won.' That's always been your problem. You assume military might somehow trumps wisdom."

"Then could you please enlighten me?" Narius said.

She scoffed again. "What do I look like, a scrivener?"

He shrugged. "What's the harm in educating me?"

Oluna regarded him, then chuckled to herself.

"Tell me, Narius, does this sound familiar? Shortly before the razing of Nekek the Bright, Marnisha, the last *ar'zhannok*, tried to flee the city. The coward had left behind his wives and children, only interested in saving himself. But King Heronus captured Marnisha and then took great delight in tormenting him. And when the king's family was eventually captured, Heronus had them all put to death in front of Marnisha, one by one, before he sent Marnisha to the Gravedigger's embrace as well.

"And that story is largely true. Marnisha did indeed flee the city, but as a distraction, as were his wives and children, for one young girl: the *ar'zhannok*'s daughter, Oranna. You see, Oranna was the craftiest and most powerful toratropic mage alive. Marnisha knew if she could survive, then one day, we might get our revenge on the Dynasty and the Imperium. So he had Oranna dress as a slave girl. When the Dynasty pillaged the city, she was taken prisoner and given to one of Heronus's courtiers, Korax Hishi, as a concubine. But Oranna used her powers to influence her rapist to fall in love with her and name their child his sole heir. She manipulated the memories of those around her to forget the child's true heritage.

"Within a generation, no one suspected that the Hishi family was ours. Similar stories played out throughout the Dynasty as members of Marnisha's court carried out their own deceptions. By the time Albanon took the throne, we had control of twelve noble families. More than enough to ensure we would have our revenge."

"How?" Narius said. "By manipulating Dalark and the Dynasty into a war?"

"Do you really think I'm going to tell you?" Oluna asked. "If there's one thing I've learned, it's that I should never underestimate you or Everys."

Hearing Oluna speak her name caused Narius's heart to twist. "I thought you were her friend. So did she."

"And I was... of a sort. Your wife is a sweet girl, no doubt about it, but so self-righteous. So self-centered. 'Poor me, plucked from a life of obscurity and given one of comfort, wealth, and power. Oh, whatever will I do?'" Oluna's expression turned wistful. "But I suppose I owe her. My granddaughter, Zivah, has been sick for so long and I didn't have the right runes to heal her. Everys not only had them, but she used them. And she did unwittingly give us the key we needed to complete our plan."

She produced a scriber and showed it to Narius. He frowned. What did it contain?

"Actually, I suppose I should be grateful to both of you, Narius." Oluna offered him what looked like an almost genuine smile. "Everys gave us one half of what we need. And you are the other half. Thanks to you both, Nekek shall shine again, and you will have the privilege to witness it.

"But my gratitude will not save you. Just as Heronus made sure the last memory Marnisha had was the death of his family, so, too, your last memory will be witnessing our triumph."

82

S panica peppered Everys with questions all the way back to Wrine, and she answered most of them. What did it matter? She had just learned her husband carried Elderreach blood within him. The fact this was only one of many stunning revelations she had encountered in the past few weeks didn't lessen its impact.

When they reached the canal in Wrine, Redtale used the long-range comm to signal they were ready to return to the forest. A few seconds later, a mound of water transformed into a doorway that led back to the stream by Papa's cabin. Challix, Rewether, and a squad of soldiers waited for her on the other side. She frowned when they saw their faces.

"What is it?" she asked.

"There's been a number of incursions over the forest in the last hour," Challix said. "Dynasty recon skimmers. And there's a large column of troops marching on the western forest through the Edge. They're at least two or three days out."

Everys's heart sank. Was Brencis going to invade the forest? Really? As if she didn't have enough to deal with as it was.

"Has the Yoreroot been notified?" Everys asked as they started back for the Shade.

Challix fell into step with her. "They have, Blessed."

"Good. I want to talk to Firestruck. I have a feeling we're going to need the Cold Light's army sooner rather than later. And then—"

"Incoming!" Redtale roared.

Before Everys knew what was happening, Redtale had thrown her to the ground and dove on top of her.

The world erupted into fire and thunder.

A blast of heat washed over her. She curled in a ball, covering her ears, but that wasn't enough to block out the roar of the explosion or her own screams. The ground bucked beneath them and it sounded like every tree around them had splintered. Then an eerie quiet fell on the woods.

Redtale slowly got off her. "Blessed, are you all right?"

Everys stared up at her and nodded. "You?"

Redtale rolled her shoulder and winced. "Think I might have caught something, but my hide's pretty thick."

The guard turned and Everys gasped. Large chunks of wood jutted out of her back. Many of the injuries were bleeding, but Redtale didn't seem the worse for wear.

Then she saw the rest of the clearing and she gasped.

Black smoke filled the air, and branches and shattered trunks were scattered across the field. People lay on the ground, moaning and twitching. She spotted Tanakept. The Maotoan lay in a heap, his chest shredded. Her stomach lurched at the sight. What had happened?

"Rewether? Challix?"

Someone groaned in response. She hurried over and found them. Both of them leaned at the base of a tree. Blood coated Challix's head and her eyes were glassy, but she was breathing. Rewether tried to rise, but he cried out and fell back to the ground, clutching his knee.

"What just happened?" Everys asked.

"Missile strike." Redtale grunted as she knelt next to Rewether to examine his knee. "You've gotta get back to the Embassy. You'll be safer there."

"I'm not leaving you or them!" Everys shot back.

In spite of her posture, Redtale looked her right in the eye. "Everys..."

Everys pulled a vial of ink from her pocket. She quickly drew her family's healing rune on Challix. As soon as it was activated, she turned to Rewether and did the same. Within a matter of moments, both of them had recovered from their wounds, at least enough that they could move. As they hobbled back to the Embassy, they passed other soldiers who rushed past them to help the other wounded. Instead of heading for the Embassy, Everys followed the medics to another injured soldier. She set to work, tracing healing runes on everyone she could.

Another explosion thundered. The ground bucked in response.

Redtale grabbed her arm. "There are more on the way. Everys, this isn't safe. We have to go."

She didn't want to, but from the expression on both Redtale and Rewether's faces, they wouldn't accept anything else. Reluctantly, she allowed them to escort her from the area.

The Shade was in chaos by the time they arrived. Fires blazed in the woods beyond the settlement. People ran through the streets in a near panic with soldiers trying to direct them to safety.

As they ran to the Embassy, Everys spotted Yllana, who sat next to another grafted, an older man who didn't appear injured but was staring vacantly, as if his mind had been switched off.

"What happened?" Everys asked.

"The Yoreroot's grove is gone," Yllana said.

Everys froze. "Tall Reach?"

"He wasn't there, but Evergreen and Stunted Root were conferring with representatives from the outer villages. They..." Her voice trailed off.

"And this man...?"

Yllana closed his eyes. "He is one of Stunted Root's grafted. This is what happens when a Cold Light is felled."

Everys wanted to do something, but she knew there were some injuries her rune couldn't heal.

Redtale grabbed her arm. "Blessed, we have to keep moving."

She hesitated, but both of her guards forced her to move.

Much to her surprise, the Embassy looked untouched, although it was clear that some of the upper branches had been scorched by the attack. The war room was in chaos as Everys entered it. No one there appeared seriously injured, although most of them looked to be in shock.

"Report!" she called out as she entered.

The room stilled, and people gathered around the main table. One of the aides adjusted the display and a tactical map appeared.

"We're getting reports of missile strikes all throughout the forest," Jorik Feyla, Overturn's second-in-command, said.

For a split second, Everys wished that Overturn was here instead of wherever the Cold Light had taken him. But she couldn't change that now. "Casualties?"

Feyla shook his head. "Too soon to determine, but I suspect they'll be high. The settlements in the forest were mostly made of wood and stone. They won't be able to stand up to the assault."

"Where did these missiles come from?" Challix asked.

"Launched from ships in both the Water Bearer's Repose and the Expanse. We can probably expect more attacks over the next few days."

"Is there anything we can do about those ships?" Everys asked.

Feyla hesitated. "We do have some antiship weaponry with us, but given the ground troops advancing on the forest from the west, I don't think we should risk them at this time."

Everys didn't like that answer, but she knew to trust her commanders. They knew what they could do better than her. She looked over at Effort, Firestruck's grafted.

"Can the Cold Light do anything about the ships?" she asked.

Effort shuddered as Firestruck occupied him. "We will do what we can, Everys Queen, but our options are limited as well."

"What about the approaching troops?" Everys asked.

"We are getting ready to move our forces to meet them, but—" Feyla said.

"No."

Firestruck's simple declaration caused everyone to fall silent.

"What?" Feyla asked.

"No. You will not risk your people to defend our forest," Firestruck said. "We are ready for what is to come. We will honor our promise. We will defeat the pretender king. We will bring this to an end."

A chill swept over Everys. Although she was looking at Effort, she could feel Firestruck's confidence sweep through the room. Even though she had no idea what was going to happen, she somehow knew that everything would be fine.

"Okay..." Feyla said. "Is there something we can do?"

"See to the wounded. Fight the fires. We will handle the rest."

Feyla's eyes darkened, but Everys held up a hand before he could reply. "We will do as you request, Firestruck."

He nodded gravely, but he didn't release Effort. Apparently the defender of the forest wanted to hear directly what was happening.

Then red lights blazed around them, followed by a shrieking that sliced through Everys's head.

"More missiles incoming," Feyla said. "Blessed, please get to safety."

Before Everys could object, Redtale and Rewether hustled her out of the room and down into the Embassy's basement. They were followed by a crowd of servants and other personnel. Shortly thereafter, she heard the sound of muffled explosions and could feel tremors through the floor. Dirt rained down from the ceilings. She closed her eyes and offered up a silent prayer that the Singularity would bring them through this too.

83

Quartus had often heard that the Cold Light's forest was a true marvel, the last remnant of the wild beauty that was possible from untamed nature.

Now it all burned before him.

He knelt on a platform in what once had been Vetranio's First Stand, a military base on the forest's border. Thousands of troops filled the base, along with their attack vehicles. Quartus's heart sank. What possible chance did anyone in the forest have against all of this?

"Isn't this glorious, Quartus?" Brencis strutted in a circle around Quartus, his hands clasped behind his back. "And this is just a fraction of the might I've brought to bear against these rebellious trees. Almost a hundred thousand troops, heavily armed, ready to bring an end to the Cold Light and to Everys. This is what the Dynasty is. This is what it should have always been."

Quartus looked over the troops. Granted, he couldn't make out their faces due to their helmets, but from what he could see, they appeared eager and ready.

"You might win today, Brencis, but we both know you're living on borrowed time. I doubt Oluna is going to tolerate a rival for long."

Brencis backhanded Quartus, which elicited a cheer from the nearby troops. Quartus nearly toppled onto his side. With a groan, he steadied himself and spit, mostly to see if he was bleeding. He wasn't. He glared at Brencis. He didn't know how, but the so-called king would pay for that too.

Brencis waved to his troops, then grabbed Quartus by his hair and pulled his head up. "Pay attention, Quartus. It's time for you to see what a real king looks like."

Brencis strode up to an audiocaster. Several camera drones, most likely from the crier guilds, swooped down from the sky. It figured. Brencis would want his victory recorded for posterity.

"My friends, the time has come. For too long, we have tolerated the recalcitrant Cold Light. First, they refused to be brought peacefully into the Dynasty by King Vetranio. Then they defied King Girai by withholding our rightful tribute. They have given refuge to Everys, King Narius's Siporan witch. They will not defy another king! We will show them why they are no match for the Dynasty. For we are strong! We are—"

Something rustled behind Quartus. He turned his head to see what it was, but there was nothing. Just the trees on the edge of the forest, the smoke rising beyond.

Brencis must have heard the same noise. He, too, looked over his shoulder, then turned back to the audiocaster. "Ahem. We are strong! We are the ones destined to—"

More rustling. Quartus twisted around to get a better look. This time, he spotted it. The trees on the edge of the forest were swaying, their branches dancing as if caught in a strong wind.

Brencis slowly turned from the audiocaster. "What in Chaos's name?"

A low moan slithered across the space between the trees and the platform, sending prickles across the back of Quartus's neck and down his arm. At first, the sound was indistinct, but within a few seconds, a voice emerged, louder than anything Quartus had ever heard in his life.

"Brencis, we do not acknowledge your authority here."

Quartus's eyes widened as he realized what was happening. Somehow, the Cold Light were vibrating the trees' branches fast enough to produce the sound. Many of the soldiers standing in front of them shifted uneasily, and Quartus couldn't blame them. If the Cold Light were able to do that, what else was possible?

Brencis, however, didn't seem impressed. He puffed out his chest and glared at the trees. "You will respect me before the day is over."

"We do not respect those who throw away their lives in vain."

That seemed to rock Brencis back a step. But he recovered quickly enough. "Is this all you have to offer? Noisy tricks? Come out and face me if you dare!"

"We shall."

There was a long pause, and then a solitary figure carrying a walking stick emerged from the treeline. Several of the soldiers shouted, and Quartus could hear flechette throwers being aimed, but Brencis held up a hand, his face painted with surprise.

"Overturn?" he gasped.

Quartus looked back at the figure and realized that it was the Ixactl strategist. He had never met him in real life, but he had heard of him often enough. But as Overturn approached the platform in a relaxed gait, Quartus frowned. Something was off about him. He appeared confident, as if the troops arrayed before him were no threat. Then Quartus spotted the vines encircling the Ixactl's arms, legs, and even his horns.

"Dented Shield, he's a thrall!" Quartus whispered.

Dark blood oozed from the vine's puncture wounds. Overturn seemed to wince with every step he took, as if he was straining against his new bonds.

Brencis actually stumbled back a step, but he quickly recovered, barking orders for nearby troops to be ready. Even still, Quartus could spot the smallest glimmer of doubt in the supposed king's eyes. Overturn walked up to the platform and easily stepped onto it. He glanced in Quartus's direction and nodded gravely. Then he turned his full attention to Brencis.

"You wanted to speak to someone face-to-face?" Overturn asked. "I'm here."

Brencis gaped at him, then snorted. "What did they do to you?"

"What was needed," Overturn said, his tone wistful. "They chose me because they knew that I had the best understanding of what a modern military was capable of. And they showed me, Brencis. They showed me what they are capable of. Let me assure you. Your troops are not prepared for what's about to happen."

"Do you really think you can intimidate me?"

Overturn shook his head sadly. "I know I can't. But the Cold Light want to give you a choice."

The Ixactl used the burnt end of his walking stick to draw a circle of ash around Brencis's feet. Brencis flinched at first, but then shot Overturn a confused frown.

"What's this?" he demanded.

"As long as you stand in that circle, you are safe." Overturn tossed the stick aside. "But when you step out of that circle, you will have two options. You will either withdraw your troops and agree to meet with our representatives to work out some sort of peace. Or you and many that follow your commands will die."

Uncertainty flickered over Brencis's face and Quartus couldn't blame him. If anyone else had said something like that, he would have chalked it up to empty bravado. But Overturn didn't look expectant. He looked sorrowful.

The Ixactl pointed back at the tree line. "I have seen with my own eyes what is coming for you, Brencis. An army that this world has not experienced for eight thousand years, when the Cold Light threw down the monsters who would be gods. If the Cold Light go to war, they will pursue you until you are either captured or dead. Retreat while you still can."

Brencis's eyes narrowed, and Quartus could practically hear the indecision warring within him. But then a smug smile tugged at his lips. He reached to his side and drew the *ur-keleshen*.

"You speak of power? I have been given power unlike anything you can imagine! It is more than enough for whatever army you've cobbled together." Brencis took a purposeful step out of the circle. "I will face whatever you have."

As if to punctuate that statement, Brencis turned and lunged for Quartus. Overturn tried to prevent the blow but only managed to deflect it, turning what might have been a lethal stab into a slice across Quartus's chest. He gasped as the pain caught up to the sight of the blood soaking into his shirt.

Brencis took a step back and held up the broken blade. Quartus's blood, which stained the sharp edge, flowed across the flat and pooled in six runes that had been carved into the metal. One by one, they lit up with a red glow. Quartus moaned as it felt like his strength flowed out of him, along with the light and color of the world around him. It all flowed into the *ur-keleshen*, forming a wicked curved blade that appeared to be made of pure darkness, a dripping shadow.

But then the runes flared even brighter, and a blast of cold air nearly knocked Quartus over. Brencis's entire body seemed to swell and his eyes blazed with red light. His mouth wrenched open as if he were ready to scream, but no sound emerged.

Brencis staggered forward. He looked at his hand, his sword, and laughed, a low resonant sound that felt like someone had dragged spikes across Quartus's mind.

"Do you see, Overturn?" Brencis's voice had become a bass rumble that shook the very ground. "Do you see what I have become?"

Overturn sighed. "I only see that you have made your choice."

Brencis's laughter shook the platform, but then Quartus felt a deeper rumbling beneath him. At first, it was a tremor that opposed the rhythm of Brencis's laughter, but it grew stronger with each passing second. Soon he heard the noise too, like a distant waterfall or the last thundering gasp of a storm before it retreated.

And then animals burst from the trees. Small ones at first, chakruts the size of Quartus's hand, but they were followed by flying wiggats.

"Vermin? This is your army?" Brencis guffawed

Overturn didn't answer. He didn't have to, because following the wiggats were packs of nerrun wolves, their muzzles flashing with teeth. And behind them were creatures that Quartus had never seen before, had never even experienced in a nightmare. The creatures loped on thick legs that ended in paws with jagged claws and mouths full of razor-sharp teeth. That was when Quartus realized what all of these animals had in common. They all had been wrapped in vines, pierced in the same way that Overturn was.

Brencis's army opened fire, managing to drop some of the wolves, but they couldn't take out the smaller beasts. Quartus rolled over to watch as the animals collided with the gathered troops, swarming over them.

"This is all you have?" Some of the confidence had bled from Brencis's voice. He fell back a step, but kept the sword up and ready in case Overturn attacked. "I have thousands of troops who will—"

His voice was swallowed by a low rumble. The trees in the forest collapsed in a crash as figures emerged from the ground itself, rising up on legs made of tree trunks with arms to match, rooted into bodies of stone by thick vines. These colossi tromped forward, ignoring the incoming flechettes as they bounded off their rocky bodies or embedded themselves in their limbs. When the giants reached the line, they tossed the Dynasty's armored vehicles away like they were nothing more than toys.

Quartus watched in stunned horror as, in a matter of moments, the Dynasty's soldiers broke and fled, the Cold Light's army pursuing them. Brencis stared after them as well, the color draining from his face. His sword, as impressive as it was, sagged in his hand. He turned to look at Overturn, who regarded him sadly.

"You were warned," Overturn whispered.

Brencis's face twisted into a scowl, and he turned to leap off the platform. But there was a pack of nerrun wolves surrounding them, each one fixed on Brencis, their eyes red and their teeth bared. When Brencis took a step toward the edge, they all growled as one.

"You had your chance to retreat and you chose not to," Overturn said. "That option has been closed to you. Now you will surrender or you will fight."

Brencis cast another look at the wolves, who responded with a new chorus of growls. Then, with a roar of his own, he lunged for Overturn with the *ur-keleshen*. The Ixactl stepped out of the way. Maybe it was the fact that he was now a thrall, or maybe Brencis's fear had gotten the better of him, but none of the king's attacks landed. Then, as Brencis overstepped a thrust, Overturn smashed a fist into his stomach then clubbed the back of his head. The sword clattered to the ground, and the deadly blade vanished into a puff of black smoke.

"Brencis, you are now our prisoner. You will be held by the Cold Light until such time as you are able to answer for your crimes. If your troops surrender, they will be spared. But those who die this day are on your conscience."

Quartus frowned. That was it? This was all that was going to happen? Brencis had tried to kill his brother, had tried to murder Everys, had plunged the entire Dynasty into death and disaster, and he could just surrender and that was it? No. Justice—true justice—had to be served. And he could deliver it in a poetic way.

He scooped up the *ur-keleshen*. As he touched the cold metal, what felt like needles jabbed into his palm. He winced, but after a second, it felt good to hold the weapon. Right. The way it should be.

"Quartus, what are you doing?" Overturn asked quietly.

He didn't answer. Instead, he stepped over to Brencis, who stared up at him with wide eyes. He started to speak, whether to plead for his life or to insult him, Quartus didn't know.

Before Brencis could say anything, he cried out, his body spasming. He thrashed and clawed at himself, screaming so loud and so long that his voice went hoarse. Then, with one gigantic seizure, he went limp, his body splayed on the platform. He shuddered as air hissed from his mouth.

"No!" Quartus dropped to the ground and touched Brencis's neck to check for a pulse. He couldn't be dead! Quartus wouldn't be denied his vengeance!

Brencis's heart still beat, but his pulse was weak and thready. If Quartus was going to finally find satisfaction, he had to do this now. He tightened his grip on the *ur-keleshen* and raised it over Brencis's chest. One stab and the cursed blade would find its sheath in the traitor's heart.

Before he could strike, though, Overturn shuddered, his head twisting this way and that. Once the seizure passed, Overturn faced him again, but his eyes seemed deeper.

"Quartus Prince. We understand your desire." As insane was it seemed, the Ixactl's voice had dropped an octave, with a resonance that Quartus could feel in his teeth. "The last time we went to war, we did so to prevent a great evil from consuming our world. We thought ourselves justified in our anger and hatred, but it led us to do horrible things, actions that changed us in profound ways. We are still paying the price. Stop before you incur a similar burden on yourself."

Quartus took several ragged breaths. He wouldn't look at Overturn or whatever Cold Light was speaking through him. They wouldn't dissuade him. He had to do this. This was right. This was just. This was the Dynasty's way, what his father would encourage, what his people would demand.

...which would cause Yusra to recoil from him. Which would leave Brencis's blood on his hands. Which would make him a monster, just like the man who lay on the platform in front of him.

The *ur-keleshen* slipped from his hands and clattered to the platform. He growled and yelled and tore at his hair. But then he turned to face Overturn.

"Take him away," he muttered.

Overturn nodded gravely, then stepped aside. One of the large creatures made of stone delicately scooped up Brencis's insensate form.

Overturn regarded Quartus critically. "You are more than welcome to come with us, Quartus Prince. There is room enough for you in the Shade."

Quartus sighed and shrugged. "Why not? It looks like you guys wrecked all of my other transportation options."

A shudder washed over Overturn, who then smiled. "Never fear, Prince. We have faster transportation waiting for us inside the forest. The Cold Light wanted to make a statement about who has Brencis and why it would be a foolish idea to try to mount a rescue."

Quartus looked back over the carnage spread throughout Vetranio's First Stand. As he did, a communications tower toppled with a resounding crash, causing him to jump. He glanced up and saw that the press drones still hovered overhead. He offered them a half-hearted wave, then winced as the pain from Brencis's beating finally made it through his adrenaline rush. He doubted that anyone watching would enjoy what they just witnessed.

"Let's go then," Quartus said. The sooner he could put all of this behind him, the better.

84

"**B**lessed, you may want to come out and see this," Trule called from the door.

Everys looked up from the scriber, glad for the distraction. She had spent the morning looking over reports from the front. Digesting the images of the Cold Light's army running roughshod over the Dynasty's forces hadn't been easy. So many lives wasted for no good reason at all.

She set aside the scriber and followed Trule out of her chambers, down a set of stairs, and out of the front door of the Embassy. As she emerged, a cheer went up among the people. Even though the Shade bore scars from the days-long missile bombardment, the news that Brencis had been swiftly defeated had lightened everyone's mood. She just wished people would stop cheering for her. She hadn't done anything. This was all the Cold Light. She'd have to thank them properly, but how did you offer a commendation to ancient trees?

Challix stood at the foot of the stairs. She smiled up at Everys as she approached.

"What's going on?" Everys asked.

"Oh, I thought you might want to be here for this arrival," Challix said, a smirk on her lips.

What arrival? She looked to the far distance for an approaching transport. But then the ground trembled beneath her feet. A massive hole opened in front of the Embassy, large vines with razor-sharp leaves whipping out and digging into the dirt around the hole. And then, much to her surprise, a transport rolled out of the hole. Once it had fully emerged, the ground closed up behind it. One of the side doors opened and a massive figure slid out. Everys's heart thrilled at the sight.

"Overturn!" she called.

Overturn turned and waved at her. That was when she saw the vines encircling him. Some of her excitement died. What would happen to Overturn now? Would he be able to return to the Dynasty and serve as the head of its military? Or would he have to remain in the forest with the Cold Light?

Then Overturn helped someone else out of the transport, and Everys's heart froze in her chest. She gasped, her hand shooting to her mouth.

"Narius?" she whispered.

But no. As she got a better look at him, she realized it wasn't her husband. He looked very much like him, but with coppery eyes instead of golden and a rakish grin that caused her to gasp again.

"Quartus!" she shouted.

He turned to her and smiled wearily. She launched herself the rest of the way down the steps and ran to him, enveloping him in as tight a hug as she could manage.

"Are you okay?" she asked.

He hugged her back. "No. I don't know what Oluna did to Narius. Or Yusra."

She pulled free, ice encasing her heart. "Wh-what? What do you mean? What happened?"

Quartus clenched his jaw then launched into the story of everything that had happened. His words tumbled out of him, faster than she could keep up at times. He described his reunion with Narius and their invasion of the palace. By the time he explained about discovering Oluna in the queen's chambers, Everys felt like she might throw up or punch someone. She wasn't sure which would make her feel better.

"Do you know where she took him?" she whispered.

He shook his head. "No. I'm sorry. Her minions were able to transport me halfway across the Dynasty's holdings. He could be anywhere."

And this happened days ago. They could be anywhere. Oluna could have even taken him out of the Dynasty's holdings entirely.

She whipped around to face Challix, who had obviously been listening in while pretending not to.

"Gather my advisers," Everys said. "This isn't over yet."

Challix rushed away and Everys led Quartus up the stairs in the Embassy. He smiled, but she could easily read the tension in his face and body. Worry practically flowed out of him and she understood why. They both needed answers about their loved ones. Shee had him come up to her quarters, where Trule found a change of clothes for him and Everys traced her family's rune on him to patch up the worst of his injuries. An hour later, they went to the war room and found her council waiting for her.

Galan walked over and gave her a quick hug. Everys smiled at her sister. When the missile barrage had started, Everys had ordered as many civilians out of the Shade as possible. Mama and Galan had been in the first wave of those who evacuated. It was good to see that they were back, safe and sound.

"How's Mama?" Everys asked quietly.

"Shaken, but she'll make it," Galan replied. "She was hoping the three of us could get together for *Ez'mazzonal* later this week."

Everys grimaced. She had almost forgotten. Everys wanted to decline, but she knew she shouldn't. Mama was dealing with so much: Legarr's death, Papa's arrest, her entire world upended in a matter of weeks.

"I'll see what I can do," Everys said. "No promises."

Galan squeezed her hand then joined P'layvo and Tolistan.

It felt strange to see Quartus seated at the table. He looked uncomfortable as well, but he offered her a shaky smile before turning back to confer quietly with Tormod.

"While I'd love to simply offer commendations for ending Brencis's war and his reign, I'm afraid we have a fresh crisis about to break." She took a steadying breath and hoped that her voice wouldn't crack. "According to Prince Quartus, Oluna has captured Narius. That means she not only has the puzzle rune, but she also has ink that should be powerful enough to cast it."

"What ink?" Hirfan asked with a frown.

"Narius's blood," Everys said, then launched into a quick explanation of what she had learned from Spanica Trentwether.

By the time she was done, silence had fallen on the room. Everyone looked positively stunned.

"Are you certain about this?" Challix finally asked. "The king has Elderreach blood?"

"I can't say for certain," Everys said. "But based on what Lord Trentwether told us and what I've learned from other sources"—she shot a nervous look at Yllana—"I'm fairly confident this is true."

Quartus nodded thoughtfully. "When Brencis was rebuked after using my blood with that *ur-keleshen*, he passed out. I think he's still in a coma right now."

That was all the confirmation that Everys needed. Yes, others might doubt, but she didn't. Not anymore.

"If I may be so bold, Blessed, so what?" Rewether asked.

She blinked at him. "Excuse me?"

"So they have the puzzle rune and powerful ink. The puzzle rune doesn't work. The Illuminates couldn't do it, even with the laser. Even if Oluna has Elderreach blood—which I'm not entirely convinced they do—what makes you think that they'd be able to use it?"

That was a valid question.

"If I may be so bold, consider the effort and energy that Oluna and her accomplices have spent in this scheme," Tormod said. "Centuries of planning, manipulating two kingdoms into a war, Oluna posing as the queen's friend to obtain the puzzle rune data, and now abducting the king? Even if the rune doesn't work, I would hazard to guess that they will at least try to cast it using the king's blood, a process I'm sure will be unhealthy or fatal for the king."

Everys winced at the thought. She had suspected that would be the case, but hearing it said out loud was painful.

"And what if they know what we're missing?" Tillmin added. "They've clearly known about this longer than we have. What if they know something we don't?"

P'layvo leaned forward and cleared her throat. "I may be able to shed some light on that. In spite of the rather chaotic past few days, we have continued working on the translation of the puzzle rune, and we may have found the answer we're looking for."

Everys perked up at that.

"Why didn't you say something earlier?" Overturn demanded.

"Until a few minutes ago, I thought our research had become purely academic! And I needed to process what the queen just shared with us," P'layvo said defensively.

She pulled out a scriber and activated it. Once again, an image of the puzzle rune appeared on one of the vidscreens.

"We couldn't refine our translation beyond what we shared a few weeks ago," P'layvo explained. "But then Tolistan had a brilliant thought: what if there was another puzzle to be pieced together? A puzzle inside the puzzle, as it were." She beamed at Tolistan, who blushed furiously. "We instructed the AI to search for such a hidden message and we found one."

She tapped a control. Bits and pieces of the puzzle rune were highlighted and broke off, swirling together to form, not a separate rune, but a piece of one.

"With this puzzle isolated, we could tighten up our translation. This is what the puzzle rune says with ninety-eight percent certainty..."

The puzzle rune once again spun apart, stretching and morphing into Dynastic.

I see the lack that needs to be fixed.
Overpower my brokenness,
Give me what I deepest desire
So long as I walk this path for you.
In my soul is certainty and delight
In what you call me to.
Unleash your power, your strength,
Reshape the world to our will.

Everys scanned the translation, an eerie sensation slithering over her. Like she was witnessing something forbidden, standing somewhere she shouldn't have been. She shuddered, trying to dislodge her discomfort.

"I love a good poem, same as anyone," Quartus said. "But what about the puzzle-within-the-puzzle? What does that say?"

P'layvo adjusted the display, and the phrase appeared. The snippets of rune transformed into words:

Cast this only where My Principalities rest.

Everys repeated that phrase several times, then her eyes widened. She knew where Oluna was taking Narius.

"They're going to Nekek the Bright," she whispered.

The other Siporans nodded.

"Would they even be able to get there?" Rewether asked. "The ruins are in the middle of the Demilitarized Zone—"

"—which is just a fading memory, thanks to the war with the Dalark," Redtale pointed out.

"That could be part of the reason they steered us into this conflict in the first place," Tormod added. "Have their enemies destroy each other and clear the way for their return to Nekek the Bright? Diabolical."

"But wouldn't the Dalark object to their presence in the Zone?" Rewether insisted.

"Why would they?" Quartus asked. "Princess—or, I guess, Empress Innana made it clear the Dalark forces wouldn't bother any of the Dynasty's troops. As long as Oluna doesn't provoke them, they'll leave the mage-kings alone."

"So they have everything they need," Everys said. "They have the rune. They have the ink. And I wouldn't be surprised if they know where to go. They'll be able to reshape the world according to Oluna's will. There's nothing stopping them."

A grim silence descended on the room.

But then Challix frowned. "Then why haven't they cast it?"

Everys's head snapped around. What?

"I'm serious," Challix said. "The king was captured how long ago? Days? A week? They've had plenty of time to get to Nekek the Bright and cast the rune many times over. So why haven't they?"

"Maybe they already have," Yllana offered, her voice laced with uncertainty.

"Don't you think we'd notice?" Redtale asked. "Would we even be able to sit here and debate this?"

"How would we know for certain?" Quartus asked. "I've seen how toratropic magic can alter a person's memories. Innana had Kavi do that to Yusra—"

"Who's Kavi?" Rewether interjected.

"They could have cast this rune and made all of us forget!" Quartus said.

"Maybe..." Galan said hesitantly. "Maybe they're waiting for the right time."

"The snippet doesn't say anything about time, just place," Tolistan pointed out.

"Yes, but what if it's a time of their choosing, not the Singularity's? A time that would be significant. Symbolic. Meaningful."

Galan's gaze locked with Everys's, and both of their eyes widened at the same time.

"*Ez'mazzonal*," Everys whispered.

Galan nodded.

Challix frowned. "Isn't that just a party celebrating community? Why would they wait for that?"

Everys offered her an apologetic smile. "In modern times, we see it as a day to celebrate community. But some traditions also claim that it was the day when the first stone was laid in Nekek the Bright."

Discussion broke out around the table. Some of her advisers were still trying to figure out if Narius really had Elderreach blood. A few of them were debating the accuracy of the translations. Challix still wondered if the rune hadn't been cast already. But Everys knew. She knew with absolute certainty that what they had figured out was true.

"I have to go to Nekek the Bright," she said.

All eyes turned to her.

Rewether frowned. "Absolutely not. If there's a mage-king about to cast a powerful rune, that's the last place you should go. We need to send in troops or—"

"We don't have any that are loyal to us outside of the forest," Overturn said. "Even if we could find some, I suspect it would take them far too long to reach Nekek the Bright. And if, by some miracle from the ancestors, they could, most of us have seen what Oluna and her ilk are capable of. I doubt they'd stand much of a chance."

"Without Tanakept, we don't have access to the chantways. That means there's only one other option that I'm comfortable using." Everys looked right at Tormod.

He squirmed in his seat. "I've warned you about this repeatedly, Blessed. As much as I want to believe the Singularity would want us to stop this, there's no guarantee."

"But we should still try," Everys said.

Tormod frowned, but then he sighed and nodded. "Very well. We can try. But I fear that we'll only have one attempt. By the time I recover, it will probably be too late."

"How many people could you bring with us?" Everys asked.

He hesitated. "You, for certain. Maybe one other."

Both Redtale and Rewether started to speak, but Quartus interrupted them both. "I'll go."

"You don't even know what we're going to do," Everys said.

"It doesn't matter."

"This might not work. You might be left here."

"You mean I wouldn't have to fight a group of crazy toratropic mages? How horrible!"

Everys narrowed her eyes at his attempt at humor. His expression was open and earnest. He wanted this, more than he was trying to let on.

"Why do you want to go so badly?" she asked.

Quartus sighed. "Because he's my brother. Because I've failed him too often in the past. Because I still owe Oluna and her minions for framing me back on the Night of Shards! But most of all, because it's the right thing to do."

Everys exchanged a look with Tormod, who nodded hesitantly.

"All right, we'll try to bring you with us. Tormod?"

He scratched at the table. "We can leave at once."

Everys almost nodded, but she hesitated. "If we're right, we still have some time. I'd like to have a night to prepare ourselves." She looked at Tolistan. "In prayer. In meditation. To align ourselves truly with what the Singularity wants."

Tormod offered her a genuine smile. "I can think of no better way for us to arm ourselves, Blessed."

She nodded. "Good. Tomorrow morning, right at the beginning of First Watch."

Quartus grimaced. "So early? I was hoping to sleep in."

Everys smirked at him. She saw through what he was trying to do, and she couldn't blame him. She was terrified of this as well. Returning to her people's homeland, reentering Nekek the Bright, to stop a mage-king? If she could refuse, she would. But she couldn't. Narius needed her. And she was going to be there for him.

No matter what.

85

Everys hadn't been able to sleep. As she lay in bed, staring at her room's ceiling, her mind just wouldn't shut down. Too many thoughts and worries and questions and imaginings collided, creating little cognitive sparks that caused her to twitch awake as they jolted her brain. Within a few hours, they would try to jump to Nekek the Bright. What would it be like, entering a city that had loomed so large in her people's history and theology? The ancient texts were filled with superlative descriptions of their home. Would she recognize whatever they found? Or would anything be left standing?

But what if they didn't make it at all? What if Tormod's tattoo sent them careening off to somewhere else, like Bastion or Utuaa or even one of the other nations, like Rioka or Erecone? What if the Singularity decided it was more important for one of them to be there instead of where she was actually needed?

Or worse, what if they were too late? Images of Narius's drained body lying on a paved floor kept assaulting her every time she was about to drift off. Would she finally find Narius, only to discover that this time, he was truly dead?

When the time came to get up, she tumbled out of bed. Even though exhaustion tried to drag her back to the warm covers, she forced herself to get dressed. But as she did, her mind woke up enough to notice that, for the first time in months, she was dressing herself with no help from the girls. Where were they?

She found them waiting outside her bedroom. Trule had assembled them all in a straight line. They stood proudly, their heads high and their arms straight at their sides. Trule stepped forward.

"I know you're going to succeed in whatever you're about to do, Blessed, but we wanted to thank you for the way you've taken care of us over the past year," Trule said. "It has been an honor to serve you."

Everys blinked back tears. But she took the time to hug each girl and thank her for her service by name. When she came to Trule, though, she pulled her chief maid into a tight embrace. A few tears escaped her, but she didn't care.

"I'll be back," Everys whispered.

"I know you will," Trule said. "And I'll have a warm bowl of palane stew ready for both you and the king."

Everys finally pulled away and headed out to the hallway. There she found Rewether and Redtale waiting for her. Rewether looked upset, as always, but she couldn't blame him. He had made his displeasure with this plan perfectly clear the night before.

Redtale, though, looked calm. She smiled. "We'll hold down the ramparts until you're back, Blessed. Go break some horns."

The two of them embraced, and then both Rewether and Redtale fell into step on either side of her, escorting her to Tormod's room.

Before they could get there, though, they were intercepted by Tillmin and Hirfan. The latter looked sour, but that wasn't much of a surprise.

"Before you leave, Blessed, we have something we feel you should have." Tillmin held out a small device, the length and width of a short sword.

She hefted it up. It looked like someone had cannibalized a digital scriber and attached it to a long box with a lens at the opposite end.

"Before I ended the Illuminates' experiments with light, Screj was building this," Tillmin said. "It's a portable laser."

Suddenly the device felt three times as heavy. No wonder Hirfan looked so upset. There was no way he would approve creating such a device, let alone handing one to her.

"When the other Illuminates heard what you were going to do, they insisted we give this to you. The mage-kings will have powerful runes and inks. You should have access to the same." Tillmin motioned toward the screen. "We've already stored a number of runes into its memory, ones that we feel might be the most needed. But you can also draw any rune on that panel if you have to."

"And it works?" Everys asked.

Tillmin nodded. "Screj and Style stayed up all night to finish and test it. They wound up accidentally flooding the catacombs, but it does work."

She bit back a laugh. She'd have to ask them how that happened when she was back. If she came back.

Everys clipped the array to her belt and adjusted it so it hung like a sword. Not the most apt comparison, but its weight gave her a little confidence.

"Blessed, if I may speak to you?" Hirfan asked. "In private?"

Tillmin's brow furrowed, but he patted Everys on the shoulder like a doting uncle then stepped away.

Hirfan watched him leave, then stepped in closer. "I was against this idea. I don't feel it's wise entrusting something like this to you given what you did in Utuaa."

Everys frowned, but she held back the retort that clawed up her throat. Let him speak his piece.

"But I also recognize that you'll need every advantage you can get." He held out a small ball that looked like it was made of gray chalk. "So here."

She hefted it. It weighed practically nothing, and it felt like it was about to crumble in her hand. This seemed familiar, but why?

"My order created this formula many centuries ago. If you throw that at a rune, it will crumble. The resulting particles disrupt the ink and stop the spell. I keep one of these on hand at all times when I'm in the catacombs just in case."

She looked at the ball again, and her eyes widened. Was this how he stopped the plague rune in Utuaa?

As if he could read the question on her face, Hirfan nodded. "Use it wisely. And use the laser wisely as well."

"I will." Those two words weighed heavily on her. That couldn't be an idle promise. She had to do as he suggested, but not because he told her. Because he was right.

With a final nod, she headed for Tormod's room. Much to Everys's surprise, Quartus had actually beaten her there. She would have expected him to have slept in or been tardy. But then, he had clearly changed and grown.

Tormod looked at them both and nodded. "The queen already knows this, Prince, but when we attempt to make this jump, I need you to keep your mind clear. If you try to direct what's happening—"

Quartus chuckled. "Tormod, I have no idea what you're going to do here. I'll go wherever you take us."

Tormod frowned, but then he nodded. "Are you both ready?"

They nodded. Tormod snared their right hands and placed them on his shoulders. Then he rolled up his sleeve to expose the tattoo, taking several deep breaths.

As he prepared himself, Everys closed her eyes and offered a quick prayer to the Singularity. *I know where I want to go, and I'm sure You know where that is too. But I know that while I may be queen of the Dynasty, You are the one who directs my steps. If this takes us to Narius, thank You. If it doesn't, may we be able to do good wherever we wind up. Whatever happens, protect my husband, if that's at all possible.*

A blast of cold swept over her, and it felt like the floor fell away. As they dropped, Quartus shouted in surprise.

Then Everys felt her feet hit solid rock. The transition was so sudden, she stumbled forward, letting go of Tormod's shoulder. Her arms pinwheeled until she regained her balance. Then she opened her eyes and looked around.

The first thing she saw was Tormod and Quartus. She wanted to laugh with relief. They had all made it! But where were they?

She turned a slow circle then gasped. Spread out before her was a massive wall, made of stones as tall as she was. It loomed over them, a hundred feet tall. But as impressive as the wall was, she couldn't help but notice the many holes that had been torn through it. Some sections had been smashed to the ground, leaving gaps large enough that dozens of transports could stream through at once.

Quartus gaped at it. "Nekek the Bright?"

Tormod nodded. "I believe so, yes."

"How did Heronus bring down those walls?" Quartus whispered. "They look like they could take a missile strike."

Everys and Tormod exchanged a look. They knew the answer all too well. It wasn't superior military tactics or better weapons or even the Dynasty's alliance with the Dalark. The true reason Nekek the Bright had fallen was because the Singularity had withdrawn His protection of the city because of their people's transgressions.

But this didn't seem the time to rehash theology or history. Tormod signaled for them to follow, and they headed through one breach into the city itself.

Everys took a moment to drink it all in. They had entered what appeared to have been a residential district, although it was hard to tell. Most of the buildings had been burned or destroyed, leaving behind heaps of tan bricks with a few bits of colorful tiles poking out. She had almost expected to see skeletons or empty armor littering the streets, but there was nothing. Cold slithered down her spine as they crept through the empty streets, passing by a deserted square with a dry fountain at its center.

They came across another wall at the edge of the district. This one had been broken through as well. They carefully clambered over a pile of stones in one of the breaches and emerged into another district filled with ruined buildings.

"Do either of you know what we're looking at?" Quartus whispered. "I mean, besides the obvious piles of rubble?"

Everys shot him a sidelong glance and shook her head. Tormod did as well.

"So then, how do we know where to go?" Quartus asked.

That was a legitimate question, one Everys hadn't considered. While Nekek the Bright hadn't been as large as a modern city, it was big enough that it would take at least a day or two to search the ruins.

"According to the ancient texts, the Scriptotum was built at the top of the highest point in the city." Tormod turned a circle and frowned. "We may need to find a higher vantage point."

Everys scanned their surroundings, then pointed to an enormous pile of rubble that appeared relatively stable. Without a word, they all headed that way.

It took them fifteen minutes to clamber up the pile. They didn't get much of a better view, although they could peek over the wall that surrounded this district as well. It looked like the city had been built into terraces, with the next highest in front of them. With no discussion, they headed in that direction.

None of the buildings remained standing, and most of the rubble had been scattered and jumbled together. Everys was about to ask if they should keep going, but Tormod suddenly lunged forward into one of the piles of rubble. With a triumphant smile, he pulled what looked like a broken metallic scale out of the rubble.

"A souvenir?" Quartus asked.

"A clue," Tormod countered. He looked over the rubble and nodded. "According to the ancient texts, the fighting was fiercest in the Merchant's Quarter. I suspect that's where we are. And if that's the case, then over there"—He pointed to his right—"would be the Scrivener's Hold with the palace complex north of that. And beyond that..."

Everys's heart stuttered. "The Scriptotum."

"Then let's go," Quartus said.

They headed in the direction of the Scrivener's Hold. When they passed through another interior wall, they discovered more destruction. Everys's heart twinged at the sight of the burned buildings. This had been the home of ancient libraries, centers of learning, repositories of knowledge and wisdom that her people had maintained for centuries. And it was all gone. None of the buildings had survived. She wasn't surprised to see that. The accounts of the destruction made it clear that both the Dynasty and the Dalark had specifically targeted this district to make sure that they had completely wiped out any knowledge of toratropic magic.

Quartus tensed next to her, his head snapping to one side. "Someone's coming."

She looked in the direction he indicated. She didn't see anyone, but she could hear footsteps, uneven and cautious on the strewn rubble.

"Stay still!" Tormod whispered, then pulled out a vial of ink. He sketched a rune on his hand, then pressed it against both Everys and Quartus before activating it. The surrounding air shimmered, and Tormod and Quartus vanished from her sight. Everys held her breath, her hand darting to the laser just in case, and hoped that whatever Tormod had done would be enough.

A moment later, a solitary figure appeared, picking her way over the rubble. Everys was surprised. She expected whoever it was to be one of Oluna's lackeys, but this was a young woman with short-cropped hair framing a heart-shaped face.

Wait. She had seen her before. That was the young woman who had emerged onto the roof in Utuaa before Hirfan pulled her out. What was she doing here?

Quartus gasped, and he popped back into existence, rushing forward.

The young woman spun around, snared him by the arm, and tossed him over her shoulder. Then she dropped a knee on his chest and held him down, her fist drawn back and ready to strike.

"Quartus?" another woman's voice called.

Everys turned and saw Yusra scramble over a pile of rubble. And she was followed by...

The strength drained out of her legs. Why was Paine here?

The woman kneeling on Quartus's chest quickly got off him. Quartus scrambled to his feet and ran to Yusra, catching her in his arms and kissing her. The two of them clung to each other. The young woman who had attacked Quartus smiled at the sight, although Paine looked positively disgusted.

Deciding they were safe enough, Everys stepped forward. The moment the invisibility rune broke, the others whirled around in surprise. And then Tormod reappeared as well.

"Everys?" Paine said. "Tormod? What are you doing here?"

"I might ask you the same thing," Everys said, injecting acid into her tone.

"We're looking for Narius," Paine said.

"How convenient. So are we." She shot a look at her brother-in-law. "Are you coming up for air soon, Quartus?"

Quartus pulled free of Yusra. But he didn't take his eyes off her.

"I was so worried about you! I thought Brencis had killed you," Yusra said.

Quartus shook his head. "He wanted to, but the Cold Light stopped him."

"And he..." she prompted.

"Is still alive," he said.

Yusra kissed him again.

Tormod strolled forward, a broad smile on his face. "This is a pleasant surprise."

The other young woman started laughing silently, then crossed over and actually punched Tormod on the arm.

"Blessed, this is Kavi. I have crossed swords with her several times over the past few years. She is quite the adversary." His smiled broadened.

Kavi waved at Everys, and she almost appeared shy.

"Believe it or not, I am glad to see you," Paine said. "All of you."

Much to her surprise, Everys believed him. And there was something comforting about hearing Paine's voice again. Something familiar, like the world was trying to right itself after being off-kilter for too long.

"So we're all here for the same reason," Everys said. "How did you know to come here?"

"We used the Dynasty's monitoring satellites," Paine said. "While Brencis had most of our forces moving toward the Cold Light's forest, we noticed one unit heading toward the Demilitarized Zone. We assumed that had to be Oluna's team, and so we headed here ourselves. You?"

Everys winced. Untangling their hows and whys could take hours, and she doubted they had the time to spare.

"Something like that," Everys lied. "Any thoughts?"

Kavi signed something, and Yusra translated: "'We didn't see any sign of them in the Lower Court. My guess is they've camped out near the palace.'"

Tormod nodded grimly. "Shall we?"

Quartus and Yusra didn't need any further invitation. They set off in the direction Tormod indicated, still holding hands. Tormod and Kavi followed next, engaged in a quiet discussion of some past adventure they had both been on. But Paine held back.

Everys fixed him with an acidic glare. "You coming or not?"

Frustration flickered through his eyes, but he pursed his lips. "Before we do, Blessed, I have something I need to say."

Really? He wanted to have a chat right that moment? But the taunt on her tongue died when she saw the serious look on his face. Yes, Paine always looked grim, but this time, there was even more weight to it.

"I do not know if we will survive this particular misadventure. My guess is we won't."

"Thanks for the encouragement," she said.

His brows twitched into a frown.

Everys winced. "Sorry. Force of habit."

"That is what I wanted to speak to you about. If things do turn out badly for either or both of us, I feel there is something I have to say."

Oh, good, here it came. More criticism. More reminders of how she wasn't worthy to be queen, how she had the wrong instincts, how she was too naive to understand the practical realities of being royalty.

"I am sorry for the pain I caused both you and Narius."

It felt like the entire weight of her body drained out through her feet at once. Had Paine just apologized to her?

A grin tickled his lips. "I know how shocked you must be to hear that, but it's the truth—one that I have blinded myself to. Narius always trusted me for guidance and counsel, saying that he relied on my wisdom and insight to never steer him wrong. I fear that I have become too sure of my own abilities as well. When you came into the palace, I was so sure that you were a harbinger of disaster. In some ways, you were. But that was not entirely your fault, and in those instances where it was, I could have helped you and been more supportive. For that, I am most sorry."

Everys's mouth worked as she tried to find the right thing to say. This was so unusual, she almost thought she was dreaming. "Well, I didn't exactly make it easy on you either."

"This is true."

Now she grinned. "And we both want the same thing, right? What's best for the Dynasty?"

"More than that, what's best for Narius. And that is you. So let's go find your husband."

86

Mother and Father glared at him from their thrones. Both looked like reanimated corpses, their skin gray and ashen and barely hanging on their skeletons. Their eyes were sunken pits, their hair stringy and thin. Yet in spite of their decrepit bodies, heat rolled off them, flowing down the steps to wash over Narius. He was roasting in their presence.

But he couldn't escape. His hands were bound in metal casings up to his elbows, the weight pulling him over in an awkward angle. A gag made of similar material was clamped over his mouth. He tried to free his hands but he couldn't.

Then he realized what was happening. This was how the royal family treated those they believed had betrayed them. When he thought Quartus had tried to assassinate both Everys and him, Quartus had been treated in a similar fashion. Narius was on trial for treason.

"Do you understand why we're here?" Father asked, his voice a whisper that pebbled Narius's skin.

He tried to answer, but he couldn't. His voice couldn't penetrate the gag.

"The Gravedigger released us from his realm so that we may address your failures," Mother said. "And correct them."

"Your crimes are these." Father leaned forward on his throne. "You were too weak, too compassionate, too idealistic. You did not live up to our expectations nor those of the Dynasty's. You allowed our enemies to see our weaknesses and exploit them."

"The foul mage-kings still operate with impunity, and you married one," Mother added.

Father nodded grimly. "Yes, you took a Siporan witch into your heart and into your bed. You pollute our noble lineage with her filth."

The litany went on, a constant barrage of his failures. At first, Narius tried to object, but he couldn't. He could barely breathe. The verbal assault continued, each accusation slicing into him. Was this really how his parents saw him? A failure, a traitor, worthy of death?

Finally, Father sat up straighter. "What is our consensus?"

"Let him die," Mother hissed.

"Guilty!" King Vetranio, his grandfather, stepped out of the shadows, leveling a finger at him.

"Traitor!" Viara, her belly swollen to bursting, joined him.

One by one, more people he knew surrounded him, joining the condemnation. Istragon, Emperor Tirigian, Favid, Quartus, Paine. All of them declaring him guilty and worthy of death.

But the last stung the worst. Everys emerged from the shadows, her skin sallow and cracked, black liquid oozing down her cheeks. As she pointed a shaking finger at him, her mouth opened, but rather than words, an incoherent shriek of rage cut through him. And as it did, her body disintegrated like leaves blown away in a cold winter wind...

Narius bolted upright on a cot, suddenly aware of the sweat that slicked his body, the dryness of his mouth, the gnawing ache in his stomach. He frantically looked at his surroundings, a simple tent with a heating unit in one corner. His mind spun through what he had just seen, but the trial blended with the other nightmares that had been assaulting him for what felt like years.

"Good morning, Narius," Oluna said.

He whipped around and groaned as pain sliced through his head. There was the enemy. There was his tormentor. As his mind cleared, he remembered. She had done something to him, cast a rune that pitched him into a series of nightmarish visions. She stood in the entrance to the tent and smiled at him.

"How are we feeling?" she asked, her voice sarcastically sweet. "Hungry? Thirsty? I'm sorry for trapping you in the holding rune, but we really didn't want to deal with you whining or trying to escape while we traveled here. That would just frustrate us. But where are my manners? Let's take a tour, shall we?"

Even though she phrased it as a question, Narius knew it wasn't. Not a suggestion either. Rather than antagonize her, he pushed himself up out of the cot. His legs cramped, protesting the sudden movement, and he stumbled forward. But somehow, he managed to regain his balance and followed Oluna.

He emerged into what appeared to be a wild forest. While he didn't know where he was at first, he recognized the trees and shrubs as those that grew in the Demilitarized Zone. His mind caught up with what he was seeing, and he realized they weren't standing in a forest. Instead, he stood on a stone floor, on which dozens of intricate runes had been carved, combining into a pattern that made his mind reel. He inspected his surroundings and spotted what at first appeared to be a stagnant pond, but then realized the edges were too straight. A reflecting pool maybe? But one choked with weeds and smelling of rancid water. His nose wrinkled. This may have been beautiful once, but decades of neglect had ruined and rotted it.

"I realize my ancestors' gardens aren't as exquisite as yours," Oluna said from his side, "but personally, I appreciate the untamed ferocity. This is what it truly means to be a Siporan. To stand amidst chaos and know that you are stronger than all of it."

She started walking, and Narius felt a tug at his chest, one that compelled him to follow. She led them on a winding path through the thicket until they emerged into a clearing. No, not a clearing. Ruins of a large building spread out before him. Most of it was nothing more than heaps of rubble, but a bit of a portico still stood, ivory-white pillars covered with delicate golden vines.

"And here is the legacy of your people, Narius," Oluna said. "From here, the *ar'zhannok* of old reigned over the Ascendancy. We imposed our will on those who needed to be governed. Had the Singularity not sent you and the Dalark to stop us, I would be seated on a throne here. But we're about to fix that discrepancy."

Again, she started walking parallel to the ruined portico, and once again, Narius was dragged after her. She eventually approached a wall that had been torn down. Beyond it was a large circular platform, one that was strangely free of debris.

"That is where the Scriptotum once stood," Oluna whispered. "Your ancestor not only razed it, but Heronus ordered all the rubble carted away and dropped into the Gravebalt Sea. This is all that remains. But it is enough. It's appropriate, I think. We will rise from the ashes of those weaklings who turned their backs on us. Let them rot. We will see a new Ascendancy reborn! Tomorrow morning, we are going to use your blood to cast the most powerful rune our people have ever known. And when we do, Nekek shall shine again."

"Nekek shall shine again!" Voices around them took up the phrase as a rallying cry, and dozens of men and women wearing robes stepped out of the early morning shadows.

"Take him away and begin the preparations," Oluna said, still staring at the circular platform. "And ready yourselves, my friends. For tomorrow, all will be made right!"

Two of the men stepped forward and clamped firm hands onto Narius's arms. He tried to put up a struggle, but his motions were feeble and they just dragged him forward, through a ruined gate, and into the ruins of the Scriptotum. And as they did, Narius offered a silent plea to the Singularity that this new, living nightmare could somehow be brought to an end.

As they approached the palace ruins, they slowed, crouching low to blend in with the rubble. Everys thought she spotted people patrolling the edge of the ruins, but she was so jumpy she could have been seeing things.

When they were almost at the palace, Kavi froze and signaled for everyone to stop. Once they had, Kavi crouched low and looked closely at the ground in front of them. Then she made some strange gestures with her hands and thrust them toward the ground.

A ripple of energy passed over the ground and, as it did, ghostly runes appeared on the ground. One of them flared and then winked out. Everys recognized it before it vanished: a glamour spell, one that had clearly been used to hide the others. She understood what half of them did: snare spells, trap spells, one that would have sent electrical shocks across a hundred-foot radius. But the rest were completely foreign to her.

Kavi turned and offered her a jaunty grin, but then her face screwed up in surprise. Everys gasped. A bright yellow plume stuck out of Kavi's neck at an odd angle. She tried to grab it, but her fingers merely grazed the feathers and she collapsed to the ground, her body limp.

Everys stared in horror. A tranquilizer dart? Where had—?

Similar darts slammed into Quartus and Paine, who dropped without a sound. Yusra dodged two of them before the third caught her. Tormod slapped his tattoo and a blast of shadows enveloped him. He vanished from the field just as a yellow-tailed dart sliced through the smoke.

Then a pain pricked her arm. She looked over and saw that a dart was stuck in her shoulder. What felt like lead coursed through her veins, and she could feel herself being pulled down to the ground. Gray swam in her vision. The last thing she saw were soldiers, wearing camouflaged outfits, emerging from the rubble piles. They stood over her, congratulating each other, as the darkness took her.

87

Awareness flickered in Everys. She was vaguely aware of the rough stone underneath her back, the way her limbs were splayed at uncomfortable angles. With a groan, she sat up and looked around.

She was lying in the corner of a ruined room. Portions of two walls met in a corner, offering her a little shelter from the wind. The rest was exposed to the open sky, which was slowly turning a bright red. Was it already so deep into Third Watch? How long had she been out?

"My apologies for the dosage," an all-too-familiar voice said. "We didn't want to take any chances."

Everys sat up. Oluna stood nearby, wearing a crimson robe with golden brocade. Dozens of runes had been embroidered into them, some of which glowed faintly. Everys recognized them immediately. Defensive runes. She looked for her pouch or the laser. Of course, all of it had been confiscated.

"You know, some of my partners didn't think you would get here in time. They said that there was no way that some girl from Fair Havens could figure out why we needed your husband or what our plan was. But I knew better. I kept telling them not to underestimate you. And here you are, just like I knew you'd be." Oluna offered her what looked like a genuinely warm smile. "You truly are remarkable."

Everys glared at her, which only prompted a laugh from Oluna. The sound was so familiar that for just a moment, Everys could see the woman she had considered one of her best friends. Reconciling everything she knew now with the woman she had met at the Queen's Court was jarring.

"Why did you do it?" The question slipped out of her.

"Do what?" Oluna asked, raising a quizzical brow. "I've done so many things to get to this moment, my dear. You'll have to be more specific."

"Why did you pretend to be my friend?" Much to her annoyance, tears actually stung Everys's eyes.

"Oh, please. What do the so-called 'Warrior's Meditations' say? 'Keep allies in your camp, enemies in your tent?'" Oluna chuckled. "We almost had everything ready to go. The Dynasty and the Dalark were nearly at war, and we were working on getting the Principality runes and the right ink. And then you came along. I could smell the ink on you the moment I met you, Everys. You survived the assassination attempt on the Night of Shards, so we knew you were capable. Someone needed to contain you, and I figured it should be me."

"So none of it was real? At all?" Everys spat.

Oluna frowned. "I suppose some parts were. Zivah is real. Thank you for her life, by the way. I almost regretted having Masruq reveal your abilities to the rest of the Dynasty, but it had to happen."

"No, it didn't!" Everys said. This time, a tear slid down her cheek. "None of this had to happen, Oluna. If I would have known who you really are, we could have worked together. With Narius. He wants to make things better."

Oluna rolled her eyes. "Do you know how many kings have promised to make things better, only to return to their warmongering and prejudice? Weak fools, all of them. They deserve what they're getting."

Everys gaped at her. "Don't you have any shame?"

"Why should I?" Oluna asked with a smirk. "Do you Siporans have any shame? We made you prosperous. We made you powerful and feared. And how did you repay us? You placed the blame for what happened here on us! You turned your backs on us, so you will have no place in our new world. I am the descendant of the mage-kings of old. I am the one who is going to reshape the world to the way it should have always been. Nekek shall shine again!"

Everys's eyes widened. She had suspected that was Oluna's plan, but hearing it stated so plainly and with such glee and enthusiasm drove a spike into her heart. A new Siporn Ascendancy, born from the puzzle rune, would be devastating.

"Please, Oluna, don't do this," Everys said. "Enough people have suffered. It's not too late. We can make a difference. But not like this."

Oluna sighed. "This is all very entertaining, but tomorrow is coming quickly. The same day that our ancestors built Nekek the Bright, we will recreate it and make it stand forever. And no amount of pleading from you will change my mind."

She daubed more ink onto her finger then drew a rune on the pavement in front of her.

"You will remain here overnight. And in the morning, you will see all of our hard work come to fruition. I grant you this one reprieve. You will witness what is going to happen. And you will know that nothing will ever be able to stop us!"

With that, Oluna activated the rune, rose and strutted away from the corner.

Everys tried to follow, but the rune on the floor flared to life and an invisible force pushed her backward. When she tried to leave by slipping under the tent's wall, the same thing happened. So Everys sat down again and waited for the morning. One hope kept her going: at least she would see Narius again.

88

Oluna returned for Everys the next day, only she wasn't alone. Instead, the mage-king led a procession of attendants, all wearing similar robes to their leader, although theirs were less ostentatious. As Oluna entered the tent, she waved her hand and the rune that had kept Everys prisoner vanished. But Everys had no illusions of freedom. That point was driven home when two of the attendants, both carrying long spears, marched to either side of her. They didn't touch her, but they made it clear from their intimidating postures that if she tried anything, they would strike quickly.

"Come, Everys," Oluna said, her voice overflowing with glee. "You are about to see the world remade. This day wouldn't be possible without you."

Oluna gave her an expectant look. Everys sighed. She considered not playing along, but she doubted Oluna would allow her to do that.

"Oh? Why is that?" Everys kept her voice flat and disengaged.

"Without you, we would have never had a clean version of the puzzle rune." Oluna produced a scriber from her robes and waved it at Everys. "And your questions about your husband's blood helped me realize the connection between the Dynasty's royal family and the Elderreach. My ancestors suspected there was a link. You confirmed it. None of this would have been possible without you."

Everys flinched and looked away, prompting more laughter from Oluna and her attendants.

They left the ruins of the palace and crossed to a vast circular platform made of interlocking stone pavers. Everys's heart hitched. Her gaze swept across the empty space. Was this really where the Scriptotum had stood? She knew from the ancient texts that the building itself had been utterly destroyed, but she had thought that maybe some remnant of the structure had survived. A column, a curved wall, something to indicate its grandeur and purpose. But no, all that was left was a small space with only a slightly raised dais in its center.

The guards shoved Everys from behind to keep her walking. As they approached the center, Everys's unease grew sharper and stronger.

Oluna glanced at her and chuckled. "Oh, don't be so grim, Everys. We won't be punished for standing here. Haven't you realized it yet? The Singularity can't stop us. All he can do is swat at us weakly as we use the runes to achieve our true potential. If he's so powerful, why doesn't he stop us? Why doesn't he act?"

Everys hung her head, hearing too much of herself in Oluna's question. While she hadn't gone to this extreme, for years she had kept the Singularity at arm's length, unwilling to acknowledge Him because of the problems she saw in the world. But now, as she stood in the most sacred place in her people's history, a quiet strength welled up inside her. She met Oluna's gaze.

"I don't have an answer to that, and maybe it's okay that I don't," she said. "If the Singularity explained everything to me, our roles would be reversed. I may not like struggling with those sorts of questions, but maybe what I'm called to is living in that tension and doing my best with what I do know."

Oluna stared at her, then snorted. "No wonder the Siporans have been downtrodden for so long. That's weakness. To use the runes properly, one needs strength. One needs the will to do what they decide is right. And that's what's going to happen today. We will use the puzzle rune to reshape the world and make it ours once again."

With that, Oluna jabbed a finger at one side of the dais. Everys's guards steered her in that direction. Another of the attendants followed and, when they reached a particular spot, the attendant sketched a holding rune at Everys's feet. When it activated, invisible bands of energy clamped onto her feet, wrists, and chest, holding her in place.

A few moments later, she heard movement behind her. Thankfully, she could crane her head to the right to see another group of attendants approaching. Two burly guards had a limp figure between them, the other person's arms draped over their shoulders. Everys's heart lurched.

"Narius!" she cried.

Her husband's head lolled up. Dark circles ringed his eyes. His torn clothing hung off his body, unable to hide bruises and welts across his chest and legs. She struggled against the holding spell, trying to break free so she could run to her husband and take him in her arms.

As the other group drew closer, recognition flickered in Narius's eyes. His breathing became ragged, and he tried to pull free of the guards holding him.

"Ev-Everys?" he whispered, his voice barely audible. "What are you doing here?"

She smiled, tears trickling down her cheeks. "I came here to save you."

His cracked lips twitched into a grin, one that sent a thrill through her. "Then I have nothing to worry about, do I?"

His quiet confidence sent strength through her arms. She strained against the spell. If she could just break free, maybe she'd be able to do something. She didn't know what, but she would gladly face an entire gathering of mage-kings on her own with no ink rather than let a single one of them touch her Narius.

"I need to tell you something," Narius said. "Something important, something I didn't tell you often enough. I love you, Everys. Nothing I've experienced has changed that at all. I love you more than my life itself."

His guards had dragged him to a spot just three feet from her. But because she was still stuck fast, it might as well have been a hundred miles. She just wanted to touch him, to feel his hand in hers, one more time. Everys wanted to scream in rage. Why couldn't she break free?

"I love—"

Then the invisible force shut her mouth and silenced her.

Oluna stepped forward, displaying a glowing rune on her hand. "Enough of the sentimentality."

Everys could only watch mutely as the attendants hoisted Narius up with a rune painted at his feet as well. Oluna strode forward. As she did, an attendant produced a jeweled dagger and handed it to her. Although Oluna approached Narius with the weapon, she kept her gaze locked on Everys, an expectant smile on her face.

But what could Everys actually do? She knew she couldn't break free. She could only glare at Oluna in quiet defiance.

Oluna chuckled and stepped up to Narius. She grabbed his chin in one hand, tipping his head back and forth while studying him, as if to find the best place to strike. Then Oluna grabbed Narius's arm and slashed the dagger across his wrist. Narius cried out and tried to yank his hand free. Another attendant darted forward, carrying a chalice. He positioned it under Narius's hand to catch his blood as it dribbled down his fingers, his hand still suspended in the rune. Everys tried to thrash against her restraints and scream at them to stop. Fire raged through her, but she couldn't do anything.

After a few moments, Oluna and the attendant walked back to the center of the dais. Oluna dipped her finger in the chalice and knelt, carefully drawing the puzzle rune in its center. The other attendants, dozens of them, stood at quiet attention.

As soon as it was done, Oluna stood up. She turned to the crowd and smiled gleefully. "Today, my friends! Today, we undo the injustice of our city's destruction. Today, we resume our rightful place in the world. Today, we remind the people of this world who its true masters are. Today, Nekek shall shine again!"

"Nekek shall shine again!" the crowd responded.

With that cry echoing through the ruins, Oluna activated the spell.

Everys twisted and pulled at her arms, trying to slip free of her invisible bonds. Panic welled up inside her. She couldn't even imagine how vile a world shaped by Oluna's would be. But she just couldn't get free!

But nothing happened. There were no flashes of light, no thunderous noise, no release of power. There wasn't even the strange buildup she had felt when the Illuminates tried to cast it with the laser.

She risked a peek at the rune. The blood appeared to be drying out, but that was it.

Everys stared at the crimson stain on the stone, confusion roaring through her. Why hadn't it worked? Oluna had cast the rune where the Principalities once rested with one of the most powerful inks the Siporans had ever known. So what went wrong?

At first, the gathered crowd waited in eager silence. But as the seconds dragged on, more and more of them started whispering. Oluna kept her arms outstretched, almost looking like a child waiting for a hug that would never come.

Finally, Oluna looked down at the rune. She shrieked and turned on Everys. "What did you do?"

Everys tried to answer, but her voice was still locked in her throat. With a growl, Oluna gestured. One of the runes on her robe flashed a brilliant red.

"I didn't do anything!" Everys's voice burst from her.

Oluna stared at her. Then she laughed, a short bark, and wagged a finger at Everys.

"Oh, but you are clever. What was it, a virus in the scriber? Did you corrupt the pattern of the rune somehow, just in case?"

Everys gaped at her. She hadn't done anything like that at all. "Why would I deliberately sabotage the research?"

Uncertainty and fury warred across Oluna's face. Then she whirled on her attendants. "Bring what she had on her when we captured her. The answer must be there!"

Two of the robed attendants hurried off of the platform. Everys twisted in the air. Narius offered her a weak smile, but she could see the color draining from his cheeks.

"Oluna..." she said.

Oluna glanced in their direction and snarled. "I suppose we can't have him bleed out and waste all of that precious ink."

She waved a hand, and another rune on her robe flashed. The unseen hands holding Everys in place released her and both she and Narius dropped to the stone floor. She scrambled to his side, tearing fabric from the end of her skirt so she could bind up his wounds. Oluna barked an order at two of her attendants to watch them. Two burly men stepped out of the crowd and loomed over Everys as she tied the makeshift bandages to Narius's wrist.

"Everys..." he whispered.

She shushed him, then pulled him close and held him. She wanted to do so much more, but she knew two things with absolute certainty.

First, she shouldn't antagonize Oluna. In her state of mind, angered and frustrated and confused, she would lash out if Everys called attention to them.

And second, if she remained patient, Oluna might bring her everything she needed to stop her.

89

There was so much Narius wanted to say, so much he wanted to do. But his wrist burned like fire and he felt woozy. How much blood had he lost? Everys cradled his head in her lap, stroking his hair, her gaze locked on Oluna, who paced back and forth in front of them.

Narius didn't care. Instead, he stared up at his wife. His incredible, miraculous, indefatigable wife. He had been so sure that he was going to die, that Oluna would spill his life out where the Scriptotum once stood. But Everys was here. She was real. That was enough for him. So he savored the way the breeze played with her long hair, the way the sunlight caressed her cheeks. If she was going to be the last thing he saw, he wanted to sear it into his mind and carry it with him into whatever waited beyond.

The two attendants returned, carrying a bag and a strange device. Oluna conferred with them, looking in the bag and inspecting the device. He could practically feel the fury boiling off her.

"Narius," Everys whispered. "I don't know if we're going to get the chance, but if we do..."

He tried to lean closer, to drink in her voice.

"There's a ball in the bag. It can disrupt runes. I'm going to try to get my hands on that device. It might be our only chance to stop them."

Wait, she was trying to make a plan? Now? He wanted to laugh—if it didn't hurt so much. He shouldn't have expected anything else. "How?"

She smiled at him. "I have no idea."

A cough rattled through his chest.

Oluna whirled on them, pulling a gray ball from the bag. "What is this?"

She stormed over to them and shoved the ball in Everys's face. Everys leaned away from it, turning her face so it wouldn't touch her.

"Soap," Everys said. "I thought you could use it after camping in these ruins."

Oluna backhanded Everys. Her head snapped around, but Everys turned back to Oluna and glared at her.

"Fine. Then what's this?" Oluna gestured toward the device. "Some sort of laser?"

"Prototype weapon," Everys said. "Redtale thought I should be armed when we came here."

Oluna's eyes narrowed. She tossed the ball, and it landed on the bag. Everys sucked in a sharp breath, but she didn't react otherwise. Oluna stared at them, clearly furious. But then a feral grin slowly spread across her lips. Narius shifted. He didn't like the predatory gleam in the mage-king's eyes.

"Bring me his blood," Oluna said.

An attendant pressed the bowl into her hands.

"Now hold her down," Oluna added.

Narius tried sit up, to raise his arms to block them from touching his wife, but one of the guards dragged him away from Everys. The other snared Everys by the shoulders and pushed her to the stone floor. Oluna knelt next to her and, after dipping her finger in the bowl, started to draw a rune on Everys that Narius didn't recognize.

"You don't want to cooperate? Fine. Let's find out what happens when we cast that truth-telling rune using your husband's blood, shall we?"

Everys's eyes went wide and she tried to fight free, but two more attendants rushed forward and pinned her arms and legs.

With a triumphant smile, Oluna activated the rune and rose. Blue light exploded from Everys's body, swirling around the two women, then coalesced into a ribbon that connected Everys's eyes to Oluna's. Both of their mouths tore open in a silent shout, although Narius couldn't miss the jubilation on Oluna's face.

Then the light vanished and Everys sagged to the stone. Oluna stumbled, her eyes darting back and forth, as if reading something hovering before her.

"No! You have to know why this isn't working! We both saw the same translation. What do you know that..." Oluna gasped, her head tipping to one side. "Wait, what's this? Everys, what did you create?"

Everys groaned where she lay. "No..."

"Oh, yes. This is... The artistry. The passion. You could have been the most powerful among us." Oluna turned to her attendants. "Scrying runes! Focus on Bastion, the Shade, Utuaa, The Stone. All the cities!"

Several attendants rushed forward, producing vials of ink, and began drawing runes around the perimeter of the platform. As they did, Oluna dipped her finger in the bowl of Narius's blood and started to draw something in front of them.

"Once again, I should thank you, Everys," Oluna said. "The puzzle rune may have failed, but you brought me something I can use to still fulfill our destiny."

Everys sucked in another sharp breath, a protest squeaking out of her. Narius frowned. What did that mean?

One by one, the attendants activated their runes. The air above them shimmered, then images appeared, almost as if they were projected onto invisible vid screens. The images were cities Oluna had mentioned, but he also recognized Wrine and Sholn and the Plissk Sanctuary Oasis. The attendants who had cast the runes stood in front of the images and began a strange sort of dance, waving their arms and twisting their hands. As they did, the imagery zoomed in to the streets, showing people going about their lives. In another, he saw Innana seated on her throne in Utuaa, sharing what looked like a tender moment with Planka. In still another, Challix and Redtale paced in what looked like a strategy room created by the Cold Light. In yet another, Auriel Zammit was stretched out in a bed, her chest wrapped in bandages.

Oluna finished her rune and looked up at Everys, glee burning in her eyes. "And now you both can watch our enemies face our justice!"

With that, she smacked her hand on the rune. The pattern blazed with a bright red light. Oluna threw her arms open again, but this time, she was lifted up from the ground, her head tipped toward the sky.

Narius stared at her in horror. She looked just like the person he had seen in Utuaa, the one who had cast the rune during the parade.

His gaze caught on what was happening on the streets of Bastion. The people on the streets stumbled and keeled over, their arms wrapped around their middles. Smoke erupted from their bodies, swirling together into a dark vortex. Narius's gaze skipped from image to image. The same thing was happening to the people in each of the images.

And then he felt it, a gnawing void blossoming inside his chest. He gasped, but the painful sensation slithered through him, consuming more and more of him. Smoke rose from his arms, his legs, his chest. He winced and ground his teeth. He looked up at Everys. Whatever she wanted to do, they had better do it soon.

Everys watched in horror as the people revealed by the scrying runes doubled over, the black smoke feeding the plague rune rising and mixing. She had braced herself for the rune to inflict her as well, but oddly, it didn't. Maybe it recognized its creator? Or maybe she was too similar to Oluna to be considered her enemy.

But Narius. He moaned and writhed, black mist rising from his body.

They had to act. They had to act now.

"Remember, Narius. The gray ball. Go!"

With that shout, Everys launched herself for the laser. Narius scrambled, picking up the gray ball. Some of the attendants shouted and started after them.

Everys scooped up the laser and switched it on. Its high-pitched hum was immediately lost in the tumult around them. Everys scrolled through the prepared runes and picked a combat rune. She clicked in the firing sequence and aimed the laser at a point on the stone platform between her and Oluna's attendants. A red speck of light appeared on the stone and quickly sketched out the rune. Within a second, a column of fire erupted from the pavement, spreading out to create a wall. Everys gaped at the result, a thick line of blue flames that was so hot, she worried it would melt the stone they stood on.

She glanced over at Narius. He had scooped up the gray ball, rolling it in his hands. Then, with all his might, he threw it at the plague rune.

The moment the ball hit the pavement, it burst in a puff of dust. The effect was instantaneous. The rune flared, flickered, and then blinked out. Oluna tumbled out of the air, landing in a heap on the stones with a grunt.

Everys looked to the scrying runes. The people in the images recovered, although they were clearly shaken.

But Oluna wasn't done yet. She stood and fixed her gaze on Narius.

"Do you know what you did?" she shrieked, and five different runes on her robes blazed with brilliant red light.

Narius rose off the ground, clawing at his throat.

"None of you understand our glorious purpose. We will not be denied until our destiny is fulfilled. We will destroy you all!"

Everys's heart seized. What could she do? She didn't know how the runes in Oluna's robe worked! Anything she tried would be worthless. If only the puzzle rune did something!

Wait. As she thought of the failed spell, she remembered the translation that P'layvo had shared, the accurate one. The words tumbled rapidly through her mind and she realized that they had all been wrong about the puzzle rune the whole time.

"'Give me what I deepest desire...'" Her eyes widened. "'So long as I walk this path for you! Unleash your power, your strength, reshape the world to *our* will.'"

That's why the rune had failed every time they tried to cast it. It wasn't about reshaping the world to the caster's will alone. It was about bringing about the Singularity's will. The person casting the rune had to align her will with His.

That was the answer. That was the solution. That's what needed to happen here.

She looked at the laser. Then, with a shaking finger, she called up the program that would allow her to manually enter a rune. She started to trace the puzzle rune into the interface. And as she did, she offered up a prayer.

I know that I've struggled against Your will for most of my life. And right now, I desperately want things to go my way, for Oluna to be stopped and for us to survive. But it's not about what I want. It never has been. I'm sorry for all the times I've struggled. I'm sorry for all the times I've doubted. When I do this, may it bring about Your will.

As soon as she had finished tracing the rune, she aimed it at the ground and activated the laser. The red dot quickly traced a tiny version of the puzzle rune on the ground.

At first, nothing happened, and Everys hung her head, sure that she was about to witness her husband's death. She could hear the attendants shouting, feel the heat of the fire. She hefted up the array and started looking through the prepared runes. Maybe there was something she could—

But then, a brilliant beam of light erupted from the puzzle rune with a thunderous roar. Oluna shrieked and fell onto her face. The beam grew thicker, expanding across the dais. In an instant, it had swallowed up Oluna in its radiance.

Then the wall of light slid over Everys, bleaching out the world. But in the split second before everything turned white-hot, she thought she saw something: a powerful figure towering over the dais. A brilliant rune she didn't recognize shone on His chest as He pushed His arms outward, as if pushing the light itself. As she gaped at Him, He looked down at her, and His lips curled into a gentle smile, one that was washed away as the light overpowered her. It sounded as if the entire world was being torn apart, the shattering of rocks and splintering of trees joining the roar with their own voices.

In that singular instant, Everys's mind opened, and impressions flooded in. Of a boundless love that had never run out. Of sheer delight of a creation continuing as it had been designed. Of the certainty that her people's story wasn't finished, that there were more chapters yet to come.

And then she was overwhelmed by strange ideas. A living rune, a being that wasn't made of light but was light, somehow drained and humbled yet so much richer and fuller for it. A family, not hers, but familiar. Promises made, promises that would be kept, in a way that no one would expect but that would reshape the world.

Then nothing. Silence. And the light that stabbed through Everys's closed eyes faded.

She risked a peek. The brilliance was gone. The rune had disappeared. And Narius and Everys sat alone on the platform. Oluna and her attendants had disappeared, and somehow, Everys knew they wouldn't be coming back. She rose, her legs shaky. She turned around and then stopped, her mind locking up.

Nekek the Bright was gone, scrubbed from existence. The ruins had vanished. Her chest heaved, not sure how she should feel. A part of her was sad. There had been so much history in this place, so much that they might have discovered or recovered or learned about her people. But at the same time, Nekek the Bright was synonymous with so much pain and suffering. Maybe it was better this way. If the rune did what she thought it did, then this is what the Singularity wanted, so it must be better this way.

"Everys?"

She whirled around. Narius sat up, and much to her surprise, he looked better. The color had returned to his skin, and he rose to his own feet, stronger than he should have been. He glanced around in confusion, then tugged the makeshift bandage she had used off his wrist. The skin underneath was whole, the cut healed. He turned to her, confusion painted across his face.

Everys launched herself at him, slamming into him with enough force that they almost tumbled to the ground. She caught his face in her hands and kissed him, savoring the feel and the taste of him, something she thought she would never experience again. There was so much she had to tell him, so much she wanted to hear from him, but for that moment, she contented herself with his presence.

He finally, gently, pulled away from her. "I'm glad to see you too."

She laughed and swatted at his arm.

He looked around. "What happened?"

Everys closed her eyes and smiled. "It's over."

Much to Everys's surprise, a small sliver of the city had survived. They spotted it from the Scriptotum's platform. Most of the ground had been smoothed over and turned to something that looked like blue glass. But in the middle of it all, a wedge of stone and brick jutted out of the ground. It appeared to be a wall from the palace, but why had this one place been spared? With no better options, they headed in that direction.

After they had clambered off the dais, Narius waited for her, then tentatively offered her his hand. She laughed at his awkwardness. He looked like an uncertain suitor meeting a woman for the first time. But then her mirth died. There was something wrong. Even though she hadn't seen him in months, she could tell.

"What?" she prompted.

He frowned, studying the blasted ground. "When Oluna cast that... that rune and the smoke started rising from my body, it reminded me of something. Something I witnessed..."

His voice trailed off as if he didn't want to finish the thought. But she knew it had to be said.

"Something you saw in Utuaa," she whispered.

He looked up at her. "Then that was you."

She winced and nodded.

"You cast the same rune on Utuaa." His voice was flat.

"I did." And she almost tried to explain it, to offer excuses as to why she had done it. But how many times had her people crafted similar excuses in this very place? So she said what she needed to. "I shouldn't have. Did anyone... did anyone die?"

He shook his head. "I don't think so. At least, Innana didn't hear any reports, and believe me, she would have known."

He fell silent, studying her face.

"Are we okay?" she asked quietly.

His brows pinched together, but then he smiled. "No, we're not. We've both been through so much, and yes, we've probably both done things we shouldn't have. But all we can do now is do better and move forward, right?"

Relief flooded through her. "And walk a new path together. I promise."

They continued to the last remaining bit of the city. As they rounded the wall, a figure jumped on Narius, tackling him to the ground. Another two charged at Everys, each one holding a brick like a weapon. It took her a moment to recognize Quartus and Yusra. Even Paine was armed, although he hung back. Everys turned to see that Kavi straddled Narius's chest.

"Get off me!" Narius barked.

Kavi scrambled away, her eyes wide. Then a brilliant smile split her face, and she hugged him tightly. Quartus and Yusra dropped their makeshift weapons and embraced Everys, both at the same time. An instant later, they let go so they could hug Narius as well. Kavi and Everys shared a nodded greeting. Paine stepped forward and offered Narius a stiff hug. Then, they looked at each other. Clearly, no one knew what to say or do.

Finally, Quartus broke the silence. "So now what?"

Narius heaved a long sigh, smiled at his brother, and said, "We go home."

"Sounds great," Quartus said. "How?"

That was when Everys heard it: the sound of engines in the distance, growing louder with every passing moment. Narius turned to look for the source, stepping to one side to peek around the rubble. He stumbled back a step and whirled around.

"Dalark soldiers!" he hissed.

Sure enough, ten transports, painted in a dark green camouflage pattern with Dalark insignias emblazoned on the side, came into view. They quickly surrounded the little island of rubble.

"Do you think you can do anything about this?" Quartus whispered to Yusra.

"I can try, but I don't exactly have my credentials on me," she replied.

As the doors to the lead transport opened, Narius raised his hands and Everys followed suit. Her stomach twisted at the irony of the situation. They had survived Oluna's scheme, only to be captured by the Dalark? Hopefully Innana would make good on her promises of friendship and cooperation!

But then, much to her shock, Tormod emerged, a gigantic grin splitting his face.

"I apologize for my tardiness," Tormod said. "I got here as quickly as I could."

As Tormod spoke, the doors on half the transports burst open and soldiers spilled out. They fanned out, their weapons up and ready, but they didn't aim at Everys or the others. Instead, they seemed to be searching for hostiles.

Narius's mouth dropped open. "What are you doing with them?"

"Oh, it's quite the tale, Your Strength." Tormod dropped from the transport. "When Oluna's minions tried to shoot me with those tranquilizers, I activated my *reshi'zhad* tattoo, hoping it would take me to safety."

"Your what?" Narius asked.

Everys touched his arm. When he looked at her, she whispered she would explain later.

"I thought I would wind up in the Shade again, but instead, I popped up in the middle of these soldiers' encampment in the Beachhead. Thankfully, they had the presence of mind not to shoot me. I pleaded my case to their commander, who was reluctant to help until he contacted his superiors. We were sent here at the express order of Empress Innana. Thankfully, that light show led us right here."

One of the Dalark soldiers, apparently satisfied the area was secure, trotted up to Narius and saluted sharply. "We are ordered to bring you to the nearest Dynasty base for further evacuation. If you'd come with us, please?"

Everys didn't hesitate. She started for the first transport, snaring Narius's hand to drag him after her. With every step, she could feel the tension flow from her body. It was over. It was finally over.

90

Unfortunately, the trip home was more complicated than Narius expected. When they eventually arrived at the recently reoccupied Firebase Forward Double-Zero, a new dilemma occurred to them. Where should they go? While Everys expected everyone to return to the Shade, Paine insisted they return to the palace in Bastion. Narius was actually relieved to hear his wife and his best friend argue about something. It was a nice sliver of normality in an otherwise chaotic situation. But when Quartus piped up and pointed out that the palace was little more than a collection of horrors spawned by Oluna and her ilk, Paine relented and agreed to go to the Shade. The group commandeered a military skimmer and Narius ordered the pilot to take them into the Cold Light forest. The skimmer's interior wasn't as lavish as Narius's usual transportation, but he and Everys found a quiet corner of the cabin to snuggle up and enjoy one another's presence.

Upon arriving in the Shade, excited individuals who were eager to celebrate their apparent victory swamped them. Just the sight of that many cheerful people was unsettling to Narius. Not that he didn't appreciate their enthusiasm, but there was just so much: meeting Everys's mother and sister, being introduced to a group who called themselves "the Illuminates," seeing that Strategist Overturn had been grafted to the Cold Light. So many people wanted to share so much. He felt far too overwhelmed to do much more than smile and nod.

Eventually, Trule of all people put an end to it all, insisting that Everys and Narius be given their privacy. She whisked them away to a rustic but comfortable room and then practically locked them inside. Finally, as the sun went down, they tumbled into bed and fell into a deep and thankfully dreamless sleep.

At the middle of First Watch, Everys emerged from her chambers, dressed and ready for the day. She jumped, startled to find Challix waiting for her with a waiting smile.

"How are you this morning, Blessed?" Challix asked, her voice light.

Everys offered a grin in return. "Happy to have my husband again."

Challix chuckled knowingly, teasing a blush from Everys's cheeks. Nothing like that had happened the night before. Both she and Narius had simply been too tired from everything. They had been separated from each other for so long, it would take a while to see how their experiences had changed each other. As much as she longed for that kind of intimacy, there were other forms they needed first.

"So, what's on the agenda today?" she asked.

Challix grimaced. "Unfortunately, quite a bit. We have several knots to untangle."

"Like what?" Everys asked. What could remain after making peace with the Dalark, defeating Brencis, and ending the mage-kings' threat once and for all?

"As wonderful as it is that your husband has returned, we have to sort through who is really in charge of the Dynasty. Traditionally, it's always been the king, with the queen serving in a more ceremonial fashion. While you certainly defied that trend before, after Narius's disappearance, you took on a more active role. One could make the argument that you are the true ruler of the Dynasty, not him, especially since he was presumed dead for so long."

Everys gaped at Challix. "That's absurd."

"Maybe, but it is a question that needs wrangling. We also have the challenge of sorting through who is part of the ruler's council of advisers. You named me your vizier, but given Paine's experience and standing, it would be legitimate for the ruler, whoever that is, to restore him to that position. Or given Paine's apparent disloyalty, you could have him set aside. During your tenure here, you included some unconventional participants in your council of advisers, such as the members of the Illuminates or the grafted. Will they continue to be a part of any future decision-making?

"And then there's the question of where to set up our seat of government. I'm sure everyone is expecting us to return to Bastion, but from what I've learned, much of that city has been destroyed. Do we return to a city in such a condition? Or do we do what the Dynasty did when Elregan was destroyed and move the capital elsewhere? We could stay here, in the Shade, but Brencis's missile barrage did a great deal of damage here. So do we choose a different city? If we do, what are the criteria that we would..." Challix's voice trailed off, and she frowned as Everys burst out laughing, almost doubled over. "I don't understand, Blessed. These are all legitimate concerns we will have to discuss!"

Everys wiped tears from her cheeks. "I know they are. I'm laughing because, in the middle of all of this, you took the time to think through all of these issues. And I love you for that."

Everys caught her vizier in a hug. Challix flinched, but then she too laughed and hugged Everys back.

"So does this mean I have your vote to remain vizier?" Challix asked.

Everys laughed even harder, then the two friends headed for the war room, their arms linked, Challix's list temporarily forgotten.

Trule and the other girls had set up a table heaped with pastries and fruits, along with an assortment of drinks. Everys and Challix were the first to arrive, and so they eagerly helped themselves to their favorites. Slowly but surely, the others arrived for the inevitable meeting. Paine first, followed by Quartus and Yusra, Redtale, Kavi and Tormod, then the rest of Everys's advisers. The last person to arrive was Narius, who seemed a bit surprised when the room erupted in genuine applause. He stood in the doorway and blushed, then looked to Everys as if she was going to save him.

She didn't. Instead, she clapped louder and mouthed the words: *I love you so much.*

Eventually, the applause died down, and everyone took their place. There was a bit of awkward jockeying as neither Narius nor Paine knew where they were supposed to stand, but eventually they all settled in. The council turned to Everys and Narius, their expressions expectant.

Everys started to speak, but then Narius did too. They stumbled over each other's words before both retreated into an awkward silence. Maybe Challix was right. This was going to be trickier than Everys had thought. Finally, Narius motioned for her to continue with a small smile.

"I want to start by thanking all of you for your help," Everys said. "This has been an arduous journey. If it wasn't for all of you, I'm not sure we'd be here. So thank you. It's my hope that all of you will be remembered as heroes for generations to come."

Most of the advisers looked abashed or uncomfortable at the praise.

"So who do I see about getting a statue erected?" Quartus asked. "I mean, I'm getting one, right? Or maybe a holiday named after me?"

The others chuckled, although Yusra elbowed Quartus in the ribs.

"Let's start with the most pressing issues first: the military situation. Overturn?" Everys prompted.

Overturn turned to her, the vines that encircled him rustling. "I'm pleased to report that over eighty percent of the forces Brencis brought to the edge of the forest surrendered. The trick now will be corralling the Cold Light's army. It's been a while since the Cold Light has had to do something like this, and the task is more difficult after Brencis's missile strike killed so many Cold Light."

Everys's heart lurched. So many lives lost, and she had had no idea.

Overturn shuddered as Firestruck took direct control of him. "We have the matter well in hand, Everys Queen. We knew that this would be our commitment when we said we would go to war for you. It is a burden we gladly bear."

"What about the Dalark's withdrawal?" Paine asked.

The strategist shuddered again, then sighed. "The Dalark are following Empress Innana's orders. But we're struggling. There's no clear chain of command that our units will recognize. I'm worried that many of the commanders are going to go mercenary."

"How about the noble houses?" Narius asked. "Any word from them?"

Challix cleared her throat. "We've tried to reach out to most of them and only heard from about a third. Those who have replied have pledged their fealty. But I have the same concerns that Overturn does about the military. Unless we can secure support from more noble houses, we could see a great deal of chaos, or possibly even a civil war."

Everys winced at the thought. The situation was probably worse than they were making it sound. But it wasn't just the noble houses they had to worry about. What about the subjugated races? She glanced at Redtale and remembered what she had said about The Stone. With Brencis gone and so much of the Dynasty pitched into chaos, she wouldn't be surprised if each of the races made a bid for independence. She doubted the Dynasty was in any position to stop them, but if that happened amid a civil war between the noble houses, what had happened to them the past few months might look like children at play.

Before she could spiral into panic, Narius reached over and took her hand, giving it a gentle squeeze. It almost felt like his strength was flowing into her. Her stuttering heart calmed, and she offered him a shaky smile.

"That is all very dire, but let's not lose sight of what we've gained. With Empress Innnana on the throne in Utuaa, we don't have to worry about the Dalark anymore," Narius said.

"But we don't know how the other nations will respond," Challix said. "If they sense that we're in turmoil, they could—"

Narius held up a hand to calm her, then smiled at Paine. "I think she's trying to take your job, old friend."

Paine offered him a weary smile, but much to Everys's surprise, didn't reply.

"Look, these concerns are valid. But let's start small. What is the first thing we have to do?" Narius asked.

That prompted a round of arguments among the advisers. Different people suggested various courses of actions, highlighting competing priorities. Within a few moments, their own discussion had spiraled out of control.

Everys sighed and decided to let them argue. Maybe they would wear each other out. Better yet, maybe they would stumble over a solution. As she listened, she snaked her hand over to Narius and squeezed his.

He smiled at her, then chuckled.

"What?" she prompted.

"When you told me what that 'puzzle rune' did, I actually hoped that things would be easier. But it really doesn't feel like much has been reshaped. It's just the same old problems all over again. So did it only wipe out the mage-kings?"

Everys considered the question. Memories of those strange ideas and concepts she had seen in Nekek the Bright flooded through her, then quickly faded. She still didn't understand what any of them actually meant, so she shrugged. "I don't know. Maybe. Would that be so bad?"

"I suppose not. I just wish that He had done more."

She glanced at the people around the table. Even though they were locked in arguments, some of them becoming heated, she didn't sense hostility. Just people who were passionately voicing their opinions and trying to find compromises between them. She couldn't help but smile. They were all here. They could all work together.

"Maybe He did," she said. "I guess we'll just have to wait and see."

Epilogue

"Everys, are you ready? They're going to be here any moment."

She shot an annoyed look at the door. He had insisted on them sleeping in this morning in spite of the impending invasion. And then he had monopolized the bathroom for far too long. Ever since he'd grown that beard, he had taken to preening in front of the mirror. He had barely left her any time to get ready. But then her annoyance melted away into a smile. Even though many of the memories of their earliest years together had faded a little, she still remembered how close she had come to losing him so many times. She'd never take his presence for granted again.

Everys finally emerged from the bathroom and almost collided with Trule. The Plissk girl jumped back and offered her a nervous laugh.

"He sent you to get me?" Everys asked.

Trule shrugged, and Everys rolled her eyes, which elicited a chuckle from Trule. The two of them swept out of the bedroom and into the hall.

Before they could make it to the dining room, though, there was a knock at the front door. Trule scurried to answer it, and Everys paused in the main hall to see who it was. She laughed when Occ shuffled in.

"How many times have I told you that you don't have to knock?" she chided him gently.

Occ dipped his head and made a halfway decent imitation of a human chuckle. "I'm sorry, Blessed. Old habits die hard."

"And how many times do I have to tell you that you can call me Everys? I haven't been queen for"—She did the math—"three years now."

"That may be, but you will always be my queen. The same is true for Narius."

Everys's grin widened. "I'll be sure to tell Narius you think that."

Occ straightened up. "No! That's not what I meant at all!"

"What's going on?" Narius asked as he came into the hall.

"Apparently Occ thinks you should start wearing my dresses and we should all call you 'Blessed.'" Everys said.

"Oh?" Narius regarded the Diradae for a moment with mock seriousness. "Do you and I need to go in the backyard so I can defeat you in one-on-one combat again?"

Occ went still. Then he rose to his full height. "Only if you want me to beat you like I did last time."

Everys and Narius stared at Occ, but then Narius burst out laughing.

"That's much better, Occ! You've been practicing."

Occ dropped back down, his upper and lower hands wringing each other. "A little. I still can't keep up such an angry attitude."

Narius ushered Occ deeper into the house, listening as the Diradae made many offers to create works of art to help them decorate. That's usually what happened when he came to visit.

Trule approached Everys. "Did his threat sound realistic this time?"

"Almost." She turned to Trule. "Has anyone else arrived yet?"

"Challix arrived at the end of First Watch. So did Yllana and the Illuminates. I think I saw the governor's transport pull in," Trule said.

That was all that Everys needed to hear. She hurried out the front door.

The cool air caressed her skin, and she paused for a moment to inhale the sweet fragrance that danced on the wind. She had never found out what flowers produced that scent. The Cold Light claimed they didn't know, but she suspected the Yoreroot had made sure that they blossomed near their home. They had been so solicitous when Narius had told them he wanted to build a home for Everys and him at the edge of the forest. They had offered to reshape the land, create a waterfall, anything to make their experience there more pleasant. Narius had refused, saying that the natural peace and beauty were enough.

He had chosen a good place to build. The forest itself wrapped around their estate on three sides. Rolling green hills spread out in front of them, between which she could catch just the tiniest glimpse of the Water Bearer's Repose's blue waters. It was hard to believe that a place like this existed.

But rather than savor the view, Everys focused on the transport that had come to a halt. A moment later, the door opened and Redtale emerged. She turned and offered a wave to Everys, who flew down the walk and threw her arms around her friend's neck.

"I wasn't sure you'd be able to make it!" Everys said.

"I was worried too," Redtale admitted. "We've been having issues with the reconstruction teams. I thought I was going to have to break some horns to get them to listen, but Rockflow knew which rocks to kick out. They caved two days ago. So, is the Prime Minister going to be here?"

Everys shook her head. "Auriel has her hands full with the trade negotiations with Rioka. She sent her regrets last week."

Redtale grunted. "Probably for the best. I know how much you hate it when she and I discuss politics at these sorts of events."

She definitely didn't like it, but she understood the need. The past four years had been difficult for everyone, what with Narius and Everys's decision to abdicate the throne in favor of forming a new government. There had been the endless negotiations with the noble houses and each of the ethnarchs, not to mention figuring out how to structure the new system to be as fair as possible for everyone while acknowledging the injustices that so many people had endured for so long.

Thankfully, Auriel Zammit had stepped forward as a genuine leader, which was part of the reason she had been elected as the first Prime Minister of what most people simply called the Cooperative. Thankfully, Narius and Everys had been able to sit out of most of the wrangling that led to its creation, although Everys sometimes had to chastise him when he got a little too interested.

Everys started to escort her friend into the house, but then she heard another transport pull up. She turned in time to see Galan, Mama, Auntie Kyna, and Tormod emerge. Redtale excused herself as Everys went over to greet the next batch of guests. Kyna tucked her hand in Tormod's elbow as Everys approached.

"My dear, it is so good to see you. Retirement suits you, it seems," Tormod said.

"You as well. You don't miss being spymaster at all?" Everys asked.

"Jumping into dangerous situations for nebulous reasons? Hardly. Besides, I have this one to keep track of now." He patted his sister's hand.

Kyna smirked at Tormod, then turned to Everys. "Thank you for inviting me. I know I may not be your favorite relative—"

"We're not actually related," Everys reminded her.

"—but it's good to be with family for *Ez'mazzonal*, isn't it?" Kyna said, as if Everys hadn't spoken. "I bring greetings from the conclave in Bastion. They send their love and thanks, as always."

Everys couldn't help but smile. One of the last things that Narius did before he abdicated was push through his Siporan Restoration Act, a series of laws aimed at helping her people. It allowed them to once again practice toratropic magic in the open, something that caused a fair bit of controversy among the other residents of the Cooperative. Most of them calmed down when they saw that there was nothing to fear, although there were still some who held on to the old prejudices. Siporans were also given a seat on the Ethnarch Parliament, which had been folded into the Cooperative's governing system, along with the Hall of All Voices and the newly formed Noble Senate. And finally, in a move that had taken some negotiation with Empress Innana, Narius had gifted the former Demilitarized Zone to the Siporan people to be used however they saw fit. Several settlements had already sprung up in her people's homeland and there was talk of trying to rebuild a capital, just one that would be far away from what people had taken to calling the Scar, where Nekek the Bright had once stood.

Kyna and Tormod went into the house, and Everys greeted Mama and Galan with a hug. Galan was already starting to gush about the new research that she, Tolistan, and P'layvo were engaged in with their new funding from Spanica Trentwether. Everys tried to listen, but she couldn't focus when she noticed how upset Mama was.

"What's wrong?" she asked.

"Nothing," Mama said, then hurried into the house.

Everys turned to Galan. "He refused to see her again?"

Galan sighed heavily and nodded. "The Cold Light were even willing to let him come here. But he refused."

Everys winced. That was a lingering wound that seemed like it might never heal. Even as the Dynasty transformed into the Cooperative, even as the Siporans found their place in a new world, even as Narius and Everys forged a new life away from Bastion and all the political games, they couldn't seem to make headway with Papa. Every time someone tried to visit him, he refused for one reason or another.

"Is he at least healthy?" Everys asked.

Galan nodded. "That's what Yllana tells me. In good health physically. They've moved him so he can take part in worship at a conclave if he wants."

"Has he?" Everys asked, a flicker of hope lighting within her.

Galan wouldn't meet her gaze. She shook her head. Everys stifled a sigh, the small ember winking out. Maybe that would change someday. She hoped so. But clearly there was more work to be done.

"What about Tilash?" Everys asked. "We invited her too."

Galan grimaced, which was answer enough. Several years ago, their brother had married a woman named Tilash. For the past several years, Everys had tried to include her in the family get-togethers, but the years their family had snubbed her had taken its toll and she had yet to accept.

"I hate to change the subject, but Mama wanted to know. Is Heronus going to be here today?" Galan whispered.

Everys winced at the mention of her stepson. "No. We invited both of them, but Viara refused. They took a trip to Elscontin instead."

Galan breathed out slowly. "That's probably for the best. Just between you and me, she hated it when Viara was here for Downcasting a few months ago. And seeing Heronus just makes Mama sad."

That was an understatement. After Brencis's defeat, Viara had divorced him. When her child was born, she had named him after the king who destroyed Nekek the Bright. She probably thought herself clever, but it hadn't mattered to Narius. He tried to do what was best for Heronus, doting on him whenever he could visit. And Everys had to admit, the young boy was charming and intelligent in a way that frightened her. Hopefully, he would take after his father more than his mother.

But the thought of Heronus quirked her mouth into a smile.

"What?" Galan asked.

"I'll tell you later," Everys promised, then led her into the house.

As soon as they stepped in the door, shadows billowed up from one corner, and three figures stepped out. Quartus naturally led the way, once again dressed in a sharply tailored suit that somehow blended traditional Dalark ribbonware and the trendier styles of the Cooperative. On someone else, it would have looked ridiculous, but Quartus somehow pulled it off. He then turned and took his wife's hand as Yusra stepped out of the portal. And finally, Kavi popped out as well, an apologetic smile on her face.

Sorry, she signed. *You know how much he likes to make an entrance.*

Quartus looked around, then his face twisted into disappointment. "Only two of you saw? We have to do this again where more people will be surprised."

Yusra swatted his arm. "Absolutely not. You'll just have to be satisfied with what you have."

"When I'm with you, that's all too easy," Quartus said, then leaned over to kiss her.

Kavi made an exaggerated gagging sound. *I think I just threw up in my mouth a little.*

Yusra ignored her and gave Everys a big hug, then greeted Galan. Then they, along with Kavi, headed for the dining room. Quartus watched them go, although he was staring at Yusra with a fondness that caused Everys to laugh.

He looked at her with a smirk. "What?"

"I'm sorry, I'm still having a difficult time adjusting to the thought of you as a happily married man," she said.

He chuckled. "Me as well. But like I said, Yusra makes it easy. She always keeps me on my toes."

"Good." Everys paused. "How are things in Utuaa?"

Quartus grimaced, prompting Everys to laugh. After the Cooperative formed, Quartus and Yusra were named as "Diplomats at Large" for both them and the Imperium. That meant a lot of travel back and forth between the two capitals, although Everys had heard that they had been spending a lot of time with Empress Innana lately.

"Tense," Quartus finally said. "Until recently, Erecone and Ksann have been content being locked in the Imperium's orbit. But ever since the Cooperative formed, those nations have been wondering if their relationship with the Imperium shouldn't be modified. Innana is none too pleased. She wants the Cooperative's word to ignore any rebellions, but Zammit wants the Imperium to use a lighter touch. I'm sure there's a way for us all to get what we want, but unless everyone is willing to sit down and talk, we'll get nowhere quickly."

Everys smiled, marveling at how mature Quartus sounded. When they'd first met, he had been so cocky and self-centered. Now, though, she could hear the burden he carried. And he did so without complaining. Well, not much complaining, and it was usually good-natured.

Quartus grimaced. "I'm sorry. Listen to me, prattling on about foreign affairs like an actual diplomat. Where's the wine? I could use a drink."

"Narius has pulled a few choice vintages out of the cellar," Everys said. "He says they're pretty good."

"'He says?' Isn't he sharing with you?" Quartus asked, his voice teasing. "Do I need to talk to him about that?"

Everys smiled, her stomach flipping. "No, it's fine. Just go ahead."

Quartus offered her a jaunty smirk and headed for the dining room. She turned to close the front door but jumped when she saw Paine in the doorway.

"Hello, Everys," he said.

"Paine."

They stepped closer together and tried to hug each other. But even though it had been years, there was still a distance between them. She had tried to overcome it, and she knew he had been trying as well. But maybe all they would ever be was cordial. And she had to be okay with that.

They pulled apart, and he offered her an awkward smile. "So... have you told anyone else yet?"

Everys's eyes widened. How did he know? Narius swore he'd let her make the announcement.

"Never fear. Your husband didn't tell me. But he has said some cryptic things to me as of late that has led me to certain conclusions."

Oh. That helped her to relax, but just a little. Had other people figured it out? They had been looking forward to surprising everyone.

"So," she said. "What have you been doing lately?"

Paine sighed heavily. "I am still... searching. I had hoped, given the chaos still nibbling at the Cooperative's edges, that the government would need my help. But even though Maotoa continues to stir up trouble for everyone, even though the Cooperative is still struggling to rebuild everything that's been destroyed, very few trust me."

Everys winced in sympathy. No one knew where Maotoa fit anymore, especially not the Maotoans, with some wanting to stay within the Imperium, others to rejoin the Cooperative, while still others advocated for independence. And Cosena and her parents weren't making the situation easier for anyone.

"In the meantime, I have been teaching at various schools. Pellio's Legacy. The Wrine Potentium. Even The Trench," Paine grimaced. "It is enough to keep me out of trouble, or so my father says."

Before she could reply, Narius came out of the dining room. "I may have to head down to the cellar and get some more wine. Quartus has already challenged Occ and Style to a drinking contest, and I'd rather they do so with a cheaper vintage than..." His face brightened when he saw Paine. "You made it!"

"Hello, Narius."

The two friends embraced. Everys smiled when she saw that Paine actually relaxed.

"Well," Narius clapped his hands together. "Now that you're here, let's go in, shall we? I think we've made them all wait long enough."

Paine nodded, and they walked into the dining room. Chairs surrounded a long table, except for a space that was empty for Occ to settle in. Their guests had broken into knots, mixing and laughing and talking in ways that Everys wouldn't have ever expected. She smiled, warmth spreading through her chest. This was the kind of *Ez'mazzonal* she enjoyed, the kind that celebrated the connections they all shared, whether as family or friends or some mix of the two.

Narius picked up a glass of wine and smiled at the assembled guests. "My friends, if I could have your attention please? Everys has an announcement."

Everys smiled as a thrill shot through her. Because this was what *Ez'mazzonal* was about as well. A celebration of what had happened, but a celebration of possibilities and certainties. Her hand involuntarily twitched to her belly.

She turned to beam at Narius. In some ways, she could hardly believe this had become her life. She still sometimes thought of herself as the shopkeeper from Fair Havens. Or the improbable queen, thrust into a place she didn't belong. Or the reluctant ruler trying to hold it all together. But in the end, she knew who she was. She knew who she would be. And as long as she could, she would continue to walk the path the Singularity drew, guided by His light, no matter what new adventures He took her on.

Acknowledgements

I may be at a loss for words. I very well may have used them all up in writing this book.

Out of all the books I've written to this point, this one may be the most personal. My life shifted in major ways while I was planning the story and writing the manuscript. I poured a lot of myself into Narius and Everys's struggles. In some ways, reaching the end of their story feels bittersweet. But I know I would have been able to make this journey, especially this leg, without the help of a lot of different people.

To the incredible students of the One Year Adventure Novel summer workshop. You were there when a throwaway idea I had in a presentation suddenly morphed into a story seed I could only call #gottabebae. You have been my constant cheerleaders over the past several years, encouraging me to take this big swing. None of you can be my Nazgûl (I checked), but I'm proud to call all of you friends.

To Jim Schroeder, who made this world that much richer by creating Spanica Trentwether and Kutnik Zavoleny as part of two different Kickstarter campaigns. When we were talking about Spanica, I had no idea how important he would become to the story overall. And while Kutnik didn't have much to say this time around, I think he's got a lot more to add to the backstory of a certain Governor-General.

To those who served as beta readers on this project, namely Katie Vincent, Chawna Schroeder, Tom Evans, and Lisa Gefrides. Your early feedback was invaluable as I tried to navigate the twisting plot and characters. I am forever grateful for your time!

To my intrepid editor, Megan Gerig. You have been one of the biggest cheerleaders for me during this project, and I appreciate all of the encouragement you've given me. You have made all three books in this trilogy shine brighter than I ever could have on my own.

To Kirk DouPonce, who created amazing covers for this trilogy. You, sir, are the best of the best!

The following people who went above and beyond in helping support me via Kickstarter to bring this book to print: Jill Williamson, Chawna Schroeder, Jim Schroeder, Anika Palodichuk, Bill Merrell, Rosie and Lydia Houze, Megan Gerig, Meghan Clark, Katrina Brinkman, and the Ohio Bremers. Thank you so much for your faith and trust in me.

To my family, who had to put up with my constant need for brainstorming sessions, who had to help me chisel out time to work on this story even as so much of our lives was changing. I can't even begin to count the number of ideas and concepts and possibilities that you helped me weave into Everys and Narius's world.

But most importantly, to the One whose will I try to follow, to the Light no darkness can overcome, to the Guide who leads me in new directions, Father, Son, and Holy Spirit, may whatever glory I gain ultimately be given to You.

About the Author

John is a PK, a pastor's kid. He grew up in Columbia Heights, a suburb of Minneapolis, with his parents and younger sister and brother. They were the terror of their local library because, every few weeks, they would come and check out crates full of books, increasing the workload of the poor librarians. In high school, though, John worked at the same library, so it balanced out.

After high school, John attended Concordia University in St. Paul, Minnesota, where he majored in theatre. Upon his graduation in 1996, he moved on to Concordia Seminary in St. Louis, Missouri. He graduated with his Masters of Divinity in 2000. He served as a Lutheran minister in Blue Earth, Minnesota, South Saint Paul, Minnesota, and Blue Springs, Missouri. He currently serves as a high school English teacher in Kansas City, Missouri, where he lives with his wife and kids.

John is a lifelong writer. He started with badly drawn comic books in the fifth grade. When he realized that he was a lousy artist, he moved on to badly written novels in middle school. He's tried his hand at screenplays (don't ask), stage plays (a little better), fanfic, teen mysteries, and religious fiction. But his first love has always been speculative fiction.

His debut novel, *Failstate*, was published by Marcher Lord Press in April of 2012, and was a finalist for the Christy Awards in 2013. He has gone on to publish four more novels with Marcher Lord Press/Enclave Publishing, two of which, *Numb* and *Failstate: Nemesis*, were finalists for the Christy Awards in 2014 and 2015. *Drawn in Ash* won the Realm Award for Science Fiction in 2023, was a finalist for the Chrsity Awards in 2023, and was a semi-finalist for the Carol Awards that same year.

John looks forward to telling even more strange tales that point people back to God and His incredible grace.

Also By...

The Failstate Series

Failstate
Gauntlet Goes to Prom (ebook exclusive)
Failstate: Legends
Kynetic: On Target (ebook exclusive)
Failstate: Nemesis

The Ministrix Duology

Numb
The Hive

The Legacy of Ink Trilogy

Drawn in Ash
The Storm's Eye (ebook exclusive)
Drawn through Blood
Drawn by Light

Cage and the Outpost of Monolith (short story)
Cage and the Warden's Secret (short story)

Anthologies

Into the Bewilderness
Just Dumb Enough (Contributor)
The Memory Eater (Contributor)
Spirited: 13 Haunting Tales (Contributor)

Kickstarter Backers

The following people helped me end this epic story by backing the campaign to bring this book to print. Without them, you wouldn't be reading these words right now. So thank you to:

Gillian Bronte Adams, Megan Archer, Michelle Arnold, Aslan's Compass, Abigail B., David Beagles, Meagan Myhren Bennett, Tim Bicknase, Vickie C., Scott Casey, Haleigh Clevidence, Edward Cloutier, Althea Damgaard, Tatianne Dobbin, Jennifer Dyer, Gretchen E. K. Engel, JR. Forasteros, Noah G, Tiffany Goldman, Chris DT Gordon, Andrew Gunsch, Michele Israel Harper, Pamela Hart, Catherine Haws, Constance Hendryx, E. A. Hendryx, Lee Hillshire, Lizzy Hite, Jason C Joyner, Angela Kim, Tonja Condray Klein, A. F. Kopp, Joel Kovach, Ryan and Kate Kuecker, La Rochelle, Tom Langemo, Becky Loader, Bob and Sandy Logan, Amanda Luedeke, Mark Lundgren, Jonathon Mast, Brian McCauley, Jill McConnell, Shannon McNear, Alex Mellen, Marie Norris, Mark Otte, William and Deanna Otte, Patty, Aaron Plattner, Tracy Popey, Mary Reed, Ashton Reynwood, Rachael Ritchey, J. Kenneth Riviere, Lisa Sauter, Rachelle Y. Sperling, G Still, Camy Tang, Kelly and Dawn Twenter, Katie Vincent, Jordan Walker, Dona Watson, Angela R. Watts, Joseph Wernecke, Tracy Workman, Jason Worley, Wyngarde, Peter Younghusband

Learn more about Vizier Paine

Want to find out more about Paine and Jesik Hollowbrook's tumultuous past? Want to see more of Vessel and Freedom? You can in the ebook exclusive novella, *The Storm's Eye*. It's available wherever you buy ebooks!

Get a free short story!

Want to find out more about the odd duo who helped Everys get back into the Dynasty's holdings, Cage and Meerdra?

Head over to John's website and sign up for the Geeky Grace Newsletter. When you do, you'll receive the short story *Cage and the Outpost of Monolith* absolutely free!

johnwotte.com/subscribe

www.ingramcontent.com/pod-product-compliance
Lightning Source LLC
Chambersburg PA
CBHW070259310726
48976CB00005B/1488